DREAMWORLD

DREAMWORLD

BOOK 5 OF THE COLORWORLD SERIES

To Cherami,
Here's to maaany
more BIG books & huge working
audiobooks! We love
with you!

Rachel E Kelly

PUBLISHED BY COLORWORLD BOOKS, WINSTON-SALEM, NC, USA

Published by Colorworld Books, Winston-Salem, NC, USA.

Web Site: http://colorworldbooks.com

ISBN-13: 978-1540761286

Cover Photograph by Richard J Heeks

Cover Design by Beth Weatherly

For the Church.

Strange! That you should not have suspected years ago—centuries, ages, eons, ago!—for you have existed companionless, through all the eternities. Strange, indeed, that you should not have suspected that your universe and its contents were only dreams, visions, fiction! Strange, because they are so frankly and hysterically insane—like all dreams: a God who could make good children as easily as bad, yet preferred to make bad ones; who could have made every one of them happy, yet never made a single happy one; who made them prize their bitter life, yet stingily cut it short; who gave his angels eternal happiness unearned, yet required his other children to earn it; who gave his angels painless lives, yet cursed his other children with biting miseries and maladies of mind and body; who mouths justice and invented hell—mouths mercy and invented hell—mouths Golden Rules, and forgiveness multiplied by seventy times seven, and invented hell; who mouths morals to other people and has none himself; who frowns upon crimes, yet commits them all; who created man without invitation, then tried to shuffle the responsibility for man's acts upon man, instead of honorably placing it where it belongs, upon himself; and finally, with altogether divine obtuseness, invites this poor, abused slave to worship him!...

You perceive, now, that these things are all impossible except in a dream. You perceive that they are pure and puerile insanities, the silly creations of an imagination that is not conscious of its freaks—in a word, that they are a dream, and you the maker of it. The dream-marks are all present; you should have recognized them earlier.

-The Mysterious Stranger, Mark Twain

One

Ezra's mind is elsewhere. It's times like these I wish my empathic ability worked at a distance and not just with skin-contact, although if I had to guess I'd say he's plotting something. The question is, what? By most accounts, Ezra is every bit the fifteen-year-old, but that makes it easy to forget that he is also astonishingly brilliant.

I grimace because he probably knows exactly what I'm thinking, which is that I want to say no to his suggestion that Nate take him home from school today. Nate's not even in high school anymore. He works at the local comic book store where Ezra hangs out, so picking up Ezra and taking him home would mean I owe the guy a favor.

I've held myself back in the past for Ezra's sake, but Nate's a creep that deserves to be put in his place. I'd gladly do it if he didn't share a bizarre camaraderie with my brother centered around comics and superheroes. He also thinks a friendship with my brother will earn him points with me, but he wouldn't even try if he knew I once ruthlessly sought after and humiliated worms like him for fun. Furthermore, I cannot stand the thought of him in my apartment.

"Don't worry," Ezra teases, catching my expression, "I won't let him sniff your underwear drawer."

I scowl at him. "He'd better not. I swear I know exactly where everything is in my underwear drawer. If even one thing is out of place I'm going to kick him in the nads and rip one of his comic books until he cries." *And that's the nicest thing I'd do…*

Ezra gives me a mock fearful look before saying, "Yeah, right. The Hulk himself could be in our apartment and you'd never know the difference. Anyway," he adds, looking serious again, "I won't even let him in the door. I have an English paper to get done."

Pulling up to the curb in front of the school, I huff. "English paper? And when was *that* assigned? Yesterday?"

Ezra gives me a blank look.

"I knew it!" I accuse. "I bet that paper isn't due for another week at least. *Why* do you have the sudden urge to stay on top of your least favorite subject?"

"You're mad that I'm *not* procrastinating?"

"No. I'm mad that you're always trying to please me. It's annoying. So just do what *you* want for once, okay? Have Nate come over. He might not be a credit to the male species but he's pretty much harmless. I trust you guys won't be doing anything more than drooling over superhero chicks and their ginormous breasts in cartoon spandex." I simper at him.

Ezra rolls his eyes.

"Maybe I should go to high school and you should go to work if you're interested in being all *responsible* and *grown up*," I add. Then I furrow my brow. "Come to think of it, if you were taking *my* classes, you'd probably have a four-point-oh and already be graduating."

The truth of that sits uncomfortably in my stomach. I'm a disorganized mess. Mom was never this frenzied. Ezra agrees, otherwise he'd be back to his old antics, like before she died. Instead he's… doing English papers weeks before they're due.

"Okay," Ezra says, although he doesn't sound as conciliatory as I'd like. "But just remember you asked for it. Nate will take me home and then we'll leave all our dirty dishes on the counter. I'll be sure to put my shoes in your study spot and shove your books under the bed along with my dirty socks. I think I might even pee on the toilet seat for good measure. Sound rebellious enough?"

"Only if you promise to tell me you hate me when I yell at you for it," I giggle. I'll take it. For now. Maybe next week he'll skip school for the heck of it…

Five-star parenting, Wen.

Ezra startles me when he leans over, grabs my arm, and kisses my cheek. With his emotions now available for me to read, I can't deny his devotion to me. *I love you* couldn't be any clearer.

"Oh yeah, I almost forgot," Ezra says with one foot already out of the car. His hand comes up with a small wad of bills. Putting them firmly in my hand, he says, "One of Nate's friends has been paying me to tutor him in math."

Before I can protest, Ezra hops out and shuts the door. He waves goodbye as he walks away. I consider throwing the money out the window, but my eyes are watering, so I stick my tongue out at him as I drive away.

Ezra gave me about twenty-five dollars. *That's* what he was plotting: how to give it to me without me being able to give it back.

He's never given me money before. This means he knows how broke we are.

Am I ever going to bring order to my life? At least enough that Ezra doesn't feel like he has to help clean it up?

I worry over it all the way to my appointment: an allergy study with a company called Pneumatikon. Although I expect typical Southern California traffic to hold me up after not getting out the door as early as I'd hoped, I arrive with time to spare. I've never participated in an allergy study before, and I don't know how strict the selection process is, so I didn't want to upset my chances by being late. I do know they offer money, and I'll put on whatever dog and pony show they want if it means being able to pay my utilities this month.

Pneumatikon, LLC, autoimmune disorder and natural treatment specialists, have their facility on a landscaped, commercially-dominated street. The bland furnishings could be in any cancer clinic in America, like the one I took my mom to on a number of occasions. For this reason I expect the waiting room to smell like cancer. It doesn't. It's new, and I welcome the chemical smell of industrial glue into my overly-sensitive nose.

I sign in with the less than enthusiastic receptionist and find a seat to fill out the forms she gave me. My shoulder bag is full of granola bars, so I have to mine through it for a pen. My hand touches the white envelope I found this morning in my stack of mail, no return address, my address handwritten. I brought it with me on the chance I'd get a moment to satisfy my curiosity and open it. I put it aside now as well, hoping that if I can get the forms filled out quickly enough, I can rip into it before I'm taken in to my appointment.

The forms are boringly standard—all good things. Medical history. Release. At the end is the compensation agreement: $500 each month I'm enrolled. That's unbelievable! This better pan out. I need that money like Ezra needs new shoes—which I will now be able to buy with this kind of cash. I think I'll even take him out to dinner.

I return the forms to the receptionist, feeling like I'm on the verge of winning the lottery, so I open the mysterious envelope, certain it's going to contain something amazing.

It's a type-written letter:

Dear Miss Wendy Whitley,

I understand your mother, Leena Whitley, passed away fairly recently. I want to convey my condolences for your loss. I had the opportunity to know Leena earlier in her life, and she was a generous and honest woman whose friendship I appreciated for too short a time.

You must be confused as to why you are only just now receiving word from me, an uncle who has been estranged to you for most of your life. It was not my idea to be absent, but keeping my distance from your family was a request your mother made years ago, and I made a promise to her then which I never broke. I may have been absent from your life, but I can assure you that you have not been absent from mine. I have wrestled with whether to make contact with you for months now and decided that in light of your newly orphaned state, even your mother would not argue with allowing you to associate with the last remaining member of your more immediate family.

I'd enjoy meeting you and your brother, and I hope you'll allow me to help you out with your responsibilities as your parents would have, were they still alive. It cannot be easy for a young lady to support herself as well as a minor while attending both school and a job full-time. I hope only to make that burden lighter.

Please take the opportunity to call me and arrange a time to get together. I would provide travel means for both you and your brother. I know the urgency of your situation and the obstacles you face. We should meet soon. If I don't hear from you, you can most certainly expect me on your doorstep at some point in the very near future. However, I wanted to give you the courtesy of allowing you to arrange the terms of our meeting at your convenience before imposing on you.

He signs the letter, Your Uncle, Robert Lee Haricott, and includes his number and e-mail. I examine every square inch of the paper, as if it will reveal its true intentions. I don't know what it means, but I don't like it. My anger grows with each second that I imagine all the awful possibilities, most of which end in this man taking Ezra from me. Why is he writing me *now*? I don't have an *uncle*. Not the kind that writes his niece letters asking for a visit. My dad had a brother though, one that Dad had a fight with before he died in a car accident, a brother that my family—my mom, brother, and I—never had contact with again. And if my mom denied that contact, it had to be for a good reason. Mom *always* looked out for us. Always.

All of that aside, the tone of this letter is just creepy. How does he know my situation? He hasn't been absent from my life? I have to consent to meet him? And then he basically threatens to show up if I don't answer? This guy has been stalking me and I don't like it.

Two

She went through this whole speech about how everyone has this energy around their body, and that if you tweak it with your own energy, waving your hands over it and stuff, it will change physical things inside the person's body," I explain to Ezra, who is turning the pages of a comic book. "She said their method doesn't even involve touching the person. Strictly-hands off. Because it interferes with energy stuff. I'll have five sessions with them, weekly. Then they do assessments to see if it has diminished the sensitivity to my nut allergy at all." I nudge him from the other side of the couch with my foot. "Are you even listening? You said you wanted to hear about my appointment the other day."

"Yeah, yeah," Ezra says, not looking up. "Crazy quack doctor practices energy voodoo. Let me guess. You're getting paid?"

"Stupid genius," I grumble, shoving another bite of homemade mac and cheese in my mouth. I made dinner tonight, which is rare. I reneged on my plan to take Ezra out to dinner— although he doesn't know that. I figured eating out would be irresponsible. But I did splurge a little, taking the night off to hang out with my brother, cook him dinner, and catch up on our week. "Anyway, to answer your question, *yes,* they are going to pay me. A butt-load. I got my first check. See?" I pull the stub out of the white envelope Dina gave me to show him. I already deposited it when I got it on Tuesday.

He leans forward to see the number, nods appreciatively. "Sweet," he says. Then he furrows his brow. "You took a read on her, right?"

I roll my eyes. "Of course. Twice. The first time when she introduced herself, I shook her hand, and again when I shook her hand to say goodbye," I say, describing my meeting with Dina, my consult at Pneumatikon. "She was excited. Actually kind of jealous, I think. Nothing that weird. Besides, didn't you hear me? It's hands-off. What on earth should I be careful about?"

"Beats me. But you just said that like it was an actual question."

"*No*," I grumble. "I just haven't *got* to the weird part yet. Because you're either totally ignoring me or jumping to conclusions."

"I'm not ignoring you!"

"Oh just shut up and let me finish," I say, getting up to put my bowl in the sink. I lean against the counter. "Once I said I was in, that I'd be a participant, she had me do all these tests. Vision, hearing, and smell."

He chuckles. "Did you bomb them on purpose?"

My jaw drops. Why would he say that? "What?"

"Did you fake how good your senses are?" he repeats.

How does my brother know about my vision? *I* wasn't even aware of how good it was until the vision test with Dina… which then led me to fake my hearing and smell aptitude once she got excited. And my hearing… Ezra knew it was good, always complaining about me eavesdropping, but how would he know it was good enough that I'd need to hide it? Deciding to address my apparent self-ignorance later and finish the story already, I say, "Stop getting ahead of me!"

"But your stories are so predictable."

"For your information, she said my vision was better than anyone she'd seen. You're saying you *predicted* that?"

"Wen, I don't know why Mom used to dumb down your empathic ability to 'uniquely perceptive,' or why she tried to make it seem like that was your only superhuman skill, but you have super-senses. Like Superman. But more realistic."

Note to self: Do not underestimate how observant 15 year-old brother is. "Well if I'm Superman, you're like… like…" I dig into my store of knowledge on superheroes for one that has an overabundant IQ.

"Batman," Ezra says.

"Batman just has money," I point out.

"*And* smarts," Ezra says.

"No. He has money to *pay* smart people to make him fancy gizmos."

"He's known as the the world's best detective! That takes mega-brains!"

"Whatever." I walk over and play with his blonde hair. Then I lean down and whisper in his ear. "We all know that you only want to be Batman so you can hook up with Catwoman." Then I jump away, laughing when Ezra whips around and tries to swat me. I know Ezra. He talks about Batman all the time, but his favorite is really Catwoman. I don't know where he got the idea that he can't have a female superhero as his favorite—probably that idiot, Nate. So he hides it.

I open the cabinet and pull out my other splurge: Oreos. They're Ezra's other favorite. I toss the bag at him. "Don't worry. It's our secret."

He's scowls at me despite the gift.

I take Ezra's empty bowl and put it in the sink. "And yeah, once I realized she was getting excited about my vision, I pretended to have normal hearing and a normal nose."

"Probably a good idea," he says, ripping into the Oreos. "What I don't get is why she even gave you a vision or a hearing test in the first place. What do your senses have to do with allergies?"

I shrug. "She said something about how energy therapy has other benefits and she wanted a good 'before picture.'"

He looks skeptical but doesn't have anything to say about that.

"Can you believe that all this time I've had superhuman senses and I didn't even realize it? I mean, I guess it's easy to overlook, what with my emotional violation being especially weird, but I don't get how it never occurred to me even once."

I plop down on the floor by the couch, wrinkling my nose as Ezra shovels Oreos into his mouth with only slightly more decor than the Cookie Monster.

"I realize you're a little unobservant," Ezra garbles, "but in your defense, you've only really had the super *duper* senses in the last year or so."

"What do you mean?" I say. Is this yet another part of myself I've been oblivious to?

Ezra's the one in disbelief now. "Really?"

I stare at him blankly.

"Wow. Okay, so make that *exceptionally* unobservant," he says.

"You haven't noticed how much more you can hear now than you used to? All these years I thought I pretty much had your range figured out, but seriously Wen, your hearing ability has increased. Remember that day I was talking with Nate outside, and you heard him tell me to hook him up with you? I was sure that you hadn't heard him, but then I came inside and you were all like 'Eeew Ezra, keep that geeky loser away from me!'"

"I *know* I didn't say it like that."

"Yeah, that's not the point. We were standing outside and down the stairs, not outside the door." He lifts his eyebrows at me.

"On the second floor landing?"

"Negatory. I mean the *base* of the stairs, the first floor. That's through a door and down two flights of stairs. *And* I was standing beside Nate's car while it was running, and that piece of junk is *not* quiet."

"Are you sure?," I say, starting to get skeptical of his account. "And I haven't always heard that well? Maybe the window was open."

"No, Wen. I've had it down like a science. I could always be sure that if there were at least three insulated walls between us, or two walls and loud music, you wouldn't overhear me. That day rewrote the rules. Trust me, you hear things now that I never would have thought you could."

"So what about my vision?"

"I wouldn't know as well, but in the few times I've thought about it, you've seen farther away than ever. Remember that day when you picked me up from the mall and you pointed out that girl coming out of the other department store entrance? It was way over a football field away and you were telling me how cute she was? I couldn't see squat but you just went on and on about every detail of what she was wearing, including the words on her shirt? I've been pretty aware of what you could see, but that blew me away. You have *never* been able to see *that* well. You've always had good vision, good hearing, but not *that* good."

"So a year then? I've only been hearing and seeing this well for a year?"

"I started noticing sometime after Mom got sick. A year and a half maybe? But who knows how long before then it started improving."

"I am so dense," I say, baffled by my own ignorance.

I stand up and fill the sink to start the dishes, wondering what it all means but needing more pieces to the puzzle. "Why didn't you say anything?"

"You never made a big deal out of it before, and I thought maybe you had always heard that well and were holding out on me. Plus, there were other things going on…"

He's right about that. Mom was dying then, and I was scrambling to figure out what I was going to do about it after months of pretending it wasn't happening.

"Why would it improve?" I say mostly to myself, elbow-deep in soap suds.

"You got me."

I look behind me. Ezra has picked up another comic book, already over the novelty of the conversation, apparently. I return to the dishes, letting my mind wander back to the brief moments that still stick from those tumultuous times. I was transitioning from irresponsible party-girl, trying to prove to my mom that I could take care of Ezra. She had planned on someone specific, I don't know who, adopting him. It was all set and ready to go when I approached her about taking him instead. She fought me on it, and who could blame her after over a year of indifference and aimlessness?

When I'm done with the dishes I pull the *other* white envelope out of my bag, the one I've been dreading telling Ezra about.

"So you are never going to believe who I got a letter from," I say, sitting on the couch next to him, the paper clutched in my hand.

I catch a glance at the cover of the comic book he's reading now: *Superman-Batman*. Very funny. I flick it with a finger.

"Batgirl?" he answers from behind the pages.

I burst into giggles. I snatch the comic book away and send my fist playfully into his stomach.

"C'mon! I'm serious! Aren't you even a little curious?" I swing the paper back and forth in front of him.

After grabbing his comic book back, he sits back against the arm of the couch as if disinterested. I catch his eyes shifting to the paper anyway as he says, "Only if some long lost relative left us a big inheritance."

I scan the paper in my hand; that never occurred to me. The mysterious Uncle has money from what I've researched. Maybe he's dying and wants to reconnect before he goes. I'd love to be in on *that* money. "You got half of it right," I reply.

Ezra throws his comic book down. "What?" He plucks the letter from my fingers.

My eyes don't leave him as he reads. He is obviously as confused as I am by it, and when he reaches the end and looks up, I say, "So what do you think? You want to meet this guy?"

"Is there actually a choice?" he says, glancing over the letter again. "Looks like he's pretty serious."

"Well, we could always move under cover of night into a cash-only motel and change our names," I say lamely, my nerves starting to get to me. "Isn't that what superheroes do? Get secret identities?" I've never thought about Ezra's smarts as a superpower before... I don't even really know how smart he actually is. Mom never wanted him tested. "You don't have superpowers, do you? I mean, maybe this is genetic or something and you have some kind of ability? Like being super genius."

"Being a math genius isn't considered a superpower."

I roll my eyes. "You would know, I suppose, since you've done such in-depth research."

"Yeah, yeah. Anyway. Yes, I think we should meet him. Maybe he's not trustworthy, but maybe he's serious. Maybe he just wants to help. Mom didn't say much about him, and I would think that if he was a real danger she would have said so before she died. Like, 'Stay away from your uncle' or something." He turns the paper over, looking at the blank backside. "I'm really curious."

Anxiety fills my stomach. "Yeah. You probably haven't considered the fact that we're barely scraping by... and I can hardly afford to buy you new clothes. He seems to have some bizarre interest in us already. What if...?" Oh please let me just be blowing this out of proportion...

Ezra catches on though. "You think he wants me to live with him? He wouldn't!" he gasps. "I wouldn't go! He can't make me; I would stay here with you!"

I slide down, twine my arm with his. I've never been more relieved to feel Ezra so bothered.

"We don't know what he wants, but it doesn't matter. We're staying together," I say, using the words I've been rehearsing for days. "The guy hasn't been around our whole lives. That's got to count for something, right?"

He pauses, squelches his worry, and then his very analytical mind moves into motion.

"Besides, if that's actually his goal, and the worst happens, I'm going wherever you are; he won't be able to get rid of me." I smile at him.

He exhales, nods as he accepts my determination. With that, the mysterious uncle is no longer a concern to him. I marvel at how easily he can push aside uncertainty. But mostly, I'm so grateful Ezra is happy living with me, that he wouldn't choose more wealthy circumstances over the helter-skelter existence I provide. He is a lot more mature than I was at his age.

I get up to grab my phone. "Let's get this over with." After punching the number, I put it on speaker so Ezra can hear.

Two rings.

"Robert here," answers an upbeat, male voice.

"Hi, this is Wendy Whitley. I got a letter from you saying you wanted to talk to me?" I say, wanting this conversation over already.

"Yes! Wendy! It's so good to hear from you," Robert says, and the first thing I notice is how he pauses between his words. "I hope I didn't startle you too much when you received my letter. I can understand if it was a bit... odd."

"Oh, no, we're accustomed to getting cryptic letters."

He chuffs softly. "So then you'll allow me to meet you?"

I wrinkle my nose and think, *no, you're not allowed anywhere near me.* But instead, I say, "Sure, Ezra and I are open to whatever you have in mind—you know, as far as meeting you, that is. Family is family, right?"

"Absolutely," he gushes.

I groan inwardly. I don't like him. At all.

"I understand you're in school," he continues, "and I don't want to interrupt your studies. I would be glad to come to you if that would work out better for your schedule."

"No, no," I blurt. "We can come to you. Monterey isn't that far of a drive. And this semester is over in a week anyway." Thank goodness. Uncle Mysterious is *not* invited to my messy apartment.

"Smart girl," he says.

What is that supposed to mean? Did he catch on to the fact that I looked up his area code to find out where he lives?

"I won't hear of it though," he says. "I'll book a flight for you and your brother. Would a week from today be okay then? What day would you need to return?"

I can't help but be grateful for the travel arrangements. My gas rationing doesn't accommodate surprise trips to Monterey. "That's fine. And we can fly back on Sunday. Ezra will still have school," I reply.

"Wonderful!" he says emphatically. "I'll e-mail you the itinerary when I have it if you will give me your e-mail address."

Once we hang up, Ezra says, "Well?"

"I don't like him." I close what's left of the Oreos bag, get up to put it away.

He crosses his arms, resists rolling his eyes. "Of course you don't. He's too excited. Too nice. Too old. Too rich. Too generous. He probably drives a car you don't like. Wears the wrong color tie. Plus, everyone knows Monterey is full of cocky rich people, right?"

"Hmph. Like *you* would know." I plop back down on the couch.

"What *would* you like him to be? Rude?"

"At least if he was rude I'd know where I stand."

"Yes... And all our questions would be answered then?"

I slide down to the floor, back to the couch and look up at the ceiling. "No, I'd probably dislike him then, too."

Three

A deafening crash opens my eyes abruptly. Then a brilliant flash blinds me. At first I think it's gunshot. But it's too loud. Bombs? Am I in the middle of a war? Another flash and a crack, like the sound of a snapping branch but a hundred times louder. The tower of pines surrounding me lights up at random intervals, interspersed with rumbles and ear-splitting snaps.

Instinctively, I bring my hands to my ears to escape the violent clamor.

Pain. Excruciating. It drills into my shoulder and filters outward to the rest of me. I think I scream, but I can't hear the sound of my own voice over the fractured air.

The pain fades somewhat and I come to. Sort of. I'm gasping for breath, filling my nose but my lungs still feel deprived. The air smells acidic. Like electricity. Then the wind shifts and it smells like fire. And beneath it all, damp earth, rotting leaves.

The crack of explosives again. It must be right next to me. It rattles my brain, dislodging the minimal grip I have on the reality around me. Over and over the litany of thundering booms and snaps derail any attempt to think. I can't gather enough moments to remember how I got here. Or even where I was last…

Whenever the white flash of the explosives subsides for a moment, the fortress of trees around me is illuminated by a vague, yellow light, enough to see by. For fear of pain seizing me again, I keep my head still while rotating my eyes as far as they will go. I see a low canopy of branches above me. I must have had the good sense to hit the ground and seek cover near this fallen tree.

Is that burning smell growing stronger? *Oh my gosh…* The light… It's from a *fire!*

Terror shoots through me, begging me to move, to escape what must be a blaze nearby. In fact… I think it's getting warmer…

But I'm equally terrified of the agony I felt earlier, hints of it still throbbing in the background, warning me to remain still. Frozen in indecision, the explosions going off right next to me only add to my inability to act. I can't think. I can't move. Why am I not dead yet?

I pinch my eyes shut, fighting for cognizance, for reason. But all I can find is panic that won't be squelched, and unrelenting noise. I know I need to *do* something but I have no idea what that is.

Move, a voice in my head says, reaching past the noise. *Move.*

Gritting my teeth to prepare for the pain, I bring my hands up again, but that small movement shears my shoulder and back in agony. Adrenaline has taken over and I scream. Hands now on either side of my face, and with tremendous effort, I push against the ground. I just need to crawl. If I can just crawl away...

But I have a red hot iron in my shoulder. It's too much, and I black out for a few moments. I slump back down. I don't think I gained an inch. My arm is being ripped off every time I float back into consciousness.

I hold still. I try. But the knife ripping apart my shoulder won't stop. I lose perception of my body, so whether I am screaming or flailing, I couldn't say. There is only agony and noise.

Help! I scream in my head. *Help me!* I fight for control of my mouth to say those words aloud, over and over, but I can't tell if I succeed. I can't tell how much time passes, how awake or unconscious I am.

No one is coming, I realize suddenly amid the haze in my head. *I'm going to die. Alone.*

I sob, and this time it has nothing to do with pain.

Suddenly, the agony which I thought was unsurpassable, doubles. I can't fit it all into my head, can't fit it all in just my shoulder—that's just the source. It electrifies every nerve, shearing my perception. I think I'm screaming, but I can't perceive any other part of myself but the torture in my back.

I black out.

I'm moving. Bouncing... More throbbing.

Darkness.

I'm cold. My eyes pop open, but I see nothing. I feel my body though, slung over someone's shoulder, I think. Am I being carried? There isn't a single part of me that doesn't throb.

The blood is swiftly pooling in my head; I'm going to black out again. But as the noise of the bombs finally fades, I wonder fleetingly where I am and how I got here. All I can recall is darkness. Unending, abysmal, darkness.

₪

I'm in a hospital. The telltale curtain partitioning my bed from the rest of the room is unmistakable. And the smell… I quail from the scent of over-bleached cotton sheets and plastic tubing. It brushes up remnants of ancient anxiety and dread.

How did I get here?

As soon as I ask the question, memories materialize: explosions and flashing lights in the woods that are more dream-like than real… It doesn't make sense why I would have been in the woods in the first place…

It has to be a dream then. I think.

I reach up to rub my eyes but pain shoots through my shoulder, and I gasp, seeing stars.

It takes me a minute to recover, but the pain seems to have cleared the haze from my mind somewhat. I remember my shoulder feeling like this before. I remember the smell of leaves and wood, then fire and ash, the haunting yellow glow of the light of a fire, the damp earth under my fingers as I tried to crawl. I also remember being carried out, bumping uncomfortably against someone's back.

I don't live anywhere near a forest though. I have not even a hint of a memory as to how I ended up in one. I must have forgotten. I've heard of people getting in car accidents and not remembering how they happened, so this must be something like that.

The sound of someone breathing nearby reaches my ears suddenly and I turn my head abruptly. I see only a curtain, but I become immediately distracted by how dirty it is…

I tilt my head. Wait. I think… my eyes… Wow. My vision has improved. I can see the grime on individual threads of the curtain. And dust. There's dust *everywhere.*

I hear the breathing again. "Ezra?" I call.

Footsteps. The face of a boy pops around the edge of the partition. It's not Ezra, but he looks like he could be similar in age. He has a toothy, slightly lopsided grin on his face, brown hair that doesn't lay right. The corners of my mouth spread automatically to mirror his smile, and I catch myself. I'm in the middle of a crisis. Why am I smiling?

"Do you know where my brother is?" I ask, testing my ability to move my hands and legs. My right arm seems to be bound somehow. My shoulder aches.

He lifts his eyebrows questioningly, stands by the end of the curtain.

"Where is my brother, Ezra?" I repeat.

The boy shakes his head.

"You don't know?" I ask.

He shakes his head, points at me, taps the tips of his index fingers together several times, and then points at me.

I blink at him, totally lost, and he repeats the same hand gesture again, more emphatically. He doesn't make a sound, and I think I finally get it. He's signing to me. I have no idea what he's saying, but at least I'm less confused. He's wearing a hospital gown as well, which means he must be sharing this room with me.

At this point, I don't know if he can hear me or read lips, so I speak slowly when I say, "Who are you?"

He points to himself, cups his ear toward me, and then nods.

"You can hear just fine, can't you?" I say, feeling silly.

He nods. Then he points to himself and mumbles something that sounds like a garbled long 'A.' He looks up at the ceiling, a little exasperated. He opens his mouth again, and with great concentration, struggles to make the sound he wants. At first it sounds like a 'T-' sound, and he repeats that several times, "T-, T-, T-"

By the look on his face though, I think that's not quite the sound he intends.

"Ch-?" I ask.

He smiles and nods decisively. Then he holds up a finger again, makes the 'T-' sound that he obviously means as a 'Ch-', and then makes a long 'a' sound that goes on a little too long, his facial muscles exaggerating the effort as he fights to form a new sound.

My mouth is open, following along as I decipher what he's saying. He moves his tongue up to the roof of his mouth several times, fighting for control, making a few false-starts. I'm on the edge of my seat, engrossed.

"Ssss-" he bursts out with finally. He looks at me with wide eyes and a triumphant smile.

I put the sounds together, Ch- Aa- Ss. "Your name is Chase?" I say.

He nods, steps closer to me and holds his left hand up, palm toward me; it's obvious what he wants. My right arm, I discover, is in a sling, so I lift my left and we high-five. But as we do, I can't help noticing how carefree satisfaction moves through me that's not quite in line with my own pleased but not quite so lighthearted attitude.

He sits on the stool next to my bed and a curious anticipation lights my body. I stare at him, confused because he's not touching me. I shouldn't be feeling his emotions. But I am. I'm sure this is not me.

Maybe the kid is just special. If I've ever felt emotions outside of skin-contact before, they've always been so vague that I've rarely noticed. They can't be separated from my own. I can pick up groups of people if they're all feeling similarly, but nobody can be isolated, and everyone blurs into indistinguishable tension in my head. One-on-one though? With this kind of precision? Never. Touch has always been necessary.

"How long have I been here?" I ask.

Chase holds up three fingers.

"I've been asleep the whole time?"

He nods.

"And you haven't seen my brother... Have I had any visitors?"

He nods, holds up one finger.

"One person? Was he a young, blonde kid?"

He immediately shakes his head. He puts his hands near his chin and pretends to stroke a long beard.

"Bearded?" I say, furrowing my brow. I don't think I know anyone like that who would visit me in the hospital.

My shoulder is still burning and becoming more insistent with every minute. I need to speak to someone who can speak back.

"How do I call the nurse?" I ask Chase.

He leans forward, presses a button on the side of my bed.

A few moments later I hear footsteps echo down the hall. Then a person in maroon-colored scrubs appears. "Hi sweetie, I see you woke up finally. How ya feelin'?" she asks in a genteel, southern accent. She stands over me, punches some buttons, straightens one of my pillows.

I don't answer right away, because Chase is apparently not the exception to my now hands-off empathic ability. As soon as this woman came within a few feet of me I felt the detached focus that I also know isn't mine. She isn't touching me… Why am I suddenly picking up people's emotions at a distance?

"I can't remember how I got here," I say. "Do you know where my brother is?" Oh gosh, my shoulder… My arm is going to fall off.

She must notice my discomfort because she says, "Are ya'in pain? Do ya need somethin for it? We took ya off the heavy stuff, to wake ya up."

"Please. But first, can you tell me how I got here?"

"You were brought here from another, smaller hospital four days ago," she says in her funny accent. I don't think I've ever heard a southern accent in person. "Yer shoulder had been impaled and you'd lost a lot of blood. You were transferred here where you could get more comprehensive care."

"From where?" I say.

She shrugs sympathetically. "'Fraid I don't know, sweetie. But yer in Missouri currently."

I do a double-take. *Missouri?* I'm not even quite sure I know where Missouri is on a map exactly. I watch her wrap my arm with a blood-pressure cuff. Her skin comes in contact with mine briefly, but it doesn't seem to change the emotions I'm picking up. Like Chase, she seems to have developed some curiosity about me.

"Who has been visiting me?" I ask, trembling with cold now. A hospital gown is all I have on.

She grimaces, hesitant. "Ahm… no one that I know of. But don't worry. I'm sure it's just because you got transferred. Yer case worker will be comin' a little later. She should be able to answer more of yer questions."

"Case worker?"

"Someone to help straighten things out," she says, and I feel the twist of her pity.

I'm about to demand that she stop tiptoeing around me, but she holds up her hands. "I don't know any more than what I was told, hon." She takes the opportunity to notice Chase as a distraction. She doesn't want to deal with my questions. "Chase, sweetie, you shouldn't be outta bed."

He signs to her rapidly.

She frowns. "Well maybe she don't want yer company. Didja ask?"

"He's fine," I say. "Please, can't you tell me anything? Chase says an older man has been visiting me. Maybe someone came while you weren't on shift. What about my brother? Ezra? Do you keep a log somewhere you can check?"

She lifts her eyebrows as she tucks in the end of my sheets by my feet. "I haven't been informed you have a brother, sweetie." She throws another blanket over me and then says, "I'll be back in two shakes." I'm about to protest, but she disappears, obviously uncomfortable with having to keep telling me she doesn't know anything.

I lay my head back and exhale frustration. What is going on? I turn my head to look at Chase. "Is there a phone in here?"

He's been watching me carefully, and he nods, pushes the edge of the curtain gathered near the wall aside and nudges a table forward. There's a standard hospital phone on it.

I'm in Missouri. I'm going to bet I can't call a California number from that thing. Should I call collect? To who?

The nurse bustles back in and hands me a plastic cup with some pills. "Ibuprofen. If it doesn't do the job, let me know."

I gladly down the pills, chase them with the water she gives me. "Why do I have a case worker?" I say. "And do I have to talk to her about contacting my brother? Does that phone allow long-distance calls?" I hand her back both cups.

"'Fraid not, hon. I'd wait for Kiera. I promise she'll be by later."

I shake my head. "You don't understand. Last I knew, I was in *California.* I've never been to Missouri in my life so I have no idea how I ended up here. I remember… having dinner with my brother… and then being in the woods…?" I shake my head. "It's all a big mess in my head. I can't possibly sit here for the next few hours waiting for this Kiera person to show. Is there any way I can make a call to a California number?"

I literally hear her heart rate speed up. Hearing heartbeats is not something I recall being able to do. I've not actually acknowledged it before now, being preoccupied with the confusion of my situation, but I have been hearing conversations and sounds and all kinds of things from all over the hospital. I even heard two people walking outside—their footsteps crunching subtly over the pavement—talking about dinner plans. Plus, the longer I'm awake, the more convinced I'm becoming that my vision has most definitely improved. I can see the streaks of the nurse's hastily-applied makeup. I can see individual particles of dirt on the floor in the corner over there…

And I can feel the nurse, talking herself out of apprehension that makes no sense to me.

"I'll see if I can get a hold of her," the nurse says finally. "I'm sorry I can't be of more help. Say, what part of California you from?"

"Pomona," I reply. "I go to Cal State Fullerton."

That definitely jolts her.

"What?" I demand, twisting my head around to look up at her.

"No reason," she says, writing something down on a clipboard she materializes from somewhere.

It's clear that she is now dying to leave the room. Her anticipation of that is tangible.

"What do you know?" I accuse.

That was the wrong thing to say. She's suddenly on the verge of panic. "Excuse me?" she says, fighting to keep cool, but she's afraid.

Why is she afraid?

"I didn't mean—Sorry," I say, not knowing what I'm apologizing for. I want this woman to stop beating around the emotional bush. "I can't remember anything that would tell me how I ended up here and it's freaking me out."

She calms slightly. "I told you what I know, hon. Ah'm sure it'll all come back to ya. Give it some time. Trauma can often make a mishmash of your memory. In the meantime, how about some real food? I betcha yer hungry."

Chase has been silently watching from a chair nearby, wide eyes, engrossed in my saga of confusion.

My eyes flash between him and the nurse. I want to demand in no uncertain terms that someone give me answers. But I'm starting to think this nurse probably doesn't know much, and what she does know, she's too afraid to tell me. I'm going to have to get my answers elsewhere.

"I'll take that meal," I say. "Do I check my own glucose or do you guys do that?"

She looks at me with confusion.

"I'm diabetic," I say, slightly questioning. They had to have figured that out, right?

She doesn't have to speak. Her resigned pity has me livid. Why can't she spit it out? "Sweetie," she says, as if speaking to a child, "you haven't had any blood sugar problems since you came in."

"I've been here three days," I say, glancing at Chase. "How is it possible you haven't had to give me insulin? The longest I've ever gone without injecting is twenty-four hours."

"I'll mention it to the doctor," she says brusquely. "But nothin' in yer chart mentions hyperglycemia problems since you arrived."

I don't like her dismissive tone. I'd probably have better luck playing charades with Chase though. His emotions indicate he may know something.

My expression must communicate my annoyance because the nurse says, "Would it make you feel better if I took a read on yer blood sugar now?" Although I can tell she'd rather do anything but.

"Yes," I reply, holding my left arm out and staring her in the eye.

"Lemme go get a meter," she says, turning on her heel and pushing one of the curtains aside before she leaves, revealing the door and hallway beyond.

My face itches, so I reach up slowly with my left hand. I meet a bandage on my cheek. I touch my head, meet stubble. *My hair is cut off?* I run my hand slowly over the entirety of my nearly-bare scalp, amazed.

I've had my limit of confusion for today. I'm so angry I grab the phone in my left hand and throw it as hard as I can. Of course, It only goes so far, caught by its cord, which is disappointing. But it gives me the slightest edge of satisfaction anyway.

Chase is staring at me, and I notice he has a pen in his hand, a notebook in his lap.

The nurse reappears, pauses briefly when she sees the phone on the floor. It must not be the first time she's seen such a sight because she steps around the phone and comes to my side without a word, full of haughty indignation though. She cleans my finger with an alcohol swab. I barely feel the prick, something that years of glucose testing as numbed me to.

"Sixty-two," she says, holding the meter up for me to see. "On the low range, but that's most likely because you haven't eaten. Pasta with pesto or grilled chicken are yer choices. What's the word?"

"Chicken," I say. "I'm allergic to the walnuts in pesto." I stare at her, daring her to challenge me on that too. I am *not* imagining being diabetic.

"I'll go put the order in, sweetie," the nurse says.

"I have a name!" I snap. "Stop calling me 'sweetie'!"

She turns around at the door. "I would have, but I don't actually know yer name."

My mouth opens. I glance from the nurse to Chase, both staring at me expectantly.

"So what... I'm like a Jane Doe?" I say in disbelief.

Her eyes stray uncomfortably to Chase. "Accordin' to yer file, yes," she says, and then she hightails it out of the room.

I whirl on Chase. "What do you know?"

He leans over a notebook in his lap, starts scribbling something.

I lay my head back, gathering in my eroding sanity as I wait. I need Ezra. Oh God, if *one* thing can go my way today, please let me see my brother's face. I can handle anything if I know he's okay... I close my eyes, drawing up the woods again. I called for help. Someone came, but it wasn't Ezra. Before the woods... It's all fuzzy. I think the last thing I remember was making dinner.

Oh! The phone call! To my uncle, the one that sent me that letter! And the allergy place! What was it called....

I rack my brain. It was a weird word. Pneuma-something. And what was my uncle's name? Maybe that's who has been visiting me!

Someone shakes my arm. It's Chase. He has an idea.

He holds up his notebook. In carefully formed letters, it says, what is the month and year?

I furrow my brow. "You want to know the date? Chase, I don't even know how long ago I was in the woods—or even why I was there... why there were bombs going off... I don't know why I'm in Missouri or why I'm a Jane Doe. My name is Wendy Whitley. I'm nineteen. I'm a college student. I live in California. I made homemade mac and cheese for dinner last I remember. Before the woods of course. God. I don't know anything." I put my hand to the side of my head, the disjointed mess of my memory seriously stressing me out.

Chase flops his notebook in my lap. He slaps the page several times, startling me. Points to the words.

what is the month and year?

Surprised at his insistence, I say, "What? Geez. Let me think... May. 2013."

He celebrates internally, taking me completely off-guard. He snatches the notebook back up, brings it close to his face, his eyebrows set in a deep V as he scribbles out a new message.

Meanwhile, I narrow down what to ask him first when he's done. Because Chase definitely seems to know something about my situation.

He tosses the notebook in my lap again.

It reads, It is Nov 2015.

Four

ightning strike often causes amnesia," the petite, curly-haired therapist named Kiera says.

"Lightning strike..." I say. "When was I struck by lightning?"

"In the woods," she says. "The lightning storm. I thought you remembered that part?"

"Yeah..." I say, recalling the crashes and flashes with a totally different perspective. "That was a *lightning storm*? Seemed more like clash of the Titans."

"It's a miracle you made it out alive," Kiera agrees.

"Two and a half years though?" I say, pushing the button on my bed to sit up a bit more. I've said the phrase 'two and half years' at least twenty times since this morning when I woke up. It's not getting any more believable.

She nods apologetically, looking about sixteen as she does it. She's probably also barely five feet tall. The maturity in her confidence, however, convinces me she's much older than she looks.

"I know it's hard to grasp," she replies. "It's best that you not dwell on what you don't know. Focus on the details of what you do know. We'll fill in the gaps together, as they come." Her voice could be mistaken for a pre-teen's.

"Focus on what I *do* know?" I frown. "What I *do* know is the problem. I know a bunch of different, seemingly unrelated things. It's like I have a bunch of split personalities and they've all been living separate lives."

She pulls a small notebook still in the wrapper out of her satchel and hands it to me. "Write them down. Everything that happens from now on and anything that comes to you. It's going to make sense eventually. I promise. Plus, I'm working on getting Claude up here tomorrow. He can tell us what he knows about why you were in the woods. That's our first step."

Claude. Right. Kiera told me that's the guy that rescued me from the woods four days ago. I've never heard of him.

"What about Ezra?" I say.

"You said you have a number for him?"

I nod. "Yeah. But I can't call from this phone. It's a California number."

She lifts her brows. "You're from California? That's not going to work."

"Why not?"

She crosses her legs, sits back, slightly nervous for the first time. "Hmm. Well… Give me a moment to come up with a response that won't confuse you."

Chase, who is sitting nearby, makes an explosive motion with his hands.

"It exploded!?" I say, shocked.

"It did not explode," Kiera chides. She gives Chase a look of reprimand.

"Can you tell me already?" I say, glad Chase doesn't tip-toe around me. As a result, he's been more helpful than all the people sent in to 'help' me. He is also the happiest person I've encountered thus far. He radiates it, and I find it easier to let go of my angst when he's near. Plus, he reminds me of Ezra with his inopportune humor. He prefers to laugh at things rather than cry over them. I need that right now.

"Yes, I'm sorry," Kiera says, and I can tell she really is struggling with what to say. She looks at the door as if to check that it's closed. In a slightly lower voice, she says, "Most of California has practically no means of communication. There was an earthquake in San Francisco a little over four months ago, worst in recorded history. Decimated the place. Destroyed the entire infrastructure. There's a refugee camp in the valley, just south, of a couple million people who stuck around after the quake. Most relief efforts are focused there, maintaining that population and arranging more permanent homes for them. A couple weeks after that, Los Angeles underwent a bout of mass hysteria. It started with a mall riot. It created a domino-effect and hundreds of riots sprouted up all over the place. Curfew was put in place and the city went on lockdown. They tried lifting the restrictions after a short time, to get life back to normal, but the riots would start up again, like an epidemic. Restrictions continued, but it was interfering with the economy. People were getting restless, frustrated. There was a mass exit of people out of the area, which was good. But the group left behind took advantage. The national guard got forced out of the greater LA area by a citizen militia only two weeks ago."

I blink at her. Not an ounce of that story sounds real. Except the earthquake. That's feasible. But LA being taken over by a guerrilla outfit?

"I can see by the look on your face that you are more confused. Do you want me to start over at the beginning?" Kiera says.

"Uh. Yeah," I say, annoyed that she felt she had to ask.

She smiles widely until a dimple forms in one of her soft brown cheeks. She stands up, steps over to me, and holds out her hand, "Hi, I'm Kiera."

I take it. I thought she meant she was starting her story over, not our brief relationship.

"I'm a therapist, and I work for the Guild," she says. "The Guild is a world-wide organization dedicated to the advancement of human capability. You've never heard of us because we've been working in strict secrecy for many years. But in the last two months, we've become more public about our influence because of the inundation of natural disasters. They started increasing several years ago but have accelerated exponentially in the last year. The Guild is made up of the brightest, most capable people on earth. In short, the world needs us. We keep the public informed about pending natural disasters and aid the government—which has been overwhelmed—in relief efforts." Kiera has a way of speaking with her hands with light, fluttery movements. It's a little distracting, so it's not until she stops that I process the scope of what she's said.

"You're saying the Apocalypse began during my memory lapse?" I clarify. "And a secret organization took over while the government was overwhelmed." Of all the things I've heard, this is the first piece of information that makes me *less* confused, not more.

"In essence," she replies. "But the Apocalypse will not succeed. The Guild will. And the Guild did not *take over* the government. They only govern their own."

"Right," I say. "And what's this about informing the public about *pending* natural disasters?"

"We have the ability to predict them with incredibly high success."

I balk. "Seriously? Like what? Earthquakes and things?"

"Yes."

"How?"

"Disaster prediction is primarily due to classified technology developed by the Guild."

"Predicting disasters is classified...?" I say, frowning. "And with all this fancy technology, does the Guild know what's *causing* these disasters? How did they get out of control to begin with?"

Kiera's expression finally lacks confidence, as does her tone when she replies, "We do not. It's a mystery."

"That's a letdown," I say. "Sooo... What are the long term plans? Are they going to stop the disasters or are we all just going to keep running from them?"

"They will be stopped."

Her conviction in that statement is obvious. "Whatever you say," I reply. I tap my chin. "Riddle me this then: the Guild is busy predicting natural disasters, talking to the government, relief efforts... but they still manage to have enough people to send you here, to *Missouri*. To be my caseworker. What's up with that?" I still can't believe I ended up in Missouri. Although if there was an exodus from California, I guess I had to choose *somewhere*. At least that part makes sense...

"The Guild sent me here because you are a Prime Human."

I stare at her. "Say what?"

"You're supernaturally gifted. When I said the Guild had capable people, this is what I meant. It is made up of what we call Prime Humans, people who have superhuman talents. The Guild, above all, takes great interest in furthering human possibility. Progress is our greatest weapon against natural disasters."

She sounds like a promotional poster. She buys what she's selling alright, but I don't think she fully hears what she's saying anymore. "Human possibility?" I say. "What, like X-men? Experimentation?"

She laughs. "Not evolution. And no iffy science. Prime Human capability arose from the energy world."

"Energy world...?" I say, and if Kiera weren't sitting in range of me I'd question her legitimacy as a therapist and my case worker. But whatever she's talking about, she buys it one hundred percent.

"Yes. A very real place, superimposed on *this* reality, giving our world life and intelligence. If you've ever heard of chakras, auras, life forces, or souls, all of these ideas came from theories about the energy world. Life force abilities are a result of realizing the power available in the energy world."

That sounds like a bunch of malarky. But something about what she's saying is familiar and I can't put my finger on it.

"Dina!" I gasp suddenly, sitting up but immediately falling back because my shoulder protests.

Kiera flinches at my outburst.

"Like energy therapy?" I burst, excited to finally be hearing something that connects to the things I *do* remember.

She nods. "You're familiar with it?"

"Yes! One of my last memories was having a consult with someone named Dina about it!" I gush as my appointment with Dina comes back to me easily and suddenly. "She worked for a company called Pneuma-something. It was supposed to be an allergy study, but she said they used energy therapy as the treatment."

"Really?" she says, perplexed.

"Yeah! She said it didn't involve skin-contact, but like, hand-waving over the body and stuff, manipulating energy. You're saying this has to do with superhuman abilities?" Okay... That part makes *no* sense.

Kiera's full lips part in amazement, and she leans toward me, says in a low voice, "I don't actually know the techniques of manifesting life force abilities, so I have no idea if what you're describing applies." Her brow furrows. "But I would advise you to not share that information, just in case. The techniques are highly confidential. Many people would like access to that knowledge."

"I don't know the techniques either," I say, and I glance at Chase who has been obediently silent. If he's here, attending this conversation with us, I'm guessing he's in on this. He must be one of these Prime Humans, too. "Like I said, she described the theory and said it was to cure my allergies, but—" My mouth parts as another part of the memory surfaces. This time I lower *my* voice when I say, "She tested me. Vision, hearing, smell, memory, personality. She *said* it was because energy therapy could have unintended benefits, but now, with what *you're* saying, the whole thing seems suspiciously coincidental."

"I would agree with you," she says, and she is clearly as flummoxed as I am.

There's more to it that I'm dying to get her opinion on, but I've never told anyone about my empathic ability. And it wasn't until my conversation with Ezra over dinner—my last memory before the woods—that I recognized my senses as far above average. But now? Now they're even better than before. I would not argue against labeling them as superhuman.

I watch and feel Kiera piece it all together mentally. I trust her, I realize. Even with her canned naiveté, her innocence and genuine intentions shine through. I'm buying what she's selling. Besides, there is no way I'm going to get to the bottom of all this on my own.

"You say you're here representing the Guild because I'm a Prime Human, and Prime Humans have superhuman powers?" I say.

She nods. "We call them life force abilities, because your life force is where they come from."

"How did you know I was a Prime Human?"

"Facial recognition."

"Really? How?"

"It's Guild technology. You were originally at a different hospital, logged as a Jane Doe. Our system picked up the alert and identified you as a Prime. We had you transferred here, a hospital with more resources."

"That's fancy... What about my face said Prime Human?"

"Your bone structure had enough of a match to your parents, which are listed in our database. That means that both of your parents had life force abilities. And that means you do as well."

My eyes widen. "No kidding." I want to ask what ability my mom had, because I remember no such thing, but I'm getting off-track and I'm more interested in how I ended up here and where I've been the *last two and a half years*.

Gah! It gets more surreal every time I think it.

I catch Chase's eye again. "And you're a Prime Human, too?"

He nods energetically.

I look at Kiera. "Okay. You're saying I inherited abilities from my parents. Does that mean you know what abilities I possess?"

Kiera lifts her dark eyebrows knowingly and grins. "You're testing me. I can understand that."

I shrug. "Seems like a pretty sure-fire way to know if you're telling the truth."

"I would think being an empath would also be helpful," she says, meeting my challenge.

I nod, impressed.

"And I am quite sure you possess an additional ability, but I haven't been made privy to that information."

"Daaaaah," Chase interjects, and it's obvious from the sound that he means to say, 'Daaaang!' also impressed with Kiera's knowledge.

"Why?" I say.

"All life force abilities are confidential until a person either releases the information to the database or they pass away. I'll look further into it tonight."

"If I tell you does it remain confidential or does telling you automatically make it public?"

"I'm your therapist," she says. "Nothing you tell me will be added to the Prime Human database."

"Okay. Does the name Pneumatikon mean anything to you?" I ask, *finally* recalling the whole name of the company where Dina worked.

She shakes her head. "I also don't know how allergies relate to the energy world. But it's not my area of expertise. With your permission I'll request a consult though."

"Sure. Do abilities ever… improve? Change?" I say.

Chase makes a sound and I look at him first. He nods with wide eyes.

"They do," Kiera says. "First, in adolescence usually, as you become more aware of them and mature in your understanding of how life force abilities work and can manifest. They can also improve gradually throughout your life. But *very* gradually. Usually too little to notice. I think both Chase and I are assuming you are asking because you have experienced a notable improvement?"

"Notable. Yeah. My empathic ability used to only work with skin contact. It has a range now. Five or six feet maybe?"

"Wow!" Kiera says, her surprise getting the better of her professionalism. She clears her throat to play it off. "That's quite impressive. I'd call it more like an evolution than an improvement. I've never heard of an ability changing that drastically, and so late in life."

"Wooooo," Chase says.

Forget confidentiality. I like Kiera. And Chase. I trust them, so I say, "I don't know when it happened. Sometime in the last two and a half years? Also, I have super-senses. Sight, smell, hearing. That's my other skill. But now my senses are at least twice as good as they were before. Before my memory loss."

Kiera gasps and she leans forward in her chair. "*All three?*"

"Three what? Senses? Yeah."

"And they all improved *that much?*"

"Umm, yeah?" I say. "What gives?"

Kiera blinks, thinking. I can hear her pulse increase. She looks at me, places her hands in her lap. "First of all, super-senses are extremely rare, and I know they are closely tied to the energy world. And in every case I've heard of, people only posses one of them. I've never heard of someone having two super-senses, let alone three." She holds up her hands. "But again, *so* not my area."

"Super-senses are rare?" I say skeptically. "That's like, the first thing you think of when you hear the word 'superpower.' There are plenty of animals with way better senses than humans, so it's not so fantastical. I'd think something like telekinesis would be more rare."

She shrugs. "Telekinesis is comparatively common. As I said, improvement within such a short time is highly unusual, but I've never personally known someone with super-senses..." She shakes her head. "I am definitely going to need that consult sooner rather than later."

"Okay. For now, can you tell me more about the Guild? Besides finding me at a random hospital and identifying me as Prime Human from my bone structure, what else are they good at?"

"All kinds of things. Anything that puts to use life force abilities. Medical advancement is a big deal. The Guild has developed and distributed a number of cures and new treatments for various ailments."

My mouth opens. "Are you—? Is that what happened to my diabetes?"

"You're diabetic?" she says.

"My whole life," I say, "until now, apparently. The nurse said my glucose has been normal."

Kiera flips through her tablet. "There's nothing about you having diabetes or receiving the cure in your file. It's widely available now, but they keep strict records of who has gotten it."

She shakes her head after another minute of searching. "I have no idea. Something isn't lining up here. That two and a half year missing chunk is going to make it really hard for me to answer your questions. For now though, it would be best for you if you kept everything we've talked about a secret. Including your name. The world is an even less-trusting place than it used to be. And there are people out there interested in getting rid of Prime Humans."

"I'm actually glad I'm not the only confused one around here," I say. "After this talk though, I can say I am slightly less-so. I'm really looking forward to meeting this Claude guy. With any luck, he can point me in the right direction."

Chase points at the side of his head and makes a circular motion with his finger, which is easy to translate.

"Claude is crazy?" I say to him.

He nods.

"You've met him?"

He nods.

"He came here?"

He nods again.

"Is he the one that you said came to see me?"

More nodding.

Kiera frowns. "I don't like that someone was able to get in to see you without being logged at the desk."

"Not like it's a prison," I point out.

"Well I'm still going to speak with them," Kiera says, standing and tucking the strap of her satchel over her shoulder. "Now that I know more about you, I'm not taking chances. If you guys will excuse me, I have a lot of research ahead of me tonight."

I nod.

"I'll see you tomorrow morning," she says as she clicks out of the room, shutting the door behind her again.

I turn to Chase. "Tell me about Claude. Other than him being crazy."

He clicks his pen, leans over his notebook. This time he draws a picture. It's a stick figure with an exaggerated beard. He draws what looks like a tent over him. Around the tent he draws lots of trees.

"Claude lives in the woods in a tent?" I say.

Chase nods. He draws what at first seems to be a bunch of L-shapes everywhere around the tent. Then I realize they're guns. He keeps drawing them, more and more of them all over the page.

"Oh my gosh, is he a prepper or something?" I laugh.

Chase smiles and nods. Then he draws a curlycue of smoke coming from the stick-figure's mouth.

"He smokes?" I say, thinking that's not a very relevant fact.

Chase draws one more thing: the unmistakable shape of a marijuana leaf.

I giggle. "How do you know he stockpiles guns and smokes weed anyway? Are you totally pulling my leg?"

He waves his hand in front of his wrinkled nose like he smells something bad.

"He smelled like weed?"

He nods.

"Why does that make him crazy?"

He stands up, pulls the curtain partition that was separating our two beds when I woke up. Then he plops back down in the chair near my bed, cups his ear like he's listening.

"You heard him through the curtain. When did he come?" I ask.

"Waah nyte," Chase says.

"Last night? What was he saying that you overheard? He was with someone?"

He shakes his head, holds up a single finger. Then he leans over his notebook for a moment while I crane my neck to see what he's writing.

Tried 2 wake U. Kept asking Y U in woods, who R U. Over & over. Left U presents.

Chase rolls his eyes. He jabs his finger at the stick figure in the picture, then makes the crazy sign again. He reaches for his backpack, unzips it. He holds it open for me to see. His bag contains a pile of various handguns.

My jaw drops. "Oh my gosh!" I hiss. "He left me *guns*?"

Chase laughs in his awkward, low gurgle, pulls them out, lays them on my bed one by one; two small guns and one larger one. I shrink away. Guns scare the crap out of me. There are actually only three, each with it's own holster. And a knife. Chase pulls it out. It's about eight inches. A nasty-looking thing.

"What the crap?" I exclaim. "Why would he give me guns and a knife?"

Chase holds his hands out, clearly in a 'told you so' fashion. Then he makes the crazy sign again.

"No kidding," I say. "And you didn't tell anyone about the guns?"

Chase waves a hand. "Nahh," he says. He writes slowly and carefully, present for you. want 2 c your face.

"Okay, okay. Can you put them back now? Geez, last thing I need is the nurse coming in here and seeing the arsenal."

Chase laughs weirdly again as he puts the guns back in the pack. Then he holds it out to me. "Fah oooo."

"Just—put it in the closet or something," I say, waving my hand at it so he'll get it away from me.

He can't seem to stop laughing at my discomfort as he walks over to the closet and deposits the pack in there.

"You think this is soooo funny, don't you?" I scowl.

He nods with a giant grin.

"You probably should have told someone about all the guns," I say. "Kiera at least. Pretty sure fifteen-year-olds shouldn't be touching firearms."

He glares at me for the first time. "Nah fiteen!"

"Then how old are you?"

He holds up ten fingers and then eight.

"Eighteen…" I say, skeptical. He does *not* look that old at all.

He points to me, then to himself, crosses his fingers, indicating we're tight. Then he writes on a new page carefully. He holds up the notebook. It says, DYAD.

"I don't know what that is," I say.

He writes again, his movements more abrupt. Apparently he can't control his motor skills that well, which is why he short-hands. The faster he tries to do it the less legible it is. He holds the notebook up.

u will.

"A dyad wouldn't be anything romantic, would it?" I say, still slightly convinced he's lying about his age even though his emotions are pretty insistent.

He blows an awkward raspberry, waves a dismissive hand. He writes in his notebook.

I chuckle. "Seriously? I mean, I'm glad this isn't you crushing on me, but I'm nineteen for goodness sake."

He gives me an odd look. Then he points to me, flashes ten fingers twice, and then two fingers.

I slump. "Right. I'm twenty-two."

Two and a half years…

Five

I touch a faint line by my eye. The beginning of a wrinkle maybe? I look different, and it's not just the oddly shorn head—although I could swear the stubble is redder than I've ever seen my hair before. Maybe it's that my skin is a little more tan. I turn my face different angles in the mirror. I close my eyes and run my hands over my cheeks. I think they're slightly less round. My body is different. Curvier? I'd like it if it didn't make me feel my missing years more.

"Who are you?" I whisper to my reflection.

Twenty-two. So much time entirely unaccounted for... It seems more likely that someone or something took over my body during that time—a terrifying possibility, but at least it's logical. How do you live for two point five years and have it all suddenly erased without even an inkling? How is that possible?

And why has no one come to see me but the loony guy from the woods? Did no one else know I went into the woods? What was I doing there?

And where is Ezra?

I finger the supple leather of the tan trench coat draped over the bathroom counter. It was cut off of me in the emergency room, and most of the back of it is stained brown from blood. When Kiera left last night, she had my personal effects delivered to my room. The coat was obviously once beautiful, but I never would have been able to afford such a coat in the life I recall. I was also wearing black jeans and a white tank over a black bra. And black combat boots. The boots are my only intact possession. I would never have chosen to wear any of these things. How did my tastes change so drastically?

I sigh. Who cares, really? After a night in the hospital—*not* passed out—my concerns have shifted massively. There is something bigger than my missing memory to worry about: the natural disasters. When Kiera told me, it was merely an idea. But the idea has taken on the solidity of reality. I've overheard people beyond my room talking. Nurses at the station, other patients, televisions.

Earthquakes, tornadoes, fires, bizarre weather patterns, drought, unrelenting rain, *freak lightning storms*… I've been up all night, tossing and turning, and listening. I can hear everything on every floor, which shocked me all by itself, but then I became distracted by the conversations. In large part, all talk is of this new world of upended lives and a constantly rising death-toll. The Guild is a common topic, but it doesn't sound like regular people know much about them. Fear is rampant, though tightly controlled and confined to private, whispered conversations. The hospital is a bedlam of gossip. Everything feels on the edge of chaos.

The disasters themselves I can stomach, but I also learned of a group called Fia. Their interest seems to focus on one thing: the eradication of Prime Humans. I need to ask Chase about it when he wakes up. I've caught that it's based somewhere in California, which is the other reason the place is off-limits. If you are a Prime Human, California is the most dangerous place you can be. Although Fia doesn't keep to themselves. They pop up all over the country, round up Primes wherever they can find them and execute them before disappearing once more. But Primes aren't the only ones in danger. Fia kills anyone who protects or sympathizes with Primes, too.

What this means is that anyone from California is a suspected member of Fia. I'm from California and I said as much to the nurse yesterday. She apparently leaked my origin to the rest of the hospital, and I've heard myself referred to more than once. And not in nice ways.

These people have lost their minds. I can't believe how easily they have put me on the side of the enemy. But if the televisions I've been hearing are an accurate indication, it's not humanity against the world. It's humanity against itself. This frightens me more than lightning storms and earthquakes.

I don't feel safe here. I begin to wonder if that's why Claude brought me weapons. If he did, then he had to have known something about me in order to think I needed to protect myself. I want to meet him more than ever.

Weapons or no, I want out of here. I'm glad Chase is sharing my room. His presence has a visceral effect on me. I feel secure, capable, and positive about the future. Even when I hear the nurses whispering about me, I'm able to keep my fears manageable.

I hear him stirring, and I open the door to find him sitting up, head in hands. My stomach quivers in anxiety to see him visibly upset. I move slowly toward his bed. "Are you okay?"

He looks up, blinks for a second; the tension definitely belongs to him. He takes a deep breath. He holds his hands palm to palm and against the side of his head to sign 'sleep.' He shakes his head and makes a face.

"You didn't sleep well?"

He pulls his stick legs over the side of his bed. He's on the unhealthy side of thin, visible through his sweats, I've noticed. I don't even know why he's in the hospital with me, I realize. I assumed he was on a team with Kiera to approach me about the Guild, but he is obviously disabled.

He shoves his socked feet into a pair of worn tennis shoes under his bed. Then he grabs a plastic bag of clothes, digs in it and pulls out a sweatshirt.

An edge of panic seizes me. "Where are you going?" I say.

He pauses before putting on his shirt, gives me a questioning look.

"I don't want to be alone," I say, sitting on the very end of his bed. "The nurses are freaking me out."

He points to the clock, then to his mouth, which he opens and closes as if talking.

I grab his notebook from the bedside table and slap it on the bed. "I don't know what you're saying."

He takes it. *Appt,* he writes. Then he points at his mouth.

"A speech therapy appointment?" I ask. Oh, so he's not just here for *me*...

He starts putting his sweatshirt on again.

"Why are you in the hospital anyway?" I ask.

He pulls the sweatshirt down. I notice it says 'Brickwood Falconry Club' above the image of a hawk.

He turns his head, points to a long scar on the left side.

He writes, *shunt out.*

"Ahh. So you had a brain injury?"

He nods and slaps himself in the back of the head over the scar, letting his head jerk forward.

"You hit your head."

He shakes his head, mimes swinging a baseball bat.

"You got hit with a baseball bat?"

He nods.

"You play baseball?"

He looks at me a little critically, and I think the answer is no, but he isn't inviting my questions so he doesn't *actually* answer. Instead he stands up. I realize he hasn't smiled at all this morning, and I'm especially on edge as a result. He's about to leave though, so as futile as it may be, I want to stall him. "Chase, what is Fia?"

His eyes go wide, and I perceive his suspicion, then his fear.

"I heard a lot of people talking about it last night." I point to my ears. "Super hearing and all. I'm a little freaked out and I don't want to be left alone."

He looks at me, hesitates, looks around the room as he considers something. Then he sighs and sits back down on his bed. He takes his notebook, and in careful letters writes:

Prime Human Insurgency Alliance = PHIA =

And then he lifts his shirt up to reveal his bare chest. There, branded in the very center is:

$$\Phi$$

I gasp, not sure if I should be afraid, but from Chase I feel fear, so I don't think Chase is from PHIA. And the look on his face doesn't say he hates Prime Humans and wants them to die. He points to the symbol on his chest, then makes the baseball bat swinging motion again and points to his scar.

"PHIA hit you in the head?" I ask.

He nods, writes, Left me 4 dead. They brand kills.

He doesn't look at me, but down at the paper. I'm speechless. And outraged—Chase's anger.

"I'm sorry," I croak finally.

He finally looks up and gives me a wan smile.

"You said insurgency... So that means... they *used* to be Prime Humans or something, right?" I say.

They still are, he writes. Not all Primes R Guild. PHIA used 2 B.

My brow furrows. Used to be? What on earth made them decide to murder their own kind?

Chase slaps his notebook shut, points to the clock.

I nod. "Appointment. I know."

He stands up, and I say, "What's your Prime Human ability anyway?"

He grins, puts the fingertips of both hands to his head and then explodes them outward.

"Reverse empath?" I say, having already sort of guessed something like that. I'd suspected Chase's effect on me was not merely my own empathic ability. "You affect the room with whatever you're feeling."

He nods, lifting his eyebrows at me and smiling. He points at himself and then me. Then he wraps his index and middle finger around each other like he did last night.

"Seeya later, Chase," I say, grinning.

Once he leaves, his effect lingers for a little while and I marvel at how noninvasive his ability is. I hadn't noticed how powerful it was until now with him gone. After twenty minutes or so, the tightness in my chest returns, growing stronger all the time until I become convinced that something terrible is going to happen. Paranoia sends me back into the bathroom, and this time I bring the backpack of weapons with me. There I listen for any sign that a crew of nurses are going to storm my room with pitchforks. This belief isn't logical, I tell myself. But I can't seem to get past it.

I hear footsteps, and I peek through the crack I've left between the bathroom and my room to see who it is. I recognize the click of heels first, so when a head of tight curls follows, I'm not surprised.

I open the door, so relieved to see Kiera I could cry.

"Oh, there you are," she says, turning around and throwing her hands out excitedly. Then her eyes go wide. "Good grief, Wendy, you look terrible. Did you not sleep okay?"

I motion for her to shut the door, and then I sit on the edge of my bed.

"What's wrong?" she asks, taking a stool nearby.

"These people hate me," I say softly. "They know I'm from California and I hear them whispering about me. They think I'm part of those maniacs, PHIA—which I also know about now. Everyone's afraid. I had no idea… When you talked about the disasters, I was thinking just… disasters, right? But it's more than that. People are losing their humanity. They're on edge. The tension is killing me. I can't stay here. You've got to get me out of here."

Kiera leaps to her feet. "They know where you're from? How? I thought I told you not— Never mind." She whips out her phone, taps a number and puts it to her ear.

It rings once. I hear the female voice that answers, *"Oh hi, Kiera. I called you earlier about—"*

"Lainey, they know she's from California," Kiera says, voice higher.

"How? Didn't you tell her not to mention it? Ignore that. I'll arrange a transfer. For now, get her out of there."

"Done." Kiera snaps her phone shut, whips around, smiling like everything is hunky dory.

"Cut the crap. I heard her," I say.

She frowns. "Oh, right. Hearing. Gather your things." She hands me the bag she came in with. "Good thing I brought you clothes."

I take it from her and go back into the bathroom. After putting on the jeans Kiera brought and managing to put my feet in the well-worn combat boots, I turn to the complicated task of getting a shirt on while my arm is in a sling.

I've finally figured out that there's no way to do it without taking off the sling, when, with my paranoid ears, I hear, *"Where are you keeping the girl who was found in the woods?"*

My head snaps up. Panic grips me. My eyes flash to the backpack of weapons. I snatch it up, but can only carry it over my left shoulder, my right shoulder unable to bear weight.

I dive for the bathroom door. "Someone is downstairs looking for me and they don't sound friendly!" I hiss to Kiera, who has her phone to her ear. I've heard her talking to someone about arranging an escort.

"Do you know who?"

I shake my head, still listening to the now-menacing voice downstairs. "But they sound like they're threatening the receptionist, so I don't want to stay and find out!"

She nods. "We'll take the stairs." Then the two of us head out the door.

Kiera knows the way, and she leads me past several nurses in the hall, all of which look at me longer than I'd like. I try not to appear that I'm running for my life, but I don't think it helps. Thankfully we reach the door to the stairs; Kiera pushes us through.

"Can you tell where they are?" Kiera asks quietly as we shuffle quickly down the steps. We have four flights to descend.

"He's headed up. With one other person, I think," I reply. "He's telling his partner—assistant maybe?—that this hospital harbors Primes, and that it should be burned to the ground once they're done. Oh my God, is he serious?"

"Guild help us, I don't doubt it," Kiera says, her voice now trembling, too. "How did they know you were here?" she whispers, but it's to herself.

"Then we need to warn the people here, don't we?" I say.

"I'll make a call once we're out," she says as we reach the first floor.

"A *call*?" I say. "The guy could have a firing squad outside ready to move into action and you're going to *call* someone?"

"What else would you like me to do?" Kiera asks, turning to me before exiting.

The weight of the weapons in the pack on my shoulder nags me with an idea. "Here's the plan: You're going to go get your car. Bring it around the front and be ready for me."

"But my instructions are to make sure you're secure!"

"Screw your instructions! We're talking about a hospital full of people they want to destroy just because *I'm* here. We're on our way out, so let's at least make it harder for the bad guys!" I push her toward the door.

Kiera protests only once more before giving up and running down one of two halls. I take the opposite direction. At the very first fire alarm I come to, I stop and yank it downward. Then I run, looking for the next one. It's around the next corner. I yank it down. I do this one more time before someone spots me.

"Hey!" says a guy in a white lab coat. Must be a doctor.

I ignore him, now running and pulling every fire alarm I see. I disappear around a corner. There are more people here, and I stop abruptly before reaching them, kneeling down to pull the zipper on the pack with my stationary arm. I pull out the biggest gun, and throw the pack back on my shoulder. I hold my arm tightly to my side and the gun in front of me, feeling zero confidence in using it as anything but a prop as I yell, "Stay away! Out of my way!"

People immediately start screaming and running, which is perfect, serving my purpose to get people out of the building and the authorities here as quickly as possible.

I alternate between screaming threats and pulling every fire alarm I encounter. People are in a frenzy, running between rooms or behind doors and slamming them shut to get away from me. I keep moving. I must be a sight. I only have a hospital gown for a shirt, not having gotten the chance to put on the shirt Kiera brought. The backpack hangs awkwardly on my arm because I can't get it to stay on my one shoulder, and a gun is held tightly in my left hand.

Gosh, I look ridiculous.

I find myself backtracking, and I nearly run right into a group of three orderlies. "Get back!" I bellow at them. They do, falling against the corner as I pass, hands in the air, fear on their faces. I keep turning around and around to make sure no one tries to take advantage of my turned back.

The reality is I'm terrified. I think if I hadn't been so on edge this morning about my safety, there is no way I could bring myself to hold a gun to people. My finger isn't even on the trigger though, not that anyone's looking. They see crazy California girl with a gun, and they scream and run.

One last fire alarm and I see a familiar hall that Kiera ran down to get out. I run full speed, the bag slapping my legs clumsily as it hangs from my arm.

I reach the lobby, a spacious, high-ceilinged room with a fountain and tower of live plants. A group of security guards is gathered near the reception desk, and I immediately hide the gun. I expect them to turn on me, but I can see their attention is on a woman in a white blouse slumped over the desk. A pool of blood has started gathering beneath her on the beige tile.

I don't realize I've frozen, staring at it, until someone screams my name.

I whip my head toward the voice, expecting to see Kiera, but instead spot a huge person launching themselves toward me. I don't get to react. They've picked me up and leapt back toward the doors before I can think. But I finally spot Kiera's fear-stricken face under the arm of the guy carrying me. She flings the door open for me and... whoever is carrying me. He's a giant of a man, not in height, but in breadth. He carries me as if I weigh nothing, running across the circular drive in front of the hospital and hanging a right. I cling to the gun in my hand as well as the bag on my arm as pain sears my right shoulder. I bite back a shriek.

I can barely make out Kiera over his shoulder because my vision is blurring from the agony. I think she's falling behind, and I hit him with the butt of my weapon. "Slow down!" I gasp. I yell Kiera's name, but it comes out more like a scream of agony. I probably ripped my stitches.

After several more paces, he stops abruptly and then throws me into the backseat of a car. I can't move, curled up on my side as I heave breaths through the agony in my shoulder. I pinch my eyes shut, but they're leaking tears.

I hear two car doors shut.

"W—Are you okay?" Kiera puffs.

The car lurches forward as I nod, and it takes all my effort to brace myself around the turns.

My thoughts suddenly turn to Chase...

"Chase!" I cry, my eyes flashing open. "Oh no! We left him! We need to make sure he's alright! Kiera—" I struggle to sit up, holding my right arm tightly, gritting my teeth, cold sweat beading my forehead.

"We're not going back," Kiera says firmly from the passenger seat in front, her face red, obviously winded. "And his appointment was off-site. He's probably not going back either. Thanks to your warning. All Primes in the area will be on high alert."

My shoulder is still burning, but at least I can talk through it now. "The bloody body in the lobby will probably warn them away as well," I say, relieved that wherever Chase is, it's better than our room where the nasty man was headed, looking for me.

"A body?" Kiera says, turning entirely in her seat. Her eyes finally fall on the gun on the seat next to me. "Good grief, is that a *gun*?" she says in a high-pitched voice. "Where did that come from?"

"Chase," I say. "Came from my friend in the woods. And yeah, there was a body. That's what all those security dudes at the desk were looking at."

Kiera covers her mouth, turns back, face-forward until all I can see is her black curls. She shakes her head, horrified.

The big dude in the driver's seat clears his throat. "Hey ladies, I'm Mike. Someone wanna fill me in on what just happened?"

Six

I apologize for the abrupt meeting," Kiera says, turning to our driver, Mike. "You were showing as the closest capable operative in the area. I couldn't believe I got lucky enough that a proprietary mission specialist was so close by. I know you're on furlough, but it was an emergency. Thank you for responding so quickly. I had no idea what kind of backup they brought and I needed to make sure I got her out of there. It was a priority level ten."

"Ten?" he says, shocked. I see him glance at me in the rearview mirror. I've gotten a few looks at his face since we've been driving. Square jaw, sharp eyes that are always scanning, hispanic, and stupidly handsome. "Who are you and why are you a priority level ten?" he asks me.

"Heck if I know," I say.

"Don't answer that," Kiera snaps. "And you know better than to ask," she says to him.

Mike grunts something that sounds and feels like annoyed affirmation.

"Where are we going?" I ask, looking out at a town that appears normal by all accounts.

"My dyad is arranging a rendezvous; we're waiting for her call."

"What about my… appointment?"

She looks back at me blankly.

"With… my *friend*?" I say purposefully.

Her eyes light with sudden recognition. "Oh! Yes. Right. We'll arrange it for another time."

"I'm not leaving here until I talk to him," I say stubbornly, picking the gun up from the seat and putting it into the backpack once more. I'm going to have to thank Claude for the timely gift— after I interrogate him about it.

"It's not safe!" Kiera says, her eyes following the gun from my hands into the pack.

I glare at her, purse my lips challengingly.

She fidgets in frustration. "Your safety is a priority level ten! How do you expect me to explain to my superiors that I kept you in the danger zone so you could talk to a crazy pothead?"

"I don't even know what a level ten is!" And then I laugh. "Well, Kiera, if you're uncomfortable with letting me stick around to chat with the guy, I expect you to pluck Mister Baker out of his wigwam and bring him to me instead."

"But—! I can't force the man out of his home! He's not exactly what you'd call cooperative!"

"Oh relax, Kiera. Just bring Mary Jane along. It'll be fine."

She huffs in indignation.

Mike laughs.

"But really," I say, "the easier solution is to swing by and let me have a chat with him before we go."

"Sounds that way to me," Mike says. "Hey, this mandatory furlough is boring the crap out of me. You bring me along and I'll back you up…" he taunts. "We can leave right now. Where is this guy?"

"I can't bring you along on anything without clearance," Kiera says.

"I've done security detail for the Council before. That takes the highest clearance," Mike replies.

Kiera's phone rings. She puts it to her ear. The same female voice from earlier—Lainey, I think I remember—says, *'I've got people waiting at the address I just texted you. Be there in fifteen minutes. They'll escort you to the airstrip.'*

"Kiera…" I warn.

She sighs. "I'm not sure we're going to make that rendezvous. She's refusing to leave unless we go see her, ah, friend from the woods."

'Tell her she doesn't get a choice,' I hear Lainey's voice say icily. *'Doesn't she get how dire the situation is? Who is going to protect her if you guys get in trouble? They've got their hands full with the hospital.'*

"I did. And she does. The thing is, I scanned for a nearby operative back at the hospital—for help since you guys were so far out—and I found one. He came in and helped me get her out safely. He's a proprietary mission specialist. And he's willing."

'*Who is it?*' Lainey asks. '*I'll see if I can get him clearance.*'

"His name is Mike," Kiera says. She looks over at him. "Mike…?"

"Dumas," Mike replies.

'*Tell me I heard that wrong. Did he just say Dumas?*' Lainey replies.

"Yesss?" Kiera says questioningly.

"*Kiera… Dumas was Andre Gellagher's dyad. Gosh, don't you check these things before you jump in with both feet?*"

Kiera's face pales, noticeable even with her brown skin. She stares at Mike, her mouth open wide.

"Who is Andre?" I ask. "And I keep hearing this word dyad. What is it?"

"So my reputation precedes me," Mike says playfully. "Excellent. Then you know I'm the badass you need."

'*Tell him thanks, but there's no way he's going to get approved to escort you guys. He's supposed to be on furlough,*' Lainey says.

"Why are you on furlough?" I ask Mike.

"An injury," he replies.

"You don't look injured," I say.

"Hmm, looking, are you?" Mike says, straightening his shoulders and puffing his chest out—as if he really needs to.

I roll my eyes. "You take up half the car, dude. You're in the way no matter where I look."

I miss the exchange between Kiera and Lainey before they hang up.

"They said no," Kiera says to Mike. Then she turns to me. "She says they'll assign us someone at the rendezvous point and you'll get your visit before we go."

"No?" Mike says, irritated. "How could they say no? It's a local mission. It's easy. It's what I'm good at. What's the problem?"

"Who is Andre?" I say again.

"Andre is the leader of PHIA," Kiera says, glancing at Mike.

It's my turn to be shocked. "And a dyad… Is that like a partner?"

Kiera nods. "Guild operatives function in pairs. People are paired with individuals intended to be their checks and balances—makes for good, autonomous, decision-making. That was my dyad on the phone."

"And mine was a psychopath," Mike says flippantly. "Which I warned my superiors of repeatedly until the guy lost his marbles and went on a bloody rampage and outed himself as the next Hitler. Can I say that I am the only one *not* surprised how he turned out?"

"Wow…" I say. "My week is just full of bizarre surprises."

"You too, huh?" Mike says, looking in the mirror. "At least you get to do something exciting."

I'm not sure I believe him about wanting excitement, because his statement was accompanied by the pangs of a tragedy, I'd say a recent one.

"Turn here," Kiera says, interrupting my observation of Mike's feelings. "We're close."

"Here's hoping Mister Baker has less excitement and more answers," I say.

"His last name isn't Baker," Kiera says. "Mike, about a mile and a half ahead. It's a grocery store."

Mike and I laugh at Kiera at the same time, catching each others' eyes in the mirror.

"Baker is slang for pothead," I tell her.

"Oh…" Kiera says.

"Who is this guy, anyway?" Mike says.

"Shh!" Kiera snaps her fingers at Mike.

"Someone who saved my life, apparently," I say as Mike pulls into the grocery store parking lot.

"Looks like getting saved happens to you a lot," Mike says. "You should request personal protection from the Guild."

"Sounds like a good idea," I say, opening my door after Kiera. "Thanks for earlier. Seeya."

After Kiera shuts her door, and before I can get out, Mike leans into the back seat, "They take requests, you know… As a level ten, you'd probably get your pick."

I don't miss his double meaning. Clearly he's asking me to request that he be my protection, but he's also saying it in a way that's sort of suggestive. "Mike Dumas," I say, "Are you pimping yourself out to me?"

He whistles playfully. "I suggested protection. But you take it how you want. I'm just letting you know, I'm for hire." He smiles at me.

I smile flirtatiously back. "I'll keep it in mind. Hopefully you've recovered from your… *injury* by then."

Seven

*I*didn't get a chance to tell you what I learned," Kiera says, opening the cooler at her feet and nudging it toward me. It's full of drinks and snacks.

"Excellent," I say, grabbing a container of grapes and feeling off about not testing my glucose before putting them in my mouth. I'm having a hard time believing my diabetes is *cured,* gone forever.

We're riding in the back of a car along with an armed man and woman who have been assigned to accompany us to where Claude lives in the woods. It's a two and a half hour trip from Lebanon where we were to Van Buren, the town closest to where I was pulled out of the woods. It's a beautiful drive, although we've passed lots of woodland areas that have been scorched recently. Kiera told me there were multiple lightning storms on the same night, spread all over southern Missouri. It was quite the phenomenon, but people are becoming less awestruck by those. The Apocalypse really is upon us.

"I was up most of the night, making calls and digging. I wish I had more to show for it," she says. "But someone with much higher clearance than me intercepted all the consults I requested."

I swallow. "What's that mean?"

"I made a lot of requests for classified information last night, and I guess it flagged something. Not really surprising. Then I got the notification that your case had become a level ten. Basically *my* immediate boss says it's out of mine and his hands. I'm to get you to the Interior Hub, and someone else is going to take over. I'm to be your therapist and help you through your transition and that's it."

I don't like the sound of that. I swallow and give her a look. "I thought you had something to tell me. But then you're saying they wouldn't let you at any information."

"Nothing that wasn't already public to the Guild in general. I can tell you that your brother isn't listed in our Prime Human Database."

"So he's not Prime Human?" I say.

"If you share the same parentage, he has to be," Kiera says. "He had a life force ability, didn't he?"

"Ezra's basically a math genius," I say. "Does that count?"

"Absolutely. In fact, most life force abilities are enhanced mental functions that allow for 'genius' capability."

I reminisce for a moment over one of my last memories of talking to Ezra about what was considered a superpower. He said smarts didn't count. But apparently to the Guild they do. If he was here I would totally rub it in his face... But he's not. The grapes go sour in my mouth.

"I did some other investigation at that point," Kiera says, "searching for information on him *outside* the Guild, and I found his social security record, his national test scores—he is definitely brilliant. He attended San Jose Science and Technology Academy at least in 2013 and 14. Records—"

"Wait, a *private* school?" I say. No way could I have afforded something like that.

Kiera nods.

"I was *not* that well off."

"If the school weren't in California, I could track down who paid for it," Kiera says. "But everything there is just really hard to get at. I can't find where he was last living, which probably means California. I also can't find credit records, so he never took out a loan. He has nothing showing in the national medical record database, which means he never had health problems. He never filed taxes. Never had a passport. He got a California driver's license when he turned sixteen, and he never got in an accident. Perfect SAT score in 2013."

I blink. I don't remember any of these things. "What does not being listed in the Prime Human database mean?" I say.

"Usually, if someone isn't listed, it means the Guild didn't know they existed," Kiera says.

"But you're saying they knew *I* existed?"

She nods. "What you've got to understand is that there is a public database, which any member of the Guild has access to. And there's a confidential database, made available only to the Council, which are the twelve people that govern the Guild. They don't make every Prime Human's business available to everyone. Everything about you remains confidential until you release it to the public database. It's standard courtesy to all Prime Humans, member or not. The only info I was given on you was that both your parents had life force abilities and that most likely you were at least an empath. I wasn't even told who your parents were to protect your privacy. My job was to approach you and offer our help."

"Alright," I say, waving my hands and getting frustrated with all this information that tells me nothing helpful. "What do you actually know?"

She pulls a hair elastic from her pocket and puts her wiry curls up in a pony tail that ends up looking more like a puff-ball on top of her head. "Knowing about your super-senses made it easier to work backward. I told you it was rare. In the public database, super-vision has only been catalogued once before: Serena Blakely in the seventies. She had two sons, Robert and Carl Haricott. Robert was childless, but Carl had one daughter in 1993 according to records, but she has been unaccounted for since 1996. His ability is shown as confidential, but since abilities are usually inherited, I would guess that he inherited Serena's sight. That then led me to assume that Carl is your father. You didn't mention him, but I figured you guys aren't on speaking terms for some reason. He is also unaccounted for currently."

"Unaccounted for?" I say. "Carl *is* my father, but he's dead. He died like twenty years ago in a car accident."

Her eyebrows lift. "As far as the Guild is concerned, your father is still alive."

"Uh…" I say. "That's not possible. My mom and my dad are both dead."

She glances at me skeptically before turning a page on her notepad. "He has been bouncing in and out of our radar for years. Never joined the Guild. Last we knew, which was in January of this year, he was living in Sacramento."

My mouth is hanging open. "That… That's just… I don't even know what to say to that. To me he's been dead. What's he been *doing* with his life that had my mom telling me he was dead?"

"Your mom…" Kiera says, confused. She flips another page, checks another fact. "Wendy, according to our records your mom died in nineteen ninety-four."

"No, she didn't. She died a year ago—I mean," I stop, calculating it based on the new date. "Three and a half years ago.

Nineteen ninety-four was *twenty-one* years ago. I would have only been a year old."

Kiera's brow furrows, and her mouth twists in a fluster. "Your biological mother wasn't a Prime. She had life force enhancement. She manifested empathic ability. And she died a few years later from leukemia."

"I am so confused," I say, aggravated that *nothing* she's saying makes sense. "Are you *sure* you have the right file for me?"

Kiera's brow furrows, her eyes scanning her tablet as her hand swipes back and forth, up and down. "You say Carl Haricott was your father. This says that the mother of his only child was Regina Walden, and she was an empath. She died in 1994."

I shake my head. "My mom's name was not Regina Walden. It was Leena Whitley."

She purses her lips in consternation. "Empaths are quite common, so I suppose it's possible that he had a child by Regina, but the chances of him having a child with *another* woman that was an empath in the same year you were born…? You have been entirely unaccounted for since 1996. You never popped up when Carl did, which implies you were missing as far as he was concerned as well. So perhaps the woman who raised you… wasn't actually your biological mother?"

I open my mouth, close it, consider that… "Leena wasn't an empath…" I say, trying to imagine if maybe she was and I never knew… No, that's not possible. And in reality… I didn't look like her at all. She was a short, delicate blonde. I never see her when I look in the mirror, and I hadn't considered it odd until now. Ezra looks like her though… Do Ezra and I share *any* parentage?

"Possible…" I say finally. "But that blows my mind if it's true."

"I also know about your uncle, Robert Haricott," Kiera says.

I snap my head back up. "Right! I forgot about him. From Monterey, right?" I recall the mysterious letter from him that I read while sitting in the waiting room at Pneumatikon.

Kiera nods. "Deceased as of June of this year though… He's also listed in the Prime Human database."

"Oh…" I say, disappointed. I admit I was hoping that maybe Ezra was with him. "What was my uncle's ability?" I say curiously. How odd it is that I come from a family of superhumans.

"Foreknowledge. Apparently of unknown scope. He was very secretive about it, and he was never successfully inducted into the Guild."

"Foreknowledge…" I say, now fascinated. "He could tell the future." Something comes over me then, a sort of tangible heaviness. The hair on my arms stands up, and for a brief moment, I smell the barest inkling of something I can't put a name to at first. But the most distinct sense of deja vu comes over me. I let it rest, hoping it will develop into something concrete, but it doesn't. When I finally let go of it, I recognize the scent that has now faded: ginger.

"Did you remember something?" Kiera asks, watching me.

I shake my head. "Just… a weird feeling." I look at her. "How did he die?"

Kiera's phone beeps and she pulls it out and looks at it.

I watch her mouth make a line as realization bumps her thoughts. "Hmm," she says thoughtfully.

"What?" I demand.

"Lainey says the men at the hospital were PHIA. And you said they asked for you specifically when they arrived, right? That means they have an interest in you in particular."

"Great. I'm a target by the Neo-Nazis," I say. "*And* I'm from California. I guess *everyone* hates me." *Good night, Wendy, what did you get yourself into that you forgot about?*

"And in answer to your question, your uncle was killed by PHIA," Kiera adds.

My mouth opens in shock again. I look down at my hands, head spinning, wondering what on earth was going on with me when I ended up in those woods. My eye catches on the backpack at my feet, the one that is full of weapons from Claude. I wonder…

"Kiera, do you have a way to track weapons? Like, if you had a serial number for a gun, could you find out who it's registered to?"

"Sure," she says. "Why do you ask?"

I'm already pulling the backpack onto my lap. I unzip it, pull out the first gun my hand touches.

"Oh…" Kiera says in recognition.

"Where are gun serial numbers?" I ask, turning the weapon over in my hands.

"Reg," Kiera says to one of our guards in the passenger seat up front. "Where is the serial number on a gun?"

"Varies," Reg says. "Sometimes it's—"

"Here," I say, handing the gun up to him. "Find it on this one."

I reach into my pack for another. "And this one, too," I say, handing up one of the smaller guns.

"What?" Kiera says in surprise. "How many do you have in there?" She leans over to get a look.

"Three," I say. "And a knife."

"Right here," Reg says, his finger on the base of the barrel. "Same for the pocket pistol."

"Reg, can you have someone look up those numbers? See who they're registered to?" Kiera says.

"Sure," he says. "One sec." He whips out his phone while I pull out the knife.

The holster is black leather and it doesn't look like it goes on a belt, but rather an ankle. It doesn't have any identifying characteristics, but the knife itself is a serrated blade with a curved end. Two of the guns have holsters. One is for the larger gun. I hold up the black strap that looks kind of like a belt, but with another thinner strap coming off of it. I envision how it goes on.

"Shoulder holster, I think," Kiera says.

The other pocket pistol has a small ankle holster.

So Claude was giving me guns *and* holsters? I'm no expert but I don't think either are very cheap. Premium leather, and the guns themselves are heavy, no plastic parts.

What if...?

"Both weapons were last registered to Robert Haricott," Reg says, handing the weapons back.

I suck in a breath as I reach up to take them.

"Haricott?" Kiera says, her eyes wide with shock. "Why would—?"

"They were *mine*, Kiera," I whisper. "Claude brought me the guns because they *belonged* to me."

"You think so?" Kiera says in a high-pitched whisper.

"Has to be," I say, pulling all four weapons onto my lap. "Claude found me wearing all of these. He must have pulled them off of me before he brought me into the hospital. Not sure why... to make sure I didn't freak people out? I don't know. Must have freaked *him* out to see someone wearing so many weapons."

Pretty jolted at the possibility myself, I rub my free hand from my cheek up to my forehead and over my buzzed head. The tan leather trench coat... perfect for concealing so many weapons.

Combat boots... Geez, everything points to me being some kind of GI Jane. Funded by my uncle?

"Wow," is all Kiera can think of to say.

I stare out of the window for a while, pondering. I kept three guns and a knife on me. For protection from PHIA? Something must have gone to hell and that's why my uncle was killed. What were my dealings with him? Did I work for him? Surely, since the guns were registered to him...

"Let's hope Claude can shed some light on this," Kiera says finally, breaking through my reverie that mostly consists of visualizing what I must have looked like with my whole getup.

I turn to her. "I don't even know who I am. This is nuts."

She frowns. "You've learned a lot in the last twenty-four hours. How are you coping?" I can sense her reverting from detective mode to therapist mode.

"I'm not," I reply. "I'd like to actually get to the coping part. I'd like to learn something about myself for once that doesn't create more unknowns."

"I'm sorry I'm not helping," Kiera says sadly.

I look at her dejected face and I can tell this adventure is not what she expected. "How is it your fault?"

"I haven't done my job."

"How's that?"

"Your scope of amnesia calls for small bites of reality, not giant gulps of information. I wasn't prepared for how much of your story was unaccounted for. I took for granted that the world is entirely new to you."

I stare at her, wondering something for the first time. "You said the Guild is made up of Prime Humans. That makes you one, right? What's *your* life force ability?"

"Confidential," she says, unblinking.

I give her an expectant look.

She stares back.

"Is it like... mind control or something? If it is I have a right to know," I say. "I don't like people in my head."

"Funny coming from you," she says, smiling. "Aren't people in your head all the time now?"

I grimace. "Yeah. I haven't quite gotten used to it. When there's a bunch of people in the room it's a mess up there. But at least I know what I'm into. If you can screw with my head, it's not cool to do it to without me knowing."

"I can't screw with your head. And besides, before, when you were living a regular life in California, did you tell people you were an empath? That you could read them?"

"No…"

She shrugs. "So you were in their heads without them knowing. Allowed you to measure your words, didn't it? Take advantage of the fact that they *didn't* know. Opportunistically."

I open my mouth to protest but she holds a hand up. "Wendy, everyone has a right to take advantage of the gifts they've been given, Prime Human or not. It's not *that* you use them, it's *how* you use them. For what purpose."

I stare at her a bit longer, but it's obvious from her emotions that she's not giving in. Besides, she struck a nerve, and I have too many mysteries in my own life to add her life force ability to that list.

"I don't think you could have broken information to me any differently," I say, getting back on topic. "Don't beat yourself up."

"I could have. But I got sucked into your mystery. I wasn't given all the information for a reason. I should have left it at that. But I want the truth as much as you do it seems."

"I can tell when people are holding things back, Kiera," I remind her. "If I didn't know you were answering my questions to the best of your ability, I never would have trusted you."

"Ah," Kiera says.

"See that?" I say. "Something occurred to you and you're holding back."

"Alright, you've sold me," Kiera says. "I couldn't have used my shrink mind-tricks on you anyway." She smiles.

"Don't you forget it. And also don't forget that you just figured something out and you're going to tell me what it is."

She laughs, then sobers. "When I got the call from my supervisor, placing your case at level ten, I realized you must be a big deal to the Guild. Plus, your super-senses…" She shakes her head. "Should have known right then. But I think they assigned me to you *because* I don't know anything. My guess is the Guild is going to graduate you to someone with higher clearance after me."

"Hmm… That's a clever way for them to hide the truth from me," I say. "I really hate liars, Kiera. Your bosses haven't earned any trust from me."

"Oh you misunderstand me," Kiera insists. "It was for your

own benefit. To make sure you had a slower transition. It's for your own safety and health, Wendy. Lightning strike makes you highly susceptible to mental illness triggers. Throwing too much at you at once could easily create more problems. Please trust me on that. They handled this the best way they could. And obviously their intent was not to deceive if they have already revealed to you through me how important you are. They haven't stopped me from digging for what I could."

"Maybe so," I say. "And I'll give them a chance, but I better get some straight-talk when I get wherever we're ultimately going."

"I'm sure you will," Kiera says. "And I'm going to feel so much better when you are at one of the Guild strongholds. PHIA scares the pee out of me."

ᒆ

We reach Van Buren and then make a turn at a sign that points to Big Spring State Park. Buildings fall away to be replaced with trees. It's not long before we reach another sign pointing to Big Springs Campground.

That's where the signs of fire begin. At first it's intermittent trees scorched on one side. Then it's a massive expanse of them, blackened and fallen.

That's where I was found. Part of me wants to take a hike and check it out, to see if anything comes back to me. But Claude offers more promise. We pass the campground, which has been completely torched, and then reach a vacant parking lot surrounded by an area that looks untouched by the fires. A river runs next to it, and a sign that says "Big Spring" points to an area overlooking the water.

We get out, and I zip my coat up over my sling to escape the chill air. I walk over to a nearby placard, which says that Big Spring is one of the three largest freshwater springs in the United States. "Hmm," I wonder to myself. Was I visiting the spring for some reason? Staying at the campground? Or was this a stop on the way to somewhere else?

Kiera comes up beside me.

"So where do we find this guy?" I ask, letting my eyes wander the area.

"I was told he lives behind the ranger station," Kiera says, pointing to a path that winds behind the park station and into the trees. "He's one of the rangers."

"Stay far behind," I tell our escorts. I don't want Claude getting jumpy with all these people storming his home. I need him loose with his lips.

"Must be closed because of the fire," I say, listening to the relative silence inside the station. "Nobody is here."

We reach a fence surrounding some utility buildings, and beyond it, a cabin complete with a pile of firewood covered with a tarp. The cabin is tiny, the roof made of wood shingles covered in moss. It's perfectly quaint—and definitely not a tent like Chase claimed.

A small breeze picks up and a horrifying scent enters my nose. I stop, putting my hand out to hold Kiera back. "Wait a minute," I say, my voice starting to tremble.

Kiera picks up on my trepidation, and her chest hollows in fear. "What?" she says.

I listen. No vital signs beyond ours.

"I smell blood," I say. I look at Kiera, guessing her stomach is probably weaker than mine. "You can stay here if you need to."

"Is it safe?" she whispers.

"There isn't anything alive bigger than a mouse nearby," I say. "So yeah."

"I'm coming," she says breathlessly, taking my arm.

We walk slowly, and as we approach the front door, it's ajar. I put my hand against the damp wood and push gently. The scent hits me full in the face, and I can't make out anything in the darkness of the interior at first. My eyes adjust though, and I push the door wider. The source of the smell is immediately clear. Slumped over a small table is a body: long, grey beard, overalls and a flannel shirt. His grey cheek rests in a pool of blood on the tabletop. Most of the blood is on the floor though. Is that Claude?

There's another body on the floor, chest down, hands clenched near his face. It looks like he crawled several feet. Crimson streaks the floor marking his trek. He wears jeans and a grey pullover, which is pushed up to reveal the skin of his back. There on his lower back is a fresh brand that I've seen once before:

I hold my breath as I take in his features: sandy blonde hair flecked with grey; a small, gently wrinkled face. He's perhaps in his fifties. I don't recognize him, and this brings me some measure of relief. But not enough that the gruesomeness of the scene doesn't seize my heart.

Kiera, meanwhile, has been deathly silent, locked in place where she stands, fists held to her chin. I look at her. "I guess this is how they figured out where to find me…" The weapon arsenal is making more and more sense now. I'm being hunted.

Kiera looks from the body on the floor to my face and then back again. She's expectant, looking at me with wide, tormented eyes.

"What is it, Kiera?" I say, stepping closer to her.

She blinks, confused. "You mean you don't… recognize him?"

I look back to the body on the floor. "Him?" I say. "Should I?" I read the affirmative answer in her emotions and I step closer to the body, crouching down next to it, looking more closely at the man's face. Maybe it's because Kiera told me I should see familiarity there, but anxiety stirs in me as I look at him. The curve of his nose… The set of his lower lip… Something there stirs my emotions even though I wouldn't call it familiarity. That's when I catch sight of a chain snaking out from the clenched fingers of his right hand.

Slowly, and with great hesitation I pinch the chain between my thumb and forefinger, my skin coming into contact with the dead man's in the process. I pull the chain gently at first, but when it doesn't come loose, I pull harder, loosening the man's fingers as it comes away.

I hold it up. It's a Star of David. My breath catches and my hand trembles. I know this necklace…

My head spins. The pendant turns and I see the familiar engraving on the back.

RWW

How did this necklace get here? In this man's hand? I look down at the him, begging some memory to jar me. But when I look at the necklace, all I can see is one face: my mother. This was *her* necklace. She was buried with it… How on earth did this man get it? Who is he?

"Who is this?" I quaver, twisting to put Kiera in view, tears starting to blur my eyes.

"I wouldn't know him if I hadn't looked at his file last night…" she whispers. "And he's older than the picture… But this is definitely Carl Haricott. Your father."

I fall on my butt, shocked, astonished beyond belief.

I look at the man called Carl. I do see it now. I've only ever seen one photo of my father. The problem is that even though Kiera told me a short time ago that the man was still alive, I'd forgotten. It didn't seem possible enough to stick I guess. But here he is...

I can't do much more than sit and stare at him for an unmarked time. I can't seem to get over the shock, the questions, and the surrealism. I examine every inch of him, finally seeing that he has a gunshot to the back of his head, the side I didn't immediately see. He was also shot in the leg—the source of the trail of blood.

I look at the necklace in my hand again, and I hear Kiera outside the cabin, making a phone call to give a report.

"We've found the body of Carl Haricott," I hear her say. "And Claude Fortner. Both executed and branded."

My father was executed... How do you mourn the murder of someone you only just found out was still alive?

"How did you get this?" I whisper to the dead man, holding up the necklace as if to show him what I'm talking about.

God. I don't even know what I feel.

I search Carl's pockets, find a few twenties, a thin wallet with a driver's license. The picture is him, but the name is David Erlich.

"Kiera?" I say as she reenters the cabin.

"This says David Erlich. Not Carl Haricott."

"Your father operated under many aliases. I've never heard of this one, but it's probably the one he was using when he died."

I remain seated on the floor and stare at Carl's face. It's completely empty, but he can't have been dead long. I keep waiting to feel something, but I can't get past shock.

Why was he here? Talking to Claude? Was he looking for me?

With that possibility, the first inkling of feeling leaks into my chest. Sadness over never knowing him... or maybe I did. But I can't remember. And that feels like a tragic loss. He looks nice, gentle and sensitive. Or maybe I just imagine it.

I look through the rest of his wallet. No credit cards. A gym membership. A discount card for a grocery store. A key is tucked into one of the slots. It looks like a post office key. There's also a small photo, old and worn. It's a picture of a woman with a baby.

She has red hair, a brilliant smile, and eyes that seem familiar. I don't recognize the baby, but it's pretty young, and chunky.

Kiera is looking over my shoulder. "I think that's you." She points to the older picture.

"And the woman is…?"

"Regina. Your mother."

I look at the photo again. I see it now. Her nose is like mine, and the set of her eyes. I look back at Carl's body, my dead father come back to life today and then murdered before I could really process it. The constant disbelief is getting overused. I'm starting to feel numb to it all.

I put Carl's wallet and its contents into my pocket. And then I turn him over, a much harder task than I expected. The dead are heavy. But I want to look at his whole face.

Once he's on his back, I say, "Can you take a picture of him, Kiera?"

"Uh, sure," she says, getting her phone out. She stands over his body, snaps about three photos of his face.

"Gosh, he looks like Ezra that way… Hair color is exactly the same—minus the grey," I say, and a shiver moves over me. PHIA is on a killing spree to get to me. And I must have known it, covered in head-to-toe weapons like I was. Which means I need to find Ezra first… if they haven't already.

Eight

Someone is knocking on the door. I squint through sleep-filled eyes and don't recognize the room. Memory comes back to me though, and I recall that last night I was brought here to the most well-fortified Guild stronghold in the world. I arrived pretty late, had my weapons confiscated, and was assigned an apartment. After no sleep the previous night I had no interest in anything but finding a bed, so they got no argument from me.

I roll unceremoniously out of bed, right arm still bound close to me, and clothed in a giant T-shirt and a pair of flannel shorts that I found in the room last night. I scuff across the carpet out of the bedroom and over to the front door, catching fuzzy glimpses of the minimalist, generic decor as I pass. I pull the door open.

A small but fit man in scrubs and a white doctor's smock is standing there holding a covered tray. He smiles at me, his eyes crinkling, indicating he might be older than he looks—which is forties or so. He's not much taller than me, maybe five-foot-nine? "Good morning," he says, his voice rich with inflection.

"Hi," I say, standing there with my lips parted, rubbing my eyes.

"I'm Doctor Lim," he says. "I'm sorry if I woke you, but it looks like it's done and you're thoroughly confused, so there's no sense in offering to come back later. May I come in?"

I shuffle aside.

He takes easy, comfortable strides to the dining table and puts the tray down. He turns around. "I'd like to check out your shoulder, if you're agreeable."

"Uhh." I look down at my T-shirt, my arm in the sling. I'm not quite sure how to let him look at my shoulder without taking my shirt off…

He clears his throat. "You should have a fresh robe in the bathroom. Should allow for your modesty and my ease." He smiles pleasantly again, sits on a chair, his posture perfectly upright. "I'll wait here."

I can't but do what he says. In the bathroom, I get a look at my red eyes in the mirror. I turn to the sink to splash water on them, but when I turn it on, it makes a humming sound but nothing comes out. I rub my face and eyes on a towel instead. Now that I'm waking up, memories of the past couple days rise out of the murkiness. My father was alive. PHIA killed him and they're after me. My mother was not my mother. My biological mother died when I was a baby. My uncle was killed by PHIA. And my brother is still unaccounted for. I was a gun-toting GI Jane. Oh, and the world is ending even though there are now bonafide superheroes. If only that were all... A hundred bizarre details search for a place to make sense.

I pad out of the bathroom in my robe, a luxurious mound of terrycloth. I'm pretty sure it's going to stay on me for the next three days.

Doctor Lim stands up, pulls a chair out from the table, and invites me to sit in it.

I do and allow the robe to fall past my shoulder to expose my bandage. I removed my sling to make it easier, and I'm having to hold my right arm up and against my stomach with my left.

I hear him snap on a pair of latex gloves and then feel him gently peel back the foam tape holding gauze in place. I've looked at the injury myself in the mirror. It's pretty ugly, a criss-cross of stitches doing their best to get my mangled flesh back into some kind of order. It's going to leave a giant scar.

"Hmm," he says with disapproval. There's not much to his emotions though. He's focused on his task in the extreme, hands moving gently over the wound. "It looks like you've ripped some of your stitches—not that they gave you much to work with. This is not up to my standard at all. When was the last time the bandage was changed?"

"Uhh, yesterday morning," I say.

"No wonder." He lifts my robe back up over my shoulder and I tug it back into place around me.

He walks over to the door where I see he's left a large satchel, big enough to fit a large bowling ball.

"Help yourself to the food. It's going to take me a moment to arrange my instruments."

I lift the lid of the tray to reveal some kind of pudding with fruit. I take a bite and realize it's rice pudding. I watch Doctor Lim pull out scissors, gauze, a tube of something with a needle-thin dispenser, a spray bottle. He's efficient and obviously has a precise way of doing things, his hands arranging the items as if they know where they go without his mind to tell them. He's clean-shaven, his hair cut close, and he's of Asian descent although I'm not sure where specifically. I'm thinking somewhere in Indochina because of his darker complexion.

"This is terrific," I say, scraping the last remnants from the bowl.

"I'll let my daughter know," he replies, lining up the instruments on a white cloth on the other side of the table. "She's recently taken up food science as one of her many interests."

My doctor's daughter made me food?

Doctor Lim goes to the door, opens it, and a young man pushes in a folded contraption. It looks like a massage chair as he and the young man set it up. It even has a rest for the person's head or face. "Thank you, David," Doctor Lim says quietly.

David takes his leave without a word and Doctor Lim says to me, "This will take me just under an hour." He sets up the last thing: an articulated lamp with a strange-looking triangular head. He clips it to the edge of the massage chair. "I'm going to take out your stitches first. Then I'm going to re-suture it with something more flexible. Also, I'm going to inject the site with a targeted growth hormone, to help the bones mend much faster. Are you comfortable with that?"

"Sure," I say, a little baffled that my doctor has set up his exam room in my apartment.

"Lovely. Face here, and expose that shoulder for me. Get comfortable and let me know when you're ready. I'm going to bring the table closer so I can access my tools."

I straddle the chair, moving around until I can both support myself against the chair while keeping my right arm tucked against me and immobile. "Ready," I say.

"Alright. Here we go," he says.

I think he switches on the lamp because my shoulder is immediately warm. And then tingly. Within seconds he touches it and it feels numb. Another moment and I can't perceive his hand at all.

"Anesthetic light," he says, answering my question before I articulate it. "New technology. And by the way, I do love to chat as I work. I hope you're up to it."

"Okay," I say, a little muffled because my face is against the headrest. I adjust my head to be better heard.

He's waiting for me to speak.

"How does the light work?" I ask.

"Frequency waves. It counteracts the nerves' signal to the brain. That's the short explanation. But I'm guessing this isn't really what you'd like to discuss, Miss Whitley."

I pause. "I'm not sure what I can ask."

"Anything you like. I understand you're short on trust these days. This is your opportunity to ask whatever you like. I am one of twelve people that has access to all information the Guild possesses."

I process what he's saying. "You—you're not actually a doctor?"

"Of course I am. I wouldn't be doing this if I weren't a physician."

"What I meant was, being a doctor isn't the main reason you're here."

"No. I oversee a specialized medical research department, but actually acting as a physician is a personal indulgence. Your shoulder was in need of attention, so it was a nice confluence of circumstances. Most days and nights find me on the Guild Council."

"The Guild Council... Right, the people that govern the Guild," I reply.

Wow. I figured I'd be handed off to Kiera's boss or something, not one of the head-honchos directly.

"Yes, the Council is entrusted with protecting and enriching our membership of Prime Humans. At present, we are the most influential and pivotal organization in the world."

I expect pride to accompany that statement, but he says it matter-of-factly.

"The most powerful man in the world is stitching up my back and letting me pick his brain?" I say.

"Power is relative, Miss Whitley. I am powerless without the operatives that compose the Guild. Further, like everyone in the Guild, I don't make decisions solo."

"Why do I get special attention? Or do all new people get personal Q and A sessions with you?"

"They don't. But you are a special case. I don't like elevating one person's life force abilities over another because the machine doesn't work without all the parts. But occasionally you need a socket wrench to fix a problem and nothing else will do. You are the only socket wrench around. I need your help."

"Why?" I ask.

"You were born with the ability to see the energy world—the manifestation of the forces that enable life force abilities. It's invisible to the rest of us. Your father saw it. And his mother."

"What invisible forces? I don't see anything a pair of binoculars or a microscope can't see," I say.

"You see life forces, Miss Whitley. And it takes practice to access. You'll have to learn how."

Life forces... Energy world... That was the new age stuff Dina and then Kiera were talking about. I'm able to see it?

Whoa.

He said I'm the only socket wrench... Kiera said I'm the only one with super-vision she's heard of since my grandmother, but my father had it too? Super-vision lets me see the energy world?

"And what do you need my help with?" I say finally.

"Accessing the energy world to discover the origin of the unnatural escalation of disasters so it can be eradicated."

He said that so naturally, like it's a perfectly feasible request.

I need you to use your superpowers to save the world.

Oh, sure, how's next Tuesday sound?

"Umm," I say. "Why would—? How—? *What?*"

"Everything in this world has a manifestation in the energy world," he explains. "The energy world can tell us things that this world can't. The disasters are more than a progression of natural ecological events. They have arisen from something, or someone, and unless we can find out what, we are merely running a race against time."

"How do you know so much about what I can do?"

"We only know what you can do because of what your father could do. Abilities are hereditary. We don't know the extent of yours, only that you have them. And Kiera reported that you also have super-hearing as well as super-smell, a combination that is unheard of. This means you are even more talented than your father. But that's always how it goes. From one generation to the next, abilities are vastly improved."

"So what about him? According to my mom he died a long time ago, but he turned up in that cabin. What do you know about that?"

"You were abducted from your father by a woman known as Sara. He searched for you for years, and it's safe to guess he eventually found you—at Pneumatikon since you said you remember going there. That was *his* organization."

Two pieces of the puzzle click together. My trip to Pneumatikon must have been the beginning of being reunited with my father... The name Sara is unfamiliar though. "My mom's name was Leena."

"We've since learned that was an alias she used to avoid detection. Her real name was Sara Rowan."

While I've sort of accepted that I wasn't biologically related to the woman who raised me, I can't place her as a babynapper. She was the most selfless and dedicated mother I knew. "Why would the woman I called 'mom' do that?"

"I don't know. But Sara could have been involved with your father prior to leaving with you. Ezra could be his and her biological son."

"What's your best guess?" I say.

"Sometimes guessing is good for finding truth. Sometimes the mind is so desperate to fill a gap in your knowledge that it will too hastily cling to a guess even when there is too little information to support it. It will begin to influence and shape things. Don't guess. You don't want to depend on and operate on false information. Stand on your own two feet and make your own decisions based on what you actually know."

"What I know is that my mom was always there for us. She lived her life for us. And she never ever treated me like I wasn't her own."

"That's a good thing to know."

"I don't know anything about my father."

"He was complex."

"How so?"

Doctor Lim pauses for the first time before answering, but I don't think it's hesitation or a lack of the right words. I think it's for emphasis, and I wait with even more anticipation. Who was my father? What did he do with his life?

"He never trusted us," Doctor Lim says. "He resented our organization, our regulation, our oversight. He always believed that the Guild's purpose was to monopolize life force abilities for the purposes of power. He spent his life working against us." He pauses his work as he says more quietly, "He could have changed the world."

It's my turn to pause, feeling that Doctor Lim is speaking *to* me as much as he is speaking about my father.

"What *is* your purpose?" I say.

"Accelerated, strategic human improvement," he says, the slight tugging on my skin continuing.

"So like… technological advancement?"

"Technology, art, medicine, science, ethics, compassion, communication… Anything that betters mankind, we take an interest in facilitating it."

"Are there Prime Humans who *aren't* in the Guild?"

"Of course. You are one example. And your father. We don't force anyone to join the Guild."

"Do most work for you?"

"Yes. But you should consider us more like an association than a company. Prime Humans find solidarity within the Guild. They can be employed within or without the organization. We own many companies, and we aim to create an outlet for every single life force ability out there. The Guild is a partnership. We want Prime Humans to have purpose so that their talents aren't wasted or misused. We also have many members who own their own business ventures, and most give preference of employment to others who are Guild members. If you are a member of the Guild, you have instant credibility with other Guild members. We look out for our own."

"Like a fraternity or sorority," I say.

"But for a lifetime and not broadcasted. At least until recent months when the Council decided to make our influence known."

"Kiera said Prime Humans come from the energy world. How exactly?"

"Prime Humans are the children of individuals who have had life force manipulation." Dr. Lim replies. "We call them the seed generation. Their abilities are comparatively weak, but their progeny, Prime Humans, see the real benefit."

I pause pensively. "So you're saying that regular people get life force manipulation, giving them weak superpowers, but their kids get the real deal… Do they ever get life force manipulation as well?"

"No."

"When I was at Pneumatikon, they were talking about using energy therapy to cure my allergies. They also gave me some tests and said energy manipulation could have 'unintended benefits.' But I already had super-senses and I was already an empath. Kiera told me I was born a Prime Human. Why do the energy thing on me then?"

"I cannot say for sure. Perhaps the individuals running the clinic didn't know with whom they were dealing. But I can tell you that Pneumatikon was a clinic that your father ran with the purpose of creating his own seed-generation that would birth Prime Humans outside of our knowledge and influence."

There is much more to this topic than he's saying. Does he realize I can tell? I have so rarely dealt with people who know I can read their minds with some measure of accuracy, so this is an odd situation for me. My instinct has always been to call out reservations and secrets in those around me, but I'm totally out of my element here. Do I *want* the people here to know my full scope? If they are holding back, do I hold back as well?

"Miss Whitley, the information you wish to know is highly classified, even among our own," Dr. Lim says, demonstrating that he knows what I'm thinking as easily as I do him. I wonder if he's an empath like me? I keep forgetting these people have supernatural abilities. They've all seemed so normal…

"The Council agreed to forgo the formalities of clearance to share anything we might know that could shed light on your past as an act of good faith," he explains. "While I am not an empath, as you suspect, my specific talent does allow me quick and concise insight into human behavior. Integrity and motives are never hidden from me. While the Council may have had reservations about sharing information with someone such as yourself who confesses no loyalty to the Guild, I do not."

On the one hand, I'm flattered that he would see me that way. Plus, I'm impressed that he can read me so well. On the other, I'm confused. "If you were going to tell me classified information anyway, why would you preface it with telling me it was a split decision? That's just going to make me distrust the Guild more than I already do."

"On the contrary, you would have been more distrusting if I'd told you things without explaining the reservations. You *expect* things to be kept from you. People distrust the *un*expected."

I sigh into the headrest. He's probably right. "Well are you going to tell me already, or keep convincing me what I would have thought and why?"

He chuckles. "Life force manipulation is lethal, Miss Whitley. Not only did your biological mother die of what we call 'seed generation sickness,' but so did your adoptive mother, Leena. Individuals who have had life force manipulation can expect to live only around fifteen years after it is done. This is the primary reason life force knowledge is so classified."

"My mom—I mean my adoptive mom—died of breast cancer," I protest. "I saw it with my own eyes."

"Yes. Seed generation sickness manifests in a variety of ways. Cancer is one of the most common. However it does manifest, the disease will be especially aggressive."

How right he is. My mom found her cancer early... The doctors were so positive that she'd be okay. But it was like treatment worked against her. And the cancer just grew. I swallow back residual sorrow. It might have been three and a half years ago, but it still feels like only a year to me, and today it feels like even less than that...

"Your father believed the seed generation sacrifice was one worth making. Pneumatikon was a clinic dedicated to manifesting life force abilities in humans."

"People did this... Knowingly?"

"I don't believe so. But he was truly paranoid about our growth and influence, so Pnuematikon was an attempt to combat us. I still have no idea if you actually had life force manipulation, or if perhaps your father realized who had shown up at his clinic and saved you from that fate. Everything surrounding your interaction with Pneumatikon is pure speculation."

Dr. Lim hasn't paused in his work, the gentle tug on my shoulder somewhat soothing as he has spoken. But on my end, his words just create confusion. Pneumatikon was performing lethal life force manipulation? It sounds like my mom might have had a good reason to take me away from someone like that.

"What about you guys?" I say. "You do life force manipulation, too, don't you? How else do you have so many Prime Humans?"

"We do. And we made the same mistakes as your father before we learned how these things work and figured out better ways. Life force manipulation, for example, we don't do to anyone who isn't already terminal and with full-disclosure. Further, ninety percent of Prime Human children come from other Prime Humans rather than seed generations now. Part of this is because the further removed a Prime is from the seed generation, the more powerful they are. So, for example, a first generation empath (one whose parent had life force manipulation) is less powerful than a second generation (one whose grandparent had life force manipulation). Abilities improve with each generation."

So my dad was creating superhumans by killing humans... Eew. I wonder what my relationship with him ended up looking like? The only memory I now have of him was from yesterday... him lying on the floor along with a blood smear. He was in the cabin of the man that rescued me from the woods... What does that mean?

"Your father was admirably driven," Dr. Lim says, guessing where my head is. "He was not opposed to risk and to taking on tasks that most people would balk at the size of. Those traits were his greatest assets as well as his greatest downfall because his risk-tolerance often strayed past lines of morality. And his independence kept him from ever working with us—or anyone honestly. Collaboration is key here. It's how we've developed the world-changing technology we have. But he discounted the benefit of that kind of partnership. He was so jaded about the world, so suspicious of everyone. I don't know that he had a friend he trusted his entire life. It's heartbreaking, really."

I inhale, having stopped breathing for a time. My father sounds... exactly like me. Isolated. And distrustful in the extreme. But I have a reason. I've been an empath my whole life. I know how easily people lie. I also know how tempting it is to take advantage of people, to manipulate them. I know how easy it is, too. I exhale a jagged breath. I'm him. And I didn't even know him.

"So what do you know about the fact that my super-senses have improved so much? Or that my empathy now has a range rather than only working with skin-contact?" I say.

"I don't know. But I find that fact quite promising. It's probable your father trained you how to access the energy world. The energy world is where these abilities come from, so if anyone could figure out how to increase the power of their life force abilities beyond the gradual improvement most experience, it would be the two of you, the ones who could actually see the energy world at work."

Man... I wish I could remember all these things he's talking about. What a wild ride my life must have become after connecting with Pneumatikon. "So... I would have known about the Guild, right?"

"In the last two months, undoubtedly. Prior to that I have to think your father must have told you of our existence. But he hid you from us well. Until you turned up in that hospital a few days ago, you had been a missing Prime from the time Sara took you from your father at three years old."

"Really…" I say, amazed. "So I knew about you… But you didn't know about me."

"We believe that prior to his defection, Andre, now the leader of PHIA, was using our resources to locate you and not reporting to his superiors about it. He hid everything he had discovered about your whereabouts from us. No records exist. He had too much autonomy, and he used the information he had access to to attack our people. We are still recovering."

I let that sink in. "So I was in cahoots with my MIA dad. And my uncle apparently. I was armed to the teeth because of PHIA." Weird.

"And you went into the woods even though you had to have known something was going to happen," Dr. Lim says. "We advised a mandatory evacuation of the area the previous day. We knew an event of some kind was going to happen across that entire area, something severe. You were knowingly flirting with death. It seems your risk tolerance rivals even that of your late father."

That does *not* sound like me. Not a lot of the pieces of information surrounding my forgotten self do. The most frustrating part is that PHIA probably knows the most about who I was. But of course, I am *not* going to them. *That* is flirting with death.

One of the things that has been bugging me since last night is the location of this facility. It just so happens it's not only in Missouri, but it is also only an hour north of where I was found in the woods by Claude. Of all the places I could be in the country, I was right down the road from the main facility of the Guild. That's far too coincidental to deny that my purpose for being in Missouri had something to do with them. But if the Guild knew nothing about me… what was I after out there in the woods?

And if I could see the energy world, did that have something to do with it?

"How did you guys escape all the lightning storms?" I ask. "I saw that they were all over this area."

"Quite a few lightning rods strategically placed," he says. "But we also evacuated as a precaution since we weren't sure of *what* kind of catastrophe we'd be dealing with. Most residents returned yesterday, just before you arrived."

"Oh…" *Why, Wendy? Why were you out there?*

After several moments of silence, I say, "How do I access this energy world everyone's nuts over anyway?"

"You must be employed by our Energy World Research department to be privy to that information. Only Guild members are allowed to work there, and only by recommendation."

I snort. "I thought you were all for sharing what you know of my past with me."

"I have no idea what you did or did not know about the energy world. Just because you should have the ability to access it doesn't entitle you to everything we know about it."

"Assuming that I knew how to access it before, and considering you told me I'm a socket wrench, why the red tape?" I shoot back.

"Because as important as you are, you are not more important than the integrity of the Guild. Protecting it means protecting the processes that keep us working together. And that means protecting vital information, such as energy world knowledge. You need us and we can help you. But we have processes, requirements."

"Assuming I knew about you, then I'm not surprised I didn't line up to join," I grumble. "My memory loss must be awfully convenient for the Guild."

"And the more we talk, the less surprised I am as well," he chuckles. "Your similarities to Carl are striking. Don't let them hold you back though. We did not create the circumstances in which you find yourself, Miss Whitley. We may be in an ideal place to benefit from them, but it was never our plan."

"Plausible deniability," I say.

"I suppose it is. But the world needs help, and the fact remains, there is a socket wrench shortage."

"That's fortunate for me, because I need some things, too: resources to track down my brother and protection from Andre—who I'm pretty sure is after me. So I might be a skeptic like my father, but I'm not too proud to make a trade."

"Guild membership will allow you access to whatever you need," Dr. Lim says. "Your brother is a Prime Human as well and we have a department dedicated to tracking down missing Primes."

"It's not like I have other prospects."

He works in silence for a moment. "Given what I've learned about you in the last forty minutes, and considering your past self obviously declined seeking Guild membership, even actively avoided our radar for some principled reason, I think it's safe to guess that your past self would call you a sellout," he says, the slightest taunting in his voice and attitude.

"Think so?" I say, the bizarreness of that two and a half year chunk of time washing over me again. But I think I also agree with him about me, given what I've learned about the version of myself that ended up in the woods.

"I do. She's not going to haunt you, is she?"

As if he's summoned her by his taunting, a shadow of guilt falls over me briefly. She indeed might. Aligning and joining were never my thing. Why all of sudden does joining a secret organization not sound like a big deal?

For a moment I flash to waking up in the woods. Residual fear washes over me. In asking myself why I was so afraid, I recognize that it wasn't the mystery of the circumstances. It stems from the second that I recognized I was alone.

I am Jane Doe.

"I think she was wrong," I say hoarsely. I take a deep breath, clear my throat. "Her father is dead, her uncle is dead, and her brother is missing—and everyone else that was with her. Not a single person she knew showed up at her bedside. She was nearly captured by PHIA at the hospital. She obviously wasn't as capable as she thought she was." My words are followed by anger. To lose my memory is one thing, but how could I also let myself lose *everyone* that knew me?

He replies with silence for a while. A few moments later, he says "I still wish I'd known her though." I can feel his genuine regret over that.

"So Andre… he wants me because I'm a socket wrench, too, I guess. But why? How does that help him?" I say.

"He would have a special interest in you because you are Prime Human Prime. The forces that guide life force abilities are within your sight and at your fingertips. With enough knowledge you have the power to… well, the sky is the limit, I believe. Andre wants to destroy humankind's ability to access those forces. Who do *you* think would be most promising to accomplish that?"

I groan. "*Why?* Why would you hate something that could help people? Enough to murder innocent people by the dozen?"

"Andre will be stopped," Dr. Lim says confidently. "We've moved everyone around to make it harder for him to locate Primes."

I hesitate before saying, "Do you think he has my brother?"

"Maybe. But given his ruthless killing spree as he attempts to track you down, I believe that if Andre had your brother alive, you would have received a demand by now. I believe it's more likely that your brother is dead, or in hiding somewhere. Only your lost memory knows."

A chill moves over me and I am silently pondering for several moments. What if Ezra *is* dead? Do I *want* to remember?

"I'm done," Dr. Lim says. "You can pull your robe up." He clicks the lamp off.

I lift my face, tug my robe up and test my shoulders a bit, feeling slowly eking back into them.

"I've brought you a protective spray," Doctor Lim says, pointing to a white spray bottle on the table. He gathers his instruments back into his satchel. "Better than bandaging. It's water soluble and will come off in the shower. Reapply after you dry. Only use the water setting on the shower for the next two weeks."

"Water setting?" I say.

He nods. "All housing units come equipped with waterless technology. But it's not good for your stitches. Use water until you've healed."

"Oh…" I say, seeing the bathroom sink with new eyes.

"If you are serious about joining the Guild, Kiera can facilitate that," Doctor Lim says, holding his satchel in two hands in front of himself. "She'll be stopping by shortly."

I nod. "I am."

"A recommendation to join the Energy World Research department will be a more involved process. You'll have to fulfill certain requirements. Security of life force research is of the highest importance."

"Like what?" I say, walking over to the sink and tilting my head to look at it more closely.

"Bi-weekly therapy sessions at first, and monthly after that. Full-time, onsite lodging here at this facility. Monitoring of all outgoing communication. Tracking device implantation. And mandatory protection detail whenever you are outside this facility."

"Tracking device implantation?" I say, making the face.

"I know," he says, mirroring my expression. "That policy is new and it's been in effect since Andre and PHIA started being so aggressive. If you are taken, we *must* be able to find you."

"I guess that's understandable," I sigh, sticking my hand under the faucet and hearing the same low hum I heard earlier, but with my hand beneath it, I now pick up the nearly indiscernible vibration against my skin.

"It's been a pleasure meeting you, Miss Whitley."

"You too, Doctor Lim," I say.

He makes a little bow and says, "Please, call me Ohr."

Nine

He's not a very doctor-like doctor," I say, sticking my plate under the vibration thing over the sink, watching how the remnants of potatoes and lettuce leaves coated in salad dressing fall off. I lift it up, perfectly dry and clean, marveling.

"I just... I can't... Ohr's on the *Council*! He doesn't make personal visits," Kiera says, throwing her hands up, starstruck. "No one on the Council does."

"He said he doesn't, but he needs me to like, save the world and stuff." I lean against the counter, wincing at the words that sound too fantastic to be real. Certainly not in the same sentence with someone as ordinary as me. I look down at myself, socked feet, wearing the robe still. "I'm thinking I really personify this superhero thing, don't you?"

Kiera stares at me, totally caught up in her own amazement. I wave my hand in front of her face and give her a look. She blinks and shakes her head. "Sorry, sorry. I just... Wow! And you... You *see* the energy world... Good grief. Level ten priority... no kidding."

"You know I still don't know what that actually means."

She pulls herself up to sit on my counter, rolls the inside of her cheek with her tongue, eyes unfocused.

"Spill it," I say.

"Trying to figure out how to put it," Kiera says.

"Well stop trying. Just say it like it is."

She shakes her head slowly. "No... I think it's better if you draw your own conclusions. Since you're joining the Guild, you'll be attending regular Colloquies, which means you'll figure out pretty quickly what made you level ten."

"Colloquies?"

"Sort of like... group discussions. Helps you learn about who we are."

"Okay… Well Ohr also said I have to see a therapist bi-weekly in order to get on the EWR team. So it looks like you get to keep your job."

"Oh… well… Do you really think so? I mean, did he say I could be your therapist?"

I raise an eyebrow. "He didn't say you couldn't. Why would it matter? A therapist is a therapist, right?"

"You might be right… It's just that I'm so low clearance, and you're like…" She waves her hands over the length of me, "a mega star."

"Mega star? Come off it."

"Wendy…" she says, struggling to keep the awe out of her voice. "If people here find out you can access the energy world directly…" She waves her hands in front of her. "Nevermind. I said I was going to let you figure it out yourself. Just, well, keep what you can do on the DL until you decide whether you want it to be public." She wipes her forehead. "Man. This is so out of my league."

"So the energy world is a big deal to Primes?"

She gasps. "Big deal? It's *the* deal. And you're like… the oracle."

"Geez. Don't blow it out of proportion or anything."

"I'm not. I'm being dead serious."

I give her a dubious look.

She lifts an eyebrow. "Don't believe me? Make your ability public info. See what happens. But remember, you can't take it back."

"Whatever," I sigh. "So, if I join the Guild, does that mean I have to have a dyad?"

Kiera nods. "Oh yes."

"Do I get to pick?"

"No." She plops on a stool, chin in hand.

"Sounded a little resentful there."

She lifts her shoulders and lets them fall. "Having a dyad that aggravates you is kind of the point. They want you to be paired with someone unlike you so that you make better decisions."

"Hmph," I say, pulling the other stool to face Kiera. "I'm curious who they'll pair me with, in that case. In the meantime, what do I need to do?"

"Oh. Right," Kiera says, sitting up and looking around as if having forgotten where she is. She stands up, looks under the counter, and by the door, embarrassed. "Crap, have you seen my bag?"

"You didn't come with a bag."

She looks at me. "Are you serious?"

I nod.

She throws herself back on the stool, elbows on the counter, forehead in her hands, frustrated. "What is wrong with me?"

"Forgetfulness," I laugh.

She looks up, red-rimmed eyes, stares past me at nothing. "Lainey is right. I am a walking disaster." She turns to me now. "I am so sorry. I swear I'm going to do better."

"Get a grip, Kiera. You forgot your bag. Big deal."

She shakes her head. "You're too nice. I'm disorganized and unprofessional. I was supposed to come here, show you the paperwork, let you know all the things you're going to have to do, and then I was supposed to introduce you to Mikel. But instead I started going fangirl over you and your meeting with Ohr. I'm an embarrassment."

"Maybe so," I say, testing the temperature of the tea in my mug. I've been thinking about ginger tea since yesterday for some reason. I haven't had it, to my memory. But I'm hoping it's some sort of gateway to a lost memory. Unfortunately the fully-stocked cabinets of my apartment only contain only Chamomile. I need to find out where to get my hands on ginger tea... "You know, the only reason I'm joining the Guild is because of you. Ohr should thank you."

She rolls her eyes. "That is such a lie."

"No it's not." I realize I like holding a mug. The weight is comforting. Maybe I'll take up tea-drinking... "I can take or leave Ohr. He's way too... otherworldly. He feels stuff, but I can't actually tell what he's thinking. I think it's because he's got this grand mission and he's focused on stuff I can only imagine. He's way up here." I hold my hand as high as it will go. "But who can relate to that? Dude is laser-focused and cool as a cucumber. I'm a working college student, I'm loud and emotional. At least that's who I remember being. But I'm only here, doing this, joining your club, because I trust *you*. I like that you're normal, that you have emotions, that you don't let your job get in the way of actually being there for me as a therapist and friend. Professionalism is overrated. It's a lie anyway. People use it to make themselves look more credible. Doesn't work on me." I breathe in the aroma wafting up from my mug. Yep, tea drinking sounds like it could be me.

Kiera looks thoughtful.

"I could get dressed and you can take me to wherever your bag is. I feel a little bit of cabin fever anyway," I say. "Do they have a grocery store here? I need some ginger tea."

"Okay," Kiera says brightly, standing. "There's a provisions building, but I don't know if they'll have ginger tea. You can make a request for it, but they usually don't stock nonessentials."

"Rats," I grumble. "Can I order it online? Is there still the Internet?"

Kiera laughs. "There is, but it's not as comprehensive as you remember. Lots of downed servers. Nothing along the western seaboard. We're in a pretty major economic recession so the online industry took a huge blow."

"Hmm. I'm also going to need a credit card if I'm going to order online..." I say, feeling my Jane Doe status strongly. "How do I get a bank account? I don't even have a birth certificate anymore. I was born in California, so getting a new one probably isn't going to happen, huh?"

"You're with the Guild now, Wendy," Kiera smiles. "We can make anything happen."

₪

The facility I'm at is called the Interior Hub, but more commonly it's called the Vault. I snorted smoothie out of my nose when Kiera told me that. Single-syllable dramatic words seem to be a thing with the Guild, but I guess the name is apt because it houses the majority of the Guild's major talent, plus the Council. It's the most well-protected facility they own. The grounds are compact, comprising ten separate large buildings and another dozen or so smaller ones all squeezed close together and nestled in the Ozarks. It's fenced in a wide perimeter three concentric times, and from the outside it is labelled as a controlled nature preserve. The Guild has somehow gotten it listed as a no-flyover zone—rare birds living in the preserve of course.

The grounds remind me of a college campus with a lot less aesthetic fluff. People are always on the go, wearing backpacks or bags. There's no dress code. Blue hair, beards, nose rings, or clean-shaven with a tie. Nobody seems to care. I see bulletin boards posting events, computer labs, coffee shops, cafeterias, gyms, and arcades.

After a quick stop at Kiera's room—one of several temporary residence rooms like a hotel—and a trip to drop off my application with the administrative office, we walk to a building as far away from the rest of the campus as possible. It also doesn't match any of the other buildings, having the most aesthetic architecture of any I've seen here. Plus, it's enormous. Contemporary angles, lots of windows and skylights. A turret atrium spirals up from the middle of the fortress. White marble face. Three fountains in front welcome us. I find the extravagant use of water odd after the ultra-conservative water situation in my apartment.

As we approach it, Kiera explains, "I served my two-year apprenticeship under Mikel. That's how most jobs in the Guild are learned. It's very different from standard education. There aren't really classes. Everything is treated like a trade. It's hands-on. And it's very intensive. Even if you have a higher education degree, or you've been working professionally outside the Guild for ten years, you still have to serve an apprenticeship to be employed within the Guild."

We enter through glass doors, and the water squandering situation is taken to a whole new level. The room we enter is the size of basketball stadium. It would be wide open if it weren't for literal walls of water separating the space into 'rooms.' Water pours down in sheets from the ceiling—which is composed of glass-encased water itself. These sheets of water pour down from all over the place and into channels below, which form a circuit of waterways. They pool beneath the transparent floor we stand on at the entrance, flowing outside to feed the fountains there.

"Whoa," I breathe, having stopped just inside the entrance to stare. It's like the whole building is made of water.

It's not only the novelty that's mesmerizing, but the movement of water. It's soothing, and stress washes out of me. I am inexplicably calm, like the sharp edges of the world have dampened.

Kiera says, "Do you feel that?"

"Relaxed?" I reply. "Yeah. This place is incredible—not really what I expected though. None of the other buildings are this extravagant. And conservation is the vibe I've been getting until now."

Kiera giggles. "It's not extravagant. It's purposeful. This is called The Water House—for obvious reasons. Most life force abilities can't be 'turned off' so when you have so many Prime Humans in one place, with so many abilities bouncing around, it can get overwhelming after a while. Water, though, particularly moving water, has a dampening effect on most abilities. People come here to decompress, escape, whatever. There are a few apartments on upper floors for people who are especially sensitive for one reason or another, and they need more constant cleansing. The other thing they put here are the mental health offices, because if you come for help, you need to be able to escape unintended influences."

"My super senses don't seem to be affected..." I point out. "But my empathic range is basically zilch. Interesting." I remember how much I've always liked rain and think maybe this is why—it gave me an escape from constant emotional connection to people and I didn't realize it.

"This way," Kiera says, pointing us to the left where instead of a water wall, there's a glass wall, and a sliding door. It says, *Neurology and Mental Health* above the door.

Beyond the doors, the decor is still minimalist. There's no receptionist, just a kiosk to sign in. Kiera presses her finger to the screen. It welcomes her by name and a directory appears. Kiera taps on Mikel's name. Then we sit on one of the two wicker benches and wait.

"Mikel," Kiera says brightly after a short while from beside me. She stands.

I look up to see a black-clad, extremely thin individual. The name Mikel said male to me, but I can't actually back that up. The person in front of me could be either. The mouth is more sharply masculine, but the eyes are more rounded, the brows more feminine. He or she has a black hair pulled into a low ponytail, and his or her slacks and blouse are gender neutral. If she has breasts, I can't see them.

"Hi," I say, standing and feeling rude for scrutinizing this person so closely.

"Don't stress," Mikel says in a voice that again, I also can't categorize. "I identify as androgynous."

"Sorry," I say meekly.

"For what? Categorization is important for mental development and function," Mikel says and offers me a half-smile. "Can't survive without it."

"Yeah, but my mom always said staring was rude," I reply.

"Ah the social conventions," Mikel says wistfully. "The earnest desire for predictability and order, but the source of so much oppression, wouldn't you say?"

"Uh. Sure," I reply.

Mikel gives another wan smile. "Would you like to come back to my office? Kiera has been eager for us to meet."

"Okay." As we walk, I say, "What pronoun would you prefer?"

Mikel laughs, which sounds definitively feminine. "I always tell my clients I'd prefer them to think of me as whatever gender they are most comfortable with."

I consider it as Mikel leads us into a water cubicle, about twelve foot square. It has a desk, a glass-enclosed computer, and two couches.

"Have a seat," Mikel says, pointing to one couch and sitting down on the other.

"It's great to see you again," Kiera says, sitting next to me. "I haven't told Wendy why I brought her here. I didn't want to make promises."

I glance from Kiera to Mikel, who looks unhappy. I can't pick up any emotions though. Maybe a little nervousness from Kiera next to me. Darn water.

Mikel stares at Kiera, whose nerves grow more and more obvious to me. Her hands fidget in her lap. I decide I don't like Mikel. Disapproving of Kiera and being publicly obvious about it seems to be a common theme among the people in Kiera's life.

Unable to take the growing tension, I say, "What is your freaking problem?"

Mikel's eyes, which are a nearly black I notice, become trained on me with the grace and intensity of a cat—I've always thought of cats as androgynous so I think that's why. "What is the last sensory memory you recall, prior to waking up in that hospital?" Mikel asks.

"Who are you that I should answer that?" I say.

I get a quarter smile this time, and Mikel puts a pale, thin arm on the back of the couch. "Mikel Stevens, director of neuroscience. I've been told that you have a problem with your memory. My specialty is memory reconstruction."

I stare back with equal intensity, not to be intimidated. "I don't need to reconstruct my memories. They're just inaccessible at the moment."

Mikel chuckles. "Human beings aren't computers, Miss Whitley. Recall is a process of reconstruction, not filing. Your memories are far less reliable than you imagine, far more fluid."

"What are you saying?" I reply, sitting back and crossing my arms. "You can or can't help me remember?"

"Mikel has never failed at helping people recover lost memories," Kiera says, leaning toward me.

"Kiera, I don't require endorsement. An intelligent person won't rely on word of mouth, but credentials. My reputation speaks for itself."

I glare at Mikel.

"Of course," Mikel says in response to my expression, "Some people operate on emotion, which Miss Whitley is obviously quite susceptible to. Should make for much easier memory reconstruction though. Even you could handle such an easy case, Kiera."

"Kiera is one of the only people I trust in this whacky place," I say. "You aren't. Which absolutely means you need her endorsement. I don't care who you've helped *reconstruct* their memories. But if Kiera spent two years under you and can attest that you're worth this fancy office and snooty attitude, I'm willing to give it a shot."

Mikel, expressionless, stands. "Out," she says (I've decided to think of her as female). "You seem to be under the impression that I need you. But I assure you, Miss Whitley, you are not that special."

I stand, glaring. "We'll see about that." And then I stomp out, Kiera behind me.

"Wendy!" Kiera says once we reach the courtyard outside. "She's a real bitch, but she knows what she's talking about!"

"I don't care," I say. "I'm not putting up with that."

Kiera groans and puts her hands to her sides in fists. "I'm telling you, you need her if you're going to remember. I'm giving you your best shot and you sabotaged it. Go back in there and apologize. Kiss her butt a little so you can get your memory back. Also, mention your super senses. Even Mikel will be impressed."

"She said you could handle it. I don't need her."

Kiera waves her hands in front of her. "She was just trying to upset you. She likes people to need her; it feeds her ego. You're letting principle get in the way of fixing your problem. Don't you want to remember what happened to your brother?"

My shoulders slump. "Of course. But I trust you more than her. Why can't you help me? Didn't you work under Mikel for years? Learned her tricks? Why do you let everyone tell you you aren't good enough?"

"Because compared to Mikel, I'm not. It's not just her methods, Wendy. I could know every single thing she knows about memory construction theory and still not be as good. Her life force ability makes her unmatched."

"Which is what?"

"Id projection. She becomes your subconscious. That's why you're thinking of her as female now. It's because *you* identify as female and she started to become it. She's a third generation Prime, super powerful, even with all that water she still takes on remnants of the subconscious projections around her. She's one of the people that lives in the Water House because she's can't control becoming the base desires and instincts of people around her."

"Well honestly, that kind of freaks me out. I don't want that person in my head."

Kiera puts her hands on her hips, scowls at me.

"Don't look at me like that. Give yourself a chance. Use your best therapist mind tricks on me. If it doesn't work after a while I'll *consider* letting that piece of work in my head."

"You're going to need to do some major kissing up to get her to work with you."

I shrug, start walking again. "Nah. I bet I can tell Ohr and he'll make her."

Kiera considers that, catching up beside me. "I think even the Council is a little afraid of Mikel. I'm not sure that would work."

"Afraid of her? Why?"

Kiera hesitates, but when I give her a look she says, "*Everyone* is afraid of her. When she's drunk she'll go on and on about senseless things. Imbalances. Possession. The id growing stronger than the ego, stuff like that. I don't think she remembers telling me half the things she's told me. I also don't know how much of it is her id projection crazy talk. When she's got it on full blast, it's like having a psychopath around. Except it's not her. It's you. Which makes it all the more scary."

"Your salesmanship could use some serious work, Kiera," I say. "I'm more convinced that ever that I do not want that... *person* near me."

She grimaces. "We'll see how you feel in a few weeks after working together. Memory reconstruction is tedious, repetitious, boring. With Mikel it's a roller coaster into your soul."

"Pass," I say. "When do you and I start?"

She stares at me, pursing her lips like she's sucking on a lemon. Then she grumbles, "Tomorrow. First thing. And we're doing it at the Water House. I don't want to risk memory contamination. After that you've got Guild Indoctrination 101."

"Seriously?" I say.

She lets out a high, tinkling laugh. "That's not actually what it's called, but I figure it would get your attention and make you eager for blood. We like Guild recruits to be passionate!"

I roll my eyes. "Exciting. Who do I talk to about finding my brother? Surely one of these Primes can help me with their superpowers."

"We don't call them that," she chides. "But we can look at the Prime Human database. I can show it to you tomorrow."

"Why not now?"

"I have to talk to Lainey."

"About what? Permission to breathe?"

Kiera gives me a look. "No, about me being the one to help you retrieve your memory, among other things."

I huff. "Does she ever ask *you* for advice?"

"All the time."

"Name one thing."

"Lainey's a proprietary mission specialist," she says defensively. "This morning she asked me what I thought about her ability to handle a new mission to hunt down PHIA."

"What did you tell her?"

"I advised her against it. She's too emotionally invested."

"If you're a Prime Human, how are you *not* emotionally invested?"

"It's not my place to talk about her personal business."

I grumble, and we reach my apartment building.

"Tomorrow morning. Eight A.M. In front of the Water House, okay?" Kiera says.

"Yep," I say, skipping up the steps to the front door. My shoulder feels amazing after Ohr worked on it this morning.

"Have you been writing in that journal I gave you?" she calls.

"Ahh…" I say, chagrinned.

She scolds me with her eyes. "If you don't want Mikel in your head, you need to do what I'm telling you."

I salute her and back through the front door.

Ten

*T*hurs, Nov 5, 2015

    Kiera's Guild Indoctrination 101 is actually Colloquies. I figured it would be a kind of new member orientation, but I think I was probably the only actual recruit in the room. Everyone else was already a member. Kiera told me I have to attend daily until I'm 'activated,' (the term for being inducted into the Guild). Once I'm a member, I only have to attend weekly. Anyway, it was a class. A facilitated discussion of a topic randomly selected from a list the Council thinks is appropriate. The topic today was Peril and Purpose. Basically, how to stay motivated when the world is falling apart.

    I expected a little psychobabble and a little motivational speaking. And there was that, but mostly there was a lot of reference to something everyone here universally refers to as "the prophecy.'" Being a noob, I had to ask what the mess they were talking about. Everyone is so overly nice here, so nobody made me feel like an idiot for not knowing something that is clearly common knowledge among them. They seemed all too happy to be able to tell me about a dude named Samuel P. Pruitt.

    Forty years ago Sam predicted the world would end within a lifetime. He had a life force ability that allowed him to see the place where he stood as it would look some time in the future. Basically, he predicted what's happening right now. It is this prophecy that everyone was so excited about in class because it means the founders of the Guild were right. It means the Council has been right. It means everything Prime Humans have been preparing for has been spot on. Turns out, the Guild has been preparing for the Apocalypse since its own inception in the seventies. Samuel was one of the founding members.

    When I kept asking questions, the facilitator told me about the library here. I went there straight after my colloquy and did some research on Sam. The Guild has meticulously preserved their history. Sam's future-telling ability was legit according to everyone who knew him at that time. He had no problem demonstrating it to people. So when he said the world would end, people believed him.

I don't know what I think of this. It feels a little kooky. A little religious even though the Guild seems to be a pretty open-minded, secular organization. It also makes me curious what else I don't know about the Guild. I think I'll be spending a lot of time in the library.

In other news, not unrelated, an earthquake hit the southern tip of Nevada. Since the Guild predicted it, people evacuated the area ahead of time, but the quake destroyed one of the dams along the Colorado River, which supplies Southern California with most of its water. The government won't spend money to fix the dam since Southern CA is basically lawless and outside of federal jurisdiction now. This tragedy stuff is happening all over, but this one hit close to home for me. I know people there. At least I think so. I hope they all left though, including my brother, because on top of anarchy, they may be facing a dangerous water shortage.

Fri, Nov 6, 2015

I started working today. It's a temporary assignment until I can get clearance to work in the Energy World Research Department, which is my goal. My job for the next three days is assisting in the routine maintenance of the public computers at the Vault, which are distributed among three different labs. Personal computers are allowed at the Vault, and we all have Guild-issue tablets, (which everyone calls their GIT), but they don't have world wide web access, only G-net, which is a mini-Internet that networks worldwide Guild servers. Guild servers are satellite-linked, not cable linked, so as disasters have systematically downed massive portions of the Internet, G-net never goes down. You can't access the Internet from G-net, and you can't access G-net from the Internet. And devices only work on one or the other. Within the Vault, the computer labs are the only place to access the Internet. So they get used pretty frequently. It was familiar work to me, which is probably why they gave me the assignment. They seem pretty interested in giving people jobs suited to them.

The Colloquy topic today was interesting: Life Force Ability Categorization and Limits. The discussion centered around the non-fantastical nature of most abilities. I get now how the Guild has managed to keep their existence so far under the radar. Most abilities have to do with either smarts or mental influence. Very few have to do with object manipulation—like telekinesis or electrical manipulation. No sonic screams, flying, or laser beam eyes. I went to the library again to read more. Turns out there's actually a Life Force Ability Encyclopedia.

Kiera showed me the Prime Human Database. There are plenty of Prime Humans whose abilities would be helpful in locating a missing person, but not when they have never met that person. It actually surprised me to find out how easily life force abilities can be rendered ineffective. Their power and scope are heavily dependent on the subject they are using it on or with. There are a lot of limiting factors, and actually most of what the Guild accomplishes is through collaborative abilities. The Guild's tight-knit community isn't just for the social benefits or for protection. I kind of suspect that if these people were just out there wandering among the rest of humanity, they would either not notice their own abilities, or if they did, they'd have no idea what to do with them. For instance, if you can hear electrical currents to such a degree that you can determine the voltage passing through a system, how does that suit you to anything but a standard electrician? In the Guild, however, you could get put in a specialized team. Maybe with someone who has megabrains and another person who directs magnetic fields. The three of you engineer highly-specialized computation systems. Where else would people like that end up finding each other?

Anyway, Kiera thinks Lainey's ability could help, and she said she'll ask. Lainey can see the connections between people, even when the people aren't together, so if I have a strong connection to my brother, she might be able to track him down that way, by following the line between us. It seems straightforward, but after what I've read, I'm keeping my expectations in check.

Last night, Castle Rock, the extinct volcano in the middle of Edinburgh, Scotland, erupted. It was predicted of course, but it's spewing some toxic ash that is making the air quality dangerous for miles. The Guild is planning to use their new air filtration chemical once the volcano stops hurling so much poisonous ash, but in the meantime, a lot of people are without homes and livelihoods.

Sat, Nov 7, 2015

Other than colloquies, it was my day off today. I mostly

spent it reading. But I also went to lunch with a couple people I've met. Being friendly is a thing here. Seriously. If you want to be left alone, do not go out in public. People will walk up to you randomly and introduce themselves. They'll ask if you're on task or a move-in. On task means you're passing through. If you say you're a move-in, they get all excited, like the possibility of making you as a new friend is the highlight of their week. It's strange. But nice. They're actually genuine about it.

The Colloquy topic was about avoiding addiction. I found out they are absolutely militant about it because to them addiction begins with a lack of fulfillment. That's why they're so adamant about giving people jobs that engage them. People often rotate through various jobs, the turnover is very high on purpose, and special assignments with your dyad are a big deal. So the discussion was about broadening the definition of addiction, a reminder that anything can become addicting, including behavior. That being said, the Guild has developed drugs that directly combat addiction, so the Colloquy spent a lot of time on recognizing when you need help. I found myself impressed with the scope of the discussion. These people are serious about fulfillment and personal improvement.

Sun, Nov 8, 2015

I haven't mentioned my sessions with Kiera before now because they're boring. She has me recounting things from my childhood. I'll tell her about something that happened to me and she'll make me start the story over again and include some detail I left out like the the clothes someone was wearing or the color of the walls or describe the look on someone's face. Most of the time I feel like I can't actually remember more than what I've said, but Kiera's really good at knowing when I should recall more. I don't know how she does it, but it's kind of crazy how much I can remember when she asks the right question. Kiera says that's why we do it—to get my brain used to digging deeper for memory pieces. She says the patterns I was used to using to reconstruct my missing memories were burned out when I was struck by lightning and I have to make new ones. These exercises are to build my tools to do that.

Colloquy topic: The Council. I thought the Guild membership voted for who was on the Council, but turns out new Council members are nominated and voted on only by those already on the Council, which I guess is supposed to keep it from becoming a political process. Council members serve on the Council for life, so it's considered a pretty big sacrifice. They don't get paid outside of a stipend. It's been that way since inception, except for the original Council. Sam Pruitt handpicked the first twelve. Council members are the only ones that have access to everything, including and especially energy world information, which I'm starting to get is esteemed like a sacred text. The energy world itself is spoken of like it's a celestial realm, a doorway to the true self and one's full potential, and the Council is extremely careful about who gets access to it. I swear the Guild's practices get weirder and weirder to me, but the people I know get nicer and nicer.

The news: A cluster of mass murders in Brazil within a three day period. I had no idea this would be considered part of the natural disaster problem, but Kiera reminded me about California. It's a psychological epidemic. Those are happening more frequently. Crazy.

Mon, Nov 9, 2015

Kiera wants me to record my dreams. Last night was the most normal one in a while. I think I was finding a book in a library. The book kept getting moved just before I'd get there. Really annoying. I guess I've been spending too much time at the Guild's library.

I barely feel my shoulder anymore. I think that growth hormone injection Dr. Lim gave me was for real. I haven't even been out of the hospital a week. I think I'm going to start running in the mornings, since my arm is cooperating already.

Lunch in the Pavilion, as usual. I met another new person, as usual. If I weren't an empath, I would seriously suspect all these people befriending me of being part of a secret plot to win over my allegiance toward the Guild. But they're just that friendly. I wonder if you grow up in and around the Guild, is friendship-making one of the gen ed requirements?

The Colloquy topic was Embracing Background Diversity. I learned another weird thing. The Guild is fond of "initiatives" (and acronyms), probably because they predict most major problems and like to get ahead of them before they even start. Today I learned about (PHPAI) Prime Human Population Acceleration Initiative. AKA (in my words) Prime Human Baby Factory. Most Primes don't even get raised by their biological parents—not really surprising after what Dr. Lim told me about where Prime Humans come from. Most of them are test tube babies from donated Prime Human gametes and birthed by surrogates. Surrogacy is considered the most honorable of sacrifices, second only to being a foster to Prime children. The Guild even pays for surrogates who aren't part of the Guild, and lots of children are raised in Guild communes. Fostering, surrogacy, and commune parenting are elevated occupations, and anyone who does them gets special privileges and concessions.

All of this baby making is because the Guild wants to increase the Prime Human population as quickly as possible. More Primes means more life force abilities in the fight against the Apocalypse. More ways the prophecy is ingrained in every part of the way the Guild operates.

I found out who is in charge of locating missing Prime Humans. I contacted them about my brother and learned that he had already been added to their list. They were already actively looking for him. When I mentioned that it was possible that PHIA has him, they told me they'd already been given all the information pertaining to him, and that if he was indeed captured by PHIA for some reason, then the PHIA recovery team would probably find him before they did—they had nothing to do with that department. PHIA recovery is classified though, so that means I get no information on any progress whatsoever. I feel like I'm getting the runaround with all these departments that aren't allowed to talk to each other.

I'm burnt out on the news already, so I've stopped watching it. Bad stuff keeps happening, and listening to it and writing it down doesn't actually accomplish anything. Plus, people are talking about stuff going on in the world anyway. I don't need to spend time keeping up with it since someone will inevitably bring it up at lunch.

Tues, Nov 10, 2015

Dreams: I was flying. It's one of my favorite repeat dreams.

Colloquy: Eric Shelding. So this is the guy that discovered the energy world and life force abilities in the 50s. If you're a life-long Guild member, he'd be like Jesus or Mohammed or something. He had a dream about the energy world and then began a quest to find it, and did. He developed life force manipulation that gave people access to life force abilities, and he published a bunch of stuff on it, tried to let the world know about the energy world and it's viability as an area of scientific study. He got huge push back, for obvious reasons, especially from the religious community who saw it as witchcraft and satanism. He was martyred apparently, by just such people, so I'd say it's pretty logical to get why, even before Andre, the Guild has always been so secret and guarded. Samuel came along not long after that with his prediction. Through him, people who knew about Eric's work began to understand that life force abilities came about for a purpose—to rescue the inhabitants of earth from certain destruction.

Heavy stuff. I kind of can't believe it's real. The bow seems a little too neat. But that's probably just me. I'm actively fighting my cynicism this time. But that's why I visited the library again to learn more. I found out there's an electronic library I can have access to on my GIT. For real?? Nobody thought to tell me this the first time I went there??

I changed jobs today. Now they have me assisting one of the handymen, Freddie, as a runner. His work seems pretty easy, and it mostly consists of changing out faulty parts in appliances all over the Vault. The bad parts are refurbished if possible, or completely recycled. I learned from Freddie that Guild appliance technology is aimed at accomplishing three things: fewer moving parts, fewer disposable parts, and less water. Easy, intuitive parts changing is the name of the game for maintenance. Time wasted on assembling and disassembling is not acceptable, so appliances are made to come apart and go back together easily.

I also made homemade tortillas tonight and watched Seinfeld reruns for a change of pace. They don't do my ultra-fancy holographic TV much justice, but after spending the day with Freddie in the Vault's Tomorrowland, I needed to feel like I was still in 2015 rather than 2115.

Wed, Nov 11, 2015

Samuel P. Pruitt, the prophecy, and the energy world come up pretty much daily. They are apparently relevant to everything and everyone at the Guild despite the fact that not once have I ever seen mention of these things on the news when anchorpeople talk about the mysterious Guild and their Prime Humans. The public knows the Guild as an organization dedicated to human improvement. This public persona is way less bizarre than their private one, which is a collection of people devoted to worshipping the energy world and stopping the Apocalypse because of a 40-year-old prophecy. Being a part of that mission is every Prime Human's ambition. To the rest of the world, however, the prophecy is more or less secret. Actually, I did an internet search for it, and it's not secret so much as it isn't broadcasted and nobody on the outside cares enough to bring it up anyway. Because the Guild made their very first official public appearance by announcing they could predict natural disasters. And they proved it by posting upcoming disasters on a website and letting the public watch them come true one by one. In that case, why would the public care if they predicted the Apocalypse 40 years ago?

Which brings me to my conversation with Dr. Lim, who called tonight to check on me. I asked him why he didn't tell me all these weird Guild things I'm learning in Colloquies, like the men, the myths, the legends, Eric and Samuel.

Dr. Lim laughed at me. "I see you've met your ancestor finally!"

Then he told me Sam was the father of Carl and Robert Haricott. Samuel P. Pruitt is my grandfather.

Yeah. I am the granddaughter of the prophet. AND I'm capable of seeing the energy world—so they say. I'm the convergence of two worshipped legacies and I auspiciously appeared on the Guild's doorstep. Sort of.

Dr. Lim said he didn't tell me right off the bat because he thought it would be amusing to watch me navigate my cynicism through the discovery.

I don't know what this means. But it feels like I've been given an enormous pair of shoes to fill.

Eleven

Pulling my laundry out of the Fiber Oscillator, I hold up my stretchy running shorts in particular and marvel at how brand new they look. I've sweated through them and then put them in this fancy waterless washer every day for the last eight days. The usual wash cycle only takes ten minutes, but I just noticed the machine also has a twenty minute cycle for delicates. In that case, will the delicate cycle make my old stuff become new again?

Wait. I don't *have* any old stuff. I have nothing from my old life. Not even a photo. It's like I popped into existence at the hospital. That was… only two weeks ago. Has it only been that long?

Yeah… this is only the second time I've done a whole load of laundry outside of my running gear.

I back up and pull myself onto the adjacent counter in the laundry room as I process that. Two weeks? I feel like I've already reinvented myself. It's not like I've remembered anything from my missing time while working with Kiera… But I have a running group, a lunch group, and a pretty in-depth knowledge of how the Guild operates thanks to Colloquies and all my extra reading. I have aspirations even. I want to work in EWR. I am passionate about CWI, the Clean Water Initiative. I use acronyms.

Today I greeted someone I didn't know, introduced myself. *Because I wanted to be friendly.*

Oh my gosh. What has happened to me? I still *feel* like myself, sarcastic, stubborn, skeptical about everything. In fact, today, during Colloquy, I caused some waves. The question posed was why, despite the prophecy, the first Council had so much difficulty convincing Primes to join the cause after their 1976 inception. Most people said things like lack of faith in something so new, fear of the prophecy, a distrust in the Council's motives, and a lack of vision.

I said marketing. It wasn't until the Council came up with the term 'Prime Human' that membership began to pick up. First, the term rings as official, so it had to have made the Guild come off as the authority on the subject of life force abilities, plus, it must have made people with life force abilities feel special, important, needed. So people jumped on because suddenly they either saw themselves differently, or they wanted to be part of an elite brand. 'Prime Human' legitimized life force abilities simply by giving them a distinction.

I could tell from the immediate discomfort around me that I'd committed a faux pas. The facilitator then tactfully assured me that the term 'Prime Human' had been coined by Eric Shelding well before 1976, when it was first discovered that life force abilities could occur naturally in later generations, not the Council. I countered by pointing out that it was the Council that decided to bring it into common use. The facilitator's answer? "The Council is comprised of individuals suited to know when and where and how to use the secrets the energy world offers to the betterment of Humanity and for the protection of Primes. To tell those possessing life force abilities who they were and what they were meant for was a well-placed and inspired action."

I was a little pissed when I left, I admit. Basically, to Guild members, the Council is a group of people in the 99th percentile of moral standards who work night and day to protect Primes and the energy world with flawless efficiency and supernaturally inspired methods. Claiming that such people use marketing psychology is like saying the Pope hires a speech writer because he sucks at public speaking. Maybe he does though. So what? Who cares as long as the message is getting through?

Yeah, I am definitely still me. A more popular me, which is a weird development. And none of these people know know my connection to Pruitt and Shelding. I've never really done large groups of friends before. Today I had three more people I know from Colloquies join me at lunch. And even after I insulted the Council by insinuating they use marketing...

I shove my small bit of laundry into a bag and throw it over my shoulder as I head down the hall back to my apartment. After losing memories of who I once was, I'm shocked at how quickly I've reclaimed an identity. Except for one thing: Ezra. Kiera told me Lainey would be willing to take a look at my connections to people, but she's doubtful how useful it will be now that I know a lot more people. She wouldn't be able to tell which one would belong to Ezra. Plus, it's limited by distance. I felt from Kiera that she doesn't agree completely with Lainey, but then Kiera seems to bow to Lainey more often than not. I might have to approach her myself—if she ever shows up here.

On second thought, I don't know why I'm accepting that. It's not like I'm trapped here. I'm just... satisfied here.

Why am I satisfied? I have no idea what happened to my brother and I'm okay with that? I have a bunch of bizarre clues about my past, dead father and uncle, guns, Claude, PHIA, but none of it puts me into a confused fix anymore. I've been over the details a million times and they're starting to get stale.

I pour hot water over my ginger tea bag and stir it slowly with a spoon as I draw up Ezra's face now, expecting desperation to follow. But I find that the hollow in my chest that usually accompanies memories of him is not nearly as deep. Not having my brother around has become normal.

Is it because I think he's dead? After hearing daily how PHIA is systematically hunting down and killing Prime Humans, and knowing that I am on their list, that they already took out my father and uncle, I think it would be false hope to think Ezra survived. He would have been there when I woke up. I'm sure of it. I haven't been desperate to confirm it because that would mean a pain I wasn't ready to deal with.

But I want closure, don't I?

No. I want Ezra to be alive. I want to find out what happened to us. But this place is making it too easy to be complacent. They *tell* me they're looking, but I have gotten zero updates. How have I been okay with that? And I'm getting nowhere with Kiera. She told me slow and steady wins the race. But if it means losing my drive to find Ezra, I can't risk it. Anger at myself grows with a vengeance. I've let myself get wrapped up in this new life. I even stopped keeping up with the outside world. I've let myself go numb. Fourteen days was all it took for me to check out of reality.

I stand up, slip on shoes and a pullover. It's chilly outside, and I work on getting my right arm through my sleeve as I traverse the grounds. It's still a little stiff, but I no longer wear a sling. Lots of people are out, all of them looking like they have somewhere to be, but the computer lab is empty when I arrive.

I sit down and pull the keyboard into my lap. The first thing I search for is lightning storms in Missouri. I want to know what kind of news coverage was generated. If my brother knew where I went, and he saw the coverage, he might actually have assumed I died and that's why he wasn't at the hospital with me.

I get a ton of hits. It turns out most of southern Missouri was *hammered* by lightning storms that night. It was a lot more extensive than I had assumed. Big Spring Park, where I was found, was part of what is being called the biggest disaster cluster ever. Most calamities, I learn as I read, happen in isolation, seemingly unconnected to other events. Recently the Guild noticed that they have occasionally been happening in clusters, where, within a certain radius, a collection of events, all of similar nature, occur at once. Four earthquakes at one time. Tornadoes in three states at one time. Sink holes in six different European countries. In this case, other than southern Missouri, there were approximately thirty other supercell lightning storms happening in different locations around the United States.

Each article is rife with stunning images of the faraway night sky lit up with thousands of veins of light. I've never seen anything like it. To me it looked and felt and sounded like the Western Front during World War II. Most of the articles address the damage that was caused, most of which was a result of fires starting and burning homes too close to the forest.

I go back to read some of the articles specific to Big Spring, but it's not until I search for 'Big Spring Survivor:' that I get a relevant hit:

> Despite the Missouri Ozarks storm being listed on the GDNS, one individual, presumed by locals to be from out of town, name withheld, was caught in the ensuing blaze. The individual was rescued by local man, Claude Fortner, 48.

Why did I go somewhere the Guild Disaster Notification System had warned people away from? I click on another article.

> Evacuations went flawlessly leading up to the Ozark lightning storm, and so far only one victim
>
> has been reported. The unnamed individual was rescued by a local park ranger who had stayed behind and taken to the Van Buren community hospital. Sources claim the individual was quickly identified as Prime Human and transferred to

another hospital. Speculation has offered a number of possible explanations for why a Prime Human would have been in the middle of the atmospheric onslaught, but the Guild has remained silent about the issue. UPDATE (Nov 2, 2015): Witness reports suggest PHIA may be involved in the individual's presence in the woods despite the GDNS warnings.

November 2nd... I quickly look at a calendar. I am pretty sure that was the day I woke up in the hospital in Lebanon. The very next day PHIA showed up. Were they in Van Buren previously to question people about the lightning storm survivor, and that's where the update came from?

Next, I search for: murders in Van Buren, MO
Nothing relevant.
PHIA in Van Buren, MO

I get the same article about the lightning storm with the one tiny update. I sigh, tapping my fingers lightly against the keys as I think.

Lebanon Community Hospital murder
Finally something.

The PHIA movement has made its way to Missouri for the first time. Yesterday, just after ten in the morning, two men in casual attire approached the receptionist's desk at Lebanon Medical Center, inquiring about one of the patients. They refused to produce identification, and when they were denied the room number of the patient in question, one of them produced a knife from his coat and slashed the throat of the receptionist, 23 year-old Shauna Carmine. Cameras show that while one looked up the information himself on the receptionist's computer, the other carved the widely-known PHIA symbol on her back before both took the elevator to an upper floor where they pulled fire alarms and threatened staff out of the building.

The identity of the patient they were after has not been disclosed, but sources say he or she escaped the premises with the help of Guild operatives. It is believed that the patient was a Prime Human of particular interest to PHIA as no other violence in the area was reported and the men escaped without further disruption.

The article includes a picture of poor Shauna—before she was murdered.

I look up PHIA itself, finding an oddly aesthetic website with well-placed white space and minimalist simplicity. Without reading the hateful words that explain why Prime Humans are unnatural and dangerous, at first glance it could be a site for a charity or a tech company. I'm actually surprised there *is* a website. Who is hosting it? And what kind of serial murder movement has the gall to actually market itself?

I do a search for Andre specifically, find a picture of a man that's maybe in his thirties or forties wearing an outfit of grey pants and grey button-up with a light pink tie. His arms are crossed, blonde hair combed back. He has a wide smile that reveals two rows of perfectly aligned teeth. He could be mistaken for a realtor. And he also reminds me of the Cheshire Cat. It's creepy. I shiver and close that window.

I read a few articles about PHIA, finding one journalist's chart of PHIA massacres. It looks like their targets were all near coastlines or major metropolitan areas. The Lebanon incident appears to be completely out of character. They had never hit anywhere near Missouri until me. How odd… The Vault is in Missouri. It's the biggest facility in the nation. Dr. Lim told me Andre's biggest weapon was having in-depth knowledge of Prime whereabouts. He must know the Vault is here… And although it would be suicide for Andre to attack the facility directly, lots of Primes live 'off-campus,' working at a number of Guild-owned facilities around the state. Yet he appears to steer clear of the place as a rule…

Except to come after *me*.

On a whim, I do a search for my name but get absolutely nothing pertaining to me. I next try Robert Haricott.

I'm surprised to find a very recent biographical article on my long-lost uncle. It's part of a series of articles called *Prime Humans Exposed.*

Little is known about the personal affairs of Robert Haricott, tech billionaire, and while living, his status as the twelfth richest man in America was not widely known. His primary business was Qual-Soft, Inc, a privately-owned surveillance technology firm that contracted with military entities. But he had stakes in some thirty companies positioned all over the United States, Canada, and the UK, all technology firms. After some digging, we find that Haricott's company was the originator of nearly all wireless improvements in the past ten years, allowing devices to transmit data over longer and longer distances. The other innovation you can thank Haricott industries for is some of the most sophisticated data-gathering toys used by the government. If you're upset about losing your privacy, Haricott industries have made it easier than ever for your correspondences to be monitored. By who? We don't know. But after Robert Haricott's death, he was immediately reported by the Guild to be a Prime Human, so it's anyone's guess.

Why have you never heard of this guy? You know the story. The Guild, per their Prime Human Protection Policy, refuses to disclose his life force ability, but we can only assume Haricott's success was due in large part to whatever supernatural privilege he enjoyed, and we were none the wiser. The man's lack of media attention ensured that his status of wealth and influence was never made known to the general populace so it wouldn't be questioned. Following his death, his privately-owned companies were either dismantled or systematically sold off. His controlling market shares of Qual-Soft changed hands. Considering Haricott was both widowed and childless, who was the lucky beneficiary of all those assets? It seems those records have disappeared with no explanation. How do you lose track of upwards of a hundred billion dollars?

One thing we do know, Haricott was reported by the Guild to be one of the first victims of PHIA, the Prime Human Insurgency Alliance. Though Haricott was underrepresented in the media, his death is nevertheless high-profile. PHIA, in most cases, has been known to operate more advantageously, taking easier targets in more public places to generate the height of fear. Cutting the Guild off at the head is either something they aren't capable of, or aren't interested in for some other reason. So why Haricott? And where, as we encounter with so many of these cases, are his relatives? Cousins, nephews, parents? Why do these people always seem to exist in a vacuum?

"Wow," I mumble to myself. My uncle was the twelfth richest man in America? How did I never know this?

I drum my fingers on the table, and it hits me for the first time that my existence as his niece must not exist for a reason. I knew that my father's name was Haricott, and my understanding had always been that I was given my mom's last name. But now… Knowing that I was *taken* from my father, not bearing my father's name must have been strategic. In fact… he's not even listed on my birth certificate. Why did that never strike me as odd? My mom said she and him were separated when I was born and she didn't want anything from him at the time. They got back together later, but my birth certificate was never changed.

She lied, I realize. My birth certificate was a fake… And my uncle… He must have known, given the letter he sent me, but he left my mom alone all those years?

Ugh… It's one thing to miss two and a half years-worth of memories, but I'm simultaneously discovering things about the distant past that are changing everything I knew about it.

I find lots of data on my uncle, a few interviews, (he apparently wouldn't often entertain them), and lots of mentions. I find an older article specifically reporting his death. He was kidnapped by PHIA, tortured, killed, and then dumped along with his bodyguard, who survived, at a hospital in Redlands, California this past June, literally, to the day, that the LA riots began. Surely that's not merely coincidence…

Trying a different angle, I search for my name and Robert Haricott together.

I get nothing. Bugged, I do a cross-search with my name and Pomona, California, where I used to live. Nothing. Not a single listing. In fact, I can't even find anyone else who shares my name, as if the name Wendy Whitley is too unusual to be shared by anyone else.

My final search is for Carl Haricott. I scan the results carefully because I won't immediately know what might actually be my dad and what might be someone that shares his name. Nothing looks promising. His alias, David Erlich, however, when I search that name and narrow it to Missouri, pops up with something: a news article from Van Buren, Missouri about the state of the town and its residents following the evacuation. It talks about some demolished property at the edge of town, no reported deaths, but a missing person. David Erlich filed a report for Gemma Rossi the day *after* the lightning storm. It says she had purportedly traveled into Van Buren the previous day in the face of evacuation orders, and she had not made contact since. He had come into town to find her.

My heart skips. Gemma Rossi is me. Once upon a time, I was an artist, and I used Gemma Rossi as my pen name. I wonder why he was using it rather than Wendy Whitley? To protect my identity? He didn't report me as his daughter either. Surely Ezra was with us. Did Ezra stay behind somewhere with Carl? Dear God, what if PHIA took Ezra when they killed my father?

Panic overwhelms me. I scoot my chair back and put a hand over my mouth. I have to find out where Ezra is. And if something happened to him… I have to know.

I look around the room like maybe a solution will appear, but all I can think of is Kiera and her telling me how long it would take to dig out my missing memory. Does Ezra really have that kind of time?

Mikel is a rollercoaster, though. That's what Kiera said. And roller coasters go fast…

I don't spare it another thought. I hop up and out of the room. I head across the well-lit grounds toward the gentle roar of the Water House—which I can hear now that I know to listen for it.

I expect it to be closed at ten o'clock at night, but hopefully I can find access to the residential floors and ring Mikel's room. When I arrive, however, the place it bustling. There are at least four times as many people as I've ever seen when I'm here during the day. I guess that makes sense. People are getting off-duty for the day and going to the Water House for some stress relief.

I look at the directory, which says the apartments are on the third floor. So I take the elevator up. It looks nothing like the lower floors. In fact, it's exactly like the residential building I'm staying in. I realize I have no idea which door is Mikel's, but I won't be thwarted. I knock on the first door I see and learn from the woman that answers where Mikel's room is. I thank her and head down the hall, reciting some possible options in my head for how to get her to help me. I am not beneath using my secret would-be celebrity status of granddaughter to the prophet and oracle to the energy world if that's what it takes.

I knock on Mikel's door. A woman opens it. It's definitely Mikel; she's wearing a pastel green nightgown, and her hair is down, framing her face. Her mouth still has that very male hardness, but the waves of her dark hair soften it, making it not as pronounced as before. Plus, she has breasts after all, the satin material of her nightgown unable to hide them.

"Mikel, sorry to bother you," I say, stumbling over my words a little because her appearance is so drastically different. "But I... I've kind of been having a breakdown and I need your help."

Mikel looks as stunned as I feel, blinking, her lips opening and closing. Then she closes her eyes, bows her head, her hand resting more heavily on the door.

"Are you okay?" I say, leaning to the side to better see her face.

"I don't take impromptu visits, Miss Whitley," she says, not looking up.

"I—I'm sorry," I say, realizing now that she is indeed having a hard time with... something. My empathic ability is a little wonky right now, wavering in and out of function due to all the water here. "I didn't want to waste time because I really *really* need your help. I was researching about my dad, and I found something. And it makes me worried about my brother. If he's in trouble I don't want to wait. So I figured I'd come to you because Kiera said you work... differently. But if—if you can't help me tonight I'll understand. I can come back tomorrow if that's better. I'm really sorry about the other day. My mouth gets away from me sometimes, and I've been really stressed—"

"Stop babbling," she snaps, holding up a hand, eyes finally flashing to my face.

"I can come back," I say, thinking I jumped the gun on this. I should have gone to see Kiera first, asked her about coming to see Mikel. She would have told me it wasn't a good idea.

"It's a little late for backpedaling," Mikel says harshly. "You've already done the damage. So get in here and stop acting like that! It's annoying." She steps to the side.

I walk past her, noticing that the majority of her decor is water features. One whole wall in her living room is a fountain, water pouring from the point at the ceiling down into a trough. She points me to a couch and I notice that she has a glass of wine in one hand now. She sits languorously on a chair, and I wonder how it ever was that I saw her as masculine.

She takes a sip of her wine. "I was feeling the vixen this evening," she explains, once again reading my mind about her gender.

I perch on the edge of the couch, but can't help sinking into it. It's a water couch beneath the upholstery, I realize.

"I was wondering if you'd be willing to help me get my memory back after all," I say.

"I can help you reconstruct your memory," she says, swirling her wine gently. "In fact, I wouldn't admit it earlier, but I find you positively fascinating. Plus, I was right. You're gaining a reputation already…" She stares at me from over her glass, and it seems a bit sensual to me. How much has she had to drink?

"Yeah, I'm kind of… a rabble-rouser," I laugh nervously.

"Defending Kiera… that was *so* cute," she says, smiling to herself. "Like a mother hen. You like her, don't you?" She chews the fingernail of her left pinkie.

"Kiera's awesome," I reply, thinking this is a mind game. I'm not going to participate. "She's treated me like a person from the beginning so I trusted her. She's pretty much why I ended up here."

"I totally understand. She's good at giving people what they want," Mikel says, running a finger over the edge of her glass and glancing up at me, her dark eyes piercing. "Like you. You love being in charge, looking out for others and having them worship you for it. She's so deferential, innocent. It makes you feel good to look out for her, to make her feel useful and needed."

"She can take care of herself," I say, an edge of defense coming into my voice. I don't like what she's implying.

"Of course." Mikel points at me, wagging her finger thoughtfully as if formulating the right words. "But you? Oh my…" She bites her lip and juts her chin slightly toward me as she closes her eyes—definitely evocative. She even half-sighs, half-moans. "The goddess wants to come out. It's so sexy. I'm not sure if I can keep my hands off of you. I do like to touch." She opens her eyes and her lips move into a pout.

I tuck my hands under my legs. This was such a mistake.

"I just want my memories back," I say, struggling not to get upset with her tactics. I don't know if she's in control of herself, but if she is, I am so over this.

Mikel perks up suddenly, sets her glass on the side table, her expression back to the brusque annoyance she opened the door with. "Yes, I'll help you. I take it you wanted to start tonight? Seeing as you showed up here unannounced at ten-thirty at night looking like a whirlwind." She stands up, takes a long wraparound sweater from off of a hook by the door.

"Uh, yeah," I say. "Tonight's good." But inside I'm thinking I bit off more than I could chew with Mikel. She's nuts.

She opens the door, turns and looks at me with raised eyebrows. "I can't actually do this without you," she says expectantly. She shoos her hand toward the door.

I extract myself from the couch and follow her. I remember what Kiera said about Mikel projecting people's ids. Was that my id just now?

All aboard the roller coaster.

Twelve

*W*e leave the Water House entirely. I rush to keep up with Mikel's billowing nightdress as she takes no thought for sidewalks, crossing the grass in her lambskin house shoes. We get a few looks, but nobody stops us. I'm more worried by the moment; whether she's going to take me to an alley to slit my throat or fling herself off of a building, both seem like viable possibilities.

She takes me to the greenhouse. It's huge and lit up like daylight inside and entirely empty but for the tidy rows of voluptuous vegetation. I was here earlier this week on a job, helping to transplant some of the sprouts, so I'm familiar with it. A small courtyard is arranged at the center of the garden, lined with outdoor furniture. She leads me there, pulling two of the chairs to face one another.

She turns to me as I approach, and before I can speak or sit, she walks up to me, puts her hands on either side of my face. She stares into my eyes, getting closer and closer, her hands relaxing until they hold me more like a lover's embrace. I don't know what to do with myself, worried that this strange moment is going to end up with her kissing me or something equally weird. But at the same time, I am hoping this is going to lead somewhere productive.

"*Look* at me," she commands.

I do so, letting her lock my eyes in place with her own. I expect it to be awkward, but it's suddenly as familiar as looking at myself in the mirror. I find myself looking deeper, searching for myself in the black pits of her eyes. And I can't read her emotions. She's a blank slate.

She suddenly releases me, and we both sit at precisely the same time, but on the cement ground instead of the chairs, facing one another.

Mikel looks around and then down. She reaches out and rubs the cement with her hands, finding it suddenly fascinating. Then she lies on her back, staring up at the ceiling. "Mmmmm," she moans, closing her eyes. "This will do."

I wait, cross-legged, unsure of what's going on. I'm about to ask when she says, "Close your eyes."

I obey.

"Think about your last memory, before the woods. Don't speak. Reconstruct as much of it as you can *in your mind only*. From the color of the room to the temperature. Don't leave out a single detail that comes to you. Including your emotions. I may prompt you, or comment, but don't reply. I will tell you to reconstruct, most likely many times if I feel you haven't given me enough. That's your cue to start that particular moment over again and do better at recalling the details of it. Begin."

I'm familiar with this exercise. It's the same thing Kiera does with me except she has me describe the reconstruction aloud as I visualize it. I close my eyes, take a deep breath and see my apartment. I'm standing over the sink, washing dishes. I made dinner, which is something I rarely do because of my schedule. I don't even know what Ezra eats most of the time. In fact, I started investigating the cabinets at the end of the week and never saw anything gone, so I was worried he was either starving himself or he was getting other people to feed him because we didn't have good food. So I gave him a food allowance so he could buy whatever he wanted, stuff he'd actually eat. But then I found like a hundred dollars in my wallet and I was sure it wasn't mine. Ezra totally denied it. But I started taking him to the grocery store myself and making him spend his allowance in front of me. We got in a fight about—

"Stop talking to yourself," Mikel orders.

She's right. I'm getting totally off-track. Apartment. Dishes. Ezra's reading a comic book. I tell him about my appointment at Pneumatikon, the tests they gave me for vision and hearing and smell. My vision was off the charts.

Ezra isn't surprised. He rips into the Oreos I bought him. "What I don't get is why she even gave you a vision or a hearing test in the first place. What do your senses have to do with allergies?"

I shrug. "She said something about how energy therapy has other benefits and she wanted a good 'before picture.'"

"Skip ahead. This is boring," Mikel says, exasperated.

I have the letter in my hand, the one I got from my uncle, Robert Lee Haricott. I did a reverse-search on his phone number and found out it's based in Monterey. That's a bit too far away for me to make a day-trip of it. I was thinking I'd show up at Qual-Soft and demand to know what he wants.

I haven't even told Ezra about the letter. I'm terrified that this is going to result in the uncle, who I know has money, making a good impression on my brother and Ezra deciding he'd rather live somewhere he doesn't have to scavenge for food and beg the neighbor's wi-fi password off of them.

I sigh. I made this decision already. Ezra deserves to know. But if I lose him, I'm going to fall apart. I swallow anxiety and turn around.

"So you are never going to believe who I got a letter from," I say, strategically sitting next to him so I can, hopefully, inconspicuously, take a read on his first impression.

I catch a glance at the cover of the comic book he's reading now: *Superman-Batman*. I flick it with a finger.

"Batgirl?" he answers from behind the pages.

I snort, snatching the comic book away and punching him.

"C'mon! I'm serious! Aren't you even a little curious?" I swing the paper in front of him.

He sits back against the arm of the couch with his book again as if disinterested. His eyes shift to the paper though, and he concedes, "Only if some long lost relative left us a big inheritance."

I hold the paper to my face again. I didn't think of that. Maybe the uncle is dying and wants to reconnect before he goes. "You got half of it right," I reply.

Ezra's grabs the letter out of my hands before I can react. "What?" he says.

I watch him read it.

"So what do you think? You want to meet this guy?" I say, when he finishes.

"Is there actually a choice? Looks like he's pretty serious."

Mikel's voice jars me out of what was so real in my head, "Summarize aloud. I'll tell you when to stop."

I open my eyes but then close them again because the details that have come so easily seem to get snagged away from me as soon as I let go of them. I can't believe how real remembering that night with Ezra was. He was right here with me for a moment…

I exhale heavily and start again. I remember what he was wearing, which was a Green Lantern T-shirt…

"Ezra agrees that we should call our uncle," I say. "He thinks Mom would have warned us to stay away from him before she died if the guy was bad news. I point out how bad off we are, and then—" A sob gets stuck in my throat. I bite my bottom lip.

"He wants to stay with me…" Mikel cries. "My brother doesn't care that I suck at everything."

I open my misty eyes and see Mikel's face buried in her hands. The warmth of shame is so strong it could be happening right this moment.

"I'm going wherever you are…" I whisper.

"Don't let him take Ezra," Mikel gasps into her hands. Then she looks up, her face somewhat maniacal. "I will kill him if he tries to take my brother."

"I wouldn't do that…" I say, afraid. But I thought about it… And hiding. I thought about that, too. Ridiculous things I could never pull off… *Would* never pull off.

I lose sight of Mikel for a moment as the scene plays out in front of me. The phone call, the sound of Robert Haricott's voice. I latch on to the cadence more than the words. His enthusiasm sounds… uncomfortable. He doesn't want to talk to me, but he's doing it. Why is he contacting me if he doesn't actually want communication?

When I get off the phone with him, I tell Ezra I don't like him. Ezra thinks I'm just cynical, which is true. But it's because of conversations like what just happened, where people mean the opposite of what they say.

"When I got off the phone with him," I say to Mikel, "it was late. We went to bed. That's my last memory. I woke up in the woods two and a half years later." I let the visual of Ezra sitting on the couch above me fade.

Suddenly, an awesome fear creeps up from somewhere inside of me, faceless and unexplained. It moves with persistence, overtakes me. This is suffocating. I can't see, and I reach for the cement, lying down.

"That's not all," Mikel gasps.

I pin my eyes shut and press my cheek to the ground as hard as I can, as if pushing against the fear crushing me, so overwhelming I can't think. I want it to stop. How do I get it to stop?

"Recon—Reconstruct," Mikel's voice stutters out of the darkness.

I don't know what that means anymore.

"Reconstruct!" she yells louder, this time the sound shoving me out of the blackness. She's lying on the ground next to me, sweating and heaving.

"I can't—What was that?" I pant.

"You," she coughs, grasping her stomach.

"No, it wasn't," I say. "I know my own emotions."

Mikel suddenly pushes herself up to her hands and knees and throws herself at the nearest potted plant—a geranium bush. She upchucks into it.

"Mikel, what was that!?" I demand, shakily pushing myself off of the ground. She wipes her mouth with the hem of her nightgown while holding her inky black hair out of the way in her other hand. Then she stands and finds the nearest chair, elbows on knees, letting her head hang as she recovers.

I wait, but a couple minutes pass by without her moving.

When I can't stand it anymore, I open my mouth to demand that she speak when she preempts me and says, "I don't recommend this." She lifts her face, her features now slack and worn in an indefinable way.

"Why?"

Honest hesitation dulls her eyes as she says, "I don't believe your memory loss is from lightning strike amnesia. It feels exactly like repression. And I have never seen anyone repress such a huge span of time. Reconstructing it has an extremely high possibility of causing mental illness."

I purse my lips skeptically. "What was that feeling at the end? Because it wasn't me."

"It came from you, straight from the coffers of your Id, who likes to torture you with guilt. That's your whole life's ambition. In this you are perfectly ordinary, Miss Whitley, and if you ask me, in two and a half years you became something you hated so you could be right about yourself. If I were you, I wouldn't want to remember. Start over. Become something new."

I furrow my brow and frown. "I want to. But my brother... I can't start over without knowing what happened. If he's alive, I *have* to find him."

"Kiera will serve you better."

"With her it's going to take years!"

"What if you find out he's dead while simultaneously splitting your Id? Or succumbing to some sort of psychosis? Or what if you find him alive and the sister he is reunited with can no longer love him like she used to?"

"You're saying you can't help me?" I say, frustrated.

"Oh I can. Your empathic ability is going to make this exceptionally easy. But there is such a thing as *too* easy."

"So you *won't* help me then," I say angrily.

She closes her eyes, makes a mental effort to restrain something—my Id poking through perhaps?

"I'm saying I advise against it. But I have a policy of leaving the choice up to the individual. I would advise you that what you are doing is selfish, not some honorable quest to find your brother. *You* can't stand not knowing where he is. What drove you to seek my help was *you* not liking how *you* felt and wanting to change it."

My face goes red with upset. "You're wrong. I came to you because I had *stopped* feeling."

"Numbness is a feeling."

"I have to risk it," I say, thinking this argument will go nowhere. "If there is even a chance that my brother is in trouble and I can save him, I can't waste time with Kiera. Because what if I do and he gets killed in the meantime? What if I wait and rely on Kiera only to realize later that if I'd remembered sooner I could have saved him? How can I live knowing that? Doing everything I can though? I *can* live with that."

She sighs begrudgingly and staggers a little as she comes to her feet. "Sometimes," she says softly in a faraway voice, "I think we take for granted the value of ignorance. The mind is not equipped with perfect recall for a reason. No matter how much we remember of an event, it will never be exactly as it happened. The edges are softer. The emotions duller. The details faded. Being unable to remember something precisely as it was protects the mind from past trauma that might otherwise consume it." She looks at me directly. "Without this failsafe, memories could easily drive us insane," she says darkly before turning her back toward me.

"I'm doing it," I say firmly.

"Not tonight," she says, scuffling toward the exit. "I need to rest from you. Tomorrow. Right here. Same time."

Thirteen

I toss and turn all night, consumed by a continual replay of my experience with Mikel. Despite my insistence, I'm not without doubts about proceeding with memory reconstruction with Mikel, especially now that I have time to think about and anticipate it. I wish she had just gone ahead with it right then and there. But then, the time to think about it was probably exactly why she made me wait.

The one thing she said about repression rather than amnesia is what's bugging me most. How does she know? If she's right, I worry the same thing: that for two and a half years I became someone I wouldn't have wanted to be, someone I *don't* want to be. Her suggestion has me reexamining the evidence. After knowing I was clad in weaponry, that I met my morally questionable father, and that I am very much like him, I worry. And I wonder... PHIA seemed to be the only ones who knew I had gone into the woods, so maybe I was in cahoots with them. I thought it odd that no one had come to visit me, but someone did: PHIA.

When I think of who PHIA is, however, what they've done, I can't see myself doing that. It makes me wonder how far I would have let them push me. Is that why I have repressed that time? Because I hate myself for what I did?

That's what the fear at the end of my meeting with Mikel felt like: terror of myself. Self-loathing of torturous proportions.

And even if I wasn't with PHIA, what about my father? Was I part of *his* cause? I don't like where this is going.

But I have to... For Ezra.

Please let him be safe.

I'm mostly sure I'm going to do it still, but this is torture. When I'm not wrestling with myself, I wonder how her ability works. How much of my reconstruction was she actually in on? Most of the time I was simply *remembering*. I wasn't speaking.

Does Id projection include seeing my thoughts in living color? And if not, how does it work? I seemed to fall so easily into the depth and detail of the memory, as if it was happening presently.

By morning I'm so consumed with anxiety, accentuated by a lack of sleep, that I don't wait for my alarm clock. As soon as it starts to get light, I find my tennis shoes. I need to run alone today.

I finish up in front of the Water House as usual, but Kiera is there already, sitting next to one of the fountains. I don't know how she knew I would arrive early.

"Hey!" I call brightly.

Her short, tight curls are bound up in a black ball on top of her head, and she stands up when she sees me. "Good morning," she says, looking as exhausted as I should feel. My eagerness to put all of this memory mess to rest has energized me despite my lack of sleep.

"What's wrong?" I ask when her irritation meets my stomach as she comes in range.

"Mikel came to see me in the middle of the night," she says, hands on her hips as she stares at me.

I stop in front of her, cross my arms. "What did she do?"

"What do you think?"

I narrow my eyes. "If her policy is to let her clients decide, then she should let them decide. She shouldn't be harassing their friends as a tactic to make the client give up what they want," I say.

"This isn't me your friend. This is me your therapist. She's only looking out for your best interests. You should listen to her."

I put my left hand on my hip. "What? You're the one that told me she was my best bet. You're the one that told me to go kiss her butt until she agreed to work with me. She tells you my memories are scary and you just roll over? What am I missing?"

"It's cold out here. Let's go inside and talk, okay?"

"Fine," I say, trouncing toward the glass doors.

We find a secluded corner and take a seat.

She wrings her hands a little. "What you need to understand about memory is that it's not locked away in some filing cabinet waiting for you to find the key. Think of it as playing Telephone. You know what that is?"

"Yeah, a message gets passed from one person to the next and by the time it gets to the person it's intended for, it's distorted."

"Exactly. Whenever you recall something, it's reconstructed. Think of a moment being a collection of pieces: smells, sights, sounds, words. When you experience a moment, you take it apart, putting those pieces in a box—a memory box. When you want to recall that moment, you have to reconstruct it from the box of pieces. But you don't have instructions. Think of it as breaking a mug and then putting it back together based on how the pieces *seem* to go together. Of course, a lot of experiences are far more complex than a mug. That leaves a larger margin of error. Now, as you experience more things, the way you put those pieces back together can change. Because you begin to perceive the world around you differently as memory upon memory is compounded, influencing your methods of reconstruction. What you know and believe right now will influence how your mind reconstructs your past."

"Okay," I say. "You're saying I won't remember things as they actually happened? I don't get it. If that's the case, why would anyone work with Mikel to recall their past in the first place? Why have I been working with *you*? Is it just me? Why?"

She shakes her head, waves her hands. "Working with Mikel will give you results. Quickly. You'll remember something, that much is certain, but the possibility of distortion is much higher in your case because whatever you've forgotten was extremely traumatic."

"People do cognitive therapy all the time to dig up traumatic memories," I point out. "It's considered healthy."

"This isn't cognitive therapy. You're forcing your Id out into the open, the thing that represents your basest desires, and you're going to let it run rampant in all of your memory drawers. Do you trust your Id to do that? Are you sure enough of who you were? Repression is something *you* did. It wasn't caused by external forces. And now you want to undo the thing you did to protect yourself. Two and a half years is a *lot* of memories to hope to reconstruct accurately when your mind never wanted it to begin with."

I cross my arms and sit back, staring up at the glass ceiling of churning water. My eyes start leaking, and once again I'm indecisive. She asked the thing I was worried most about: Am I sure of who I was?

I'm not, and that is the scariest thing I can think of—to not truly know what you're capable of. What was I doing with

Carl, my father, the guy who was giving people super powers at the cost of their life? What were my dealings with Andre? Why was he the only one that came for me? *Where are the people that knew me?*

For a moment the pendulum swings and I think I am going to take her advice. But naturally my thoughts turn to Ezra, the person who will pay for my decision one way or another. And I can't turn my back on him. Strangely, it is that conviction that calms me. What Kiera proposes is terrifying. But there is no amount of scary I wouldn't go through for my brother, the person who made my life finally mean something.

"I'm doing it," I say. "I've thought it through and there is no way I can live without knowing the truth."

Kiera rubs her forehead tiredly. "I wish I'd never suggested Mikel."

"Well you did. I have to act on what I know. I can't *unknow* that she has the ability to help me."

"Too bad," Kiera sighs. She waves her hand and stands. "Well come on. Your activation starts today."

"Really?"

She nods. "You are being initiated into the Guild. You'll have a series of tasks to complete with your dyad—which you're being assigned to today."

"I'm getting my dyad today? For real? Do you know who it is?"

She shakes her head as I follow her out. "Hopefully someone who does a better job of backing you down than I do."

ℵ

"Oh my gosh! Chase!" I gush, coming into the small conference room.

He stands up with a bright smile and hugs me. He's so thin I'm afraid I'll break him.

"Wen-ee," he manages.

"Just call me Wen," I say. "It's easier and that's what most people call me anyway." Then I raise my eyebrows at him, fist on hip. "So. How'd you know?"

He crosses his fingers and grins mischievously.

Someone clears their throat and I turn to Henderson, the gentleman who brought me in here along with Kiera. She's my membership facilitator, but he's the guy that reviewed my application and supposedly had a hand in choosing my dyad.

"Why do I get the feeling you guys had assigned me a dyad before I ever agreed to join?" I say.

"Because we did," Henderson says. "Possible dyads are under review years beforehand. Chase was in your hospital room as a test run. To see if a possible dyad partnership was possible— should you choose activation."

"Possible? I thought you get assigned someone and you don't get a say."

"You don't. But until the assignment is officially made, we may put two people together to see how they mesh. Years before activation, in most cases. Not yours, though. We had a very short time to come up with possibilities."

"How did Chase know you were experimenting and I didn't?" I ask, giving Chase a look.

He crosses his arms haughtily but playfully, then points to himself. "'Mart," Chase says.

Henderson smiles. "He was moved from another hospital and given no explanation as to why so I'm sure that had him suspicious. Chase just turned eighteen, had chosen activation, so he was at least expecting a dyad assignment would be made soon. The dyad we had intended for him was killed by PHIA a couple months ago, so we'd been on the lookout. I'm sure it wasn't that hard to deduce that being placed in the same room as you was strategic."

"Well I like your choice," I say. "So what now?"

"Business as usual," Kiera says, "until you receive your first assignment."

"Actually," Henderson says, "her activation has been accelerated. Unification is tonight."

Kiera's face goes blank, speechless for a moment before saying, "That actually happens? I thought it was a rumor."

"No, it's just rare," Henderson says. "Certain life force abilities entitle membership. All that's left is the pomp and circumstance."

"What's tonight?" I say, not wanting to miss my meeting with Mikel.

"Unification ceremony," Kiera says. "It's short and sweet. Here. Eight o'clock. But be here fifteen minutes early to prepare. You shouldn't miss your meeting." She gives me a disapproving look.

Chase links arms with me. "We 'ang owww," he says, pulling me toward the door.

"We can until after lunch," I say, letting him guide me toward the door.

"Think about what we talked about," Kiera calls. "You can still change your mind."

"Can but won't!" I call back.

I hear her sigh.

"Whaa?" Chase says, walking us into the sunshine.

"I'll tell you all about it. But let's get breakfast. I'm starving."

Fourteen

"*U*ngg*," I mumble to the person shaking me awake.

"Uuuu*p*," the voice says. "Uuuuu*p*." His p's catch in a puff of air.

I pull a pillow over my face.

"Wen-ee," he says. "Wen-ee!"

My brain wakes up enough to recognize Chase's voice. "Whaaat?" I grumble, refusing to open my eyes.

"Uuuu*p*!" He yanks the pillow off of me.

I reach out haphazardly and push him. "G'way," I say.

Something smacks me on the head. A magazine maybe? My eyes pop open. Chase is standing over me with his notebook in-hand.

"What was that for?" I say.

He holds the notebook up and jabs the words on it with his finger.

Mikel.

I sit up abruptly. "Crap!" And then I remember I told Chase to wake me up from my nap in time for my appointment.

He crosses his arms and rolls his eyes.

"Sorry!" I say, digging my feet into my shoes. I push my left hand into a jacket, leaving the right side draped over my injured shoulder. "Thanks! You can let yourself out? I gotta run."

He shoos me with his hand.

I bound out the door, walking quickly down the hall and out into the night, once more headed toward the greenhouse. I'm still waking up, recalling the, as promised, short unification ceremony a little over an hour ago. It was way less cult-creepy than I imagined. Chase and I were given ten minutes prior to the start to come up with a physical or mental task for each other to complete in under ten minutes that would highlight our particular limitations. Normally, apparently, dyads have been working through assigned tasks for a while and are getting to know each other. So with our activation being accelerated, it's a good thing we already know each other to an extent.

Chase's task for me was to hang from a bar by my hands for five minutes. My challenge, of course, was that I couldn't possibly use both my hands with my shoulder not quite recovered. So I had to use one hand. Five minutes is a long time to hang on to a bar with one hand. My left arm is still feeling it.

My task for Chase was to sing a popular song. Of course, Chase can hardly talk, so the expectation was he was going to fumble through his chosen song, but he blew everyone—all fifty-eight people present—away when he sang *Fight Song* flawlessly, as if his speech handicap weren't present. Kiera said singing uses a different part of the brain. Nevertheless, it brought tears to my eyes; it felt like a sign.

After our tasks, we had to say a few words about why we chose that task for our dyad and how we intended to fill in for our dyad's inabilities. Chase signed his words, and someone mumbled a translation to me. He said he was glad my shoulder was broken because otherwise he wouldn't have known what task to give me. I'm way too capable. And then he said maybe that was my flaw— taking too much on because I can do so much. So he was going to always be willing to take up my slack when I need it. I said I chose singing for Chase because of his brain injury, obviously. And I said Chase didn't really need someone to be his voice since the singing proved that—but he needed a family. And I'd lost most of mine. So I'd be his.

Dr. Ohr Lim was the Council member in attendance, and he stood before me and said, 'Wendy Whitley, as a member of the Council, I represent the interests of the entire Guild membership. As you have chosen to unify yourself with us today, we would ask that you state your allegiance, here and now, so that we may forever hold you accountable to our common cause of human progress. Do you take that cause as your own, and in so doing swear to protect Prime Humans, to place their benefit above your own, and to exert yourself toward their betterment from this point on?"

I replied, "Yes."

Ohr welcomed me to the Guild, everyone cheered, and he told me he would be recommending me for the Energy World Research (EWR) department pronto. Chase and I headed back to my apartment, where we spent a few minutes talking about PHIA and how getting my memories back may really help with tracking them down. He was totally on board with my memory recovery with Mikel.

I let myself into the greenhouse when I arrive and see Mikel already in the courtyard. She looks like she's meditating. I don't disturb her when I get there; I sit and wait.

"We will begin by backtracking to your initial appointment at Pneumatikon," she says, her eyes remaining closed. "Do you agree that you would have gone to your follow-up appointment with them?"

"Yes. How do you know about—"

"Then you will draw up the memory of your initial appointment," she orders, "but not the events, just the place, its sights and sounds and smells at first. I will prompt you from there. Do not speak aloud. Close your eyes and begin."

I make myself comfortable in my chair, drawing my knees up under me.

The waiting room is on the small side, also empty. The chairs are upholstered in a flower print, and it's a tasteless combination of puke-pink and forest green, too well-matched to the series of impressionist prints on the wall depicting flamingos. The plants are fake and could use a serious dusting. The carpet has been newly-installed, and it's the industrial kind that makes me wonder why they didn't just put down tile. The door to the back is slightly ajar...

"That's where we need to go," Mikel says, her voice slightly quavering.

I follow a faceless white smock down the hall.

We stop in a huge room. Treadmill, weights, an entire wall of filing cabinets, two desks and computers, other diagnostic tools I don't recognize. A huge white poster with lines of black characters is on the wall: a vision test poster. I look down and see a yellow line taped on the floor. Next to me, a closed door. I wonder what's behind it.

I can't take my eyes off the door.

"Go in," Mikel says.

I reach for the handle and open it. Beyond the door is Dina, the woman who interviewed me at Pneumatikon. She's standing in the middle of an exam room, staring as if she expected me. She holds her hand out to shake mine, and I am suddenly overcome with trepidation.

I take a step back.

"Stay," Mikel says. "Let the memory start here."

I hold my ground even though I want nothing more than to leave.

"Dina Gregor," Dina says, smiling at me now, her hand still extended. "You can call me Dina."

"Nice to meet you," I lie, hoping she'll quit with the hand-shaking.

She does, waving her arm toward the nearby chair. "Would you like to have a seat?"

"Reconstruct," Mikel orders.

I open the door again, and beyond is Dina, holding a pillow. "You'll be more comfortable if you use this," she says, handing it to me. I take the pillow, put it on one of two chairs in the room before sitting down.

"Reconstruct," Mikel says.

Dina's holding the pillow. "You'll be more comfortable. This will take at least a half-hour." She doesn't hand it to me, instead placing it at the head of the odd-looking exam table that reminds me of a massage table.

I stare at it, the same dread washing over me. I walk toward the chair.

"Stop," Mikel says. "Do the thing you don't want to do."

I take a deep breath, staring at the pillow as Dina says, "It could take longer if conditions aren't optimal."

Indignation comes over me. She thinks I can't relax? I walk over to the table.

"An attendant will be with us while I work, and the session will also be video-taped for teaching purposes," Dina says as I hop up onto the table. She leans around the door into the hall. "Derek, we're ready for you."

My chest quivers, my eyes fastened on the doorway as a middle-aged man walks in carrying something, but I'm too busy staring at his face and hoping I can warn him away. Dina is up to no good. He should get out.

"Reconstruct," Mikel says.

He's wearing blue jeans and a white polo and carrying a radio. He's silent as he plugs in the radio.

"Lie back," he says, smiling.

I shake my head.

"Reconstruct," Mikel says. "Stop resisting."

Derek offers me a smile as he plugs in the radio. I lie back as harp music filters gently into the room.

For Ezra, I think as the lights dim, and tension slowly leaks from my chest and out through my feet.

Dina's face is over mine suddenly, startling me.

"Let go," Mikel says.

Dina's silver hair is pulled back today. She has graceful features, a long, sloping nose and high cheekbones.

I avoid making direct eye-contact, so I glance over them quickly. Then I do a double-take and my eyes dart back up to hers for a second look. They're almond-shaped, brown, slightly hard. My chest has constricted in panic though. I could swear her eyes were different a second ago. Black and empty. Like death. They look normal now…

"Reconstruct," Mikel says, but I can hear my panic reflected in her voice.

I pause, calming myself before trying again.

"Stop with the emotion," Mikel instructs. "Just… think visual. What you see, hear. Like you're watching it instead of living it."

"You look quite comfortable already," Dina says from over me, "but we're going to go through some relaxation techniques to get your energy really pliable. Keep your eyes open, but I want you to focus on your breathing, concentrating on in and out."

I focus on the sound of her rhythmic voice. "In… and out… in… and out. Try to breathe slowly… and evenly. Enjoy the sound… and the feel… and the sensation of air moving in… and out."

I follow her instructions exactly.

"Now I want you to concentrate on the sound of my voice while you watch my pen," Dina says softly.

The pen pops into view, not far from my face. I gladly focus on it, letting everything else blur.

"Concentrate your visual efforts on the pen; keep your focus on it as I move it closer, not letting your attention waver. The pen is the only thing you care about right now. Release every other focus. You care only about the pen and the sound of my voice."

The pen draws slowly closer to me. Before it gets too close, and thus too uncomfortable to focus on, it vanishes. *What a neat trick.*

"Now you can go back to breathing. In… and out… Close your eyes," Dina whispers.

Peace finally settles over me, and I'm content to lie here, enjoying it and forgetting everything else going on.

Dina's voice interrupts me, "I want you to focus on your breathing. Feel it. In… and out. I'm going to be silent now and let you enjoy the relaxation."

I become distracted by the fact that cool air comes in through my nose, but I exhale warm air. I love how my chest expands each time, making more room for my insides. It gives me chills of pleasure down my neck and arms. With each breath, I am more and more refreshed, as if I'm stretching out muscles that have been hibernating, releasing lingering emotions that have been trapped in my crevices.

Sounds start to get uncomfortably loud, however. The harp music is grating. Vehicle noise from the freeway jumps forward. Someone's yelling. A baby is crying. Doors creak. Toilets flush. The whine of electricity moving through the walls becomes as loud as a stadium of people.

And then heartbeats. Several of them hammering out a rhythm, one fast, one slow, and mine, which is somewhere in between. I listen to them as I would a song with heavy bass until the smell of new carpet distracts me. Dina's perfume is heavy, and Derek's shaving cream lingers strongly. The tang of electricity reminds me of work where I fix computers.

With so much to take in, I have no concept of time. The menagerie of sense swirls around and through me, trapping me in its rhythm.

I feel something against my skin: like static. It moves from my chest outward, pulsing slowly. I could be getting a massage, but no hands touch my skin.

Once the tingling fades, my mind is left entirely uncluttered, empty even. Someone's erratic heartbeat steals my attention, the sound of anticipation or anxiety. Coupled with new perspiration from somewhere, I think it means the latter. My own pulse speeds up in response. No... I can *feel* the anxiety. And excitement like fluttering. But this isn't me. This is someone else. Who is touching me?

Confusion clangs inside my head, and suddenly the sounds, smells, and sensations clamor for my attention. And the feelings, too. Like a crowd of people forcing their way through one door all at once.

It's too much.

At the same time, impatience claws inside my head, making my efforts to manage the din around me agonizing. Before, I had no trouble pushing sounds back, one by one, so I could listen to them individually. But it's not as easy as before. I want push it all out of me by getting up and shaking out my legs, but I can't get out of my own head.

"Wendy," Dina's voice booms into the noise, and I anchor myself to it.

"Yes," I say, hoping she will keep talking.

A new burst of excitement nearly derails my control, and I wince.

I want to know who is touching me, feeding me their emotions, so I open my eyes.

Something is close to my face. Too close. But it moves away and I realize it's the pen. I'm back where I started. The sensations of earlier came with me though, impatient anxiety and giddy anticipation. I can't get control of my senses now. It's so loud. I put my hands over my ears, fighting to concentrate so I can put the sounds in their place, in the background where they belong.

I blow air out slowly once it all fades, careful to control my thoughts so they don't jar the latch I have on the sounds. I push myself up on my elbows.

"Lie still and allow yourself time to adjust," Dina says.

I turn my head to find her on the other side of the room by a small desk. She's writing something down.

"That's a 'light hypnotic state'?" I say, slightly questioning, slightly accusatory. I don't know much about hypnotism, but I find it hard to imagine something even heavier than what just happened.

The pits and valleys of Dina's face are strikingly visible. Her makeup looks awful. Is that her pulse I see under her skin? Holy cow. Does the hyper-alert state of hypnotism I read about take time to wear off?

She crosses her arms and shrugs. Derek is here, too, also taking notes. "The point is to get you relaxed," Dina says. "Some people require a deeper hypnotism than others to do that."

I think she might be insulting me. But I don't care. The memory of the session is still so fresh, not to mention the fact that my senses are most definitely improved.

Dina's been watching me intently. "Are you all right?"

I'm too busy looking around, astonished by the unending level of detail I discern. I follow a single minuscule piece of dust swirl up to the ceiling, down to the floor, and then back up to rest precariously on the edge of Derek's notebook paper. I look up to his face. The irises of his eyes look like blue pools that someone dragged a brown-soaked paint brush through in a zig-zag pattern.

I blink. More dust. I brush it with my hand. I never could see this level of detail before. I'm ten feet away from Derek and

Dina, but I can see them as well as I could if I were standing only inches away.

Dina steps closer to me. "Is everything okay, Wendy? What are you experiencing?"

She's pulsing red with impatience and I wince away from her, disliking the jitters she seems to be emanating.

"Um…" I start, unsure of what I want to say.

"How are you feeling?" Dina asks, now hotly jealous.

I look down the length of me. I know these feelings aren't mine, but I can also see that no one is touching me.

I come up on my elbows again, but Dina puts her hand on my wrist.

My breath is knocked out of me. Except I felt no fist in my stomach. I only know I can't quite figure out how to inhale. I'm blind. I blink, but there's nothing. I don't know if I moved my eyelids at all.

I can't hear.

I reach for my ears, to make sure they're still there, but I discover I have no arms. No legs.

I've been ripped out of my body, and I've been suspended in an abyss. There is nothing to perceive here.

No sooner have I intuited this than the walls make themselves known. I sense their presence. I can't see them, but I know they are there. But they're moving toward me. I know it. Soon they will collapse on me…

Closer. Closer. Inch by inch.

Soul-clenching Panic.

At any moment I will be condensed into nothing.

Unable to find my mouth, I can't even scream.

I want to fight. I want to breathe. I want to perceive *something*.

Where is my body?

The walls aren't solid surfaces. They're vines that can reach inside of me and obliterate even the thoughts in my head. They will erase me.

My mind!

A sudden shift in perception. I'm thinking. I'm here! Which means I can fight. So I yell it in my head. *I'm here! I'm here! You haven't erased me!*

The vines fall away and I get it: This is not *me* I feel. Not my panic. Not my terror. Not even my lack of sense.

The foreign emotions release me, and I'm empty. A blessed relief. My heart palpates erratically. I shiver. Dina's hand on my arm moves out of the darkness and into my sight. I look up to meet her eyes, but they are completely empty. Her mouth is petrified into an 'O.'

It takes me a second to get my words to my mouth. "Dee-ah?" I slur. I stare fixedly at her face to figure out what's wrong.

I listen, stunned to hear only silence from her body. No heartbeat.

She falls to the floor.

"Oh my God!" I say, panic having revived me fully. "Her heart! Help her! Her heart! Help me!" I look around but I don't process anything. I leap to the floor, but my body moves clumsily and I more or less fall instead.

I spend a moment struggling to get Dina on her back so I can start CPR. I finally close my eyes and concentrate. Digging my shoulder into hers, I manage to get her rolled over. I put my hands on her chest, but I'm too weak to exert enough force.

Derek's at the door. "Lisa! Bring paddles!" he shouts. He comes to my side, puts his fingers at Dina's neck.

"It stopped," I yell at him. He's wasting time with diagnostics! "Her heart stopped!"

Rather than helping me do CPR, he goes to the door again. "LISA!" he yells.

Forget him. I put my hands to Dina's chest again, determined. I use all of my weight, this time getting it right. Resignation falls over me because of what I don't feel: her presence. Even unconscious minds have a pulse of emotional life. I know this because I held Mom's hand as she died. Her heart stopped and I felt her life seep out through her skin. The emptiness was unmistakable. Dina's is, too. She's gone.

Shock revives me a second time, but it's Derek's. He's back with paddles, and this time he grabs my wrist to get me out of the way.

I freeze in place though, and what energy I had left gets sucked right out of me. I slump forward just as my vision goes dark again.

"Noooo!" I scream, and within only moments of the blindness, I hurl myself away, scrambling with no perception of whether I'm putting any distance behind me. But my vision clears and I feel the floor under my hands and knees finally.

Outlines of people emerge from the darkness. Dina's on the floor. Is someone on top of her? The wall is at my back, and I collapse against it, heaving.

Once I'm no longer suffocating, I search for an escape. People are everywhere though. What are they doing? What has happened? What did I just feel?

My body shakes, so weak I can hardly hold myself upright. I start gasping, well on the way to full-blown hyperventilation even though I don't know how I have the energy. I do my best to wrap my arms around my legs. I put my head in my knees so my lungs can't get out of control.

When the reflex subsides, I turn my head to find a terrifying sight: Derek is passed out on the floor near Dina. I can hear his heart though, easing my sudden panic. I take several calming breaths before processing that someone else, a woman, is here. Defibrillator paddles in hand, I think she has given up her resuscitation attempts.

I perceive there are other people in the room, but right now all I care about is that Derek's chest keeps a steady rhythm. The memory of darkness that eviscerated of my sense of self sends my pulse racing. The terror is too fresh, and nausea is quickly moving up on me. Unable to hold my stomach, I vomit on the floor. I hold my head in my hands in an attempt to squeeze out the memory. *Forget. Forget!* I tell my brain, but it's like an aftertaste that lingers in my mouth. I can even smell it in the air. I reek of it.

Desperate for reprieve I listen to my breaths. I listen to the heartbeats in the room. I focus on Derek's, counting them, nervous in the interim of time between each one.

Something tickles my cheek. Tears. I rub my face. My mind engages again. Dina touched me… What I felt was her. She died. Then Derek. He started to feel it, too, but I escaped. Or *he* did? My lips twitch, and I force the words out, to test them, "They touched me," I whisper, "And I felt…" I stare at Derek's slowly-rising chest. "I felt Dina die."

I shake my head. That's not what death feels like. Mom was at peace. What I just experienced was nothing like that. It was the strife of a hundred-year war. It was unending. Until it was gone. Did I make Dina feel that? Why? How? And how did I survive enduring that with her?

I have been lied to. I see red as I look at the people in the room. This is *their* fault, not mine. They did something to me while I was hypnotized.

But why would Dina have touched me if she knew what would happen?

"I don't know!" I wail. "I don't know!"

A hefty blond woman is in front of me now. She's afraid of me, and her fear punches my overwrought chest.

"What happened?" she little more than mouths.

What do I say? Maybe energy healing doesn't agree with my superhuman abilities? Maybe I should have told Dina and she would have known...

Known what? What if none of this is their doing? My empathic touch and super-senses could have gone haywire.

"All *I* know is that you shouldn't touch me," I reply venomously. I know I don't trust these people. There is a lot of damning evidence against them.

"Oh believe me," the woman says, wide-eyed, "I have *no* intention of touching you."

I shudder, slouching as my head keeps slumping to the side. I rest it against my knees, leaning into the corner, comforting myself with its solidity and imagining myself pushing right through it and out the other side. Out there is a space not permeated by the terror this room just experienced. It's sour and dank here. Out there is sunshine and birds chirping. Life.

Will I ever reclaim it? Will they ever let me leave? With Dina dead and Derek nearly so, what happens next? Will I go to jail?

Ezra.

What will happen to him? I begin to sob in sorrow over a future that will surely take him away from me...

No! I flail, reaching for my brother who is nowhere to be found.

Recognition. Sudden and intense. It yanks me right out of my memory and transports me to another...

I test the gun at my hip, turn the key, and push the door open into a darkened office. My eyes move over the row of filing cabinets. It will take forever to go through those. I'll start with the computer.

I bring it to life and go to work on circumventing the password. I smile. Whoever set this thing up only gave a password to the user's account and didn't even set one for the admin. So I take the back door in. I use my name to search, and a video file immediately comes up. I double-click on it.

It's a shot of a room I recognize but can't place. There's an exam table in the middle, and on it is me, unconscious. A man in shabby clothes walks into the frame. He's bearded and slightly hunched. He walks right over to me and tugs on the sleeve of my shirt.

"Hello?" he says. He shakes my shoulder. "Wake up!"

He checks over his own shoulder briefly before taking my wrist as if to check my pulse. He freezes where he stands, his hand still on my arm. Then, after a few moments, he collapses nearly on top of me before slumping to the floor.

The video flickers, the same scene reappears, but the man's body is gone. A woman walks in this time. She's scantily-clad in a miniskirt and silver heels. She walks a little more confidently than the last man, not even hesitating to put her hand on my shirt over my stomach. She looks over her shoulder, but then back to me. She places her hand on my forehead. She's completely still for several seconds before collapsing.

The scene resets again. My brother walks into the frame.

I stagger backward in the chair. "No!" I plead, the anvil of instantaneous dread dropping so suddenly I think I'm going to suffocate. But my eyes are locked on my brother who has rushed to my side on the screen.

"Wen!" he says, reaching for my arm. "Wen, are you—"

His voice is cut off. He's not moving. His hand is locked on to me.

"No Ezra!" I scream at him. "Don't touch me!"

But my warning can't travel into the past.

Ezra collapses to the floor. The video stops.

Wrapping my arms around my middle, I choke on my breaths. Shock mixes with anger. Fury. Murderous wrath.

One name comes to mind: Andre. I will kill him for this.

The dark room dissolves, and I blink, doubled over, into the lights of the greenhouse.

Fifteen

"*ethal* skin…" Kiera says, struggling to believe it. "Are you certain? Wendy… That—"

"Doesn't sound possible," I say, bringing my knees up into my chair and wrapping my arms around them. "I know. But I remember it. All of it. It's as real as waking up in the hospital in Missouri."

"I wouldn't be so quick to—"

"Believe my own memories?" I say. "I figured you'd say that. And maybe if the memory wasn't so powerful, if I couldn't still taste it in my mouth when I think of it, I'd go along with you."

"False memories can feel just as real," Kiera says. "They're made the same way as real ones. They can even include *mostly* truth. Memories can be distorted in a million ways."

"You know what else makes it so believable?" I say "That it's so *unbelievable.* How do you make up something like a death touch?"

"Easily," Kiera says. "Metaphor is a huge part of our psyche."

She seems to have an objection to everything. And her logic is circular. She's telling me to only accept what I want to accept. I stare at her. "Kiera, do you believe my brother is dead? Be honest."

She hesitates, but the look on her face cannot be mistaken, even without my empathy. I wait for her to say it though.

"Yes," Kiera replies, her brown face creasing in compassion. "I'm so sorry."

Even though I think I've accepted it, too, her confirmation brings more tears to my eyes. "Then why does it matter what the hows are?" I whisper, looking away.

"Because the truth matters."

I shake my head. "You don't get it. Ezra was my responsibility. I fought with my mom to be able to keep him with me after she died. I was supposed to protect him. So even if what I remember isn't true, his death is still my fault. What's the point of letting myself off the hook anyway? He's gone and that's going to be true no matter how I remember it."

Kiera sighs.

"Mikel says she's done," I say. "She wishes she didn't see what she saw."

"No, she wishes *you* didn't see it."

"Untrue. She thinks the memories are real."

Kiera sighs again. "We can work on digging up the details and the rest of your memory. You need a clearer picture of how it all came to a head."

I nod, although I haven't decided if I *want* to know more.

"I'm here for you," she says. "Whenever you figure out what you need, *please* let me know."

"Okay." I don't look at her, hoping she'll leave now. I know she showed up this morning because Mikel must have said something, but I don't want to talk.

She's still watching me, so I say, "Please go. I want to be alone."

"I don't think I can do that," she says. "You're in a vulnerable place. But we don't have to talk. Pretend I'm not here." She pulls a laptop out of her bag and puts her feet up to sit the length of the couch.

I roll my eyes vaguely. If there's no talking involved this might work.

My eyes fall to my hands. My skin killed people. What the hell? Hand waving can make people's skin *lethal*? It doesn't seem conscionable. It seems too simple to be real, and in the time I've spent reading up on life force abilities, I've definitely encountered abilities that are powerful enough to be seriously abused, but nothing so outright deadly.

It seems that Dina's energy therapy is what caused it as well as the improvement of my senses and the evolution of my empathic ability. But I've touched plenty of people since waking up. Nobody has died. Did that lethal effect go away? Why not my improved senses? It doesn't make sense.

This was supposed to bring me closure, but I am more confused than ever.

Later in the day, the sound of my phone ringing jars me out of a numb haze. I don't get up, but Kiera does, snagging it off the counter and looking at it.

She walks it straight over to me, showing me the screen.

It's Dr. Ohr Lim.

I take it. "Hello," I say.

"Miss Whitley, my deepest condolences."

"Thank you," I say robotically. I hope he called for more than well-wishes. Those are basically useless.

"I'm not just calling to offer sympathies," he says, reading my mind.

I exhale with relief.

"I may have a few answers for you. A *few*."

I glance at Kiera. This has to be her doing. "About what?" I say, interested.

"I've received word from both of your therapists, and I can offer you a few explanations about the things you remember that will help you be slightly less confused about them."

"My supposed death-touch," I say, looking at my free hand again. "Please tell me you know something about that."

"I do. It's a side-effect of channeling, which is the ability to share your life force abilities with others. Your father possessed this ability as well."

My mouth falls open.

"It's quite rare. We have a few channels among our membership, but none are lethal. I believe the lethalness depends upon the intensity of the channeled ability. In your case, given the power of your own life force abilities, this made your skin deadly."

On the one hand, I like that I was right, that what I remembered wasn't made-up. On the other hand... holy crap. "I never killed anyone prior to Dina," I say. "So why, all of a sudden, would I be lethal?"

"I don't believe you were a channel prior to Dina. I told you Pneunmatikon practiced life force manipulation, which is called hypno-touch. That is the method used to manifest life force abilities in humans. I believe your father had you undergo hypno-touch in order to *make* you a channel."

"Why would he do that?"

"Because you were more powerful, could likely see more of the energy world than him. He was going to use you and your ability to obtain his ideal world where anyone could have a life force ability."

"But… He would do that? To his own *child*?"

"He did as much to Regina and Sara, your mother and adoptive mother. And hundreds of other people."

My stomach turns.

"How did he know I'd become a channel?" I ask. "Can you like, choose what ability to give someone with, ah, hypno-whatever?"

"Hypno-touch. And no. Performing hypno-touch on a Prime Human, however, will make them a channel fifty percent of the time. It will also vastly improve their abilities. For him it would have been a calculated risk. And since he was a channel already himself, that probability was likely quite a bit higher."

"Speaking of risks, I thought hypno-touch was lethal," I say. "Kills you within fifteen years? Where does that leave me?"

"It is. Although, with Primes, that time period is all over the board. The life force ability seems to determine the effect of hypno-touch quite a bit. I've seen that life span be as short as a few months, but I've also seen Primes completely immune to the sickness."

"And you know this because?"

"Like I told you before, we fumbled our way through understanding how it all worked. Mistakes were made. But now we know."

"Alright," I say. "And so what about now? Why aren't I lethal anymore?"

"I don't believe you are a channel anymore. I can see that you might have been motivated to maintain the monopoly on what you could do. Because channeling is a powerful gateway. When even one Prime channels another, new talents emerge, even new abilities. In your case, channeling would allow *anyone* to see the energy world using you. Energy world sight in combination with other abilities… one can only imagine what new talents would emerge. Being a channel would make you a priceless commodity, Miss Whitley. And having assessed your character, I have no trouble believing that you would have done what it took to keep such power out of the hands of others. I have no trouble believing that you found a way to undo your hypno-touch."

"But my senses are still improved. My empathic ability still has a range, which didn't happen until *after* I'd had hypno-touch."

"You see, and likely hear and smell, the energy world. There is a reason it is held sacred by Primes. As I told you before, it *is* the place where life force abilities originate. Do not underestimate the amount of knowledge you can and likely *did* gain about that place. Do not underestimate what you were able to do with it and gain from it—including the real possibility that you could enhance your own abilities at will. Frankly, Miss Whitley, there is nothing about your case that surprises me. I *expect* you to be the exception, to every rule."

I take a deep breath, consider it. "How would I know if I was still a channel?"

"In my experience, you channel simply by touching the person you want to share your abilities with. I know what you're thinking. How do you touch someone to channel to them if your skin will kill them? The answer is I don't know. I know your father wasn't lethal to everyone, but he was never a member of the Guild, so what he knew about channeling stayed with him."

"Hm," I say. "Well I've touched lots of people here. They haven't died, and nobody has mentioned suddenly having super-senses, or reading emotions. So maybe I'm not one anymore."

"I think that should give you adequate assurance."

"It does. But the one thing about the memories I have now that I'm not sure of is the timeline of my brother's death. The first one, of Dina, I'm sure must have happened around two and a half years ago, back when I first came into contact with Pneumatikon. The second one, where I saw my brother…die. I'm not sure when it happened. But in the memory I knew it was Andre who did it. I knew I was there to get information about myself, but I'm not sure why. I also knew where I was in the memory. But currently, I only know it's familiar."

"I can't give you any leads on that. Only you can search the memory for clues that will tell you when and where you were."

I sniff. "Yeah…" I'm not sure why it's only just now happening, but the pain of loss seems to have held itself at bay until now. Maybe because Dr. Lim's information erases the last of my doubts about the legitimacy of my memories. I thought I was sure of Ezra's death before, but now I'm even more certain. Is that how mourning death works? Denial is shed in steps? I don't remember this with my mom, but then, I was holding her hand when she died. With Ezra, I don't have his body. I've simply lost hope a little at a time, and then a lot.

"If I happen upon any more information that I feel relevant, I will pass it along."

"Thank you," I manage, choking on the sobs building in my chest.

"Anytime, Miss Whitley. I'm sincerely sorry for your loss. I know it's a past memory, but the pain is real, current, as if it just happened. Be sure to take time for yourself."

"I will."

"But not too much," he adds. "Find your purpose. Embrace your second chance. We all owe that to those who have gone before."

Sixteen

Pouring boiling water over the teabag in my mug, I close my eyes like I always do and inhale the wafting scent of ginger. I don't know why, but ginger is like coffee to me now. I need to smell it in the morning to wake up. Kiera procured them for me, and I cried the first time I steeped one and the scent hit me, like I'd found an old friend. I began to wonder if I had and I just couldn't remember them.

Mixed with the scent of ginger are flowers, lots of them. Frankly, the scent is so rich it's sickening, a little too organic and sweet at the same time. Sympathy flowers and various gifts have been showing up at my apartment on the regular for two weeks now as people become aware of my brother's death.

I'm coping really well. I took about a week off of working, but for the past week I've been at the Energy World Research (EWR) department, perfecting meditation—probably good for mourning. I think I'm ready to resume therapy with Kiera again to get back the rest of my memories. I'm certain I've remembered the worst of it, so the rest should be easy, right? In fact, I don't think I've felt this calm and well-adjusted since before waking up at that hospital. Who would have thought?

They sure made a good choice in Chase for my dyad. He hasn't let me retreat. In fact, in the past two weeks he has thrown a video-game party, movie night, and board game party all at my apartment. Every time I've dreaded it, but each time I have enjoyed every second.

Too bad he wasn't around when my daughter, Elena, died. I was sixteen and lost. I was abandoned by the boy I thought loved me. I was such a mess then. I went out every night, got caught up in the emotions of others to escape my own. It was a different kind of substance abuse, and I did it to hide from myself every single day. But Chase doesn't let me hide. He gets me out and with people—

I grip the mug in my hands more tightly, a sudden hot wash of familiarity pouring over me. With it, I bristle with growing acrimony.

I set the mug down and whirl on Chase who is asleep on the couch.

"Chase!" I yell. The kid has practically lived here since we became a dyad. I've let him because I know he doesn't have a family either, but now I know... I know what he's been doing.

His head pops up. He rubs his eyes. "Whaa?" he says.

"How dare you!" I say, arms crossed, staring down at him. "Manipulating me with your ability? It gets more powerful the more people you have around, huh? That's why you've been throwing all these parties!"

His eyes are now wide open, and I can tell by the sudden, cool defensiveness I pick up from him that I've caught him. He fumbles around the couch cushions, finally dropping to his knees to look under the couch for his tablet. He's not supposed to use it to communicate because he's supposed to take every opportunity to either work out his motor function by writing or his word formation by talking. But when he wants to get something out quickly he uses the tablet.

I'm fuming, and I swear if Chase were any older I would probably have said a lot of nasty things. But he looks too close in age to my brother. And this kind of move is exactly something Ezra would have done to 'help' me.

He holds the tablet up: **My fault**.

"Yeah it's your fault!" I say. "You can't do that to people, Chase! All you've accomplished is masking what's underneath!"

He shakes his head as he types furiously.

No. My fault you remembered. I told you to go to Mikel.

"What? That was *my* idea. I wouldn't take it back. I had to know what happened. But this isn't about that! This is about why it's wrong for you to trick people's emotions."

My ability can help.

"No. It can't. Not in this situation."

You knew what I could do. You're just mad because you think you should suffer for him.

"No," I say desperately, uncrossing my arms so I don't look so combative. He has no idea... He has no clue how much damage he can do with his ability—which is so similar to mine, so I should know. "I think I should feel what *I* feel. Not what you or anyone else *wants* me to feel."

Why would you want to feel bad?

"I don't. But I've been here before, Chase." I sit on the coffee table. "It's addictive to be able to change emotions at will. It seems harmless. And it was so easy for me to let you because I spent so long in the past losing myself in what other people felt. But one day I woke up, realized that I was addicted and that I'd wasted my time chasing the next emotional high. And life had totally passed me by because of it. I almost lost everything."

He tilts his head at me, furrows his brow before leaning over his tablet.

You DID lose everything. What is the point of letting yourself feel bad now? You can start over.

I stare at the words on the screen, and I don't know how to answer. I only know that the idea of having someone around who can toy with my emotions makes me sick to my stomach. And it upsets me that Chase doesn't see it that way. In fact, who is *he* to decide how much I've lost? Who is he to decide what's good for me? He's just some kid who doesn't know how to feel anything but happy-go-lucky all the time.

"You don't know what you're talking about," I say tightly. "In fact, I'd say you're doing this to escape grief over *your* family. I'm telling you, Chase. It's going to bite you in the ass."

He glares at me, types quickly.

That advice hasn't worked out that great for you.

I suck in a breath. "Get out," I say, a storm gathering swiftly in my head. The rain has already started as tears come to my eyes.

He bends over his tablet.

"GET OUT!" I scream. And then I go around the apartment, gathering up everything that's his: socks, backpack, the stack of board games he brought last night... I throw all of it in the hall.

He apparently has taken my order seriously, shoving his feet into his shoes, passing me with a death stare, tablet under his arm.

I slam the door once he's through. Then I pace, infuriated. The nerve! What a know-it-all little twit! He manipulates me and then he thinks I should *thank* him?

I stop, heaving several breaths that keep wanting to explode into sobs. I can't figure out why until I realize that I could have had this same argument with Ezra. He was always trying to help me in ways that weren't remotely helpful.

God. I miss him.

My breaths staggered and painful, I stumble to the bathroom, catching myself on the jamb. I catch sight of my reflection. I got a new haircut yesterday because my buzzed hair had grown out so much and was starting to look shaggy. It makes me look so normal, adjusted. Happy people do things like care about their hair.

I got a haircut yesterday when I found out only two weeks ago that I killed my brother. What is *wrong* with me?

Tears starting to fall in earnest, I dig through the cabinet under the sink. I know they're here. Chase brought them and made me cut his hair with them: clippers. I locate them finally, snatch them out of the case and plug them in. Then I run them over my head, back to front on the shortest setting. Then I toss them in the sink and give in to my sorrow, falling to the floor and weeping like it will never end.

Seventeen

I hear their whispers outside of my apartment; they obviously don't realize how good my hearing is. Or they've forgotten.

"She's not ready for outside demands right now," Kiera says.

"I heard she was fine. And now she's not? You're coddling her," a voice I recognize as Lainey's says. I've never met her, but I've heard her through the phone plenty of times when Kiera's talking to her. "Therapists don't coddle. They help people cope."

"I'm not just her therapist. I'm her friend," Kiera says defensively.

"You know you can't be both."

"She needs a friend more than a therapist right now."

"She needs a purpose, not a friend."

"It hasn't even been a month since she learned what happened," Kiera hisses.

"We need what she can do, what she can remember."

"She can't do it like this."

"Says who? Where is her dyad anyway? He's the one that needs to be in there, kicking her butt back into existence."

"She made him get lost."

Lainey groans and huffs. "So how is the memory reconstruction going?"

"It's not," Kiera says. "I don't think she *wants* to remember anything else."

"But it might help us. We need PHIA's location."

"Again, she's recovering. She'll remember when she's ready."

"Kiera," Lainey says through gritted teeth. "You need to request reassignment. You're too close to this."

"Like you and the mission to find PHIA?" Kiera snaps. "Andre is your *brother!* How you can possibly have tricked yourself into believing you can handle this case is beyond my comprehension. If you don't take my advice, then you can expect me to return the favor."

"I wasn't even raised with him!" Lainey says in a low voice. "He's nothing to me but some shared DNA! He's a serial killer!"

"I'm done with this conversation!" Kiera says. "You obviously don't care about my opinion. You do whatever you want. You always have. So don't be surprised that I'm doing the same!" I hear my door open and then slam shut. I hear Kiera breathing heavily, probably standing just inside the door. I hear Lainey stomp off and then Kiera collapse on the couch.

Ahhhh. I guess it's no wonder Lainey is such a piece of work, being related to Andre and all. You can't escape your DNA. Kiera told me yesterday that Lainey was coming here for business. I don't care to meet her. If she looks like Andre it's going to make it that much easier to dislike her.

"Good morning, Wendy," Kiera says, drawing the blinds in my room.

"What's up?" I say. "I see Lainey has arrived."

"Hmph," Kiera says, plopping on the end of my bed. "I figured you heard that."

"Andre's sister, huh?"

"Yeah. Only by blood though. Different surrogates."

"Surrogates?" I say, sitting up, stuffing a pillow behind my head.

"Yeah they share a donor."

"Oh yeah, I forgot about that," I say. "The baby factory."

"It is a little bit. Increasing the Prime Human population means better technology, less illness, more opportunity. It means making the world a better place. It's unorthodox; people aren't used to it and it changes what's normal. Families outside the Guild that raise Primes have waited for forever. The situation couldn't be more ideal for those kids. And kids raised within the Guild have wider opportunities, a wider family, more security because of who they belong to."

She's right; it does seem a bizarre family structure, but what do I know? I don't have a family anymore.

"I take it *you* were born from a surrogate?" I say.

She nods. "Guild born and raised."

"And your ability is?"

"Still not going to tell you." She smiles. "So what about your memory? Are you ready to try again with it?"

"No," I say. "But I'm ready to take Andre down. I want in on the same team as Lainey."

Kiera grimaces. "You're obviously welcome to apply, but the Council handpicks that team. I doubt they're going to approve you. You're even closer to Andre than Lainey."

"At the rate Andre's going, eventually *everyone* is going to be too close to him," I point out. "And then who will they assign?"

"Someone who doesn't have a two and a half year memory loss and traumatic memory recovery," Kiera replies sternly. "Someone whose psychological health won't risk the mission."

I blink at her, unused to her being so... harsh. Looks like she's at least partially taking Lainey's advice to heart. I guess there's something to this dyad thing after all. I should probably call Chase and make up. Maybe. He's so much like Ezra, and now I'm going to be seeing it all the time if he's around.

I turn away from her, letting out a staggered sigh. "You're probably right," I say, tears starting to wet my pillow. "But thinking about and plotting against Andre makes me feel something other than numb or sad."

Kiera stays quiet.

"I don't want to remember anything else," I say. "I don't think I can take it. And honestly..." I pause because I want to be sure what I say next is what I actually still feel. "I don't want to know who I was anymore. Especially now when there's obviously no one to go back to."

I haven't told Kiera what the past week has been like for me. I've been close to finding a disaster nearby and finishing myself off for real this time. It seems that everything I am, all these talents and abilities and legacies, have cost me everything. The Wendy I was, who never trusted the Guild enough to join when the Guild could have protected her brother, also cost me. And now she has nothing that I want anymore. She lost everything I cared about. I don't trust her. I don't want her around. I want her gone. The thing that has stopped me was looking around and marveling at how foreign this life would be to her. Few people get an honest opportunity to drop an entire life and pick up a new one in a different place with different people and completely different opportunities. So I'm going to give it my best shot.

"I'm starting over," I say.

Eighteen

*A*re you sure you don't need any help?" Kiera asks, leaning over the counter, watching me roll chicken, ham, and goat cheese inside a piece of pizza dough.

I shake my head. "Go be social," I say. "It's a little too crowded in my head, and a task keeps me from getting burned out on it."

"Wen, do you mind if I turn on the TV?" Jackie asks from the living room.

"Of course not," I say.

The news comes to life on the TV projection and Kiera says in a low voice, "I'm really proud of you."

I busy my hands with another stromboli. "Just doing what my therapist tells me. Figured I'd moped around enough."

She smiles. "I know it's been tough. I get why you were mad at Chase—you needed to make this step on your own—but he was only trying to help. You should have invited him." She turns around and looks at the room. Xander and Leticia are playing cards at the dining room table. Jackie and Aamir are lounged on the couch, feet propped up on the ottoman. Imani and Justin are lying on the floor. More people are supposed to show up later, closer to midnight to watch the ball drop in Times Square. New Years' parties are happening all over the Vault tonight.

"I did," I reply, "but he isn't talking to me."

'*A Guild spokesperson said in a press conference today that the sink hole problem in northern Ireland is getting worse and that they have no explanation for the cause,*' the anchorman on the television says. '*He said they're sending new operatives out to assess the problem from a different angle, although he declined commenting on what that angle might be.*'

I pull another piece of dough toward me and begin flattening it by hand.

"He will," Kiera says. "Chase doesn't seem like the type to hold a grudge."

'*The National Guard along with the Guild have declined to comment on their long-term plans for southern California, but undercover operations reveal that paranoia increases as resources have grown thin. What is to be done about what is sure to become a humanitarian crisis remains to be seen,*' the anchorman continues.

I grit my teeth. The California crisis always gets me. Why is nobody fixing the dam? And how on earth can a psychological epidemic go on this long? It seems really suspect. It has to be Andre's doing. I want to take Andre down. I wish I could, but the Council's not going to let me anywhere near an operation like that.

Why is this kind of news on anyway? It's New Year's Eve. We're on the cusp of a a new start. Aren't we supposed to be watching parades and coverage from New York?

'*Let's not forget the earthquake damage to the aqueduct system that feeds most of LA area from Colorado. Those people have got to be seeing a dangerous water shortage. We're also talking about a major coastline, Dave,*' the anchorwoman replies. '*I think before starvation, we're going to see another disaster. My question is, if the Guild predicts something is going to hit there, will evacuation be forced? And how many lives will be lost trying to get these people out of a place they don't want to leave?*'

I slam my pot on the stove and everyone jumps and looks up at me. I grin. "Sorry guys! Lost my grip on it!"

'*That's a great question, Raelyn,*' Dave, the anchorman, says. '*I think this is a situation where only time will tell. We'll be following the situation closely. Another great question though: Who is The Human Movement?*'

'*The Human Movement? I've never heard of them,*' Raelyn says.

'*That's what a lot of people are saying, but their protests have grown both in size and reach, drawing the attention of some important people. We thought the Prime Human Insurgency Alliance, or PHIA as they're commonly known, were the only ones out for the Guild. Turns out, a new force is on the scene,*' Dave says.

My curiosity piqued, I edge around the counter to see better.

The scene shown is a crowd of protestors with the White House in the background. They're chanting something unintelligible, while in the foreground the narrator says, '*They call themselves*

The Human Movement, and their message has caught like wildfire since they made their first appearance two weeks ago. Every day, all over the country, protests of all sizes have gathered in front of government buildings demanding that the Guild show themselves, cooperate more extensively with public and private relief efforts, and share their technology in an effort to more effectively face disaster calamity world-wide. Today, they've gathered an estimated three-thousand protestors and growing in front of the White House, in opposition to the Guild, who, they claim, is trespassing on the rights of the American people. Our reporter, Audrey Lancaster, spoke with their organizer to get the full story.'

'I'm here speaking to the founder of the Human Movement, Gabe Dumas,' the blonde reporter on the television practically yells into her microphone. Behind her is the chanting crowd being held back with makeshift barriers to keep them from pressing into the space where she's doing the shoot. Next to her is a man much taller than her, tan, dark hair. His head is bowed, which blocks his face as he leans closer to her to hear. *'The crowd here has grown in the last hour, swelling into the street where local law enforcement have been forced to close off traffic. Mr. Dumas, thanks for your time. Can you tell us a little bit about your cause?'*

'Certainly, Audrey,' the man called Gabe Dumas says, his voice full of expression. *'The Human Movement's interests are simple: transparency and collaboration.'*

'Transparency of Guild operations?' Audrey asks.

'Transparency of anything would be a welcome start, Miss Lancaster,' Dumas says, glancing up at the camera briefly a few times. *'Currently, any information on Guild day-to-day goings and comings is entirely unobtainable. Where they buy their groceries seems to be just as hush as what and who governs them. Such secrecy is unacceptable. A refusal to collaborate with either government or civilian efforts to mitigate disaster impact sends the same message the term "Prime Human" does: These people see themselves as superior to the rest of humanity, that our simple-mindedness and limited skill are of no consequence, of no use. Frankly, Miss Lancaster, I take offense to being viewed as a damsel in distress, in need of rescue by a vigilante that won't take off their mask.'*

Still hunched toward Audrey, Dumas finally looks up for longer than a second at the camera, this time staring directly into it with remarkable intensity.

"Good lord, why is he so handsome?" Leticia says, who has come up behind me from the table.

'*All of your protests have taken place in front of government buildings. Interesting that you would choose the White House as your gathering place,*' Audrey says, '*Seeing as your issue seems to be with the Guild rather than government.*'

'*Indeed!*' Dumas says, a sardonic smile on his face. '*I looked "Guild" up in the phone book for an address, you know, so we could bring the party to the proper place—I didn't want to inconvenience anyone else with our raucous gatherings—but there was no listing. Can you believe it? The most influential organization in the world doesn't have a spot in the yellow pages. I'm befuddled. My only solution was to go door to door.*'

'*You have been able to gather quite a following in a short time,*' Audrey says. '*To what do you attribute this?*'

Dumas seems to have recovered from his dripping sarcasm as he replies, '*I think we'd all like a hand, not to mention a say, in our own fate. The Guild seems to believe the comic books, that superheroes, by virtue of their superior skill, have the right to operate outside of laws and ordinances and without consent or the restraints of democracy. It turns out I'm not the only one that disagrees with their philosophy.*'

'*It would appear so,*' Audrey says. '*Back to you, Dave and Raelyn.*'

"What an idiot," I say, jerking a drawer open and getting a spoon out. "Doesn't he know Prime Humans are literally *hunted* by PHIA? And he wants the Guild to make the address to the front door public information?"

The eyes of everyone in the room are on me. Dave and Raelyn are exchanging superficial banter in the background.

"I've heard that name before," Kiera says, tapping her chin. "Dumas."

I pause. "You're right…" I say, racking my brain.

"They sure do get around," Leticia says. "It's like an epidemic already. Minneapolis, Portland, Tallahassee. All three of those have had Human Movement protests in the last two days. They already have a hundred thousand followers on social media. But this is the first time I've seen the founder."

I have no idea how Leticia knows that until I remember that she actually helps run one of the Guild's social media pages—which I've learned doesn't actually interact with people. It's purely informational. In any case, she'd have to be up on stuff like this.

"There was a piece on him in last night's news," Justin says. "He's from Southern California."

I jerk my head toward him. "In case you were wondering, California was not long ago a perfectly legitimate place to be from where people did normal people things like start families, watch football, and sell awesome tamales on the street. Being from there doesn't mean jack squat. Something is up. Those people are being held hostage."

"I don't think he meant—" Kiera starts.

"Slow your role. I'm not saying being from California is bad," Justin says defensively. "I was only drawing a possible connection to PHIA. This might be a new angle, a more subtle angle Andre's taking. And since PHIA is based in California…"

"Whatever," I say, chopping the onions a little too violently. "Then you should have said, 'Maybe he's PHIA in disguise.' Saying he's from California is meaningless."

"Maybe so," Justin replies. "My bad. Jumping down my throat about it was uncalled for though."

"Wen, it was harmless," Jackie says.

"Breathe," Kiera says under her breath so no one else can hear.

I rub my forehead. "Yeah, you're right. Sorry. The guy… he just makes me mad. And I'm freaking out because I don't have any paprika. I swore I got some, but I can't find it."

"I have some!" Xander says, jumping out of his chair. "Want me to grab it?"

"Yeah, that'd be great," I say. Then to Justin, "I'm really sorry."

"No problem," he says. "How about we watch something a little less…" He struggles to finish the sentence.

"The news," I finish.

"Right," he says. "Jackie, what else is on?"

"Mike Dumas," Kiera whispers to me, leaning over the counter again. "That's where we remember the name. The guy that helped get you away from the hospital?"

"Oh! Right!" I furrow my brow. "Andre's dyad partner. Geez. You think Mike and this Gabe guy are related? That'd be crazy…"

She pulls a tablet out of her bag, thumbs through some things while I put the tray of Stromboli in the oven and scoop the onions into my saucepan. I drizzle them with oil and turn the heat on. I still can't decide if I like these fancy cooking surfaces. They never feel hot. Neither does the pot. It's not until the contents start sizzling that I believe it's working.

"Oh. My. Gosh," Kiera says in a low voice. "Mike's mother was Alma Fuentes. She died when Mike was little. And Mike was raised by the Dumas family. Adoptive family members listed are mother, Marisol, father, Daniel, and their son, Gabriel."

"Whoa."

"You aren't kidding." Her eyes narrow as she scrolls slowly through something. "It looks like Gabe is a Prime, too—spontaneous origin."

"What does that mean?"

"It means he has a life force ability, but nobody knows where he got it. Neither of his parents have life force abilities."

"I didn't know that was possible."

"It's very rare. But life force abilities have been around as long as humans. Sometimes people are born with them already."

"What's his life force ability?"

"Confidential."

I roll my eyes. "Why? Can he like, control the weather or something? Laser beam eyes?"

She chuckles. "I told you, all life force abilities are confidential until the person says they can be listed in the directory. Has nothing to do with how powerful they may be."

Xander appears again.

"Thanks." I take the paprika from him.

He leans forward. "It was still an asshat statement on his part. He doesn't get out much. Don't hold it against him."

I smile at him. "I won't."

"He's got a fascinating history," Kiera says after Xander returns to cards with Leticia. "Born with Spinal Muscular Atrophy, of the lethal variety. Spontaneous recovery at age six."

"How is his life force ability confidential but his medical history isn't?" I say.

Kiera shrugs. "He must have made that part of his medical history public information at some point. Anyway, he went on to earn a bunch of degrees. He has PhDs in biology and physics. He speaks, on record, twelve languages." She looks up. "Pretty incredible."

"*Twelve?*" I say. "His life force ability must be some kind of genius thing. How old is he?"

"Thirty."

"Thirty with double PhDs, twelve languages, and running the anti-Guild movement," I say. "Gosh, I want to talk to Mike. First his dyad partner becomes a Prime Human-hating psychopath. Then his brother wants to take down Guild security measures. What's Mike's ability? Giving people personality disorders?"

Kiera taps on the screen a few times. "Uncharacterized mental suggestion."

I raise a questioning eyebrow.

"Means they aren't sure of the scope. He probably can't control it enough to test. It also usually means it's really powerful."

I give her a skeptical look. "Andre and Gabe are anti-Guild and they were both closely associated with Mike, who can put thoughts in people's heads. Maybe *he* is the ring leader."

"Now that Gabe is out causing a fuss, the Guild is going to look into his background and find this same connection," Kiera says. "In fact, I'm sure they know it already and that's why Mike's been on furlough."

I shake my head. "You said I need something to occupy myself with, and since you won't sign me off for full-time energy world research, and Ohr won't sign me off for PHIA intelligence operations, I'm going to spend my time doing some investigation of my own. I'm going to feel Mike out myself."

"Suit yourself. But first I hope you're going to finish cooking. Those cordon bleu strombolis smell amazing."

I'm no dummy. I can tell Kiera doesn't think I'll get anywhere, and her food compliments are her way of changing the subject so she doesn't have to tell me so. It doesn't matter though. In the five weeks since remembering my brother's death, this is the first time I've felt like doing *anything*—without someone being in my head influencing me, that is. And she doesn't know that when I decide to do something, I always find a way.

Nineteen

*D*r. Lim's residence is in a building almost identical to my own. My hands are clammy and my stomach is bubbling with anxiety when I get there. I stand in front of the door for several minutes, battling doubt.

This is nuts. I'm placing a pretty big bet, and I have no clue whether it's going to pan out. I could be ruining my future here at the Guild. I could be throwing all of it away on oversized aspirations. I should just do my time, work my way up, gain trust and practice giving it. I'm just impatient, that's all…

When I think about turning around though, panic fills my chest, the kind I used to feel after my daughter, Elena, died when I was sixteen. It crept up on me whenever I went home. The only thing waiting for me there was numb misery. So I started *not* going home. I started going out all the time just to find other people to feel. For a year I accomplished nothing. I *became* nothing. Except bitter.

My brother saved me back then. And though his death is on my hands, I know beyond a doubt how disappointed he'd be with me if I let guilt consume me again. I have a second chance, and not in the usual sense. I can completely remake myself. I can start over as if I have just been born. If I can just let go of who I remember being… If I can let go of wondering what I became… If I can forget who I thought I should be… Then I can have the confidence to face the person on the other side of this door and get what I came here for. I can throw myself at this second chance with everything I've got in me.

I take a deep breath and press the buzzer.

A young woman answers the door. At first I would guess that she's a little older than me, but there is a timelessness to her appearance that makes her suddenly look as if she could be forty as easily as twenty. But I'm guessing she's related to Ohr just based on her ethnicity. She has high cheekbones and a small mouth, flawless bronze skin, and long black hair so straight and silky that when she tilts her head a little, all of it, especially her bangs, immediately sweeps to the side in mesmerizing fluidity. Such is the only acknowledgement she offers when she sees me. She recognizes me, and she's wondering why I'm here. All of this is clearly available to read in her emotions.

Surprised by her astuteness, I realize that she knew I'd pick all that up, thus why she didn't waste words with a conventional greeting. I also finally notice she's wearing an entirely black outfit: black skinny jeans, black fitted knit shirt, black flats. It enhances the exoticness of her persona.

"I'm here to see Dr. Lim," I say, holding out my hand. "But we haven't met."

She meets my hand with her own smaller one, and her mouth curves just enough to resemble a smile. "I'm Shiah," she replies. "Ohr is my father."

"Right!" I say, brightening with recognition. "The cook! You made that rice pudding. It was delicious!"

"Thank you," she says, bowing her head slightly. "My father isn't here. He's traveling."

"Oh…" I say, downcast. "When does he get back?"

"Undetermined. He oversees the Prime Human Population Acceleration Initiative, which comprises thirteen clinics, world-wide. He makes rounds to each of them every other month. But he has a particular interest in your affairs, and he informed me before he left to be available to you, should you seek his assistance."

I stare at her a moment, mostly because I'm too busy basking in her placidity, emotions that are nearly identical to Dr. Lim's: self-possessed, completely confident but not arrogant. It's like she's planned out what to feel ahead of time. It's also like she knew I was coming, or maybe she had just already determined how she'd deal with me if I showed up.

She waits, humored by my interest. It's then that I become insanely curious about her ability, which I would bet is identical to her father's, and I would also bet it explains her easy mental state.

"Precise, nearly infallible memory recall," she replies.

My mouth opens. I didn't voice my question…

"Experience," she answers. "I have encountered exactly four other empaths. Each of them reacted exactly like you. They each wanted to know what my life force ability was that resulted in my state of mind."

"It's kind of awesome," I say.

"I don't know any other way," she says. She pulls the door open a little wider. "Would you like to come in?"

"Please," I reply, walking past her.

The first thing I lay eyes on is a gallery of two-foot canvasses covering the wall straight ahead. Each one is a painting of a tree, or some part of a tree. Some are up close; others are far away in the context of some larger natural scene. And each tree is drastically different. Each one has... *a personality?* Whatever it is, they pull me in, and I walk closer, restraining myself from reaching out to test the texture of the paint. The styles are all different as well. Some are done so realistically they could be photos. Others are impressionist. One is even cartoon-like.

"Which is your favorite?" Shiah asks from behind me.

"This one." I point to a squat, desert tree. It looks more like a bush, devoid of leaves. Instead its foliage is a thick collection of spindly green twigs.

"That was in southern Arizona," she explains.

"Did *you* paint them?" I ask.

"Yes. Every time I travel to a new place I paint a tree I saw there."

"That's a neat tradition." I eye the walls of thirty or so paintings. "You've been to a lot of places. And you're very good. So many different styles though. Your versatility is unheard of. They're really all yours?" I turn to look at her.

She nods. Nothing in her emotions indicates she's lying.

"How do you decide what style to use?" I ask.

"I try something different each time. It's my way of... distorting memory so each place can have it's own... soul."

I don't know what that means, but it sounds poetic, and she seems convicted by it. I move closer to the paintings, trying to make out the brush strokes.

"It would be hard for someone like you to understand," she explains, once again preempting my thoughts.

I turn to find her standing several feet behind me, hands behind her back, feet spread slightly. It's exactly how I've seen Dr. Lim stand.

"I have a perfect memory," she says. "This is my attempt at creating something that isn't perfect. I know that doesn't really explain it for you. But you'd have to be in my head with more than my emotions to grasp what I mean."

"I guess so," I say.

"What did you need assistance with?" she asks.

I look around, having momentarily forgotten.

"Kiera says you have been adapting socially," she says. "Are you satisfied with your progress?"

I grimace slightly at her robotic mode of speaking. "Not really. I want to be more involved, but everyone thinks I'm too much of a head case to do anything. I'm surprised they haven't relegated me to working the provisions counter or the coffee shop. Probably because I'm not that nice. Those people are so happy and content, like handing you your bag of groceries is their most favorite thing ever."

She makes two noises that sound like a chuckle. "You have to realize that no task is considered 'relegation.' They're happy because they enjoy doing it. Some people genuinely like interacting with other people. People do what they love here. They wouldn't assign you to the provisions counter because you wouldn't enjoy it."

"Surely there are some things done around here that nobody wants to do."

"If there's a job nobody wants, it becomes automated."

I didn't know that... So they have a machine that cleans the toilets and opens the mail...? I'm getting distracted with questions again, so I say, "That's great and all, but I've spent the last two months reading up on the history of the last two years and getting in shape and watching way too many sitcom reruns. I want to do something I actually enjoy, but nobody will let me."

"My father says you've requested to be on the PHIA recovery team. However, you told him that the only reason you were seeking Guild activation was because you wanted resources to find your brother and protection from Andre. The first goal has been laid to rest. Joining the PHIA recovery team is contrary to your second goal."

"That was before I knew what Andre did to me," I say, barely remembering saying those things to Ohr in the first place.

"Okay," she says, sitting on a stool nearby. "But you can see how at this point we don't actually know why you choose to remain affiliated with the Guild. Motives are important because they predict future actions. And my father has the responsibility to ensure that the possible actions of one member don't put the entire body at risk."

"My reasons weren't all that honorable before," I reply derisively, "so I didn't think motives mattered all that much to you, so long as I chose to join the club."

"Whether a motive is honorable is subjective. The goal is to have one so that we can all know what drives your actions. If we can help without endangering the whole, then the Guild has served its purpose."

"Fine," I say, crossing my arms, exasperated with arguing logic and getting nowhere near what I came here to discuss in the first place. "My reason for wanting in on the recovery team is to destroy PHIA. They're nasty people and they deserve to die. And I would think my super senses would make me great at reconnaissance. But Ohr said no because I'm a socket wrench or whatever. Except that Kiera won't let me do that for real because energy world stuff is top secret. and it requires passing a psychological assessment that she won't clear me for because I told her I don't want to seek memory recovery, and she thinks that's unhealthy. Look, it's cool. I get it. I'm here because I have an alternative to those two things and I want to see if you'll let me do it."

"Oh!" she says, genuinely interested. "You should have said so from the beginning."

"I tried but... you went all motives and logic on me and I got distracted by my questions because it was sterile and weird and—" I pin my lips together. "Nevermind."

She crosses her legs, props her elbow on her knee and waves her hand. "Understood. You have my attention."

"Cool. Okay, so recently I learned about The Human Movement, and even though they aren't hurting Primes—yet—they're growing an awful lot and you guys don't need yet another group out there after your lunch money. I want to be involved in whatever you guys cook up to deal with that. I'm really passionate about this, and I'm ready to contribute."

She tilts her head pensively, her hair swinging in a uniform motion. She blinks twice and then says, "What makes you think we intend to even acknowledge The Human Movement?"

I pause, looking at her with confusion. "Have you... kept up with them?"

She just continues to stare at me expectantly.

"Their message is connecting," I argue. "Like, *for real*. They had their first protest a month and a half ago in Reno. Practically nobody showed up, but the right person did, because Gabe Dumas got interviewed by the same guy that does the Prime Humans Exposed website, which, if you didn't know, gets something like half a million hits a day. After that, Prime Humans

Exposed started publishing on their website when these protests would be happening. It blew up. Ten turned into one hundred, which turned into one thousand practically overnight. They've sponsored seventeen protests in the last two weeks. I think DC's final numbers were thirty-eight hundred. Yesterday, Dumas was personally in London, his *first* international protest, and there were over four thousand people present in front of Buckingham Palace. You're telling me you guys are going to *ignore* that kind of growth?"

Shiah's only response is to lift her eyebrows.

I cross my arms. "You ask me, I think he's using life force abilities to gain that kind of following that fast. First of all, I know he's a Prime, and when you watch his videos, people act like they're at a rock concert, not a protest, and he's the lead singer. He's got major fan love, and there's no real explanation when he hasn't had time to actually *garner* that kind of adoration. Secondly, the attendee numbers are hard to believe, at least in the time frame THM has been around. I'm not buying. I suspect someone from the Guild is helping him. You guys have a real problem on your hands."

"Or an opportunity," she replies, unbothered.

I'm about to ask her what she means, but she says, "Your zeal is commendable, but your most useful post is in energy world research. And dealing with The Human Movement would require too much time outside of Guild facilities. It's too dangerous for you."

I purse my lips. So they *aren't* going to ignore THM… Why did she let me go through all that explanation just to tell me no?

Well, it was exactly what I expected anyway. I take a deep breath, raise my chin slightly. "First of all, I never declined working in energy world research. I just don't like the conditions being placed on dealing with my memory loss. If I'm a socket wrench, you all should stop giving me the same conditions as a common hammer. And secondly, you can either let me do this, or I'm leaving the Guild to do it myself."

The only indication of surprise on her part is to shift slightly on her stool. "An interesting strategy," she comments. "Weighing your importance to us against our need to follow caution… You don't remain docile in unfamiliar situations for long."

"And you don't get riled easily, do you?"

Her mouth curves slightly upward. "No."

"What's your conclusion?"

"The balance is in your favor."

I clasp my hands together. "Perfect!"

"I would caution you not to abuse your power," she says. "The Guild has enough resources that we will eventually learn to fashion a new socket wrench."

"Maybe," I say, "but they won't be the granddaughter of Samuel P. Pruitt who can also access the energy world in three dimensions, which even Eric Shelding couldn't do. I'm a one-of-a-kind combo, and you all know it."

She laughs quietly but delightedly. "And not modest, either. Perfect. In the meantime, you'll need to refine your assets. I'm going to bypass the psychological requirements and put you through to the energy world research team. All other conditions will be in place, especially the tracking implant."

I blink. I had no idea this girl had that kind of clout. Isn't she just Ohr's daughter?

"You're going to put me in a top secret department when I just blackmailed you?" I say.

"Yes."

"Why?" I say, brow furrowed in consternation.

"I have my own bets to make," she replies.

"I threatened leaving, which means I have no loyalty. I could get all your secrets and then go spread them to the masses."

She smiles vaguely, hands clasped over her knee, emotions like the surface of a placid sea.

I roll my eyes. "Holding your cards. Fine. Anyway, details. I know I'm supposed to have a bodyguard when I'm out and about. I'm requesting Mike Dumas."

She assesses me shrewdly. "Requesting?"

"Demanding," I say.

"Considering his relation to Gabe Dumas, plus his past affiliation with Andre, you don't consider that ill-advised?"

I shrug. "I consider it strategic."

Her eyebrows lift slightly. "It's a good strategy," she says appreciatively. "I don't believe Mike is a threat to the Guild, but in terms of psychological strategy it's quite ideal."

"Psychological strategy?"

She tilts her head again and there goes her amazing hair. "Of course. If you're going to represent the Guild in our efforts to deal with The Human Movement, you're going to be delivering quite a few public statements, your bodyguard at the ready. It's going to be a bit of a slap in the face to Gabe Dumas to constantly see his brother aiding and abetting his enemy, won't it?"

I'm stunned again, too many questions coming to me at once. "Public statements?"

"Yes. The Council has taken an interest in The Human Movement, for the same reasons you pointed out. The plan is two-fold, and they've been looking for a personality to carry it out. You've volunteered yourself, and I believe you are well-suited to the task. Further, what safer place in public than front and center, on camera, in sight at all times?"

My face blanches. I'm *suited* to the task? This girl barely knows me! "Umm. What is this two-fold plan?"

"First, to appear at prominent THM protests and issue a statement for the media. Second, to host an interview series. You'll interview Prime Humans so people can see who they are and thus who *we* are."

My jaw drops. I take a step back. "You're joking."

"No. But if you have something else in mind, I'd appreciate hearing it," she says. "You have obviously studied the movements of THM prior to making your proposition."

I blink at her for a moment. What on earth? I came here to get in on some investigative work and she instead proposes that I become a public personality? Is she mental? "I was thinking more like... undercover stuff. Recon. Befriending Mike and Gabe and finding out who the Guild mole is."

She laughs, and it's a pretty sound that's way too short. "Oh Wendy, firstly, Mike and his brother are not on speaking terms— for obvious reasons. Secondly, I don't believe Gabe Dumas is as complex as you imagine. THM's demands are clear and we aim to answer as best as we're able. That's all. No subterfuge necessary."

Except she wants to flaunt Mike's affiliation with the Guild in front of his brother... That is *not* a strategy I would have thought the Guild would devise. They're too... proper. Who *is* this woman? Does she really have the clearance to pull this plan off?

"Public 'statements'... touchy-feely interviews... Sounds more like a marketing strategy," I grumble, recalling my argument with my Colloquy facilitator, Rickard, about the Council using marketing strategies.

"Everything is a marketing strategy," she replies, surprising me. Again. "To win people, marketing is necessary. A strong, representative voice to deliver the pitch is key."

I'm floored. I said this same exact thing, and here it is coming out of the mouth of the daughter of someone directly on the Council. Rickard can eat it. "I know," I say.

"I know you know," she says, unmoving. "That's why I'm picking you."

I stare at her for a few beats, wondering several things: Did she hear about my argument with Rickard? And why would she say 'picking'? As if I just interviewed for a job?

"But I have no experience with something like that," I say weakly, doubting my protests are going to make any difference. Shiah couldn't be any more sure of herself.

"That's what we need. Low-profile. Young. Innocent. Someone difficult for Dumas and his followers to sink their teeth into. Someone that can represent everyone that's *not* the Council. You have a willful, no-nonsense, independent attitude. Members of the Guild have been increasingly viewed as sheep, children without a voice and in need of constant protection. But they aren't. They are intelligent, free-thinking individuals, and you are going to be their voice."

I want to keep arguing, terrified as I am of the task of making myself someone people take seriously, but I just bargained for the opportunity to be involved. I had no idea I was going to get myself in this deep, this quickly. I want in on taking The Human Movement down, and if this is the only way they'll let me, I guess I'm going to have to figure out how to 'be a voice.'

"And in between," Shiah says, "energy world research. Enough to keep you satisfactorily busy, you think?"

"I am seriously starting to wonder if this was your plan all along..." I say, "You only wanted me to think helping you with THM was my own idea."

"You can obviously choose to believe otherwise, but I simply have the ability to spot the merit of a good idea and adopt it immediately. I don't quibble over where the idea came from as most do. And neither will the Council when I tell them."

"You're going to tell them it was *your* idea, aren't you?"

She smiles wanly.

"Shiah the shark," I say, pushing off of the couch. "You're kind of terrifying, but for some reason I really like you."

"Thank you," she says, escorting me to the door.

"See that?" I say. "It's like nothing affects you. If it does, it's nothing but a blip on the radar and then it's gone. I'm having trouble figuring out why perfect memory would produce such controlled emotions."

"My learning curve is exceptionally quick. I dwell far less on emotions because I've learned—and I remember clearly—when they are and aren't helpful." She stands with the door open.

"I *can* tell that there's more to it than you're telling me," I say. "But I'm worried that if I stay here any longer, you're going to rope me into more crazy schemes. Anyway, do I have my people call *you* or are *your* people going to call *me*?"

She experiences a sudden thrill, which courses through me in turn. It feels as if this meeting was something she's been waiting for. Like me, she's been impatient for something to happen, and me walking into her apartment was exactly what she needed today.

She's smiling at me, her hand on the open door, waiting for me to finish taking a read on her. "Report to the E building tomorrow morning," she says. "The Energy World Department will be expecting you for more than meditation."

As I walk away from her apartment, my own elation puts a bounce in my step, but I'm also in a little bit of shock. Part of me doesn't know what just happened or how. The larger part is on top of the world. I did it. And it worked out even better than I imagined. I'm going to do something, and it's going to matter.

I promise, I won't waste my life this time, Ezra.

Twenty

I suck in a breath, nearly losing my nerve and backing away from the subject lying on the table. She doesn't look like a human being anymore. She looks like... like she's encased in a purple, liquid cocoon. Frightened, I glance up, wanting Jonas' assurance, but instead a kaleidoscope of color meets my eyes. Hues and patterns shift all around me so quickly that I can't make out anything solid, not even the floor. I've been suspended in a psychedelic fantasia.

And then I'm falling, but the floor catches me, and my butt plops onto the very normal beige carpet. I blink, staring at its fibers for a moment before looking up and realizing the room has returned to normal.

Jonas is leaning across Seraphina, my subject, to stare at me on the floor with wide-eyed curiosity, his wavy blonde hair falling forward.

I take a deep breath. "I think—"

"You were successful?" Jonas says in his thick, Norwegian accent. He tucks a lock of hair behind his ear, his eyes as wide as saucers.

I nod. I can't believe I did it... They said I should be able to but... I don't know what I expected to see, but I was *not* prepared for *that*. What *was* that?

Jonas grins, thrilled as he comes around to help me up.

I hold up a hand to stop him. "Give me a sec. I'm still... remembering gravity."

"How did it appear?" he presses, sitting cross-legged on the floor next to me.

"Like a Lisa Frank poster," I reply.

"Lisa Frank..." Jonas says, confused.

"Forget it. You'd have to see it," I say. "Next example. You ever looked in a Kaleidoscope?"

He nods excitedly.

"Like that, but it's the whole room and constantly changing. Psychedelic. I lost my feet because I couldn't figure out where the ceiling and the walls were. But before that was Seraphina. She was covered in this purple liquid—well, it looked like liquid. It flowed all around her, like she was swathed in it. And it was illuminated, like a light bulb was behind it."

"Thrilling," he breathes, completely in awe. I'm in major awe myself. I think maybe I didn't actually believe all the hype before and that's why actually *seeing* the energy world is such a shock. It's a real place. The energy world is *real.*

I roll onto my knees and come to my feet. "You should have warned me how disorienting those colors shifting all over the place was going to be. I might have stayed upright if I'd known to expect it."

He laughs. "How would I inform you? It has never appeared to me. I only smell it."

I listen to Seraphina's vitals to be sure she's okay. She's been placed under hypnosis to achieve the hyper-alert state I've been told is necessary. It's supposed to help me, the practitioner, see the energy world quicker or something. I guess it's true since it only took me about a minute to do so. And then all I had to do was open my eyes. What a trip. My gosh, I can't believe what I just saw! "You study the energy world, don't you?" I say. "Gather data on its makeup?"

Jonas looks at me questioningly. "I have much data on the olfactory landscape of the energy world. But from where would I have gathered other data?"

"Uhhh... I don't know. This is your department, isn't it? And the Guild is super advanced. You're saying you don't have any info on what that place looks like?"

"No," Jonas says, coming to his feet as well. "No, we do not. You are it, Wendy. Origin of all visible data from the energy world. And I could not have more thrill over this!"

He claps his hands and goes to the nearby counter to fetch his tablet.

I can't believe what he's saying. They have out of this world life force abilities that they claim come from that crazy alternate reality, and they don't know anything about it? How the crap have they gotten this far without such rudimentary information? And... how do they know that messing with stuff they can't see is safe? My gosh, I totally get why I'm so important now. The whole Sam and Eric legacy was not an exaggeration. No wonder Shiah was willing to push me through to start working here. I can't believe Dr. Lim didn't from the get-go.

I stand over Seraphina and murmur some instructions to bring her out of hypnosis. It's one of the things they've been teaching me the past few days.

"It sounded like a success," Seraphina says, sitting up.

"We are going to stride hugely now," Jonas gushes, hastily tucking a stray lock of hair behind his ear again. He holds his hands wide. "Huge." Then he starts furiously typing.

I lean against Seraphina's table and cross my arms, working through my confused surprise. How has the Guild seen my father and his mother have abilities like mine, and never been privy to any of what my family saw? At all?

I suppose I've fallen for the hype in Colloquies. In reality though, Eric Shelding may have *found* life force abilities by discovering hypno-touch—energy therapy done under hypnosis that gives normal people abilities—but he never actually saw, heard, or smelled the place. After joining EWR, I found out it wasn't until he did hypno-touch on my grandmother that anyone understood that the energy world could be visible to someone with super-sight.

Jonas apparently has super-smell. And spread around various Guild facilities are two others with super-smell—all related to Jonas—and two women (twins) with super-hearing. Last is the most common energy world sense—touch. There are six of these—people with an extraordinary proficiency for hypno-touch. They feel life forces with their hands better than typical practitioners. One of them works with us in our branch of EWR, and three others are all engaged in creating the seed-generation. They do hypno-touch on terminal disease victims. The other three are not members of the Guild. But all of these individuals, I've learned, are first-generation Primes (their direct parents had hypno-touch). That means their senses pale in comparison to mine.

One of the most interesting classified facts I've learned in EWR is the concept of Invisibles. These are Prime Humans who no longer have their life force abilities. They've lost them somehow. But additionally, they are rarely affected by the life force abilities of others, making them, for all intents and purposes, invisible to those possessing life force abilities.

And Andre, I learn, was confirmed to be one of these Invisibles. *That* is why they have had so much trouble tracking the guy down. They're having to do it without life force abilities and are totally sucking at it.

The EWR's interest in this is, of course, why? What in the energy world causes people to lose life force abilities and also become immune to them?

Actually, EWR has a *lot* more questions than answers. I assumed the Guild knew more, because they seemed to know so much about what I'm capable of. But apparently my family took the secrets of that world to their graves. And I was about to as well.

That's some serious conviction.

I rub my face, wishing I had someone who knew me before my trip to the woods to consult with.

They're all dead.

I sigh. Right... That's why I chose to join the Guild... That's why I'm here right now, making myself and what I can do available to them. Because the paranoia and rebellion I inherited from my father and apparently his mother got everyone killed. My suspicion is my old self rearing her ugly head.

I can't let that happen.

"Are you ready to go again?" I say.

"Absolutely. Clear your mind," he instructs, coming over. "Focus on—Oh, Seraphina, you are awake. Wendy, would you like to put her under?"

"Just lie down, Seraphina," I say. "I got this, Jonah. I want to try it without her under hypnosis." I close my eyes as Seraphina lies down, but focus on my hands. I'm going to skip all the breathing mumbo jumbo because thinking about the sensation of movement over them is how I got to the energy world in the first place, not breathing. It's actually super easy.

Jonas falls silent, waiting, his hands near Seraphina's stomach while mine are at her chest. He's got to achieve his own hyper-alert state, and it's my goal to do it faster than him.

I feel the tug on my hands shortly, and I open my eyes, but this time I keep them rigidly focused on the purple liquid beneath my hands, which I now realize are also covered in the same substance. It extends from my hands to my arms and chest and down to my feet. It's not liquid, either, I realize upon my second look. It's composed of something strand-like; purple, illuminated, and wrapping around our bodies. But Seraphina's seems to flow toward her chest in a whirlpool. I move my hands gently, side-to-side, to see the interaction. But I get caught up in the resulting sound, an enthralling string symphony, but more synthesized, more alien, no sharp sounds, no whine. Beautiful.

I describe it to Jonas, but I don't know that I do an adequate job. I also describe the purple strand-like substance enveloping the body, which I believe is the life force everyone keeps mentioning. I assume it's the most important part, seeing as this cocoon is the source of incredible superhuman ability.

Once I've described it in as many ways as I can, I take a nervous breath, determined this time to let my eyes only see a sliver of the room at a time. So I look past Seraphina's head, down at where I know the boring carpet is. It's not beige though. It's orange, a lot of different oranges. The disorientation, I realize, comes from the fact that the orange fluctuates hues as I move my point of view; even the mere shift of my head can change it. It's still the carpet with the same texture; it's just a different color. With this in mind I look up, slowly, identifying objects first: the wall, a desk, the computer monitor, a framed piece of art. They are all still the same shapes. But everything is a completely different but ever-changing color. And every bit of it is glowing like it's backlit.

Now that I'm prepared for it, it's a lot easier to keep my balance when I know the same objects and space exist. The difference between our world and this alternate one is literally the colors and the light. Life forces, it seems, are the only variation. They encase the body rather than the body itself being a different color. In fact, I can't even see Seraphina's body beneath her life force.

I describe all of this to Jonas, and as I do so, I can't help wondering how much my past self had learned about this energy world that I'm going to have to relearn. And how, I wonder, are these colors going to tell me the source of natural disasters?

Twenty-One

*T*hat sounds super boring," Kiera says when I explain the interview series show idea to her.

I shrug. "Maybe that's the point. They want the public to know that Primes are as plain as everyone else."

"They're not going to have an audience at all if they don't spice it up."

"Shiah said it's supposed to give The Human Movement the transparency they want. Spicing up what's really vanilla isn't transparency. It's creating a false perception—and THM will call out any move like that."

She's unconvinced, but she says, "Well I can't believe you waltzed in there and blackmailed her. What if she'd said no to all of it?"

"I would have done exactly what I said. Gone to find out for myself."

She shudders and shakes her head. "I don't know how you could stomach that. I love being part of the Guild."

"You've been around it your whole life so it's your family," I say. "But it's not mine. I don't have the same loyalty."

"But you could," she says. "If you'd start thinking of it as a circle of friends instead of a means to an end. I don't even know what you're after at this point." Kiera walks over to my freezer and refills her cup with ice. "Which is why it blows my mind that you're already on the Energy World Research team… I hadn't even gotten notification that my professional opinion was being disregarded."

I sense a bit of resentment, but Kiera needs to get over herself, so I don't comment on it. "They need me," I say, glancing briefly at the television. Yesterday, after my meeting with Shiah, I decided I better be more up on the goings on—especially if I'm supposed to make public statements at some point. I can't stand the same tired newscast banter, though, so I decided I'd keep it on mute and listen in when something new pops up—like now.

Kiera turns around, lifts her eyebrows. "That so?"

"Yep," I say, once again ignoring her tone. Sitting on a stool, I press a button on the manual control panel for the volume. I still can't bring myself to use the voice command. It feels pretentious.

'—*predicted to hit within a two-month period,*' the newscaster is saying as a red strip highlights an area from the Caribbean all the way to the North Carolina coast. '*The Guild has supposedly appointed an official ambassador to the White House, who delivered the news to the President yesterday. Congress is currently in an emergency meeting, and we're waiting to hear more details.*'

Four talking heads appear.

First to speak is an older man, grey hair slicked back, blue suit, '*A systematic evacuation of coastal areas is the obvious solution here. But we don't have the housing anywhere inland to accommodate that kind of move. Is the Guild working toward narrowing down the area at all? Do we know* what's *coming? Hurricane?*'

A woman with long brown hair replies, '*We don't know any details yet. The report we've gotten is exactly the map we've shown. And the timeline. Usually these things come with a little more information, so we're either not getting it because the White House doesn't want to cause a panic, or because the Guild has decided on a new method to deliver information. I think this new ambassador position is evidence of that, and it comes at the heels of some pretty disparaging criticism from the public about how they've handled things in the past—blindly throwing information out for people to translate how they may.*'

A short man, sleeves rolled up, says, '*How they've handled things in the past is to eliminate the middle-man. They've saved time and that equals lives. This is the first time we've gotten a report not directly from the Guild, but from a White House representative. If these things have to start going through a legislative filter, it's going to mean greater loss of life. I think this is a poor move on the Guild's part.*'

The woman rebuts, '*You're ignoring the fact that Prime Human violence has increased more in the last two weeks than at any time since they outed themselves five months ago. Mistrust is rampant, and the Guild Council, in my opinion, is doing this in an effort to protect their own. And they have every right to. Every* time they make an announcement about some impending disaster they get criticized for not going through official outlets, for hiding in the shadows, for acting above the law—especially in cases of PHIA massacring their people.'

'The massacres only happen because PHIA knows where they hide out,' a skinny guy in glasses says. 'Because PHIA's leaders used to be affiliated with the Guild. The violence is a Prime Human matter, and it's a separate issue from the Guild's responsibility toward the people of this country to abide by the same laws—'

'A Prime Human matter?' the woman interjects. 'Since when are serial killings not a human matter? If we're going to talk about what kind of transparency and process the Guild owes the rest of us, we've got to talk about what those demands are going to cost the people providing it!'

'You're twisting my words,' the skinny guy says, pointing at the camera—and the woman presumably. 'What I'm saying is that there are processes to these things that should be carried out so that people don't lose their faith in the United States' government's ability to manage what's going on. If the government hands any significant amount of power over to an organization that hasn't been put to a vote by the American people, you're going to end up with panic, which is going to cause more violence as people follow suit and begin taking things into their own—'

'I need to interrupt here, because we've got the person on the line who arguably started this debate several weeks ago,' the grey-haired gentleman says. 'Gabe Dumas, founder of The Human Movement is ready to weigh in. Mr. Dumas, have you been listening to the discussion, are you aware of what's going on right now at the White House and the recent appointment of a Guild Ambassador?'

'I have, and I am, on both counts, Mr. Dearing,' says the unmistakable voice of Gabe Dumas. Even over a less-than-quality connection, his command of the articulation and annunciation of language is obvious.

'Any thoughts on why the Guild has chosen this time to alert White House officials of a disaster prediction rather than make the announcement themselves as they have in the past?'

'We first have to ask ourselves why it is the Guild hasn't fed us their predictions through the bureaucratic machine until now. The government has utilized scientific and technological consultants since its inception, so the Guild could have chosen to take on a consultant position while maintaining the secrecy of their existence. *Given their dedication to secrecy and general reticence about any matter outside of disaster prediction, that scenario seems rather ideal. But they didn't take that course. They considered it and intentionally decided against it. What they actually chose was to maintain a distance, making their predictions directly to the public to gain their own credibility, meanwhile passively waiting for the government to sufficiently cripple itself in the public's eyes to the point that they have to allow the Guild some measure of decisive power. As to your question, I anticipate that the news we'll hear shortly from the White House is that this latest prediction is of a cataclysmic nature, that it is going to be so titanic that when it's over no one will remember we even had this conversation, caught up as they will be in the ensuing havoc. And that is exactly why the Guild chose to partner themselves with the government at this time rather than any other. Beware, on the other side of this latest calamity is a world more desperate for our clandestine superhero, the Guild.'*

In the short moments following his words, I recognize that all of us—the four talking heads, Kiera, and myself—have hung on Dumas' every word. He's so very good at delivery, his volume, word choice, rhythm. He can lull you with the sound of his voice. I blow air out through pursed lips as the woman makes a comment about the Guild's 'coming out' five months ago, how it wasn't planned, but they were forced to because of PHIA, who had begun massacring them after the fall of California.

'Ms. Lichtman,' Dumas says, *'We have still never been given more than a vague explanation as to why PHIA is out for Guild blood, but I am certain it's more complex than we've been led to believe. I'm not interested in justifying PHIA's actions, not by a long shot. But I'm out to discover who the Guild actually is, and I believe their enemies can tell us a lot more than their spokespeople.'*

'Thanks for your time, Mr. Dumas. I'm sure we'll be hearing more from you again soon.'

The talking heads return to their debate, arguing what the Guild's strategy might be. I lower the volume, biting my lip pensively. He is *so* good. He can twist anything the Guild does to paint it negatively. Gabe Dumas is definitely going to be a problem.

"I don't understand why that guy is getting so much airtime," I say, putting my chin in my hand. "THM's not helping things get better. They're making it harder with all those protests all the time."

Kiera shrugs. "The media loves controversy. They'll allot airtime to stir the pot."

"Gabe Dumas showed up what, like a month ago?" I say. "And now he's suddenly an expert on government-Guild cooperation? It's sickening that the media is *purposely* endangering the world by giving him attention. People need to come *together*, not have another reason to pick sides."

"Where does someone like that come from?" Kiera says. "I mean, how do you wake up one morning and decide you're going to start a movement to take down a group of people who want to make the world better?"

"He's going to see right through this interview series idea," I say, shaking my head. "We need something better."

"It's not like the Guild is the only group that keeps secrets," Kiera says, still indignant. "The government is corrupt and secret and incapable of helping anyone. Politicians have been bought by private companies for years; where was Gabe Dumas' umbrage then? Nobody has even heard of the guy until now. He spent the last ten years of his life as a college professor. You don't go from an academic to protest organizer and critic with the gall to take on the most influential organization in the world without an explanation."

And you don't go from college student to energy world savior either... But here I am. Gabe Dumas at least has the educational background to not sound stupid. In fact, that's probably why so many people have taken him seriously. And I'm sure his fetching looks and charm haven't hurt either. I, on the other hand, have zero skill with public speaking. I assume they're going to give me statements to read at these protest events, but how is that going to win public opinion?

"People *like* him," I reply to Kiera. "People aren't going to like me. Not if I'm delivering pre-recorded messages."

"You signed up for this," Kiera says, holding up two hands.

"You don't have any advice after analyzing him that might help me... find an angle? Why is he doing this?"

She crosses her arms, thoughtful. "He's obviously brilliant... Both academically and socially. His areas of interest, especially now, seem pretty broad. I don't believe you can win an argument with him, not that the Guild would let you attempt something like that... I know it sounds cliche, but be yourself. It's going to be your best weapon."

I roll my eyes. "You are kind of a crappy therapist, Kiera," I grumble. "Has anyone ever told you that?"

"Yeah."

I look at her in surprise.

"But I'm good at my job."

"Those two facts contradict each other," I point out.

"I'm a recruiter, Wendy," she says, her brownish-green eyes giving me an expectant look.

I stare at her in confusion for only a second. "Oh! For the Guild? You're *not* a therapist then?" I ask, straightening to combat the immediate irritation gathering in my shoulders.

She waves a hand. "It's what I initially trained for, but it's supplementary to what I do now. Turned out I was better at... well, this. Getting people like you to see the value in becoming part of the Guild, getting them to find their place here among us."

I can't believe what I'm hearing. Tiny little Kiera with a head of tight curls, and a dimple in her cheek when she smiles really widely is telling me she was part of a scheme to get me to join the Guild. I struggle to think rationally, but I can't get past affront. "Why are you telling me this now?" I say between gritted teeth.

"I have a new assignment. I leave tomorrow morning." She sighs. "I didn't want you to find out from someone else. This is always the hard part—telling people I've been grooming them. It's the same thing *you're* about to do in public though. I guess that's the other reason I chose now. Because I think you can finally understand."

"I..." I look down at the floor, struggling to find words past the shock. "You were my friend for hire. That's what you're saying. How can you possibly compare that to making statements at press conferences?"

"I'm still your friend," she says emphatically, sitting on the stool next to me. I lean away instinctively. "Everything I did and said was genuine. I wasn't just assigned to helping you get your life back, I *wanted* to. And look at you! You're about to go out and speak on behalf of the Guild! And you're utilizing your life force ability. I'm staggered by how far you've come, not just as someone who was put under my care, but also as your friend."

I look away, shake my head. "You don't know what a friend is."

She stands up, aggravation finally coloring her emotions. "A friend is someone who helps you reclaim life. I do that for a lot of people. The Guild noticed I was good at it. So they made it my occupation. I love what I do, and I get to do it all the time. You don't get it because you won't stop seeing the Guild as an organization bent on power. Think about who you are, Wendy, who you want to be. The Guild is here to help you be that person. That's what it's about. That's *all* it's about."

I wish that for once my anger wouldn't translate into tears, but it does anyway. I wipe my eyes and turn my glare on Kiera. "Fine. If you're coming clean, then tell me about your life force ability."

She blinks at me, struggling to keep her squeamish reaction from me. There's no hiding though.

"You've been using it to get me to like you, to trust you, haven't you?" I say. "You and Chase. You're both the same, thinking you can use your abilities on people without consent. It's not right, Kiera. And it's certainly not what friends do to each other."

She puts her hands on her hips, looks up at the ceiling. "My life force ability is as much a part of me as my food preferences. I can't change it at will. My life force ability is *me*."

"You have a duty to tell people how it can manipulate them. At least Mikel was open about her head shrinking."

She shakes her head. "No. That's society's way of thinking. Only they would single out a person's life force ability and speak of it as a disease that requires full disclosure." She looks at me. "Our life force abilities are who we are as much as any other trait. That's why the Guild makes disclosing them optional. I have no more obligation to tell you what my life force ability is than I do what my favorite color is."

I give her a pitying look, because it's becoming clear that she's either ashamed of her life force ability or she depends so heavily on it that she doesn't know who she is without it. "I have always made it a point to know my friends' favorite colors," I point out.

She half-sighs, half-huffs. "I gotta go. I have some packing to do."

"Blue," I say as she opens the door. "That's your favorite color."

She pauses, her back toward me. "Sky blue. I'd say good luck out there, but I don't think you need it." She closes the door.

Once she's gone, I'm alone with my questions. Like, does it matter that the Guild hired someone to recruit me?

I slump. Probably not. It would be naive of me to think they wouldn't or shouldn't. They have a purpose and their actions are intended to meet that purpose. That's how I saw them before and that's how I see them now. Kiera is a person, though, who purported to be my therapist and my friend, but in reality she was after something other than friendship. She thinks she can be both, but she can't. The moment she made a choice to deceive me, she decided not to be my friend. I have no idea how she disguised her emotions from me so thoroughly in the last month though. Surely whatever her ability is has something to do with it.

As I mull it over, I keep coming back to her words about what the Guild is. And then I remember her counsel to me: be yourself. It's advice used so frequently that it's lost any value. How odd that it should be the thing that gives me an idea though. The idea, at first, is so ridiculous that I don't take it seriously. But I keep getting pulled back to it. So I start picturing it, how it will go, what the reaction will be, and how I will handle the backlash. I think I can do it... I really think I can.

Then it becomes brilliant. Because it is the one way I can imagine to stop The Human Movement in their tracks.

Twenty-Two

A thick cloud of hairspray descends upon me, and I inhale before I realize it. I start coughing and then sneezing. I hold my mug of ginger tea away from me so I don't splash it on myself.

"Sorry!" Jaina, my stylist says. "Should have warned you it was coming."

"It's fine," I say, setting the mug down and reaching for a tissue now that my nose is surely going to turn into a faucet. "I'm just really sensitive to hairspray. And I wasn't paying attention." I sneeze again.

"Gosh, I'm sorry!" Jaina says, nervous. "Can I get you some water?" She starts fanning me with her hand, then fumbles about for an actual fan.

"Relax," I say. "I'm seriously fine. But if you're going to be so on-edge, we're going to have a problem. I can pick up every blip you're putting out and I'm going to be a basket case before I ever leave this hotel if I have to fight your nerves as well as my own."

"I'm sorry!" she says again.

I exhale impatience. "What is wrong? You were fine a second ago." I really don't have time for a jittery stylist. I need to go back to memorizing these remarks the Council provided me with.

She clears her throat. "Didn't you see the forecast?" She indicates the television that's on low in the background.

I shake my head, give her a questioning look.

"Humidity's at ninety percent here in St. Louis. It's probably going to rain before the day's out. I should have let your hair naturally spike instead of styling it down."

I blink at her, wondering why that issue should be causing her this much stress, how it can possibly even *be* an issue in the face of… well, *everything*. "Jaina. My hair is not even two inches long." I struggle to keep the condescension out of my voice.

"You'd be surprised how much more of an issue humidity is to shorter hair. Curls every which-way..." She shakes her head disapprovingly. "Without the weight of hair to help, it's entirely up to the product to do the work. You should never work against short hair." She gives me a wide-eyed confident stare as if she's let me in on an industry secret.

"Holy. Moley," is the nicest thing I can think of to say. "And here I am, worrying over the five hundred and forty eight words I have to memorize..."

To my utter disbelief, she totally misses the sarcasm, instead taking it as a statement of validation rather than the blustering expression of irritation it's meant to be. She starts talking about starting over, wetting my hair down, and then giving it a little mousse to keep its texture.

She makes a move toward me and I hold up both hands to keep her at bay, my tablet nearly falling off of my knees. "Don't touch me, Jaina, or I swear you're going to lose a hand!"

She freezes in confusion.

"What is *wrong* with you?" I snap. "How dense can you be? And how can you possibly stress *this* much about a few hairs being out of place with something like a hundred *million* people being displaced from their homes and countries? Geez. Get some freaking perspective, woman. And go find somewhere else to be."

She scampers off, and I make a few exclamations to myself before realizing I'm not alone. I hear her heartbeat before I see her, and I turn in my chair to spot Shiah propped casually in the door opposite the one Jaina disappeared through.

She stands there calmly, watching me, and I wait for her to berate me or something for yelling at Jaina. But my gosh that woman is exasperating. Shiah's wearing another black outfit. In fact, I've never seen her wear any other color. This time it's a little more dressed up. Black, tapered slacks. Black, cropped jacket over a black camisole. Her black shoes have about an inch wedge, just enough to suggest formality. Her sleek black hair is pulled back in a simple business ponytail. I have never in my life looked as swanky as Shiah does, and she accomplishes it with so little. She doesn't even wear makeup.

"An interesting choice of apparel," she says, having assessed my own outfit, which directly contrasts hers, I realize. "You didn't like the one that was selected for you?"

"I can't take myself seriously in that pantsuit," I reply.

The left side of her mouth curves up. "One might argue others can't take you seriously in jeans."

I look down. "They're not *jean* jeans. They're white denim, which is way classier than blue denim."

"It's a bold color choice."

"*White* is a bold color choice? I mean, aside from it being after Labor Day, white really isn't all that scandalous."

She inhales and exhales serenely as if she has nothing else to do in the world but stand there and breathe. She is the most composed person I have encountered in my entire life. "I support your choice to establish your individuality," she says, and her eyebrows lift slightly as if she's implying something additional. But I have no idea what that might be.

"Thanks," I say. "I at least went with the pantsuit *theme*." I stand up and grab my matching white twill jacket from the nearby chair. I pull it on over my lacy purple tank. I hold my hands out and turn around. "See. Edgy class with a professional flair."

"Very feminine. I approve," she says. "You've taken quite a bit of autonomy, though. Most wouldn't have usurped a decision like a prescribed wardrobe without at least complaining about it first."

I turn around and look in the mirror, tugging my jacket down and admiring my reflection. "Kiera told me to be myself. I think it's important that I come across as authentically as possible."

"That's why I chose you," Shiah says.

That's the second time Shiah has mentioned choosing me... I'd like to tell her it wasn't her idea, but if I'm honest with myself, that's a total lie. She basically took what I had planned and twisted it to suit what she actually wanted. I think she *wants* me to think most of it was my idea though...

I still think it's crazy though. I'm nineteen as far as experience is concerned because I lost my memory. Who in their right mind makes a nineteen year-old a spokesperson? Shiah doesn't even know me...

And I haven't memorized my speech...

"I wouldn't be dependent on memorization," she says, taking a seat across the cabin.

I snap my head around. Can she read minds or something?

"This will likely be the only time you receive your remarks ahead of time," she continues. "What you say needs to be relevant to Dumas' discourse. He has been adhering to a similar message since it's a new crowd in a new city each time. But we strongly believe Dumas will not ignore your presence once he realizes you will be a fixture at his protests. That means he will start addressing you specifically. You'll need to be prepared to respond. So you'll wear a wireless communicator and your responses will be relayed that way."

This news doesn't surprise me. In fact, the Council and Shiah have no idea what I've been planning. In the last three weeks since I dreamt it up, not only have I watched every video The Human Movement has posted online and read every interview with Gabe Dumas available, I've also been mentally preparing myself to handle what I'm sure is going to cause major waves. After today, I'm not completely sure I'll remain as spokesperson. I'm reasonably sure I will. But I'm also aware that I could be seriously pushing my luck on how much the balance Shiah told me about is in my favor.

"I'll keep that in mind," I reply. "But this is my first appearance. I want to get it right."

She merely nods and sits in one of the open chairs in the room, turning her attention to her tablet before I can cast a scowl her direction.

I put aside my GIT and tune into the news on my internet-enabled tablet. I have watched more news in the past three weeks than I have in my whole life. But I figured it was part of my job description as a Guild spokesperson.

Currently, the Caribbean Evacuation is dominating the media and has been for weeks now, which is no surprise. It's the result of a tectonic event projected to impact the east coast from North Carolina down the the Caribbean, the same disaster Dumas criticized the Guild for filtering through the White House. Although after finding out that the event would require major international cooperation to evacuate some hundred million people—more than half of those from islands—in two month's time, I have no idea how anyone would think the Guild would have even considered their usual avenues to deliver the news. I'm kind of surprised they didn't go directly to the UN.

It looks like the ongoing efforts are nowhere near becoming manageable. In the first days after world governments revealed the gravity of the upcoming disaster, and evacuation plans were hastily distributed, every coastal city looked like it was in the middle of a military occupation, with soldiers on every corner with rifles. In several places, including Miami, the fleeing residents overpowered military peacekeepers and then proceeded to ransack every business for provisions on their way out of town. Florida had to open up every lane of every freeway and road as north-only routes just to manage the traffic at a crawl.

Now the waves of island evacuees have begun, but the people are being directed to the same places as mainland evacuees. Those people are already feeling the crunch of a lack of resources, so unending trains of new evacuees are wholly unwelcome. Most of them don't even speak the same languages or dialects, so cooperation isn't easy to come by. Mainland evacuees have started to abandon the camps and head further inland, leaving a string of violence, theft, and general mayhem as they search for a home. The most common image or video in the news is that of the constant stream of people on foot who have disembarked from a vessel—fishing boat or container ship, every seaworthy vessel is being utilized to get people off the islands as quickly as possible.

Surely hundreds have lost track of their families in the chaos. I wonder… If I was in northern California with my uncle, did I get separated from Ezra somehow after the San Francisco earthquake? Perhaps that's how he ended up getting taken by Andre.

I sigh.. Sometimes I wish I knew the details of our separation. But most days I don't.

I wonder… Are life forces like souls? In the EWR department, we always speak about them scientifically. Life forces. Energy. Resonance Spectrum—that's the terminology they use to talk about the different colors objects project. In the three weeks I've been working there I have never once thought of life forces as souls. If they are, does that mean that I might be able to see a soul… without a body?

A breaking news story pops up on my tablet: the water crisis. It's been a growing problem since the disasters began picking up in frequency, and with the influx of refugees and the appearance of refugee camps, the problem is becoming worse. But it looks like the Guild has announced they are close to a solution although no details are given. I have no doubt that whatever it is, it's going to be earth-shattering. I don't know why the Guild even *needs* a spokesperson like me. If we keep doing what we're doing, people will eventually accept that we aren't the devil. And with the economy falling swiftly into ruin, the government will collapse. The Guild will be all that's left standing.

"Is there even going to be news coverage?" I say, sort of to myself, sort of to Shiah. "No one is going to care with all the other crap going on…"

She looks up, tilts her head, her ponytail swinging to the side, her expression pondering, like she hasn't considered the necessity of news coverage before. But she doesn't reply, looks back at her tablet.

I stare at her for a moment, sort of annoyed but mostly confused because she doesn't seem concerned. Although being as cool as a cucumber is Shiah's MO, I've discovered.

"How do you guys do it?" I say to get her talking. "How does the Guild know disasters are coming? Is it a life force ability? Someone that can predict the future?"

"Premonition is a rather common life force talent," Shiah says. "But no one, save your late Uncle Robert Haricott, has ever managed to master it. It requires significant mental discipline."

I notice she didn't include the famous Samuel Pruitt in that judgment… Maybe she considers Samuel a given. "My uncle mastered telling the future?" I say.

"Oh yes. He accomplished an extraordinary amount of good with it, too."

Humility washes over me, and I wonder how much I knew him…

"Our most dependable assets are of the raw intelligence variety," Shiah continues. "They have developed technology and mathematical constructs to be able to predict disruptions in human behavior on a grand scale and translate it into geological and meteorological implications."

I raise an eyebrow. "Blah blah blah… Big words… No to precogs… Humans act weird… Something about the weather… Your uncle was unusual. That's pretty much all I heard."

She mirrors my eyebrow with her own.

"On a completely unrelated note, where's the bodyguard I requested?" I ask.

"You mean demanded?" she says, smiling. "He'll meet up with us shortly. He hasn't been briefed on anything other than that he's up for a possible personal protection selection. The Council is extremely hesitant about giving him this assignment, given his multiple connections, and I'm supposed to be making a last ditch effort to convince you to take someone else as your protection."

I laugh at her straight face. Shiah is such a trip. I swear she knows she's funny but she never actually laughs at herself—which is what makes her funny in the first place. "Okay?" I chuckle.

"It is callow and unnecessarily dangerous for you to allow Michael Dumas to take upon himself your personal protection. Not only is it base to place him in a likely position of emotional conflict, but it's a dirty move, one which the Guild would never employ as a tactic."

"Hmm, those are some strong accusations," I say, remembering that it was Shiah herself that called it 'good strategy.' I take it she and the Council don't always agree.

"Indeed. Something to consider."

"And you?" I say. "You still think it's a good idea?"

"No doubt, Mike Dumas may decline the job if he so chooses," she replies. "No need to place his supposed emotional burden on yourself. As for the rest of it, I disagree with the word 'unnecessarily.' It's dangerous, yes. But we need more guts in this campaign for acceptance. We don't have enough of it among our ranks."

I wonder how much Shiah is going to regret going to bat for me against the Council when today is over.

"By the way," Shiah says, coming to her feet, "your first Prime Human interview is tomorrow. She lives here in St. Louis."

My mouth opens. "You're telling me this *now*?"

Her mouth curves upward again. Shiah must really be in a good mood—however that translates in her world. "After a public appearance in front of five thousand shouting protestors, a simple interview with one Prime Human in front of one camera is going to feel like PR kindergarten."

"*Five* thousand?!" I squeak as my stomach drops to my feet.

"You know as well as I that THM protests where Dumas is physically present are extremely well-attended and organized— that's why you will only be attending events where *he* is. Besides, his message is growing in popularity. And St. Louis has been relatively untouched by the disaster epidemic. The people here have yet to feel a need for the Guild, so they can afford to protest it," Shiah says, standing and motioning me toward the door.

I barely hear her. I'm following on her heels, desperate for the air outside so I don't feel like I'm suffocating. We're flanked by a huge group of protection operatives as we make our way down the hall though, so I get no such relief.

"Get yourself together, Wendy," Shiah whispers to me when she notices my state, and I glance up to see that we've arrived in the lobby. In front of us are more operatives, glass doors, and vehicles lined up outside. I don't have to think, I'm simply escorted into the nearest one.

Someone is already inside, dressed in a black sport jacket, white collared shirt and black tie. Before I can get out a greeting, he says, "Well, well. If it isn't Miss Level Ten herself. To what do I owe this pleasure?"

"Mike Dumas," I say, sitting in the captain's chair adjacent his, noticing that Shiah got into a different vehicle, and also recognizing Mike's immediate attraction toward me. "Glad I could make your day. You did tell me you were for hire. I assumed you were serious."

"And I assumed you'd forgotten me. What's your level ten self doing here?" Mike's extreme flirtation is all coming back to me now... This, I can handle.

"Well..." I say, wishing I'd planned what I would say to Mike when I saw him. "You are looking at the new Guild-appointed Human Movement relations spokesperson. And *you,* Mike, I have selected as my personal security detail until the foreseeable future."

Mike's face freezes in an open-mouthed, staggered expression.

I can't help biting my lip. Maybe I was too quick to think Mike would want to do something like this. I barely know the guy. I spent all of fifteen minutes with him. Gosh, he's huge... I definitely want someone as intimidating as him backing me up.

"Shit," he breathes. He grimaces, making an effort to reel in his shock. "Ah, sorry. I'm behaving like an ass and you're offering me the first real job I've had since..." He looks at me directly finally, clears his throat. "I'm *really* sorry."

For a dreadful second I think he's going to say he can't take the job, but instead he says, "I apologize for hitting on you right off the bat. It was unprofessional and I know better. I was told I was going to be put in a pool of possibles for a protection gig. I was expecting to audition, so I got my cocky game-face on because that's how you win those jobs. So when you jumped in looking like a million bucks, I was just... in that frame of mind. And now I feel like a complete idiot."

"It's okay," I say, laughing a little nervously because Mike went from counterpart to subordinate within moments. I'm not sure how to deal with his underling personality.

He clears his throat. "Okay, yeah. So I'm honored that you'd hand-pick me, but I gotta come clean here. I know you know my connection to Andre, and if you were picked for this spokesperson job, you are surely smart enough to have realized I'm related to Gabe Dumas, founder of The Human Movement. I'm pretty much effed on every side, which is why I've been sidelined for months. Nobody trusts me. I can't even believe you're sitting here offering me a job that has anything to do with The Human Movement. So my question is how much did that affect your decision? I'm not saying I can't do this job, but personal protection is about trust, and I want to make sure you trust me otherwise this won't work for you."

"Actually, that's *why* I picked you," I say, feeling with almost complete certainty that Mike Dumas actually has no subversive connection to Gabe Dumas. He is clearly distancing himself from any affiliation whatsoever. He's a terrible choice for a spy. Nobody trusts him, and he knows it and has even accepted it. I'd bet a hefty sum Mike is completely Guild-loyal—just like Shiah said. I can check any suspicion about him off my list.

His brows lift. "Would you mind clarifying?"

I cross my legs, clasping my hands over my knees. "I picked you because you have more intimate knowledge on Gabe Dumas than anyone else. And I've seen you in action so I knew you were capable."

"I don't mean to second-guess you, but that seems... stupid. You want to consult with me about my cousin, that's one thing. But we're talking about your personal safety. Why on earth would you take the risk to trust me?"

I tilt my head and stare at him. "I'm an empath, Mike. I know when someone is lying to me."

He blinks, sits back in his seat. "Well damn. Okay. You are one ballsy VIP. I can't think of a single Council member that would do what you're doing. This should be fun. I take it we're headed to the Arch then?"

"Yes. And for the record, the Council hates that I'm doing this."

He looks at me curiously. "How did—? Nevermind. Not part of my job. Speaking of my job, have you ever had personal protection detail before?"

"No."

He nods, sits up straighter, buttoning his jacket, and I swear I can see yet another persona fall over him. "Then let me give you a quick lesson. You lead. I trail you because not only can I block you from behind, I can also spot threats ahead. I'm your shadow. When you go through a door, I go first. I will be with you at all times. *All* times. You don't enter any room without me checking it out first. You don't get into any car without me okaying it first. You don't shake anyone's hand or accept any packages or items from anyone directly. Everything goes through me. I'm like your unseemly wart that won't go away. I'm stuck to you no matter what you do and no matter how much you don't like it. It's my job to protect you and that includes annoying the hell out of you if that's what it takes to keep you safe. Do you understand?"

Okay, forget the subordinate personality. Before I can stop myself, I say innocently, "So what? You take showers with me, too?"

I watch him, unsurprised that he actually *considers* the shower idea. He can't help it. That's exactly why I said it; a past version of me made power-plays second-nature. Mike recovers within seconds though and laughs. "No. But I will check out the shower before you use it."

"And where do you sleep?" I say disappointedly. "At the foot of my bed like a good guard dog?"

"Level Ten," he says, "I know you think I'm hot. And you know I think *you're* hot. But the only way this works is as a completely platonic relationship."

"You keep calling me Level Ten, though. How am I supposed to keep it platonic if you're using pet names?"

He laughs. "I call you Level Ten because I have no idea what your name is, actual or alias."

"Oh," I say, wrinkling my nose. "Wendy Whitley. That's my name."

He pauses thoughtfully, and I'm about to ask him why, but he replies, "I wouldn't have pegged you for a Wendy."

"What? Why?"

"I don't know. Haven't you ever met someone and found out their name and thought it sounded weird to call them that?"

"I guess. What name *wouldn't* have been weird?"

"Ashley. Sara. Whitney. Mariah. Any of those."

"Mariah?"

"Yeah. Or Gina. Maybe Celeste."

"Gina? Why Gina?"

"You just look like a Gina."

I lift my brows, considering whether to point out that my biological mother's name was supposedly Regina. I decide against it. He doesn't need my life history to do this job.

"Doesn't matter anyway. Would you prefer Wendy or Ms. Whitley? Or something else?"

"Call me Wen."

"You got it. You made a good choice, Wen. I know I have a lot of damning connections in my past, but there is no one more qualified for this business than me. Plus, I know Gabe better than anyone. He's turning out to be a real pain in the Guild's ass, so whatever I can do to help your campaign, I will."

"I can see that," I say, sitting back in my seat. "And one more thing, if you use your mental suggestion ability on me I'm going to punch you and then fire you."

He laughs, although it's somewhat nervous. "I'll do my best. Keeping things strictly platonic should definitely help for what *you're* worried about. But you should know that my ability is part of what makes me good at my job. I can influence you to move in a situation to ensure your safety. Mostly though, I'll be using what I can do on *other* people instead."

I regard him suspiciously. "Fine, but just so you don't think I'm joking about anything else, I fired my dyad *and* my therapist for using their mind tricks on me. You're pretty to look at but that won't stop me."

"You can't fire your dyad. I should know."

"Well I did," I say.

He whistles through his teeth. "It's starting to sound like you have quite a bit of the Council in your pocket. So... what made you of level ten importance? How on earth does an eighteen year-old become a spokesperson for the Guild?"

I don't answer, a little surprised at his gall. He was all apologetic not ten minutes ago, and now he thinks we're on sharing terms?

"Don't get me wrong," he says, noticing my expression. "I'm not just being nosy. Knowing what makes you important will help me protect you. Helps me know who might be after you."

Catching my hesitation, he adds, slightly irritated, "If you don't trust me, then why the hell did you pick me?"

He's right of course. But I didn't pick him because I trusted him.

He sits back, crosses his burly arms, and sudden recognition comes over him. "This is some sort of PHIA recovery strategy, isn't it? Put a high profile Prime in public as bait and wait for Andre to bite. Why the hell am I being kept in the dark about it? That's a dumbass strategy. Why THM events? The Council's just giving my brother more fodder by... Wait. They think he's connected to Andre, don't they? I *told* them he wasn't." He snorts, shakes his head. "A waste of time and I'm not interested in being a part of it. You can take this job and shove it."

I stare at him, waiting for him to finish. "Are you done whining?" I say when he finally takes a breath.

"Yep. You can drop me off here," he says, looking out the window, hand on the door.

"Turn around and look at me," I order.

To my surprise, he obeys.

"First of all, I might be young, but I'm *not* eighteen," I say. "Second, I see the energy world, Mike. The *only* person in the Guild who can. I'm the daughter of Carl Haricott, the *last* person who could see it. I'm also the granddaughter of Sam Pruitt."

His eyes have grown wide. "Daughter of Carl Haricott? You... You were on our list of missing Primes. You were..." He laughs humorlessly. "You were a myth. Andre and I used to joke about it... Finding you would be like finding the Holy Grail. Wasn't gonna happen. Are you shittin' me?"

I frown. So that's what he and Andre did when they were dyads... They searched for missing Primes, and that's why Andre knew where I was when the rest of the Guild didn't. And what about Mike? He seems to not know Andre found me. "No. I'm not," I reply, irritated. "I wanted to be on the PHIA recovery team, but they wouldn't let me. So I took my second choice, which was to bring Gabe Dumas' movement down. So this is exactly what I told you it was."

He clears his throat twice. Looks down at his feet. Shifts in his seat. "This was... unexpected," he says. "My bad. I'm shoving my foot in my mouth for the second time in fifteen minutes..." He blows air through his lips, then looks at me apprehensively. "You sure about this?"

"What exactly?" I say.

He waves his hand. "Putting yourself in danger for one. Making me your protection when I disrespected you twice already for another."

"Do you want this job or not?" I say, getting aggravated. "Because if you do, then you don't get to question my decision to do this. In fact, you don't get to question anything."

He seems at odds with himself, but he says, "Yeah, you're right. I'm sorry. Again. I don't know what my problem is— probably still expecting to be treated like I'm contagious. Ignore me. I can follow orders *and* keep you safe. I swear it."

Geez. This guy is manic. "Good, because it looks like we're almost there. You have my back?"

"Wen," he says, holding his hand out to me. I turn, take it, and he says, "You have my word, I will protect your life with my own. You follow my instructions and I will follow you into any life-threatening situation you choose."

About five different flirtatious replies come to mind, but I suppress them. I have no idea what has come over me, except that I hate being doubted—*and* ordered around. Flirting my way into the position of alpha has always been my response to overconfident men who want to tell me what to do or expect women to fall all over them. Logically I get that Mike telling me what to do is a different situation, and it's for a very different purpose, but I can't seem to suppress my instincts.

My gosh, how am I thinking about stuff like that with what I'm about to do? Maybe it's the nerves. Flirting eases tension. Right? How does my speech go again? Where's my tablet? Holy crap, I'm going to lose my lunch… And Jaina was right about the humidity. I'm going to have an afro by the time this is over.

Twenty-Three

*B*ack when my empathy was reserved to only skin-contact, I could often feel the effects of it even at a distance. The energy or vibe of the group, if it was large enough, would seep into me until I was hopped-up on pure human emotion. Now, however, with my new distance empathy, that effect is instantaneous, less like a gradual buzz and more like a shot of epinephrine to the arm. I'm bouncing on the balls of my feet from inside the St. Louis Arch's visitor's center, located underground beneath the feet of the Arch, which means the crowd itself is literally on top of me.

We were brought here by an alternative underground entrance, and on the walk Shiah informed me that St. Louis is actually the birthplace of the Guild. "Really?" I said. "That's fitting then, huh? Since Dumas has been looking for the right place to 'knock' per se."

She laughed. "Oh Wendy, it is *more* than fitting. The funds needed to complete this visitor's center were supplied by one of the founding Guild members in the seventies. Within days of completion, in fact, the Guild alliance was forged right here, in one of the rooms beneath the Arch. Thus the Arch commemorates not only the gateway to the west, but also the gateway to the future."

"Whoa," I replied. "Did you plan for this to be my first event for that reason? Because we will be metaphorically and actually 'answering' from our own door?"

Shiah walked silently for a bit, and I recognized it as nearly identical in emotional experience to what Dr. Lim did once: used silence to create emphasis.

"I did not," she says finally. "After all, Gabe Dumas chose the city as well as the location—this is the first time he won't be demonstrating in front of a government building. I simply looked up where he would appear next in the timeframe I was looking for. It didn't take any trying on my part."

We walked in silence after that. Everything began to feel... destined, like the universe had approved of my efforts and was ushering me down the hall. Confidence fell over me in waves. And as soon as the elation of the crowd hit me, I was ready. I've been ready for an hour now.

Mike, however, has been totally on edge; pacing the front doors and checking around corners.

I have strictly ignored him, closing my eyes and letting the pulse of the crowd take me over as I wait, listening to their chants. I've not heard Dumas speak yet; he always delivers an opening and a closing address. We arrived *after* the first address, but I listened to it on the way over. His message was the same, a demand for more Guild transparency, an end to the monopolization of technology and information, collaboration between Primes and Humans, and an end to the term 'Prime Human.' The chanting from the crowd has cycled between 'All Humans are Prime,' 'Secrecy is slavery,' 'Cooperation, not collusion,' and finally 'We are The Human Movement.'

The crowd seems to calm on it's own, but I can hear the faint sounds of a microphone being tested. It's nearly time.

"We have been knocking," the astute, unmistakable voice of Gabe Dumas blares through speakers above. "And again we have gotten no answer."

The crowd shouts and boos.

"But sooner or later, we will! My friends, they have heard us... They *have* heard us. But they pretend they don't, lying to themselves that one day we will go away... Will we?"

The crowd shouts a resounding chorus of "No!"

"We won't. As we raise our voices, we have called upon those afraid to question their saviors, and told them, 'Now is the time!'"

The crowd cheers in a deafening roar.

"Our message resounds, and our numbers grow. Today the Humans of St. Louis have called together the biggest gathering of Human supporters yet seen!"

More raucous cheering.

"We finish this demonstration five thousand, seven hundred and twenty-two strong!"

The crowd explodes, electrifying me so that I have to take deep breaths to keep from sprinting.

"Five thousand, seven hundred and twenty-two *Human* strong!" Dumas booms over the crowd.

"Now," Shiah says, having appeared next to me. "Are you ready?"

"I was ready an hour ago," I say, boldly striding up the ramp that will take us above ground. Mike is behind me, his head on a swivel, and with the crowd I can't read him specifically, nor do I care to. I'm in a zone. I know I *should* be nervous. I know this is the craziest thing I've ever done by far. I know I shouldn't possess the skill necessary to pull this off. But I don't *feel* any of that. I feel a compulsion to move, an unrelenting drive to do what I came here for. How can I possibly be afraid? It's going to be easy.

Once through the doors above ground, one foot of the arch is directly in front of us. A short stair climb is the quickest way to get to the same level as the protestors. Dumas is staged at the other foot, about six hundred feet away, his sea of supporters separating us. Surrounding the sea is the media, more than I've ever seen at any of his events. Cameras, microphones, and well-groomed reporters. No wonder Dumas was so sure THM has been heard by the Guild with that kind of media presence.

A flood of black suits precedes our small group, and a couple of men trail us, each carrying a speaker. A small stage is waiting for me, nothing more than a raised platform. I've already been fitted with a microphone as well as my GIT, but I'm not going to use it. In fact, I shove it in the sound tech's hands once she's done. For one thing, I remember the whole speech—including the parts I added at the end. For another, I'd be shooting the Guild in their big giant ignorant foot if I give those sanitized remarks after this crowd was just wooed by the master. I'll sound like a politician, or worse, a robot politician. Instead I'm going to filter my words through this insane amount of energy and passion lent by the crowd, as well as lean on the uncanny feeling that I am in exactly the place I should be at exactly the right time.

As I step up onto the small stage, Gabe Dumas is directly across from me. If I didn't have more than exceptional vision, I wouldn't be able to make out his features, or realize he's laughing as he helps his sound guys wind up cords while the massive crowd begins to disburse in chorus' of varying chants. I don't know that anyone, other than the portion of the crowd positioned closest to us, realizes we are here. Most of them seem to want to get as close to Dumas as possible.

With a nod from my sound guy, undeterred, I lift my chin. "Knock, knock, knock," I say, the immediate sound of my voice lost in the amplified version of it booming though the speakers behind me.

It's like a wave. The whole crowd of five thousand turns in a uniform ripple. Their sudden and universal confusion nearly knocks me back.

Gabe Dumas stops, a loop of black cord in his hands as he stares and then squints to see better.

"The Guild is here," I say, nearly laughing to myself at the double-meaning. I throw out my hands wide though to capture the attention of those who are still searching for the origin of the voice. I fully expect the crowd to stare dumbly at me, which they do. "I can see by your faces that you weren't expecting an answer today," I say, as the confusion of the massive crowd crashes against me, tangibly forcing me backward a step. Whew. A chair would be nice right about now.

"Sorry we didn't RSVP, but we're a skittish group," I explain. "We don't like to announce to the uglies out there where to find us. Of course, all of that is about to change. I hope you're ready."

The crowd shifts uncomfortably and nobody knows what to do. A few stray shouts pop up, but they stay quiet for the most part. And Dumas moves to the very edge his own stage, likely frustrated that he can't see that well. I just wait a few more moments, letting them get an eyeful of me.

"So now that you've had a sec to get over the shock," I say, forcing myself to stand still, center-stage, "and I've got your attention, let me introduce myself. I'm Wendy Whitley. I'm twenty-two years old and I will be personally attending your Human Movement parties. My official title is Human Movement Liaison, which basically means I speak for the Guild. I am here to make sure we have a voice at your get-togethers. Seeing as you've been inviting us for over a month, I'd appreciate it if everyone could make sure, when they see me or my muscle…" I wave at the suited guards around the stage's perimeter, "Or anyone else that's with me, that you act like we're human, too, like we are invited, and not like we're trying to save you against your will." I put my hand over my mouth in mock horror.

I start slowly pacing, noticing that the crowd is shifting in the middle; Someone is moving through it. Not wanting to get distracted, and assuming my people can handle whoever it is, I continue, "Nobody get uppity and pull any kamikaze moves. My dudes are trained and you're probably not. So that won't end well for you." I pause, making stern eye contact with as many people in the crowd as possible, this time looking for who is approaching and realizing that it's actually Gabe Dumas himself. My protection shifts, creating a wider perimeter around the stage to prevent him or anyone from getting closer.

I put my hands on my hips. "Alright, so now that I've laid my ground rules, I want to say thanks for inviting us. In case you're wondering how you ended up with me, a public speaking noob, with, I'm told, a 'bold' outfit choice, an overabundance of sarcasm, and too much independence for her own good, rather than one of the older more experienced Guild members, it's because at the Guild they don't force people to do anything. They encourage everyone to find a way they can contribute. What this means? I volunteered. I'm here because I want to be, because I think it's important, because I chose to put myself at risk—which, by the way, is why you don't have more information on Prime Humans. Nobody forces them to disclose their abilities even *within* the Guild, so they certainly wouldn't force them to *outside of* the Guild. But that discussion is for another day."

Dumas has finally emerged, stopping at the edge of his assembly, a respectful twenty or so feet from the perimeter established by my guards. He puts his hands on his grey slacks-clad hips, his pale blue shirtsleeves rolled up to his elbows. I'm more grateful than ever that I ditched the pantsuit.

"Today I'm here to be Human with you, to share some of *my* secrets." I stop and put my hand solemnly to my chest. "No matter who gets in front of you from the Guild, they are all individuals. We each have our own talents... motives... fears... stories... Here's a snippet of mine: I was born with life force abilities, but I knew nothing of the Guild. I was raised by a single mother along with my younger brother, who was also born with a life force ability. My mother died of breast cancer, and I was left to care for my brother until I was reunited with my father. I spent my time avoiding association with the Guild, valuing my independence. A few months ago, Andre Gellagher, the nasty PHIA guy that likes to kill people, got a hold of me and my brother. And then he murdered my brother. He recorded it and left it for me to find.

"I was on the run from Andre along with my father, but we were separated once more, and Andre found him before I could. He tortured him in an effort to get information on my whereabouts, and then he killed my father, the last remaining member of my family."

I hang on to the microphone for dear life as I speak things I had battled with whether to say earlier. I had decided not to, but I guess that changed somewhere in the last fifteen minutes. The crowd is deathly silent, still locked in perplexed disbelief. Gabe Dumas stands erect, expressionless, eyes intense but with the attraction of a magnet. I have to make a concerted effort not to watch him as I speak. But it seems that staring at him is the only thing keeping my tears at bay. My knuckles are white, and my heart is pounding, not from nerves, but from the power emanating from Gabe Dumas. I don't know what it is, but it's tangible, and it keeps my emotions together when I should be falling apart. He's an anchor.

"I had lost everything," I say, having found new energy, and I manage to cast my eyes among the crowd once more. I pace slowly the length of my small stage. "After my escape from Andre, I was found by the Guild who protected me. I was lost though, believing that the things I could do were better off in the grave because they had cost me so much. It was then that I realized it wasn't what I could do that was the problem, but that I had isolated myself from a group of people offering a community, a family, a circle of protection, and a purpose."

I gain speed and stop my pacing, instead focusing on the sea of faces. "I didn't want to repeat the mistakes of my past, so I became a member. And I currently work in the Energy World Research Department. The energy world, as many of you know, is the place where life force abilities come from. And I am the only person alive capable of seeing it. That is why PHIA wants me: because Andre believes I can undo it all—this world of superhuman ability. The Guild wants me because they believe I have a chance at uncovering the cause of the natural disasters and putting a stop to it. And I want to be here, in front of you, because I want to show you my face, so you can no longer say you don't know who we are or where we came from. We are just like you, but we are targets. And right now the only protection we have is our own. You can change that though. You are The Human Movement. You comprise billions, but too few of you will stand with us; too few will stand up for us; too few are willing, during this time of so much uncertainty, to make yourself a target for PHIA. Yet you demand we expose ourselves. A stalemate exists, and someone has to break it. So here I am. I have a massive bounty on my head. PHIA's prized target. The Guild's prized talent. I'll be coming to *your* parties. Where will you stand now?"

I let my eyes fall on Gabe Dumas again, and he bows his head slightly. And then he smiles. *He smiles?*

I turn and hand my microphone off to an attendant as Mike takes my hand to help me off the stage. We head for the steps that will take us back to the doors leading to the visitor's center. Mike stays close, the light pressure of his hand at my back. I hear him issuing orders to secure both entrances—there is a second one beneath the other arch foot. But I've fixated on the crowd's chaotic mix of emotions. They've erupted into sound, not cheers, but not jeers either. Mostly… confusion and questioning. I listen for Gabe's voice, but if he's speaking I can't pick it out.

Shiah made it inside ahead of me, and she stands in the very center of the expansive lobby when I come down the ramp, her face completely devoid of her reaction. I'm going to stop and plead my case, explain my logic, why I completely hijacked what was supposed to be a very sanitized and scripted delivery, but Mike urges me onward. Before I pass Shiah though, I see the left side of her mouth curve upward.

Twenty-Four

I'm aware that I have imploded everything. I've heard pieces of Shiah's unending string of phone calls. I don't need to listen to who she's talking to. Her side of the generally repetitious conversations tells me everything I need to know:

'*Yes, I'm aware of what this means.*'

'*What is your suggestion?*'

'*Have you spent any time considering the situation beyond your initial reaction?*'

'*She's resting. You may interrogate her tomorrow. After the interview.*'

'*It will remain on schedule.*'

'*I'm handling it.*'

'*If you do that you'll discredit* all *of us.*'

'*No sign of him...*'

'*Our team is prepared.*'

'*I have received phone calls from all twelve of you, each with differing opinions. Are you issuing an order? Then make sure you all agree. Please do not waste my time with castigations. Public sentiment will have the final word.*'

'*If you must.*'

Security moved us from our previous hotel to one right across the street from the arch. With my exceptional hearing and a great deal of concentration I can pick up the members of the crowd milling around near the arch:

'*Who is she?*'

'*It can't be real.*'

'*She's fresh. Normal. I like her.*'

'*They'd never let someone that high-profile...*'

'*A decoy.*'

'*Do we even know if she's from the Guild?*'

'*Dumas didn't hang around for rebuttal.*'

'Dumas was floored. Did you see him?'

'I heard he had an interview right after...'

'There's no way protests are going to be safe now...'

'The energy world is bogus. They've been spouting that from the beginning.'

'You think it's real?'

'Who is this Wendy Whitley?'

I've also heard news crews:

'—here at the Gateway Arch where a young woman appeared at the end of the latest Human Movement protest. She claimed to be a voluntary spokesperson from the Guild, although it's unclear what portion of her voluntary capacity was sanctioned by the Guild organization itself. She also claimed to be a high-profile Prime, capable of accessing 'The Energy World,' where, she asserts, life force abilities are made. Not only did she chide Dumas and his followers for demanding an audience, but issued a challenge that, in effect, said, "You've been asking for us. Here I am. But you know my presence here puts you in danger. What will you do now?"'

They interview a few of the attendees, each one agreeing with being completely taken by surprise. One person, a young man by the sound of his voice, says, *'Dumas has a contender, for sure. What she just did blew everyone away. We haven't even processed what it means yet. Even if it turns out she's not who she says she is, we gotta ask the question, "What if she* had *been?"'*

'Do you hope she is?' the reporter asks.

'Hell yes. I'm a huge Human Movement Supporter. This is my first event with them and it was awesome. Being out there with so many people who think like you do... It was amazing. Makes you feel invincible to have so many people beside you.' He laughs. *'So I know it sounds kinda backward when I say I think we need this new blood as much as the Guild obviously does.'*

That takes the cake for me. I've been in heaven for at least a couple hours now. I've been lying on the couch in our suite of rooms, basking in a haze that fluctuates between utter contentment and awed disbelief.

I can't believe what I just did...

Oh my gosh, I did that. I did that*!*

I've never felt this way before... starry-eyed over myself.

I let my ears wander, catching snippet after snippet of newscasts and conversations, all revolving around Wendy, the girl from the Guild.

"You are a freaking badass, Wendy Whitley," I tell myself before popping a handful of M&Ms from the bowl on the coffee table into my mouth. "That might have been your best idea in your entire life."

"I'm glad to see you have no regrets," Shiah says, taking a seat in the armchair across from me. "I take it things are going well across the way?"

"The plan has proceeded without a hitch."

"Mm," she says, and I can tell she's amused.

I sit up. "Hey, sorry I made you look dumb in front of the Council. I know you vouched for me, convinced them to give me a shot. And I was going to do it like you said, honest. But then I heard this short interview with Dumas after that whole east coast oceanic earthquake prediction, and he was already twisting things the wrong way, and I knew we had to do something way different. We needed to call his bluff, make him and his followers really think about what they were asking."

"Gabe doesn't bluff," Mike says from somewhere behind me.

I sit up and look over the back of the couch to find him standing near the window, peeking through the sheer curtains into the grounds below. I throw an M&M at him when he doesn't look at me. "Oh really? So why didn't he address his followers after I spoke?"

"Because he is a chivalrous ass. He'll respect you for having done such a good job capturing the crowd. He appreciates anyone willing to take him on. For another, you were obviously not planning to stick around for a debate, so he wasn't going to start one for the sake of having the last word. He'd consider that underhanded and beneath him."

"*Will* he respond?" I ask, patting myself on the back again for making Mike my bodyguard.

"You can count on it."

"*How?*"

"Hell if I know. But if I were you I wouldn't get sucked into it. You're in deep enough with committing to be at the events he personally attends. That's going to be enough to keep your head going in circles."

"His post-event interview is supposed to air on the local seven o'clock news," Shiah says. "In about five minutes. And I agree with Mike. Gabe Dumas is not to be trifled with. He is a skilled orator with a wealth of knowledge to back up his reasoning. Focus on issues, not on him."

I frown. I think they're underestimating me.

"As to your apology, I would accept it if I hadn't already known you were going to… creatively circumvent the prescribed remarks," she adds.

"How'd you know?" I demand, surprised.

"For one thing, the speech you were given has four hundred and sixteen words, not the five hundred and forty-eight you told Jaina you were memorizing. Secondly, I am intelligent and observant, and I never discount patterns of human behavior. You are not a pantsuit-wearing mouthpiece. You are a revolutionary, and even when you choose your loyalties, you are not content until you have shaped them to your liking. You embody the spirit that the Guild needs to be seen possessed of. And that is why I ensured that you would have the opportunity to be seen." She pulls her tablet back into her lap.

"I knew it," I say, narrowing my eyes at her, but it's more good-natured than annoyed. "I knew you had something cooking. It's a good thing I like you so much, Shiah Lim. I usually hold it against people when they keep things from me." I playfully throw an M&M at her.

To my surprise, she catches it one-handed without even looking my way and pops it into her mouth. "Maintaining your esteem is not something I have the luxury of actively seeking. But I'm glad it has worked out that way anyway." She gives me a small smile. "We must tread carefully at this point," she warns. "The Council is upended, to say the least." She turns the TV on, flips to the right channel.

I prop my feet on the coffee table, expecting to have to wait until Dumas' interview airs to find out how my appearance was received. But a reporter is on the screen, on site at the arch talking about the crowd's reaction to my appearance. I'm the number one news story. And according to the anchor, Wendy Whitley is the trending topic on social media.

Wow. That was fast.

I lean forward.

'*Today St Louis residents turned out at the foot of the Arch for a protest organized by The Human Movement,*' the anchorwoman says. A video appears of an overhead view of the crowd chanting 'All Humans are Prime!' It's an impressive sight, heads and signs bobbing as people face Dumas' stage at the foot of the Arch.

'*The Human Movement, an activist group committed to breaking down the veil of secrecy surrounding the Guild,*' annihilated their own records for attendance, boasting nearly six thousand attendees. With every protest, The Human Movement has petitioned for the Guild to show themselves, a plea that has gone unanswered and unacknowledged by the Guild. Until today, when a young woman literally upstaged Dumas, claiming to be a spokesperson from the Guild.'

And there I am. Standing alone on a small stage in my white jeans and jacket, in front of one foot of the St. Louis Arch, '*Let me introduce myself. I'm Wendy Whitley. I'm twenty-two years old and I will be personally attending your Human Movement parties.*'

The anchorwoman returns. '*She went on to describe her background and decision to join the Guild—which was mostly due to a tragic run-in with PHIA. Meanwhile, her sudden and clearly unexpected appearance left Dumas and his audience stunned.*'

I come back on the screen. '*I volunteered. I'm here because I want to be, because I think it's important, because I chose to put myself at risk.*'

The anchorwoman: '*She continued her very personal delivery, and what she revealed next utterly staggered supporters of The Human Movement. And it has not stopped there. Word has spread like wildfire, and everyone wants to weigh in on the question: "Is her claim real?"*'

I appear once more, this time the camera has gotten a much closer view of my face as I speak. '*The energy world, as many of you know, is the place where life force abilities come from. And I am the only person alive capable of seeing it. That is why PHIA wants me: because Andre believes I can undo it all—this world of superhuman ability. The Guild wants me because they believe I have a chance at uncovering the cause of the natural disasters and putting a stop to it. And I want to be here, in front of you, because I want to show you my face, so you can no longer say you don't know who we are or where we came from.*'

The anchorwoman clears her throat, turns to her co-anchor. '*Is it real? That's what everyone wants to know.*'

Her co-anchor, a clean-shaven guy in a red tie, says, '*So far the Guild hasn't corroborated her claim, but recent sources have insisted that another high-profile Guild official was accompanying Miss Whitley.*'

They flash a quick shot of Shiah offstage, arms wrapped around herself as she watches me from behind with an unreadable expression.

'*Like all Guild officials, no one knows the woman's name or position, but she is believed to have a tacit connection to the illusive Guild Council. She was spotted off-stage, so we have evidence to suggest that Miss Whitley was at least present under the auspices of the Guild. Her authority as spokesperson is still unknown.*'

'*We'll keep you informed of all developments as the story unfolds,*' the first anchorwoman says, '*and shortly we'll hear what Gabe Dumas had to say after the conclusion of his protest today.*'

A commercial break ensues. "Well," Shiah says. "I guess we got that media coverage after all." She smirks at me.

I roll my eyes.

"Of course you did," Mike says. "People are dying to know more about the Guild."

Shiah chuckles. "So *scandalous.* Is she or isn't she? Whoever she is, her face is everywhere. Her mystery holds us spellbound! The illustrious and exclusive Guild has finally shown their face! *Her* face!"

I wrinkle my nose. "Please. I could be some crazy off the street." But inside I'm hoping I'm wrong. I hope people believed me...

"Exactly," Shiah says. "You are, which makes you the kind of public figure people can grab on to."

After a commercial, the anchorwoman comes on and says, '*And now, our exclusive interview with Gabe Dumas. What did he think about being upstaged by Miss Whitley?*'

He is suddenly on-camera, wearing the same button-up I saw him in at the protest. '*It was fantastic,*' he says, nodding and smiling exuberantly, eyes wide, cheeks still red from his performance. '*Absolutely marvelous.*'

'*You weren't a little disappointed that your success at achieving such record-breaking numbers is going to be minimized now that people are distracted by something more interesting?*' the interviewer prods.

Dumas makes a face. '*Heavens no. This isn't a popularity contest. This is activism. I'm not interested in standing for hours shouting in front of government buildings and public monuments indefinitely. The more immediate goal has been to evolve this into more than a one-way dialogue. That finally began today. I couldn't be more thrilled.*'

'*Alright. So let's talk about Miss Whitley. It sounds like you buy her credibility. You believe she is who she claims?*'

'*Oh definitely. Without a doubt.*'

'*What makes you so confident?*'

'*Because her bodyguard is my brother. And I know with a certainty that my brother is in the employ of the Guild.*'

The interviewer gets caught in his own shock for a few seconds too long before saying, '*Your brother works for the Guild? He's a Prime Human?*'

'*Yes, and if you insist upon labelling those possessed of life force abilities that way, then yes again.*'

'*Interesting. That's quite the coincidence then that the Guild would choose someone so closely associated with you to guard their, in Miss Whitley's words, "prized talent."*'

He huffs. '*It is most definitely not a coincidence. It was purposeful. In my opinion, it was also overkill—although on the plus side I didn't have to spend any time wondering whether to take Miss Whitley seriously. I think, however, that I would have bought her story even without my brother's presence as confirmation.*'

'*Why so?*'

'*If you have to ask that question, you obviously didn't listen to her speak. Her remarks were completely off the cuff. If she had prepared anything ahead of time, I doubt she used it. When a person speaks honestly, it's very easy to spot.*'

'*Alright, so assuming Miss Whitley is who she says she is, how will you be handling her challenge? She said she's going to stalk your events, which means that PHIA is probably going to as well. How do you think your constituents are going to handle that probable danger?*'

Dumas reclines somewhat in his chair, hands clasped over his stomach, his face full of delight as he looks into the camera, his dark eyes full of fire. '*I can only hope Miss Whitley is doing me the honor of watching this interview, because I want to convey my deep appreciation for her unmatched bravery. The Guild ought to elevate her as an example for the lot of them. And really, that was enough for me to be thoroughly impressed with the woman. But for her to paint a target on herself and then metaphorically hand the paint can over to us as a call to test our merit was the most elegant strategy I've encountered. And my constituents, if they truly believe the words they've shouted with vim, will recognize that, too. We stand by Miss Whitley, and we are committed to breaching the segregation PHIA has created no matter what.*'

'*Those are extremely complimentary words from you, Mr. Dumas. Have you changed sides then? Are you now a Guild supporter?*'

He laughs but doesn't answer, and when the interviewer just looks expectantly at him, Dumas leans forward and gives him a look of disbelief. '*That was an actual question?*'

'*So that's a yes?*' the interviewer asks.

Dumas stares at the guy with his mouth open, and it's easy to see that he's struggling for a response he thinks will be appropriate. He holds up his hand to keep the interviewer from speaking again and sighs heavily before answering as if it's a burden to say, '*No. I have not "changed sides."*'

'*Your hesitation to answer implies—*'

'*That I found the question imbecilic,*' Dumas barks. '*And offensive. And ignorant. And a testament as to why I detest interviews with the media. Let me make this exceptionally simple for you: I am a fan of Miss Whitley. I am a fan of anyone who lets bravery govern them instead of fear. Whether they are Guild or human, no matter what "side"—*' Dumas makes air quotes, '*they are on. The Human Movement is about Humans, ALL Humans. I'm not looking for points on a scoreboard. I'm looking to make one team, not two. To remove the shroud of secrecy, no matter who you are or what abilities you may or may not possess, helps that cause. To recognize the merits of those who oppose your ideals also helps that cause. Until now, the Guild hasn't shown enough of themselves to even begin to assess their merits. Am I a Guild supporter? No. But I'm more optimistic now that I know they aren't as oblivious as I'd feared. To have made that woman their spokesperson was a move so profoundly in-touch with the needs of the world right now that I can only applaud them. Now we might get something done.*'

The anchors appear again, giving instructions on how to follow the story as it unfolds, but Shiah lowers the volume, turns to look at me expectantly.

"Hmm," is all I can think to respond with.

"'Hmm' is right," Shiah says, tapping her chin. "Championing you was not what I predicted, but it is most definitely in his best interest." She smiles to herself lightly. "I love being wrong…"

I don't hear an ounce of sarcasm in her statement, and before I can ask her about it, her phone rings.

"Yes, I've seen it," she answers the phone with.

'*Is she going to be able to handle this?*' the feminine voice on the line says.

Shiah glances at me and I nod.

"Yes, although at this juncture I'd advise you not to make a statement," Shiah says. "It's too little too late. If you do it now people will know you were waiting to see what came out of the wash before signing your name to it."

'*Too late. Your father had her added to the roster of publicly declared and verified Primes on the website hours ago.*'

Shiah laughs. "Because my father understands what this will do for us. That's perfect. It's there for anyone that's looking, a tacit connection but not an opportunistic public endorsement."

'*Yes, although I imagine Dave is going to get a herd of questions at his next press conference.*'

"And then Dave can corroborate incidentally. Instruct him to speak matter-of-factly. It needs to appear that Miss Whitley's affirmation was a given, not an afterthought."

'*The Council will still need to speak to her. There are precepts to adhere to.*'

"I'll bring her in myself when we return."

Shiah hangs up and looks at me again. "Anything more than 'Hmm' to say now?"

"I'm having a hard time deciding whether I like that he likes me," I say, rubbing my temple pensively with a finger, "whether that will help or hurt."

"Help," Mike says. "If Gabe doesn't like you, he will railroad you like he did that interviewer. He will run circles around your arguments and make you question that you know anything at all. If he likes you though… He'll make sure you have a voice."

I grimace. "I think I'd rather he didn't like me."

"Only because you want to be in control all the time," Mike says. "You want to earn your place on your own merit with no help from anyone."

"I've barely spent a day with you. You don't know me!" I snap.

Shiah chuffs in amusement. "Yet somehow he does."

I glare at her. They are seriously ganging up on me?

"I commend your skill at your job, Michael Dumas," Shiah says. "Discerning what motivates your charge is of underrated importance."

"Whatever," I say. "I just don't like Gabe Dumas having any control over whether or not people listen to me. Because it makes me and therefore the Guild seem weak."

"Gabe makes everyone seem weak," Mike says. "It's just a fact of life."

"I'm going to prove you wrong," I say.

"No doubt."

"I am!"

Mike looks at me. "I'm not arguing."

"Yes you are. I'm an empath and I know you think I'm full of it."

"So what. I'm not your advisor. I'm just someone that knows Gabe really *really* well. You don't need my approval so why are you picking a fight to gain it?"

I wave my hand at him. "You're right. Go do your guard dog thing. But stay out of my bed." I smile sweetly at him.

He gives me a dry look but turns for the door to one of the rooms in our suite.

"Your youth is showing," Shiah says.

"Turns out, I still think of myself as nineteen," I reply flippantly, tossing another M&M into my mouth.

She sighs, and the first inklings of her losing patience begin to appear.

"There has to be an alternative," I say, wanting to change topics as much as she probably does. "I don't want Dumas doing me any favors."

"You'd rather he expose your shortcomings? Your inexperience and lack of knowledge?"

"I can handle it."

"You can't even handle your bodyguard doing it."

I lay my head back and rub my forehead. "Mike is different."

"Why?"

"I can't explain it. He just is."

She thinks about it but doesn't seem to come to a conclusion. Rather, she shifts gears. "At this point this debate is irrelevant because Dumas *does* like you. Don't try to make him hate you; it will look as childish as it is. But if you want to own whatever part of the spotlight Dumas offers you, capitalize on it. If he compliments you, accept it graciously and take charge of the issue at hand. There is nothing to lose and absolutely everything to gain in being seen as a credible person by your opposition. And for the

Guild's sake, if you have any loyalty to it whatsoever, do not make this about you. If Gabe Dumas softens toward the Guild because of his respect for you, own that respect for all of us. When you go out there, no matter how much you want people to see everyone at the Guild as an individual and you as merely a piece of it, they won't. *You* are the Guild now in their eyes. What you do reflects on the entire organization."

I sigh. "Yeah. I got it."

She turns more fully to face me, her jet black ponytail whipping threateningly. "Do you?" she demands, eyes flashing. "The Guild may consist of tens of thousands, but the public only sees *you*. Do you understand that pressure?"

"Yeah, yeah, I got it!" I say, irritated.

"Then who are you from this point on?" Her eyes pierce mine with an intensity I didn't know she possessed. It's intimidating and I wish she'd stop.

"I am the Guild," I say.

She stares at me still.

"I am the Guild!" I repeat.

"That's exactly who you are," she says, finally unlocking her eyes from mine. "Don't forget it."

Twenty-Five

"**Just** have a conversation," Shiah says. "That's all this is. And it's not live. So you don't need to get nervous. If you stumble over words, start over. If you word your question poorly, start over. They'll cut everything else. And keep it short. We don't need a biography. We want to know about her life force ability and something that makes her human and relatable. These are going to only be long enough to fill commercial breaks."

I nod, more comfortable now that I know I don't have to follow a prescribed list of questions. They've already made me record a very brief title sequence. It took me fifty times to get it right, so my confidence is pretty low. But I can talk to someone. I'm good at that.

I'm already in the hot seat, on a set similar to the one I saw on television last night where Gabe Dumas fawned over me. I'm still mystified by that, not quite sure how to navigate someone who may make a pattern of flattery. I wonder if I'll ever get close enough to him to read his emotions… That would make it really easy because then I could sniff out his tactic and use it against him. I've done that enough times that it should be second nature, even without my empathic ability. But Gabe Dumas is a new kind of challenge, and I'm not confident enough to act blindly.

A young woman enters the set. She could be my age or older, dirty blonde hair in layers just past her shoulders, big, bright green eyes, and an enviably perfect smile. I stand up to greet her, holding out my hand. "I'm Wendy."

"Erin," she says, shaking my hand. Her grip is loose, but she seems immediately distracted by something. She even turns away from me, moves her chair to the right a few inches, then back, and then forward again.

I look at Shiah, who is standing just off of the set. She nods encouragingly.

I lean to the side to catch sight of what Erin's looking at. "What's up?" I say. "Do you need a different chair?"

"No. I'm fine. But this one thinks he's funny." She picks the chair up, shakes it, rattles it against the floor.

"The chair?" I ask, confused by her bizarre behavior.

She laughs easily and turns around. "I'm sorry. I must look crazy, giving a chair what for." Then she plops down.

I hold up my hands. "I wasn't going to say anything. But yeah, it was totally crazy."

She smiles and her eyes laugh. Her face seems used to it. "It'd probably help if I told you about my life force ability first."

I shrug, curl a leg up under me. "Fine by me."

She leans forward, hands clasped between her knees. "I see dead people."

I blink at her, thinking this is a joke, that she used a line from the movie, *The Sixth Sense*, to be funny. But her emotions state that she's serious.

"Really?" I say, my brother coming to mind without effort.

"But not whoever I like," she says, as if she knows where my head has gone. "Whoever's around me. Usually there's a lot of them. Like an entourage. A lot of regulars. But most show up to see what the fuss is about. When they find out I can see them, they usually hang around a while, thinking I can give them a voice. But once they realize I'm not interested in giving them a new lease on life..." She laughs a little at her joke. "They usually go away."

"Can you speak to them?" I ask, fascinated.

"Oh yeah. You saw me do that. So can you and everyone else. But they can't speak back."

"You said that one was being funny. He wasn't talking though?"

"The regulars know I don't like sitting on them. So sometimes they take my chair to aggravate me or get my attention. It's not that either of us feels it, but could *you* sit in a chair if you could plainly see someone sitting in it?"

"Probably not. Do they sit on *you*?"

"Yeah. But I have a few who look out for me, keep the riffraff from causing too much trouble."

"When you say you see them, how much do you see?"

"Depends on what they can project. From what I gather, it takes practice to project yourself once you're dead. Most of them barely get more than a shadow out there. If they get something out there at all, it's usually blurred, like a memory." I notice her attention has moved from my face to somewhere over my shoulder.

"Do people seek you out a lot? Living people, I mean, who want you to check on their loved ones?"

"They probably will now, assuming you guys are going to air this. But at home people ignore it. The novelty gets old. And I get tired of it, too. On the rare occasion that someone new finds out what I can do, they inevitably ask for me to check and see if this or that person is hanging around them. I'm always glad to look, but like I said, with most of them there's not much to see." She's still staring over my shoulder. I can't resist the urge to turn and look, but of course I see nothing, just the corner of the set where a few pieces of spare furniture and room props are stacked.

I turn back to find her staring at me. I try not to flinch from it, but it's hard. "Alright, so now we know what makes you a Prime Human, but what makes you Erin? What do you do when you're not preoccupied with ghosts?"

"I'm still working that out. I'm in college, still haven't settled on a major, although things are pretty serious out there, so I'm not in a huge hurry. My parents are dentists, so that's a possibility, but I figure I'm better off trying out an array of things so that whatever demand there is when the world is done going to pot, I'm in a position to fill it."

"Ah, that's why your teeth are so perfect," I say. "I can't keep my eyes off of them."

She rolls her eyes. "Yeah. Perks of being in a family obsessed with teeth."

"Besides being my interview guinea pig, what's the gutsiest thing you've ever done?" I ask.

She's staring over my shoulder again, but she answers, "Entered a beauty pageant."

"Tell me about that."

"I don't know what came over me. I had heard about it at school and had this wild idea that I wanted to win it. I went home and told my mom and she was really skeptical, didn't want me getting caught up in vanity and all that, plus, she had to have worried I'd be let down. But she eventually let me do it. I was surrounded by girls who had done stuff like that for years, so I knew realistically what I was up against. I think I won because I was brave enough to think I could do it, and because I didn't try to be them."

"You won?" I say, surprised. "Because you stood out then?"

"In a way. People are this weird mix of a desire to never see anything change but at the same time being so relieved when they finally see something a little bit new. So I did a little singing routine, wore all the outfits. I didn't really do anything unusual. So I think I was enough of what the judges were used to seeing while being different enough to satisfy the novelty aspect."

"You think that's always the best course? Mostly predictable but a little bit different?"

"Obviously not," she laughs. "You would be the example. Of course, your sphere is a lot bigger than mine was. That might be the factor to decide how different to be."

"I guess we'll find out," I say, smiling at her. "Thanks for taking the time and being brave enough to meet with me."

"My pleasure," she replies. Then she turns to the camera man. "This next part is not on-air."

She waits until she sees the red light turn off and then she faces me again. "Sometimes, and I really mean once in a blue moon, I see someone who has near perfect projection. They never waste time with bothering me. They're always watching someone, trailing them. I always think of them as guardians. But anyway, you have one. He's been standing right over there." She points to the corner I looked at earlier. "Maybe the best projection I've ever seen."

My heart thumps into overdrive, and I turn like I'm going to see the person she's talking about. I'm also sort of afraid and I'm not sure why. I naturally think of Ezra, but some part of me hopes it's not him. I don't know that I want him spending his afterlife following me. Don't they say that ghosts who hang around people and places have unfinished business? I don't know. I don't know anything. In fact, I wasn't even sure if I was certain of an afterlife before. I'm still not sure of it even though this girl is telling me she sees people who have died.

"Do you want me to describe him?" Erin asks.

I clear my throat. "Um. Yes?"

She gives me an understanding look. "I don't have to," she says. "It's not like you can do anything with the information other than maybe look over your shoulder every now and then and wonder if he's still there." She smiles. "Ghosts, on the whole, are pretty useless to us living people."

"Then why do you call some of them guardians?"

"Well… I think it's probably possible to hear ghosts. But I don't have that ability. And I would guess that the ones who can project their appearance really well can also project their voice. And people who are attuned to hear it can make it out. Yours is standing a good ways away from you, but he's obviously focused on you. I've seen the guardians stand really close to people before and move their mouths like they're speaking. And while the people they're speaking to don't actually acknowledge it, I think they hear it somehow, or in the very least sense it. Also, a couple of times I've been really overwhelmed by a bunch of weak projections giving me a hard time, and when I'm about to lose it a guardian shows up and sets everyone back in line."

"What does mine look like?" I ask, though my hands are shaking. I tuck them between my knees.

"He's under six foot. He's wearing a tailored grey suit, no tie, the top button of his white shirt undone. He's an older guy, maybe in his early fifties. Salt and pepper goatee." She laughs as she watches over my shoulder. "He's stroking it now with the barest smile on his face. I think he knows I'm talking about him. He has these really deep, wise-looking eyes."

Erin's attention falls back to my stunned face, and I swear, with every particle of me, that she is not lying. So she's either delusional and has bought in fully, or she's telling the complete truth. But I have no clue who she is describing.

"I don't recognize that description," I tell her when it's obvious she's wondering if I know who the person is.

She sits back, a little disappointed. "Well, like I said, it doesn't actually matter. But it must be at least nice to know that someone is watching over you."

I turn around again, staring at the dusty corner and seeing nothing. I give a little wave though. "Thanks, whoever you are."

Erin gives a little gasp and I whip around to find her wide-eyed. "He signed, 'You're welcome,'" she says. Then she gives a little start. "He disappeared."

"Disappeared?"

"Yeah, he must be saying he's not going to say anything more. They can turn their projections on and off." She shakes her head in wonder. "Your guardian knows American Sign Language—or at least how to say 'You're welcome' in it. This trip has definitely turned out more interesting than I expected."

"That's an understatement." I turn to Shiah, having almost forgotten she and Mike are still here. "Who am I interviewing next?" I say. "This is pretty freaking cool."

But Shiah is bent over her GIT. At first I think she hasn't been paying attention, but she strides over to us, holds her tablet up to Erin. "Did he look like this?"

Erin nods in definite recognition. "Oh yeah. Definitely."

Shiah next turns the tablet my direction. I see a man that fits Erin's description precisely, except in the photo he's wearing a navy suit.

"Who is he?" I ask, wondering how Shiah knew so instantly.

"Robert Haricott," she replies. "Your deceased uncle."

Twenty-Six

*S*hiah sighs, puts her hands on my shoulders. This is the first time I have felt her experiencing any anxiety, let alone this much of a hefty dose. She looks me in the eye though. "Wendy, your goal is to go in there and tell them what they want to hear." She holds up a hand to keep me from speaking. "Your goal is to go in there and tell them what they want to hear," she repeats.

"But Shiah—"

"No!" she hisses, putting her hand over my mouth and shaking her head emphatically. "Quiet. You don't get to ask questions or have a suggestion or state your opinion this time. There are twelve people in that room, and each of them is motivated by one thing: protecting the integrity of the Guild in order to protect everyone in it. Most of them have been around since the Guild's inception and it was because of them that the Guild now has over twenty thousand members. They fiercely guard and protect the membership, and while they won't state outright a belief in a Prime Human superiority, they don't always discourage the attitude because it means some level of disassociation from the outside world, which breeds solidarity and unity within. They do *not* want that to disappear, because if it does, so does the Guild. And if the Guild disappears, Wendy, all hope of bringing the natural disasters to an end is lost, and the world descends into chaos and destruction.

"So if you value your world and the people left in it, you will recognize that if *you*, the one person alive able to access the forces that power life force abilities, end up on the outside, you will be discredited, defamed, and you will be left without the resources to do what you need to. They *will* protect their own, Wendy. Even at the cost of losing your talents. To stay inside the boat, you don't tell them how to make a better one. You tell them you belong to the Guild and you are committed to furthering its purpose to protect the Prime Human population so it can do its work."

Stunned into speechlessness, I stare at her.

She nods, pulls open the door to a hall leading to the conference room, and prods me in the back.

I came into this pretty confidently, planning to use the same tactic with the Council that I used with Shiah: It's my way or I'm out. But Shiah said that won't work. And after that speech, I believe her. I'm completely rattled now and I have no idea what's going to happen or what I'm going to say. I also now don't really know why Shiah was so adamant about helping me become a public personality if what the Guild actually wants is to continue hiding under a rock. My head is teeming with questions as I walk timidly down the hall so that I barely notice the murmur of conversation coming from the room ahead.

I do notice, however, that conversation stops once I appear, and I stand in the doorway to a room far more modest than I had imagined. I expected opulence, but instead it's probably half the size of a high school gym. The furnishings in my apartment are a lot more luxurious than these. It's nothing more than a standard conference room approaching the need of an update.

"Welcome, Wendy," the woman nearest me says.

"Hi," I say, turning my attention to the brunette wearing glasses, a blue blazer and skirt. She's so normal…

"Have a seat," she says, pointing to the chair next to her.

I oblige. How I imagined the Council is suddenly shattered as I glance around the table at a group of older men and women who could be anyone I've met out in public. I see Dr. Ohr Lim as well, smiling wanly at me, hands clasped in his lap.

"The reason we wanted to meet with you is to get to know you better," the woman says. "We take a genuine interest in each of our members; we want to know how to help them lead fulfilling lives so they can tap into their full promise. Additionally, when one of the members takes on a role in public, they must understand that the things they do and say reflect on the Guild directly. Once you become a member, you take upon you the burden of that responsibility, because while your will is yours alone, your allegiance belongs to a higher purpose." She smiles warmly, and it seems to accompany genuine concern, if not for me directly but for the people she's talking about protecting.

"I understand," I say, afraid to say anything else lest I incur Shiah's wrath when she finds out.

"Good." The woman nods and then looks around the table. "Shall we introduce ourselves now?" She doesn't wait for an answer, instead looks back at me. "Councilwoman Debra. Twelfth chair. A pleasure laying eyes on you, Wendy."

The gentleman next to her slides his chair back and stands. "Councilman Malachi. Eleventh chair."

They each follow in succession, and although they count down and stand in order, they aren't actually sitting in that order. I realize I have no idea what the chair number actually means...

"Councilwoman Maryann. Tenth Chair."

"Councilman Ahmed. Ninth Chair."

"Councilwoman Sarah. Eighth Chair. "

"Councilman Dawud. Seventh Chair."

"Councilwoman Sri. Sixth Chair."

"Councilman Kassapa. Fifth Chair."

"Councilwoman Abigail. Fourth Chair."

"Councilman Paul. Third Chair."

"Councilman Abram. Second Chair."

"Councilman Ohr. First Chair."

Debra turns back to me.

"Is there going to be a quiz on that later?" I say.

She chuckles. "No. But I am sure you'll encounter each of us from time to time. We'll be sure to introduce ourselves again."

"Thank you," I say. "I'm lucky I remember anyone. Everyone I meet these days is new."

"I know one day faces will start to repeat and it will no longer be a faceless crowd—within *these* walls of course." She smiles.

"Yeah, about that," I say, "Thank you—for letting me have the opportunity to do my part."

She nods, and behind her, Malachi says, "How do you view your part? What purpose do you see it fulfilling?"

One of the other women adds, "What motivated your decision to act against the parameters that were set?"

"To what extent can we expect you to adhere to direction?" says another man.

Debra holds up a hand to keep anyone else from chiming in, but she's obviously awaiting my answer.

"I just want to be an example to other Primes," I say, hoping it's the right thing. "Because I think they're used to hiding and they don't really know how to exist now that people know about the Guild. Guild members look out for each other, and I want to convince them that that's still true even with how things have changed. If I can go out there and face the world, so can they. We have all these crazy talents and how are we going to change the world with them if we're afraid of the world? I ignored direction because I knew you would never ask me to put myself out there like I did. If it was going to happen, I had to be the one to do it. I have no intention of calling anyone else out. But if I can put myself on the line and make people see us differently, I'll do it."

"Do you realize how many more resources will be required to ensure not only your safety at these events, but the safety of everyone in attendance?" another man asks.

"Well…" I say hesitantly. "I can't think of a better way to extend goodwill than to use your resources to protect your opposition. It says you place value on more than Prime Human lives—even Humans who reject what we stand for."

"As you can see, ladies and gentleman," Ohr says, "Miss Whitley understands the stakes and the delicate balance that must be maintained. Shiah has done her job well. We would be no better served than to allow both of them to continue in their work."

I pick up quite a bit of annoyance, but nobody argues— nor do they acknowledge him. Apparently I have been a contested subject prior to this meeting. Instead, one of the women who hasn't spoken yet, but whose voice I recognize as the person that called Shiah after the Dumas interview, says, "We encourage you to play to your strengths, Wendy, and would like you to know that we value your spirit and strong sense of duty. There are only a few things that we ask, that simply must be adhered to when you speak to anyone not belonging to the Guild either publicly or privately."

I lift my eyebrows expectantly.

"One, you will not ever refer by name to anyone from the Guild without first written permission," she explains. "Two, you will never criticize members of the Guild Council or policies that have been put in place for the protection of Guild members. Three, you will not recruit any Prime Human belonging to the Guild to participate in your Human Movement appearances."

"But that's… counterproductive," I say. "The point is to motivate Primes to not be afraid, and you're telling me if someone comes to me and genuinely wants to be a part of that, I have to tell them no?"

"This is precisely why you also have the interview series. Participants are chosen on a voluntary basis only. So if someone wants to participate, invite them to be interviewed for the series. The reason for this is we currently do not have the resources to protect so many Primes who might choose such a dangerous public occupation. One Prime Human girl and thousands of Humans are going to be quite enough for our armed operatives to handle."

Something about that seriously doesn't sit right with me. I just can't articulate it, and I don't want to for the sake of keeping out of trouble. I need to nod and get out of here...

"Lastly, you will not privately correspond with Gabe Dumas or any of his constituents."

Now I am literally biting the inside of my cheek.

Debra is watching my face though—well, everyone is but she's the closest—and I have to say *something* or she's going to know for sure that I'm holding back "His *constituents* are exactly who you want to win over," I say. "Can you explain how that's going to work?"

"You are free to interact with them in public as much as you want, preferably in front of a camera as that will ensure that the most people can benefit. You are even free to interact with them on social media platforms, provided it's not a private communication."

Every eye in the room is on me, and I'm about to explode with stuff that is going to get me in a *lot* of trouble.

Shut up, Wendy. Shut up Wendy. Shut up, Wendy, I chant mentally.

"I realize this seems harsh, controlling even, but it's for your own protection, and it's to help you. Your campaign is already notorious for its transparency. The integrity of your words in public are best preserved if they are never countered in private. And the best way to ensure that is to *only* speak publicly. If you can't say it publicly, it shouldn't be said."

I feel lightheaded with unspoken words. Actually, that's me holding my breath. *Deep breaths. Not too deep. They're watching.* I literally have no idea how I'm going to get out of this room without skewering myself...

"Do you agree to these terms?" the woman asks.

My hands are wound so tightly in my lap they're a sweaty mess. I'm going to cry if I don't yell first...

Ohr catches my eye then, and he gives me the same apologetic look he gave me in my apartment when he explained I would have to have a tracking device implanted if I joined the EWR team.

That simple look makes all the difference, and I exhale heavily. *Someone* in this room hasn't completely lost their mind. And that's enough for me to say, "Yes."

"Wonderful," the woman says, and everyone scoots their chairs back. I practically leap to my feet.

"Before you go," Debra says, and I have to stop myself from making a run for it from whatever she's going to say next. "We've gotten regular updates on your progress with the EWR department. With all the data you've been providing, the team over there has hardly slept, assimilating it all. Nice work."

"Thanks," I say barely above a whisper.

"And another thing," Malachi says.

Oh Gosh. Not another thing.

"Dyads are purposeful. They can help you," Malachi says. "We've all had our fair share of arguments with our dyad partners. You must learn to cooperate, to counsel. It's because of this fundamental skill that the Guild has been able to develop the technology we have. None of it is a solo effort. We know how to get along and it makes us far more capable."

I nod.

Debra smiles at me, and I take it as a dismissal. Thank goodness. I make a beeline for the hall, resisting the urge to run. When I get to where I left Shiah and find her still there, waiting nervously, I storm past her, desperate for air.

But even when I reach it I can't stop. I break into a run, the red behind my eyes blurring the people I pass into nothing. Meanwhile, my head is swirling with the injustice I was just forced to agree to.

'*No contact with any constituents...*'

They want to silence me.

'*If you can't say it publicly, it shouldn't be said...*'

They want to censor me.

'*You can't recruit any Primes to help...*'

They don't want me infecting their own... They might as well have publicly disavowed me.

They want to keep me both under their thumb as well as at arm's length so that they can benefit from me until... Until when?

Until I destroy myself in public? Until Humans fall down and worship them? Until Gabe Dumas throws in the towel and The Human Movement is no more?

Their promises of protection and solidarity and belonging and a brotherhood of cooperation and respect only apply if you're willing to comply, if you're willing to play by their rules. I just told the public that Primes are no different than them, that Primes are only afraid and that's why there is so much secrecy. But the Council obviously has zero interest in their membership taking my demonstration as an example. They simply hope that my performance will create a bait and switch to convince people that the Guild is more open than it is—than it ever will be.

And the thing is… the Council is *convinced* of the rightness of all that. All of them… there was no subterfuge. They truly believe what they say. They *live* what they say.

Except for Shiah… I think. She sees what I do. She tells me things nobody else has the guts to say out loud. She knew what I would encounter in that room, how hard it would be to keep my mouth shut. She knows yet she stays. *'If the Guild disappears, Wendy… the world descends into chaos and destruction.'*

Is this how the world is supposed to work and my logic is so broken that I just missed it? Am I simply *wrong* to believe the world can exist without walls and secrecy between people? Am I simply another naive idealist?

Maybe. My survival has depended on my conformity. I've had to do as they do to benefit from association. I joined the Guild to escape isolation on the outside, to find protection and a sense of purpose again.

'Your past self would call you a sellout.' That's what Ohr said to me when I told him my reasons for joining the Guild were self-serving.

But now I know *everyone's* reasons are self-serving. That's how the whole system keeps working.

I come to a staggering stop in a little group of trees outside the water house, gasping, hands on my knees.

My past self would call me a sellout, would she?

"She was wrong," I say, swaying and letting myself fall against the nearest tree.

'Your father resented our regulation, our oversight,' Ohr told me. *'You're so much like him…'*

"Where did that get you Carl?" I scream into the trees. "Where did that get *us*?! You were wrong!"

The trees don't answer, but the sight of them, towering high above me reminds me of that night I woke up in the woods, watching yellow light flicker against surrounding trunks. I was alone. I was a Prime Human less than an *hour* away from the Vault, in the *middle* of a disaster. Dr. Lim mentioned that the disasters might be caused by someone and that I should be able to see as much in the energy world. It's clear that I *had* to know much more about it than I do now. What if... what if somehow, I knew enough to cause those lightning storms, and I did it in an effort to wipe out the Guild's facility?

What if I became my father after all? And like my father, I lost everything and everyone because I never opened my mind or my heart to people who offered me a family? So what if it's not *ideal*. Idealism ruined my life.

I sink down to the ground, face in my hands, my eyes overflowing. "I was wrong," I sob. "I was wrong, Ezra. I am so sorry..."

Twenty-Seven

*W*en? What wong?" Chase says, his face full of concern.

I throw my arms around him, which knocks him back. I can tell he's bulked up a little, but he's still on the skinny side. "I'm sorry," I say.

He returns the embrace. "Me too."

I finally let go and get a decent look at him only to realize he's not alone. A young woman with waist-length light brown hair is looking on from his couch.

I bite my lip and grimace. "Oops. Sorry. Guess I shoulda called first."

"Don be siwwy," Chase says. "We watt da news."

"Seriously?" I say, looking from Chase to the girl. "That is a terrible date, Chase. Next time you need to call for better advice."

He gives me a look. "You see?"

"What?"

"Wook," he says, pulling me further into the room.

I lean my head to the side to make out what I'm seeing on the projection. It looks like a satellite image, and even though it's familiar, I can't tell where it is.

"Is that…?"

"Forda," Chase says. "Satawite imash. No more Forda. No more Cooba. No more Damaka—Damay—"

"Jamaica," the girl on the couch says. "And the Dominican Republic. Bahamas. The only island left in the Caribbean is Puerto Rico, but… it moved."

"Moved?" I say, sinking down abruptly onto the edge of the coffee table.

"About two hundred kilometers south."

The map blips and changes suddenly to become its former self, complete with Florida and all of the Caribbean islands.

"They've been replaying it over and over in time-lapsed images," the girl says.

Sure enough the first image to appear is of the ocean somewhere. There's no telling where because it's just a blue expanse with the occasional passing cloud formation. Chase points to somewhere in the middle of it where the only indication of something happening is that the water changes hues slightly in one area, and that change gradually bleeds south. Suddenly the image goes dark.

"They switch it to nighttime view," the girl explains.

The oddly-colored water is highlighted in green, and it continues swelling in size until it abruptly stops. The image presumably zooms out, and I can now see the lights of civilization as the only indication of continents. It looks like the shape of the United States, but there are no lights to illuminate the Florida peninsula or anywhere near it.

"It's still there," the girl says. "But everyone was evacuated in time. No people, no lights."

"Wow. They actually did it."

"It's a miracle," she says. "If people are still fighting our efforts after this, they're just as bad as PHIA. They even got West Africa evacuated, so the resulting tidal waves in the next few weeks as the plates settle won't harm anyone."

The green illuminated area in the North Atlantic looks much smaller now that it's zoomed out, more of a jagged pattern overall. Another green smudge has appeared somewhere north of South America. It creeps slowly outward, away from the continent, spreading into a giant smudge. The next image is lit by daylight, and the green smudge suddenly appears as cloudy water—a white underwater cloud. Several images later and Cuba and Haiti are dissolved into the white cloud. And then the other Caribbean islands. At the same time, the cloud pushes north with a vengeance, colliding with the tip of Florida and liquifying it. The cloud consumes the peninsula like a terrifying, faceless leviathan until it stops, short of Georgia, leaving the panhandle intact.

Meanwhile, the cloud to the south has come close to, but not touched the island of Puerto Rico. However, a progression of images shows the island literally jumping south from one image to the next. The final image appears, the one I walked in on. The cloud is in the middle of slowly dissipating back into the blue depths of the ocean.

"This all happened last night?" I say.

"And this morning," the girl says. "Where have you been if you're just now finding out?"

"Camping," I mumble, hoping she's going to stop asking questions.

"Camping?" the girl says. "In this weather? It's freezing."

"I got a room for a few nights at the Water House," I say quickly.

"Oh," she says. Everyone apparently knows there are rooms available for people to make overnight stays when they really need it. It's typically understood as a 'do not disturb' environment. I was there for a week after my meeting with the Council. It was Mikel that found me outside in the grove of trees and told me about it. Making up with Chase was my first order of business when I decided to reenter society.

"I don't know how long you were there, but earlier this week the Guild was pushing hard for the evacuation to get done sooner," the girl says. "The timeline prediction got pushed up for some reason. Anyway, one of the Council members got involved, addressed the UN and challenged them to get every able ship down to the Caribbean to pick up evacuees and take them anywhere, as long as it was away from there. Governments stopped worrying about making things organized and documented and just started loading people up, no paperwork, no names. Evacuees didn't even know what country they would end up in when they got on a ship. It was grab and go. People were packed in like sardines."

I stare at the new world map on the screen, thinking this is the confirmation I've needed. All week I've spent wrestling with what to do about my Guild membership. Part of me hates this place. And the other part of me... the practical part, sees what the Guild is accomplishing and wants to be a part of it. How do you argue with a system that works? And how can I want to dismantle a system that's accomplishing so much?

"Basically, what they're saying is that part of the Caribbean plate was shoved underneath the North Amiercan plate. They're estimating over a hundred million people were saved because of our prediction team," the girl says soberly.

A hundred million people... How do you argue with a system that can save a hundred million people? I don't miss how the young woman said it, too: *our* prediction team. *Hers.* Mine. *Ours.*

"You okay, Wen?" Chase says.

I cannot tear my eyes away from the TV as it pans over a camp of evacuees now, eventually finding their faces, which are careworn, tear-streaked, terrified even. But alive.

I see Shiah's face in my mind.

'*Who are you from this point on?*' she asked me after St. Louis.

'*I am the Guild,*' I told her, knowing that's what she wanted to hear. But I could tell from her face that I didn't sound convincing.

'*I am the Guild!*' I shouted at her.

'*That's exactly who you are,*' she answered. '*Don't forget it.*'

I look up at Chase finally. "I am now."

"I saw you. In Sain Woo—Woowis."

"Yeah?"

"Awesome," he says. "You famous now!"

"Your speech is tons better," I say. "Can we chat?"

He turns to his friend. "Wainey? Would you mine?"

I start. "*You're* Lainey?" I say, seeing the girl with new eyes. I didn't picture her as so young.

"Yep," she says, standing.

"Wait," I say.

"You guys have stuff to talk about," Lainey says.

"That can wait," I say. "I'm more interested in finding out how things are going with tracking your—with tracking Andre down." I can't believe I almost said 'with tracking your brother down.' She probably would have punched me or something. She already doesn't seem all that impressed with me.

"It's confidential."

I roll my eyes. "That is bogus. I *own* confidential."

"You *would* think that, wouldn't you?" Lainey says, crossing her arms and cocking a hip. "Milking your insta-fame to its fullest? Not everyone cares who you are, you know. You aren't *owed* special treatment."

"Wainey, don be diffi—diffi-coot," Chase says. "You come ere to fine Wen anyway."

Lainey rolls her eyes and huffs. "I can tell that was a dumb idea."

"Aww, Lainey, like Chase said, don't be difficult," I pout. "I'll give you an autograph if that's what you really want." I don't mind rubbing my status in her face because she started it, and I can tell it makes her jealous. When I got back from St. Louis, and before I met with the Council, I was most definitely mobbed by fellow Primes, and this afternoon I had to hide my face in a hoodie to get over here without being stopped by someone. As for confidential, I know she must want to talk to me about Andre. Why does she have to act like she doesn't?

Her cheeks turn red and she makes a disgusted sound. "Don't be gross. Kiera said you were reasonable. But you obviously glutton yourself on being obstinate."

"I'm an empath, Lainey," I reply. "I only dish out what I pick up."

We stare each other down. We're about the same height, and, to my chagrin, obviously of similar personality.

"Wadies," Chase says, putting himself between us. "What dis? Sit." He grabs Lainey by the arm and pushes her back onto the couch.

He comes over to me and I hop to the side. "I got it," I say, sitting back on the coffee table where I was before.

"Now," Chase says, looking at Lainey. "What you wan?"

"Michael Dumas," Lainey says, her voice taking on a deeper, business tone. "I'm being restricted from access to him. But for some reason *she* was able to secure him as her bodyguard. And I want her to ask him some questions for me."

I didn't see that coming... But it still gives me a *lot* of satisfaction. "I'm sitting right in front of you," I scoff. "You catch more flies with honey, you know."

Her only concession is to look at me with questioning eyebrows.

"From my understanding, he's already told the Guild everything he knows," I say. "You have questions they haven't already asked?"

"That's just it. Other than basic information, basic assignments, his file is blank."

"I guess he doesn't want anyone knowing his business," I say, knowing that anyone within the Guild, at any time, can keep their past confidential.

She huffs. "Exactly why I want to question him. Why? Does he have something to hide? Where are his mission debriefings? Where is *anything*? Doesn't he want Andre caught as much as the rest of us? Why would he withhold information that could be helpful?"

She makes a good point, and knowing she's having to go about finding Andre the Invisible without being able to fully utilize life force abilities, interviewing and investigating are the only tools she has. It strikes me then how the Guild is not set up to accommodate scenarios where life force abilities are not a viable tool. They've kind of shot themselves in the foot with this one...

On the other hand, I can also sympathize with Mike for wanting to keep his business from the public domain. "If you have a history of being partnered with a psychopath, I'm guessing you'd end up taking a lot of flack from people," I say. "So I don't blame him for wanting to shut the door on his past for good."

"It's selfish," Lainey replies.

"Mike is Guild-loyal and doesn't deserve to be continually interrogated," I say, getting defensive on his behalf. "And you have plenty of Guild resources to do your job. If you can't do it, maybe Kiera was right and you're too close to this."

She bristles, her face growing redder by the moment. She shifts her attention to Chase, exaggerating the turn of her head to dismiss me entirely. "Chase. Thanks for hanging out."

She doesn't wait for him to reply. She whips around and exits the apartment.

"Reeow!" Chase says, obviously going for a cat sound but doing a terrible job.

I laugh. "I've missed you. So, about that fight..."

Twenty-Eight

*H*ow many supporters can he reasonably expect?" I say, running my hand appreciatively over the super-soft knitted hat I found in the wardrobe selection in my dressing room on the plane. It's nearly February in Salt Lake City where we're headed, and we're going to be outside. "For one, it's like ten degrees there, and for another, a hundred million people kept their lives because of *us*. Are people still arguing?"

"As a matter-of-fact, yes," Shiah says, handing me an alternative hat, one that's not white though. "You've obviously not been keeping up with things as you should."

"I'm trying to be like you," I say, tossing the blue hat she gave me on the vanity. "Monochromatic. I'm branding myself. Anyway, yes, I've been a slacker. It won't happen again though."

"That's why I brought you the white boots. But last time you wore a purple camisole to offset all the white," Shiah points out. "It looked great. Stick with the theme. Besides, the park is covered in snow, which will be great for you if things go south and you need camouflage, but terrible for the people watching to actually *see* you."

I purse my lips disappointedly. "But I really like the white hat. It's so soft. I think it's cashmere."

"Fine. Then contrast with a scarf," Shiah says. She rummages through the box.

"So people are still dogging on us even after the last minute save getting everyone out in the nick of time?" I say.

"The buzz is that people are demanding to know how the timeline shifted. People question if we handled it in the best way. *Should* we have known sooner? They have no way of knowing or judging since they have no idea how disaster projection works." Shiah emerges with an orange scarf and a red one. "The predictions themselves have been somewhat unreliable lately and people are noticing."

"Unreliable?" I say, brow furrowed.

"Yes. For several months, timelines have, at times, been inaccurate. Calamities are happening sooner than predicted. Grid scientists have been scrambling to determine the source of the discrepancy."

I'd like to say that sounds disturbing or suspicious, but we're talking about pinpointing the exact *day* a disaster will hit. The fact that the Guild can even say what kind of disasters is coming is unreal.

"Such errors could easily be forgiven," Shiah says, "But the last minute rush this time meant all but throwing people off of the boats at the nearest location without regard for the number of evacuees those areas had initially agreed to take. Places like North Carolina, Virginia, Suriname, and Guyana got hit the hardest because they bordered the safe zones. The aftermath of the whole thing has completely upstaged the miracle. Resettling that many people is going to take years. In the meantime, finding food and shelter for them is going to put a tremendous burden on locals. A fair bit of anarchy has already begun. It's only going to get worse."

She's right about that. As far as I know, the Prime Human interviews I've done haven't gained much attention amid the news from evacuee camps; I'm secretly glad for that. I've done three more in the last two weeks, all at the Vault; they make me cringe because on the whole, Prime Humans who live at the Vault are a privileged bunch who might be super smart and talented, but are kind of out of touch with life outside the walls. I think it's high-time for me to make an appearance again. I don't want the world to think vanilla interviews set to emotional music and strategic video editing are the sum of who we are. Shiah has implied that the interviews were a trade-off. The Council wanted them. Shiah wanted someone in front of a crowd. So a deal was struck.

I select the red scarf and wrap it around my neck. I don't think I've ever worn a scarf before, having lived in Southern California my whole life. "I look like a murdered snowman," I laugh, standing in front of the mirror to get the full effect of my weather-appropriate ensemble. I'm wearing white pants and a white turtleneck sweater, but the chic look is totally hidden under the long white puffy coat.

"You could do the orange." She says from behind me.

"No way," I say. "Red heads don't wear orange."

From the mirror I see the corner of her mouth quirk. "I believe a week and a half ago you screamed at your stylist for having such petty concerns when the world was in an upheaval."

"Yeah... I did, huh?" I reply. "Well the world being in an upheaval isn't going away anytime soon. My job is to convince people to stop fighting progress, because if we can do that, the upheaval part will go away sooner. Step one is making people like me. And as stupid as it is, people's first impression—which is based on appearance—matters."

"While we're on the topic of the upheaval part..." Shiah says, "How is progress?"

I pull off all my outerwear and lay it over a chair until we land. "I went into EWR three times last week during my... break."

Shiah sits in the vanity chair backwards, puts her chin on the top of the chair back, her inky tresses falling forward fluidly. "That didn't answer my question."

"Aren't you connected with the Council?" I say. "They get updates on all my progress."

"I'm the *advisor* to the Council," Shiah says. "And I have far too many other endeavors to stay up to date on EWR every moment."

I had kind of assumed Shiah's position was something like that. After meeting them though, I have no idea how Shiah pulls off the things she does. Something occurs to me just then. "Who is your dyad?" I ask.

"I don't have one," she replies.

"What? Isn't it a requirement?"

"Not for me."

"How is that?" I ask, frustrated by her curt answers.

She looks at me for a while, but, as usual, I have no idea what she's thinking.

"The Council is my dyad," Shiah says finally. "Don't concern yourself with that right now. It's irrelevant."

I am so confused, but Shiah's look says she's not going to get into it, so I say, "If you're not actually on the Council should I even be telling you about my work in the energy world?"

She shrugs. "My motivation for asking had nothing to do with the particulars of your findings."

"I knew that," I say, sitting on the sofa on the other side of the small cabin.

"I know you did."

"I swear, Shiah, it's like you can read my mind."

"I can't. But I can make near perfect guesses based on past observations—which I recall in perfect detail. Human behavior is predictable."

"Do your predictions ever fail?"

"Of course. Such as Gabe Dumas championing you after your first appearance. But my data was corrupted."

"You are such an android. What data?"

"Interviews that had been conducted since his first appearance. Interviews with Mike Dumas after the emergence of The Human Movement."

"Mike gave you false information?"

"I wasn't the one who interviewed him. And it wasn't false—to him. It was filtered through his own biases and perceptions."

"Speaking of Mike, Lainey came to me and said his file is blank. She was looking for info on him."

Shiah lifts her chin off the chair back. "Did she? I'll speak to her superiors about her circumventing protocol."

I give Shiah a look.

She just stares back at me, the lights reflecting off of her dark eyes. Shiah is one of the few people I've encountered who is unafraid of any amount of eye contact.

"Shiah."

"Wendy," she replies, "Mike is a superior bodyguard and an excellent source of intel on Gabe Dumas. You should content yourself with those two things."

Of course she would immediately know I'm fishing for more information... I keep my eyes locked on her, though, pressing. "What's the story with him and Andre? I know they were assigned to find missing Primes. What happened?"

"Mike is *your* employee, not mine. And even if he was, Mike has been cleared of his past as far as the Guild, and therefore I, am concerned. All parts of his past are confidential until he releases it. If you want further information about his background, you'll obtain it directly from him. Lainey has breached policy by coming to you instead of him. But I suspect you bringing her up is your way of trying to get at the same information she is, but letting her take the shame in asking."

"She claimed she was being kept from him," I say, ignoring her accusation. "Therefore she *couldn't* question him directly. So I guess I'm more interested in why that is rather than about him specifically."

She gives me a patronizing look. "Wendy, how does the Guild handle disciplinary matters?"

"It goes to regional supervisors first, and if the matter can't be settled there, then the Council directly. The Council decides what, if any, disciplinary action is necessary. Once that part is over, that's it. The record is expunged from all databases at every level."

She crosses her arms, and looks at me expectantly.

"Which is why Mike's file is blank, I'm guessing," I grumble. "Because his entire history involves Andre since they were dyads."

Shiah nods in affirmation. "Lainey already requested communication with him, which he declined. She was already given all relevant information about Andre. I know you have educated yourself on Guild policies, therefore you know all of this. Trust me when I say that I cannot be manipulated into divulging information that is not mine to reveal. I will see through any attempt, so please don't waste my time in the future."

"Know it all," I grumble, leaning back on the couch and frowning. "So you're saying I have to get my info from the source."

"That's the *only* place you're going to get it. But I'll be the first to tell you that you should let it be. Let Mike do his job. Don't let your attraction to him ruin his opportunity to prove himself and your opportunity to be professional and mature."

I sit up. "I am not—" I stop and fall back, crossing my arms. It's no use denying it.

Shiah leans her chin on the chair back again. She smiles lightly.

Nothing gets past Shiah. "It's not about that," I say. "I just…"

"Have to know his deep dark secrets or you just can't cope," Shiah finishes. "Except that itch only applies to men whom you have laid claim to."

I make a sound of protest, but it's hard to deny the things she's saying. "He's freakin' hot, Shiah!" I whine.

She chuckles. "That he is. But you know as well as I do that it's not your attraction to him so much as his attraction to you that has you striking first to gain the upper hand."

My mouth is open in disbelief. "How do you know these things?"

"I told you. I observe people and retain those observations in perfect clarity. I figure people out very quickly."

"This is going to get annoying."

"Helping you avoid mistakes is annoying?" she asks genuinely.

"No, I guess not," I reply. "I think maybe… that was my past self being annoyed. I don't actually want to relive my past mistakes, and definitely not with Mike. Sometimes… my former self tries to assert herself. I'm trying to do things differently this time, but I guess old habits are easy to fall back on… especially when trying to fill in the gaps created by missing two and a half years."

"Understandable," Shiah says. Then she spins her chair around to sit with her legs crossed and looks at me directly. "Don't lose too much of yourself, though, Wendy. I didn't pick you to conform. I picked you to push boundaries."

I think I'm starting to get that about Shiah, just based on what she told me before I met with the Council. Shiah has an angle in this public relations campaign, and it doesn't necessarily jive with standard Guild culture.

"I get it," I reply. "Balance. I'm figuring it out."

She smiles. "Are you ready?"

"For round two? Sure. Talking about the history of the Guild's formation should be easy. I spent my first two weeks at the Vault reading up on that."

She nods once. "You'll speak at the end. Just like last time. We'll adjust your remarks as needed depending on what Dumas says during the event, but I'll be in your ear to help you with that."

I nod.

"He hasn't gotten much media coverage lately," Shiah says. "His last event was cancelled because of the subduction, and he's taken a bit of a break in the week and a half since, probably because people have been caught up with the Caribbean disaster and the ensuing mayhem. But once things calm to their usual levels of hysteria, we want to have already gained traction."

"Traction: check," I say.

"Remember, Wendy. Issues. Not Dumas."

"Oh my gosh, you and Mike…" I complain. "I can handle this!"

She ignores my outburst. "I'm not concerned on that front. The biggest X-factor this time is PHIA. Your security alone has been quadrupled this time, an exit plan put in place in the event that things go south. Armed operatives are already on-site ahead of us, screening the area."

"What do your android instincts predict? Will PHIA show?"

She frowns. "They have a flair for dramatic and decisive violence. And this is the premium opportunity, so I'm treating the situation as if they will. I advised the Council to have the recovery team in place as well. With any luck, Andre will be captured. The just as likely alternative is that he doesn't show. He has not been particularly active lately—a change from his usual pattern. But I'm quite happy with either scenario."

I rub my hands together. "Win-win"

"It's imperative that you follow Mike's lead, no matter what he tells you," she instructs. "As far as capable bodyguards are concerned, he's the best there is. He *will* keep you safe so long as you let him do his job."

"Yeah, yeah," I say, raising my hand, palm toward her. "I know. I swear I will do exactly what he says."

She snorts. "Don't make promises you can't keep, Wendy."

Twenty-Nine

It may be only twenty degrees, but that was the warmest welcome I've ever received," Gabe Dumas says, eyes alight with the excitement of the crowd he just expertly stirred into a frenzy. I watch him on a monitor inside a clubhouse at Liberty Park where a makeshift security office has been set up. He's right. It was a *very* warm welcome. The crowd chanted 'Gabe Dumas' the entire ten minutes prior to him getting on stage—which isn't a stage at all. It's a small raised pedestal in the middle of the crowd. No room for pacing like St. Louis.

"I thank you, Salt Lake," he continues, his tone so personable it seems like he's sitting down to have a small conference with a few people rather than a few thousand. He turns slowly around to make eye contact with all of them. "To know so many here have taken an interest in their rights does my heart good. It's been an especially tough couple of weeks for us human beings, hasn't it?"

The crowd murmurs in agreement, and Dumas' expression can only be described as solemn as he says, "I would first like to thank the Guild. Their recent feats in the Caribbean should give us all cause to triumph. I want to thank them, publicly, for their significant and irreplaceable part in preserving the lives of some hundred million of our fellow Humans. To think that we could have just as easily been mourning the deaths of those same hundred million right now... It's unthinkable. I cannot fathom what it would feel like to lose that many people at one time so tragically. But I think it puts our current struggles into perspective—namely, how we are to make sure those countless survivors will have a life. The heaviness of my gratitude is in no way diminished by my history of criticizing their methods."

His delivery is quieter than usual, and I've watched every single speech he's ever given. This is different—as is his position, literally, of standing in the middle of the crowd. Having seen footage of all of his events, it appears he just keeps simplifying things. I admire his style, and it seems to be working. The crowd is enraptured with him as always, those closest to him even placing their hands on his feet, and others beyond them reaching. He starts turning this way and that to touch the hands of anyone who extends a hand for him, if only for a brief moment. The intimacy he has established just in touching fingertip to fingertip... I find myself wishing I was among them.

Dumas crouches down, still brushing their fingers, still looking at the crowd as if what he is about to say has only just now occurred to him. "In fact, saving one hundred million lives has grotesquely widened the Guild's deficit of accountability."

Still crouched, he stares further into the crowd, as if questioning them, contemplating their reactions, nodding just as if validating their confusion. "We all watched our televisions as bodies of land were swallowed up into the sea, and we felt the debilitating sense of our own powerlessness. Suddenly we no longer were the rulers of our Earth, but she the ruler of *us*. How had a comparatively tiny organization, known only as the Guild, been endowed with such vast capability that they could see the scope of this event with such accuracy? They prevented the deaths of an incomprehensible number of people! I think there was a moment in the face of such a miraculous rescue that we of The Human Movement wondered what right we had to fight any of it."

He bows his head, his hands at rest at his sides, seeming in deep contemplation.

He stands suddenly and swiftly. "We are surely in the hands of gods," he yells, "individuals with such power that they must deserve our adulation and worship... Our blind trust." The tone of Dumas' voice is suddenly bursting with outrage, and the next part he says with definite affront, "The gods..." He shakes his head with disgust. "As all gods, they are silent. Mysterious. Unapproachable. They choose who lives and who dies. Yet we know them not!"

The crowd erupts, and Dumas lets them stew for a minutes. Then he calms them with nothing but the lift of his hand. "We don't know their number. We don't know their identities. We're told they are benevolent, interested in Human survival, and we are asked to simply trust them. When we ask to see their faces, they respond that we must *blindly* trust them. They perform miracles, and we can't shake their hands to thank them. We can't ask questions. We can't learn. We can't know. We must simply...

believe that they are who they say and that they will *do* what they say all while the earth crumbles beneath our feet."

He huffs in genuine frustration, looks down for a moment before looking back up. "We imagine what powerful beings they must be… We tremble in awe. The irony is that with all of their obvious power, they still claim that they are so vulnerable that any amount of transparency will endanger their ranks. They plead for their own weakness while simultaneously accomplishing feats of wonder."

The crowd rumbles with indignance. Dumas shakes his head in disbelief once again, holds a hand out, but not to still them. Instead it's as if he is leading an orchestra—one of human voices. Chanting begins somewhere to his right, and it is met with another group at his left. They converge, but it is rhythmic, their words alternating in a way that seems as if it should have been choreographed.

I realize suddenly that I have held my breath. His skill is incredible. I am witnessing some kind of power that I can't name.

He stills them by lowering his hand slowly. "Something isn't right, my friends," he says. "These messages are not congruent. If you demonstrate the power to save one hundred million people, you certainly have the power to save your own… If you pretend you can't, you are hiding something. If you honestly *believe* you can't, you are missing something. *You are no god.*"

He then jumps down into the crowd, which has erupted into cheers and chants. He raises his hands and begins clapping out a rhythm that they immediately respond to. The way they align themselves to his tempo so easily astounds me.

Shiah looks expectantly at me.

"What's your advice?" I ask her.

Now her mouth twitches. "Turning over a new leaf of maturity, I see."

"Just using all my assets," I say. I turn to Mike, behind me. "Thoughts?"

"Good luck," he says gruffly, his eyes still on the monitor. He's been wound tight since he met up with us at the airport. He gave me the same lecture about security as Shiah did, and then I surprised him by not arguing. He's been hovering extra close, entirely focused on spotting possible threats. Clearly he is not thinking about public relations strategies.

"Issues, not Dumas," Shiah says. "What you have prepared is an excellent starting place for answering the question he has asked. Don't skip ahead or you'll get caught in a war of words."

"You don't think it's worth pointing out that those hundred million people weren't evacuated by Prime Humans, but by *Humans*?" I say. "It *was* the collaboration he's been wanting and he didn't even mention that just so he could keep complaining."

Mike chuffs but doesn't comment, his eyes still on the screen.

"That's exactly the type of thing that's going to get you into a war of words," Shiah says. "And it's a straw man tactic that will make *you* look the fool, not Dumas. He has questioned the Guild's power in his remarks, not a lack of collaboration. *Current* issues, Wendy. Past ones are irrelevant."

"Fine," I say, crossing my arms and plopping on a chair in front of the monitors where I will spend the next hour and a half waiting and listening to the Human Movement chanting while resisting the urge to run around the building due to the energy of the crowd—which may rival that of St. Louis. Like last time, I'm ready for this, and I let Dumas' words bounce around in my head, examining the angles, acknowledging them and formulating my resulting convictions. From that I pull out the words I will say.

ןּ

Dumas spends the next two hours in and among the people. He shakes hands, hugs, puts his ear to those who wish to speak to him, laughs, joins the chanting, but always stays on the move. Like all of his protests, his objective seems to be to personally interact, in some way, with every single person who has come to hear him speak. The vigor of the crowd follows him as he moves through it, although he leaves a wake of excitement behind him, creating an inexplicable rhythm of energy only perceived if one watches the details, as I am on the monitor. He winds them up, one by one. As I feel the effects of it, I wonder how he does it. I marvel at his power to inspire them with so little—because he does. It invigorates me with passion each time. It has to be a life force ability. It just has to be, but I'm not sure how exactly I would define it.

When he's done, having made his way back to his platform for closing remarks, the crowd is back to pulsing out his name again.

He waits. The energy peaks. Then settles, and he says, "The Guild. What a phenomenon they are. A few months ago, an ordinary-looking man in a suit and tie, whom nobody had heard of, stood in front of a cluster of microphones and cameras and told the world an organization existed that could predict natural disasters because their members possessed superhuman abilities. Since then, Guild predictions have become as important to everyday life as knowing the balance of our bank accounts, having milk and bread on hand, or clocking in at work. They play an integral part in our existence, and they seem to have slipped seamlessly into that role. So seamlessly that we barely acknowledge that we know slightly more than nothing about them. We've taken what little information they've given us about themselves as truth because, well, their predictions, which prevent countless deaths, don't fail."

Dumas has a questioning look on his face as he says, "Who *are* these people? *Are* they people? An alien race perhaps? Artificially enhanced humans? We've been told they have a 'vast' membership, but I couldn't tell you how that adjective translates in terms of numbers. Twelve? Twelve hundred? Twelve thousand? Twelve million? We've been told they have superhuman capability, but what's considered 'super'? How powerful *are* these people? They say these capabilities originate from the 'energy world,' but what is that? It's merely a name. Is it another planet? Another dimension? Why does nobody care?"

Dumas' mouth forms a frustrated line for a moment. "The catastrophes. Another phenomenon. *What* is causing them? Their scale and scope and frequency doesn't match any time in recorded geological history. Something is happening, and the only thing people seem to care about is where the next one will hit. The earth moves beneath our feet, rearranging itself, and we don't stop to ask why…"

He sighs, puts a hand on his hip. "Then St. Louis happened. The Guild was made flesh in the form of a young woman… brazen, humorous, intelligent, raw, so painfully human. I was shocked, perhaps more than anyone, because, to me, 'The Guild' had been nothing more than a cardboard cutout that I talked *about* and not *to*. I spent my time convincing people that cardboard should not be trusted, could not be dependable, and should never be revered no matter what it claimed it was able to do. We shouldn't ever accept blind worship. We should demand to know the force behind the curtain. Once hidden in a vast sea of possibility, in St. Louis the Guild's true form leapt out of obscurity and stared us all in the face, making jokes and firing challenges at us. To me, the Guild finally became... *real*. Miss Whitley, in a mere five minutes, changed who the Guild was to all of us. And I finally figured out who they are."

Dumas rotates in a slow circle on his podium, and his silence feeds the crowd. They seem to grow louder with noises of anticipation.

He clears his throat and raises his voice, "I believe the Guild when they say their ranks are made up of people just like Miss Whitley. Just like my brother. They look and talk and act like you and me. How else would they have been able to hide their existence so well?

"But now they set themselves apart from us. They have elevated themselves, labelled themselves, and said, 'We are different. We are special.'"

Dumas smiles and shakes his head. "That's precisely why I believe them now. I believe they are exactly what they say. Their exclusivity is such a very Human thing to do. The more they separate themselves, claim they aren't the same as us, insist on special consideration, insist on a label like 'Prime Human,' the more Human they become. Oh, *the irony* of their absurd, everyday humanity..."

The crowd chuckles collectively.

"Now that I know who they are, my objective has shifted. Now I want them to come down from the clouds and join the rest of us.

"I assume that at the close of my remarks we will be hearing from Wendy Whitley, our liaison to the Guild. Now that we know what we're dealing with, it's not that hard to guess what her angle will be, considering she's only Human... She'll probably charm us with her humanity, give us insight into some obscure aspect of the Guild. She'll give us a bit of herself, she'll step down a little closer to our level, enough to make us believe our voices today have accomplished something. But it will be superficial propaganda, but enough to appease our curiosity for a season. Enough to earn our tolerance of continued Guild obscurity. We will relegate ourselves to the role of dependent child rather than equal."

Dumas clears his throat. "This is not okay. We've already been children once. We didn't know how the world worked. Cars moved on their own. Food appeared at our dinner table. Televisions could create moving pictures. People built skyscrapers. It must be magic. Santa Claus was easy to believe in. We were content not to understand. But one day we grew up, and it became necessary to either know how things worked or be helpless. To be independent, capable, courageous, moral, kind… these are things we developed because we understood independence allowed us choices. We wanted that choice so we let go of dependence.

"By their secrecy the Guild demands your dependency. This will steal your choice, and ultimately your freedom. The cardboard cutout wasn't working, so Miss Whitley is the newest distraction. Her purpose is to make you feel like the Guild is transparent. She looks and talks and acts like you. She will make you see yourself *in* the Guild and therefore give them your trust."

He stills his hands, turns in a slow circle to scan the crowd, which is insanely quiet.

His eyes are hard when he raises his hands again. "This is an illusion they hope you will fall for."

I catch my breath as the crowd explodes. Their rapt attention has transformed into chaos. From my place in the clubhouse, I hear voices even louder than they were in the last hour.

"The Guild is not our master!"

"Secrecy is slavery! We are not slaves!"

"Hu*man*! Hu*man*! Hu*man*!"

Mixed into the chants are shouts that maybe only my ears can make out. They are threats and insults toward the Guild and Prime Humans. They are declarations of loyalty and predictions of our downfall. They're rabid.

A hand falls on my shoulder, startling me, and I look up to see Shiah. "I don't think it's a good idea for you to speak now," she says. "We can do a press conference later once it has cleared out."

I stand abruptly. "No!"

"It's not safe," Mike says, stepping forward.

"I don't care," I say. "This is what I signed up for."

"They won't hear you," Shiah says.

"You don't know that," I say. "Backing down is what he wants."

"He has already set you up for failure either way," she replies.

"The only failure is letting *that* be the last word," I insist, stabbing a finger at the monitor.

She gives me a disapproving look. "You are not going to fall prey to his tactics. *We* will not fall prey to it."

I throw my shoulders back, put my hands on my hips. I step toward her. "He thinks he knows us. He thinks he knows *me*. And if we falter now he will be right!"

"You are not speaking now," Shiah says firmly, her eyes tightening as the only indication that she's growing irritated. In the background, the roar becomes louder, threatening.

I cross my arms and plant my feet. "I am, too. You gave me this job and I am doing it."

"You're not capable," she says matter-of-factly, not moving, hands clasped behind her back in a completely non-confrontational stance, so unlike the words coming out of her mouth.

"*Yes I am*," I reply venomously.

"He accused you of being a pawn," she says lightly. "He knows what you're going to say and you haven't even said it yet. You don't have any earth-shattering news to distract people with this time. Now all you've got is your anger. You're too volatile. You are not what the Guild needs right now."

I suck in a breath, shocked. Not what it needs?

She stares me in the eye as if summing me up. Her bodyguard has moved closer and everyone in the room has taken a step toward us. Mike is right behind me now, and I can feel he agrees with Shiah.

"I am *nobody's* pawn," I growl, lifting my chin. "I am doing this and *no one* will stop me."

Three men move closer to me and one of her hands snaps up to halt them. Her eyes stay on me though. She stares at me for about fifteen seconds and I stare back daringly.

"You're right. I won't," she says, flicking her fingers at the surrounding muscle. "That's not who we are. But be prepared. Your history indicates that when you return to this building you will likely no longer be our liaison."

She pulls the communicator from her ear—the one she was going to use to help me when I went out to speak—and lets it fall to the floor.

I glare at her, exhaling hot breaths, indignation at her presumption that she can predict my actions with so much accuracy rippling through me. She's as bad as Gabe Dumas. Neither of them knows me. Neither of them grasps what I truly stand for. I understand the Guild. I comprehend its purpose better than every member I've met. "You have sold me short, Shiah Lim," I snarl. "*You* forgot. I *have* no history. Your data is corrupted." I turn on my heel, heading for the exit.

Mike has preempted me, pushing open the doors ahead and scanning the area with his weapon drawn. "Backups, thumbs out of your asses and do your job!" he growls into his communicator. "Nobody relieved you of duty."

Just like that, we're surrounded, but I don't pause in my step, tossing the end of my red scarf over my shoulder. I barely feel the ground beneath me, a fire in my chest building with each foot that brings me closer to the stage that's been set up for me. It's been blocked off, and operatives have been maintaining the space for the duration of the protest. I don't see anyone, don't even comprehend the shouts aimed at me, telling me to go home, that I'm not needed. Their hatred for me flickers like a candle compared to the inferno in my heart.

They are simply… wrong. I have been underestimated on both sides. The Human Movement and the Guild both. They all think they know why I am doing this. But neither has grasped why I am even a member. So much of myself I have had to give up to become part of the Guild. Even more I have had to let go of in order to speak for Prime Humans. I fought for this. I have sacrificed. Since I woke up in that hospital, when PHIA made their move on me… all of the revelations of my past and the revelations of what I mean to the Guild… meeting so many wonderful Prime Humans and realizing what made them that way… watching disaster after disaster and understanding what has made the Guild what it is… I have been molding myself so that when moments like this happened, when people questioned my purpose, I would know it with certainty. And after today, they will never again question who I am.

I nearly lose patience with the attendant who is testing the microphone attached to me, and when she's done, I leap up the steps that will elevate me. Without pause, I meet the sea of greedy eyes that are hungry for my downfall.

Not today, I say to them with my own. *Today you will know me.*

"You came here today to feel," I say abruptly, catching sight of my breath in the frigid air. I recognize in a millisecond that I forgot to put on my coat, but I don't feel cold in the least. I refuse to shy away from their jeering expressions. I don't look for Dumas. He is as irrelevant to me as his words. "You came not really knowing why the Guild makes you uncomfortable, makes you angry, makes you sad…. But a man showed up, looked you in the eye, and he put words to your emotions. Suddenly you understand yourself… Suddenly your life is a little less murky. The things you feel… they don't torture you. Instead… Instead they give you purpose. Purpose is that thing that comes to us when confusion finally leaves."

I gesture at the wide sea of them. "Have you looked around you? To your right and your left, your front and your back... they all share this same feeling with you. Can you honestly say you have ever felt so much belonging before?"

I look at them, each of them, challenging them to answer. "You can't. I know you can't because I feel it too. I'm an empath, and the spirit here is magnificent. Validating. *Empowering*," I say fervently. "Do you feel that? It is the sense that you could face the most terrifying darkness imaginable. You could fight with your last breath. Outnumbered and outgunned. Nevertheless you are *fearless*. And you would do this, even and especially for the people around you today that are no more strangers because of this purpose you share. When you wake up tomorrow, and you begin fretting once more over the events in the world, do not be fooled by your mind, by your memory. It *will not* give you this moment back. But that does *not* mean it never was. It is up to *you* to have faith that it was, and allow that faith to guide you more confidently into each day."

"This feeling..." I say, holding a hand up in front of me. "This power..." I hold my other hand up. "This is *your* Guild." I clasp my hands together tightly to show them.

They watch me, spellbound, amazed. I have them.

I keep my hands bound in front of my face, on display for them. "You need this more than ever. You need kinship and alliances during a time in history when we are facing extinction. What's happening here and has happened at Human Movement events all over is called hope. It arises when people stop feeling alone and start feeling capable."

I lift my chin slightly and maintain my solid stance. "That's why PHIA isn't here. They attack when you're feeling most alone, not when you are invincible as you are now. And people are invincible when they belong to something. And you belong to The Human Movement."

My clasped hands still out for them to follow, I square my shoulders now and raise my voice slightly, "We are all agents. Of something. The only way we have ever accomplished anything as a human race is through alliances such as these." I shake my bound hands and speak more rapidly. "In 1976 Prime Humans realized they were different. They recognized that they each had been born with a similar potential that could better the world. They also realized that *together* they could not just better the world but change the face of it. So the Guild was forged, and suddenly, they belonged to each other. This power you are experiencing right now… it is the same power we wield." I hold my clasped hands higher.

I look entreatingly into the faces of the gathering. "It is *not* about the IQ or the superpower. It is not the technology. The resources. Throughout history, far more people with genius-level brains have lived and died in obscurity than those that have done things like changed the theories of mathematics and science and technology."

I pace down the stage, my hands ever bound together. "The ones who never accomplished more than survival did not have this." I hold my bound hands out to the crowd. "They had no one to tell them who and what they were, what they could *do,* what they owed the world. But Prime Humans? They became powerful because they belonged to something other than themselves. They became bigger. They weren't *born important.* They *became* important because they *believed* who they were told they were. Bigger. Part of a purpose. And seeing themselves as bigger made problems seem smaller. So they *were* smaller."

"*This* is the power we wield," I yell, holding my hands high above me. "The power by which we dreamt up technology to predict natural disasters. It is the power that allowed us to save one hundred million. It is the power that will allow us to save seven billion… even though we are grossly outnumbered. And outgunned. Nature would have us. But it is impossible to win against *this*." I shake my joined hands.

I spread my feet, standing firm in one spot, unmoved, unintimidated. I bring my hands lower, in front of my chin. "How we do that isn't a secret. It's not mysterious. It's not magic. It's… simple. It is the same thing you have right here and now, today, for this moment with those who surround you.

"Mister Dumas is right: We *are* human. We aren't hiding who we are from you. We are a guild. When someone becomes part of the Guild it is called Unification. *That* is the thing we will fight you and anyone else to protect. We are powerful because we are agents of the same cause—the cause of accessing our potential and using it to change the world. We protect the membership because we cannot afford *this*." I hold my clasped hands in front of me and let them separate slowly. "Picked apart," I say solemnly.

"Separated." I spread my fingers on both hands and stare at them. Everyone is.

There is stillness, all of us looking at my hands for the several moments, lost in the despair I have spelled out.

I pull my hands to my chest protectively, clasp them again, my eyes on the floor of the stage.

I look up, reveal my bound hands once more, wave them to the crowd. "This is sacred to us. It's our legacy. It's our family. To be part of it is a privilege, but one that demands all that we are. Because only potential is inherent. Capability is the thing that requires a fight. And it is something we earn together within the Guild, *because* we are a guild. The Human Movement has this, too. Right here and now. Grasp it tightly. And ask yourselves, what is *your* purpose? How will *you* change the world?"

I make a small bow and descend the steps. When I reach the bottom I finally let my hands fall to my sides. Mike quickly takes up his usual residence at my back. The crowd explodes, but the vibe is totally different than it was when I walked up.

"No words," Mike murmurs to me over my shoulder once the crowd is behind us.

"Thank you," I say, head held high, certain that Shiah is regretting her words. I notice, as we walk through our gauntlet of protection, that there are tears in everyone's eyes. One of them raises his hands, clasps them together in front of his face, and immediately, the whole line of them follow. I stop, stunned as I look around to see that every single person in the vicinity has clasped their hands in front of them, just as I did only moments ago.

My eyes fall on Shiah, who is standing in front of the double doors, waiting, and her expression is entirely unreadable. She does nod at me to turn around though.

I do, and although I am surrounded on all sides by my own protection, there is an entire sea of clasped hands behind them— those of the crowd raised up high for all to see. It's a salute.

My mouth falls open.

Mike nudges me in the back. "We have to move," he says.

I start walking again, catching up to where Shiah is. Her bodyguard, Brad, opens the door for us. "Well done," she murmurs while simultaneously handing me my coat as we walk through. "Very well done." She looks over my shoulder to Mike. "Let's get her out now. The car is waiting to take her to the airport. Go ahead and I'll meet you there."

Mike touches the small of my back, turning toward a side-door once we are inside and back out to a sidewalk headed in a different direction than we came in from.

I'm reeling. It's like my own words have suddenly hit me, like I've only just now realized what I said. It's just like St. Louis actually. I've tapped into something outside of my consciousness, except I relinquished myself to it even more surely than before. I always know what I want to convey, but the actual words don't come until I'm up there, and the emotions of thousands hit me squarely, and suddenly everything is clear and simple. I'm in awe of myself. Again. How do I do it? Where does it come from?

We've reached the car, and suddenly I recognize Mike's growing agitation. I look at him when he opens the door but he doesn't speak, just motions me in. I sigh, taking my seat. He shuts the door, his attention, for once, not on our immediate surroundings.

Once he's in the vehicle with me and the door shuts, dulling the roar of the crowd at the park, I pick up the loud chatter from Mike's communicator in his ear, '*We've got an altercation going on with some of the attendees but we're handling it.*'

'*Any more action and you get your men out of there. We aren't referees,*' says another voice.

Our driver pulls into the street, and I toss my coat to the side. "Everything okay?" I say to Mike whose head is oscillating to look out of every window.

"Not until we're in the air."

"They're not coming," I say. "This isn't their style."

Mike ignores me.

I sit back in my seat, grab my bag from the floor and retrieve my phone from it.

There's a text message from Ohr with one word: Perfection.

I smile at it, about to text back a thank you when my heart leaps terrifyingly out of my chest with Mike's sharp and sudden fear.

I snap my head up. "Mike! What's wrong?"

He has his eyes closed, his head bowed in his hands. His heart rate has increased dramatically, surely from adrenaline.

"Mike!" I punch his arm that's like iron. I listen to see what he's getting from his communicator but it's quiet.

"It's fine," he says, lifting his face, hands shaking. "It's fine."

"It is *not* fine!" I snap. "What is going on! Don't lie to me!"

"It's fine," he growls, mentally pulling his dread under a weight to suppress it.

"Stop the car!" I order the driver.

"No!" Mike says. "She's not in charge. You get this car to the airport or I'll make sure you get fired."

I look back at him, eyes flashing. "And *you* are fired if you don't tell me what's going on. Right now!"

His face goes into his hands again. "Oh shit… Oh shit…" he mumbles. "Something is going on…"

"Mike," I say, making an effort to calm my voice and not scream at him. "*What* is going on? I don't hear anything on your communicator. Is Shiah safe?"

"Yes," he mumbles, sitting back in his seat, running his hands back and forth over his thighs. "But Gabe is not."

Thirty

urn the car around!" I say to Jerry, our driver. "NOW!"

"No," Mike says, shaking his head. "My job is to keep you safe. Safety is ahead not behind!"

"Screw your job!" I yell. "Your brother is more important than your job, idiot!"

"He can handle himself," Mike seethes, his eyes wild. "This is *my* call, not yours." He leans forward. "Airport."

"*No*, he can't," I say, livid that he's being like this, that he would abandon his flesh and blood for his duty. I have no idea how he knows Gabe Dumas is in trouble, but his emotions don't lie, and I'm not going to argue hows and whys right now. "Jerry," I say calmly to the driver, "head back to the park. Mike does not outrank me and he has no say in your job."

"Miss Whitley, are you certain?" Jerry says. "Your plane is supposed to be in the air in forty-five minutes. Shiah's car is already en route."

"I'm certain."

Jerry makes a U-turn.

"Don't do this," Mike says, but inside I can tell he wants to. He *really* wants to.

"I'm doing it," I say, sitting back in my seat. "I've lost my only brother, Mike. I'm not letting you lose yours today. I'll be fine. You've got this. Where should we take the car? On the east side? Do we still have guys there? Can you redirect them?"

Mike stares at me for five seconds and then shakes off the rest of his protest. "I'm not sure where Gabe is exactly, so no. Jerry, drop me off at the south, near the pond. And then get her to the airport."

"Uh uh," I say. "You are *my* bodyguard, and you are not leaving my side. We're going together."

"Don't be stupid," he says. "I'm not taking you into probable danger."

"Instead you're going to go alone and get accused of abandoning your post? Mike, I know your history. This job was your chance to redeem yourself. They're going to can you for sure if you go in there alone, and I won't get a say. This way it's *my* idea. It's on me, not you. *I'm* going in there after Gabe, and you're my bodyguard. You go where I do."

He glares at me and then slams a fist against his door. It reverberates through the car. "Dammit! That dumb bastard!" he heaves.

"Before we get there, tell me what we're getting into," I say.

He slams his fist into the door again, furious. "Dumbass!" He takes several breaths to calm down. Then he turns to me abruptly. "Pull that gun out of your boot."

I raise an eyebrow as I reach down. I didn't tell him I had it. An edge of the butt is showing only if I stand a certain way. Mike is awfully observant to have noticed let alone figured out it was a gun.

He holds his hand out and I put the pocket pistol into it.

"You know how to use a gun?" he asks, releasing the clip— something I have no idea how to do. Looks like it's loaded.

"No," I reply.

"Here's the safety," he says, showing me a tiny lever beneath the barrel that he flips with his thumbnail. "This is a semi-automatic, so you'll have to pull the slide back to load." He demonstrates. "Once you do, you can fire continuously. Keep your palm firmly here." He exaggerates putting the back of the gun to his right palm. "It'll absorb the kickback if you fire. Keep the gun up and aligned with your vision. Tight and controlled." He hands the gun back to me. "Your boot is a good spot to stash it. But don't pull it out unless I tell you to."

I tuck the gun back where it was.

"I'm taking the lead," Mike says, already scoping the park out as we approach it. "That means you follow me. And you do exactly what I say. If you do I promise you'll get out unscathed."

Jerry pulls the car up slowly to the sidewalk near the pond.

"Jerry, keep it right here," Mike says. "With any luck we'll be back quickly."

"Let Shiah know I'm handling some business with Gabe Dumas," I say. "Mike is with me. I'll contact her as soon as I'm back."

Jerry gives me a skeptical look.

"She's not going to like it. But you make sure you tell her this was *my* idea."

"Come out my side," Mike says, opening his door and stepping out onto the shoveled sidewalk.

I follow, pulling my coat back on and wrapping my scarf back around my neck as we exit.

Mike immediately leads us off of the sidewalk. I do exactly what he says and stick close to his back as he plows a path through the snow that's nearly a foot deep.

The sun is going down, bringing with it colder temperatures that freeze our breaths in clouds around us. I think we're walking next to the pond, which is a sheet of frozen white. We walk beneath trees, and beyond them is a shoveled concrete area surrounding a decommissioned fountain.

We slow when we reach the trees near the back of a building with river rock accents all the way around. By the smell I think it's a restaurant. We can see people passing through the park nearby on foot, leftovers from the protest. Some of them pass near the building but don't stop. Mike waits for an opening and then the two of us run to the rear of the building, taking cover near the dumpster.

"You sure he's here?" I whisper, Mike's shift in stealth and certainty baffling me. I can tell he thinks this is the right place. How does he know?

He nods, so I employ my super hearing to make out what's going on inside.

First I just hear clanking and a light crash—kitchenware maybe? Then I hear a woman crying. Rushed footsteps.

Mike reaches for the handle to the rear entrance, but I grab his arm. "Hang on a second," I hiss. "I should be able to tell you where he is."

Mike pauses, and I close my eyes.

The first thing I hear is a wheezy male voice inside, not on the other side of the wall, maybe toward the front of the building, *'We need to wait until the place clears out. The Guild should be just about out of here if they aren't already, and then we can work without their interference.'*

'Bernie says their team started combing through the place a couple minutes ago,' another voice says nervously. *'Thought they were on their way out and then they turned around.'*

'They don't need to be here,' Gabe Dumas' voice breaks in from a place closer to the back of the building where we are.

'They didn't. Their being here is your own fault,' says a baritone voice from near where I heard Dumas.

'*Turned around?*' wheezy says. Back to the front of the building. '*What for? The VIPs are out already, aren't they?*'

'*Saw both of 'em drive off. Maybe they're looking for PHIA?*' says Nervous from the front.

'*What exactly are you hoping to accomplish?*' Dumas asks.

'*Getting rid of Satan's messenger,*' says Baritone.

'*Satan's messenger... That's a new one for me. What are we waiting for? This assassination is taking an exceptionally long time,*' Dumas says impatiently.

'*Why would they be looking for PHIA? The thing's over. The Prime's have gone,*' Wheezy says.

'*Let's calm down,*' says a female voice. '*It's not the time to lose face. They're probably making sure everyone gets out. We've got time. Dumas'whole team is here so no one's going to be reporting their disappearance any time soon.*'

'*Will you be killing my people as well or do your moral mandates exclude putting to death associates?*' Dumas says tiredly.

The weeping woman picks up her volume. I think she's in the same room as Dumas.

"What's going on?" Mike's voice says loudly in my ear. "We need to get moving!"

"He's in a room here in the back," I say. "Him and his team. I think there's one guard with them. In the front there are at least three, two men and one woman. They're getting nervous because the Guild has started combing the park."

"Dammit," Mike says under his breath. He reaches up to tap his ear.

"Hold on," I say, pulling his hand back down and digging my phone out.

Shiah answers on the first ring, "Wendy." She doesn't need to say anything more. I hear the disapproval and protest in her voice.

"Get our people out of the park," I say in a low voice. "They're endangering us."

"Is that so? I was told Gabe Dumas was in some sort of trouble and you were spearheading a rescue mission. I would love to retrieve the team as soon as you are clear."

"Just do it!" I hiss. "The bad guys have, max, five people holding Dumas. I've got super hearing and a badass bodyguard. Fewer is better."

"What am I going to tell the Council this time? If you're not dropping bombs on stage you're diving into danger."

"Nothing. As far as they're concerned I'm boarding the plane. Now can you please do this?"

"As you wish," she sighs. And then she hangs up.

Mike tries the rear door to find it predictably locked.

"Front door?" I say.

"Doubt it," Mike says as he begins scanning the side of the building. He walks around the back, eyes up and then down, looking for something, though I can't say what. He runs his hand over the river rock foundation and loosens a stone near the bottom. He works at it, jiggling the five inch stone it until it comes free.

He walks over to the three cars parked in the rear lot. Mike leans over a luxury sedan and peers inside.

"Stay close," Mike says. He looks around, and when he verifies that no one is nearby, he grips the rock in two hands above his head. Then he slams it down onto the windshield with enormous force.

The windshield cracks and the alarm sounds. Mike drops the rock, which I notice now has blood on it. He takes my hand and we run back to the side of the building.

"What are they doing?" he whispers.

'Sounds like out back,' Wheezy says. 'My car doesn't have an alarm. Yours, Jon?'

'Probably just some snow from the trees fell on it,' Jon, aka Nervous says, and it's followed by footsteps heading our direction at the back.

"Someone's coming!" I whisper.

"The back?" Mike asks.

"Yes!"

"Perfect. Stand on that side of the door. Don't move until I say we're clear." He stands on the other side where the door will open and I hear the deadbolt turn. I nod emphatically at Mike, who stands ready.

The door barely opens before Mike grabs the guy coming through by the shirt and flings him around his own body and straight into the stone wall on his other side. The tall man's face plows into the jagged rocks so fast he doesn't get a chance to utter a sound. He falls to the ground, face bloody and completely knocked out. Mike grabs the keys that have fallen out of the man's hands. He clicks the button to disarm the alarm. The car falls silent.

"Stay behind me," Mike says as he tugs my hand, letting us in through the now-open back door.

I have no problem with that order, huddling against his back as he lets the door full shut behind us. My adrenaline has worn off to be replaced with claustrophobia. We are now no longer in the open but enclosed in a dimly lit hallway, along with a bunch of people with sinister motives. I time my breaths with Mike's, determined to align myself with his every move.

In front of us are the bathrooms. The hall to the left leads to the front of the restaurant. To the right and around the corner lies the kitchen, most likely where Dumas is.

"Gabe's at the back?" Mike mouths softly over his shoulder.

I point to the right.

He turns around to face me. "Draw your weapon," he whispers. "As soon as we turn the corner, put your back to me and aim to our rear. They're going to head this way when our friend out back doesn't show. Let me know as soon as you hear them."

I nod, reaching down to my boot, my hand shaking.

He wraps an arm around my back, pulling me closer. "Don't be afraid," he whispers next to my ear, giving me chills. "I will not let anything happen to you."

"What about you?" I tremble.

He releases me with a self-assured grin. "This is going to be easy. You'll see." He turns toward the back, motioning me to follow, but I'm already there. He creeps to the corner, peeks around the edge for merely a second. Then he turns the corner completely. I follow, but turn back to face the doorway as soon as he does and draw my gun, holding it out in front of my line of sight, just like he showed me.

I hear a scuffle, a smack, and then a voice behind me that is undoubtedly Dumas', "Mike? Miss Whitley?"

"Quiet!" Mike hisses as I hear him drag the body of his second victim to the side.

I don't turn around to see, but back a few more steps into the room, gun trained on the door, and I listen.

"What's taking Jon so long?" I say to Mike, repeating the words I hear from the front of the restaurant. "Probably making a call... Just check on him... Fine... Someone just got up from their chair." I keep my eyes on the door, gun gripped firmly in my hands. "Just one."

Mike appears next to me immediately, puts his hand on the top of my gun to lower it. He guides me to the door with his hand on my back and we stop there. "Footsteps," I say. "One set."

"When they stop at the outside door, squeeze my hand," he whispers.

I close my eyes. The footsteps move casually, come to a stop at the same time I hear the first slip of metal against metal as they turn the handle. I squeeze Mike's palm. I don't see him leave; I only feel the slight breeze against my face as he moves faster than I can blink.

I hear the exterior door shut and then a soft grunt. That's it. Then the certain sound of a body being dragged down the hall. I back up, gun out once more as I wait with bated breath, praying that Mike is the one that made it out of that scuffle. Sure enough, Mike appears, dragging with him the body of a third victim, a smaller black man dressed in, surprisingly, a priest's habit.

"You knocked out a priest, Mike?" I say with horror.

He looks up and grins at me, eyes wide with excitement, obviously enjoying himself. "I'm no respecter of religious zealots, Wen," he says. "Guy outside had a big old cross on a chain. I think this is some sort of religious group."

"It is. They believe the Guild is a legion of angels and the Human Movement is a legion of devils. They're doing God's work," scoffs Dumas' voice behind me, and I turn around, getting my first view of the room and the people in it. It's a kitchen, and it's occupied by five conscious people other than Mike and myself: Gabe Dumas, two women, and two men, all bound.

"Lovely to see you, Miss Whitley," Dumas says when my eyes fall on him, an enthusiastic smile spread across his expressively handsome face. It's weird to be this close to him. His hands are bound behind his back and he's sitting up straight on one of the stainless counters next to his staff, ankles crossed casually as if being kidnapped is an annoyance that's merely passing the time.

"I told you to stay quiet!" Mike hisses at him. "Are there only two more?" he asks me, stealing my attention.

"I'd say so," I reply as I close my eyes.

"The Guild has cleared out, I think they were making sure PHIA wasn't causing problems for THM," I say, repeating what I hear. "I wish they wouldn't do that... Wasting time and resources on that trash... Public sentiment's important. That's why we're here, to handle things in the shadows... Okay, well call Bernie. Tell him to keep scouting the area. No witnesses... Crap..." I open my eyes while lifting my weapon and hissing,

"Footsteps right—" But Mike isn't next to me. I spin in a circle, but he's not here.

"Wh—" I start, but Dumas chuckles at my confusion just as I realize what's going on. The footsteps I heard were Mike's. He went to take them head-on.

I consider following but change my mind, instead training my weapon on the door again and shaking my head. Mike makes knocking people out look stupidly easy. I actually hear an exclamation of surprise this time, a feminine one. Then a scuffle, a grunt, and the clatter of chairs followed by a crash. Another crash and the definite crack of someone's bone breaking. I wince at the sound. Finally, jogging steps and Mike's barely-winded face.

He doesn't pause, snagging a knife from a knife block.

"You first, Lelani," Dumas says to a quavering dark-haired woman with tear-stained cheeks next to him.

She hops down, but only when Dumas nods at her encouragingly does she turn for Mike to cut through her bonds.

Dumas, I notice, is looking at me curiously. He opens his mouth, but I ignore him by putting my back to him and digging my phone out of my pocket to dial Shiah.

She answers immediately again. "I would not be in the least bit surprised to hear that Wendy Whitley has accomplished her mission?" she says good-naturedly.

"Glad to hear you are done underestimating me."

"I have never underestimated you, Wendy," she says matter-of-factly.

Her words to me during the protest indicate otherwise, but it suddenly hits me what she's telling me. She was totally playing me... "You!" I say. "You set me up!"

"I have always believed in you, and I told you, I can size people up easily. I know your weaknesses. And weaknesses point the way to strength and ability."

"You... did that..." I say, my thoughts going back to less than an hour ago when I totally stole Dumas' audience from him. I can't articulate what I'm feeling all of a sudden at this most inopportune time... Capable. But it's more than that. I should have failed out there. Nineteen in spirit. Inexperienced. Emotional. Awkward. But I didn't. Shiah exerted the right pressure in the right way, and it allowed me to beat the odds.

I don't know how to thank her for bringing that out of me... But it expresses itself in the form of tears in my eyes.

"I've got Jerry bringing the car to the front of the Liberty Grill," Shiah says. "Five minutes."

I sniff and clear my throat to erase the evidence of crying before I turn around. "Tell him to look out for a guy skulking around. He's the only one Mike hasn't beat up."

"Are you and Mike hungry? Want me to have something picked up?"

"Oh my gosh, yes," I reply. "I'm famished. Burgers? Do they have In-N-Out this far east? I haven't had one since California."

"Consider it done," she says.

"Mike? Burger?" I say.

"Two," Mike says, working on Gabe's bonds now.

"Two burgers for Mike," I tell Shiah.

"You got it."

I hang up to find Dumas' staff staring at me with differing expressions of disbelief. The blonde woman, Rita, whom I've seen lead protests in other places without Dumas, is glaring at me suspiciously, as if *I* was the one holding them captive. Dumas himself seems annoyed, rubbing his wrists.

"Let's get the hell out of here," Mike says. He looks at his brother. "I don't think I've ever seen you shut up so well. Keep it up. You're coming and we'll drop you off wherever you want. I'm not leaving you here for those freaks. I don't want to have to come back."

I expect Dumas to retort, given his expression, but instead he throws his arms around his brother to embrace him. With my exceptional vision I can see his body tremble. It stirs something in me to see them together, Gabe so obviously affectionate toward Mike. It's pushing up tears again. I am *so* glad I insisted that Mike come back here.

Mike removes himself from the embrace when it becomes prolonged. Dumas' eyes are red now, and from where I stand I finally discern his extreme relief. At first I think it's from being rescued, but then he says, "I have been so worried about you, Mike."

"Let's go," Mike says gruffly, turning away and touching my back to urge me to the door.

I don't argue, knowing we need to get out of here quickly. Mike takes us out the back entrance. It's dark now, and we pass Jon, Mike's first victim, still passed out and bloody on the ground. Mike produces the keys from earlier and presses the panic button to set off the car's alarm before tossing the keys on the man's chest.

Jerry is waiting at the front as expected, and Mike opens the front passenger door for me first. I climb in and he shuts it before letting Dumas' staff divide up among the available seats and cargo area.

Once everyone is loaded up, Dumas says, "The police station."

I motion to Jerry and he pulls into the darkened street.

"Shut up," Mike says from behind me, and I think it's in response to Gabe, who was probably about to say something. "Nobody in this vehicle wants to hear a damn thing from you. But you *are* going to listen. For once in your life you're going to listen to me. It's only because of Miss Whitley that you're alive. I was going to leave your sorry ass to face the consequences of your own stupid decisions, but she's the one that insisted we turn around and make sure you lived to deliver nonsense to the masses another day. No protection detail, Gabe? What the hell kind of bullshit is that? You figured you could spout the shit you do in public and nobody was going to want your blood? I can't do this every week, Gabe. My responsibility is to Miss Whitley's protection, not yours, dumbass. Don't go out in public again without someone good having your back. You have people working for you that rely on you. You have a duty to protect them from the hell that's going to be raining down on you."

I hear a sigh, Dumas' I think. In the silence of the vehicle a lot of drastically different emotions are whirling around. They are all so strong—which is understandable considering what just happened. I so wish I could pick up just Gabe Dumas', but I don't know him well enough to isolate them from the roar. I can pick Mike out, though, and he's enraged.

"You have my heartfelt apology," Dumas says in his notable cadence. "All of you. Rita, Soren, Lelani, and Garrett. What I allowed to happen this evening was solely my own fault. It was irresponsible. And I apologize to you, Mike. And you as well, Miss Whitley. I agree with you wholeheartedly and will ensure that my people and I are adequately protected from now on. I thank you as well for coming to my rescue. You put yourself in unnecessary danger and I appreciate that."

"You're welcome," I say, although I hear the question in my tone. I'm surprised at the depth of his humility. That sounded honest...

"Miss Whitley, might I ask you a question?" Gabe says.

"No," Mike says. "You can keep your overactive trap shut until we drop you at the curb."

"Gabe Dumas, if you have a question for me, you can feel free to ask me on any social media platform or at any public event," I say and it tastes like perjury on my tongue. "I have nothing to say to you personally," I finish, relieved to have the ugly words out of the way. I hope I never have to say them again.

"Very well," he says, his voice discomfitted. I latch on to it, searching for his matching emotion in the car so I can isolate him. "If I'm not permitted to ask questions, I will at least leave you with my approbation. Your remarks today have had me in contemplation since—part of why I failed to adequately observe my surroundings. Thank you for always forcing me to analyze myself."

I don't reply, determined to stick by my promise to the Council that I would not interact with Gabe Dumas outside of the public eye. But I have questions for him as well, so it's incredibly hard. I bite the inside of my cheek and let go of chasing down Dumas' emotional rhythm. I let my aggravation join the chorus of everyone else's in the car until we pull up to the lights of the police station.

Mike hops out to open the back, and suddenly the implications of tonight's events occur to me.

"Mister Dumas, may I ask a favor?" I say when I hear him open his door.

"As long as it's in my power and it does not violate my convictions, I will gladly grant any favor you ask," he says eagerly.

I think I've pinpointed his emotions. His anticipation is so over the top at my asking him for something that I wonder if it's actually real. I guess he feels so indebted to me for saving him that the possibility of evening the score is incredibly appealing.

"Do not mention what happened tonight in public," I say. "I'm not interested in being seen as your rescuer. I am also not interested in Mike losing his job as my protection—which may likely happen if the Council finds out what transpired. There is no one I trust more than Mike to do this job for me. So if you have any remorse for putting me and everyone else in danger, you can make it up by doing your part to make sure he keeps his position. I'd appreciate if you'd keep the night's events in confidence."

He sighs again, his disappointment obvious as it sinks down into my stomach like a weight. What was he was hoping for? Gosh, I wish I could ask him…

"You have my word, I will not bring it up publicly," he says, and without an ounce of doubt I believe him. He doesn't even consider the possibility of breaching his promise. It's a non-issue, and though he was clearly disappointed with the favor I asked, he is still thrilled to be able to give me something.

"Should a time come when I am asked something and the answer would require referencing this evening, however, I cannot lie," he adds solemnly. "It is against my principles."

"Fair enough," I say, marveling all the more at his mental clarity.

He gets out, shuts the door. His emotional flavor leaves with him, and the loss is almost tangible. He's a powerful presence, I realize. If he weren't meek and shaken over the night's events, what would he feel like then?

"Gabe," I hear Mike say from outside the car. I can see him in my sideview mirror though, standing a few feet away from his brother. "Please don't do this to me again."

"I'm sorry," Gabe blurts, desperation in his voice. "I abandoned you that day. Forced you to leave. I know you were afraid of me, and I... *I* was afraid of me..." A sob escapes his throat and from here I can see his jaw trembling.

Mike takes a step back.

Gabe notices. "Can you call me?" he asks, recognizing that his time with Mike is spent. "I can give you my number." He reaches into a coat pocket. The anxious lines on his face bring tears to my eyes for the third time today. "I need to talk to you about—"

"No," Mike interrupts. "You chose one thing and I chose another. This is as important to me as your cause is to you. You need to respect that." And then he goes around to the driver's side.

"I might have chosen a different side but it never required disowning my family," Gabe says after him, pain coloring his tone.

Mike ignores him as he opens the rear door.

"This is why I fight them, Mike. What's happening right now isn't right," Gabe says as Mike gets in. "You're all I have left now, but I've lost you after all."

Mike stops with his hand on the door. "That's *your* choice." He pulls his door shut. "Let's go," he says, tapping the back of Jerry's seat.

Jerry pulls into the street, headed for the airport. My heart is breaking though. At first I think it's Mike's emotions, but a large portion of the sadness is my own—for Mike. Dumas is correct: this isn't right. But it's necessary, and Dumas just proved that. He clearly has an overly idealistic perception of the world, and it nearly got him and his staff killed. It's the same ideal he's been demanding the Guild embrace, but it took the Guild to save Gabe Dumas from himself. The irony of what just happened is unreal. I hope Dumas is smart enough to recognize it. I also hope he recognizes that the strife between him and Mike is his own doing.

Gabe Dumas doesn't seem to consider consequences much. He blindly follows his convictions without considering how they will impact others. His lack of consideration is infuriating. I swear if he puts Mike under the stress of something like this ever again I'm going to make him pay. In the meantime I think I'll just bury him in public. If I can make his cause go away, then it will be better for everyone, Dumas included.

Thirty-One

knock lightly on the door adjoining my hotel room to Mike's. It's early, but I haven't been able to go back to sleep, my head spinning through the questions I've been reserving for Mike. We arrived in Chicago late last night and everyone else crashed. I have three Prime Human interviews this morning, and growing. After my performance in Salt Lake, Shiah has been inundated with volunteers.

But I need to talk to Mike before the day gets too busy.

His door opens almost immediately, and his shirtless body is in front of me. "Are you alright?" he says, scanning the room over my shoulder.

"Yeah. I'm good," I say, having trouble tearing my eyes away from his chiseled chest. I catch sight of a large scar on his abdomen. "I need to talk to you."

"Oh," he says, uncertain.

"My place or yours?" I smile.

"Yours is bigger," he says.

I move out of the way so he can come in.

He hesitates. "Let me get a shirt," he says, sniggering, and I realize I'm looking at his body again. He doesn't wait for me to answer, but turns into his room while I back toward the couch to get a final look. Gosh, he's a specimen. I take up a cross-legged position at the end of the sofa, contemplating as I have many times since taking him on as my body guard, what it might be like to have something more. I like him more all the time.

Mike reappears with a white undershirt on, but rather than the couch, he makes a beeline for the coffee maker.

"How did you know Gabe was in trouble?" I ask his back, seeing no point in beating around the bush.

He fills the pot in the sink and dumps it into the machine before replying, "Because I sensed it. I have a connection to him that strengthens when we're close. I can feel what he feels then. I felt his fear and recognized what it meant." He turns around, leans against the counter, and looks at me, expecting more questions.

My brow is furrowed. "How? You're not even biological brothers. Just cousins, right?"

"Yes. And I don't know. I think it must have something to do with my ability and the fact that until recently, we'd always been close. But it's always been there. Ever since we were kids. When we're far apart it fades into a vague perception. I can locate Gabe no matter where I am though. I know his direction from me at all times. That's how I found him so easily at the park."

I put my chin in my hand. "So weird... How are two people so close but end up having totally different ideals?"

"Probably because we're totally different people. Sometimes I wonder, if I wasn't cursed to endure his emotions, and if we hadn't been related and basically thrown into the same family, would we have been friends?"

"Does asking that make any difference?"

"No, but sometimes he behaves so... backward, and it seriously frustrates me. I basically have him with me all the time in a lot of ways, but I still don't *get* him, you know?"

"Yeah. But you care about him, a lot. I could see it and feel it when you were together."

His face turns pensive. "I do. But I'm tired of caring about him being compulsory."

I'm not entirely sure what that means, and even though he's too far away for me to read, I can tell it's a vulnerable statement.

The smell of freshly-brewed coffee fills the air after a while, and he says, "Other than Gabe, I've never told anyone all that I just told you. If you could... keep it in confidence..."

"Of course," I say quietly, my heart reaching across the space between us.

"If people knew that I..." Mike shakes his head. "PHIA, THM... I have direct connections to both."

"You'd have the scarlet letter, even more than you already do," I say.

He nods. "Thank you, though. For making sure he was safe. Fact is I care about Gabe, and that's obviously not going to change.

I don't want to think of what it would have been like to lose him. And you made the whole thing easy. Your skills in reconnaissance are a serious asset. If you ever get out of... the PR business, and you aren't the most sought-after talent in the world, you should do spy work." He grins.

"You're allowed to care about him," I say, bothered that Mike sounds like he'd stop caring about Gabe if he could. "He's your brother. Just because you don't agree doesn't mean you shouldn't mean something to each other. And I *do* know what it would have been like for you to lose him."

He catches on to my tone immediately. "No, I know. That's not what I meant. It's a struggle for me to be connected to him in a lot of ways, even without him being the founder of THM."

"Oh..." I say, not having considered things beyond the current situation, probably because I take it for granted. I'm connected to everyone around me because I'm an empath. So if anyone understands what it's like, I do. Has he forgotten that? "So, this connection, does it go both ways?"

"No."

"Hmm. Okay. So are *you* alright?"

"With what?"

I roll my eyes. "Mike, you know what I mean."

"I'm fine."

I purse my lips. "I hate that he's upset you so much."

Mike shrugs, turns back to the coffee maker. "I knew what I was getting into with this job."

He's deflecting me now. "So is it just you and Gabe?" I ask.

Mike tosses an empty sugar packet in the trash. "Just us," he says, punctuating the words, his cue that he's not saying anything more about it.

I have to restrain myself from my instinct, which is to get up and make a direct come on. When I'm trying to be close to someone and they hold back, it brings out the worst in me.

I exhale heavily, fighting the itch. It would be a lot easier to let go if I weren't so attracted to Mike. And considering how strong the urge is, I'm now certain my attraction is a lot more than a passing crush. Of course, I did stay up a lot of the night thinking about how well we work together. I had the time of my life with him, saving his brother. I love having him near and not just for protection.

Mike seems intent on staying by the coffee maker, and now that his back is toward me, cutting me completely off from what he may be thinking, I can't take it anymore.

I stand up and walk over to him, finding his emotions predictably in full retreat from attraction. I lean against the counter and find his face. "Mike," I say, "why are you hiding by the coffee maker?" I know the answer of course, but I want to know if he'll own up to it.

His hands are wrapped around the mug, which he raises to his mouth for a prolonged period of time.

Watching him is torturous, because now that I'm even closer to him, and the chemistry between us is clear and present, my feelings for him are putting pressure on my chest. I want to touch him, his arm, his face, something. But I ball my hands into fists instead, longing turning to irritation.

"Don't you already know the answer to that?" he says finally.

It's my turn to stare, and my heart retreats, bit by bit. "I didn't ask the question to find out the answer," I say. "I asked to hear you answer it."

"That doesn't make any sense."

I puff impatiently. More deflection. I cross my arms and head back over to the couch. "You can stand over by the coffee maker to avoid me reading you all you want, Mike. Eventually you have to stand at my shoulder again."

He turns around entirely, putting his back to me. "What part of platonic don't you get?"

"What part of me being an empath don't *you* get?" I plop down on the couch. "You can't hide. Trying only makes me mad."

"I'm not trying. I'm just not acting on it."

I roll my eyes and shoot eye daggers at his back. "Again, empath. You don't get to feel things without me feeling it, too. Pretending I don't feel them doesn't actually work for me, so you don't get to delude yourself into pretending either. This is supposed to be a trust relationship, right? That requires honesty last I checked."

"What's the point of telling you how I feel if I'm not going to act on it? It will make for either awkward situations or too much temptation."

"Hey, you wanna keep having conversations like this with me, keep hiding. That's all I'm saying. I've been doing this empath thing for a while and deflection pisses me off."

He sighs heavily, hanging his head. "Wen, you're not being fair. You're asking me to compromise myself, and I'm just trying to do my job, which is to keep you safe."

"I'm not asking for anything but honesty."

He remains silent.

I grind my teeth. I'm clearly not getting anywhere with him today.

"Why don't you live at the Vault?" I ask, propping my feet on the coffee table. I've got to get my head elsewhere. The truth is I respect Mike, even if he infuriates me. I do want something with him, but I don't want to twist it out of him. I don't want to begin a relationship on the basis of manipulation. I don't have a lot of experience with that, so I'm going with my gut here that says I've taken the conversation as far as it can comfortably be taken for now.

He faces me once more holding the mug in both hands in front of him like a shield. "Because I don't want to."

I struggle to keep the aggravation over his curt answer out of my voice when I reply, "Why don't you want to?" I swear I need to stop analyzing his every move as an emotional bulwark. I'm going to drive myself crazy.

"Too many people I know," he replies.

"Why is that a problem?"

He leans against the counter and crosses his ankles. "Think about it."

"Is it because of your connection to Andre?"

He lifts an eyebrow.

"They think you're secretly on PHIA's payroll or something? PHIA cooties? PHIA spy? Seriously?"

He takes a careful sip of his coffee.

"If you'd spend enough time there they'd get used to it and stop thinking dumb things like that," I say. "If you hide it makes you look guilty."

"Maybe. But I'd rather avoid it so I don't have to deal with it at all. Besides, I've never lived at a Guild facility. I like having a little more freedom."

"I like freedom. That's why I decided to start crashing Human Movement events."

"I believe that. Good thing you're so good at it so you can keep jumping ship on the weekends."

"Yeah, hopefully Shiah and the Council can stop being afraid I'm going to say something over the top that brings the whole Guild crashing down."

Mike laughs. "Shiah is *not* afraid of what you'll do. She has your number. You didn't see her while you were speaking. Hands in front of her mouth trying to shield the most enormous smile you've ever seen on her face. And she was crying. *Crying.* Wen, I've known Shiah a long time, and she almost never cries."

"Yeah..." I say. "I realized what she did after the fact."

"Shiah..." Mike says, shaking his head. "She knows what to say and do to get people performing at their best. For you, that was telling you that you couldn't do it. You hate when people tell you that. You get all crazy-eyed and scary." He sets his coffee down, puts his hands on his hips. "*Go to hell, Shiah! I'm going out there and kicking Gabe Dumas' ass!*" he mocks in a high-pitched voice. Then he turns to the side as if talking to a completely different person. "*Mike, eff your job of protecting me from crazy people. You take me to the den of the crazies to rescue your backward-ass brother or I'm firing you!*"

I laugh at his performance, but I'm thinking about Shiah again. I'm the one that underestimates *her*. I've got to stop that.

"While Shiah may not be afraid of what you'll say, I do agree that the Council is," Mike says.

"Really? Why do *you* think so?"

"You're too popular, too fast."

"I didn't know that could be a problem."

"If you continue on this track, becoming the most beloved Prime Human both inside and outside the Guild, it will give you a lot of power. Primes have been looking to the Council as figureheads for years. They're like a bunch of pious monks to everyone in the Guild. But now there's you. And piety is *not* your MO. You are far more interesting and relatable. Plus, you're the gateway to the energy world. Passionate personality *and* the basis of their veritable religion? Primes are watching you even more than humans are. You locked yourself in from day one, and the Council couldn't get rid of you even if they wanted to. You're gaining so much favor among Primes that it's going to make the Council obsolete. Pretty sure the Council is terrified of your status getting to the point where it could too easily tear the Guild they've built apart."

I suppose he's right about that. But if they're upset about giving me too much power, they only have themselves to blame. It could have been more than just me, but they refused to let me be more than a one-woman show.

"The Guild has to change if it's going to survive in the open," I say. "Or it's going to be torn apart with or without my help."

Mike leans casually against the counter again, taking his coffee in-hand once more. He chuckles, remembering, and it fades into a thoughtful look as something occurs to him that he doesn't share. If this keeps up, I may end up changing my mind about Mike.

"Well anyway, now that I've learned her secret weapon to keep me in line, what's she going to do at Dumas' next event?" I say. "He's probably going to accuse me of killing kittens or something, and when Shiah tells me I can't keep my cool over his kitten-killer accusations, I'm not going to fall for her manipulation." I throw my hands up. "I'm ruined now."

"No, *Gabe* is," Mike says. "You felt him, didn't you?"

"Not really. That car was swimming in emotion. Like a cesspool. I tried to. But I don't know his mind well enough. The most I got was that he was majorly frustrated. Why do you say he's ruined? You think he'll give up now?"

His eyebrows lift. He takes a sip, ruffling my impatience. "Give up? No. But Gabe is totally addled. Not only did you make one kickass argument that connected with his own following, but then he required the Guild's help to survive, which basically invalidated his entire transparency and openness argument. I'm not saying he's going to throw in the towel, but his ego took a major hit. He has both times you've spoken. You challenge him. You push him. He's going to become obsessed with what comes out of your mouth. Obsession is always Gabe's undoing."

"He sounds like a head case," I say. "But even if he wasn't, he's a lot less scary than you and Shiah have made him seem. All that talk about not taking him on in an argument, that he's smarter, quicker. He's smart, but his ideas are flawed. No matter how brilliant you are, if your argument doesn't hold water, you're done."

Mike stares into his coffee, thinking about something that I desperately wish he'd share.

Shiah bursts through my front door at that moment wearing a black silk nightgown. "TV," she orders. "He's on." She notices Mike, and her eyes move suspiciously from him to me.

I reach for the remote on the coffee table.

"Thirty-two," she says once I turn the TV on.

'—the ethics of your proposal. How much progress can we reasonably expect from the Guild if they can no longer ensure their members' safety. Your response?' the interviewer asks.

Gabe Dumas runs a hand down his face, which is more exhausted than I've ever seen it. No doubt he had a late night at the police station filing a report. There's no telling how much sleep he eked out. 'How did I get this interview?' he asks.

'Excuse me?' the woman asks.

'This television spot. This is the morning news, right? How did I manage to garner your network's interest to hear me speak about issues I've addressed repeatedly at my events?'

'Um, Mister Dumas, are you hedging the question?'

'No. I've addressed it before, and I hate repeating myself. What I would like to know is why it is Miss Whitley from the Guild—the heroes everyone loves so much—never appears in front of a camera except for my events. If I can gain media coverage so relatively easily, I am positive they can as well. They simply choose not to. Their absolute obsession with inaccessibility is tiring.'

'Mister Dumas, are you declining comment?'

'You know what I think?' Dumas says, sitting back in his chair, preoccupied with his own thoughts. 'They are behind my continual media coverage. I'm given free access to it because whenever I get in front of you media people I lose my cool and make a scene.'

He glances at the now-silent interviewer who wears a sullen expression that says, 'Like now?'

'Let's talk facts. I have what, maybe half a million supporters if I'm lucky?' Dumas says, speaking more quickly. 'Those are not numbers that garner exclusive television interviews on a weekly basis. I'm the opposition, and there is obviously power the Guild wields in having one. It gives them credibility and legitimacy. It rallies their supporters, puts them up in arms to watch me get attention. They watch me yell and make accusations and they get upset. They mobilize. The Guild, meanwhile, keeps themselves entirely apart from it all, above it, letting you media people do your magic to rile the masses. I think I will take a page out of Miss Whitley's book. I'll do interviews when she does.' He stands up and walks off the set, leaving a slack-jawed interviewer, but only for a moment because the surprised news anchors take the camera instead.

I mute it and turn to Shiah in shock. As usual, she's unruffled, maybe even a little satisfied.

"He's right, isn't he?" I say, reading her emotions clearly for once.

She looks at me and can't help smiling.

My jaw drops. "You! You're the mole! All along, you're the reason THM is as big as it is! It was a strategy! You're something else, Shiah Lim," I say. "Who else would think to put their rival in front of the world rather than stifling their voice? How do you think of these things?"

"I am unafraid of failure, unlike most, because I know it's temporary and eliminates incorrect paths," she explains. "If Dumas is truly on the side of right, he deserves the chance to speak, does he not? If he's on the side of wrong, his words will fall on deaf ears. He will negate himself. Truth will have the final say. Why then should I fear his voice? I don't fear truth. I fear it never having a chance to be recognized because we have never entertained the opposite. Dumas will cement our cause, one interview, one event at a time."

I stare at her, floored by her wisdom. It's counterintuitive. It's fearless. It's beautiful. It's… faith that right will prevail.

"Shiah…" I say, struggling for the precise words to express my awe.

"Classy," Mike says.

"He figured it out *much* faster than I thought however…" Shiah mumbles, staring at the screen in contemplation and tapping her chin, just as she did the last time Dumas did something she didn't expect. "I am impressed, to say the least."

"Who cares," I say. "You are incredible. It's a privilege to work with you."

"Thank you," she says, taking a seat at the other end of the couch. "And now we strategize, because Gabe Dumas, as usual, keeps up with us."

"Strategize?" I say. "You said he'll negate himself."

"Eventually. If we want to move this along, he's going to continue to require your help getting there."

"Me?" I say.

"I told you, Wen," Mike says. "Addled. Obsession. Undoing. '*I'll do interviews when she does.*' That's the start of the obsession."

Shiah nods appreciatively at Mike. "How do you feel about being interviewed?" she says to me.

"Fine, I guess. But isn't it going to be immediately obvious that I've started doing them because he wants me to? And he's going to realize that he was right? That you've set him up?"

"Of course. But it will force him to decide whether he will continue taking our favors for the sake of airtime, or whether he'll decline airtime out of principle. He's going to be put in a difficult position. An uncertain Gabe Dumas is one we can handle."

"He's going to do exactly what he just promised," Mike says. "Do interviews when Wendy does. He's not going to back out of that commitment no matter what."

"Okay…" I say, uncertain.

"Perfect. In the meantime, we've postponed the interviews today. PHIA attacked one of our labs here in Chicago. Burned it to the ground. Nobody was hurt, but wherever they leave their symbol, panic ensues. We'll be flying out in a few hours."

"Uuugh, really?" I say, still bothered about Dumas and suddenly wishing I could be alone so I can sort out why. "I swear I'm going to bring Andre down."

"You likely will not find time to do that," Shiah says. "Because you have two interviews in Roanoke, Virginia."

I rake my hands down my face, unable to hide my lack of enthusiasm. "Is there a gym in this hotel? I need to go for a run before we load out."

"Downstairs," Shiah says, standing. "I have a call to make, but be ready to go at noon."

Mike guzzles the rest of his coffee, and jogs into his room, obviously to get ready to tail me.

I hop up and dig through my suitcase for my running gear. I pull it on quickly in the bathroom and splash water on my face. When I come out, Mike is ready.

We head silently downstairs, and when we reach the gym I head for the nearest treadmill. Mike takes the one next to me.

"Mike, can you go lift some weights or something? I need you out of my range. I need my own head for a bit."

"Sure," he says, and I can feel his accompanying concern as he steps down. He watches me as he heads for the other end of the small gym.

I press a button and begin an easy pace. My head is so noisy, the kind of noisy I've felt whenever the things going on don't agree with my conscience. Amid the noise, I keep hearing Gabe Dumas say, 'I'm the opposition.' I picture the look on his face as he recognized what that meant, that he'd been used to create his own downfall. The Guild used him to rally support. And they did. That support almost killed Dumas last night.

And that bothers me. I don't want Dumas dead, clearly. I don't want his opposition though. But Shiah does, I've learned. Shiah's strategy is brilliant, and her faith in truth is admirable, but the fallout bugs me.

Why though? Is Dumas in the wrong or not?

I wrinkle my nose. He's wrong. So that's not it. When Dumas revealed that he respected me, it irked me that I might somehow owe my success as a public relations agent to him. But Shiah and Mike told me it was immature to reject support, even if it came from the opposition. I get that now. But this... making Dumas look a fool upsets me for other reasons... reasons I can't figure out.

Maybe... maybe it's because Dumas himself is not the deplorable human being I imagined. He's principled. He's convicted. Honestly. How can I fault him for that when being principled and convicted is something I've fought for since I joined the Guild? For that alone I would respect him. But there's something else... He intrigues me. I want to figure him out. I have never in my life wanted to read someone's emotions as badly as I do Gabe Dumas'. I think because he's such an odd duck. He functions differently than most. I want to know what moves him, beneath it all.

I press the button to accelerate and catch Mike out of the corner of my eye, lifting a bar of weights over his head and then back to knee-level. My heart flutters with more than exertion. And then there's Mike. I don't think it's loneliness making me want him. Since I outed myself in St. Louis, I've become more of a celebrity within the Guild than without—just as Mike pointed out. I was asked out at least half a dozen times in the week prior to Salt Lake. I haven't had a romantic relationship since before my mom died—at least as far as my memory tells me—because I was breaking myself of bad habits, not to mention I kept so busy with school and work. But now... I feel ready. Apparently Mike is not.

So I run out my disappointment with him and the unsettling situation with his brother. For an hour I run until my legs are threatening collapse, until I let go of aggravation because I can't focus on anything but the exhaustion. I slow to a stumbling walk, take the towel from Mike, who has suddenly appeared next to me again, and wipe the sweat dripping from my face.

I step off of the treadmill and nearly fall from the weakness in my legs, but Mike catches me.

"Sorry," I say, finding my feet. But Mike doesn't let me go, the heaviness of his intention in my chest weakening my legs again, but for a different reason.

I look into his face. His eyes are on my mouth, but he glances up when he feels me looking at him. He has one hand behind my back, and he brings the other up to touch my face. He touches my cheek, then my lips, breathing heavily.

I can't speak; my mouth has gone dry. My heart is banging the inside of my chest so hard it might knock me over. I'm drawn to him by an inexplicable magnetism.

Mike battles uncertainty, but my own nearly overwhelming need for his lips on mine is much louder in my head. It takes everything in me to resist. I don't want his regret later, and with that I resign myself to the disappointment. "If you aren't sure, you should let me go now," I whisper. I can't open my eyes. If I look into his face, I may not be able to fight the urge to lean in closer.

His response is immediate. He lets go of me while simultaneously moving my hand up to the treadmill bar in case my legs are still questionable.

When I open my eyes, he's across the room. He starts pulling weights off a bar and putting them away.

I let myself sink down onto the floor where I finish dredging the sweat from my skin, trying not to breathe too heavily because his smell is mixed with my own now…

"And that's why it's a good thing he doesn't live at the Vault," I mumble to myself. Clearly, Mike and I can't be around each other for more than twelve hours or we start giving into the attraction that's been present since the day we met.

I stand up once Mike puts the last weight away. I pour myself a cup of water from the cooler and down it in a few gulps. Mike is behind me when I reach the door.

"I really expected to spend a lot more time preventing people from killing you," Mike says as we wait for the elevator. "I can't handle all this idle downtime."

I chuckle. "Where's PHIA when you really need them?"

"Andre was never good with timing. He's emotion-driven. Spontaneous. I swear the guy came up with the majority of his plans on the fly."

"Really?" I say, turning to face him. "If that's true, why hasn't he been caught already?"

Mike has a wide stance, hands clasped behind his back, looking militant. "I'm not the guy in charge of that. I'm barely allowed to think about Andre, let alone come up with a plan to capture him."

I turn back around as the doors open. "I'm not allowed to either. But maybe you and I should come up with one anyway. I know someone who would be all over the implementation."

"That so?" Mike says as the doors close.

"Lainey Flynn. She's on the PHIA recovery team? Says she's tried to question you about Andre before…"

Mike grunts. "Yeah, I remember."

I wait for him to continue, trying to give him the opportunity to broach the topic, but he doesn't.

The ass.

"Are you opposed to coming up with something to track Andre down?" I say as the doors open to our floor. "We need to do *something* with our downtime. If we don't we might as well throw in the towel and make out in the elevator right now. It's inevitable."

Aaaand there I go… Saying things I know I shouldn't. Why does he have to be so distant and make me come at his shell with a sledge hammer?

Mike steps out, looks right, left, and then motions me to follow. "I guess I have no choice. It's either come up with a plan to capture Andre, or make out with you in the elevator…" He makes a face. "I'm so torn."

I laugh and head down the hall. "Go think about it in the shower. We'll reconvene when we're on the plane."

"Thinking about you in the shower is *not* a good plan, Wen."

I reach my door and turn around. "Oops," I say. "I totally didn't mean to suggest that. I meant, you know, a shower is a good place to weigh decisions."

He rolls his eyes. "Sure you did." He swipes a key card in the door. He reaches behind me to open it and then nudges me through, shutting the door between us.

I turn toward the room, a smile still on my face, and find Shiah staring at me. "That is not a good idea, Wendy," she scolds.

She holds out a mug of steaming tea to me.

I don't ask how she knows about Mike and me; the woman knows everything. I take the mug and frown at her. "Don't worry. He's not so sure either. You can tell me later what the problem is. Right now I'm covered in sweat."

"I don't need long," Shiah says, following right behind me as I snatch new clothes out of my suitcase. "It's a bad idea because Gabe Dumas is going to fall for you at the end of all this, and that's going to convince him to join the Guild. We need him."

I stop and turn. She has shocked me for the second time today, but this time I cannot believe what I'm hearing. Literally. Surely when she says, 'fall for you' she means something other than the common meaning of the phrase.

"Shiah," I say, setting my mug down and crossing my arms. "Please tell me you did not just say I'm a... a Guild prostitute."

"I did not tell you you're a Guild prostitute," she says flatly. "I told you Gabe Dumas is going to fall in love with you. So hard that he will follow you anywhere, even into Guild membership. He is an extremely valuable asset. If you are already taken by his brother, he's not going to be inclined to come anywhere near you. Unrequited love is not something that motivates people. Date *anyone* else. No one else will daunt him. Except Mike."

I rub my hand over my short hair, grimacing because sometimes Shiah says the weirdest things like they are totally normal. "Shiah, let me be *really* clear with you right now and set some of your bizarre android instincts straight. If by some iota of chance you're right, and Gabe Dumas thinks I'm the love of his life one day, I have zero interest or conviction in using his heart—or anyone else's—against them. I don't do that. And no one, not even God Almighty, will convince me to. I will date whomever I want and it has nothing to do with my mission to promote the Guild. If you want Gabe Dumas to join the Guild, find another offer he can't refuse, one that doesn't involve manipulating his feelings."

"You misunderstand me," Shiah says. "It's not going to take trying on my part or yours, therefore it's not manipulation."

"Oh no. I understand you perfectly. *You* are the one that doesn't understand. If you tell me to not date Mike because I need to make Gabe think he's got a chance in hell, that's one hundred percent manipulation."

She just smiles in that knowing way that can sometimes bug the junk out of me. "You win," she says. "I'll let it go. But

I'm telling you up front: getting involved with Mike Dumas is a mistake. Do with that what you will. Now go drink your tea. You need it."

"Whatever," I say, so done with this weird conversation. I snag my mug and turn on my heel for the bathroom, desperate to get away from Shiah and her strange motives that make me uncomfortable at every turn. She's elevating Dumas so he'll fall harder and faster… And now she's hoping he'll fall in love with me so she can recruit him? I shiver with disgust in the bathroom. Shiah is equal parts brilliant and totally out of touch.

Thirty-Two

I dig my phone out of my backpack and look at the screen.

Game night tonight? My place. I promise to keep my mind to myself. I'll make cookies…

The text is from Chase.

I smile and text back: EWR is expecting me. I have to work until 9.

My phone dings again. On a Saturday? Suuuuuck. his reply reads.

Duty calls, I type. Then I pause and sigh. I don't actually want to go play games. I don't want to go to work at the EWR either. But I haven't seen Chase much, and if I don't see him now it will be another week before there will even be a possibility…

I can come after? I hit send.

He texts: Good plan.

I toss the phone back and rub my face. I want to go back to my apartment and sleep off the jet lag and replenish the membrane that usually protects my mind from being too heavily bombarded by the emotions of those around me. I feel raw and vulnerable with it so thin; I am in serious need of some alone time.

I lay my cheek against the glass of the car window to absorb the warmth of the sun, hoping it will inject me with some of its energy. We're nearly to the Vault, and this will be my only break. I get to clock in at EWR and then put in quality time with my dyad. Tomorrow, I'm back at the EWR. Then my weekly Colloquy. The day after that I'm back on the plane, headed for Raleigh, North Carolina where The Human Movement has their next big event not even a week after Salt Lake. Shiah has been exclaiming over the location ever since it was announced yesterday on THM's website. Apparently Dumas has surprised her yet again. Since the mass evacuation from the Caribbean,

Raleigh is probably more dangerous than southern California. Although Shiah has insisted that the danger can be managed with adequate preparation—which she has had her head buried in since then.

Two days after that, I have my first spot as an interviewee. Shiah went all out. Her intention is to flaunt the Guild's connections and influence in the most ostentatious way possible. She has me scheduled to be on Good Morning America. With a move like that, her message to Gabe Dumas seems pretty clear to me: 'Sure, we got you on TV. We can get on TV, too. As much as we want. With whoever we want. We *own* television. We own *you.*'

I roll my eyes just thinking about it.

"The pace is only going to continue to increase," Shiah says, typing something on her GIT. She tucks a stray lock of black hair behind her ear. She's doing that mind-reading prediction thing again. She told me about the interview an hour ago, but somehow she knew my head was back on it.

I give her a dirty look.

The corner of her mouth perks up, but she maintains focus on her device. "By the way," she says. "Jonas is going to ask you out tonight at work."

I don't reply at first, analyzing the possible reasons for her telling me that. "Dare I ask how you know that?" I say dryly.

"Analyzing behavior patterns."

"Really. What kind of patterns could you have possibly observed considering Jonas works in the EWR department at the Vault and I haven't even been back there in five days?"

"You told me he emailed you. Twice. Asking when you'd be back."

"The EWR department basically revolves around me and the stuff I tell them about the energy world. So it's natural they'd want to know when I'd be back," I say.

"They know what day to expect you back *at work*. They are kept up to date on that schedule. Jonas asked when you would be back in general."

I roll my eyes. "Whatever, Shiah. I'm not interested. So if this is your attempt to play matchmaker to get my head off of Mike, you should let it go."

"This is my attempt to prepare you for his approach ahead of time so you can think about how to let him down gently," she says. "You're tired and worn down and you're frustrated about Mike. You're itching for someone to take it out on. I know exactly how it will go on the spot if you don't think about it now, and you need to preserve your work relationships."

I turn back to the window, my indifference turning into outright belligerence. I am so over Shiah's constant preempting. "Do you think you can maybe *not* be so helpful all the time?" I say acerbically.

That surprises her and she thinks about it for a moment. When she can't figure it out, she asks, "Why?"

"Sometimes you have to let people screw up. It's good for them," I say, closing my eyes against the sun once more.

My answer jars her. I have no idea why. And I don't care. I'm in a mood and I'd like to just wallow in it for a while. Maybe I'm not actually tired. Maybe I'm still unhappy with the status quo. Maybe I'm still bugged about making a fool out of Gabe Dumas. Or maybe it's Mike.

Maybe all of the above.

ℕ

"Do you have plans later tonight?" Jonas asks from across the room.

I've learned how to see the normal world at will while I'm still in the energy world by letting my eyes blur. And I do so now in order to look at Jonas. He's bent over his note-taking at the desk. From here I can see him writing down what I told him: how life forces, which appear to be composed of strands, move in a clockwise direction around the chest swirl. I've been trying to figure out what it looks like beneath the strands, like how they might attach to the body beneath, but I can't control them well enough. They slip out of my fingers whenever I attempt to part them.

"I'm going over to Chase's for a game night," I reply, moving past the irritation that Shiah was right, because instead I'm annoyed that Jonas asked the question from outside of my range. It was purposeful. Normally, if someone were going to ask me out—such as the guy that has been running at the same time as me in the morning whenever I'm here—I would feel it for a while

before they actually got up the courage to ask. Jonas, it seems, being aware of this, has been careful to keep his distance, as if I wouldn't notice, as if I'm too dense to know he did it in order to avoid being vulnerable to me when he asked.

"Chase?" Jonas says, not pausing in his writing.

Oh my gosh. How does he not know my dyad's name? I've introduced them.

"Oh wait. He is that skinny boy?"

I bite the inside of my cheek, trying really hard not to read into his statement. What's he trying to say? Is he trying to insult Chase? Is this a language-culture mixup and I should not take it personally? Jonas may mix up the order of words in a sentence sometimes, since English is his second language, but his meaning has never been confused before...

"I would not have thought you went for the boyish ones," Jonas says.

I am floored. Who the hell does he think he is?

"I'm only saying this because you're my friend, so please don't be offended, but don't you think it would be better if you associate yourself with a more mature crowd? Because you are a public figure now, you have to represent us with strength, and people will unfortunately see your youth first."

Every bit of restraint leaves me then. This guy doesn't know who he's messing with. "Oh..." I say. "I hadn't thought of that... Sometimes my youth gets the best of me!" I laugh demurely. "I was only going because Chase is my dyad. I'm trying to be supportive. It's tough, you know? Being paired with someone who's still a teenager." I look over my shoulder at Jonas who is busy trying to look occupied with his clipboard.

"Oh... He's a nice kid," Jonas says. "But I have a duty to look out for you. In EWR we have a reputation. You know this. It is not easy to be seen as shaman. We have to stick together."

Is that so? He's *such* a prince. "That is *so* sweet, Jonas," I say. Sarcasm leaks out in my tone despite my effort to restrain it. I'm shocked that Jonas doesn't pick up on it.

"It is my pleasure," he replies.

For the remaining ten minutes of my shift, I have different conversations with Jonas in my head, deciding which tactic to use, because I'm not spending the rest of my career in EWR circumventing Jonas' egoism.

I simultaneously weave my hands through Dawn's life force to see if I can get it moving in a different direction. I've learned that I can't be too rough with them or the usual musical sound becomes a discordant, fingernail-scratching cacophony that sounds anything but healthy. That's my cue to stop. I've already been told about the dangers of hypno-touch—the top-secret life force manipulation that creates superhuman powers in people and creates the seed generation. I've been told it involves pulling strands forcibly. I avoid anything that feels like that.

Jonas comes over briefly to record Dawn's vitals, and I catch the unmistakable twist of irritation, which is easily translated: he's offended that I rejected him.

I was doing so well... I was actually considering just *talking* to him about his assumptions. But then he had to go and act *entitled.* And some things can't be solved with conversation. Sometimes you have to *show* someone. I am not going to let this pass. We're going to be working together for a while, and he needs to know that I am not just a woman of words. Plus, I will be doing all the women at the Vault a favor.

In my time at the Vault I have come to recognize that Primes chosen to work in the EWR department have veritable rock star status. Everyone wants to be friends with them, to take them out for lunch, to rub shoulders with someone so close to the energy world and the sources of the life force abilities we all enjoy. And Kiera was absolutely right about how people would react to learning my identity. After St. Louis, I was actually approached for my autograph, and five people asked to take selfies with me. I've found extra rations in my bag after visiting the provisions counter, and after seeing the inside of other residences I realized that my apartment is one of the biggest in the entire campus. Of course, my status is due to more than working in EWR, but I've noticed my colleagues enjoy their fair share of fawning. And Jonas, I know, gets asked out practically on a daily basis. He's a good-looking guy, playing up his high-profile role with a bizarre hipster look: exotic long hair, faded jeans with holes, and argyle sweaters. Just weird enough to be sort of eclectic and mysterious. And desirable to the starstruck young Prime Human girl.

Jonas is exactly why I have become so cynical about men and their mind-games. They can't ever be straightforward and vulnerable, and if a woman rejects them, they denigrate her at first mentally, and then to their friends. Jonas asked me out expecting me to say yes because I've seen other women want him. And I'm betting that he's asking me out to boost his own status. It's not like I've felt a deep-seated attraction from him in my weeks working here. Even if I had though, it wouldn't make his reaction any less disgusting.

I pull my hands from Dawn's life force to come back into the regular world. "All done," I tell her. My subjects are never under hypnosis anymore. I just don't need it to observe the energy world like others do.

Dawn sits up. "Progress?"

I shake my head. "Still can't figure out how to get the strands to do what I want. I wish I knew what makes them swirl around."

"We'll figure it out," Dawn says, hopping down from the table. "Tomorrow?"

I nod. "I'm here in the A.M. I have Colloquy at one."

"See you then," she says and leaves the room.

I walk over to the desk where Jonas is looking at the screen that gives the running record of Dawn's vitals as I touched her life force. I know he's looking for correlations, but when I lean over and prop my chin up on my elbows, butt in the air, and cleavage in his face for good measure, he stops what he's doing immediately.

"I've been thinking about what you said earlier," I say. "And you're right. I need to make sure people take me seriously. It would probably say a lot if we were seen together. Want to go with me to Chase's?" I say. I bite the tip of my pinkie in the corner of my mouth and then let my voice go a bit higher when I say, "We can… watch a movie at my place after. If you want." I look down at the desk shyly.

He does not attempt to hide his pleasure. "That sounds like fun." He reaches out to touch my arm. "You are a gorgeous woman, Wendy. You don't have need of boys. You can have any man you wish."

It's really hard not to snatch my arm away, but I can't just sit here and let him touch me so I stand up and smoothly extract myself.

"Wrap it up," I say, giving him a winning smile and holding the door. "Don't make me walk there by myself."

He taps a couple of keys eagerly and comes to my side.

"Tomorrow, I want to do an outdoor session," Jonas says conversationally as we walk down the hall toward the elevator. "I think we can find new data. The natural world behaves different from the manmade one."

"Whatever you want," I say. "You've been at this a lot longer than me, so I trust you know what you're talking about."

My compliment produces the expected satisfaction on his part, and I roll my eyes in the darkness as we approach Chase's building.

"Wen!" Chase yells excitedly when he opens the door. The party is already in full-swing behind him, and my nose tells me alcohol has made its appearance among his guests.

I give Chase a hug. "You remember Jonas," I say.

"Whassa Jonas," Chase says, reaching out to shake Jonas' hand.

Jonas takes it but his attention is on the living room where the 3-D projector is being put to use with a video game. "Is that the one Dax has been working on?" he says, coming fully into the apartment to see it better.

"He named it finally," one of the girls standing nearby says. "Absolute Zero. He lets Chase play out the bugs." She turns her attention to me. "Wendy!" she gushes. "Chase said you might make it!"

I have no idea who the girl is...

"Shoot, that's hot," Jonas says, mesmerized, watching the true 3-D monsters leap at Cindy and Drake, the two people taking their turn at the controls. I've played it before. Chase is good friends with Dax, who is considered top five, Guild-wide, in programming skill and he's only sixteen. Developing the game is his hobby because the Guild isn't funding any entertainment projects right now with the world where it is. Gaming parties are a regular thing with Chase. That and falconry, his other love. He has a pet hawk that he takes outside the Vault's walls on a regular basis to hunt.

"I call the loser," Jonas says, squeezing between two girls on the couch.

Wasn't he *just* telling me I should hang out with older crowds? He looks right at home.

"How you?" Chase says, closing the door behind me.

"Tired," I reply, tucking my hands into the pockets of my jacket and hoping the girl who greeted me isn't going to come over and interrogate me about the energy world or ask for a picture.

"I make them treat you normal," Chase says, noting my skittishness while leading me over to the kitchen. Then he looks questioningly at Jonas and then back to me.

"Long story," I murmur. "I'm teaching him about life. What's new with you?"

"Got a job," he says, grin wide and ecstatic. His anticipation has me leaning toward him eagerly. No doubt this is why he invited me over in the first place.

"Doing what?"

"Hoomahn Moomen even seckoo—seckurr—ittee." He puts his fingers to his head and makes the explosive motion with his hands to indicate his life force ability. "Kowd Kontoll."

"You're working in crowd control at Human Movement events?"

He nods emphatically, crosses his fingers—his sign for our dyad partnership.

"Seriously?" I say, stalling because I'm not sure how I feel about that. I'm not sure if he's equipped to smartly handle that kind of danger. He has zero experience, and our next stop is Raleigh, a veritable war zone.

"I hab skillz," he says, making the explosive motion at his head again.

"You do," I say, trying to be happy for him. I guess he's right... He can sway emotions of the people around him, calm them or excite them. For crowd control I guess it's pretty darn useful as a security measure. Aside from his safety, I'm bugged because I'm not entirely sure of Chase's scope. Just how much *can* he move a crowd? And if there isn't outright danger involved, *will* he? Is he another one of Shiah's tactics to win this public relations war with Dumas?

My phone dings, and, grateful for the distraction, I pull it out of my pocket.

It's a voicemail from Mike. I don't remember my phone ringing...

"Sorry to cut it short, but I gotta go," I say to Chase. I don't actually have to. I can call Mike later, but I can't stand here and act like I'm thrilled about Chase's new position. I'm going to end up saying what I really think and it's going to end in a fight. Again.

"Aweady?" Chase says. "Jus' got here."

"I know," I say, guiltily. "It's just..."

"I know. Bizzy all time, but you show up. All dat matter," Chase says, putting a hand on my shoulder. "I see you in Wawee—Wahh-wee." He grumbles at his inability and tries again. Fails again.

"Don't hurt yourself," I say. "I know what you mean. I'll see you in Raleigh, too." I turn to go.

"Way way!" Chase says, turning around and grabbing a plastic container from the counter. He shoves it in my hands. "I may cookees. Take dem. Cewebwate!"

"Thanks!" I say, struggling to keep upbeat. I look to the living room where Jonas is in the middle of his turn at the game. "I'm going, Jonas. I'm sure Chase doesn't mind if you stick around though."

Jonas glances up, shoves the controller at the closest person, and hops up—to my disappointment. Being reminded of Chase's highly manipulative ability, and how much I detest it, I've lost my appetite for making entitled douchebags look like morons.

I catch Chase's eye as we leave, and he gives me a questioning look again. I roll my eyes and just before I close the door, the girl, whose name I still don't know, yells, "Wendy!" She raises her hands in front of her face, clasps them together. Behind them I can see her smile. The rest of the room follows suit, game paused, clasped hands raised in front of determined faces.

The gesture catches me totally off guard, rocking me suddenly to my core. At the Vault, I have associated the majority of people's reactions to me as a result of my access to the energy world—a purely superficial fame. But this is more than that. I have taken for granted that they've been watching me speak for them—even though Mike told me as much. I warm, humbled that I have created this kind of unity within the Guild. I've rallied them and brought us closer.

I raise my own hands and clasp them in return, touched and proud to call these people my family. What a great end to a crappy day.

While Jonas and I cross the grounds toward my residence building, and Jonas chatters about the flaws in the game's 3-D interface, I'm grasping for any way to get rid of him. After such a nice moment at Chase's, I desperately just want to end this night gracefully. But if I can't keep him from coming up to my apartment, it's going to be that much harder to dismiss him in such a way that I'll still being able to work with him. As I listen to him talk, I wish I could stop up my ears. He's back to implying that such social gatherings at Chase's are necessary after all. EWR needs to be 'accessible' as Jonas puts it.

I spot the entrance to my building all too soon, and I stop and turn to Jonas, his arrogance apparently having no end. He's no longer hiding his intentions at all, acting like he's already got this in the bag, like his self-assured, superior attitude is actually appealing to me.

If he would just not think like a cocky SOB for more than five minutes, I could move on with my life. But it's like he's pushing to see just how much of his conceit he can get away with. No way am I shirking the opportunity to teach him a valuable lesson. The Guild doesn't need a guy like this, and the delicacy of EWR's status among Primes certainly does *not* need this jackass expecting to be worshipped.

I make a detour, pulling him to the side of my building instead, into the shadows. I move in closer to him, putting my hand on his abdomen and moving my hand upward, letting my lips part and my breath tease his neck. I push him against the wall and press against him.

"Whoa," he says, putting hands on my arms. "Upstairs first?"

I put my mouth on his ear lobe. "Nope," I say, caressing his chest up to his neck.

"You are naughty," he gasps when I tug on his waistband suggestively. "Are you always aggressive?"

I answer by putting my my hand up under his ridiculous argyle sweater and sliding it up.

"It's chilly," he says. "Are you sure you want this happening out here?"

I tug on his waistband again. "Jonas, Jonas," I moan against his neck, thinking to myself there is no way I'm letting him in my apartment. But I say, "Are you saying you don't know how to warm it up? Let me teach you." I push his shirt up again, this time managing to convince him to take it off by kneeling and bringing my lips tortuously close to his stomach and breathing my way up to his chest while pushing his shirt up at the same time.

He tries to put his hands on me, but I push him back aggressively against the wall. "No. Let me," I say, letting my hands wander all over him, teasing, purposely working him into a dizzying lust with barely any contact.

He finally relents, letting me have my way, but he's losing control with every moment. I know where to take him, can recognize the moment when he will relinquish his control to me and I can get exactly what I want from him—which he will soon find out is not at all what he was hoping for. The more arrogant they are, the faster it happens, and Jonas is nearly there mentally after only a couple minutes. This is so easy.

At the exact moment that I turn my head to whisper my next request in Jonas' ear, I hear footsteps on gravel nearby that stop abruptly. It's unmistakably the sound of someone coming upon us. I whirl around, having no problem seeing into the darkness and spotting an outline I'd know anywhere.

"I can come back later?" the embarrassingly familiar voice says. It belongs to Mike.

Thirty-Three

W"*ho* is there?" Jonas says behind me, incriminatingly shirtless. His hand touches mine as he makes a move to stake his claim.

I snatch my hand away. "Mike," I say, taking a step toward him. "I was going to call you when I got home…"

It's a good thing it's dark. My cheeks are on fire.

"I can tell," Mike says, hands shoved in his pockets uncomfortably. He's too far away to read, but I can tell from the look on his face that he'd rather be anywhere else, and if I hadn't heard him, he wouldn't have stuck around to get my attention.

"I was!" I say, stepping forward because Jonas has moved closer to me again.

"I can come back tomorrow," Mike says. "You're busy."

"Yes, she is," Jonas says, snaking his arm around my waist.

I don't think. I react, lifting my arm and whirling, letting my elbow slam into Jonas' face.

"What the hell?" Jonas says, doubling back. "What was that for?"

I'm not sure how to answer at first. My plan for Jonas is ruined, and I either have to tell him what I think of him right now and deal with the consequences at work, or apologize and tell him it was just a skittish reaction. But I'll still have to solve my problem with him later… And in the meantime… who knows what Mike will think. What a mess.

I'm running out of time to turn this around… And if I ask myself, the only person's opinion I care about at the moment is Mike's.

"I never gave you permission to touch me," I say to Jonas. "And you sure as hell don't speak for me. You're lucky Mike showed up, because I was planning to spell out exactly what I think of you. You might be in EWR, but you're a disgrace to

Prime Humans and to the Guild. Giving me advice about who I should associate with… That you think I or anyone else owes you a thing simply because you're some Guild celebrity… You disgust me. I don't tolerate scum like you. You better rethink your life, Jonas, because you now have my attention. You no longer get to be ignored."

"You're crazy!" Jonas says, backing up and holding his nose. That's exactly what I look like…

"I guess I am," I say. "Now get out of my face, and don't let me hear about you abusing your status anymore, or I'll finish what I started here tonight. And I'll make sure you get kicked out of EWR. Don't you forget who *I* am."

Jonas has been slowly backing up, at a loss. I can tell he'd like to fire back some insults, but my threats have stuck, probably and especially the one about kicking him out of EWR. I'm pretty sure I could make it happen if necessary though. I know how disciplinary hearings work, and I could bring an arsenal of proof of his abuse of position by way of the many women he's toyed with.

"I'm outta here," Jonas says. He turns to go, and under his breath I hear him say, "you crazy bitch."

"Super-hearing, idiot," I say to his back. "See you at EWR, Jonas!" I slump though. This is *not* going to help my work environment. Ugh, Shiah. Why does she always have to be right?

I turn to a stunned Mike, and now I *really* don't know what to say. I cross my arms. Uncross them uncomfortably. I have no idea what he's thinking.

"I'm curious. How exactly would that have gone if I hadn't shown up?" he asks finally.

Unsure of what he's going to think, I hesitantly pull a permanent marker out of one pocket. "I was going to convince him to let me, ah, do a little doodling on him in the dark."

"Doodling?"

I shrug, look away even though Mike probably can't see my face very well in the dark. "I wanted to make sure the next girl he lays the moves on knows exactly what she's getting into. Figured he needed to be properly labelled."

"Hm," he grunts, and we stand still in the silence for a bit. He clears his throat. "And what makes you think he'd let you do that?"

I bite the inside of my cheek, embarrassment coloring my face again. Do I really have to spell this out?

I sigh. Why do I care so much what Mike thinks anyway? If he can't handle the truth then he's not the guy I thought he was.

"Experience," I reply. "Giving dirtbags what was coming to them was my specialty once." I cross my arms challengingly. "I gave all that up a while back, but Jonas kept asking for it."

He bellows with laughter.

I let the corner of my mouth curve upward.

He tries to clear his throat through the sniggering, wringing his face with a hand. "Wendy, The Perv Police," he chuckles. "Did you have an outfit? One that you changed into so you could be civilized nerd girl by day and roving vigilante by night?"

I grimace. "Stilettos?"

He hoots with laughter.

I cross my arms and bite my lip through my smirk. I love seeing him finally act with so much abandonment.

I walk over to where he's standing on a gravel path. I didn't realize it was back here. He must have been using it to get to my building when he came upon me. When he's done cracking up, I say, "In all honesty though, I'm glad you interrupted me. I probably wouldn't have gotten away with that if I'd followed through. Pretty sure Jonas would have gone and whined to someone important. I could have lost my job."

He leans against a nearby tree, tucking his hands into his jeans pockets. "I doubt it, Level Ten. You're not replaceable at this point. In either of your positions."

I hold my breath, because he just used his non-platonic nickname for me. It's backed up by the chemistry of mutual attraction between us.

I keep still. And silent. I'm not going to be the one to make the first move. He already knows where I stand.

He looks into my eyes for a moment. "I'm still glad I saw it, though," he says, his voice low. My chest gets heavy with the weight of his growing attraction. It's so hot out here... I don't think I can keep my distance if he keeps staring at me like that.

"I'm glad I saw it because it made me jealous as hell," he says, pushing off of the tree. "I said to myself, 'Could have been you, dumbass.'"

I suck in a much-needed breath as steps even closer. He reaches out, touches the length of my cheek with the side of his thumb. I can't stop myself from responding, reaching up and running my hand softly along his outstretched arm. He reaches for my waist, closing his eyes and inhaling deeply. So I close the distance between us, run my free hand from his chest to the back of his neck.

He shudders under my touch. From his emotions, I know he has dreamt of this moment a hundred times before, and it has finally been made reality. The release of so much pent up emotion has me unsteady on my feet. I grip his arm to keep myself upright. It just keeps coming though. So much longing. So much relief at being able to be close to me. I had no idea he felt this strongly…

"Why did you wait so long?" I whisper, truly not understanding why he has been so adamant about keeping things professional in the midst of these kinds of feelings. This isn't just attraction. This is something way more serious.

It was the wrong question to ask apparently. Suddenly and unexpectedly, he catches himself, as if only just now realizing what he's doing. He releases me and steps back. "I'm out of line."

"No, you're not," I insist, trying to close the distance between us again.

He reacts with inner turmoil, backing up again and running into the tree, so I stop where I am.

"I'm sorry," he says. "I don't know what came over me." He groans, reaches up and grabs his hair in his hands. "*Dammit*," he hisses, seemingly to himself, the depth of his sudden aggravation rivaling that of the attraction I felt from him only moments ago. "Dammit. This isn't how this was supposed to go." He glances at me, but then looks away, almost frightened, as if I'm going to lure him back into a moment. "I totally let myself go. I think it was seeing you over there—and then talking to you—It was my fault for coming out here, thinking I could talk to you without—"

He steps to the side, away from the tree and turns his back to me, arms crossed, head bowed. "I'm sorry," he says again, and it's clear that he's keeping his back to me to avoid my face, to keep his feelings at bay.

He doesn't want me to see him like this.

A lot of responses come to mind. There are two halves of me: one that wants to take control of the moment, make Mike forget whatever his hangup is and give in. The other side of me is furious.

"Why?" I say through gritted teeth. "If this is about your job as my bodyguard…"

"I shouldn't have come here," Mike says. "That's the real problem." He turns back around, his stance back to the usual confident and reserved front I'm used to seeing. And his emotions... How can he suddenly feel like a totally different person from the vulnerable one that stood in front of me only a moment ago?

His instant indifference punches my heart. How many times am I going to let him reject me after I've made my feelings available? No one has *ever* gotten a second chance like him. I confessed one of the most shameful pieces of my past. I never made him feel badly for not being ready. Against my better judgment I let him hide his emotions without prying. But this is the second time he's touched me and then taken it back. And after discovering the mountain of feelings he's been harboring... how can he stand there and pretend that it was just a minor slip?

Why do I feel so betrayed? This is normal guy stuff. This is how they are. This is how *everyone* is. They all play games. Can't ever be exposed. Can't ever let the girl know their real feelings. Can't look weak. Gotta play it cool.

Mike has never been special, but I've treated him like he is. Was I seriously just blinded by muscles and good looks? That is *not* me.

Why do I feel like crying?

Get it together, Wendy!

I take a long breath. Swallow. "I didn't listen to your voicemail yet. But if the fact that you came to the Vault is any testament, you actually needed something important."

Mike crosses his arms, spreads his feet, still seems to be avoiding looking at me directly. "Not really. I came here to meet with Lainey. Figured she'd finally leave me the hell alone once she realized I didn't know anything that would help her. Don't bother with the voicemail; I didn't leave one. I was just calling to see if you were home. Since I was here, figured it'd be rude to not at least stop by and say hi. I gotta run though. I'll see you in a couple days."

"Yep," I say tartly, crossing my own arms. The truth is I want to scream at him, but what's the point of that?

"Have a good night," he says and then turns and walks away.

I watch him disappear, and when he's out of sight, I pull out my phone, look at the list of voicemails. The one from Mike is a minute and a half long.

"Didn't leave a voicemail, my butt," I mumble. My thumb hovers over play, and I sigh. Am I done with him or not? What does it matter what the voicemail says? Whatever it is, it's just going to make me angrier—if that's possible. It's just going to get under my skin, make me confused and frustrated. I am done with angst. Mike is not who I thought—nor who I hoped, apparently.

I stab the delete button and shove my phone back into my pocket.

Thirty-Four

Welcome to hell, folks," Franklin, the head of security says from the other side of the small terminal. He's pacing in front of his team with a menacing expression. I spotted Chase among them earlier, shadowing one of the senior officers. "This isn't St. Louis. It's not Salt Lake. It's not even California. *This...* is the armpit of the Apocalypse, ladies and gentlemen. If you think you know what to expect today, go back to the plane. I don't need you. Because this is the crater of the volcano. Anything—and I mean *anything*—can happen here."

"The risks are not news to me," Shiah says into her phone from beside me, and Franklin's motivational sermon fades into the background. "I was aware of them before we even came. Did you expect our arrival wouldn't cause a stir?"

I don't bother to listen to the other side of her conversation. It's more of the same stuff I've been hearing since we left the Vault yesterday. The indecision and skepticism I've been enduring from the entire group has felt like emotional volleyball. It's founded though. Raleigh was a major evacuee checkpoint during the Caribbean crisis. North Carolina was the closest North American safe zone, so while at first they efficiently handled a constant stream of refugees, when the Guild moved the deadline up every bit of order that remained went to hell, and the eastern part of the state fell into anarchy. Raleigh is on the edge of that chaos, a sort of gateway between structure and bedlam.

I'm not convinced this will go well for us. Evacuees, which have settled in and around the Raleigh area, may sing the Guild's praises for saving their lives, or they could just as easily denounce us for having turned their worlds upside down when we moved the deadline up and they were dumped on North Carolina shore without a thing to their names. Locals will hate us, most likely, for obvious reasons.

It could also be a little of both, and that might be more dangerous than anything.

"We expect there will be," Shiah continues. "It would be ignorant to assume otherwise, and I am not ignorant. You however, have demonstrated your lack of foresight—"

She sighs. "No, Councilman Abram. I'm not insulting you—"

I almost listen in. Almost. But it doesn't take much imagination to guess what Abram is saying. Shiah's indignation is growing though. She is nothing if not totally in control of herself at all times, so if she's aggravated, it's purposeful and she's about to flip the script.

"Councilman Abram," she says, and her voice becomes completely serene, gentle even.

"Here we go…" I chuckle softly.

"You are within your responsibilities to call me and offer your guidance. You are not within them to have an emotional outburst when I state that some things have escaped your consideration. You are wasting my time by even conversing about it. And you are wasting your own with worrying over things that have been delegated to me. Your time should be devoted to handling the relief effort in northern Europe to keep those people from freezing to death. All of you unanimously agreed to give me this responsibility, and I have demonstrated repeatedly that I am more than capable of handling any level of complication. Your opinions, therefore, are illogical. I suggest conferring with the rest of the Council if you think changes need to be made. But I surmise they will tell you the same thing. I can only assume you know this, which is why you came to me directly. Good day, Councilman."

Shiah hangs up, puts her phone in her bag.

I snort and smile. "Shiah, I love you."

She tugs her shoulder bag higher and gives me a half-smile. "I love you, too, Wendy." She tilts her head thoughtfully and then she looks me in the eye—as is the norm for her. "I care about you a great deal, actually. And I think very highly of you. You always seek to act honorably, and you balance skill and humility with exceptional grace."

I open my mouth, touched. "Wow," I say. "Thanks."

"And I apologize for not telling you that sooner," she says. "That was my error. Sometimes my mind is so busy it forgets to remind me of subtleties, like the fact that people need affirmation on a regular basis."

I lift my eyebrows, ever amazed at Shiah's unembellished words. Flattery isn't in her vocabulary, so when she speaks, her words are resolute and declarative. I trust her character judgment more than anyone else's I've ever met.

Mike approaches me once Franklin's group dissolves, taking his place at my shoulder. I didn't talk to him on the plane; Franklin had everyone memorizing the map of downtown. He sent me a text message yesterday though, to which I didn't reply. It was another apology for letting things go the other night. I don't care. I'm moving on.

At the moment though, Mike's in bodyguard mode. He's always been really good at that, separating himself from his attraction to me while he's on duty. He's good at being a bodyguard in general, actually. Sometimes I forget he's back there, because I can turn right or left unexpectedly, and he's never underfoot. I'm less upset with him today, plus, Shiah's got me thinking about compliments, so when we stop at the doors to exit the terminal to allow Franklin's men to form a corridor of protection, I say, "You are fantastic at your job, Mike."

"Thank you," he says, putting his hand on the small of my back to motion me toward the car. I don't pick up anything but his usual detachment as he keeps his eyes and ears open for potential problems. Not that I should be paying attention, but I guess I'm still hurt after all, enough to care what he's thinking.

Franklin wants our caravan consolidated this time, so Shiah is riding with us. I make my way back to the third row to give her room. Mike climbs in beside me, and Shiah sits in front of me, her bodyguard, Brad, in front of Mike. In the front passenger seat is an additional bodyguard. Two SUVs are ahead, two behind, all loaded down with our protection and logistics teams. I can't help but notice a semi take the head of the line, and I assume it has to do with our security. Maybe there are more guys riding in there. Or barriers that are going to be set up. Shiah wasn't kidding when she told Abram she had this covered.

"I offered Gabe Dumas shared use of the balcony of the capital building to deliver his remarks," Shiah says as we pull away. "That way there is only one point of delivery, and protection can be concentrated. I believe I was right to assume you wouldn't take issue with that, Wendy."

"That was nice of us," I say, grabbing my water bottle out of my bag and leaning against the window. "Did he take the offer?" I twist off the cap.

"Readily. One other thing. Due to the heavy concentration of evacuees living here now, it's safe to guess many attendees will speak Spanish as their primary language. Mister Dumas offered to translate for you in exchange for the favor."

I nearly choke on the water in my mouth.

Mike pats me on the back. "You okay?"

I push his hand away. "Shiah, tell me you're kidding."

"At no point have I ever kidded with you about anything."

That's true... But this is crazy. She can't possibly think this is a good idea.

"You trust him to translate for me?" I say.

"Trust? What's to trust?"

"He could... I don't know... take liberties with translation!"

"Mike speaks Spanish. So do two other people on the protection team. I speak Spanish as well. It would be absurdly foolish for him to attempt such deception, not to mention way outside of his prescribed behavior patterns."

"And it's *not* foolish for him to deliver words that oppose his own?! If you speak Spanish, why can't *you* translate for me?"

"Because I am not an orator. And this is good strategy."

"How is this good strategy?!" I shrill, frustrated that I only have the back of Shiah's headrest to yell at.

"How is it not?" she says. "It paints us as united. It paints us as humble. It paints us as trusting. It paints us as an organization that can and will work with anyone. You can handle yourself through it. There are zero reasons this isn't a good thing."

I frown, cap my water. Crazy, counterintuitive PR campaigning is Shiah's speciality. I have no idea why I question it anymore. "I'm inclined to agree," I say, "but I'm also inclined to wonder what the heck Dumas is getting out of the deal. I'm assuming he made the offer *after* getting invited to use the balcony. So he has some other reason for offering."

"To see what you do," Mike says.

I glare at him. "What I do? I'm going to speak, and he's going to repeat the same thing in Spanish. Where's the mystery?"

"Just look at you," Mike laughs. "All worked up about the whys. You don't speak from a script, which means that knowing Gabe is going to be translating for you is going to affect what you say and how you say it. He wants in your head. He wants to push your buttons."

I throw my water bottle forcefully into my bag. "Aaaaaaaaagh!" I groan. "Why does he still have a following? He spends all his time trying to bug me!"

"Which is why he will inevitably lose," Shiah says.

The sights outside my window capture my attention just then. We're driving through what probably used to be a rural farming area, but now it's covered as far as the eye can see in temporary housing: anything from tents to clapboard shacks to shelters composed of arrangements of random trash. Old tires seem to be a popular element.

"Hold tight everyone. We've got a blockade a mile ahead," our extra bodyguard in the front seat says as the SUV rolls to a stop. Mike unholsters his gun.

Unease creeps over me, and I lean forward to peer through the windshield. I can't see anything but the rear of the SUV ahead. "Are we going to be able to get through?" I ask the car.

"We are prepared," Shiah says confidently. "Franklin knows the plan."

"The plan?" I say.

"The biggest problem in these camps is access to clean water first, and food second," Shiah says. "And it's the same story in every place that's taken on evacuees. There isn't enough infrastructure to support such an enormous influx of people. You can't travel through a refugee camp without being hijacked for what resources you have. I made sure we had something to offer so we would be allowed to pass peacefully."

"Could have just taken a helicopter in," Mike grumbles.

"Oh! The semi!" I say.

"It will take them a little while to unload it."

"Hope it came with a forklift," Mike mumbles. "Or this could take hours."

I roll my eyes at him. "Seriously? Shiah thought to bring along a *tractor-trailer's* worth of donations to make sure we got to our destination, and you don't think she planned how to get it unloaded quickly?"

"I always think ahead," Shiah says quietly. "At every moment of my day I am planning for the next moment, next hour, next day, next week. I don't know how to *not* think ahead."

Silence fills the car, but in my head it is not quiet. Shiah's angst clenches my chest, but it's followed quickly by resignation. I've never felt her disquieted like this. I marvel over it, wondering why a comment about her planning ahead would cause her distress…

"One day I will explain it to you," she answers, startling me with her discernment of my internal questions. Or maybe she didn't. It was kind of a natural continuation of her earlier words.

"Jordan Lake is nearby and supplies most of the area's water," Shiah says, back to her usual unruffled self. "Evacuees have started accessing it directly, and it's being put to use without proper water treatment and waste water disposal. It's going to become contaminated."

"Yeah, the impending water crisis is making headlines more and more," I say. "Drought in the mountain west… Contaminated water sources from earthquakes… People living in tents without bathrooms…" I sigh. "This is so stupid," I mumble. Why am I in a war of words with Dumas when there are things like water shortages, millions of starving homeless people, Europe plunging into an ice age, constant fires and tornados, wide-spread mass violence, and tsunamis hammering Asia constantly? This whole Human Movement thing is ludicrous.

"It is necessary," Shiah says, preempting me once more. "Focusing on mere survival shrinks the mind. That's when people do terrible things to each other. Dumas must be heard. And so must you."

I don't understand… I don't even think I can grasp the logic anymore, not with my spirits sinking lower as I stare out over the fields and fields of makeshift shelters. Things are getting so dire… I've been searching the energy world for clues as to a solution. That's what they keep insisting on—that the energy world can tell us the problem. The energy world can point us to the source. But the energy world is nothing but a bunch of colors. I see those pretty colors. That's it. The mystery eludes me.

Is the prophecy immovable? Are Prime Humans misguided to think *they* are the solution? What if the disasters never stop?

"However," Shiah says, and I hear her voice change. I know her pretty well by now, and I would bet she's about to tell me something big. "Water has always been the Guild's primary environmental concern. For years, ever since the disasters first began increasing in frequency, we've been focusing our efforts on making sure there would always be enough water. And we finally have a solution. On that semi, in addition to provisions, are the first water purification kits to be distributed as part of the Guild's Clean Water Initiative—what will be the most widespread humanitarian effort the world has ever seen. The kits will allow these people and others to disinfect their own water—any water, no matter how contaminated, no matter the source. It will purify and separate the sediment with one drop per gallon before breaking down and becoming completely harmless."

"Whoa," I say. "That's incredible. And that truck has the first distribution?"

"Yes."

There is clearly more to it. Mike was right; arriving by helicopter would have been much safer and faster. But Shiah wanted me to see these camps. She wanted me to be upset and motivated.

"*You* will be announcing the debut of our Clean Water Initiative," Shiah says quietly.

My mouth opens in surprise. I want to ask her if she's joking, but I'm sure I'll get the same response as before. "Uhh… Shiah, isn't that something someone on the Council would announce?" I say. "Like, at a UN meeting? That's *huge* news. In fact, I shouldn't say any of the things I've already prepared. I should just say that and then drop the mic."

"Outside of disaster prediction, it is the most significant technological development of our day," she agrees. "That's why it needs to come from you."

I exhale my confused impatience. "You're going to have to explain your logic to me."

"Attendance at Human Movement protests may be relatively small, but they are merely the brave few who represent a much larger portion of the population. Everyone wonders the same things Gabe Dumas voices whether they attend a THM protest or not. As you said in Salt Lake, he speaks what many people wonder but are too busy trying to survive to say or think about: that we are masked vigilantes, swooping in to save the day and then disappearing once more, all in an effort to establish our supremacy. He claims that this problem would be solved if Humans could know their savior beyond news reports and third-party exposés.

"You are the most well-known Prime Human in this nation. You are no mystery to the masses. You're also a twenty-something, a youth, someone who will be around to see the future. *You* are going to bring water, the most necessary commodity on earth. Something as big as that requires someone both as important and as unmysterious as you."

I pause, trying to imagine myself that way, but I feel like an imposter. We're giving people the power in any situation to scoop water out of a creek or a toilet and be able to drink it. It's mind-blowing. But I had no hand in that. Humility is heavy on my shoulders.

"And very soon," Shiah says, "the ocean and salt-dead bodies of water will serve water needs as well. We are very close to a quick and inexpensive method of removing salinity. *This* day is going to pave the way and set the stage for *that* day, which will change everything."

"Oh hell," Mike says. "Next you're going to tell us the food synthesizers are nearly done."

"Wow," I breathe. "Wow." I can't think of anything else *to* say. This is a big deal. This is a big freaking deal.

After a pensive pause, I say, "I take it you have news coverage for this event then?"

"Yes," Shiah says. "And whoever misses it will hear it on Good Morning America and then again on late night TV the same day."

Everything is just so timely with Shiah… How does she do it? How does she make the stars align like this? I'm interviewing right after I make the biggest announcement in history, with the biggest news show in America, right after Gabe Dumas said he wasn't doing more interviews until I did. And it all coincides with the release of this miracle chemical that will create clean water for everyone? Not to mention Gabe Dumas is going to be repeating what I say today, which means *he* is debuting the information to the Spanish-speaking population from his own mouth… Shiah is basically using him as a voice for the Guild under the guise of a favor.

"Damn," I breathe. "You continually leave me in awe of you, Shiah."

"Planning is what I do," she says, unbothered this time.

Thirty-Five

*A*llow me to introduce myself," Dumas says to the growing crowd, standing on the balcony just outside the glass doors in front of us. "I am Gabe Dumas, and I represent a group of like-minded individuals who believe in the power of a united humanity. Our purpose here today is to be heard. By our government. By our neighbors. And of course, by the Guild."

Gabe Dumas then repeats the same message in Spanish. Meanwhile, I cannot get over the size of the gathering. I couldn't even begin to guess the number... six thousand? Eight? Ten? They stretch beyond the grassy place and streets in front of the capital building, wrapped around buildings surrounding the block. I can even hear them beyond where I can see, so many who are attending don't even have a view of the stage.

We arrived before the crowd, for security reasons, and ever since then I've been preoccupied with reading the general sentiment as they've trickled in. At first they seemed confused and greatly apprehensive. I'd say they weren't quite sure about being here. But slowly, as the gathering swelled, they grew in confidence. They grew in excitement, mirroring the state of Dumas' gatherings in the past. I wonder, have all THM events progressed like this?

"The message is clear," Dumas continues. "We demand collaboration with the Guild collective. We demand the sharing of technology and information. In times like these, we cannot afford to hoard our assets. We need to solve the imminent problems of the day. We need all hands on deck. Whatever their membership, the Guild cannot possibly see to the needs of a hundred million Caribbean refugees. But seven billion humans can."

His translation commences, and I wonder, how did the people in the crowd learn about this gathering? I listened to them as they arrived, and the majority speak Spanish, so I think it's safe to assume they are mostly evacuees. It's not like they have easy access to the internet, and the language barrier would at least slow down word of mouth from the locals.

"Hold your posts, undercover team," I hear Franklin say from nearby. "Dumas is going in. We've got a couple hours to go. Eyes open. Report any problems immediately."

"That was fast even with the translation time," I say. "His opening remarks are usually twice as long."

"He hates being so far away from the people he's speaking to," Mike says. "Up on that balcony… made him feel like he was talking down to them, like he couldn't fully connect. He was antsy to jump in to the crowd so he made it short and sweet."

"Well I hate this part," I say, bouncing on my toes. "The anticipation is like needles. By the time Dumas makes his closing remarks, every one of my nerves is so on edge that even my clothes are uncomfortable."

Shiah, who stands next to me, says, "Dumas rightly assumed most of these people don't know what The Human Movement is about—taking it back to the basics. I would suggest you do the same. Say who you are and then deliver the announcement, however it comes to you."

"Yeah, I think he's right to assume they don't know what he's about. Something weird is going on," I say, crossing my arms as I fight to absorb the energy of the crowd. "At first it felt like every one of these people just happened to wander in. Then they realized they weren't the only ones and so they stuck around to find out what the deal was. As soon as Dumas started speaking though, they were laser focused on him as if they'd found their purpose in life… Thousands of people, from all different places, thrown together, living in the middle of anarchy, and they gather in front of the Raleigh capital building totally confused about why they're here? There's got to be a life force ability in effect."

"Of course there is," Shiah says quietly.

I turn to face her. I'm not really shocked, because she's implied as much before, but I *am* annoyed that I never get to be in the know. "What?"

"We sent in a few telepaths ahead of today to help stir up attendance. A couple of Prime Human operative additions to security detail, such as your dyad, Chase, will ensure that the group doesn't get out of hand. The most important additions to the team are two people: one who has an ability we call beacon—they draw people to them; the other, an amplifier—someone who can increase the range of a target ability. The attendance is therefore no surprise. But as for Dumas…" Shiah tilts her head just so. "You are right. There's something to him which keeps his audience enraptured and pliant. I've noticed it every time he's spoken. And he gets better at it every time he speaks. It's one of the reasons I picked him."

"Picked him?" I say quietly. "What do you mean?"

"You don't think THM was the *only* group after the Guild when we came out to the public, do you?" she replies.

I turn back to the glass doors ahead, lips parted in confusion. "I don't understand."

"Religious groups, political groups, corporations, human rights, charities, and everything in between. There has always been someone around to oppose us. THM, however, was the only group started by someone who had nothing to gain. It is the only group who is a worthy opponent."

I don't sense an ounce of arrogance in her statement. "But you… You elevated them to… to oppose us? I don't understand."

"We must keep our own power in check," Shiah says quietly, and it seems as if she is speaking to herself.

I wait but she doesn't continue. "I don't get it," I say.

"Leave the planning to me." She turns to look at me finally. "For you, today is the most important. There were nearly one hundred million evacuees," she says quietly, but her words are backed with palpable gravity. "One hundred million. As if becoming homeless and starving weren't traumatic enough, entire cultures have been lost because homelands were submersed into the ocean. They have lost intangible things, things that define them. Parts of themselves that their children will never see. Their identities are in flux, and no matter where they go now, they are hated, because they need more than local communities can give. So they are being forced to choose between death and violence. Who is the Guild to them when they can't even provide for their families? What do they care for a savior when their survival is still in question?"

Helplessness squeezes my chest. I've thought as much on any number of occasions.

"We need to be heard by these people even more than Dumas," she continues. "To them, demanding more has become more necessary every day. Questioning a savior who only half-delivered is something they do amongst themselves already. Dumas will easily win their hearts, and they represent an enormous population—one that will determine the future more than any other group."

She moves behind me and turns me bodily to face the glass doors ahead again, beyond which is the balcony and beyond that, the massive gathering of refugees. "These are the survivors of the future, Wendy. You are looking at the people that will come out better than anyone else by the time the Apocalypse concludes because they are in training for survival that much sooner than the rest of us. In the midst of that, they are remaking themselves. They will build a new culture and history, new morality. We must be a voice in their lives. It's imperative that they know we haven't forgotten them, that we are actively working to turn things around for them. They need to take your message back with them to their camps and it needs to spread. Previously, your appearances have been about THM. But today it is about the world. The Guild does not campaign, Wendy. Without THM we would not have cause to be here. This will be your most important appearance yet."

I exhale deeply, my nerves making an appearance even over the usual confident state crowds put me in. "No pressure," I laugh humorlessly. "So we're using THM's campaign as our trojan horse..."

"It's a delicate balance," Shiah says. "And I wouldn't say Dumas gains nothing. Without our efforts, how would these people have known to show up? And how would he keep the peace once they did?"

The crowd erupts, and a correlating thrill shoots upward from my stomach to my chest. I've let go of any fear, and excitement funnels through me. I have no control over how I feel with the crowd infiltrating me like this.

"If you'll excuse me, I've got to return a phone call," Shiah says, and she walks deeper into the large room, away from the doors leading to the balcony.

The chanting begins, but it's in Spanish. It's then that I bother to notice Mike standing nearby, ever on alert. I motion for him to come closer, which he does. "The balcony issue aside, what does Gabe feel like when he's delivering his remarks?" I ask.

"Gabe is completely in control of himself when he speaks. He's committed. And completely unafraid. Even now, while he's in and amongst those people, he sees himself as one of them. It doesn't occur to him that they may not agree. He assumes he's right. He assumes that the words he says cannot be denied."

"Why do you think they believe him?" I say. "These people didn't really know why they came here. But Gabe started talking and all of a sudden their world makes sense to them."

His brow furrows for a moment. "It's always been like that, I guess. Gabe at the science fair. Gabe in debate club. Gabe's valedictorian speech. When he's in front of a group, he owns it. I told the Guild this when his movement first started. I can't explain it. He's just charismatic that way. Maybe it's that his will is so strong, and they sense it."

"The Guild's database shows him as being a Prime of spontaneous origin. What can he do?"

"Count. He can count anything in seconds. And he is freakishly good at learning new languages. I can't think of any language he doesn't know at least somewhat."

I frown. That's interesting but not really helpful.

"What are you trying to figure out?" Mike asks. "You're going to do fine. You don't need to think about what Gabe's doing."

I bounce on the balls of my feet some more. "Nothing. Just amazed at his ability to turn a crowd, that's all." I step toward the glass doors, looking out into the crowd as Dumas makes his way through it, shaking hands, leaning in to hear someone speak to him, smiling, yelling an answer… He's got a giant bodyguard trailing him this time though, a built black guy who looks like he could even take Mike on. "I see he's finally got some protection," I say. "Guy looks like he could rough someone up."

Mike sniffs, but I sense he agrees. "Yeah, I know the guy. Used to train at the same gym with him years ago."

"Really?" I say, turning around to face Mike, but he's still looking past me, through the glass.

"Name's Porter Tranwick. He was in the military when I knew him. I haven't kept up with him all that much, but he's top notch. Couldn't have picked someone better. I don't know much about the rest of his team, but they seem solid."

I feel his relief, and I can't help but smile a little. Every time Mike expresses concern for Gabe, it kind of makes me melt. Maybe it's that it makes Mike more human… "How do you think

Dumas found him?" I say. "Did they know each other then as well?"

Mike shakes his head. "No… They might have met once…"

"But what?" I say when I can tell Mike's holding something back.

He clears his throat. "I used my life force ability."

I lift my eyebrows.

"I didn't know it was going to be Porter. But that's how it happens sometimes. I needed Gabe to have protection. So I willed it."

"You… *willed* it?"

He shrugs. "I know it sounds stupid. But I don't have a better word for it when I use it long-range like that. If I have something in mind I want to accomplish, I meditate on it, send it out into the universe. And a lot of times the universe delivers. In this case, it looks like it got a hold of my old buddy and sent him out to help my brother."

I smile again.

"What?" he says gruffly.

I punch him in the arm. "You love him… It's just really cute."

"Of course I love him," he huffs. "I told you as much. I also don't want to jeopardize my job. If he's protected, I don't have the distraction of worrying."

Just like that, I've forgiven Mike for the other night. Why can't he be this open all the time?

"Hmm," I say, turning back around to watch Dumas wind his way through the crowd, making contact with every person around him. It's kind of effortless, the way he moves. Like he's part of them. Like the whole thing is synchronized and the crowd knows where he is at any given time. And they don't press on him either. They make way, but without stepping on the people behind them. It's uncanny, actually, and I furrow my brow, studying it. The group moves in response even before Dumas moves. I can't tell who is determining his path: Dumas or the crowd.

"What was that 'hmm'?" Mike demands behind me.

Why have I never watched Dumas in a crowd before? Well… I've never had the opportunity to look down on it before like this. I step right up to the glass.

"Whoa," Mike says, putting a hand on my shoulder. "We have eyes below, not up here right now. No reason to expose yourself before you have to."

"Do you see that?" I say, pointing. "Look at them. Look how they move around him."

I finally have Mike's attention, and he steps next to me, watching for a minute or so before saying, "They're kinda like water around him."

"That is... bizarre..." I mumble, mesmerized by the movement. It strikes a familiar chord in me suddenly, and I struggle for the connection for a while. I've seen this before... not this exactly, but something like it...

Where have I seen this?

It's not the crowd. I've obviously seen plenty of crowds by now... It's the movement.

It's the pattern.

"Mike," I say suddenly when it finally hits me. "I need you to hold really still. Don't move until I tell you, okay?"

"What are you—?"

"Shh!" I insist. "Nothing you need to worry about. Just hold still. I've only done it like this once before. I need to concentrate. I'm not sure if I can get in the right zone, with this crowd, but..." I'm babbling now. I need to shut up and focus. "Just let me hold your arm. Keep it still," I say, letting my hand rest lightly on his jacket as I close my eyes.

I take controlled breaths, fighting against the crowd in my head to find the place where I can click over. They call it hyper-alert, and for most I understand it's a scale. You achieve it slowly and gradually. For me it's always been instant. Once I find the right emotional note, it switches me over like I've found the right frequency.

There it is. Wow. That was a mere second, as if the energy of the crowd transported me on its own. I can hear it—the energy world. That's how I know I'm there. It's much louder than usual... like a room crowded with innumerable melodies. If I hadn't come here for a specific purpose, I'd probably examine it more. But I open my eyes, careful to remain very still so as not to fall victim to the vertigo of shifting colors.

The first problem I encounter is the glass. It's nearly opaque blue. I took for granted that glass would be anything but transparent as it is in the normal world. But that was silly. Everything in the energy world has always been a different color, different texture. Here the glass looks like a wall of static, which changes hues as I shift my head.

I can easily push away the energy world by unfocusing my eyes, but how does that help me see the crowd?

I nearly make Mike accompany me outside to the balcony, but I notice, in the practice of pulling the energy world in and out of focus, that I catch a glimpse of the purple lights of the life forces of the crowd for a split second between 'worlds.' So I stare intently at the crowd as I let my eyes adjust back into the energy world.

Bingo. The blue static of the glass disappears. In fact, it only fades back into view if I think about it too much. So I don't. It doesn't take much effort to maintain once I lock focus on the purple mass of wonder going on below.

"Holy… Wow…" I breathe, watching what looks like an ocean of illuminated purple. Upon each person's head is a swirl, precisely like the one on peoples' chests. I've noted and described both of these swirls repeatedly while working at EWR. But now each swirl bleeds into others next to it, inseparable, at least as far as I can tell. The connection between their life forces, in fact, makes a bigger picture on the whole: that of one huge crowd-size swirl, arms of connected life forces spiraling outward. At the center… Gabe Dumas. I know because I unfocus my eyes for a moment to verify. He is somehow binding thousands of life forces, creating a synchrony of movement among them that's reminiscent of the movement of one singular life force.

Does he know he's doing that?

Surely not. I don't think *anyone* knows, save me.

What does this mean?

I can't look away.

It's so… beautiful. It's the most stunning thing I have ever seen.

Harmonious.

Perpetually flowing.

It could pick me up and carry me away at any moment.

I exhale in release, and with that I don't perceive my body any longer. I only perceive myself as part of the grand life force in front of me.

One.

Someone jerks my arm suddenly, and I nearly lose my footing. A life force moves in front of my face. "Wen!" the person yells.

Frightened, I push their chest to get them away from me, and as I do, the lights of the energy world fade. Solidity of the normal world knocks me completely out of my ethereal state, and I stumble backward, arms flailing.

"I got you," Mike says in my ear, and indeed he does. Again. He holds me upright as I gasp for air. My head spins, like I just rammed it into a brick wall. The energy world... that was moving. This world? By comparison it feels like slamming on the brakes after sticking my head out the window at a hundred miles an hour.

It's then that I notice the number of people gathered around us, Shiah in particular. She has her arms grasped about herself, and she's staring like she knows what happened. Admittedly, I'm not quite sure what *did* happen. I know I went into the energy world. I know I saw the crowd as a swirling life force with Gabe Dumas at the center. But this feeling in my chest? The sensation that suddenly everything is moving in slow motion? I don't know what that is.

"What happened?" Mike says, holding one of my elbows, concerned that I haven't found my feet yet. I have. But I'm worried that at any moment the earth is going to start spinning again and I'll be knocked off balance once more. I can hear Mike's pulse. It's elevated compared to those around us, but it still seems excruciatingly slow.

"I—Um—" I look around, pretty sure I shouldn't be saying what I just saw in front of all these people. I'm bound by the Council, by EWR mandate. "Research," I say, but it sounds more questioning than definitive.

"What? Research?" Mike says, totally confused. "You were totally unresponsive," he says. "Did you hear us talking to you?"

Man, I want to tell him... I want to tell someone... I know who I want to tell: Gabe. I want to ask him if he feels what he's doing. Most of all... I want to go back there... I look over my left shoulder, noticing only then that Dumas isn't out there.

I worry for only a second, because suddenly the door to the stairs opens, and Dumas, followed by his bodyguard, Porter Tranwick, appears, face flushed, a smile emblazoned there as if he just had the time of his life. I believe it. I did, too.

He stops when he encounters our odd gathering. His face changes to one of curiosity as his eyes shift among the group, coming to rest on me. Behind him, his bodyguard, Porter Tranwick, senses the tension in the room, and with one step closer to Dumas, his somewhat reserved presence becomes menacing. Mike responds instantly, hand on his weapon, body in front of me.

"You're done already?" I say, putting my hand on Mike's arm and stepping slightly out from behind him to get him to stand down. The tension in the air is way too high right now. Tranwick looks like he's in the mood to maul a bear. I want to see if I can get something out of Gabe though. Plus, he usually churns the crowd for a couple hours at least. Is he taking a bathroom break or something?

Dumas tilts his head, his eyes boring into mine, his mouth curved in amusement. "Already, you say? El Cielo, Miss Whitley. I was exercising consideration. I was concerned you'd be cross with me if I went too much longer. Especially after you so generously allowed me the use of the facility's balcony for my remarks..." His expression changes suddenly. "Oh wait, was that sarcasm?"

"No..." I say, totally lost and distracted at the same time. Did he just use the word 'cross'? That's kind of adorable. Crap, did I just call Dumas adorable? Why would he think my question was sarcastic?

"I believe your fans await your closing remarks, Mister Dumas," Shiah says, suddenly appearing at my side.

Dumas hesitates, obviously perturbed at being dismissed, but he quickly accepts that there's nothing he can do about it. He heads for the balcony, and Shiah turns toward me. "Are you okay, Wendy?" she says quietly. "You stood in the same spot for an hour and a half. I was this close to having you airlifted out of here and to a hospital. But your vitals were good according to our paramedic on standby. What happened?"

She's definitely rattled, but probably not as much as me. An hour and thirty minutes? I stood in one place for that long? It felt like five minutes! I stare at her with open-mouthed shock.

"I take it you don't recall even an hour passing," Shiah says, accurately translating my expression. "What did—" She stops abruptly, closes her eyes and then opens them. "Now isn't the time. You have about three minutes, five minutes max, before you have to go out there." She points to the balcony. "Are you ready?"

I look from Shiah's face to Dumas' back. He's saying something in Spanish, and the crowd seems to be cheering between every phrase. His closing address is going to take forever at that rate.

"Yeah, I got this," I say.

She examines my face for signs of uncertainty, but I have none. Though I have no answers for why the last ninety minutes suddenly felt like no more than ten, or why nobody was able to get me to come around, the power of the crowd hasn't left me. And I think this may be the most hyped-up crowd yet. After my experience in the energy world, I am more connected to them than any other group before. I could do this with my eyes closed.

Shiah nods once. "I believe you." Worry leaves her entirely and the corner of her mouth curves slightly. "Bring them water, Wendy."

Thirty-Six

Pause whenever you've completed a thought," Gabe Dumas instructs me as soon as I step through the doors and onto the enormous balcony. "Don't concern yourself with my ability to remember what you've said. My memory is exceptional." He grins at me, hands clasped behind his back. "But the crowd's attention span is not as long as my memory. So I'd pause often for translation." He puts his hand over his heart. "I promise I will do the best job I know how to accurately communicate your meaning, tone, and intent."

"I have no doubt you will," I say, realizing I believe that. "I do have an additional request though."

He lifts his eyebrows in the same excited way he did the last time I asked him for a favor after we rescued him in Salt Lake.

"Hold my hand," I say as the technician finishes positioning my microphone.

His enthusiastic expression turns into bewilderment. I can't feel his emotions though. Not with this crowd. Not that it matters to me *what* he's feeling. I'm undaunted and self-assured. Nothing, not even possibly giving Dumas the wrong idea, concerns me. I have a goal and a message to deliver.

"Pardon my hesitation, Miss Whitley," Dumas says, finally finding his words. "That particular request did not seem to be in the realm of possibility. You caught me off-guard. I'm not opposed to it, but I find it worth mentioning that I don't think I've ever seen you less in need of hand-holding than right at this moment."

I chuckle. "You'd be correct. But I am about to change the world with my words, Mister Dumas. As my translator you get to own a part of that. Forever. There are cameras everywhere. What is about to happen is going to be aired all over the nation and eventually all over the world. I don't intend for you to own any of the Guild's success without relinquishing, if only for this moment, the idea that we are at odds. If you can't put aside your opposition to me and my cause for for the next few minutes, I'll have someone else stand in to translate."

I expect him to think about it. I even hope he'd be slightly put off by my arrogance. But instead he raises what I can only translate as a devilish eyebrow. "My, my, Miss Whitley. You do ever put my brain in knots. How can I refuse?"

"Excellent," I say, holding out a hand.

He takes it in his own, and I nod to the sound techs as we walk toward the railing. I have not looked behind me to Shiah and the ever-lurking Mike, because I don't care if I'm meeting disapproval. I am preoccupied with my plan.

We stop in front of the railing, and I feel Gabe's eyes on me. I pause, close my eyes only briefly, and with the aid of Gabe's life force so close—which is why I needed his hand—I pull myself instantaneously into the energy world.

Gabe's hand tightens on mine, and I assume he's prompting me to speak, so I squeeze back to tell him I'm getting there. But he seems to be hanging on to my hand as if making sure I know he's still there. I decide to ignore him, because I need to regain concentration. I need to watch as I speak.

I look out on the brilliant purple sea below. The crowd is still now. Composed of separate life forces without Dumas threading his way among them. But I keep my attention trained on them as I begin:

"Being here with you has been an unrivaled experience. I've felt your energy, your desire for purpose. I've felt Gabe Dumas connect with you, awaken some part of your souls that has been suppressed by constant tragedy. Your need to hope for yourselves again is infectious and inspiring."

I squeeze Dumas' hand to signal him to translate. When it takes a couple seconds longer than I expect for him to start, I look his way as he clears his throat and says, "Es verdaderamente maravilloso estar entre vosotros hoy."

I glance at him, because not only did that sound totally robotic, but he can't possibly be done.

He squeezes my hand, takes a concentrated breath, and this time, his voice changes timbre, reminiscent of the melodic delivery I'm used to from him, "He sentido su energia, su deseo para la finalidad. Me he sentido Gabe Dumas conectar con usted, despertar alguna parte de sus almas…"

He continues. I watch the crowd. At first they seem to be confused by our seeming camaraderie. As Dumas speaks, however, his tone becoming more earnest, they settle in rapt attention. Eventually, they begin to move a little, not any substantial distance—maybe just shifting their weight.

"My name is Wendy Whitley," I say when he finishes. "And I am a member of the Guild, an organization dedicated to the improvement of life. My life. Your life. Lives that have not even been born. Every life."

I wait as Dumas speaks.

"I am a Prime Human," I continue. "I have felt with you today because I am an empath, capable of feeling the emotions of those around me. I also have what's called Energy World Sight, which means I am the *only* Prime Human capable of fully experiencing the forces that power life force abilities, the abilities which grant superhuman capability."

I squeeze Dumas' hand. I've been waiting for something to happen with the crowd each time he translates, but it seems that strange interconnected spirals forming a larger spiral only happens when Dumas is *part* of the crowd. Up here, away from them, I think they would *like* to move that way, but physical distance prohibits them. He must feel it, too, and that's why he was impatient to get off the balcony.

"I'm here because I volunteered to be the liaison between the Guild and The Human Movement," I continue. "I'm here to remind you that we are always near, that we are always listening even if we don't always reply."

It's hard not to be disappointed that my experiment hasn't gone the way I'd hoped. For a brief moment I consider taking Dumas with me into the crowd. But I'm pretty sure Mike would tackle me before I made it… And afterward, I'd get it from Shiah. And the Council. Bummer.

I continue watching though, because in the mysterious world of energy you never know what could happen. "Today," I say, "as I was thinking about what I wanted you to know about me, what would even matter to you in your world of constant change, danger, uncertainty, I was drawn by the memories of my past. I grew up in Southern California and was forced to leave when chaos took over there. After the deaths of my brother and my father, I realized that everything I knew and had cared about was gone."

I signal Dumas, whose delivery increases in intensity. He's fully engaged now, and the crowd's energy responds. Now that I'm paying more attention to its nuances rather than what's visually happening, I sense it. They react to simply the lift and lull of his voice.

My turn again, and I say, "I had to let go of my past self or I was going to drown in the sorrow of my loss. I gave up who I was, what I stood for, what I wanted out of life. I've been rebuilding it ever since. I've struggled against past instincts. I've battled past demons. I've moved into an apartment that contains none of my things and has technology I only halfway know how to use. I live in a state I'd never even visited before. I abide by rules that my past self would have snubbed her nose at. I did all this because I knew I needed refuge or I was going to die like the rest of my family and friends."

I wait for Dumas to deliver his translation, astounded that his voice even catches at one point.

"Like me, you have been thrown into a strange land," I say. "Pulled from the imminent threat of death, you sometimes ask yourself if you are a fish pulled from the jaws of a shark but thrown on land, miles from water. Death is still coming for you… unless you can find water again. And fast."

Dumas launches into Spanish, picking up his pace. Eyes are wide. Mouths are open as they wait for the resolution I've been building up to.

He ends, and I pause before continuing, looking out over the ever-shifting crowd. Their movements seem agitated, but their emotions flutter with ever-growing excitement.

"Agua," Dumas murmurs from next to me, unbidden. "El Cielo… Que han resuelto la crisis del agua…"

I know the word 'agua,' and 'crisis' is probably exact. He's figured it out…

"As I speak to you," I say, "trucks have been dispatched toward your camps carrying bottles of a substance called Purus. One drop will purify a gallon of water for drinking and solidify the sediment so it can be easily separated. It will be made freely available, and it means you are no longer tied to overcrowded areas. You are no longer dependent on dwindling clean water sources. You, like me, can remake your life. You can rebuild. We are the Guild. We may be made up of Prime Humans, but we were not formed *for* Prime Humans. We are here for *you*. For the future. For all."

It's clear that there are many bilingual people in the crowd. Shock and relief ripples over them even before Gabe Dumas delivers the first sentence. But once he does, the murmuring grows in pitch. Gasps and exclamations fill the air as people grasp the message. I unfocus my eyes to see them past their life forces. People start crying, hugging each other.

The most common word I hear among the interwoven Spanish is 'Agua.'

Water.

My own tears have begun to flow freely; it's difficult not to just sob. Dumas is squeezing my hand again, but I can't tear my eyes away from the people below, their exultant relief. The loud chatter and beaming smiles. I'm laughing and crying and smiling all at once. I have to wipe my eyes with my free hand over and over just to see. When I do, the energy world is back in view, but it's different. Above the crowd is a haze, like steam maybe, but more opalescent, with hints of reflective color moving through it. It seems to be coming off of the sea of life forces—off of the people themselves.

I have no idea what it is precisely, but it must have to do with what I feel right now, through them. I also know it's time to go. I raise my right hand to wave. Dumas follows, lifts our joined hands as well, and we stand united for another five seconds before I release his hand and have to close my eyes a moment to center myself back in the normal world again. It's not nearly as dizzying as before, so it doesn't take but a moment. When I open my eyes, Mike is right there, ready. But I barely catch his expression as he moves to put himself between the crowd and my back.

I meet Shiah at the door. She's looking over my shoulder in visible consternation as she offers her arm. "Just beautiful, as always, Wendy," she says without looking at me, leading me back into a room set aside for prep. She motions for Mike and Brad to stay outside the door, and she shuts it.

"Am I in trouble?" I say, collapsing on one of the couches. What a rush.

"For holding hands with the enemy?" Shiah says. "That was quite brash of you, but I doubt anyone is going to be complaining. Dumas included."

"Then why did you kick everyone out?"

"Because you saw something earlier. I'm guessing it had to do with why you asked Dumas to hold your hand."

I frown. "I don't know if I'm allowed to tell you, Shiah. I mean, I want to. I *really* want to. But it's EWR stuff. And I'm a rules girl these days."

"We can discuss what information I'm privy to later, but let me start off with a statement. I know the assumption has been that you are not a channel. But I'm almost entirely convinced now that you actually are. And I believe you just channeled Gabe Dumas. You *showed* him the energy world, Wendy."

Thirty-Seven

I sit up abruptly. "What? How do you know that?" I demand.

She perches on the arm of the couch. "Earlier, when you were hanging on to Mike's arm and staring at the crowd for over an hour, you were looking at the energy world, weren't you?"

"Y-yes," I say hesitantly. "The way Dumas was moving the crowd... It looked like... It was familiar. I wanted to see it... on the other side."

"And when you took Dumas' hand, it was to use him to go into the energy world, wasn't it?" she says intently.

I nod, grateful that Shiah seems to have at least some knowledge about how my energy world sight works. "I wanted to see them move as he spoke. It wasn't the same though. Until the end. Then something weird happened with their life forces, but I was too caught up in the moment to figure out what it meant."

"His face, Wendy," Shiah says. "I saw him on the camera feeds and that's what makes me think so. Right before you started speaking his eyes got huge. He fell back a step. He was gasping during your opening remarks in shock. That's why he stumbled through the first line. When he came back, his face looked like yours when you were staring at the crowd earlier. Then, at the end when you let him go, he fell against the pillar behind you. Then I couldn't see because his bodyguard got in the way. Wendy, have you ever touched someone while you've gone into the energy world?"

"Sure. With Jonas the other day, we went outside and that's how I figured out I could enter the energy world without my subject on a table under any kind of meditation. I held his arm while I looked outside for the first time." That was an incredible experience, actually. Before today while watching the crowd-sized life force, the sky in the energy world was the most beautiful thing I'd ever seen. Its a menagerie of colors both on and off the spectrum, and it fluctuates and undulates like a lava lamp.

"Held his arm?" Shiah says, pensive. "You touched his skin? And he didn't mention anything? Didn't react?"

"No, he had a jacket on. Thank goodness. The thought of touching him makes me want to hurl." I grimace. My coworker relationship with Jonas still needs some patching up.

"Just like Mike earlier?" Shiah says. "You didn't make contact with his skin?"

I shake my head. "Come to think of it, I don't think I've ever touched anyone's *skin* while I've been in the energy world."

"Until now," Shiah says, her face distant, arms wrapped around her and resting on her knees.

"So I'm a channel? How? Your father said I wasn't. Because it would have had to come from the hypno—I mean the life force manipulation I had done years ago. Which would mean I'd be dead already. He said I had to have figured out how to undo it. And besides, nobody has died, and I've touched plenty of people's skin."

Shiah stands, arms still folded, and she paces slowly, eyes on the floor.

Meanwhile, I listen within the building. Particularly I listen for Gabe Dumas. If he saw the energy world through me, wouldn't he say something to one of his people?

I catch his voice finally: '*I'll leave it to your discretion, Tranwick, but I'd like to make my way out the same way I came in.*'

'*Understood,*' a rich, deep voice—Tranwick's I'd guess—says. '*My team will continue scouting. We need to be ready when they give the clear.*'

'*Garrett, I need books,*' Dumas says. '*If it must be one of your online pathetic excuses for a library, so be it. My urgency has superseded my principles.*'

'*Awww, you hear that Lelani?*' a voice, maybe belonging to Garrett says. '*Gabe's going to make a deal with the library devil finally.*'

'*There's always a woman behind it,*' a feminine voice answers—Lelani, I guess. A pause, and then she says, '*Oh wow. Whitley's going to be on Good Morning America the day after tomorrow. They sure managed to keep that under wraps until the last minute.*'

There's a pause for a few seconds, and then someone laughs loudly. If I had to guess, I'd say it's Gabe Dumas. My suspicions are confirmed when as soon as it quiets he says, '*You don't say?*'

That woman... I would give my right arm to have but ten minutes with her undivided attention. Ten Minutes! *I don't need my right arm much anyway.* Her *though... I need inside that head of hers.*' He sighs wistfully. '*Her continual distance and dismissal is suffocating me slowly.*'

'*Distance? She held your hand in front of six thousand people,*' a woman with a surlier voice than Lelani says disdainfully. '*You need to stop falling for her garbage. I warned you about the interviews from the start but you didn't listen until she came on the scene. Why is it everything I say goes in one ear and out the other?*'

'*Eight thousand, seven hundred and seventy-six at the end—and those are the ones that were in sight,*' Gabe says, seeming unperturbed by the woman's chastisement. '*And I don't listen to you because everything you say these days is negative.*'

A scoff. '*Gabe, that girl is the* Guild,' says the same grumpy woman. '*No matter what you wish and hope and want so desperately to believe, she's Guild, through and through. Everything she does out there serves her master. And making you feel like she's even remotely on your side is the result of the talent and resources behind her. You know how much of our campaign has been dependent on them. Today's numbers... After how much pushback we got going into the camps on foot to promote, the attendance doesn't match. That was them. They got bodies in the street. We are being played. And the girl is owning you. As if being their Triple Prime Human Deluxe who can see the forces of the universe weren't enough for us to have to combat, she's also an empath. Why didn't she mention that in St. Louis? More Guild secrets, because that's who she is. At least it explains how she's a twenty-something with that kind of stage presence. She's been cheating. She rides the energy of the crowd after you've riled them up. She's a cheater. Just like all of them, she's using her advantage to push support for the Guild using* our *platform, and now she's using* you *directly.*'

Silence fills whatever room they're in, but it's not long before Dumas says, '*You don't even hear yourself, Rita. The Human Movement is about stopping the exaltation of the Guild, to realize that they and us are all human. We aren't different species. We aren't working for different things. I want them seen as people, not gods, and treated as such. And our events are about taking that message to as many people as possible. What does it matter* who gets the bodies in the room? Are we not still heard? What does it matter if the Guild shares a stage with us? I can't think of anything that brings them closer to our level than that. Of course they benefit from the spotlight. They have every right to. They helped create it! And today? They made an announcement about the most humanitarian technology the world has ever seen and they did it at *our event!*

'*They haven't silenced us, Rita. They haven't silenced us at all. They've given us every opportunity to be heard. They've simply spoken louder thus far. But we can turn it around. If we can't do this... If we can't convince people that the exclusiveness of the Guild is no longer necessary, then we weren't right to begin with. I don't hate the Guild; I don't think the general membership is made up of liars and usurpers. If you feel that way, you probably ought to go see about PHIA recruitment. The Human Movement is not for you. I wish you wouldn't though. I do appreciate your insights. I may not act on them directly, but I do internalize them. I quit interviewing, didn't I?*'

'*Yes, but your terms are counterintuitive,*' Rita says, and it's clear from the fact that she's not up in arms after Dumas' speech that the two of them spend a lot of time openly criticizing one another. '*And if you didn't care about the source of the spotlight, why did you deliver the ultimatum to begin with?*'

'*I'm a louse in front of the media,*' Dumas says dismissively. '*I intend to improve. But I stand by the ultimatum, and I am still pondering the meaning of their quick response to it. Miss Whitley has not interviewed until now because the Guild doesn't do interviews. It would shred their persona of mystery and make them too accessible. So why now? If you've got a probable answer, I'm interested to hear your opinion.*'

A door opens. '*Mister Dumas,*' Tranwick's unmistakable voice says. '*A moment please?*'

'*Certainly,*' Dumas says, and then the door shuts.

'*Dear god, what's the fastest way to get food poisoning?*' Rita hisses. '*He's going to make us watch GMA for research. And he's going to gush the entire time. If I'm going to lose my breakfast I want it on my own terms.*'

'*Only because you aren't the subject of the gushing, Rita,*' Garrett says. '*Come off it. Dogging* her *is not how you get him to notice you instead.*'

'*Shut up, Garrett!*' Rita whispers. '*He's just outside the door.*'

I come back to the current room where Shiah is sitting on the other side of the couch instead of the arm. She's waiting on me.

"Hey," I say. "How long have you been staring at me?"

"What did you learn?"

"If he saw the energy world, he gave no indication," I say. "But there's only one way to really know... I have to go there again and touch someone's skin. Do you have clearance for EWR, Shiah? It'd be nice to know once and for all so I don't have to talk around it when it comes up."

"I have as much clearance as I want," she says. "But the EWR department is something I've steered clear of, although my father would like it otherwise."

"Why do you steer clear?"

"Energy theory is not developed enough. It's a waste of my time."

"Really?" I say. I did not expect that answer at all. "You think it's bunk even though it's the origin of life force abilities?"

"It's not *bunk*. It's simply irrelevant as a basis for decisions until it provides reliable and concrete information. EWR spends their time feeling around in the dark. They attempt to ascertain the laws of a world they can only observe through a tenuous sensation in their hands. In essence, energy world research is as viable as afterlife research."

I laugh. "Tell me how you really feel, Shiah. I do see it, you know. It's a real place."

"I have no doubt the energy world is every bit as real as this one," she says. "But if you are the only one who ever experiences it, the scientific method can never be exercised."

"If that's true... Why have the EWR department at all?"

She stares at me, assessing. I think the crowd must have disbursed, because they have finally faded enough that I can pick up her feelings. She wonders if she should answer my question, or maybe she wonders if I can answer it myself. I'm not sure which.

"If I am a channel though... that changes everything, doesn't it?" I say.

"It does. The energy world can be observed and tested across disciplines if you are. And that means..." Shiah rubs her hands over her face, conflicted. Wait, Shiah is conflicted?

I hold up my hands. "Okay, how about we stop the speculation and test it first?"

She nods. "Yes. You're exactly right."

"Take my hand," I say.

Her hand falls in mine and I close my eyes. It takes me a few seconds longer than earlier. I guess the crowd really does make it easier.

I open my eyes to the shifting lights of the energy world-overlaid room. And it doesn't take but a moment of feeling Shiah's emotions to tell that she's seeing what I do. Amazement. Awe. Shock. These are all things I felt the first time I saw it, too.

She lets go of my hand abruptly, hurling us back into the comparatively dark 'real' world. Shiah is breathing heavily, her heart rate accelerated.

She pops out of her seat, paces the room in front of me, and I can feel her mind at work.

"I'm a channel," I say, letting the words settle on my tongue. "Oh my gosh... And that means I showed *Gabe Dumas* the most restricted information on the planet."

Shiah yanks the door open. "Brad, tell Franklin I want Gabe Dumas brought to me. Immediately."

"He and his team left probably twenty minutes ago," Brad says. "Do you need them... retrieved?"

Shiah pauses, frustrated. Her urgency is kind of frightening, and though I don't know precisely what's going on in her head, I trust her unequivocally. So I step forward. "Mike, go alone. Find Gabe. Tell him this: he has those ten minutes, no arm necessary, if he'll come back here. We'll make sure he and his team get out of town safely."

I give him a look when he hesitates, but with no protest from Shiah or anyone else, he nods and heads for the stairs.

"No arm necessary?" Shiah says as she shuts the door again.

"Gabe Dumas would give up his right arm to have ten minutes of my undivided attention," I say, smiling at her. "He's going to get a kick out of wondering how I knew he said that. Now, you tell me the plan."

"First, I need to reschedule the helicopters."

I snigger, "Helicopters? You're kidding."

"How else did you think we'd get out of here? I don't have another tractor trailer waiting behind a bush." She taps a message on her phone.

"I don't know. I figured we'd drive out. You don't think they'd let us pass after what we just did?" I sit on the couch again.

"If you give more, people tend to automatically and immediately expect more. See, that's the real problem with the Guild that Dumas has yet to realize. That's the thing the Council is coming to realize but is at a loss for how to handle, and is the *primary* reason we still exist behind a curtain. We have to constantly outdo ourselves. We have elevated ourselves. We've made promises. We've set our own standard. Now, if you call yourself a Prime Human, there is an immediate expectation for you. You better practice *exactly* what we preach. Should we fail to deliver improvement often enough, we will be the natural target of blame for all hardship we *didn't* prevent. We will fall from grace. One day, if we don't evolve, the very people we help will destroy us because we will have made ourselves irrelevant." Her head is still bent over her phone, as if her words are casual declarations. But they're not. At all.

"Um. If I weren't more concerned about what we're going to say to Dumas, I would totally ask you more about that," I say, floored, "but Mike's going to locate him in like ten minutes. We don't have a lot of time. Can I reserve you to continue this discussion on the plane later?"

Shiah puts her phone down finally and takes a breath. "It's not unrelated. If it were, I would not have said it. Let's hop back to your previous question. You asked why we had an EWR department if it couldn't produce useful data. The reason is because everyone needs something to believe in. Hard, observable data has never been enough. Humans need the Guild. And the Guild needs the energy world. In both cases the mystery, the obscurity, the enigmatic promise that someone or something out there moves things outside of our control... People crave it. They psychologically need it. Because without it, it's just them. It's... just... them. And that, Wendy, is the most terrifying, most debilitating idea to us humans. Ultimate responsibility. Self-Governance.

"Until right now, EWR has been nothing more than a point of worship for Prime Humans. The department is classified and mysterious, not just because what little is known is actually dangerous in the wrong hands, but also because if Primes *knew* what little was known, how much the Council operates on the fallibility of human judgment, they would lose faith in the system. Most of them would go their own way, searching for another idol. And all that we *do* accomplish within our great collaboration toward a better world would be lost. See, that's the great mystery to it all. It's not the Council or the energy world that accomplishes feats of wonder like Purus. It's the everyday members. The Prime Humans who believe, with all their hearts, that they serve an ultimate destiny of triumph, that their privilege of life force power comes from a world reserved for only a few, and that their beloved Council makes their decisions based on 'research' the energy world tells them. This perception is what enables the Guild, Wendy. Until now."

"Until now?" I say.

"You are a channel. Through you, any Prime Human can come face to face with the source of their own ability. Through you any Human can see the inner-workings of Primes. It will demystify everything. And now Gabe Dumas has seen it. He can describe it, in public, to anyone he chooses. If the Council finds out... If Primes find out... EWR... I have considered it from many angles, and the risk is too great. And now is *not* the time to destroy the integrity of the perception of the Guild. It would be too much, too fast. First, you must not let anyone in EWR know you are a channel. As for the Council..." Shiah purses her lips. "I need more time to assess the efficacy and timing of telling them. And second, you *must* keep Dumas from sharing what he's seen with anyone."

"How?" I say, frightened by her intensity.

Shiah sits finally, across from me. She leans forward. "Wendy, Gabe Dumas has feelings for you. He has respect for you. He sees you as a worthy opposition *and* a worthy ally. And most importantly, he trusts you. Even more than his own brother despite the fact that *both* of you are employed by the Guild. I need you to use this. I need you to protect the Guild by protecting the sacred things that keep its wheels moving toward progress. We need much more than the development of Purus before this disaster crisis is over. Do you understand? Will you do whatever it takes to gain a promise from Gabe Dumas that he will never share what he saw today?"

I stare at her blankly, wrapping my head around all the words she's said. It's going to take me a lot longer than today to grasp it all, but an affirmative answer is eager on my tongue. And only because it's Shiah. It's her I trust. Not the Guild. Not Primes. I would do whatever she asked, because her wisdom is unsurmounted. She perceives my thoughts without my words.

She preempts my questions before they have fully formed in my head. She grasps my struggles without me saying. And her timing and ability to plan is so spot-on that it's like she can choreograph reality to culminate into a grand finale of her choosing. And now she's asking *me* to participate in that?

"Yes, of course I will," I say.

She smiles. "Good. A promise is all you need, Wendy. In past interviews, Mike was vehement about that one quality: Gabe's word is ironclad." She stands up and heads toward the door.

"Wait, you're not staying?" I say. "I'm not supposed to have private communication with him. I figure having you around is like having the Council in the room, right?"

"There are exceptions to every rule, Wendy. Wisdom is knowing when those exceptions are." She opens the door. "I'll have him sent in as soon as he arrives." She shuts the door behind her.

With her confidence gone, I'm visibly nervous. I realize I am terrified of being alone with Dumas. I'm not sure why. Is it because now it's just me? Do I lack confidence entirely and that fact has escaped me because every time I've been around him I've hidden my own self-doubt behind the more palatable emotions of others?

That's got to be it. I'm a total fraud. And he's going to realize it now. This was such a bad idea... Not only does he have classified energy world information, but now he's going to know I'm an emotional puppet. Whatever perception he had of me that allowed me to gain his respect is going to be lost. And with it, the whole 'make Dumas obsessed and bring down his operation' idea is going to be trashed. I'll ruin everything.

Where is my ginger tea when I need it?!

There is no way I can do this. Shiah needs to handle this. She is far more capable than me anyway.

I stand up to go find her just as the door opens to reveal Mike. And behind his shoulder, Gabe Dumas.

"Shiah informed me you were to have strict privacy," Mike says, his face expressionless. His words are so devoid of feeling that it's only when he stands there without letting Dumas in that I realize there was the barest hint of a question in his tone.

"Yes. Thank you, Mike," I say quietly.

He nods once, steps to the side, says nothing more as Gabe moves past him into the room.

It's only once he shuts the door that my eyes come to rest on Gabe Dumas, who has been watching me as intently as Shiah often does. I'm alone with him. I am alone with the leader of the resistance movement.

"Hello, Mister Dumas," I say, having no clue what I'm going to say after the greetings are out of the way. "Thank you for coming."

"Miss Whitley," he says, his dark, piercing eyes not leaving mine. He breaks into a smile. "The thanks is all mine. This is an unmatched pleasure."

Thirty-Eight

My eyes involuntarily lock on to Dumas', and we apprise one another. He tilts his head a little when my eyes meet his, eyebrows arching, unsurprised that I haven't yet spoken beyond an initial greeting. This is the first time I've been allowed to experience Gabe Dumas' emotions exclusively. He knows what I'm doing. And he makes no move, either physically, verbally, or emotionally to obstruct my probing of his mind. He seems not only willing, but welcoming of my violation, which makes it not feel like violation at all. I'm an honored guest here.

So I start poking around as his intellect shifts into gear—he is obviously drawing conclusions about my interest in his emotions, and I examine every blip of that movement. The impression that keeps reverberating back to me, each time I taste some new emotional thread of his, is genuine, effortless authenticity. I'm wandering around in there, looking for some sign that Gabe Dumas is not what he seems—some indication that the things he obviously now knows about the energy world have bred a subversive plan.

I get nothing even remotely indicative of that. What's more astounding is that when I search for signs of self-deception, I feel only brazen determination. I have never felt an adult with such an honest mind. In all my years of sensing emotions I have accepted that everyone—other than young children—close off some part of their consciousness either by deliberate or subconscious choice. Mikel would probably agree with me. Shiah is a different case, because while she doesn't *hide* what she feels, she does *control* it. She decides what to feel and when.

Gabe just feels. He's unafraid of what any of it may mean. He's living right in there, all systems go, no secrets, not even from himself and certainly not from me. The more I look at him, read him, follow his emotional rhythm and the effect it has moving through his body—*my* body—the more those emotions indicate that Gabe

Dumas has a *serious* attraction toward me. That draw grows with every passing moment. It expands his chest until it physically aches.

I expect him to shy away from that, to attempt to hide it, but he doesn't. He embraces it like some new curiosity that needs to be shaken and tested.

I can't seem to tear myself away from his intoxicating mind to speak. I want to live in there. I want to learn the ways of his positively fearless soul. I gather all this about him in under fifteen seconds although it seems like far longer. His character didn't require any searching. The entire procession is right there on display.

Something inside Gabe Dumas is softening to the point of incoherency—which seems like it ought to be a foreign emotion to him considering how quick I've already ascertained his intellect to be. In fact, behind his oozing emotions, a part of his brain is analyzing the feelings and drawing conclusions. And the conclusion to him is startling. He retests it again, unable to deny the growing warmth within him.

I marvel that I know so much about what's going on in his head in play-by-play detail. I've learned his emotional symphony lightyears faster than anyone before. As a result, everything he's done and said in the past makes perfect sense. It all falls into place as the man behind The Human Movement, Gabe Dumas, earns my utter respect and deepest admiration. He's extraordinary. One-of-a-kind.

The intensity of his attraction grows so powerful that I can't properly breathe or separate myself from it. I can only look away, fighting for control of my own emotions that have gotten carried away with his.

He closes his eyes as a result of mine leaving. He takes a labored breath, coming to a resigned but not necessarily disappointed conclusion. "I can only assume it's obvious to you," he says, "but I'm not capable of feeling something that strongly and not speaking my mind. It's why I keep getting myself in trouble on television. But even so, I hope you won't be offended for me to speak what I know you feel. I adore you, Miss Whitley. You have occupied my thoughts regularly ever since you first appeared across the lawn in St. Louis, and even more so every day since. You intrigue me more and more. And after tonight I fear I shall not sleep but instead strive to conjure again and again the feeling I have when you look at me as you just did."

I stop breathing, blinking in surprise. He's right. His feelings are no mystery, but I have never before had someone volunteer to expound on, let alone admit aloud, what they actually feel to a veritable stranger. Considering who he is, and who I am, this is utterly inconceivable, yet it just happened right in front of me.

Why? Why would he put all his cards on the table like that?

I remember that I'm still standing in the same place I was when he walked in, so I take up a spot on the couch just to shake up the air. I've run an emotional marathon through Gabe Dumas' mind. What happens now?

"Would you like a seat?" I say, motioning to the other end of the couch and wishing there were some other piece of furniture to point him to in the small room. Sharing a couch suddenly feels way too intimate.

He obliges and then looks at me expectantly, waiting. I can tell he desperately wants to ask me questions. Lots of questions. And above all, he wants to know how his words sit with me. But I'm the one that called this meeting, so he sees it as rude to assert himself more than he already has.

Oh my gosh. I already know him well enough to translate all that.

"How do you do that?" I ask him when the silence seems to reach a fever pitch and I can't figure out what I need to say first about why we're here. All the while Gabe has been impatient for me to speak as if it's the only thing that matters to him in the world at this very moment. It leaves me breathless but excited with anticipation.

He raises his eyebrows. "Do what?"

"Just... do stuff like tell me you adore me without even pausing or deflecting? I don't sense a single shred of self-conscious fear or apprehension or worry. Even in a regular, everyday situations between people... Without the welfare of thousands demanding objectivity and detachment, that's unheard of in my experience. But considering who I am and who you are, it seems downright impossible that you'd be bold enough to be so open about it. I can't figure out how you manage that."

Dumas smiles. "Just how nuanced are the emotions you read?" he asks as he turns something over in the background of his mind.

"Depends on the person and my experience with them. Yours practically write your exact thoughts out. By far the most nuanced emotions I've ever encountered. But anyway, you haven't answered my question."

He relishes pleasure in my answer before he says, "Indeed, Miss Whitley, you are correct. I was simply considering a response."

"You have to *consider* a response, Mister Dumas?" I ask, smiling—which comes easily. "You've never had a problem coming up with one instantly before…"

"With narrow-minded interviewers who only ask the same questions over and over, of course not," he says. "Your presence, however, is taking its toll on my intellect. Furthermore, as usual, you ask a question I haven't considered before. So I have to think about it. There are a lot of factors working against me at the moment." He smiles expectantly at me.

I hold my breath for a moment to subdue the explosion of butterflies in my stomach. I need ask something before he turns the tables and puts the spotlight on me instead. "You've never considered it weird that you can spout off your feelings to strangers when other people have such a hard time doing it with people they've known for far longer?" I ask.

"Do *you* have a hard time spouting off your feelings?" he asks, watching my face intently, full of begging inquisitiveness. "It seems like it would be easy for someone like you who can so readily know of someone's intentions."

I called it. He's going to figure out how to get me to own up to the truth one way or another. But I'm not sure what that truth *is* yet… *Or maybe all these emotions are just too crazy to be real…*

"You'd think so," I reply. "But believe it or not it's more of a handicap than anything. Because people are notorious liars. Not just with others but with themselves. They live in self-denial. It's hard to trust anyone when you know that no matter what they say, it's not the thing they *want* to say. It's not the thing they *need* to say. It's hard to put yourself out there when you know you aren't getting the same even if the person is well-intentioned."

"Interesting insight," Dumas says, considering it. "So you expect honesty but you don't always give it?"

"True," I reply, surprising myself, but then, in Dumas' emotional climate of honesty, it's hard not to act on it. "Like I said, it's not all roses. I can't fully appreciate anyone and can't fully be myself because I know that it's not reciprocated. It's a self-destructive cycle." I shrug. "Maybe if I could ignore it for a short time and get past the preliminary falsities of a relationship I could push through their barriers, but I'm also impatient and demanding. I analyze emotional waves, *looking* to take offense at the first sign of even the vaguest dishonesty. It doesn't take long for me to despise people. I'm easily frustrated."

"Do you despise me?" he asks quietly, leaning toward me ever so slightly, his eyes stealing mine again.

"No," I reply softly, a dizzying flurry taking hold of my chest.

"Miss Whitley, what I saw earlier… I assume that was your doing. Why did you show me that?"

"It was," I say, grateful for his reminder as to why we're here right now. His emotions are almost brutally intense. I'm losing myself in them. "And it was accidental," I answer without thinking. I can't seem to help coming clean. How can I lie when he's been so truthful with me? I have no idea how I'm going to exact the promise Shiah wanted.

He sits up. "Accidental? How so?"

"Because I didn't know I could show it to other people. I was using you to see the crowd in the energy world—that's actually the main reason I wanted to hold your hand. It was the first time I'd touched someone while there." More confessions… What has come over me?

"Yet you weren't surprised by my question, which implies that you knew you had shown me. Which means showing others was at least in the realm of possibility, or you were alerted somehow as you were showing me. Which is it?"

I wave a hand. "Look, I'm not going to go into the details of something you shouldn't have seen in the first place."

He sits back. "Then why am I here?" he asks, annoyed by my deflection, which is a relief after so much heavy chemistry. "You want something from me, clearly, and I'm guessing that if that was indeed a slip-up, what you want is my silence about it. Again. You are asking for silence. You can't seem to ask for or give anything else."

"You are the opposition," I snap. "I owe you nothing! And you would be *nothing* without the Guild's intervention on The Human Movement's behalf. Any success you see? It's a ruse, Mister Dumas. We made you what you are. So you either promise you will keep silent about what you saw, or attendance at your events will dwindle into nothingness."

He stares at me, stone-faced, calculating, but this time it's full-speed. I can't keep up with it; it's positively dizzying. He comes to a sudden mental halt, and he slaps his thighs with his hands as if mentally wrapping up our meeting. "I don't take kindly to threats, Miss Whitley," he says calmly. "And I can't ever seem to turn down a challenge either. Nothingness, you say? I'll be sure to quote you on that at one of my future events."

He stands up, almost turns to go, but something else occurs to him. "You say The Human Movement would be nothing without the Guild... But who would *you* be, Miss Whitley, without *us*? That's the thing I wonder about you more than anything."

His outrage at my threat is clear, but he's right on that count. I wouldn't be a public figure if I hadn't stumbled across news coverage of his event months ago. I wouldn't have considered outing my life force ability if I hadn't seen what a brilliant orator he was and known it was going to take someone of equal guts to contend with him. In fact, everything I've done that's been considered brilliant was because I was making sure I outdid him. It's a humiliating realization, but underneath it all is the overall truthfulness of his question beyond what he even realizes.

Shiah's words come back to me about using Dumas' campaign to promote our own. She said Dumas would cement our cause. *Truth will have the final say*, she told me after Dumas realized his success in achieving a public presence was due to the Guild. This, I realize, was Shiah telling me how important The Human Movement is to the survival of the Guild. He is our platform to evolve into something greater. Just like his exceptional skill pushes me to break barriers with public declarations of my past and my identity, The Human Movement pushes the Guild to change the way they do things a little at a time—like letting a twenty-two year old girl take the stage and talk about being a target of PHIA. And then interviewing with Good Morning America— something the Guild also has never done.

I rub my face as the realization of what Shiah has been after all along comes crashing down on me. I know what I need to do, but I'm terrified of doing it.

Dumas, who has been waiting on my reply, gives up finally and strides toward the door.

"Wait!" I say, standing quickly.

He turns, and I can tell he's relieved that I stopped him.

"I do want your silence," I say, taking a couple steps closer to him, putting my shaking hands behind my back. "I wish it weren't always that way. I know how frustrating it is. Believe me. *I know*. I'm sorry I threatened you. I forgot what I know about you for a second because sometimes when people point out stuff you know is true, it stings."

I look down at the floor and sigh to formulate my next words. When I look up, Dumas is smiling kindly, and he's back to inviting me into his mind as if I didn't just threaten his life's work.

"Silence isn't easy to maintain," I say. "And for you I know it's especially difficult. So what would be worthwhile to you in exchange?"

He walks up to me until he is a mere three feet away. His smell, like rain on cracked earth, invades my nose and hijacks my train of thought. The draw between us is back in full-effect. I know what he's going to ask even if I couldn't already sense it in his emotions before it comes out of his mouth.

"A moment of unabashed Wendy, unhindered by duty to her newfound family," he says, his voice quiet but rich with refinement. It's the first time I've heard my first name spoken in his expressive cadence.

I look up, my mouth so dry I can hardly answer, "Okay."

His mouth turns down slightly at my visible discomfort. "Why are you frightened?" he asks gently.

I'm sweating now, and I take two deliberate breaths before resigning to the fact that they aren't helping at all, and stalling isn't helping me arrange my thoughts. "Because I know what you want to know," I say, swallowing, which also doesn't help. "And I... don't know if I can handle the implications of answering honestly."

"You think too much," he says, this time his frown turning around, his mood lighter, more playful.

I laugh twice, shedding an ounce of discomfort in the process. "Says the man who thinks constantly while simultaneously talking and feeling and calculating."

That was the wrong thing to say, at least as far as helping me regain confidence. Because he melts, then he sighs. "El Cielo, I love when you do that." He notices my resulting grimace and says, "That makes you uncomfortable? When I express how I feel?"

"No way. I am absolutely not uncomfortable when you confess your adoration," I say.

He lifts an eyebrow, one side of his mouth curved upward. "You use sarcasm to divert discomfort. I can't possibly put you on the spot now when the idea of being up front with me is so distasteful to you. I've lost my appetite for blackmailing you into honesty with my political clout. Furthermore, I'm growing more concerned that you are going to break my heart, and that's why you are so hesitant."

My nerves diffuse and I sigh. That he would care so much about my comfort makes me suddenly and desperately *want* to confess my feelings. "And you are very considerate, trying to loosen my nerves, and holding your feelings in reserve so they don't overwhelm my ability to discern my own," I say. I look him in the eye. "Thank you for that. Ask the question I know you've been dying to ask now. I'm ready."

"After reading my thought-emotions, and after I repeatedly made you uncomfortable with my declarations, what did you think of me?" he asks.

"That you were the most extraordinary man I'd ever met. And then, after what you said to me, I thought, 'Why is he doing this, knowing what it may cause?'"

"What would it cause?" he whispers.

"Feelings I don't know that I can handle," I reply.

"What feelings?" he asks, every part of him openly begging that what I will say is what he so desperately hopes.

I cannot leave him wanting like that, not when he has offered so much of himself to me. The need to give him what he asks overtakes me. I cannot leave this space without putting my whole heart out for him. Fearlessness washes through my soul, and I reply. "Waking up tomorrow and realizing that I am in love with my nemesis."

His breath catches and he closes his eyes. Between the two of us, the temperature of the space has increased two-fold. I'm wearing a white turtleneck sweater, and I'm sweating. I'm also fighting desperately against touching Dumas.

His eyes open suddenly. "I'll go now," he says. "Because if I stay I will ask to touch you. And if I touch you I may never leave."

"But what if I said yes?" I say, stepping closer to him. "Unhindered Wendy, remember? I've already put aside what happens when I leave this room. Can't you?"

He looks up at the ceiling, exhales a staggered breath. While his body language says indecision, his emotions clearly communicate that there is no way he's going to turn me down. So I take another step closer to him, well inside his personal space.

"Aye, mi encantadora doncella," he groans softly, looking into my face. "You are torturing me. How am I going to continue living my life as it was if my heart occupies two places? How will I navigate the three interviews I have on television tomorrow without breaching your trust? They're going to ask me about you.

They always do. And all I will be able to think about when they say your name is the softness of your skin and wondering what you felt about me when you woke up."

"You think too much," I say. "And you forget who you are. You are Gabe Dumas, and you can handle anything. Why are you stalling? You've already said yes to me with your emotions. And it's been way longer than ten minutes. We've got to come out of this room sooner or later or they'll be coming *in.*"

He looks down at me with a mischievous grin. "Perhaps you haven't gleaned this already, but I'm what many would label a disgustingly over-the-top romantic. I love to prolong longing, and so my ideal fantasy is that of forbidden love. I'm stalling so I don't forget this moment tomorrow. I've got to have something to last me through the indefinite number of days that will commence before I can stand this close to you again."

He sobers as the reality of imminent separation plunks heavily between us.

Unwilling to let that ruin the moment, I reach out and lace my fingers with his, which are lean and warm. I didn't pay attention to how they felt earlier when I held his hand. I was completely caught up in wanting to see the crowd in the energy world. But now the texture and weight of his hand is all I pay attention to.

But then Gabe puts his other arm around me, resting his hand on the small of my back. I can't think; I can only bask in the intoxication brought on by having him this close. And maybe it would be a simple embrace to anyone else, but for us it's more. Beyond the door to this room, everything that we are has drawn lines between us. Yet here we are inexplicably drawn to one another by things stronger than ideals. The moment is a conquest—one where love has surpassed beliefs. I'm mystified by the mere existence of the moment, and maybe he's right; the forbidden nature of it makes the weight of his hand draw the emotion out of me so powerfully.

Gabe brings our joined hands up to his mouth where he inhales the scent of my palm. My heart dissolves and I lean into him. I run my free hand up the length of his bare arm, memorizing the divets of his inconspicuous, but substantial muscles.

He still hasn't made a move to kiss me, and needing him ever closer I let my face fall against his chest. The weight of his hand rests against my hair and I look up, expectant.

He brings his face close, but he only rests his forehead against mine, our noses nearly touching. He caresses my cheek down to my neck, his eyes closed as he breathes me in. My lips are aching for his, but when I lean in to make sure he knows, he pulls his face away. I'm disappointed, until he kisses my forehead, letting his lips linger there.

"Wendy, I don't need to sleep on it to know. I love you *now*," he says.

My overwrought heart feels like it has burst. "Then why aren't you kissing me for real?" I whisper, drunk with his words as they bounce around in my head, rustling up dizzying stirs of exultant happiness through my whole body.

"Ahh," he says, amused, hugging me to his chest again. "You know why. I'm going to very much enjoy imagining what your lips would be like on mine for the foreseeable future. Besides, I think you are going to have quite enough to defend when you face my brother. What will you offer *him* to keep quiet?" He experiences an icy shot of genuine worry along with those words.

"Mike? Why would—? Oh. *Ohhh*… Oh my gosh." I lift my face from his chest. "Oh, crap. He's right outside! He felt everything you did! What am I going to do?" I plead.

"So he told you then…" He sighs. "I honestly have no idea, Love. I am unaware of what your dynamic with him is, but no doubt you carry some status and authority. He's always been a man who can take orders. I'd try that first."

"Seriously?" I push away and put my hands on my hips. "Your brother has given me some serious intel on you for months now, stuff campaign managers can only dream of obtaining about their rivals, but when I need the same from you, your advice is to order him to stay quiet?"

He crosses his arms. "You know, his bizarre synesthetic connection with me only flows one way: toward *him*." His eyes flit up and then down, and the first hints of genuine uncertainty filter through his chest—and consequently mine. "I know my brother quite well, but even to me his actions still retain a lot of mystery. His Guild membership, for example. I didn't even know he was employed by a secret organization until a few months ago. Yet he'd been part of it for ten years. If my brother can keep that kind of secret from me for ten years, then I obviously don't know him all that well, and he obviously has a lot of respect for his superiors if he unwaveringly kept their order to keep the Guild a secret from his own family that long."

"This sucks," I say, shifting my feet, dread beginning to take me over. "This really, really sucks."

"I take it there are further complications," Gabe says. He sighs, and then in a robotic voice says, "Are you involved with him?"

I look up. "Why would you say that?"

"I will take that as a yes."

"It is not a yes!"

Gabe rubs his forehead, and his heart sinks a thousand leagues. "As much as it wounds me to say it, you owe me no fidelity. Outside of these walls I can't be anything to you but Gabe Dumas, founder of The Human Movement. Whatever it is you haven't talked through with him though, you need to. Force the issue if you have to. Pursue something with him if the mood strikes you. In fact, I implore you to not hold back. You and I have no future, only chance meetings if your overseers let you for the sake of yet another secret they want me to keep. Make no mistake, I will keep the ones I have already agreed to. But I have to continue my work. And you have yours."

He steps back, toward the door, leaving me with my mouth open in shock. "You tell me you love me and then you tell me to get with your brother in the same five minutes?" I say. "What am I missing?"

"Only that Mike loves you," Gabe says. "Has loved you. Even before me. And Mike actually has a chance with you that I don't."

"You're acting like you're interchangeable," I say, flabbergasted that I am once again being rejected, and after the most genuine moment I've ever had with someone in my whole life.

He shrugs, his back to the door now. And his face is utterly devoid of the expression of happiness I saw only a moment ago. He is shockingly resigned. "You got what you brought me here for, didn't you? Why are you disappointed?"

"I didn't—I mean, I did, but then you were... I didn't expect..." I flounder. I started this meeting intent on following Shiah's instructions, that I'd get Dumas to promise. And I did. He's not stupid though... He knows that everything that has transpired was based on his promise as currency. If I were him, and I was faced with that harsh reality...?

"I know," he says, holding up his hand.

"I meant the things I said," I say, close to tears, wanting to step closer to him again, but his hand between us says a definitive no.

"Goodbye, Wendy," he says. "Thank you for far more than the moment of unabashed Wendy I'd hoped for."

I can't find my voice as he turns around and opens the door. He shuts it behind him, and I stare, completely at a loss. But Shiah appears within moments, and with her comes the memory of the prophecy she made, '*Gabe Dumas is going to fall in love with you.*' She warned me against getting involved with Mike. '*Date anyone else*,' she said. '*No one else will daunt him. Except Mike.*'

She was right. She was ridiculously right. And for the first time I think she also knew *I* would fall for *Gabe*. She didn't tell me because she knew how I'd react. Her advice wasn't just about strategy after all.

She walks up to me and uncharacteristically but genuinely puts her arms around me while I fight tears over could haves, should haves, and impossibilities.

I only partly succeed. It's stupid. I just basically met, got to know, fell in love with, and then broke up with the guy in the space of half an hour. This should *not* be affecting me this way.

"You're an empath, Wendy," Shiah replies. "You can take a read on someone's character in less than a minute. You recognized what you wanted immediately. It's not petty, fleeting, or less viable simply because it was short."

"Do you think the recovery time will be as short?" I say into her shoulder.

"It's going to add a whole new angle to this campaign," she says. "So forgetting and letting go is likely going to be impossible."

"Wheeeeee," I say, letting go of her and wiping my eyes. "So what's *your* advice on keeping Mike quiet?"

Thirty-Nine

The sound of helicopter blades disrupts any opportunity to speak with Mike. Gabe, who apparently chose to come without his team and only his bodyguard Tranwick, opted to make his way out of the city without our help. I worry about him as Mike draws his gun, and our line of protection herds us out of the building and toward the street where the first of several helicopters has landed to pick our team up. I don't get to see much of anything in the streets surrounding us because Mike has me running, crouched over under his arm.

The door of the helicopter slams shut and we are immediately lifted into the air. It's too loud to talk, but Mike's emotions from beside me spell out clearly his disapproval. He's practically shouting it at me, and after a while I realize he's taking advantage of my inability to properly talk back to him. He's yelling at me without me being able to defend myself.

Coward. He's going to hear it. I might even fire him for good measure.

I consider all kinds of vindictive things as we fly through the darkness toward the small airstrip to the west that we came in on. We didn't use the Raleigh-Durham airport. It's already shelter to thousands of refugees, as most public facilities in this area are now.

And then my thoughts return to Dumas and where he might be. I close my eyes, hunch against the wall so Mike can't see my face. I spend the rest of the trip warding off Mike's growing acrimony though. He's making me more furious by the moment.

As soon as we land, I am hot on Shiah's heels, coming beside her, leaning in, and mumbling, "Permission to lay in to my bodyguard in private once we are boarded?"

"He is *your* employee, not mine," she replies, distracted with her GIT. "Let me know the status of the sensitive information afterward though, please."

"Done," I say, falling back.

The plane has already been secured when we reach it, so we board immediately. I expect Mike to disappear once the hatch is in place, but he doesn't. He follows me even more dutifully than before. That sucks. I really wanted to be able to call him a coward. I open the door to my private room and stand to the side, motioning him in.

He is all too eager.

"Shut up," I snap as soon as he opens his mouth. And then I get in his face. "Don't you *dare* pull crap like that with me again! You will *not* scream at me emotionally while I can't get away or reply. And furthermore you get *zero* say in what I do. It's above your pay grade. It's out of line. And I will *not* tolerate it!"

"That's how you're going to play it?" he growls. "Use your rank to shut me up because that's the best defense you have, isn't it? I seriously expected better from you. But I'm not sure why. Not after what I've seen you do in the past." He scoffs. "You're despicable. You don't represent the Guild. You sure as hell don't represent me. Do us all a favor and step down before you make a mockery of everything we stand for."

I cross my arms. "Excuse me? Getting involved with your brother is *despicable*? What makes him so objectionable to you, Mike? Because he thinks the Guild could do for more honesty? Because he sees our privilege and knows we could be doing more with it? Who the hell do you think *you* are thinking you're better? Thinking *we're* better? If I have feelings for Dumas it's because he's got more integrity than the entire Council put together. For you to defame him by condemning me for realizing that is what's despicable. It's vile, because I know he would never degrade *you* like that!"

Mike blinks, taken aback. His outrage stutters, backpedals, chokes forward again only to be met with bewilderment once more. He lets his hands fall to his sides and he says, "What did you meet with Gabe for?"

"That is not your business," I say.

That irritates him, but he says, "Be straight with me. Did you seduce him to gain something?"

"Seduce him? No!"

"But you met with him alone… to get something from him, right? You used his feelings for you to gain the upper hand?"

"I met with him to discuss a piece of sensitive information I knew he had possession of. The rest is… complicated."

"Uncomplicate it," he growls, crossing his arms again.

I wouldn't have guessed this level of jealousy from Mike, but it seems like the only explanation for his venom toward me.

"I don't owe you an explanation," I say. "You and I share nothing. That was *your* choice."

He scoffs. "You think *that's* what this is about? How oblivious can you be to what you are? Let me be really clear then. Taking advantage of my brother's feelings is something I will not tolerate. I no longer work for you. I quit. And I will expose you for exactly what you are. I did it to that piece of trash, Andre. And I have *no* qualms about doing it to you either." He leans into me. "I'm taking you down, Level Ten."

At first I'm livid. But as I translate the meaning of his words, however, I get the first inkling of realization that this entire fight is one huge misunderstanding. I can't help laughing, a bit hysterically, mostly out of relief. I hold up my hands in surrender. "Mike, I think we have totally talked past each other."

"Then start talking *at* me," he glares.

"Okay, okay," I say. "Sheesh. Stick that temper in your pocket for a sec. You're making me nervous. Alright, let me see if I can explain without breaching confidentiality. I had you bring Gabe Dumas because I realized he had a piece of sensitive information. Like super big deal stuff. Stuff that could bring down me *and* the Guild, except I don't think he realizes that, even now. So I wanted to talk to him and see if I could get him to agree to keep it secret. And yes, I knew going into it that he had feelings for me, and that for some deranged reason he'd come to respect me. My hope was that it was enough to get him to promise me he'd protect the information he had. I also knew, from overhearing him talk with his team earlier today, that he, quote, 'would give his right arm for ten minutes of my undivided attention.' I hoped that was what was going to seal the deal for me—that he'd get to ask me whatever it was he wanted to ask me and then he'd feel indebted to make the promise."

I sit down in the nearest chair, disliking that I have to share the next part. I can't look at Mike as I say it. The captain allows me to stall momentarily when she comes over the speaker, telling us to prepare for takeoff, so Mike takes another seat nearby and looks impatiently at me as the plane jerks into movement.

I clasp my hands together. "It was the first time I felt his emotions alone, without crowds or cars full of people to get in the way." I sigh. I don't think I can go into detail with Mike about this part. "I fell for him, okay?" I say, hoping the awkwardness deflects him from asking questions. I'm wringing my hands now. "And we had a moment, and I totally forgot why I had him there in the first place," I say in a rush. "Until he brought it up. And I had to come clean. I needed him to keep quiet. He was frustrated by that, and I got... well you know me. I tried to threaten him, mostly because I was totally caught off guard by what I was feeling. He didn't buy it, countered by getting up to leave, and I asked him to stop. Apologized. I asked him what his silence was worth. He told me he wanted me to be honest about how I felt. So I was. He promised. And then he left."

Mike is working through the information, coming down from his temper little by little. "Dammit," he says, putting his face in his hands. "I jumped to conclusions. I *lost my head.* I'm sorry."

"No, I am," I say. "I should have considered how you'd translate it—what was happening in the room—what it would 'look' like. Especially after what you saw me do to the last guy I thought deserved a lesson." My face goes red from the memory.

"I should resign," Mike says, looking up and staring at nothing. "I obviously can't handle this post."

"No!" I insist, fearful of that possibility. "You can't quit!"

"What I *can't* do is be objective. I just threatened you, my charge, the person I am supposed to give even my life for, without having facts. I've been worried this would happen, that I'd jeopardize your mission, that I'd put my brother ahead of my responsibility to the Guild. I thought I could handle it. But I've chosen him over your safety not once, but twice now. We haven't even been at this two months. I'm sorry. I have to resign."

"Mike, don't do this!" I cry. "I don't want a mindless drone for a bodyguard. I want someone to question me. I want someone who knows me, who knows *him.* I want *you* behind me."

The plane's engines drown out the cabin for a moment as we speed down the runway for takeoff. There is silence between us during that time, and Mike, unfortunately, does not seem to be conflicted. He's not going to change his mind.

The engines quiet into white noise and Mike looks at me. "You don't want me behind you. Do you know why I kept rejecting you?"

"The same reason you're trying to quit now."

"No. I rejected you because I knew since you first hit the stage in St. Louis, that Gabe was going to fall for you, that he was already doing it, little by little. I told you, didn't I? That obsessing over you was going to be his downfall? I also knew that if I started something with you, you were going develop a thing for him too. That's how it's always worked with us. The girl always ends up with feelings for both of us. Always. So I rejected you so you wouldn't start wanting him. I wanted you all to myself. I was just prepared to wait until this thing was over, and with you under strict orders to avoid private contact with him, it was unlikely you'd ever have a chance to develop a thing for him."

We sit in silence for a while, but I sense Mike has other questions, and he's been arguing with himself about wether to voice them.

"Did you listen to my voicemail?" he asks finally.

I roll my eyes. "You mean the one you didn't leave? No. I deleted it."

He grimaces. "Yeah... That whole night was kind of a disaster."

I wait for him to continue, but he's locked in an internal battle of sorts. Whatever it is he wants to say isn't coming easy.

"Mike?" I say, hands clasped in my lap. "Let's not stop being honest. Aren't we friends? I care about you. I really do. Whatever it is you're struggling with, I want to help you if I can."

"Are you Gemma Rossi?"

I sit back, shock as my first reaction. Where did he hear that name? What does it have to do with anything? "Yes," I reply. "It was the name I used when I used to do art."

He exhales in recognition. "Do you remember the Detritus Benefit?"

More shock. Where is he getting all these things about my past?

"Kind of. I was sixteen at the time. What do you know about it?"

"I was there. I met you."

"What?" I gasp. "I don't remember that."

"It wasn't exactly face to face. I came across you while you were in a crate in the back, crying."

My head spins. "Crate...? I remember the crate. I don't remember meeting *you* though, or anyone for that matter."

"What *do* you remember?" he asks curiously.

I rack my brain, digging past the haze that surrounds that time in my life. There's just sadness though, and anger. My mom showing up to support me, but I can't remember anything she said. "The cloud sculpture I made is probably the most memorable," I reply.

Mike sucks in a breath.

"And I know I must have gone into the back because I remember waking up in the crate," I say. "Everything in between though is a total blackout. Doesn't really surprise me though. It was a really tough time in my life."

"That cloud lived in my parents' house for six years," Mike says. "Gabe and I bought it for our mom."

I'm stunned into silence, blinking and trying to recall more to corroborate his story, maybe explain why I can't remember much at all. But it's all blank…

"Gabe met you, too," Mike says, leaning over, elbows on knees, hands together. "But only your voice, just like me. You never came out. We talked to you for a while, and you weren't impressed with him. That wasn't new. Gabe has a tendency to turn women off with his overabundant confessions. Gabe and I had a bloody fistfight afterward like a couple of animals. I knocked him unconscious. When he woke up in the hospital with a concussion, he'd forgotten what had happened that night, including meeting Gemma. I remembered it all though. I took his forgetting her as a sign that she was meant for me and not him. I was so sure I wasn't going to have to steal her from him, like I'd been doing with others—just to hurt him, I might add. I was desperate for hope. I was through with the ridiculous love triangles. I was sick of letting my anger at being tied to him get the better of me. I wanted out. So Gemma became that hope. She disappeared though. No record of her name outside of art circles—which she disappeared from after that day, too. The mystery bred the fantasy and the obsession to find her. I realize—*now*—that I conjured all of my delusions."

"Mike…" I say, my heart breaking for him, but also floored by the coincidence. How has my memory been wiped of everything from that night, and how have I never noticed?

More missing memories… What the hell is going on with my head?

"You're probably wondering how I figured out you were Gemma," he says, staring ahead at nothing. "It was Lainey, actually. Like I said, I met with her the other day, answered her questions. I still don't know what exactly cued her, but when I was done, she said, 'I can't breach confidentiality obviously, but you need to look into your charge's history. I think there may be a connection to her past in there somewhere. It's worth looking into.' So I researched you, starting where I met you in Missouri. I connected the dots based on the story you'd told everyone about how you came to join the Guild. News articles about the lightning storms. I combed them all, looked in Guild files, found out where your father was found, drew more conclusions, more research. Long story short, I found the missing person's report for Gemma Rossi filed by your father's alias. Shocked the hell out of me. All along… I'd been your protection and had no idea you were the girl from six years ago."

I have my hand over my mouth, no definitive reaction coming to me over the amazement.

"So now you get why after we return to the Vault, I can't be your bodyguard anymore. I love Gabe too much. I love you too much. I swore I was going to stop hurting him—because that shit only comes back to haunt me anyway. And I think, Wendy… Maybe… Maybe I had it backwards about you. Maybe Gemma was the girl that would finally choose Gabe instead of me."

I pull my knees up into my chair, feeling even worse than I did after being turned down by Gabe. I wish I could tell Mike he's wrong. That's how much his confession stirs the parts of me that have cared about his from the beginning. But the reality is… I want Gabe over him. No contest. And even if he never wants me, it's still the reality. Mike deserves someone who wants *him* that much.

Mike's standing over me. He's tugging me by the arm, and I realize my hand is still pressed against my mouth as I try to hold back tears. I don't resist, but as soon as my face reaches his chest I burst into sobs. He holds me tightly, stoic as he lets me fall apart over his plight and my own that he doesn't even realize. I force down the words I want to say. I want to beg him not to go. But that's not fair. Mike has been one of my only real friends, and it kills me that I can't give him what he wants and needs.

When I finally quiet and he releases me, he says, "So, Good Morning America in two days…"

"Yeah," I sniffle, wiping my eyes. "I'm so excited. And I just can't hide it."

He chuckles and it becomes wistful. "I think you might be more excited to know that Shiah was on the phone while you and Gabe were 'talking' and she was telling the network you wouldn't be appearing unless Gabe was put on for the same spot. I'd put my money on her winning that bargain."

My mouth opens. "The *same* spot? Is she crazy?" I roll my eyes. "Forget I said that. This has Shiah written all over it."

"What's the matter? You get to sit next to him for an entire fifteen minutes, maybe more with commercial breaks."

"I'm an empath, Mike! I do well at events because I can use the crowd. If I'm next to Dumas, no crowd to drown him out, he's going to railroad me with his emotions."

"Nah. He's totally in love with you. Your biggest problem is going to be making sure he doesn't stare at you adoringly and give your contraband romance away."

"Mike, he basically said we were a non-item before he left. He said that once he left that room he was going back to being my opposition. In fact, he said like three times that I should go be with you. He's not going to be gazing at me adoringly, Mike. He's going to have it all under control, but he's going to lock me in an emotional fight on the inside and then probably an intellectual one on the outside. I can't multi-task like that! This is going to be a disaster…" I whine.

Mike taps his chin. "So that's what that was about at the end. I figured he was just sad about having to leave… You told him we had a thing?"

I nod and grimace. "I didn't deny it. He asked me outright."

"That dumb bastard. He wasn't even going to fight for you with me in the picture." He sighs. "There was a time when I would have considered crushing him that thoroughly and easily the ultimate victory…"

I tug his arm. "Help me, Mike. How do I do this?"

He puts his hands on his hips and stares at me, pensive. "First of all, you're going to let the stylist do whatever they want to you instead of fighting them the entire time. Hair, lipstick, perfume, the whole nine yards of feminine arsenal. And you're going for ultra-prepared. I'm assuming they've sent over a list of questions?"

"Uhhh list?" I say.

"Where's your tablet?" he says.

I pull it out of my bag.

"Check your email," he says.

"Seed Questions for GMA," I say, reading the subject line of one the most recent ones.

"Let me see them."

I tap on the email and hand it to him.

His eyes scan the screen. His pensive look turns into a smile. "These will work perfectly. Count on the media to dig for dirt. This is nothing new for you. The words you come up with at the protests are you, not the crowd. Confidence is the only thing you lack. I suggest seducing Gabe backstage beforehand. Should give you a boost, plus it will knock him off his game."

I grimace. "I am not going to seduce him, Mike. Can you imagine if someone caught me?"

"You can seduce me instead if you want. In front of him." His eyebrows lift excitedly. "It'll put him in an instant bad mood and he'll make a scene in front of the media again."

"That's awful sweet of you, Mike," I say, rolling my eyes at his halfway serious, halfway playful suggestion. "We'll keep it as a backup plan. I was thinking something a little less questionable."

"Ah, fine. I'll go over the questions with you, give you his probable answer and then give you a list of do-nots to keep you out of defense territory. I don't want to tell you what to say or he'll know it's me saying it and not you."

"Perfect," I say, smiling as he takes his seat once more next to me. "By the way, this is why I need you as my bodyguard. #IntelOnDemand. That's my code name for you."

He laughs. "My code name is a hashtag?"

I grin. "I've been getting better with the social media stuff this past month. Shiah has someone push most of my posts, field my messages, so I don't have to stay on top of it all the time, but she likes me to get on there regularly, say something trademark Wendy." I roll my eyes. "I dig the hashtags though. It's fun to try to come up with something clever."

"Well #IntelOnDemand has a phone number, you know. #IntelOnYourCellphone."

I frown. "#NotTheSame."

He squeezes the top of my hand affectionately. "I know, bonita."

Forty

Good morning, Wendy," Ohr says, smiling warmly at me, hands clasped behind him. "It's been such a long time since I've seen you, but I've eagerly kept up with your appearances, so it seems not so long. You look well."

I fight to get past my shock as quickly as possible. We're in a room backstage of Good Morning America, and I did *not* expect to see him here. Council members make it a point to stay far away from the public eye.

Plus, with my interlude with Gabe Dumas two days ago still fresh in my memory, and anticipating seeing him shortly, I worry Ohr will see the evidence of my breach of trust behind my exterior. He's going to see the fact that I couldn't stop thinking about Gabe all day yesterday. Shiah would if she didn't already know. And Ohr is Shiah, the prequel.

"Hi," I manage to say finally. "How are you?" It comes out less cordial than I intended, probably because I was simultaneously thinking 'What the crap are you doing here?' while I said it.

"I'm quite well, thank you," Ohr says. "Mike Dumas," he says, looking over my shoulder. "Shiah tells me you perform your job judiciously. Your commitment to duty given the difficult circumstances of your past and present situation has been exemplary of the behavior we prize in all our members."

"Thank you, Councilman," Mike says, equally as nervous. "I appreciate the confidence, but I'm actually resigning after today."

Ohr's brow furrows. "Yes. I know. May I ask why?"

Ohr asked for permission, but I don't think it would be advisable to decline, and I can't help holding my breath until Mike comes up with an answer. "I've found myself incapable of thinking objectively," Mike says.

"I understand you share a one-way empathic connection to Gabe Dumas," Ohr says.

"That's correct."

"We weren't made aware of this when you were activated, nor were we made aware of it when you were interviewed repeatedly about your ties to The Human Movement."

"Yes, Councilman," Mike says with deference.

"We keep running into lies of omission with you," Ohr says. "Are you aware of how split the Council's decision was to allow you to serve as Miss Whitley's protection?"

"I'm not."

"I didn't expect so. And it so happens that I was one of the few who voted in vehement approval. I also made several conciliations I didn't want to on other issues in exchange for gaining majority approval. One of those concessions was that Miss Whitley would not be allowed to recruit other Prime Humans to help her. She would have to work solo. My internal reasoning was that having you as personal, real-time insight into the actions of Gabe Dumas would greatly outweigh any potential benefit of Miss Whitley's having a team to back her up in front of the public. And when I learned that not only could you share what you knew of Gabe Dumas by virtue of familial attachment, but by a veritable mind-link as well, making you, for lack of a better word, the ideal spy, you can imagine the efficacy of my previous judgment was solidified."

"I wasn't aware of that," Mike says, and then he sighs, knowing exactly what I do: Ohr is going to strong-arm him into keeping his position as my bodyguard.

"Until now," Ohr says. "Furthermore, you are probably also not aware of the vast impact of Miss Whitley's campaign on our membership in such a short time. Colloquy attendance is up twenty-two percent. Intra-Guild employment is up twenty percent. And the percentage of Prime Humans of Unification age who are members is at an all time high of ninety-six point three percent, which is up from previous highs of only eighty-one percent. Membership monetary contributions are up twelve percent. Michael Dumas, this is improvement the Guild has not seen since it was first organized. You have been integral in accomplishing that, and so I would like to know to what post you see yourself better-suited to should you step down from your responsibility as Miss Whitley's protection, especially now that you realize the primary reason you were instated in the first place and the import of Miss Whitley's calling."

I certainly didn't know any of that. Wow! I'm feeling pretty humbled, but it's hard to ignore the fact that Mike has deflated behind me. I want to intervene, but I don't know what I can say that's not going to get us in trouble. Ohr can't know the real reason Mike wants to step down, which means that Mike has no real defense.

"I see your point, Councilman," Mike says. "I discounted my value as a source of intelligence. I discounted Miss Whitley's responsibility as well."

"Which is why I came here to make sure you no longer discounted either," Ohr says. "If you'll take a moment to consider all the talents you possess, Mike, I think you'll see, as I do, that you have been unwittingly building up to this role. Your physical skill ensured your viability as an exceptional bodyguard, which meant placing you within close proximity to Miss Whitley and therefore Gabe Dumas would be seen as more natural and less suspect. There is no one, Guild-wide, who is a suitable replacement for you. Will you neglect to serve the Guild in your greatest capacity in favor of less challenged loyalty?"

Mike, suddenly aggravated, says, "And what of my life force ability, Councilman? The trade-off of being connected to Gabe is that he neutralizes my mental influence when he is in-range of my reading him directly. If he's near, he counteracts my ability. It makes me less effective at keeping Miss Whitley safe and in helping her at all with my life force ability. My understanding has always been that our greatest capacity to serve the Guild comes from putting our life force abilities into regular use for the betterment of those around us."

"He neutralizes your life force ability as well?" Ohr says, visibly intrigued. "Yet another omission, I see. I'll overlook this one as well because I think that now is the time you may want to start searching for understanding of the origin of this connection to Gabe Dumas rather than running from it, as I ascertain you have in the past. That's why you joined the Guild, wasn't it? To separate yourself from him? I know you were extremely close to him growing up, and I know when he began The Human Movement rather than joining the Guild, you were more relieved than you admitted to anyone aloud. I fear, Mike, that your sole reason for your Guild membership is not principle, but escape."

It's obvious to me, from Mike's internal reaction, that Ohr has struck a nerve of truth. So it's no surprise when Mike says, "Understood. I'll remain as Miss Whitley's protection for as long as you need. My motivation has always been to serve in the Guild to the best of my ability. My allegiance seems to be constantly put into question by forces outside my control, but I won't be deterred."

Ohr relaxes his stance, transforming from exacting authority to a more casual counselor. "That, I believe, is why you struggle to prove your allegiance. You sound like a promotional brochure, Mike, not a human being with needs and desires. None of us serves the Guild without a personal motive, without the promise of gaining something for ourselves: status in our field… belonging… companionship." He lifts an eyebrow, glances briefly from Mike to me and back again, and one side of his mouth curves up, precisely like Shiah's often does. "Life is nothing without personal aspirations. You are not made to serve the Guild, Mike. The Guild was made to serve *you.* If we have nothing or no one here that gives you purpose, then you will forever be for sale to the rest of the world."

Ohr makes a little bow and says, "Have a wonderful day. And Miss Whitley, I can hardly wait to watch your interview."

Then he exits.

I whip around. "Did he totally suggest what I think he suggested?"

Mike sighs in frustration for probably the fifth time since Ohr showed up. He looks like he has something sour in his mouth. "Of course he did. He thinks I should make a move on you. He thinks I'll never be loyal until I do. And he thinks I haven't already spent a lifetime trying to understand the connection I share with Gabe. He wants me to spy on my brother constantly and if I don't I'm going to be put on indefinite furlough, just like before."

Someone knocks on the door.

"Yes?" I say, turning.

A man with a clipboard and headset appears. "We need you in the holding area."

"Okay," I reply.

"Forget everything that just happened," Mike says, touching me in the small of the back to urge me forward. "You have a job to do and your frown is ruining your ass-kicking persona." He checks beyond the doorway and then motions me through.

"Okay," I sigh. "But I really am sorry, Mike. I wanted you to stay, too, but not because you were guilted into it."

"He's right anyway," Mike mumbles behind me as we follow the attendant at a distance down the hall. "It's hell for me, but this is where I can do the most." Then he shakes his head. "Those numbers… Wow, Wen. That's really something to be proud of."

I try to smile back at him, but I hate sometimes that Mike falls so easily into alignment. He was just accused of having no real loyalty and he swallowed it, determining again to try harder to prove himself. Mike has more loyalty than I do, that's for sure. I'm always questioning everything the Guild does, everything they ask me and others to do—like now. Mike never does. He never thinks about leaving or fighting them on their decisions. He just obeys.

The attendant leads us onto a set, *the* set, the one that overlooks Time's Square. He gives us a moment to enjoy the view. I step close to the window to find that the threat of rain earlier has delivered. Below, however, is a massive crowd of people huddled under umbrellas. I don't even have time to feel bad for them though, because as soon as I appear, they start waving excitedly.

I wonder, for a moment, why I don't feel them more, but I answer my own question immediately: it's the rain blocking my empathy just as the water house does.

I hold my hand up to wave back, smiling. But no sooner have I acknowledged them than I notice a young man in the front. He's holding a sign that says:

My Puerto Rican family still lives. I believe.
#GuildFist

He then holds the sign in the crook of his arm and clasps his hands together and raises them up. Like dominos, the crowd follows suit, one after the other. They've even closed their umbrellas to free their hands. They raise their hands in the Guild fist, looking up at me.

I suck in a breath, instinctively wanting to turn to look around for who they are saluting, because it doesn't feel like it should be me. But it is. I trademarked that sign.

So I lift my own hands up, clasping them together in front of me. I bow my head though, because their tribute doesn't belong to me; it belongs to everyone else at the Guild who actually does the work. I just talk.

The attendant gets my attention, and then asks me to stand and wave at a camera for a few seconds. After that, Mike resumes his place while I get outfitted with a microphone.

Mike shifts his weight behind me in response to a nearly overwhelming burgeoning of anticipation and impatience. I recognize he's been holding it back from me until now. It surprises me, because he's always made a practice of keeping his feelings in reserve with distractions like scanning every square inch of the area around us when he's actively protecting me. "Feel that?" he whispers. "That's him. I'm going to stop holding him in check in my head as often as I can afford to. So you have more #IntelOnDemand."

"Weird," I say quietly. "Second-hand emotions. They don't feel the same as him."

"They won't. They'll change in intensity depending on my distance to him. And I've spent a lifetime suppressing him, disguising him, ignoring him. Chances are I've managed to internalize some of that distortion."

Gabe Dumas appears with his own bodyguard, Porter Tranwick, moments later, looking attractively energized. My heart skips upon seeing him, already setting me up to be an emotional mess. He is not yet in my empathic range, and I intend to keep it that way for as long as possible. Second-hand emotions, however, are a lot less invasive. I have to actually pay attention to pick up on them. Right now he endures sudden amazement when he lays eyes on me.

"Good morning, Miss Whitley," Gabe says with a smile, having been stopped a ways away by the sound tech. "You are looking... perfectly lovely."

"Thanks," I say, heart skipping to his exultant expectation. He's looking pretty darn good himself in nothing but a simple, white dress shirt with the top button undone and a pair of contrasting black slacks.

Ugh. My life.

Mike's breath reaches my ear, having leaned in, but before he even speaks, he clenches in second-hand conflict, which turns to profound aggravation. "Allow me to scramble my brother's brain for you," he murmurs so quietly only my ears can possibly make it out. "Smile like I've told you the funniest thing you've heard all day."

I grin, knowing exactly what Mike's doing, and my expression is met with sudden and gut-wrenching disgust—Gabe's.

"Gabe's biggest flaw is his jealous insecurity," Mike murmurs. "Considering his looks and brains and charm it's mind-boggling, isn't it? I don't even have to touch you and he throws a conniption."

He's totally right. He's caught up in a tempest of loathing, his ordered thoughts sinking swiftly into its sea.

Then Mike places his hands lightly on my upper arms, and Gabe huffs audibly now, shifts his feet, crosses his arms, looks away—or he tries to.

"By the way," he adds, so close to my ear that it gives me goosebumps. "That dress has already scrambled his brain without my help. Well done listening to wardrobe."

I turn my head slightly toward him. "Thank you," I whisper.

Mike lets go of my arms and stands at the ready once more behind me.

I stare at Dumas, who keeps his expression stoic but feels daggers toward Mike. As soon as he senses my eyes on him, however, he looks at me, wondering what's caught my attention.

I give nothing away, instead looking around the room as if I've concluded some assessment of him, which drives him into a tantrum of frustration.

A blonde woman, whom I know is named Jessica, appears from a doorway to my left. "Gabe Dumas and Wendy Whitley!" she says excitedly, striding in our direction.

I turn to face her as she approaches me. Her perfume hits me first, and then she gives me one of those awkward girlfriend hugs where we only use our forearms and go cheek to cheek. I try to be gracious about it, but those hugs annoy the hell out of me.

"It's so great to meet you!" she says exuberantly. Then her eyes give me a quick scan. "You look amazing," she says under her breath, giving me a knowing look, but she quickly and efficiently fights back envy. Ugh. Maybe I let wardrobe go a little far with this over-the-top white dress that hugs every curve. Girl drama is the *worst*.

She darts over to Dumas next, and he responds before she can get a word. "Jessica," he says in an octave lower than his usual tone. He takes her hand in both of his. "Gabe Dumas," he continues. "What a privilege it is to be with you today."

She melts, staring up into his dark and engaging eyes. She's even shorter than my five-foot-six frame, so she has to crane her neck slightly, making her look even more smitten. "My, my, you are even more handsome in person," she says. He just smiles at her warmly.

She reverts back to business easily though, clapping twice and saying, "Take a seat, guys. We have ninety seconds of commercial left." She steps up onto the platform where the set is arranged: a tall, round dinette table with three stools. She waves us up. I take the chair directly across from her, and Gabe takes the one that faces the camera directly.

"Okay guys!" Jessica says, smiling easily with a set of perfect, white teeth. "Easy stuff. I know you guys prepared, went over the questions, right? We're live so watch your language. I'll ask you individual questions, but feel free to interrupt each other if that feels natural and not awkward." She holds up a warning finger. "No fighting though." She laughs. "But I'm sure we don't have to worry about that. You guys are pros. Look into camera one. Brian will count us down, and then you look at me."

"No problem," I say. Beside me, however, Gabe remains silent. I don't search for him. I'm ready for this.

"Five... four..." Brian says, standing next to camera one, holding up fingers, "three... two... one." He points at us.

I turn to Jessica and smile, but it looks like they're playing a clip as an introduction first. It's a montage of Dumas and myself at different THM events. It ends with Gabe and I in Raleigh, joined hands raised above our heads right after the Purus announcement.

"Wendy Whitley and Gabe Dumas, away from the crowds and sitting at the same table for the first time!" Jessica says, signaling that the camera is now on us. "Wow, you guys," she gushes. "Thank you *so* much for being here and giving us the opportunity to get better acquainted with what has appeared to become quite the dynamic duo. First, the news. The news, you guys! Purus. Give our viewers the run-down in case they missed it."

"Purus is a new chemical developed to make water potable," I reply. "One drop will purify and sanitize one gallon. With the exception of salt water, any source of water can be cleansed for any use. The Guild is providing it to all disaster zones for free."

"This was a pretty quick response to the water crisis," Jessica says. "I think every time we hear of some new Guild technology, we're blown away by how fast they can develop it. It makes people wonder what the Guild can accomplish—what can we expect from them in terms of solving the problems facing our world today. Gabe, I think we all feel similarly to THM in that respect. Would you agree that's one of your movement's ongoing demands?"

"Oh absolutely," Gabe says. "I'm as thrilled as the next person over the release of Purus. But frankly, this is becoming ridiculous. The world is falling apart and we have *no* idea what the Guild is doing behind the scenes. We'd all like to be and *need* to be a little more prepared for the future, but how can we do that without knowing what resources are and will be available? I'm not diminishing their contribution. Not by a long shot. But I *am* saying they could be handling this better. They could be helping *more* if they'd allow the rest of us access to what they know."

"First of all," I interject, wanting to be sure I get my say in before Jessica moves on to the next question, "Purus has been in the works for years. We didn't watch the news a month ago and say to ourselves, 'Well, I guess we better figure out how to give people clean water.' No, clean water has been one of the highest priorities for the Guild since its inception in the seventies. Preparation for what is happening right now is what started the Guild in the first place."

Jessica tilts her head, and I can tell she wasn't prepared for my answer. Just goes to show how much she *hasn't* researched the Guild.

"Are you implying that the Guild *knew* about the impending Apocalypse *before* it started happening?" she asks.

"Of course they did," Gabe says. "They have the ability to predict disasters, don't they? We have never been told the scope of that prediction, so there's no reason to think that they don't know more than they've said."

I clear my throat. "Actually, the the global disaster notification system is as accurate and up-to-date as we can make it. We don't know any more than what we've shared with the public about when and where disasters will strike. What I was referring to was a prophecy made by one of our founding members who possessed the life force ability of foresight. *He* predicted the apocalypse. The Guild was formed to combat it. That is our primary purpose. So it should come as no surprise that we spend the majority of our resources on preparation."

"Wow," Jessica says. "Why have you chosen to reveal the existence of this prophecy now?"

"Existence of the prophecy hasn't been a secret," I point out. "It's been hinted at and referred to many times in articles and on our website. It's out there if someone wanted to look further into the Guild. I suppose it hasn't been referred to as a prophecy in other places, mostly because the word has a hocus pocus feel, and people don't take that stuff seriously."

"Fair enough," Jessica says. "I guess we've all got some research to do."

"As for what you can expect from the Guild," I say, "I think you, me, and everyone shouldn't revolve our lives around what the Guild may or may not do, because as Mister Dumas has pointed out—and I would like to second—we are not gods. We're going to do everything we can to help, but we're not interested in dependence or even in power. As I've pointed out at past THM events, it is our close-knit exclusivity that gives us strength and ability, and we're going to stick with that model as long as it continues working."

"Thank you for that insight, Wendy," Jessica says genuinely. "I want to backtrack now and get into a little more detail about this THM-Guild dynamic. Let's take a look at where it all started."

We turn to the monitor on the set, and there am I, poised at the center of the stage in St. Louis, the foot of the arch at my back. I'm in the middle of explaining who I am.

The clip concludes, and Jessica says, "I've kept up with you guys, and the progression of this thing is just fascinating. Gabe, I want you to take me back and tell me what it felt like the moment Wendy appeared on the other side of the crowd in St. Louis where thousands had gathered thinking they were only going to be hearing from *you* that day. What was your very first thought?"

"'Who is that talking? I can't see a thing,'" Gabe answers immediately from beside me, unamused with Jessica's interest in our *dynamic.* He hates focusing on anything but issues.

Jessica laughs. "Oh that's right. You were at one foot of the arch and she was at the other. I guess that's pretty far, right?"

"Six hundred and thirty feet," Dumas replies. "Same distance as the *height* of the Gateway Arch."

Impressed by his recall, she locks on to that. "So six hundred and thirty feet separated you, and you got off the stage and started walking through the crowd. When you finally laid eyes on her and figured out who was talking, what was your very first impression?"

"Confusion."

"How so?"

"It didn't add up. She was this absolutely beautiful, articulate, humorous, fearless young woman standing on a makeshift stage with zero fanfare, saying that her protection detail was going to rough up anyone that got uppity, and apologizing ahead of time for being an inexperienced public speaker, (which hasn't inhibited her ability at all, by the way). She could have been one of my constituents climbing up on stage and playing a joke on everyone—which I considered when she first started speaking. She was so strikingly different from every other recycled spokesperson we'd seen from the Guild that it didn't seem possible that such a self-assured, obstinate organization like the Guild could have enough precocity to send someone like that out to represent them. But I saw my brother standing closer to her than anyone, and I knew she had to be from the Guild after all."

"Yes! Your brother," Jessica says and then she turns to me. "Give me the dish, Wendy. Whose decision was it to make Mike Dumas your bodyguard?"

"Mine," I reply.

"What motivated that choice?"

"Taking Gabe Dumas down, of course," I say, smiling.

"Ahh, so you you wanted to get under his skin. I'm curious, how did the whole thing start? You said in your first appearance that representing the Guild was something you volunteered to do. It wasn't an assignment they gave you. What led you to volunteer?"

I sit back more comfortably and clasp my hands together on the table in front of me. "When I made the decision, I'd recently survived a second attack by PHIA and then learned they'd murdered my brother and my father. Plus, I'd been partnered up with someone who had also lost his entire family to PHIA. He showed me the symbol they branded on his chest after they'd murdered his family, beaten him with a baseball bat, and left him for dead. Not long after that I saw Mister Dumas interview on TV. When he presumed that he had a right to be able to look up my address on the internet, I felt like spitting in his face."

Jessica's mouth opens and she grins scandalously. "It sounds like you have quite a bit of animosity for The Human Movement."

"I don't," I say before she can launch into another question. "But you asked what motivated me at first. That was the start of it, and the rest all came together. In reality though, the only thing that separates my ideals from those of Mister Dumas is experience. I was once exactly like him in how I saw the Guild. It took losing my brother and then my father to teach me the importance of association and loyalty."

"I beg to differ," Dumas says, sidelining Jessica again. "Miss Whitley assumes that losing loved ones would bring me over o her way of thinking. But I've lost both my parents to PHIA. I've lost contact with all of my extended family and friends in California and I have no idea if they are still alive. I've even lost two and a half years of my memory due to PHIA, and considering the state of the world, that was like dying and waking up in a completely different reality. I've lost a considerable amount, but here I sit, still of the belief that all of us have to work together, now more than ever, because we simply don't have the luxury of time to test an alternative. The real difference between Miss Whitley and myself is that I'm able to let go of what I've lost and prioritize our dying world, while her actions along with the Guild's have been about self-preservation."

My hands have balled into fists in my lap as Dumas has spoken, and I've focused intently on what he's said so I don't interrupt and demand to know about Dumas' memory loss. He lost two and a half years?! No way in hell that's a coincidence. No way. I want to shake him right now and say 'me too!' and then compare notes to see if we can piece together what happened.

"Wendy?" Jessica says.

I look up at her, obviously having focused to the point of zoning her out. I've got to get a grip, shove my insane curiosity to the side. "Sorry, can you repeat the question?"

"What had your attention?" Jessica says, shifting gears instantly. "Obviously something Gabe said struck a chord with you. What was it?"

"Um, his memory loss… I was… trying to figure out if I'd read anything about a life force ability that could do that—erase memory."

Phew. I pat myself on the back for that save.

"And?" she says.

I shake my head. "Not to my knowledge." But Dumas is immediately suspect.

"Okay," she says, turning back to Dumas. "It sounds like you've been a target of PHIA then. What do you think their interest in you is?"

"I'm sure it has to do with my brother," he says, but I swear I can feel his eyes, or at least the majority of his attention on me with heavy intensity. "Considering he works for the Guild in a high-status capacity, and given the Guild has entrusted Miss Whitley's safety to him, I have no doubt he's higher on PHIA's list of targets, which would bleed into anyone associated with him."

The stress in my head builds to a fever pitch. Oh my gosh, he has got to stop breathing down my neck with his emotional inquisition. I can't think straight. I've got to jar him out of it. "Maybe," I say, crossing my legs the other way, just to move. "But I think it just as likely they'd be after Mister Dumas directly. He *is* a Prime Human after all."

Jessica sits back, looks at Dumas, aghast. "You're a Prime Human, Gabe?"

That did the trick; he releases me from a portion of his demand as he looks at Jessica like she's sprouted horns. "Heavens no." His eyes shift to me, equally taken aback. "What would make you claim such a thing?" He's trying to answer that question himself, and he comes to the wrong conclusion because he's back to mentally grilling me. I think he believes I know something about him I haven't shared, and it relates to his memory loss, and claiming he's a Prime Human is evidence of that. He's got to stop though.

"The crazy counting. The language proficiency. The above-average memory," I say, counting them off on my fingers. "And I've seen you move a crowd, too. You were a professor at a college before this, not a motivational speaker. How did you get so good? It's because you have life force abilities. Spontaneous origin. But you have them. That makes you a Prime Human. I didn't realize that was news to you."

"That's your label. Not mine," he says, crossing his arms, growing in aggravation. Maybe he'll back off for the rest of the interview now.

"Interesting twist though, you have to admit, Gabe," Jessica says. "The leader of the Human Movement is possessed of life force abilities."

"It would only be a twist if The Human Movement were opposed to life force abilities, which it's not."

"You've never mentioned them before. That seems a little like you don't want the association."

"Nobody ever asked. I certainly haven't hidden it," Dumas says, hammering me once more with suspicion. "And it has never come up because I don't consider myself any different from anyone else with talents."

"I'm glad we've gotten to the topic of life force abilities," Jessica says, "because that *is* the crux of this whole thing, right? Wendy, we know that one of yours is seeing the energy world, but what else can you do?"

"I feel what the people around me feel," I say. "I also have super-senses."

"Super-senses?" Jessica says. "Like superman?"

"Not quite that good. But I had no problem seeing Mister Dumas from six hundred and thirty feet away in St. Louis. And I can eavesdrop on anyone in the same building as me as long as the room isn't lead-lined."

"Really!" Jessica says.

"No, I made up the lead-lined part," I smile.

She laughs.

"That's how you did it!" Gabe exclaims suddenly.

"Did what?" Jessica says, eyes wide with a probable juicy story.

"Listened in on Mister Dumas and his team yesterday," I shoot, once again pushing his invasive emotions off of me.

"You didn't!" Jessica gushes. "Learn anything good?"

"Oh yeah. For one thing, Mister Dumas hates technology."

"I do not hate technology," Dumas interjects.

"It must be part of the reason he goes after us," I say, ignoring him. "For instance, the idea of using an online library is offensive to him."

"I prefer *actual* books in a place I can physically walk into," Dumas says.

"*Also*," I say before Dumas can get another word in, "Rita, one of his team members, has a serious crush on him."

"That's petty," Dumas says.

"Rita…" Jessica says. "She's the cute blonde one that leads some of his other protests, correct?"

I nod.

"Well I can see why," Jessica says, eying Dumas but ignoring his look of aggravation.

I hold up my hands to acquiesce. "No argument. Rita has good taste, at least as far as looks go. But she obviously needs to buck up some courage."

"Rita," Jessica says, looking toward camera one, "Go for it, honey. The world is ending. You got nothing to lose."

"Here's what you do, Rita," I say, copying Jessica and looking at camera one, "Tell him you found a library." I look at Jessica. "Quick, what's a super-intimate must-see library in New York?"

"Oh, oh, oh," she says, leaning forward and tapping the table with her hand as she racks her brain. "I know the perfect one. The Grolier Club. In Manhattan!"

"Bingo, Rita," I say, looking at the camera again. "On your way, pick up something with mango. Anything really. It's his absolute favorite. If you can't find something quick, go for some churros. He's a sucker for those, too." I turn to Jessica. "They have churros in New York?"

She shrugs. "Meh, sometimes."

"Okay, scratch the churros," I say back to the camera. "Mango all the way. Give it to him at the library while you're showing him the philosophy section." I sit back in my chair, satisfied.

"That was a boorish salmagundi," Dumas says with disgust.

"You sure have his number," Jessica giggles.

"Just the best intel available," I say.

"Thank you for that performance," Dumas says, at the climax of his aggravation thus far. "Now that you've thoroughly embarrassed Rita on national television, she's going to quit, and I'll be left without one of my advisors."

I wave a hand. "You ignore her anyway and you know it."

"That is not the case at all," Dumas says.

"Let's talk about yesterday's event now," Jessica says, seizing control back. She motions to the monitor where Gabe and I appear side-by-side, standing on the balcony of Raleigh's capitol building. '*Pulled from the imminent threat of death, you sometimes ask yourself if you are a fish pulled from the jaws of a shark but thrown on land, miles from water. Death is still coming for you... unless you can find water again. And fast.*' I conclude my words and Gabe then begins his translation and the clip fades.

"It was clear you were holding hands during Wendy's delivery, *and* you translated for her. What was that like and how did it come about?"

I hold my breath. This question was on the list as well, so I'm not surprised to hear it, and Dumas should be prepared to answer it without touching on sensitive topics, but I still worry.

"She asked me to hold her hand so we could present a united front because she was going to be delivering big news," Dumas replies. "She said, and I quote, 'I don't intend for you to any of the Guild's success without relinquishing, if only for this moment, the idea that we are at odds.' And then she proceeded to threaten me with finding an alternative translator if I didn't agree. I couldn't very well turn that down, could I?"

"She's certainly feisty!" Jessica says. "Some might argue that Salt Lake was more of an emotional roller coaster, but to me Raleigh tops them all. You held her hand through the most emotional moment your events have ever garnered. How did it feel?"

"Even the word breathtaking doesn't do the experience justice," he says simply but not without emotion. He seems to have *finally* let go of interrogating me mentally.

Jessica smiles at him for a moment, sensing as well as I can that he means it, although she has no idea what he's actually referring to. He was seeing the energy world, and breathtaking is the best you can do for a descriptor. She turns to me. "Why, Wendy? Why did the Guild decide to make an announcement of that magnitude on a small stage, in the middle of dangerous territory, at an event hosted by those who want to see them dissolved?"

I take a moment to answer, because I think it's the most important question she's asked, one I've been hoping she *would* ask. I've even practiced the words, because I knew I wouldn't have the energy of a crowd's emotions to give me power.

"We chose that place because of the people who would be there to hear it. They're facing a future without a lot of things the rest of us take for granted, so it was a no-brainer that they should be the first ones to see relief," I say. "But I don't actually think that's the question you're asking, because if THM *hadn't* been there, I'm betting you wouldn't have asked it. But THM *was* there, and so then the announcement gets placed in a political context, and then people start automatically seeing it as a strategy. It's the same thing they've been analyzing all along because they expect that the Guild is out to find the biggest stage, to reach the widest audience, and that we're doing it so that we can gain control and crush the opposition. But you know, I take offense to being seen that way, as a pawn for the Guild to play in this fight for power that doesn't actually exist. I spell it out, over and over: we're out to do the most good we can, to meet as many needs as we're able, and we *can* do it because of *how* we do it. I know I speak honestly for the rest of the Guild when I say that. *That* is the message that I am charged to deliver, and I will continue to say it as many *times* as it takes in as many *ways* as it takes. So here we go: In order to continue to aid millions despite our small number, we have to do own the things that will maintain the integrity of our roots that have gotten us this far. In that, we have to act in our own best interest. It's what we've always done. It's how we've survived. It's how we are successful. None of what you have seen us accomplish would have happened without our Guild being exactly what it is. You don't have to be popular to make a difference. In fact, no one who has ever changed history has done it by doing what people expect or by what the majority demands. We intend to change history. We expect it's going to make us as many enemies as it does friends. But we are undaunted."

Jessica has her chin propped on her fist.

Dumas is engaged in a high-speed analysis, but he pauses it to say, "And everyone keeps asking me why I esteem Miss Whitley the way I do. I daresay she could even turn PHIA into an ally if given time on their stage."

"No doubt, Gabe," Jessica says. "The two of you have been a delight. We hope to see you again on Good Morning America. Where is the next event?"

"Chicago," Gabe says.

"And then Berlin," I say.

"We'll be following your journey," Jessica says, grinning widely once more. "Thank you guys!"

Forty-One

*M*iss Whitley!" Dumas demands from behind me as I walk briskly toward the dressing room.

"Miss Whitley!" Dumas says again, his voice rising. "What the devil was that!? Speak to me this instant!"

"Mike," I murmur. "He's making a scene."

"Hold up a sec," Mike says, and I pause and turn in the hall to see him walk right up to Gabe only to have Tranwick intercept him.

"Porter," Mike says, almost in greeting.

"Whassup, Big Mick," Porter Tranwick says with a twinkle in his eye as he stretches to his full menacing height, which is about six inches taller than Mike, who stands at five-ten. "You know how this goes."

"So do you," Mike says, getting about five inches from Tranwick, unintimidated. "He shuts his mouth or I shut it for him."

"That ain't yo place, man," Tranwick says, his voice deep and smooth. He rubs his bearded chin and says, "'Course, maybe I'm wrong. Maybe you signed up to be her dog, too." He tilts his head. "She got you in the fights on the off-days, man? Make a little money off you on the side?"

"Stand down, Tranwick," Gabe says, annoyed as he circumvents the man's enormous body.

Mike steps in front of him. "Back off, Gabe. Miss Whitley is not interested in speaking to you right now."

"I don't give two shakes," Dumas says. "She lost my consideration when she pettifogged her way into negating my presence during that interview. And she used someone unavailable to speak for herself to do it!"

"I *had* to," I snap, stepping forward. "Because you were acting like a badgering two-year-old! There was no other way to get you to back the hell off!"

"*Me* back off?" Dumas says, flabbergasted. "I answer a simple question about PHIA and your response is to paint me as a liar for not proclaiming myself as a Prime Human! And then you proceed to mock me with a grossly inflated play-by-play of a private conversation!"

"No," I seethe. "I'm talking about you jamming your emotions down my throat. Don't you *ever* manipulate me that way. I will take you *down*. Every time. With *pleasure*."

"Aw naw, G-man. You don't want none of that," Tranwick says, shaking his head, having taken the 'stand down' order seriously as he leans against the wall, ankles and giant brown tree trunks for arms crossed casually as if we are a source of entertainment. All he needs is popcorn.

Dumas steps back, staggered, but I've gotten his attention. "Oh," he says, and his intellect gains speed. "I wanted you to... You were holding back about—"

"I don't want to hear it right now," I stop him.

"You will hear it! You said you were—"

"Shut your overactive mouth!" I yell. And then under my breath, through gritted teeth, I say, "Not here."

He blinks, *finally* getting it. "Apologies," he says quietly. "For earlier. Sincerest. I didn't realize I was causing you so much distress. I was simply communicating my—"

"Oh my gosh!" I say, aghast. "Do you even know *how* to close your mouth?"

"Nope. He doesn't," Mike says at my shoulder. "And Shiah's here."

I spin on my heel to find her black-clad figure coming my way in a hurry, her ebony hair wound into a knot on one side of her neck. I can't help but notice for the second time today the black dress she's wearing. It's quite similar to my own white one, which is a lot more daring than her usual high-swank, low skin clothing choices. She looks fabulous in it, and I asked her about it this morning when we left the hotel. She ignored me, as she does sometimes, instead firing back the interview seed questions to test my preparedness.

"The Council," she says breathlessly when she reaches us. "They want to meet with you immediately." She looks over my shoulder. "And you as well, Mister Dumas."

I look from Shiah to Gabe and back again. "They caught it, too, didn't they?" I say, knowing the Council must be interested in the fact that Gabe's memory loss coincides with mine.

She nods.

"Someone enlighten me, please," Dumas says.

I turn. "I have to go. I would suggest you come."

"The conditions are still in effect, Wendy," Shiah says. "He'll have separate transport."

I close my eyes and gather patience. "Fine," I say.

"Separate transport?" Dumas says begrudgingly. "Conditions? This veiled communication is entirely unacceptable. I have no desire to speak to your Council. I need a private word with Miss Whitley and then I'll be on my way."

"That won't be possible, Mister Dumas," Shiah says authoritatively. "You touched on something in the interview that indicates you may unwittingly have information about PHIA. The Council is requesting a word with you to determine what, if anything, you may know that might be helpful. Should you consent, you'll be taken to their location separately, as one of the conditions of Miss Whitley's position is chaperoned communication with you."

"Chaperoned?" Dumas says, dumfounded as he looks at me, and I easily translate that he's thinking about our visit two days ago that was the exact opposite of chaperoned. I only hope he has finally learned the virtue of silence.

He has. He shakes off amazement, squares his shoulders and says, "Let's crack on then."

"My father will accompany you," Shiah says, walking next to Dumas behind me as we continue down the hall. "He's a big fan of yours."

"I didn't realize I had fans among members of the Guild," Dumas says.

"Actually, other than my father, there are two other Council members that are," Shiah says in the matter-of-fact tone only she can produce.

"Your father is on the Guild Council and he's a fan of mine? Pardon my ignorance, but that seems like a conflict of interest," Gabe says.

"Oh most definitely not. Seeing you activated as a Guild member is among their primary goals for the year."

I smile and cough on my suppressed snigger. The elusive Shiah is up to something.

Gabe bellows in laughter. "Is that right? I do believe I'm going to enjoy this meeting then."

I bite the inside of my cheek to control my chuckling. It's evident from his emotions that Gabe does not suspect a bit of subterfuge on Shiah's part.

But I know her better than that.

뇌

It's pouring outside, and we load up under an awning, leaving Gabe Dumas and several Guild protection operatives behind to wait for the next car. I don't know how our driver can even see. But the sound of the pounding rain has me confident my conversation with Mike and Shiah will be kept confidential. I lean toward Mike first and ask, "Did you know about Gabe's memory loss?"

"Yes. Is that what this emergency meeting is about?" he replies.

"Partly," Shiah says, her head popping up between the two of us from the third row. "The other reason is to offer him Guild resources to continue his campaign safely. Tech, extra operatives, transportation. That kind of thing. He can't afford the kind of resources he's starting to need."

"There's no way he would allow that much Guild oversight," Mike says.

"We've discovered that Dumas' technology specialist, Garrett, is a member of PHIA," Shiah says. "He's been working undercover, we believe to get to Wendy. We recently instituted a new top-secret software designed to locate members of PHIA. Six programmers defected with Andre, so the software scans website and public software codes in search of signatures—signatures of those Prime Humans known to have defected from the Guild. The Human Movement website was written by a just such a former Guild member. And we know Garrett is Dumas' man in charge of that."

"Seriously? That's genius strategy," I marvel.

"Why would someone not wanting to be found 'sign' their code though?" Mike says.

"No, not a signature like that," I say. "Everyone arranges their code differently. Think of it like handwriting. No two people write exactly the same way. The same goes for code. Even if you don't write your name on it, it still smells and sounds like you." I shake my head, impressed. "Whoever thought of that and then had the skill to write that spyware is friggin brilliant."

"Thank you," Shiah says. "I wrote it."

My jaw drops and I look at her. "I would ask you if you're kidding, but you don't kid. So instead I'll say, why did I never know you wrote code?"

"It has never come up," she says. "And I do a great many things you don't know about."

"I believe that," I say. "But tell me about your conversation with Dumas earlier. Why did you tell him we're trying to recruit him?"

"To witness his reaction myself."

"Ah, Shiah research," I say. "To keep your 'data' up-to-date."

"I also wanted to influence him *not* to accept the Guild's help if possible," she says.

"Why?" I say. "If he's had someone from PHIA so close to him, doesn't he *need* help?" I gasp in horror. "I just outed him as a Prime Human on national TV!" I squeak.

"The Council will bring up your revealing Dumas' Prime Human status as a breach in your agreement."

"Crap," I say.

"In answer to your question, I have many reasons, but primarily I do not want to see The Human Movement any more intertwined with the Guild than it already is. I believe my efforts were fruitless though. Dumas will not refuse."

I turn to Mike. "You didn't think Gabe's memory loss was worth mentioning before?"

Mike frowns, indecisive. "Some things that are Gabe's business to tell should stay Gabe's business to tell." Behind his words I sense a tumultuous pain, an unresolved conflict.

I turn back to Shiah. "I'm guessing the Council didn't know Dumas shared a memory loss almost identical to my own either?"

"You have memory loss, too?" Mike says, shocked.

I nod. "When you met me at the hospital, I had just woken up from it the day before."

He gasps. "What day did you—"

"October 29th," Shiah replies. "The same date you reported in as well."

"Wait. What?" I say, looking between Mike and Shiah. "The same what?"

"I lost six years," Mike says. "But not all of it from what I can tell. My memory is a mess of holes. My timelines are all screwy, so I have a hard time putting my past in order. I remember some things, but they could have happened six months ago or six years ago. I can't tell."

I stare at him with open-mouthed shock. *Six years!?* How could I not know that about him? How has it never come up? Have our conversations really been so shallow that something as huge as massive amnesia never made it into conversation even a little? I turn to Shiah with wide eyes. "You *knew* Mike had missing memory and you didn't tell me?"

"Just as it wasn't Mike's business to report Gabe's memory loss, it wasn't my business to report his," Shiah replies. "I told you his past was confidential, but he was free to share it with you if he chose."

I look at Mike.

He holds up his hands. "You never asked! And how was I supposed to know you were missing memory as well? You never mentioned it either!"

I slump in exasperation. Sometimes the Guild's need for confidentiality in every realm is a serious hindrance.

I glare at Shiah. "I think you could have at least mentioned that I wasn't alone in my missing memory."

She shrugs. "Maybe. But then you and Mike and Gabe are not the only ones, so I wouldn't make any assumptions. More and more people have discovered that they have lost memories. All of varying lengths and from different time periods. A Guild-wide investigation was launched not long after you joined to interview every single person who had forgotten a span of time in order to find out the connection. It's been kept confidential to avoid panic as well as to keep from alerting whoever is causing it. When you meet with the Council, I believe you will learn more."

"What the hell…" Mike says. "I gotta say, I'm not sure the Council handled this in the best way…"

I can't disagree. "Well, Mike. I'll tell you mine if you tell me yours. Maybe it will help one of us, me, you, or Gabe, piece together the past."

"Gabe doesn't want to remember," Mike says, and I can feel an old trauma resurfacing.

Compassion for Dumas seizes hold of my heart. "I said that, too," I reply. "After learning my brother was dead and the circumstances of it… I didn't want to know anything else. But as soon as Gabe said he'd lost memories and it was the same length of time, it woke up my desire to know again. I think… I think he'd feel that way, too, if he knew so many people suffered the same kind of loss."

Mike exhales heavily. "I don't think knowing his story will help you. If Shiah's right, and this memory loss is widespread, the coincidence could be due to both of you having something to do with the Guild and Primes. Gabe's memory loss starts two months before yours."

"He was emotionally interrogating me during the interview just because I hung on his statement about losing his memory a little too long," I say. "He wants to remember, Mike. Don't you?"

He looks at me, indecisive. "Wen... Andre was my dyad during the entire six years I'm missing. I remember very few things, but not enough to convince me that I was never in line with him. They say memories are what make you. What if mine made me a different person? One that was just as twisted as he was? Some days—most days—I'm glad I can't remember. If I became a sick bastard like him, I hope I never remember. If he was a sick bastard and I was stuck as his dyad for some reason, it couldn't have been a good situation. I don't want to remember that either."

He turns to his window, staring into the tempest, and I think he's not going to share. My excitement sinks by degrees each silent moment. But then he says, "It was at the end of this past October. Gabe and I woke up in our parents' house in Bakersfield. It was burning. Smoke was so thick... But their bodies were nearby. Along with a girl, twenties. Neither of us recognized her. Blood was all over the floor. On the wall was a giant PHIA symbol painted in it. Neither of us knew what it meant at that time. We dragged the bodies out even though they were already dead, throats cut."

I wrap my arms around myself, chilled from his residual panic.

"Houses were burning everywhere when we got outside. Looked like a brush fire had descended from the hills, but there were no people, no sirens. It was eerie. We got the car out of the garage, went in to town, found that empty, too. No phones worked. Gabe's the one that caught the date, first on a calendar in a convenience store, then on a newspaper. It was something out of the Twilight Zone. Gabe started insisting we had to go back to the house, we had to see what we could save before it was all lost.

"So we went back. Gabe jumped out of the car before it even stopped, dove into the house that was all but demolished. I went in after him to get him out of there. I kept shouting at him that it was too late. He was going to get himself killed. He wouldn't listen, and I nearly passed out again from the smoke. I had to crawl out or I was toast. So I laid there on the street where the bodies were, hacking and coughing like I was still inside. My arm burned, but there was no injury. 'He's going to die,' I thought. I'm going to feel my brother burned alive. Because not only do I get Gabe's emotions, I feel what he does when we're close. Physically. I prayed he'd pass out first.

"Suddenly he was collapsed beside me, passed out but still breathing. So I searched the bodies. No ID on the girl, but she was wearing a chain with a wedding band on it. The engraving said 'Body and Soul.' That was it. Gabe came around and I showed him the ring. He stared at it and I could tell something about it rang a bell. He wouldn't talk about it though. He was a mess, like no version of him I'd ever seen or felt. I knew the Guild was the only way to get him *and* myself some help. Without a working phone I had to activate my GPS implant. I tried to explain to Gabe that I was getting him help. I worked for an organization that could help us figure out what had happened. But all he heard was 'I've been a secret operative for years without your knowledge.' He started yelling. Saying everything was on me. That everyone was dead because I'd brought my enemies into his life. I couldn't defend myself against any of the accusations because my head was swiss cheese. I couldn't even figure out what my most recent memory actually was. And I was willing to bet he was right anyway.

"Gabe wouldn't come with me when transport arrived. I kept saying, 'I'm getting you help. We'll get your memory back. Just come with me.' And he just stood there, staring. I tried to take him bodily, but he threw me off of him and pulled this crumpled note out of his pocket. Inside the paper was a ring like the one we found on the girl. And the note said 'You failed. Your child is dead.' And it was signed 'Φ' in blood. He holds the ring just so, and inside you can see the engraving, 'Body and Soul.' Same as the girl's. 'I woke up with it in my pocket,' he said."

I'm speechless. And Mike won't look at me, but his anguish is obvious.

"That was his wife lying in her own blood in the street with our parents," Mike says, his voice trembling. "And he had a note telling him his child was dead, signed by the same people who'd written on the wall in blood over our parents' dead bodies. And neither of us could even remember him ever being married, or having a kid, but that only seemed to make it worse for him. God, I was sick. But then he pulls out this ziplock of orange something, mostly melted. Attached to it is this note. It says, 'To Little

Mickey. It's written in the gummy bears.' It was signed with a lipstick kiss. Same color the dead girl had on. Same shape of her mouth. He told me he found it on my bed. 'Your favorite flavor,' he said, and I could feel his loathing of me. I told him we'd sort it out. It couldn't be what it looked like. I couldn't believe it. I'd had a thing with my brother's *wife*? And then he said, 'You actually think I want to remember *anything*?' Then he told me to leave. So I left him there to bury our parents alone. To bury *her*. I shouldn't have. But I couldn't take it. He hated me. He hated me so much. Being near him was only making it worse. I was afraid of him, of what he'd do to me. I was afraid I'd let him. So I left. And it wasn't until he made his first Human Movement appearance that I had any idea what he'd been up to."

My hand is over my mouth and tears are in my eyes. I have my own awful story, but it sounds like Gabe Dumas' is far more tragic. A wife, child, parents. And he lost them all. To add insult to injury, he has evidence that his wife wasn't faithful. After what Mike told me about his connection to Gabe and the history of their relationships, it even sounds probable, maybe even inevitable? I don't know. But it's absolutely heartbreaking. I don't blame him for not wanting to remember. So why does he want to now?

I sigh heavily. "This is horrible. We've got to take down PHIA. They're behind this. They've got to be stopped."

"I just thought of something…" Mike says, turning to look at me. "The Detritus Benefit. Neither you nor Gabe remembers it, but it sounds like it's a separate memory loss from your most recent one. Gemma Rossi is actually one of my last complete memories. That's probably why it's stuck so well. Before I made the connection that Gemma was you, I only remembered that I was there looking for a missing Prime. But now… it's too coincidental. I had to have been there searching for Carl Haricott's daughter. I found her and I never knew. If Andre really is somehow behind the memory loss, it's totally reasonable to assume he was behind that one as well… Shit, he even knew you were in that hospital you woke up in, didn't he? That's who you were running from when you lost your memory. I'm telling you, I think *you* are the correlation."

Shiah has remained silent, but she's been thinking, quietly assimilating the information. I don't sense surprise on her part, but then, Shiah rarely feels surprised. Something about her expression though…

She sits back, "We're nearly there."

"Where?" I say.

"Co-op city. It was purchased by the Guild several years ago. It was going to be an east coast base of operations, but the Guild has been systematically moving all coastal operations inland."

"They bought a *city*?" I say, looking out the window into the heavy rain, for what, I can't say.

"It's more like a full-service housing development, originally built as a cooperative."

We make an exit off the freeway and the first thing I notice through the grey is a group of ten or so high-rise buildings. They stick out because they are all identical, as well as the tallest things in the area by far. We wind through these, eventually ending up in front of a huge high school, six stories tall, that doesn't look to be in session. We pull around to a side entrance where the car stops. The place looks vacant. I'm not sure if my hearing is accurate right now with the pounding rain outside, but it also sounds empty.

The protection operative in the front hands back umbrellas, and I tug my white trench coat tighter around me as Mike and Brad get out and scope the area before opening our doors. Shiah leads the way and places her palm on an inconspicuous console. It lights up and then the door opens on its own.

I look up and around as we walk through it, thinking nobody would ever suspect the Guild owned the place.

"They're not here yet," I say, now certain the building is empty but for us. We walk down a hall that lights in succession as we proceed. It still looks like a typical hall in a high school. Closed classroom doors break up the long locker-lined walls.

"Other than my father, the Council will not be physically present," Shiah replies, making a turn and stopping in front of a set of double doors. She stands in front of them, waiting, and I hear the faintest sound, like electricity suddenly activated, and probably only detectable by my ears. After a couple seconds, the doors open on their own, revealing a wide hall lined with benches. This is the first place we've been in this building that looks like it's seen an upgrade any time in the last fifteen years.

"Then why are we here?" I say.

"Because this was the closest fully-functioning projection room."

Since she's not offering any more, I'll have to go with it. However this is going to work will soon be apparent.

"The Council will meet with you first," Shiah says. "Mike and I will wait here and receive Gabe when he arrives. Through there," she says, pointing to a simple door at the end of the hall.

"Advice?" I say.

She gives me a half smile. "I think you've got a handle on it."

She's probably right. Not wanting to look like I'm hiding behind my coat, I take it off and hand it to Shiah before walking down the hall, my heels clicking on the tiled floor. Unlike the last time I met with the Council, I walk with confidence. I know who I am this time, what they stand for, and how I fit.

The balance, I now know, is even more in my favor.

Forty-Two

I'm shocked to find the entire Council through the double doors, sitting not at a table this time, but in a circular arrangement of chairs. Well, almost. Ohr is missing. There's even a gap in the chairs where he should be. I pause in confusion for a moment, activating my ears more fully, listening, but there is not a single heartbeat in here.

"Hello, Wendy," Debra says from her place closest to the entrance, smiling as warmly as the last time I met her. Even her auburn hair is wound into the same bun I recall. "Welcome. I'm glad you made it safely through that unearthly downpour. Going from that oddity into an abandoned school has probably cast an unsettling light on this meeting that we would have opted against, given the import of what we have to discuss. But these days the necessity of swift action makes for less than ideal situations, doesn't it?"

"If the Caribbean is any testament, yes," I reply.

She seems pleased by my answer, maybe even a bit surprised. I'm close enough that I should be able to take a read on her, but I get nothing.

"In explanation as to why you cannot hear our vitals or sense our emotions," Debra says seeing my perplexed expression, "this is merely a projection. A hologram, if you will. None of us are actually here, but as I said, the weight of this meeting requires at least the sense that we are all together at once."

"Super important face-to-face meeting," I say. "Got it."

Debra chuckles. "I'll jump right to it then. The reason you are here is because Councilmen Ohr has ceded his seat on this Council. To you."

I blink. Stare around the room at the eyes staring back. One woman I know as Sarah is smiling quietly, and so is a much older man next to her, whose name escapes me. I don't know how I feel about this… I don't know how I feel at all.

"Excuse me?" I say, having trouble finding my breath through the disbelief. "Are you talking about an Abdication?"

Debra's face lights up. "Yes. You've educated yourself, I see. I am most impressed. Most Guild members are not versed on Council administration basics, let alone the more obscure exceptions."

"I had a lot of free time when I arrived at the Vault," I say. "I wanted to know what I was getting into."

Debra nods in approval, glances around the room at the others, who have varied expressions, some like hers, others quite delighted, and others still sullen and unreadable.

She turns back to me. "Are you aware of the conditions of approval for an Abdication?"

"It only has to be approved by a majority vote, rather than the usual unanimous vote required for new Council member instatement."

"And what would you guess the reasoning is for that?"

"Probably because being on the Council carries a lot of inherent power and prestige. If someone is going to give that up, they probably have a darn good reason, likely a more selfless reason. Plus, once you Abdicate, you give up your seat completely, whether or not your choice was voted in. The usual selection process is nomination-driven. So I'd think, in theory, Abdication should have less obstacles because of the motive behind it."

"What are the conditions on who can be selected to receive the seat?" Debra asks, clearly intrigued with my knowledge.

"Anyone who is not related, either by blood or marriage or adoption. Not a dyad, and no one who shares your classification of life force ability."

"Well," Debra laughs appreciatively. "One would think you'd been prepped for this meeting."

"I discussed usurping the empire with Shiah once," I say. "I was researching loopholes on how I could do it."

Debra's expression changes instantly to shock.

I hold up my hands. "I'm totally kidding." I look around at the plethora of expressions, most entirely unimpressed.

"Sorry," I say, sheepish. "I wasn't aware humor wasn't allowed."

Debra reverts to her good humor of earlier. "It is. It

doesn't happen often though. So we often miss it when it does. But back on topic, you are probably *not* aware of what exactly happens once the Councilperson has declared their intention for Abdication."

"No. There are several different voting methods though."

"That's because the Council currently presiding has the ability to determine how they'd like to carry out a vote. In this case, we have chosen to vote with you present, and without a secret ballot. In this way you and each of us have the benefit of knowing where everyone stands. That comes with its own complications, as you might imagine, but the trade-off is that we are only allowed one vote, whereas in other methods there are many voting sessions, many discussions."

"Okay," I say. "And how long do I get to decide whether I actually *want* the seat?"

"As long as you would like, but you are to remain in this room. Once you have been informed of the voting method selected, you are prohibited from contact with anyone else."

My brow furrows. "Why would you tell me the voting method before even asking me if I wanted the seat in the first place? Now I can't talk to or get advice from anyone."

"The opportunity to request more time was as soon as I informed you," Debra says.

I stare at her and move among all the faces in the room, wanting very much to cooly inform them that it was totally underhanded of them to spring this on me and then not give me an *actual* opportunity to discuss the proposition with people I depend on for advice. Especially Ohr. What was his motivation, and how on earth does he think I can pull off a majority vote from these people who are looking at me like the mere idea of me being selected is a disgrace to the job? And choosing to vote in front of me seems like a power play, a method of intimidation. It's clear they never guessed that I'd know what Abdication was, and they hoped such ignorance would intimidate me as well. They expect me to shrink, probably because that's what I did last time. They obviously don't know that intimidating me does the exact opposite.

So now the question is, *do* I accept?

I wish I could ping Shiah. She's the only one whose opinion I actually care about in that area. I wonder if she knew this was the reason they wanted to meet with me? I bet not.

She mentioned they'd ride me about bringing up Gabe's Prime Human status on national television, and they obviously don't care about that at all.

Okay, so what *would* Shiah do?

She'd determine if the timing was right. She'd weigh benefits and risks. She'd assess these people and probably know exactly what to say to get their vote.

She is the one that needs to be on the Council. She may be related to Ohr, but she's not related to me. Which means that *I* can Abdicate to her.

Perfect. I'm sold.

I square my shoulders. "I accept," I say. "What's next?"

Debra now wears a solemn look as she says, "You have the opportunity to speak. Afterward, we vote."

I would have preferred a Q and A, but some words are better than no words. What words though?

The Council's interests lie in keeping the Guild together. I have to say something that will demonstrate that this is my interest as well. I've spouted a lot of things at events to convince people of our inclusivity, our normalcy, our common interests with the rest of Humanity. I've tried to erase the perception of lines. But I know that within these walls, those lines have to remain distinct.

Shiah said that Humans need Prime Humans and Prime Humans need the energy world. Something to believe in…

I know exactly what to give the Council to believe in, and I know how to get their vote.

"I am guessing that I don't have a lot of fans in this room as far as votes go, which doesn't surprise me in the least," I start. "I'm twenty-two, and if I can remember what I've read, being voted in would make me the youngest person to ever be put on the Council by about fifteen years. With the exception of the very first Guild Council in nineteen seventy-six, I would also only be the second case of someone being voted in that was not raised under Guild oversight. Ohr would be the first, go figure. I would also only be the third case of successful Abdication. Basically, I'd be a unicorn. So I have pretty realistic expectations for how this is slated to go."

I spread my feet, clasp my hands behind my back as I've seen both Shiah and Ohr do and look at each person in succession as I speak, "I'm used to being a unicorn by now though. I know my value, and I know my responsibility toward the Guild and myself. I also know a great many things you wish you did. Like what your life force looks like when it's next to another person's, when people touch. The exquisite beauty of the sky as it reflects the colors of the life forces below. And I've seen the seemingly inseparable connection a crowd shares when Gabe Dumas moves among them. I've seen what happens when that many people feel the same thing at the same time, and I've heard the music of souls. I've smelled the pure intent of goodness on Shiah's life force. I have seen, just in the last two days, the incredible possibility of what I *can* see.

"Two days ago I discovered that I retained the ability to channel this ability. Everything I see can be shared with anyone who touches me while I am in the energy world, and with this realization I have felt the weight of what this means. The promise *and* the danger. I've been pondering how to handle the discovery, because my sense of morality has begged me to take care of who has access to the world I see. As I stand here, I can tell that my experience and my ability and my intent have been weighed by all of you, and you've found me wanting. Let me inform you that the feeling is mutual. From your bait and switch to keep me from consulting with anyone, to your choice of voting method—not to mention the fact that, given the 'import' of this meeting, you could have and should have met me on equal footing, in person. But you didn't because you didn't want me to take a read on any of you, which might have helped me figure out what to say. You have chosen to take away any possible advantage I might have had. As if the odds aren't *already* stacked against me. Where once I walked into the Council room at the Vault and was impressed by the lack of opulence, now I am frankly disturbed that even among the Guild's Council, political games like this are taking place. I admit, I had a higher standard for you. And it sucks that I was wrong. That you would be intimidated by my ability to read your emotions indicates you have something to hide. And that doesn't sit well with me.

"What I can do has the power to change the face of the entire Guild. It is not a game, and therefore has no place in your strategy to maintain the status quo. It's the basis of everything we all hold dear. And I will not allow you, who clearly lack forthrightness and honesty, to determine what to do with the knowledge my channeling ability will bring without me having a say. You either vote me onto the Council, and give me the opportunity to help determine who will see what I do and how my ability may benefit others, or I will channel no one, and I will resign from EWR. I will pursue energy world research on my own however I see fit."

I clasp my hands behind my back and wait, scanning the faces that are a mixture of outrage, surprise, confusion, and disbelief.

"How do we know you have this ability you claim?" Abram all but sputters. He is one of the few Council members who has chosen to accost me when I'm at the Vault to question the words I've said at events. I am not counting on his vote, even a little.

"You don't," I say. Then I tilt my head. "Too bad you didn't make this a face-to-face meeting. I could have shown the energy world to all of you." I look around at the walls. "It's a shame I'm now stuck in this room until you guys finish voting." I tsk-tsk. Then I say, "Now you have to decide if you're going to take the bet that I'm lying." I turn my eyes on Abram's, unafraid of his disdain, challenging him.

Abram looks like he's been slapped. But elsewhere are wide eyes, pondering faces, and on a very few, imperceptible smiles.

Debra's face is a mixture of calculation and disapproval, and she says, "Councilman Abram, you know this process does not provide for inquisition or rebuttal. Such was agreed upon beforehand. We will take our vote now."

Debra looks at me. "Councilman Ohr Lim, has opted for Abdication, selecting you, Wendy Whitley, to replace him as the first chair on the Council of the Guild. You must obtain at least six votes to be placed in his stead. Our vote will be final. Should you be selected, you are charged to remain on the Guild Council until death, or until you choose to Abdicate your position. Do you accept?"

"Yes," I reply.

Debra turns to the group. "All in favor of Wendy Whitley taking the first chair on this Council, raise your hand."

I count them.

Nine hands.

A thrill moves through me. I did it! I did the impossible.

Debra turns to me. "Councilwoman Wendy Whitley, as of this moment you are hereby appointed to the first chair of the Guild Council. Please take your place." She smiles at me. "The chairs behind you are real. You may place one in the gap for yourself.

place another at the head, please. We have immediate business to attend to, as you know."

"Nobody get up," I joke, as I drag the heavy Oak chairs into place in my heels and body-hugging white dress.

And then I take my place, a twenty-two year old girl among a bunch of seasoned vets. Holy hell... I'm on the Guild Council.

I'm on the Council!?

And Gabe Dumas is my very first order of business as Councilwoman Wendy.

Forty-Three

Hello, Mister Dumas," Debra says, her cadence exactly the same as she used with me. It's so bizarre to suddenly be on this side of it rather than where Gabe is. "Please, have a seat." She holds a hand out to the chair I placed moments ago.

He doesn't budge, instead looking directly at me, his face devoid of a reaction. After five excruciating seconds, his eyes move slowly among the other members of the Council, which, I just now notice, have changed their projections. They have completely different faces than they did only a moment ago... That's some fancy tech.

Gabe, having assessed each of them in turn, finally looks up and around the room. "This was a planetarium before. Are you using it as a holographic projection room?"

"Indeed, Mister Dumas," Debra says. "Very astute of you. Councilwoman Wendy is the only person who is bodily present with you at the moment."

"Pardon my ignorance perhaps," Gabe says, "But holographic projection seems a bit outdated given the level of technology you've demonstrated in other realms. Virtual reality seems more your speed."

"Some of our members have dabbled in virtual reality development in their spare time," Debra says. "But there are a great many needs in the world to tackle before we officially expend our resources on unnecessary luxuries like VR. I believe Councilwoman Wendy described our purpose with succinctness during the GMA interview."

He smiles. "That she did. I must say, though, this projection doesn't leave much to be desired as far as visual and audio experience goes. It's astounding."

"Thank you. Would you like to take a seat or would you prefer to stand?"

"I'll stand for now," he says, putting his hands on his hips and looking delicious as he does so.

"My name is Councilwoman Debra," she says. "You of course know Councilwoman Wendy. The names of everyone else will remain classified."

"Of course," Gabe says in an overly conciliatory tone.

"The reason you are here is two-fold: First, our surveillance and PHIA recovery teams have discovered that Garrett Stimple, who is your technology specialist, is an undercover member of PHIA. We detained him while you were en route to this location, and will be holding him for questioning."

Gabe looks pensive. "How long will you be holding him?" he asks.

"That's not your concern. We simply wanted to make you aware and to let you know that we have the situation under control."

He crosses his arms. "No formal charges. No due process. Why am I not surprised?"

"I assure you, Mister Dumas, we are not wrong," Debra says. "Mister Stimple was a former programmer for the Guild, and he defected with Andre. Our assumption is that he joined your cause to gain proximity to Councilwoman Wendy. We cannot tolerate such a threat so close to one of our operatives. Due process or not. If he has information about the location of Andre and the rest of PHIA, we must have the opportunity to acquire it. Lives depend on it."

"I don't even know why I'm here," Dumas says. "You have clearly placed more value on your agenda than anyone else's. It's no less offensive to me to bring me here to break the news than it would have been for you to storm my hotel room and take Garrett bodily in front of me."

"Mister Dumas, I don't understand," Debra says. "He was a threat. We removed him with no bloodshed and no harm to anyone either on your team or ours. Are you opposed to us pursuing members of PHIA to protect our members?"

He looks up at the ceiling, sighs, and then looks back down. I haven't missed that since looking at me when he first arrived, he has entirely avoided me.

"I am opposed to you refusing to go through the proper legal channels," Dumas says. "By demonstrating your lack of respect for the laws that the rest of us follow, and because of your revered status, you have stated unequivocally by your actions that the law is ineffective and unnecessary. By so doing you sow unrest, discontent, and anarchy, which only breeds more violence. And one day, Councilwoman Debra, those seeds will burst forth with such vengeance that the threat of PHIA—which has not caused any substantial violence since before the Caribbean disaster I might point out—will pale by comparison."

He looks at me finally. "Oh you will be fine, for a while, locked away in your co-op city towers and your underground bunkers and hidden bases. But where will that leave the rest of us? There are not enough of you to protect us, Ladies and Gentleman. You don't hoard the life boats when the ship is going down. There are enough, but only enough for *all* of us in this case."

"We did not bring you here to lecture us," Debra replies. "We brought you here to offer additional assistance in keeping you, your team, and consequently our own operatives safe."

After his lack of concern over the threat of Garrett, however, Debra sounds like she has little belief that Dumas has any interest in help.

"Ahh. I see. What kind of assistance?" he asks.

"Facial recognition devices, which will allow you to scan anyone you employ or who attends your events. You would know immediately if they are a member of PHIA. Communicators that cannot be hacked. A secure server for correspondence within your team, and with ours should you need it. Perimeter monitors, for when you are not hosting events, which will enable your protection team to know who is going and coming. Counter-surveillance technology. Advanced, non-lethal weaponry."

"That's quite a goody bag," Dumas says. "Sure."

There is silence for about four seconds, and then Debra says, "You are requesting the resources I mentioned?" Like me, and probably the rest of us, she didn't expect that.

"Yes. It all sounds very helpful. And secure. I wouldn't want Miss Whitley to feel insecure at my events." He smiles at me. And then he looks at Debra. "And if it will prevent you from kidnapping more people for questioning, I'm in."

"Okay," Debra says, apparently choosing to ignore his kidnapping comment. Meanwhile, I'm floored that Shiah was right. I can't believe he's accepting the Guild's help, not to mention trusting us. We could use all of that technology to track his every move and record his every word...

On second thought, Dumas isn't subversive. He doesn't actually have anything to hide. This is the reason I respect him so much, the reason I have such strong feelings for him. Why would he care that he's being watched by us? And he made it clear only two days ago that he didn't care that the Guild was getting him interviews, getting him an audience, and spotlighting his events… Accepting Guild technology in no way actually violates his principles.

I envy him… I wish it were possible for the Guild to live that openly. I think we could. One day. But not today. I had to blackmail them into making me a Council member for goodness sake.

"We'll have a technology consultant contact you to make arrangements for delivery," Debra says. "On to our second issue: your memory loss. We have reason to believe PHIA is behind it. We would like to learn the circumstances of your missing memory, to ascertain what, if any, help it may lend us in finding them."

His brow is furrowed as he listens to the request. Without hesitation he replies, "On October twenty-ninth, two-thousand and fifteen I found myself on the floor of my parents' home in Bakersfield, California, along with my brother and the bodies of my parents and an unidentified woman. The house was burning down, and we escaped with the bodies to discover the neighborhood as well as the city had been abandoned, likely due to the brush fire that was consuming our development. It was at that point I discovered the date. The last memory I recalled was having lunch with my brother in Los Angeles. It was there, he had told me over the phone when he called to set up the lunch, he would tell me about an idea he had that he wanted me to take part in. I remember what I ate for lunch—my last meal as it were: salmon with a creamy dill sauce. Waldorf salad. Raspberry iced tea. But I do not remember what it was he had called the meeting for in the first place. I even remember the date: March fifteenth, two-thousand and thirteen. I recall nothing between that date and waking at my parents', which brings my total time missing to approximately two years and seven months."

October 29th. That's the date Shiah said everyone lost their memories.

"I have reasonable evidence to suggest that PHIA was behind the murder of my parents and the unidentified woman," Dumas continues. "They painted their symbol on the wall of the house and on a note, which I found in my pocket, that said 'You failed. Your child is dead.'" Dumas' face remains impassive as he speaks, but I can't help the pang of compassion I feel.

"To this day I do not know who the woman was, but I buried her body along with my parents in an unofficial grave in Greenlawn cemetery in Bakersfield marked with large stones. Should you feel so inclined to identify her or to apply forensics to gain further evidence of the circumstances of their deaths, you have my permission to exhume the bodies—not that I expected you to ask, but I do have an interest in keeping people honest and law-abiding if it's in my power. So in this case, I am ensuring you are within your legal rights."

"Thank you, Mister Dumas," Debra says. "Is there anything else?"

"Yes. I still have the note, which I had intended to have DNA tested to determine if the source came from someone indeed related to me. I also have a blood sample from the woman. But I have chosen to spend my resources on more relevant causes, namely The Human Movement. I would be amenable to handing those samples over to you, as well as one other piece of evidence that may be helpful. A satellite phone. I retrieved it while sorting through the ashes, so it's badly damaged. I don't know whether any part of it is still viable, but I suppose if anyone can squeeze blood out of a turnip, it would be you people." He smiles wanly.

"That is extremely helpful. Thank you, Mister Dumas," Debra says. "I must admit I'm surprised at your cooperation. What has motivated you today to not only accept our technological resources but relinquish to our possession the things that may be the only clues to your missing time?"

"The fact that you have to ask implies that you wouldn't understand even if I told you."

"Mister Dumas has chosen to hide nothing either personally or professionally, that's why," I say. "When you hide nothing, you have the luxury of extending trust even to those who oppose you. You have nothing to lose because you've already given it all."

Dumas avoids my face again, but the draw toward him is so strong that I have to shift in my seat to dispel it.

"Miss Whitley—er, *Councilwoman* Wendy—obviously has a finer grasp on what I am about, as she should seeing as it's her job," Dumas says. "To her words, however, I would add that extending trust is much easier when someone of integrity is part of the receiving end. It sealed my decision as soon as I walked into the room."

It's obvious that he's referring to me, but he is *still* not looking at me.

"Thank you, Mister Dumas," Debra says. "When should we expect those items of evidence?"

"I will put them into Miss Lim's hands at my earliest opportunity."

"Very good," Debra says. "Thank you for your time."

"Excuse me," I say. "But the proper way to thank someone who has extended the kind of trust that Mister Dumas has is to return it, at least in portion."

All eyes are on me. Abram, in particular, looks like he'd like to choke me. Good thing he's not really here.

"Councilwoman Whitley, we will, in private, determine what, if any, information Gabe Dumas may be entitled to," Debra says. "You have not been recognized by the floor person. Reserve your comments."

I stare back at her. "I do believe, Councilwoman Debra, that you have had more than adequate time to gather information and to determine its relevance to Mister Dumas, as well as its sensitivity."

"We have. We corroborated Mister Dumas' belief that his memory loss was likely due to PHIA. If you would like to negotiate further information, you will have adequate time when we convene to discuss such issues. That time is not now."

"No, you determined what information to give him up front, regardless of whether or not he returned the favor. Are you saying you did not discuss what to reveal should Mister Dumas demonstrate complete compliance?"

"It depends on how worthwhile the information he has provided ends up being. Councilwoman Wendy, you are out of line. Defer your questions to a more private setting. You are not the floor person, nor have you been given the floor."

I plow ahead. "By Guild law, Prime Humans, regardless of Guild membership status, are inherently entitled to certain rights, Councilwoman Debra," I say. "Do I need to remind you what those are?"

Debra shoots daggers from her eyes at me. "Certainly not, Councilwoman Wendy. But Mister Dumas did not request an advocate when he was asked to appear before us."

"Only because he didn't know his rights," I shoot back.

"He was not informed because this was an informal meeting. If it had been an official Inquisition, he would have been given a detailed explanation of his rights, which is the typical situation that would warrant an advocate." Debra looks like she's going to burst an artery.

"Typical or atypical, every Prime Human has the right to an advocate when they appear in front of the Council, *for any reason*," I say. "I spoke out of turn to ensure that Mister Dumas' rights were not violated, which I am within my own right, as a councilperson, to do at any time."

I turn to Dumas, who at some point chose to sit down, arms crossed, a look of pure amusement on his face. "Would you like an advocate, Mister Dumas?"

"How can I refuse?" he says.

"Who would you like to appoint?"

"You seem to be doing a fine job. Is that allowed? Having a Councilperson as advocate?"

"Of course," I say, smiling.

"Then I would like to appoint you, Councilwoman Wendy."

"I accept," I say, looking around the group, grateful for the first time that I don't have to endure the sum of their disapproval at once. "Here's the thing, guys. The other day when I discovered I was a channel, it was through holding Mister Dumas' hand at the protest in Raleigh. It was purely accidental, but the damage was done, and Mister Dumas has access to highly sensitive information about the energy world. He also now has knowledge that I am able to share my ability, something, frankly, even I don't want the world to know right now. I have enough of a target on my back as it is. Mister Dumas, so far, has no impetus outside of me asking him, as a favor, to keep this information private. Unless we give him one. Shiah, Mike, and I all agree that Mister Dumas' word is ironclad, and he has reinforced his integrity here before you today by his compliance and willingness to aid our investigation. I propose that we explain why we believe the memory loss is due to PHIA as well as the conclusions that have been drawn in exchange for his silence about the energy world and my ability to share it." I look at Dumas. "Would you be open to such an exchange?"

"Absolutely," he says, humor written in the creases of his eyes.

I look at Debra. "Floorwoman?"

"Mister Dumas," Debra says, "If you will step outside a moment, we will discuss it."

He stands up without a word and leaves.

"This is preposterous," Abram says. "Councilwoman Wendy should be charged with violating classified information."

"She told us it was an accident, Councilman Abram," Sarah says. "And even if it weren't, this is not the time to discuss it. We need to come to an agreement on what classified information can be shared with Mister Dumas. The most obvious piece of information is that the memory disturbance affected a number of our own."

"I don't think it prudent to share how widespread the disturbance was," Dawud says. "But I believe it's safe to reveal the common threads."

I raise my hand. "I think I need to be quickly briefed on the status of the whole thing, seeing as until today I have had no knowledge that this memory disruption extended beyond just me."

"You'll receive access to all classified files to get yourself up to speed on your own time," Malachi says sternly. "Now we need to ascertain how we will acquiesce to your demands on Mister Dumas' behalf."

"Oh stop it, Councilman Malachi," Sarah says. "She's not looking for a list of names and dates and circumstances. There is time for a quick briefing on the tentative conclusions that have been drawn."

"Do tell," I say, leaning toward Sarah.

"First of all, most disturbances were so minor that individuals did not notice the absence of their memories right away," Sarah says. "It came to them only when circumstances needed them to recall something and they realized they couldn't. Second, six years seems to be the maximum time lost, but only one of those cases includes complete amnesia. The others are selective. Third, in occurrences of drastic memory loss such as yours, each person 'woke up' on the same date, October twenty-ninth of last year, indicating to us that this is the date the memory disruption occurred, across the board. Also, the drastic cases coincided in proximity to lightning storms that were part of the lightning disaster cluster. Fourth, the inaccuracies in our prediction timelines—such as the hastening of the Carribbean disaster—first began right after October twenty-ninth. We have since recalibrated the Grid to accommodate, but still do not understand what caused the change in previously charted patterns. The fact that it coincides with the memory disturbance, however, indicates a connection."

Sarah takes a breath. "Fifth, the memory disruption was almost exclusively limited to individuals with high clearance. Although that may be because we simply haven't expended many resources to search for occurrences in people outside of the Guild. You and Gabe Dumas are a good indication that there may be many more though. It is worth noting that every member of this Council has suffered some amount of disruption. Until today, of us, Councilman Ohr had the most drastic disruption. He lost the five months prior to the October twenty-ninth date. And finally, on October twenty-ninth, our primary and backup servers were hacked. So thoroughly, in fact, that we have no idea what information, if any, was taken or deleted from our databases. We believe we have all forgotten something very important, and someone went to great lengths to ensure we would never remember."

I sit back. "Wow." So the lightning storm I was in might have actually caused my memory loss after all and *not* repression. And storms happened all over southern Missouri where the highest population of Primes can be found… To erase their memories?

"Councilwoman Wendy," Debra says. "What, of this information, do you believe should be shared with Mister Dumas in exchange for his silence?"

"What you just told me. Except for the part about Ohr specifically. And the Grid prediction timelines shifting."

Abram laughs.

Malachi says, "Not a chance."

"Why not?" I say. "It's all general."

"I am not consenting to telling Dumas that I have missing memory," one of the men says.

"We don't need Dumas thinking the Council is compromised that way," another woman says.

"Dumas doesn't need to know our servers are insecure."

"Dumas has no right to know even the most remote information on the victims of the disruption."

One of the men, of east European origin, who has come across to me as the quiet pensive type, says, "We aren't talking about what information Dumas has a *right* to know. He has no right to any of it. But an exchange must be made, and we have to weigh the risks of that information being made public. Let us get back on track."

"Well said, Councilman Kassapa," Debra says. "Does anyone have anything of use to add?"

"He's quite brilliant," one of the other women, much older with short, grey hair, says. "There is almost nothing we can leave out of the account Councilwoman Sarah gave that will not raise his suspicion of a gap in information. If we leave out our servers being hacked, he'll wonder why we don't have concrete documentation of past events to cross-check against our memory. If we say our servers were hacked and we don't know what's missing, he'll wonder why no one of high clearance can cross-check to ascertain. If we say high clearance individuals suffered, he will surely draw the conclusion that we are included in that classification. If we leave out dates, he will wonder why we left out such rudimentary information that could have easily been gleaned from interviews. Whatever we choose to leave out, he will know is the most sensitive, most specific, most pertinent. And if he chooses to breach his word and share the information publicly, he will attack from the angle of the missing information first. He will attack from the vulnerable side. For that reason, I am seconding Councilwoman Wendy's suggestion with the added caveat that we leave off the lightning storms. It would allow him the possibility of locating the other scenes of massive disturbances. A well-rounded story is best. It leaves little room for attack."

That gets a few pensive nods.

"What assurance do we have that he will keep his word?" sputters Abram. "None! This is not acceptable!"

The older lady replies, "His behavior patterns indicate he is trustworthy. Furthermore, as I said, he is intelligent. He knows his movement gains the audience it does because of Councilwoman Wendy's presence. If he were to breach trust, he risks losing that support. He knows this. I don't believe sharing the information about the memory disturbance would benefit him enough to take that risk."

I'm pretty indignant that any of them would think Dumas would breach his word, but then, they don't know him like I do. It's still hard to believe. Even without being an empath, he demonstrates in action and word a consistent motive and belief. I keep my mouth shut though. It looks like the group is going to agree.

"We have a second to the motion with an amendment. Let's vote," Debra says. "All in favor of the amended motion?"

Nine hands, plus my own. The *same* nine hands as before. Looks like Abram and whoever that other old guy is are going to be a problem for me.

"We have a majority in favor. I will alert Shiah to have Dumas return. Sarah, will you deliver the information as you just did, minus the details about Ohr and the disasters?"

"Certainly," Sarah says, and within moments, Dumas reappears and takes his former seat, looking around the room expectantly.

"Mister Dumas, it has been decided that you will receive all of the general conclusions we have that likely relate to your memory loss, minus certain specifics that might lead to identifying members of the Guild. Is that acceptable to you in exchange for your silence on both Councilwoman Wendy's channeling ability and your knowledge of the energy world, as well as your confidence as to the information we are about to share?"

"Absolutely."

Debra looks to Sarah, who repeats what she told me almost in exactness, minus the details we agreed on. And I feel good, really good. None of this would be happening if I weren't on the Council. It's only been an hour, and I've already moved us toward more transparency.

"Fascinating," Dumas says at the conclusion, and by his expression I can tell he is immersed in contemplation. "You've given me quite a bit to consider. Should I come across or think of further relevant information, I'll be sure to pass it on."

"We would appreciate that," Debra says. "Thank you for your time today."

He stands and bows his head. "Anytime," he says, and I watch him as he leaves, hoping he realizes that I did this not out of principle, but for him, to make up for always demanding silence, and because I know what it's like to lose that much time. I hope it brings him closer to answers, and to closure. It does for me. My brother is dead because I didn't protect him, but at least his death could be the catalyst for my better decisions. I'm making something really good out of those decisions.

Forty-Four

When I finally stumble out of the holographic room, I'm worn down, cranky, and starving. It's been five hours of discussing everything from who should spearhead construction of the residential buildings in the Guild's new property in Iowa, to whether people in northwestern Europe should be evacuated now or whether we should continue humanitarian assistance until the technology in the works to heat the waterways and ground is ready. But the looks on the faces of the two people waiting for me beats all.

Shiah cries as soon as she sees me, not sobbing or anything, but silent tears tumble down her lovely bronze skin. She has her hands clasped under her chin, and when I get close enough to her, she grabs me and hugs me tightly, caught up in more abandon than I knew she was capable of. Pride and affection and gratitude all mixed up.

She pulls away, hands on my shoulders. "I am *so* proud of you, Wendy. I knew you had it in you. I knew you did. You believe that, don't you? I didn't foresee this, and I'm sorry, I felt so bad about it once my father arrived and told me he'd Abdicated. And then I was mad, because I knew they weren't going to play fair. And I worried and I worried, and then I realized I was worrying over nothing. I hope it doesn't sound condescending, but I've loved mentoring you, and I didn't want it to end."

"Oh, it has *not* ended," I say. "It just got kicked up a notch. I'm on the Council now, and I get a definite say in the fact that you aren't leaving my side."

"Well done, Wen," Mike says, and he hands me a steaming styrofoam cup. One whiff and I can tell it's my tea.

"Oh my gosh," I sigh, closing my eyes and inhaling. "You're a lifesaver."

"My mind is so blown right now," Mike says. "All we got to see was the message pop up on Shiah's tablet from Councilwoman

Debra to have a bulletin created informing members of the Council seating change. Gabe was out here, waiting, and he got to see us dance around and hug each other like five times. And then he goes in, and when he came out, he was laughing his ass off. And he said he wasn't going to tell us what had gone down to get us back for earlier, jumping around in front of him without saying what as up. But the second time he came out, he told us and that's when Shiah figured out how you must have gotten the vote. But it's not the same. I'm dying for the play-by-play."

"And I am glad to share it, but I'm so hungry I'm going to pass out if I don't get calories soon." I frown. "I swear they were just testing my endurance. Every single one of them had snacks, and they just sat there and ate their virtual sandwiches in front of me."

Shiah laughs, and then she says, "Okay, food next. But first, bathroom?"

"Gosh yes," I say. "Maybe it's a *good* thing I didn't have anything in there. I'd have to pee ten times worse."

"I've got your coat," she says. "There's one this way."

I follow her, still getting used to the excitement pouring off of her as I sip my tea. In the bathroom, complete with adolescent graffiti on the stall walls, as I'm washing my hands, Shiah says in a low voice, "I have a surprise for you. *You* are going to see Gabe this evening, before your interview tonight."

I step back. "How?"

"Debra wants me to go to Dumas' hotel to retrieve the evidence discussed. But you're going in my place, disguised as me. Brad and Mike are both in on it. I think it should give you about an hour safely."

"What about the driver?" I say, thinking this is ill-advised but hoping I'm wrong. I would *love* to surprise Gabe at his hotel room. On the other hand, I almost forgot about my appearance on late night TV in the midst of the day's excitement.

"The plan is for Brad and myself to be dropped off at Dumas' hotel, and for you and Mike to be taken to *our* hotel. Then Brad and I would get a taxi back. But instead, you and I will surreptitiously switch coats and shoes in the car. Mine has a deep hood, and it's dark, so you should be able to hunker down into it and pass easily for me. Meanwhile, I, wearing your hat and coat, will be sitting in the third row, out of the driver's sight. I have perfect confidence that I can manage to avoid his direct line of sight and Mike and I have a distraction planned for getting through the lobby detail. When you return with Brad, you'll go through the side entrance. My goings and comings don't have to be catalogued by security like yours do. After that, we leave for your interview."

I look at her, seeing her black dress with new eyes. "You've been planning this, haven't you? That's why you wore a dress that could be hidden under your coat, wasn't it? How would you know...?" I say, my head in knots at how she would know Debra would tell her to go to Dumas' hotel.

She laughs. "I am not *that* good. I had a different plan originally, one far less seamless. One that involved needing Dumas' participation. But when Debra sent me the message, it was perfect." She raises an eyebrow. "Circumstances do seem to want to move in your favor, I must say."

I throw my arms around her. "Thank you," I whisper.

"You deserve every bit of it. I am so hopeful now, Wendy..." Her eyes tear up for the second time. Such an outpouring from Shiah in such a short time... I'm going to relish it. "Let's go," she says, patting me on the back. "We'll pick something up for you on the way."

ℼ

I stand behind Brad, who knocks on the door of room two-twelve, which I've been told is Dumas' room. I have no idea if he's alone in there, or if he shares it with his staff. And I'm nervous again. Every time I'm about to be alone with him, every bit of my confidence dissolves. It's especially pronounced this time, because it's mixed with a layer of dizzying anticipation. Because now I'm daydreaming all kinds of things for how our reunion will go. And then I'm worried, because last time he said there could be nothing between us. In the end I decide I'm just going to go in there, be his friend, and let things fall where they may.

I hear the door open, and Brad says, "Shiah requests a private word with you, Mister Dumas. I'd like to make sure your room is secure, if that's alright."

"Certainly," Gabe says in his distinct cadence, pulling the door wider and stepping to the side. Brad walks past him, and then Gabe's eyes turn to me in pleasant greeting, then widen as he immediately recognizes me under Shiah's black hood. He says nothing though, instead waits for Brad to finish walking the perimeter, sweeping with his handheld surveillance detector.

"Looks good," Brad says, motioning me in. I step into the room that looks to be, thankfully, only occupied by Dumas.

Brad shuts the door behind him, and once more I'm alone with Gabe Dumas. And I don't want to be anywhere else. And neither does he.

Gabe rubs his chin with a close-lipped grin. "Do you realize that I have never once laid eyes on you in any other color but white?"

I look down at Shiah's black coat and laugh. "It's a good thing, too. Made the disguise that much more effective."

"Indeed. The two of you, white and black. It's such a distinct combination. I always *expect* to see you in white, so now my head's in a kerfuffle, even more than your presence usually engenders. Tell me, do you wear any other color outside of the public eye?"

"Shiah doesn't," I say. "She's always in black. On my off-days I prefer jeans."

"Would you like a seat? Take your pick."

I catch his eye, and for a moment I consider asking him if he's one of the options to pick. And in dark blue jeans, a white undershirt, and his ever-expressive eyes that don't like to leave me, it's hard not to. Really hard. But I didn't come here to seduce him. I came to be with him. I just want to be in the same room without the expectations of thousands watching us play out a power dynamic.

I sigh and look around. The choices for seating include a bed, another bed, and an office chair.

I choose the office chair because I'm still in my white dress from earlier. On the desk is an open computer, the browser showing the satellite image of a city.

I remove my coat, throw it over the back of the chair, and sit, legs crossed, and say, "There. No more kerfuffle."

He takes a long look at me. "No. Kerfuffle still in effect."

"In case I forget," I say, pleased to have distracted him so. "I'm supposed to come back with the evidence you agreed to hand over."

"You intend to stay long enough to forget?" Gabe asks with reserved hopefulness.

"I don't intend to leave until I've forgotten," I say before I can stop myself, looking him in the eye.

He exhales almost with a groan. He closes his eyes. Far too long for my liking, especially because he's struggling to control his emotions. I'd rather he didn't. I'd rather he be the Gabe Dumas I met in Raleigh.

He takes a seat on the bed furthest away from me, out of range, brings his knees up to sit cross-legged. "Wendy, I cannot think of anyone else I would love to see more right now, and your mere presence has me awash in all sorts of daydreams, but might I ask, why did you come here?"

His words jar me. Shouldn't it be obvious to him why I'm here? Without the confidence of his emotions near, I'm a wimp, and I immediately feel like a complete idiot for thinking he'd want this visit. I kind of want to cry. But as I watch him, the look on his face, I know he meant what he said. "Because I missed you," I say.

His face once again reveals his struggle. "You missed me," he whispers. "What about me did you miss?"

"Everything," I say. "I've missed everything about you. Your eyes, your mouth, your hands, your mind, your body, the way you move, the way you never, ever lie to me. Mostly, I love what you do to me."

"What do I do?" he asks, his voice cracking.

"You make me live." I close my eyes, let his smell, which has permeated the room, fill my nose. Then I exhale, exhilarated. "I feel... more alive with you than anywhere else."

I open my eyes and look at him. "I figured it out on the way over. It started when I saw you interviewing on TV on New Year's Eve. You pissed me off so bad. I was banging pots, slamming drawers. And I told my friend, Kiera, that someone had to take you down. So I blackmailed Shiah into letting me."

He lifts his eyebrows at me, but I continue, "Something in me latched on to you. They kept telling me, Wendy, focus on issues, not Dumas. But I couldn't. I had to outdo you. I had to out-strategize. Out-think. When I finished my speech in St. Louis, and the buzz started, I had the best feeling I'd ever had in my whole life. And I was hooked. Hooked on you, on listening to your every word and figuring out what I could say in response. I was addicted. The feeling you create in me, the drive, the passion... It's not who I started out as. This isn't the person who joined the Guild. You pushed me into becoming who I am now."

I clear my throat and swallow because my mouth is going dry, and my chest is over-expanding with my billowing emotions. I've never been this honest and vulnerable with anyone in my whole life, and it's terrifying and thrilling all at once. I'm stuck in the roller coaster, unable to stop myself, but I don't think I would if I could...

"And now that I know you," I say, "and I realize what it was that drew me, I love you so much I can't breathe. You are what I never knew I wanted. And even on the other side of the fence I saw it. Even over there you were helping me become a force that makes me feel worth my salt, that makes me not feel like a fraud when I'm out there speaking. You inspire me to own who I am, to stand for what I know, regardless of who is in front of me. *You* do that. So yes, I've missed you. You don't have to do anything. You can sit there and keep your distance from me if that makes tomorrow easier for you. I just want to be with you."

He's falls back on the bed, knees bent. He rubs his face. "Wendy..." he says, his voice aching. "You should know I came over here because I'm hemorrhaging and I hope that distance will prevent you from having to feel it. I will never hide from you, but everything in me hurts, and I don't want you to feel guilty for making me feel that. I want you with me. Always. I want you." He turns his head to see me. "I want you more than I want *this*." He waves his arm around the room. "This life, this cause, this world, this sound and fury. I want you above all. But—" He struggles against tears.

"I know about Mike and your wife," I say, wishing I could go lie next to him and give him comfort. "About your past. But I don't want him. I don't. He knows it. I know it. He even helped me get here tonight."

"No," he says gently, reaching toward me, but letting his arm fall to the bed. "No, I know. And I'm glad *you* know. I have... never had a woman spend *so* much time with my brother and still choose to sneak out of the house to see me and then insist, in so many... *humbling* words that she loves me. Especially when we are... rivals. Especially when so much stands in the way of us ever being together. That you still would choose me, the illogical choice, the nearly impossible choice, over him, the easy, logical, and more desirable choice... I believe you..." He closes his eyes, takes several staggered breaths.

He sits up again, runs his fingers through his hair until it stands charmingly on-end. "The obstacles I mentioned are not just our ideals—and those are obstacle enough. I'm going to give you a bag of evidence tonight, which I've agonized for months over. To pursue it or to let it fade along with my memory? I relinquished it to the Guild because they asked, and it didn't feel like a decision. It was passive. I thought it was finally out of my hands. I was grateful that in the end I didn't have to make a decision. Except I've been thinking about it for a few hours now, and I realize I *did* decide. To choose passively is still a choice. Apparently having someone ask was all it took to push me. So I have to own that decision now and all that may come with it."

He looks at me questioningly. "Am I correct to assume he shared his account of the events in Bakersfield?"

I nod.

"There are some things my brother doesn't know, which I discovered after he left Bakersfield. One is that the ring found on the woman didn't fit her. It was too small. Now obviously if it did belong to her, she was wearing it on a chain for a reason. Logically, that reason would be that it didn't fit her anymore. But it still leaves reasonable doubt that she was, in fact, married to me. Which means that whoever the ring *does* belong to may still be out there. The ring I found in my pocket fits me perfectly. I even had a visible tan line that matched it exactly.

"The question then becomes, why was I not wearing it? Perhaps for the same reason that its matched pair was not being worn either? That is the most logical conclusion. My wife and I must have been estranged, and if we were, chances are she was not in or around that house or me when the supposed PHIA massacre took place. So where is she?" He points to the computer. "When you came, I was choosing the best route to go into California, on foot if I must. I have to go back to Bakersfield and then LA, the last place I remember living and working. There is bound to be someone still there that knows me, that knows *her.* And if there are physical records still, I will comb through them all. If we were estranged, evidence suggests that we were not yet divorced. And if there was a child involved…" He hangs his head, runs his fingers through his hair again. "I don't know how old the note in my pocket was… Could it be that the loss of the child is what separated us? I believe I have a duty to find her, to reconcile if at all possible. I believe in upholding commitment above all else, no matter the cost. Memory or no, child or no, I'm almost certainly married."

Tears have been coating my throat, and I sniffle back the ones I've kept from spilling over. "I understand," I whisper, leaning back in the chair to stare at the ceiling so I don't have to see him so far away from me, not just physically, but in other, more permanent ways.

He stays silent and still. The room is so heavy it could be underwater. At least I feel like I'm underwater. It matches the continual rain outside.

"Gabriel?" I say, still staring at the ceiling. "Why does this only make me love you more?"

I don't expect him to answer. I'm more or less asking myself the question, but he replies, "Why did you call me Gabriel?"

I contemplate it, the easy answer being that I simply don't like the name Gabe. But I could have called him Gabriel at any point. I've known that was his full name since Kiera looked him up that very first time. But this time it felt so wrong to call him simply 'Gabe' that only 'Gabriel' would come out.

"Because you are so much more than one syllable," I say, giving into my tears. "So much more…"

"I don't know if it means anything at all, but I'm sorry, Wendy," he says.

"For what?" I say. "For consistently showing me that you are everything I believe you are? For, without condition, acting out the ideals you proclaim to thousands? Don't apologize for that. I don't want you to do or be anything other than who you are."

He scrapes his face again. "May I make a confession? You may not like it."

"You never have to ask to tell me the truth."

He glances at me briefly. "I forgot about forgetting for the first couple of months. There was so much heartache surrounding it all, so much hatred for Mike. I think I wanted to believe he'd done what the gummy bear note implied because it was just more of the same thing I knew with him. It made it easier to shun a forgotten past that, no matter how you sliced it, was bound to be painful. It wasn't until you came into the picture that I started to revisit the decision because I was feeling things I hadn't felt in so long. And then two days ago in Raleigh with you, I came away and everything was ripped wide open because of my automatic fears about Mike. I started thinking about it again, and that's how it came out during the interview. Because it came out in the interview, the Council got involved, and now here we are. And I finally feel ready to take on my past. All because I fell in love with you. I've always been of a mind that the people we fall in love with, no matter the impermanence of the relationship, have the opportunity to change us more than anyone else. You've changed me, Wendy. You've made me believe I can love, regardless of my connection to Mike. You've made me believe that it *did* happen. I want to learn that love story. Because of you."

"Thank you for telling me that," I whisper. "It makes it all worthwhile." And I mean that. I didn't want to walk away from here tonight thinking it was all a waste.

"When do you leave?" I ask after a little while. "What happens to The Human Movement?"

"I'll wait until after you get back to me about the DNA testing and the phone," he says, his voice still catching. "I want to have all the information possible. Hoping that process is shorter rather than longer. As for The Human Movement, I'm leaning toward having Rita replace me. After your comments this morning, she seems to have acquired a renewed vigor for the cause—and bringing you down." He grimaces.

"How all good rivalries start," I say. "I look forward to sparring with her." That's not entirely true. I look forward to *wanting* to spar with her. Right now my heart is broken and the idea of sparring with anyone but Gabriel sounds about as engaging as the Council's discussion today about Purus delivery routes. I sit up as it occurs to me that I don't recall us talking about California. That place has to have a serious need for Purus by now, yet the Guild and the national government ignore it, as if it has fallen completely off the map. I wonder...

"What do you think about being the one to deliver Purus to California?" I say. "If you're already going there..." I put my chin in my hand, thinking.

"Assuming the hows were worked out, I have no problem with it," he says.

I wave my hand. "No, I'm thinking something bigger. Also, something that could help Rita. We could outfit you with a camera, and you could do video from wherever you are, prerecorded for events. Or something like that... I need to spend some time with Shiah, brainstorming. But my gut says you have a huge opportunity here, and it would allow you to still stay closely connected with The Human Movement. Plus, California could get some of the help it needs."

"I've considered lots of ideas for how to keep myself relevant to the movement," he says skeptically, "but I don't have the resources for any of it. My entire staff is made up of volunteers. My protection operates on a significantly reduced fee. But our events are growing so much that we're in need of increased security, so we have to spend money on actual venues now. We do have some private donors—which is another thing I worry about losing if I disappear, but I'm going to approach them individually, explain the situation and have a plan to present. With any luck I will—"

"Oh stop, we don't intend to let THM dwindle," I say. "We wouldn't let a lack of funds be your downfall. You taking Purus into California would be as big for us as it would be for you..." I start cycling through lots of ideas, and I get excited. "I need to talk to Shiah," I say, sitting up. I grab Shiah's coat, tug my arms into the sleeves. "I have to go, but promise me you will not disappear without talking to me first. Can you wait until we see each other in Chicago?"

He's staring at me, a look of what can only be translated as esteem on his face. "I don't think I could ever say no to you."

I look at him expectantly. "Is that a yes or a no?"

"Yes, of course," he says, chuffing softly. "It's just that I love watching you get so decisive and commanding. Am I correct in assuming that the Council is selected by vote and that you were voted in only today?"

"Yes."

He nods, chuckles softly. "I concluded as much. By the looks on your people's faces outside, the outlook was grim, although I had no idea what was going on at the time. Shiah was on a rampage, yelling about breaching integrity and the Council's obsession with old ways. Is she like that often? She's quite terrifying. Overturned a table and a bench. Then she punched Mike."

My jaw drops and I stop buttoning the coat. "She punched Mike?"

"They didn't tell you?" he says, eyes sparkling with amusement. "Her bodyguard and Mike were preventing her from attacking her father. She kept screaming at him, 'You set her up!' She came at him to slap him, and Mike stepped in her way, so she laid back and punched him instead. I think Mike liked it though." Gabriel sniggers.

"Wow," I mouth. Here I've been all this time thinking Ohr and Shiah were on the same team. But it looks like Ohr was betting on me *not* getting voted in. Why would he Abdicate at all? What was he hoping to gain?

"Look at those wheels turning," Gabriel says, smiling. "The indomitable Wendy Whitley has sniffed out injustice and is on the case to right it... I believe you're going to change things, you know. You are the heart and soul of the Guild. Thank goodness they have you or they would whither into irrelevance." Then he frowns. "If they don't let the world destroy itself first."

I look at him and then step toward the door. "Gabriel, the heart and soul of the Guild is the members."

"So you keep saying. But when I think of the Guild all I see is you in my head. When it attends my events, it's always you. I even met the elusive Council. But you were the only one that showed up. The rest of them... they're phantoms."

We have a short moment in front of his door in which I get to experience the Gabriel I came here to see. The one with a soul so free it makes anything seem possible. I've certainly come away enlightened with lots to do. I came here with a different purpose, but as usual, Gabriel Dumas delivers the unexpected.

I can't help throwing my arms around him, and he says, "I'm supposed to wish you luck on your interview tonight. But you don't need it. You can be sure I'll be watching though."

"Goodbye, Gabriel," I say.

"Wait. You forgot," he says, slightly smirking. He grabs a black, plastic ziplock from the desk and hands it to me.

I smile and shake my head at it as I take it. "Mission accomplished, I guess."

Forty-Five

The prodigal daughter returns," Ohr's smooth voice greets me as soon as I enter the sitting area shared by our suite of rooms.

I stop short, finding Shiah sitting on the bar, still in her black dress, ankles crossed, tossing nuts into her mouth with a little too much intensity. We've been caught.

"Where have you been without your bodyguard?" Ohr asks, standing somewhere between the bar and the couch.

"Brad was with me," I say, deciding in an instant to play this like I haven't been caught sneaking out. I put the package from Gabriel into Shiah's bag, and then take off her coat and hang it up—Shiah is an extraordinarily neat person. A place for everything and everything in its place. She's a minimalist, and I found out that's why she dresses in black. She detests cluttered rooms, cluttered closets, and, as she refers to them, cluttered decisions, like choosing on a daily basis something as arbitrary as color. I also pull out the outfit for tonight's interview. It's a dress as well, but I haven't even looked at this one yet.

Concluding my service to Shiah by putting her coat where it belongs, I turn around with the garment bag. "I was visiting with Gabe Dumas."

"Visiting with Gabe Dumas," Ohr says as if that doesn't compute.

"Yes," I say, reaching into the bathroom to hang up the dress. "What brings you here?"

"In Moshiah's coat?" Ohr says.

"It's less conspicuous," I point out. "I felt it'd be safer to pose as Shiah. Again, what brings you here? To explain why you put me on the spot today?" I fill a glass of ice water at the bar, coming purposely close to Shiah on my way to the couch. I pick up her approval.

"What private business do you have with Gabe Dumas?" Ohr asks.

I lean against the fridge. "The details of my meeting are classified until I have discussed them with the rest of the Council and we determine what level of confidentiality they merit."

Eesh. I sound like I'm on the Council or something...

His brow arches a bit. "My, how quickly the tables have turned. Be careful, Miss Whitley. Pride will earn you no cooperation among your fellow councilmen and women."

He's right. I am definitely flipping the script. It was only this morning that he strong-armed Mike, and I stood there and let him, because he's Ohr. He was on the Council. Now... the Council has lost a lot of my respect, now that I know how they operate. And Ohr is apparently no different if Shiah was furious at him. "Why did you Abdicate?" I ask, glancing at Shiah, who looks on with no apparent intent to intercede. She looks so much like him, the high, graceful cheekbones, The almond eyes that seem to emanate calm no matter the emotions underneath. But they are different. Strikingly.

"To give you the best chance for a place on the Council," Ohr says. "If I had known such a move would create so much animosity from you, I might have rethought it."

"Bull," I say. "If you wanted me to have my best chance, the least you would have done was informed me ahead of time."

"You received a majority vote. Did you not *wish* to be on the Council? You didn't have to accept the selection, you know."

Ugh. I am so over these games. I can get my information from Shiah. I don't need him. "Why are you here, Ohr? Either get to your point or get out. I have to leave in half an hour."

"To first ask you a question."

I take a sip of my water and I wave my hand for him to go on.

"I'm told you demonstrated significant knowledge of Council procedures today. But are you aware of your supplementary requisite duties as a member of the Council?"

"Supplementary requisite duties..." I say. "My required duties outside of the Council now that I am *on* the Council?"

"Yes."

"Not in detail, but I know there are lots of rules about interacting with the rest of the members, like dating for example. I know I'll have to speak at Colloquies on a regular basis... Oh, and shadowing. That's off the top of my head."

"Yes, that's all correct. Do you also recall the requirement that you donate a portion of your ova toward the Prime Human Population Acceleration Initiative?"

I pause my glass on its way to my mouth. Now that he says it, that does seem familiar. How did I forget that? "Right," I say as my mouth goes dry despite the fact that I just swallowed water. "I have to donate some of my eggs so more people can be born with my abilities." My stomach feels queasy. I down the rest of my water in one gulp. Now I remember. I read about it after Kiera explained surrogates and the Prime Human adoption system. All of it unsettled me. Kiera said it sounded wrong to me because I was used to a different cultural dynamic. I figured she was right, and I didn't think too hard about it because I figured I just needed to get used to it. But I guess not thinking about it isn't the right way to get used to an idea.

"I'm pleased that you were already aware of it," Ohr says. "Those raised outside of the Guild often find the emphasis on population increase to be off-putting. It's important for Council members to set the example for the rest of the Guild. Gamete donation is simply another measure we take to ensure the survival of the Guild."

I lean forward and set my glass on the table. "And you're here because you oversee that department—population increase. And you want to make sure I set an appointment."

"I oversaw it while on the Council," Ohr replies. "Now another Council member will oversee *me,* because I head the department. But yes, as this is now my primary responsibility, and since I am actually in the same city as you, I felt there would be no better time to broach the topic face-to-face. As I said, I always expect those not of Guild birth to need extra sensitivity. I am indeed relieved that you are so amenable."

I wouldn't call it amenable. I'm definitely going to have to spend some more time on this one, now that it's relevant to me. I wonder how long I can stall?

"I understand you will be at the Vault for the next five days before your trips to Chicago and then Austin," Ohr says. "We've streamlined and advanced the donor process, which means that we can start the process and then harvest your eggs within a much shorter timeline. The procedure is quite simple and will not even require a day of your time, which I know is now extremely valuable. You may have other plans I am not aware of, Councilwoman, but this week seems to present the most ideal opportunity. You can check one more responsibility off of your list before returning to your campaign and Council responsibilities."

I look over at him, still standing comfortably in the same place he was when I arrived, hands clasped behind his back, a pleasant look on his face as if nothing is wrong in his world. He's close enough to read, and his emotions say as much. He's hopeful that I will agree, but not overly so, as if this is just something he's checking off on *his* list of responsibilities.

"Sure," I manage to say, because what else *can* I say? I did know this before I agreed to be selected to the Council. I conveniently chose to forget it. And it doesn't matter anyway. I would have accepted selection even if I'd remembered. Some things are worth compromising.

"Thank you," Ohr says genuinely. "What day shall I expect you?"

"I get back tomorrow," I say. "I'll be busy all day. But I can see you the day after. First thing. And then the end of the week before I go to Chicago." *Let me get this over with...*

"That would be perfection," Ohr says. He steps forward then, offers his hand.

I step forward and take it, feeling like I should be thanking him for Abdicating, but I'm still unsure about his motives. But then, do motives matter all the time? Dumas takes our help despite the fact that he knows we do it to further our own cause... And I'm gladly taking Ohr's place...

"Thank you, Ohr," I say. "For Abdicating. I'm excited for what I can accomplish."

"You are welcome," he says, and he smiles widely and appreciatively. "I believe I made a wise choice."

"Good night, Moshiah," Ohr says, hands clasped behind his back as he heads for the door.

She's silent as her eyes trail after him until he shuts the door behind him. Then she slides off the counter and heads for the coat closet. "Well done," she says. "But I admit I didn't expect you to relinquish your ova so readily. Go ahead and change."

I give her a look because I'm dying to know about her and Ohr, plus, I need a little hand-holding after my veritable second breakup with Gabriel.

"We'll talk when we return," Shiah says, putting an understanding hand on my shoulder.

I nod, taking a committed breath. Nothing like easing heartbreak with a little interview in front of millions.

Most days I can't believe the life I've managed to acquire.

But today is the first day I've felt like I don't own my life anymore. It owns me.

⎇

"I totally botched that," I say once we're in the car and headed away from the studio.

"No, you didn't," Shiah says. "It just felt that way because it was a totally different format from your usual."

I sniff. Yeah, my 'usual format' has always involved Dumas. It felt so wrong without him.

"You were funny and charming and still completely sharp and on point," Shiah says.

"My favorite part was when he tried to passive aggressively dog you about your age," Mike says. "You immediately whipped out the stats. Damn, I didn't even know that stuff. The median Prime Human age is fourteen? The median Guild member age is twenty-four? How on earth do you know that stuff off the top of your head?"

"I didn't take Guild unification lightly," I say. "I wasn't going to be taken by surprise if I could help it. I did a lot of studying before."

"Wen, it still blows me away that you made it onto the Council in less than four months of joining, but you've one hundred percent earned it. The time you've obviously put in to educate yourself so you can speak about the Guild confidently... The research you've done about THM so you can be totally coherent when people ask you about it... You have a dedication to the things you take on that I admire. It's an honor to work for you."

I turn to look at him. He's not usually so verbose in his compliments. I wonder if he's just trying to make me feel better since he knows something happened between Gabriel and me? "Thanks, Mike," I say.

"We're here," Shiah says. "I don't think I've ever been so tired in my life."

"This has been the longest day *ever*," I agree as Mike and Brad step out of the vehicle.

Shiah and I lean on each other through the lobby and onto the elevator. She's not usually so physical, but I'm not going to complain. It's a relief to have her near. When we reach our suite, and Mike and Brad split off to their own rooms, Shiah and I flop onto the couch. We put our feet up almost simultaneously.

"It feels like everything is about to change," I say. "I'm not sure why."

"It is," she says. "The status quo changes every single day for you. It looks like you've only just now noticed."

"It's not every day I make it onto the Guild Council," I point out.

"Among other things," she says, and then she yawns. "I am feeling a step behind you these days. You are changing too quickly. It's going to take me some time to recalibrate."

I laugh. "Sometimes your choice of words reminds me that the way you think isn't like the rest of us. Other times... you totally pass as human."

That was the wrong thing to say. Her resulting sorrow has me wrapping my arms around myself before I realize it. I look over and her eyes have welled up. My guilt increases five-fold and I reach for her. "Oh gosh, Shiah, I'm sorry. I don't think sometimes... I didn't mean it in anything but a positive light.

"I know," she quavers with her hands over her face, her head against my chest as I wrap my arms around her. "Please, don't apologize. Let me feel this for a moment."

I'm not sure what she means, but I keep my mouth shut, holding her. Her wordless affliction gathers like heat in my chest until it overflows, pushing upward as she lets herself sob. As I feel it—partly as a spectator because I know it's not me—I recognize that she isn't trying to turn it off. She's... letting herself cry even though I sense that she has the power to push what she feels aside. Even as I gather this, her distress begins to subside, pulling away from her. She recognizes the effort to retain it has become contrived, so she lets the pain go. Sooner than she wants.

Sooner than she wants?

I don't understand her emotional trek.

She sits up, wiping her eyes. "I know," she says. "I know I confuse you. And if my father could only feel this moment between us, when two planes of experience have passed close enough to touch each other, but neither can truly see the other, he might finally understand."

"I—"

"Don't understand," she says. "I know."

"Will you—"

"Explain it to you? I will. But you will only grasp it in part."

"Okay."

"But first, I would like to know what was happening in your head while my father was making a play for your eggs earlier this evening," she says.

"Well when you make it sound disturbing like that…" I say, wrinkling my nose.

"No matter how palatable I phrase it, it doesn't change the reality," she says.

"True. And that's where my logic was when I agreed. It still kind of disturbs me, but I figure it's only because test tube babies and surrogates isn't how reproduction has been happening for thousands of years. The whole Prime Human Reproduction Acceleration Initiative is just a more palatable way to say 'baby factory' anyway, and that has this whole soulless, robotic feel to it as the only real argument against it. But when you consider that these kids are *wanted* for their probable contribution to the world, I think that's what makes it okay."

"It's still a big thing though," she says. "In fifteen years or so, a bunch of versions of you will be walking around who can do what you do, but better. And knowing how much you have to think about how best to direct your powers for good, their world will be even more complex. Sort of feels like uncorking a bunch of grenades and sending them into the future."

I can't tell if Shiah disagrees with the reproductive practices of the Guild or if she's being a devil's advocate, but it's still a good point anyway.

"You have to have faith in the next generation, I guess," I say. "I don't think the world is ready for a bunch of supercharged versions of me who can see the energy world right *now*. But fifteen years from now? I'm on the Council. I'm in the best position to help get us there. If I don't believe I can sort this whole thing out—the disasters, the Prime Human-Human dynamic—then why am I even here?"

"That is wisdom," Shiah says, nodding. "Yet another example of your rapid growth. Soon I will not be surprised at the things you say."

"The other thing was that I didn't want to come across as rebellious," I say. "They're already watching my every move. I need to be seen complying with as many procedures and policies and rules as I can, because when things that matter the most to me come up, I need all my leverage reserves to negotiate. You can't get anywhere if you don't compromise." I grimace. "I have suddenly, and against my will, turned into a politician."

Shiah laughs lightly. "Politics have their place. The goal is to have the most honest, most self-sacrificing politicians to engage in the game. You fit that bill."

"So do you," I say. "That was my plan, you know, to Abdicate to you once I was instated. I have to wait a year, right?"

"I would never accept a selection," Shiah says firmly. "And I would ask you to do all you can to ensure that I am never nominated."

I'm at a loss. Shiah practically *is* on the Council with how much influence she has in her position as advisor. They defer to her regularly, they listen to her, and I can only guess that, like me, they see that Shiah has uncanny intuition about people that allows her to be able to pull things off that others can't. I am obviously missing something. A huge something.

"Alright, now *you* talk," I say, turning toward her on the couch and pulling my knees up.

"And now I talk," she agrees, copying me. "I have the ability to recall any moment of my life experience in perfect detail. The sights. The sounds. Smells. Sensations. Emotions," Shiah says. "Down to the tiniest iota of detail, limited only by the capacity of my senses. I can recall it in my head, over my skin, in front of my eyes, as if it is happening this very moment. I am my very own source of virtual reality. On demand. At any moment."

"Seriously?" I say, imagining that.

She gives me an expectant look.

I roll my eyes. "Yeah, I know you're serious. It's an expression, Shiah."

She rolls her eyes back at me. "I know it is, Wendy."

I lean away and hold a hand up, grimacing. "Ohmigosh, I didn't know your eyes could do that. That was *so* weird."

She rolls her eyes again.

"Ahh!" I say, scooting down the couch and and looking away. "Stop, stop! You've corrupted my Shiah-data! Now I have to go recalibrate!"

She giggles at first and then it explodes into uncontrollable belly laughter, and then we are both howling, bowled over each other.

"Wait, wait," I gasp. "So can you do other faces, too? Like…" I sit up. "Can you be like ultra sultry? You look like hell on wheels in that dress. But you still walk in it like you're an accountant."

"Pshh," she says as if offended. She stands up and pulls my pumps out of the closet—hers don't have as much of a heel. She tugs them on her feet, pulls the pins from her hair and shakes out her black mane, standing with hip cocked, chest out just enough, her dark eyes on me like she can devour me with them. Then she struts over to me, leans over slowly, her hair falling in a curtain as she meets juuuust the right angle to reveal the perfect curve of her breasts. "Like this?" she purrs.

"Um, yeeeah," I say, a little hot, because not only does she *look* like she's making a genuine come-on, but she *feels* turned on as well. I think I might actually be reciprocating.

She doesn't move, but instead brings her face ever-closer, her mouth open enough to be inviting. I'm actually having a hard time looking away from her perfect mouth as I take a deep breath, swallow, and say, "Last I checked, I was straight, but dang, I kind of want you to kiss me right now."

"Kind of?" she breathes.

I think about it, and as I do I perceive her sort of retreat emotionally, to let me figure out how I feel. I think I said it half-joking, half-serious, mostly because I'm unsure how I feel about it, but I do *want* to know. I want to know if I'd feel anything more than what I do right now, which is safe with her. Totally safe.

"I do," I say, reaching up to put my fingers through a lock of her hair. I've wanted to touch it ever since I met her. It feels as silky as it looks.

She moves her lips closer and I tilt my chin to meet them. Oh gosh they're soft. Like rose petals. She brushes them against mine, and the gentleness of it entices me to sink into them. And for a few seconds I enjoy having her so close. How many times I have looked at her and thought how gorgeous she is, how much I love her. She doesn't just inspire me; she leaves me in awe of her constantly. I internalize every word she says, even the ones I don't understand. But they do something inside of me, and then they come out at exactly the right time. My God, she makes it so easy to love her. This moment, which I recognize is devoid of any kind of lust, is the most vulnerable moment of my life, but with her it doesn't scare me. At all.

Her lips leave mine, hovering only inches away. Slightly breathless, she's heavy with an inexplicable emotion that she bathes in, letting it linger as long as it will stay. I tuck her hair behind her ear, because I can't help touching its flaxen perfection, and I want her to know the kiss wasn't weird for me. She falls onto the couch next to me, laying her head on my lap, her hair spread all over me.

The thing I marvel over most, as I brush my fingers through Shiah's hair and stare at nothing across the room, is how completely normal it all feels. I do wonder what it means. Do we have something together? Or was it just a moment? Does it have to be more because it felt so... unfettered? Yes, that's the word I'm looking for. Unfettered.

I've kissed men plenty of times, and it's never been as easy as kissing Shiah just now. Kissing a man is a hot mess. There's always this edge of lust and anticipation overshadowing the affection and sweetness of it. And expectation. There's always the uncertainty of expectation in the background, wondering how far things should go, and what the other person wants... I didn't wonder any of that with her.

So I stop trying to figure it out. There's no existing label for it. Just love. Pure, unencumbered, unconditional love.

"Thank you for being you," Shiah says finally, and then she yawns again.

I look down at her, curled up on my lap, totally at ease and content, and I feel like crying because my whole self just wraps around her. There is no one, not even Gabriel Dumas, who makes it so easy for me to love them. And I don't know why. It's her. Who she is.

Her eyes fall closed, her emotional awareness blurs, and I ponder my future as she fades into slumber. I'm still raw from losing Gabriel, and maybe I'm trying to let go faster but I think it was for the best. I doubt a relationship can last when ideals are so much at odds. I'm sure the sneaking around and the secrecy would get old. And I don't think Shiah is right about him; he won't join the Guild. Not even for me. Well... Maybe I'm wrong about that. He said he could never say no to me. But I would never ask him to do something like that. It would be asking him to be someone he's not, and that's not a version of him I want.

I look down at Shiah. I could do tonight every night and be happy, I think. Being with her is the easiest thing in the world. I don't need anything else. I am... completely at peace with her. I love her odd little phrases, feel a victory every time I make her laugh, and every moment I've ever had with her since we met has come so easily. She's been my best friend, my confidant, and a lot of what I think about the world now is because of her. She's my immovable rock. She turned me into this... this fearless and undaunted person. It seemed like it didn't even take trying, because whenever she is near, all of the voices in my head that have been telling me I can't, leave at once. She gives me some kind of power that makes the things I imagine become reality, because with her… doubt is nonexistent.

Tears fall from my eyes just from thinking about all of these things. I could spend the whole night reliving it all. I worship her, I realize. I worship Shiah. And that doesn't make her my equal. It makes her my guide. My teacher. My master. She is the head and I am her hands. To me, Shiah is… perfection. I would follow her anywhere.

And strangely, that is what makes something with her entirely out of the question.

So tonight was… just love. And I'm not going to overthink it. Definitely not tonight.

I remember then that she forgot to finish telling me about why she doesn't want a Council seat. She started off my telling me about her ability, which sounds absolutely nuts. She can walk around all day, every day, in a haze if she wants. Forget walking. She could do it from the comfort of home.

But she doesn't. She's the most active, busy, involved person I have ever met. She's always going or coming, and a moment like this, where she's asleep before I am, is rare. It's just after three A.M., but this is exactly what I've seen her do every night: engage herself every second until she can no longer keep her eyes open. Shiah never checks out of her life. And I need her more than ever.

Her hair wound in my fingers, I lean down and touch it to my face as if it will release some of its innate power. And maybe it does, because emotion overwhelms me and a sob escapes my throat. "Thank you, Shiah Lim," I whisper.

Forty-Six

Crap, are we late?" I ask Mike who is standing over me. I rub my eyes and move to stand up only to realize the weight of Shiah still lying on my lap. My neck has a wicked cramp and my butt is numb. Our team is in here, gathering up our belongings that we should have packed last night.

"Getting there," Mike says. "Brad and I would have checked on you sooner if we'd known you weren't ready."

Shiah rouses with all of the commotion. Once she realizes what's happening she sits up abruptly. "What time is it?"

"Six," Mike says.

Shiah leaps up, looks this way and that, frantic for about four seconds. Then she stops, stills her hands by her sides and closes her eyes, casts away all stress as easily as shaking dust out of a rug, and for fifteen seconds engages her brain in quiet but methodical thought.

Mike and I glance at each other several times. He gives me questioning looks and I wave my hand for him to be quiet.

She opens her eyes and says, "I'm going to go shower. I'll be out in five minutes." Then she walks into her room.

I look back at Mike once her door shuts, and he's staring at me.

"What?" I say, worried he sees the kiss I shared with Shiah written on my face.

"Just… wondering how you're doing."

I stand up, nervous for a second and then indignant that I have anything to be ashamed of. "I'm okay."

He tails me into my room when normally he'd wait outside the door.

"I need to shower, Mike," I say.

He groans. "Seriously?" he hisses, glancing briefly behind him to the door leading into the living room of our suite. "I've been super patient. All through last night. Figured you'd tell me when you got a second to breathe. But I'm dying to know what happened yesterday. I felt him from here like he was in the next room. That was some seriously powerful emotion. I had to call someone to watch my post so I could go lose it in the bathroom. What the hell happened between you two?"

"Oh," I say, awash with relief followed in quick succession by the air getting pulled from my lungs. The hollow it leaves behind deepens before I can stop it. I had forgotten... How?

The interview of course, but then Shiah. She made me forget. So easily, too. How does she know what I need so exactly that she can make me forget such profound heartbreak? And even now, when I expect I should be hiding in the bathroom with the sound of the shower to drown out my sobs, I'm in control of myself even though the air feels heavier. I rummage in my suitcase for a pair of jeans. "It's over."

Over. That word is too simple to be this painful.

"Over?" Mike whispers, completely at a loss. And then he's mad. Really mad. Furious even. "What did he do?" he growls.

"He's going to find his wife," I say matter-of-factly, jeans and T-shirt in-hand. "Because he's got pretty compelling evidence that the dead girl wasn't her."

"What evidence?" Mike demands.

"Not now, Mike," I say tiredly. "I have to get ready. It's a long story."

"Everything with him is," Mike scoffs, crossing his arms. "Why does he have to make an issue out of *everything?*"

"Wendy!" Shiah calls from the other room. "You are returning to the Vault as Councilwoman Wendy. Blue jeans are *not* appropriate!"

I look down at the clothes in my hands and shove them back in the suitcase. "I wasn't going to wear jeans, Shiah!" I shout back. "Geez!"

"Yes you were," she says, her wet soapy head popping around the door frame, a towel wrapped around her.

"Did you seriously get out in the middle of your shower to tell me that?" I say, aghast.

"They're taking the bags down as soon as you're dressed. You would not have had the opportunity to change if I'd waited until I was done to tell you. And paparazzi are outside this morning."

"I was going to shower..." I say.

"No time," she says, disappearing.

"How does she have time to take a shower and not me?" I grumble.

"Because you take the longest showers on the planet," Mike says. "What do you do in there? Plan your speeches?"

I ignore him, grabbing the backup white outfit I brought from the closet: mid-calf pants, silk blouse, and a blazer. Good thing. I came to New York with no idea that I'd be leaving as a Council member. And paparazzi? What the crap? That has never happened before.

I change in the bathroom, run a little mousse through my short hair—which I've come to love for it's chic simplicity—and emerge from the bathroom.

Shiah is there, and before I can say anything she says, "Hold still." She reveals a tube of lipstick and runs it over my mouth. Only when she puts the cap on do I catch a glance at the color: fire engine red. She adjusts my collar so it's standing up and hands me sunglasses with huge lenses that look like mirrors.

"I'm on my way to the airport," I say. "Why all this fuss?"

She hands me my white heels. "Because in the time it will take us to get from the hotel to the car, you are going to have about a thousand pictures taken of you, and you're running on three hours of sleep. Let's go."

I hop after her, tugging my heels on one-by-one. "A *thousand*? Why? What changed?"

Mike hands me a newspaper. It's the New York Times.

On the front page:

Poised to Win Hearts: The Guild's New Councilwoman

It heads a shot from Good Morning America. It's me right before the interview, standing and making the Guild Fist to the crowd in Time's Square through the window, my head bowed solemnly.

"What?" I say, confused. "Since when does the media know who's on the Council? And who took the picture?"

Shiah snags the paper from my hand. "Since a public Guild figure became a Coucilmember. You can read it in the car. We have a schedule."

I skip to the bed for my bag. "You did it, didn't you? Shiah! What is the harm in telling me these things ahead of time?"

"I just did," she replies. Mike and Brad take their place, Shiah dons a wide-brimmed black hat and shades, and the four of us make a procession out of our room and downstairs to the lobby where security is already engaged with a crowd of reporters. Flashes blaze to life even though we haven't reached them.

"All smiles. Own it," Shiah says quietly from next to me, and then she falls back behind me.

Mike pushes open the glass door for me, and he's probably got his eyes everywhere, but I can hardly see or think with all the commotion. And shouting. I make out words, but no phrases. And the clicking. Clicking and flashing and yelling. Do they actually expect me to be able to answer any of them if they're all screaming at the same time? Thank goodness for the sunglasses. I look up, because that's the only direction that *doesn't* have lights flashing in my face. At least it's not raining anymore, although the sky is ominously grey.

An open car door is in front of me, but I turn and wave before getting in. I slide over to make room, but the door shuts abruptly, and the car jerks into motion with only me inside. Instantly I'm on alert. The protocol is that if there's danger, I'm to be driven to safety, protection or no. The car is jerking through the early Manhattan traffic, so that seems to be what's happening.

What about Mike and Shiah and Brad? What happened back there? Are they okay? I grope around for my bag to get my phone.

"What's the status, gentleman?" I say to the driver and extra protection in the front. Where is my bag?

I groan. Shiah discreetly took it from me to make sure my hands were free for the crowd.

I lift my sunglasses up and look to the front again when I don't get an answer, and a face is there to greet me, leering. Blonde hair carefully parted and combed, like a Ken doll. Perfect teeth. I don't recognize him. At first. And then...

I gasp. "Andre." My breath leaves me, I'm hot all over. I'm dead. I'm still breathing but I'm dead. He's going to kill me. Long before the Guild can locate me by my GPS implant.

I scramble for the door handle, but it won't unlatch. Oh my gosh, I'm locked in a car with Andre with a *child lock*?

"Hello, Councilwoman," he says, grinning widely as the car sways this way and that through traffic.

What is there to say in a moment like this? Especially when I discern Andre's utter hatred for me as it fills the car? Do I plead for my life? Do I die with a snotty reply on my lips?

"You," Andre gushes grotesquely, pointing his finger at me. "You are a brilliant woman."

His tone and words don't seem to match his emotions, but then, I realize, the hatred isn't his. It's mine. I've never felt this kind of loathing toward another human being.

"What do you want?" I say, wondering how long it will be before Mike realizes the car has been hijacked. Andre switched our driver somehow, because this is definitely the car we've been using in New York. In fact, my coat is in here, which I told my team to be sure was left out of my luggage.

I catch myself from doing a double-take when I see my boots, too. I look back at Andre immediately, afraid of staring at them too long. He's been occupied with pulling something up on a tablet fortunately, which he hands back to me now.

I take it without really thinking because all I can visualize is my boots, and what they should still contain, as long as Andre was too stupid to check. I always keep my pocket pistol in them. I just have to find an opportunity to reach into them discreetly…

I look down at the tablet, and every strategy for reaching my gun leaves my head immediately. On it is a video. Of my brother.

I sink back, hand over my mouth, my gut clenched so tight I feel nauseous.

"Oh God," I breathe. It's Ezra. It's him. A much older him. But there's no mistaking it. I'm looking into a future that should have been. An Ezra I should have known. I assume I did, but I don't remember it. And I may never.

He's leaning over a bunch of papers at a desk, scribbling. Behind him the walls are plastered with maps. They cover every inch of space, and the maps themselves are covered with lines and markings in different colors and incoherent characters. If Ezra knows he's being taped, he gives no indication. He turns around, his back to the camera as he stares at the maps, rocking forward and back in an office chair.

There's a timestamp on the video. It's today: 02/25/2016 03:52:36

It's California time.

"Lately he's been staying up all night," Andre says conversationally. "Very motivated. But, considering what's at stake, it's no wonder."

This video is fake, but I can't look away.

"What's he working on?" I ask barely above a whisper, hoping that at some point I'm going to figure out what angle I should be taking. I hate being so completely at Andre's mercy.

"He is developing an equation to locate all Prime Humans."

"Based on what?" I ask, thinking the idea sounds too far-fetched to be real. Even my brother, who is so smart it blows me away, can't possibly have had that capacity.

Andre chuckles but I don't look at him. "If only you could remember…" He tsk-tsks. "You'd be so proud! It's based on his own theory, which he developed months ago, before your brain, er, left the building per se." He laughs again. "The technical implementation, however… that's going to remain my own secret," he adds proudly.

I don't want Andre thinking he's gotten to me as profoundly as he has, but I can't stop watching Ezra, how different he looks. It's like having more time with him even though he's gone. I want him to turn around, but he just rocks back and forth, clicking the pen in his hand over and over. I'd always snatch his pen away when he'd do that and shove a pencil at him. 'This pen never did anything to you,' I'd say. 'Stop abusing it!' He'd always have some comeback prepared. But now… that clicking is the most beautiful sound in the world.

I'm crying. Dammit, I'm crying in front of Andre. My heart ripped in two, I take the tablet and slam it several times against the window until it's shattered beyond repair. And then I throw it at Andre. He ducks, it hits the seat and falls to the floor.

Andre looks from the tablet to me with annoyance.

"You were hoping I wouldn't remember what you did," I snarl at him. "You were hoping you'd be able to use him against me again. But I won't let you, you piece of shit."

His eyes narrow. "Get control of yourself, Councilwoman. I've left you alone for months because I have an agreement with your brother that as long as he works for me, I will not lay a hand on you. I could have killed you at any time. I can kill you now. But that would not get what I need from him. I've grown impatient though, and I have given him two weeks, as of today, to complete his task. If he does not, I kill you, and there is no hole you can hide in where I will not find you. I have people everywhere, moles buried in so many holes that you and the Council can never hope to eradicate them all. And even if you should I have an army of Humans waiting in the wings."

He's lying. He has to be. My brother is dead. I watched him die by touching me. It was a video, too, just like—

I stop, mid-memory, realizing suddenly that something is amiss with it. The memory of watching my brother die, which

I was never able to nail down the timeline of... it can't be real. I know this because I just saw an older Ezra on Andre's tablet. But in the memory of his death, he's still the fifteen year-old Ezra I remember. But that's not how I should remember him. Unless Andre's video is fake to the point of even age-progressing Ezra. Either that or I've mis-remembered him... And if I've misremembered that part, how much more does my head have wrong? Is the memory real at all?

A wash of overwhelming relief that I might not have been the one to end his life is followed by instant panic: What if he really is alive? What if Andre is telling the truth?

Oh God... I'm going to be sick. I don't know what I should believe.

"I have every confidence that your brilliant little brother will give me what I need," Andre says, now that I'm not throwing anything else. I glance out of the windows to find that we've stopped at the curb in front of a bustling JFK airport terminal. "If you hope to see him alive again, *you* will also give me what I need. In two weeks time you will make an announcement at one of your public appearances that Prime Humans are the cause of natural disasters. You will say that humans have been unnaturally tinkered with, and their offspring are aberrations that are disrupting nature. Nature is rebelling against *them* and Humans are getting caught in the cross-hairs. You will tell them you know this because the energy world has told you. You *will* do this, or when your brother has finished his work, I will kill him. And I will drop his dead body off in front of the Vault."

I stare at Andre, horrified. That would start a war. A genocide. A bloodbath. He's insane. He's absolutely evil. And everyone knows you don't negotiate with disgusting psychopaths. He seriously thinks I would agree to something like that? Especially with his half-assed evidence that my brother is alive? And even if he was, why on earth would I trust Andre's word not to kill him when it's over, especially when he thinks we are 'aberrations'? What an absolute moron.

I have no idea if the video was genuine or if my memory is, but it doesn't matter right this moment. Andre isn't going to hold anything over me or anyone else ever again. "Why do you hate Prime Humans?" I say, nearly on top of my boots—I've been edging slowly toward them. I always keep the gun in the left boot... "Seeing as you *are* one?" I add.

"I don't hate them. I pity them. They shouldn't be." He reaches for something at his feet, and I take the opportunity to reach in my boot. The gun is in my hand. Andre is going down.

"They are the result of children playing with things they know nothing about," Andre says, looking at me again, a shoulder bag in his lap. "It's simply the unfortunate reality that they must be disposed of."

"You were kidding yourself if you thought I would fall for that kind of blackmail," I say. "You obviously don't know who you're dealing with."

He narrows his eyes at me. "Neither do you, apparently."

"I guess I'm about to find out," I say, lifting the gun and releasing the safety in the same motion. "Hands up," I say, the small barrel trained on a very surprised Andre.

"Put your hands up now!" I scream at him when his shock delays him from following my order. "Both of you!" I scream when I see the driver's hands shift from the wheel. Only then do I realize that the driver is *my* driver: Jerry. Jerry is PHIA?!

"Get out out of the car," I say when they comply. "Slowly."

As their doors unlatch simultaneously, and I'm about to open my own, I remember that I can't get out through my door. They must remember as well, because both of them leap from the car as soon as their doors are open.

"Idiot, Wendy," I mutter, leaping over the armrest and out of the passenger side. They are not getting away. No freaking way.

"Stop!" I yell, kicking my heels off, hot on their heels.

They don't. So *I* stop, remember to keep my gun up as I place my feet. Then I shoot. I tag Andre. And then I aim at Jerry. I shoot, but miss. There are too many people around—all screaming and running now—and I'm a complete amateur.

I turn my glare on Andre, who is struggling for his feet. "I wouldn't do that," I snarl, coming to stand over him.

He rolls over, and I see I've caught him in the side. It's probably not a fatal shot. I keep my gun on him.

"He'll die," Andre threatens, gasping. "If I don't come back, they'll kill him."

"Lies," I say, keeping the sight of my small pistol right over his ugly face. "You are full of them."

"You want to take that risk?" Andre taunts, hand gripping the bloody wound at his side.

"You're not going to own me or anyone else anymore," I say, hearing the gasps and shouting going on around me. But I don't see them. I don't care about them. I don't see anyone but Andre.

He holds his hand up. "Your memory," he coughs. "No one else can tell you who you were. No one else remembers. If you kill me, you'll never find him, and you'll never remember."

"And if I let you live you're going to tell me all about myself, is that right?" I scoff. "The problem with liars, Andre, is that no matter what they say, their truths are as worthless as their lies."

Andre sneers up at me from under his eyebrows, "You'll never find your child without me... You don't even remember *him* do you?"

I grit my teeth. Lies. All lies.

"Fuck you, Andre," I say, and I keep my eyes on his face as I pull the trigger.

Forty-Seven

It's just me," the pair of arms that have been fighting to pick me up say in a soothing, gravelly voice. "Shhh." The arms wrap around me, attached to compassion and softness and intense relief. So instead of fighting them off, I sob into them, tucking my face into a hard chest.

"I need backup now!" the chest rumbles loudly against my ear. It's Mike.

I grab for his shoulders. "Mike," I cry. "Find Jerry. He got away! My brother. He might be alive."

"Okay," he lulls, keeping me folded against him. "We're not out of the woods yet. I need you to be ready in case we have to move quickly."

"He might be alive, Mike," I bawl. "What have I done?"

"Where is my backup!?" Mike says into his communicator. "I need an ETA!"

"What you had to do," he says quietly, keeping my flailing arms still. "I'm so sorry, Wen. I've never dealt with that many cameras, and then the guy that tried to push through the line... I should have known it was only a distraction. I overreacted and... I'm sorry." His residual panic bleeds into me, and I hang on to him like I'll never let go.

"You did so well," he croons when I start crying again. "Don't believe anything he said. Andre is the best liar there is. He says the things that will eat you from the inside."

"Don't let me go," I say.

"I won't. But I might have to pick you up. There's too many people..."

"Am I in trouble?" I say, frightened as it sinks in that I just killed someone point blank.

"For executing the leader of PHIA in front of hundreds of witnesses? Ummm, I'm not sure. Public relations are Shiah's area."

"Where's Shiah?" I say, looking up.

Mike buries my head again. "Don't," he says. "Everyone has their phones out, and I don't want to see you in the paper tomorrow with Andre's body."

"I'm not ashamed," I say, lifting my head again to see shocked faces all around us.

"About damn time," Mike says with relief, not to me. "Up we go." He pulls me to my feet, which are bare, and guides me toward a car approaching the curb at a breakneck speed. Shiah hops out before it comes to a full stop, followed by Brad scrambling after her.

She throws her arms around me as a flood of uniformed bodies swell around us. "You're okay," she says with the most intense relief, but her heart is hammering. "Thank you. Oh thank you. You're okay…"

"Car, car, car," Mike prods, nudging both of us.

Shiah takes charge suddenly, puts her shoulder under my arm as if I can't walk on my own and heaves me toward the car. Once we're all in, Mike says, "Can you get us clearance to drive onto the tarmac, Shiah?"

"Damn straight," Shiah says, whipping out her phone.

"Are you hurt?" Mike asks me while Shiah barks at someone.

I shake my head, the shock starting to wear off to be replaced with numbness. "He said he had my brother, Mike."

"You can't trust anything he says."

"He said I had a child out there, that I'd never find him on my own."

"Do you *really* think you'd have a child out there you don't know about?" Mike says.

I look out the window at nothing. "No. But…"

"Wendy, I'm telling you. You have to let everything he said go. You have to. It's over. *He's* over."

"If my brother's alive, he's in California," I say.

"Now that Andre's gone, PHIA is going to fall apart," Mike says.

"He said they have moles in the Guild. He's right! Jerry—He's PHIA. Andre said he hasn't come after me because he had an agreement with my brother. Mike, if my brother really is dead, why has there been practically no movement from PHIA since before I joined the Guild?"

"Because they *can't*. The Guild has relocated everyone. The intel Andre had is outdated now."

I shake my head. "No, Andre's about creating fear. Even if he couldn't find Prime Humans, he'd kill at THM events just to stir the pot and scare people. Did you know he wanted me to make an announcement that Prime Humans were the cause of natural disasters? It's because he wants Humans to turn against us. Fear, Mike. That was his weapon."

"It's a valid concern," Shiah says. "The Council needs to issue a Guild-wide investigation to weed out PHIA informers. You've cut off the head. We need to act quickly on the roots."

Shiah's phone trills.

"I'm going with you to the Vault," Mike says. "If PHIA's on the inside, you need twenty-four-seven protection."

Shiah hands her phone to me.

"Yes?" I say into it, expecting it to be someone from the Council. Where is my stupid phone?

"Wendy! Thank the stars you're alright. I was terrified. The video on the news was pitiful. I couldn't tell if you fell over because you were injured or exhausted." It's Gabriel. My heart leaps into my throat.

"I'm on the news already?" I groan.

"Afraid so. But don't concern yourself with negative reviews." He sighs. "The spin is ever in your illustrious favor. Not only are you everyone's favorite Guild darling, but now you're the fearless and exacting protector of your kind. Good grief. There's already speculation that you drew Andre out purposely to trap him. You're the benevolent, fierce goddess to the masses."

"Well gee, Gabriel. You don't have to be so dejected about it," I smile, content to hear his voice.

"It's an odd thing, to be both in awe of you but convicted to the dissolution of your organization. It seems like you keep a go-to list for ways to make my life harder every day." He chuckles "Rita is yelling at the television, 'The woman is a murderer! How does nobody see this!?' If she finds out I stepped out to call you she's probably going to burst an artery and quit. She absolutely loathes you."

"She's just mad that she's spineless. Maybe one of these days she actually *will* quit and stop filling the universe with her negativity. How do you have Shiah's number anyway?"

"Oh… She left it out when she went to the loo at Co-op City yesterday. I took liberties. She doesn't strike me as an absentminded person, so I tend to think she left it on purpose. Unlocked no less. Is she mad? I could have stolen all the Guild's secrets while she was indisposed!"

He just called the bathroom a *loo?* That is so cute… I look up finally to see Mike and Brad and Shiah smirking at me. I kind of forgot where I was for a second…

"No, I'm sure it was purposeful," I say. "Well it was nice of you to check in on me. I've got to go, um, strategize."

"I know," he sighs. "I was stalling. I love hearing your voice. Maybe you could arrange to be in danger tomorrow so I will have an excuse to call again."

Butterflies flutter in my stomach.

He clears his throat. "My apologies. That was… not fair."

"I don't mind," I say.

"Well I do. You don't deserve to be strung along."

You can string me wherever you want… I think wistfully.

"Goodbye," he says.

"Bye." I end the call and hand Shiah her phone back.

"I don't mind," Shiah breathes mockingly, fluttering her lashes.

I shove her, and she giggles.

My phone rings now, and Shiah is already holding it out to me. The ID says it's Debra.

"And so it begins," I sigh, sitting back in my seat to get comfortable. "You guys can make fun of me some more at the end of my fifty-eight phone calls."

"Councilwoman Wendy," Debra says, standing at the head of the conference table. "While we are all *deeply* grateful that you did not suffer injury or death, your actions were unsanctioned by the rest of this Council. You've stated that you felt that the consequences of ending Andre's life were outweighed by those of keeping him alive. Can you expound on your reasoning for the rest of us?"

I lean forward, put my elbows on the conference table. "He was blackmailing me. As a member of the Council and spokesperson for the Guild, I felt that his influence over my actions while he remained alive was too risky."

"That is not a valid reason," Malachi says. "If you felt your ability to perform your duties was in jeopardy, you should have come forward to the Council and we would have appointed a temporary replacement in your stead until the crisis had been managed."

I laugh drily. "No, you don't get it. If Andre had remained alive, I would not be sitting here with you. I'd be in my helicopter, which I would have commandeered from the flight deck, along with my bodyguard, a sack of badass weapons and super sick tech gear. I would be on my way to California where I would then interrogate every person I saw until I located Andre's hideout, and searched the whole place for my brother, all while unloading my machine gun on anyone that looked at me funny. So don't feed me a stupid line about *coming forward* to tell you I'm unfit to haggle with you."

"She admits how volatile she is!" Abram says.

"What keeps you from doing that *now*?" Maryann says. "If this is about your brother and not Andre, why would killing him change your urgency?"

"Because now I'm found out," I say. "Now there's video circulating social media and on every network showing me blowing Andre's brains out. So I'm here in a disciplinary meeting with you, and everyone in the Guild and in America is going to have eyes out for me. Not much of an opportunity to take things into my own hands now that I've blown it all to heck, is there? That was the point."

"This is ludicrous," Abram says, waving his hands wildly. "She's sitting here and *telling* us she'd be stealing resources if we weren't here to stop her!"

"Oh I'm sorry," I shoot back. "You're mad because I'm telling you the honest truth? What exactly were you expecting to hear that would make my actions more *okay*? I'm being as truthful as I can because I know what I did is going to cause major waves and I'm ready to face the consequences. What *should* worry you is if I'd fed you a line about Andre being on his way to bomb a school or something and that's why I killed him. I took Andre out because I don't want me or anyone else to fall prey to his lies. And I don't want him to have the opportunity to do what he really wants, which is to turn Humans and Prime Humans against each other with lies about Primes causing natural disasters. I don't want anyone exercising that kind of leverage against the Guild."

"So you're saying you regret your actions?" Debra says.

I push my mug of tea forward and let my forehead fall into my hands and shake my head. These people... I swear I have explained this to each of them in turn on my flight here, individually. This probably would have gone a lot better if I'd just said, 'Andre was evil. Andre deserved to die. The end.'

I look up. "I regret nothing. I knew what I was getting myself into. I weighed having him alive with having him dead. I chose to take the consequences of killing him in the open upon myself. Stop arguing with me about things I don't disagree with you on."

"Do you agree then that your actions are unbefitting of your office and warrant stripping you of your Councilship?" Malachi says.

"Absolutely not," I say, unsurprised by the suggestion. He already said as much to me on the phone earlier. "I put my duty to the Guild ahead of my fear, ahead of my personal feelings, maybe even ahead of my own brother. I also knowingly jeopardized my seat on the Council itself. If that's not the kind of action *befitting* a councilperson, then please, explain to me what is."

There's a sharp knock, and then Shiah appears. "Pardon the interruption," she says. "We've got a sizeable, unannounced THM protest happening at JFK. I've got it feeding into projector two."

"Activate projector two," Debra says, and the floating image comes to life.

'*—started gathering an hour ago, and airport security has been unable to regain control of the crowd, which is blocking traffic through the terminal. Several flights have been cancelled, others rescheduled to accommodate the logjam. Police have already used tear gas on some protestors, who began harassing a taxi driver.*'

The image shows a rowdy crowd, makeshift signs that say things like: Murder is a Crime, Justice 4 All, Prime Human MENACE, Prime=Slave Master, Fight Prime Supremacy.

I've seen footage from lots of THM protests, but none of them have been this disorderly and borderline violent. It's a bedlam. These people are out of control. But intermixed with the shouts, is the most common THM chant: Hu*man*, Hu*man*, Hu*man!*

"This isn't The Human Movement," I say, hands gripping my tablet.

"I believe it is," Shiah says. "This is a reactionary protest without Dumas' presence to quell them."

She's right. He's nowhere to be found. And a giant banner emblazoned with The Human Movement indicates that these people identify as THM. A fire blazes to life in the middle of the crowd, which spreads to accommodate it. Someone hangs a crudely-stuffed dummy from a stick and holds it over the fire. It's wearing a white coat and pants.

"Ouch," I grimace.

"Look," Shiah says, stepping forward and pointing to someone in the foreground, athletic with long blonde hair, screaming and holding a sign that says, 'The Devil Wears White.'

My mouth falls open in outrage as I see who it is. "Oh my gosh, it's Rita," I say, recognizing the blonde immediately. "Shiah, get Dumas on the phone."

"Already on it," she says, putting her phone to her ear.

But no sooner has she done that than an anchorperson comes back on and says, *'We've got Gabe Dumas on the line, hopefully to shed some light on this latest development with The Human Movement.'*

'Mister Dumas, hello. Can you tell us why it is you aren't present at the protest at JFK?'

'Because I'm on my way to Chicago, currently,' Dumas' voice replies over the line. *'And as you know, the majority of THM protests are not led by me personally.'*

'Are you aware of the situation there? That police have been dispatched to keep control of the crowd?'

'You are the fifteenth phone call I've received in the last thirty minutes. So yes.'

'Is there a reason you chose not to be at this particular protest?'

'I am not present because my schedule wouldn't allow it. I don't have a private jet to travel at the speed of sound, which means in the interest of conserving resources, I drive to most of my appearances—as I am now. Logistics and planning are still being put into place for this Sunday, and they require my oversight, which meant I needed to leave New York before the protest began. I left it in the hands of one of my team members.'

'Mister Dumas,' the anchorman says, *'we're not used to seeing THM protests require law enforcement's intervention. The tone is much more heated and combative, which we attribute to the atmosphere of outrage on the part of The Human Movement toward Miss Whitley's public assassination of Andre Gellagher. Is this a new strategy we can expect at future events?'*

'I personally do not approve of the strategy,' Dumas says, *'and while I can encourage a climate of respect and openness and*

discourage any demonstration of hate and fear, I can't control either, especially if I am not present. My goal is certainly to maintain an air of civility now as well as in the future, but I don't control my supporters.'

'Do you feel that your message of peaceful collaboration with the Guild has been betrayed by the demonstration at JFK?'

He sighs. 'As much as I would like for all Human Movement supporters to go about expressing their beliefs in ways that won't risk probable violence, I am not The Human Movement. We are. And a lot of us are frustrated to the point of what you're witnessing at JFK. The media's entirely unbalanced coverage of yesterday's event is disheartening at best and infuriatingly perverse at worst.'

'It appears that neither Miss Whitley, nor any other representative of the Guild is present at JFK. Has your amicability with the Guild dissolved?'

'The Guild does not attend all THM protests, only the ones I am present at. But either way, they were not told ahead of time about the JFK protest. The event itself came about last minute, and was solely organized by my associate, who obviously chose not to inform our Guild correspondent. I hope to continue to have the Guild's presence at Human Movement protests, and I still expect to see them in Chicago. But I have no doubt this protest at JFK will create tension. And maybe it's time they saw the raw emotions of the people.'

'Can you give us a quick synopsis of your feelings about Miss Whitley's decisive justice at JFK yesterday?'

Dumas huffs. 'Your word choice is exactly what has Human Movement supporters so upset. Miss Whitley's quote-unquote "Justice." In case everyone forgot, justice does not belong to the Guild, nor Miss Whitley. Now, I have no doubt that her actions were based on more complex motives than simply justice, but that's irrelevant. It's clear from every single detailed video of the event that Andre was rendered helpless by Miss Whitley's first shot. He was captured at that point, and he could have answered to his crimes. So her second shot was nothing short of murder. And murder is illegal in this country, no matter who does it or for what reason they do it. It doesn't matter what heinous crimes the victim is responsible for. There is a justice system in place, and the Guild and its members are not exempt.'

'Thank you for your time, Mister Dumas.'

'You are welcome.'

I stand up. "He's right."

Shiah mutes the volume.

"Of course he is," Malachi says. "Which is the problem. Which is why your actions were *not* in the Guild's best interest."

"You don't know that," I reply.

"Councilwoman Wendy," Sarah says, "We have always walked a fine line to maintain our own jurisdiction and govern our own. But your act was in direct opposition to the law. We are now going to have to assert sovereignty on this matter. Seeing as you claim to have thought through your actions, you can be the first to offer a suggestion for how this should be handled."

"You're making it too complicated," I say, crossing my arms. "We don't need to claim *sovereignty*. I'll turn myself in."

"What!" Abrams sputters. "We can't have a member of the Council indicted for murder!"

I suppress rolling my eyes. "It's the only solution, and I already said I accepted the consequences."

"And if you are convicted?" Maryann says.

"Then I go to prison." I simper at Abram because I can't help it. "And if I'm in for more than three months, you get to replace me."

There's silence as the group considers it.

Sarah is the first to speak, "If it were that simple, I would agree. But if you are indicted, you are going to be questioned under oath. Everything surrounding PHIA and Andre is sensitive information. And what of the demands he made? When the prosecutor asks what Andre wanted from you, how will you answer? I voted you onto this Council because I recognized your commitment to maintaining your integrity at any cost. But I'm afraid, in this case, the mere suggestion that Prime Humans are responsible for the disasters could accomplish exactly what Andre wanted without you needing to affirm its truth. In fact, choosing to shoot Andre to keep the information from getting out may be a very easy motive for the prosecution to latch on to." She shakes her head. "These are very murky waters."

I place my hands on the table and lean over it. She's right. I sigh heavily, considering, weighing the consequences. I've gone about this campaign with the truth grasped firmly in-hand. I've believed that if I could be the one brave enough to speak the truth in public, it would change not only how the Guild interacts with Humans, but how Humans interact with the Guild.

I believed the truth would unite us. And it has, but separately. THM is stronger because of it, but so is the Guild. They have grown in strength and commitment. Our membership has increased. When I came home to the Vault today, they were waiting. Thousands of Prime Humans left their posts, lined up along the road leading from the main gate to the parking deck. All of them had their hands clasped solemnly in the 'Guild Fist.' We *have* grown stronger, but we are still vulnerable, even and especially to lies.

So in this case, the truth could destroy everything. It could end up killing all the people who can solve the disaster problem. The truth could destroy the world. The truth is a weapon… and this time we don't have the strength to wield it.

I look up finally, and it takes me a second to find my breath and speak. "What Andre wanted me to say was a lie. And I will not perpetuate such a lie, even if it takes lying to do it."

Even though I am prepared to carry out the plan, the words still feel dirty. Incriminating.

Dear God. What have I become?

Sarah looks at me with genuine compassion. "Then I move that we allow Councilwoman Wendy to return to New York to face her crimes."

"I second," says Maryann.

"All in favor?" Debra says.

It's unanimous.

Forty-Eight

*B*ecause of your high profile, you'll have a bail hearing," Shiah says, her back to me as she rummages underneath the counter for something. "I've asked that no special treatment be afforded in terms of the scheduling, so the hearing won't be until tomorrow. You'll be in jail for one night, but they've agreed to allow Mike to stay on duty outside the building once you've been arrested. He'll have two others with him, on patrol."

"And the arrest is going to be in public, right?" I say, glancing through the window and down at the landscape below. We're on our way back to New York, and I'm in awe of myself. Again. I'm actually looking forward to being arrested, but at the same time I'm agitated. My schedule is totally up in the air.

Shiah gives me a look over her shoulder. "What kind of PR advisor do you take me for? Of course it's going to be in public. They'll be waiting for you as soon as we land. And I put in a call. Lots of cameras. Lots and lots."

I can't help smiling that Shiah, as usual, has everything under control. After the Council meeting, she hugged me from behind and said, "Have I told you lately how awesome you are?" And she's been upbeat ever since.

But I'm still on edge. I hate that I'm pretty much going to be sidelined. I am going to miss at least one Council meeting if not more, and there is so much to *do*. One of the things I learned once I was put on the Council was that the Guild has been heavily experimenting with various disaster-prevention technologies. During the subduction, for example, they used anti-tsunami technology to protect the Gulf coastline, and it worked! But that was never made public because if the world knew the Guild had any capability in preventing disasters, the demand would start in earnest. People would stop at nothing to find us, to take technology they know nothing about. It must be strategically used, because it can create what is known as The Ripple Effect, which basically means it will heighten the intensity of other disasters occurring elsewhere. This is something Guild scientists are frantically trying to understand, because as of right now, they have no explanation for The Ripple Effect. The ethics of the decision to keep those technologies quiet is constantly on the table with the Council, because it gets harder and harder to use any prevention technology without people finding out, because now all eyes are out for us thanks to THM. What are we doing that we aren't telling the public? I *need* to be part of that conversation.

There are other things I'm missing. I was supposed to make my first Colloquy appearance as Councilwoman Wendy tomorrow morning. And I have been wanting to experiment with channeling at EWR. And Chicago. I might miss Chicago and talking to Gabriel about his plans to go to California. Nevertheless, how is it I have become someone who sees getting publicly arrested as a fun challenge?

"When do I meet with my lawyer?" I ask.

"I'll be representing you," she says, turning around with a package of coffee grounds in her hands.

"You… have a law degree?" I say, skeptical.

She sniffs in retort, stares at me. "Wendy, I have been groomed from birth in every discipline deemed even remotely useful for serving on the Council. I passed the Bar when I was ten."

My mouth opens in shock.

"The medical boards when I was thirteen," she continues. "Doctoral degrees in philosophy, business, Psychology and Sociology, and Anthropology by the time I was seventeen." She counts them off on her fingers. "And those were the required disciplines. I study the other sciences on the side. I speak twenty-eight languages. With the exception of one person, I can infallibly tell when someone is lying to me. If I've watched anyone speak for at least fifteen minutes, I can determine which words of their story are the most true, or the most false. I can read people's minds without even being in their heads with enough accuracy to call myself a telepath. You are unequivocally guilty. But conviction will be impossible because I will be representing you. The mere fact that I will have a say in juror selection makes the whole thing laughably predictable, and it hasn't even started."

I lift my eyebrows in amazement. I don't doubt her. Not one bit. But wow!

"Who can you *not* tell if they're lying?" I ask.

She dumps the coffee grounds into the coffee maker and presses the power button. "My father." She turns back around. "But only because he is the only person in the world who shares a portion of my life force ability's power."

"Why don't you want to be on the Council?"

"Because I will *not* have my ova harvested."

"Because you are afraid of what your children can do?"

"My children would never be children. They would be gods. But gods without the freedom to choose."

I tilt my head. "How so?"

Shiah comes and sits on the couch, facing me. "Because their judgment would not be hindered by the bias of flawed memory reconstruction. I know you are familiar with the process. You reconstruct memory based on biases you have acquired, and each memory you make is built upon those flawed memories of the past. If you're playing a game of telephone, the message is completely skewed at the end because it had to be reconstructed through so many different lenses of perception."

"Kiera used that example…" I say.

"Because I taught it to Mikel who taught it to her. It is the most pointed and universal example of the fallibility of Human memory. But *my* memory? There is no reconstruction. No deterioration. You often compare me to a robot, and that's because I am."

"No," I say emphatically. "You have emotions. I've felt them."

"Of course I do. But I have the ability to change them at any time, at will. Because I can recall any situation I have felt them, relive that moment, and trick my body into manufacturing them. But that's not what concerns me. That temptation can easily be managed. What becomes increasingly difficult for me, and will be impossible for them, is experiencing uncertainty. Uncertainty is the thing that drives free will. And it exists because humans cannot recall the experiences of their past in unbiased light. They can barely remember them at all, in fact, so they move on instinct, on emotion, on the egregiously small and imprecise data they retain from their pasts. This allows them egregious amounts of uncertainty. It means they fail, over and over and over again."

Chin on hand, I begin to grasp what she's saying. I begin to grasp, in small part, what Shiah's life is like. And I begin to see my own in comparison. "I hate failing," I say.

"I hate *not* failing," Shiah says. "I hate that I can have a situation before me and see it from so many perfect angles of my experience and realize that choosing the wrong thing is impossible. *Choosing* is impossible. The thing was chosen long before the situation arose. It was foreordained."

"You can't... choose wrong for the sake of experiencing what it's like?"

She gives me a calculating look. "Could *you*? If you knew beyond a doubt what the implications of a particular action were, could you act against what you know to be true? Could you do that while knowing that your actions would ultimately harm others? Could you *purposely* and *deliberately* harm people f*or the sake of knowing what it's like*?"

"Oh..." I say softly.

"Every decision has implications, no matter how small. The only reason people make choices that harm others is because they simply don't know better. They want to, and they try, so hard. But by their very makeup they are guaranteed to fail repeatedly. Some of them give up. Some try their whole life. Most fall somewhere between the two. But none of them are condemned. How can they be when they've been given nothing but uncertainty? When everything they think is based on the inaccuracies of their memory?"

"I see your point... But it sounds... hopeless," I say.

"Oh Wendy, no," Shiah says, shaking her head. "It is not. What's hopeless is living a life without ever knowing who you would have been if your actions weren't already determined. Hopelessness is being trapped by your nature. Trapped in an existence where factual knowledge is the only way to improve yourself. You can't act in opposition to yourself. Perfection? That's stagnancy."

She reaches for my hand, her eyes on mine. "Hope is in Humanity. What I wouldn't give to feel it. And I would give all that I am to preserve it." Tears come to her eyes, and the love I feel from her is so powerful it makes me cry.

"You fail," she says. "Over and over. But sometimes you win. And those wins have more power than all the many wrongs. They move not just one of you, but all of you forward. You all change. Together."

She touches my face, wipes my tears. "The vast majority of you don't even recognize it happening, you even vehemently deny it, but that's only because you can't accurately remember who you were, so how can you possibly know how far you've come? Your imperfect memory of yesterday is, ironically, the very thing that gives you such power. If I were to have children, I would want them to have that. Not this. Never this."

I lay on her shoulder, link my arm with hers to have her closer and wishing and pretending that she never has to leave my side. It's probably due to being an empath, but I know who she is now. I know on a profound level that Shiah means all that she's said, that she knows it with the kind of certainty I may never experience. I suspected that she was special before, that her ability to remember, which seemed cut and dry at first, gave her an edge. But this is beyond my wildest expectations. And I love her so much for believing in the essence and makeup of me, a human, so much that she would choose my pitiful experience over her own.

My heart pounds loudly, and a magnetism gathers between our skin so strong that it feels like it's pulling the breath from my lungs. "I love you, Shiah. If I could give you my bumbling human experience, I would."

"I love you, Wendy. I will fight for you and all of Humanity, Prime or otherwise. It is the one thing I believe I have an actual choice about."

"What makes you say that?"

"Because my experience is limited to this sphere and to the dimensions of my own five senses. I don't know the implications of championing Humanity to the function of the Universe. That's why I take no interest in the energy world, in the afterlife, or in anything else that might give me additional data to dispute my belief. I gladly embrace ignorance because the feeling of closing my eyes and reaching for and believing in something I can't see is exhilarating. It is the one choice I get to make for *me*."

I sigh, further enamored with her. She says it's for *her* but it's still for *us*.

"I think they call that love," I say, goosebumps dotting my arms and tears now freely falling. "When you choose to believe in someone like that. I guess it's a good thing for us you're on our side then. I don't want to think of what it would be like if you believed the imperfection of Humanity was ultimately a menace to the universe."

"You are correct. On both counts. But I am not without opposition. My father does not agree."

I sit up and look at her. "He hates... everyone?"

"Not in the same sense that Andre hated Prime Humans." She sighs. "He would say that he loves humanity so much that he has dedicated his life to helping them achieve perfection. What that means is he wants to fix what he sees as broken. To him, I am the means to that." She frowns. "That's why he named me Moshiah."

"That means…?"

"Savior."

"Wow."

"Exactly. And that's why he Abdicated. He wants so badly to get me on the Council that he chose you in hopes that you would fail the vote. The Council would have nominated me in that case. I'm understood to be the next in line."

"You could have turned it down."

"Turning it down would have been seen as traitorous. I've been in and around the Council my whole life with the expectation that I would one day serve. And my father knows that I have my sights on you and your advancement. I could not have turned it down and remained in my place of significant influence. So he used you against me. And he knew that either way he'd win. If you lost, he would get my stem cells. If you won, he'd get stem cells from the person who can access the energy world directly."

"He did all that in hopes of getting some mini Shiahs? Even that has limits."

"Think bigger. He wants to isolate the genes that enable my life force ability and use stem cell and gene therapy technology to 'repair' the genes of everyone else."

"Oh my gosh…" I breathe. "He wants to give everyone *your* life force ability?"

"Yes."

"Why doesn't he use his *own* stem cells?" I say. "You share the same ability after all."

"According to understood life force ability theory, mine is more powerful, more precise and infallible. He says his memory does degrade over time, but I believe that may be because he doesn't use its full capacity as frequently as I use mine. I don't know. I believe that other than his research, he spends most of his time recalling things that keep him in a constant state of zen. He doesn't allow himself to be sad or to get upset at all. He believes it's not useful. Why would he choose to let himself feel badly if he can instead feel good? It's a drug with zero inhibitive side-effects. He's brilliant. He's successful. And he's powerful. And content. He believes everyone should have that. He sees what I do, what I accomplish, and he realizes logically that my capacity is greater, that my children would likely have incomprehensible ability, so he won't settle for less for forwarding his vision."

"So *he's* the robot then," I say.

"A robot committed to advancing humanity by whatever means necessary. Because while he plots how to convince me to hand over my eggs, he and his team are busy developing the technology. Stem cell therapy could allow everyone, regardless of birth, to pick their life force ability from a catalog. If he can't have his primary goal, he'll take that as his second."

I fall back against the couch, thoughts going a mile a minute.

"That is the future, Wendy," she says, translating my shock accurately and watching my face to see what I think about it.

My gut reaction is to rebel against something like that, but if I'd spent any time on considering the future beyond the apocalypse, I could have assumed this is where things would go. You can't put this many insanely brilliant people in one place and not expect them to make advancements so reality-altering that it takes your breath away. And you can't lose your breath without asking yourself if there is such a thing as too much too quickly.

"I don't know how I feel about that," I say finally, "but I'm kind of regretting that I started the process for my obligatory donation this morning before we left…"

"There's still time. Will you refuse donating?"

I slump. "Probably not. I feel like there are more imminent problems that require me being on the Council. So I doubt I'm going to make an issue of it. For now."

"I have stayed far away from my father's research, but if he has made his first forceful attempt to get me on the Council, then he is close."

"How do *you* feel about it?" I ask. "I get that you don't want people having *your* ability, but what about other life force abilities for everyone? Yay or nay?"

She pulls her knees up, rests her chin on them and stares across the cabin. She's doing that 'get your attention dramatic pause' thing.

"My grandfather participated in the Cambodian genocide. Are you familiar with it?" she asks.

"Um, no," I say, confused what her statement has to do with my question.

"In the early seventies my grandfather, Phen, got a job at a university in France, so the family relocated. They allowed Phen to send his son, my father, who was already brilliant at thirteen, there to receive his medical education for free. It was in France that my grandfather became indoctrinated to communism, which soon led to his association with the Khmer Rouge, the communist party in Cambodia. The family moved back to Cambodia when my father was fifteen to help kickstart the revolution.

"Phen was placed in charge of teaching medicine to army medics and prison staff. And his zeal for the Kampuchean revolution was such that he sent my father into one of the prison camps as a medic at fifteen. There my father administered care to prisoners, which, he learned, were being tortured and starved. But they were enemies to Angkar, the organization of the revolution, so my father did his job, which he came to understand was to keep the prisoners alive through their torture long enough to get their written confession of treason against the party. Once the document was received, all prisoners were taken to the killing fields where they were executed and buried in mass graves."

I stare at her in appalled silence. I know I asked her a question, a really important one, but I can't remember what it was anymore...

"The egregious violence and suffering took its toll on my father, and he took great pains to contact Phen, only to find out that his mother had died—from hypno-touch sickness, but they didn't know that at the time. Phen told him that his mother's last words were to her son, to honor her by being loyal to Angkar and to do all he could to ensure Cambodia's freedom from capitalist regimes.

"My father served in prison camps for four years. On occasion, when a prisoner was in especially ill health, my father was brought in to sit through the interrogation. Beating and systematic suffocation were the most common forms of torture. Sometimes the interrogators would burn them. And then they'd demand a confession, in the prisoner's own hand, of their treason against the party. They were beaten. Interrogated. Beaten. Interrogated. Thrown back into the cell. And then it would start all over again the next day. The goal of the written confession was to 'justify' their inevitable extermination. He watched the interrogators work systematically to force a confession, any confession, of any form of treason from people who clearly had no connection to the enemy. And my father's job was to keep them alive through it all.

"The guards and interrogators were perhaps the most psychologically manipulated of all. They were indoctrinated by way of written biographies. They were made to confess their failings on paper, to see themselves as deficient and therefore in need of Angkar, which didn't fail, which never erred. If Angkar arrested someone, they were guilty. The confession was only a formality. And so the interrogators and guards saw the prisoners that way, as enemies, no matter how unbelievable their testimonies or how many psychological tactics had to be used to twist the truth to resemble espionage. A prisoner's memory was there for the molding, to align with the accusation and therefore the will of Angkar, which had already condemned them."

Shiah pulls her slick black hair over one shoulder, revealing the tears in her eyes. She pauses to allow herself to feel the words she has said. I recognize this as something I've felt her do often. Now that I understand her ability, this act reemphasizes how profound it is that she champions the flawed nature of humanity. It would be so easy for her to see people through rose-colored glasses, to only choose to feel the good. She stays engaged with the full range of emotion, so she can *be* human.

"The Khmer Rouge used the flaws of the human mind to reconstruct the memories of their followers to exact obedience," she says. "And *all* of this came about *not* because someone took joy in torture and devised a system to do it all day, every day, but because someone decided what society needed and then concocted a plan to make it happen. In the case of the Khmer Rouge, the decision was that society needed to rid itself of class distinctions that had oppressed so many and install, instead, a more simplistic, self-sufficient, agrarian society, in essence a return to Cambodia's roots."

The sound of the plane bleeds through the ensuing silence, and after letting myself ache for Ohr and his experience, I say, "So now he wants to install perfection so that people don't screw up like that anymore?"

"Yes. He witnessed more suffering in four years than you or I will witness in our lifetime. Although I suspect he endured most of it in his virtual reality of peace. But that doesn't answer your question."

"I totally forgot what my question was. I'm too horrified."

"You asked if everyone should have life force abilities on demand."

"Right!"

"I don't know."

My brow furrows. "Then what did the story have to do with anything other than to make me feel bad for your dad? Why don't you know?"

"Because I don't want to know. Again, my knowledge has gaps where the energy world and life force ability theory are concerned, which means I don't have the facts to make a determination. I place my faith in humanity's ultimate goodness, to be able to handle anything, to figure out even something as monumental as this. I wash my hands of being the one to decide, because I have successfully created my own personal ideal: to be as clueless as the rest of you. What I believe? I believe in *you*. I side with *you*. And whatever you determine, that is what I dedicate myself to.

"Finally, I told you the story because that's what I *do* know. The story illustrates one of countless instances in which someone determines what's best for humanity. It's a battle fought every day all over the world. Some believe in progress. Others believe in traditional values. Some believe conformity breeds unity. Others believe individuality is their god. No matter *what* the ideal, history has proven over and over and over again that *forced* adherence to an ideal undoubtedly fails. The more it is forced, the more it rebels, transforming into hate, into intolerance and oppression, into the most heinous acts of violence humanity can dish up. I tell you this because you are in a position of power and influence with which to force just such an ideal. So tread carefully.

"Also, I told you so you could understand my father. I want you to see him not as an enemy, but instead as the opposition, in the same way you see The Human Movement. If my father weren't forcing the issue of making all humans Prime, would you even be asking this question about life force abilities on demand?"

"Good point," I say.

"There are no enemies. There are only people of differing experiences and opinions. Pushing and pulling toward balance."

"So do you know what I'm going to choose?" I say.

"Nice try," she laughs. "But no. I don't know because *you* don't know. And your rate of change has been increasing so much in the time I've known you that it's challenging my capacity. Have you ever actually stopped to notice how dramatically far you've come in only three months?"

I pause, because I haven't. I really haven't. "I guess I've been seeing it as things *around* me changing quickly, and I've had to adapt. Not the other way around."

"Has adapting always come so easily to you?"

I purse my lips. "No... When everything was gone from my former life, I realized that I needed to find something to care about. And since my old self lost everything, I decided to start making choices that were opposite to what I would have chosen in the past. One of those was to stop agonizing over every decision. And to trust people. You popped into my life at the exact time I started testing that. It worked out." I smile at her.

"Ah!" she says excitedly. "That's what I suspected! When I met you and you tried to blackmail me, I wondered at your bravery. Was your memory loss empowering you? How else might it benefit you? Would it challenge my own ability? Would it affect your predictability? A door of possibility opened up, because I was being confronted with so much I didn't know. I was uncertain. It turns out my suspicions were right though. Your memory loss hit the reset button on your memory reconstruction patterns."

"How so?"

I've rarely seen Shiah so thrilled. She sits cross-legged across from me, a throw pillow clutched in her hands, leaning toward me as if we're sharing gossip at a slumber party. "By the time people are adults, they have accumulated so much faulty, bias-laced memory that it becomes harder and harder for them to experience anything without automatically and unconsciously applying a preconception. Their memories begin to take on a pattern, a pattern that perpetuates itself. This makes adaptation extremely difficult because none of their accumulated data is helpful. So they shy away from new situations.

"But for you? You were literally stripped of everything and everyone that might have set expectations for you in the past, and plopped into an entirely new world. Nothing from your past was going to help you. And there was nothing familiar around you to fall back on. So you stopped looking backward. You stopped relying on your faulty data. And you've begun accumulating new data, but also *intentionally* resisting old patterns. You've been remaking yourself—just as you said in Raleigh. You're like a child but with adult capability, and it has absolutely fascinated me. That's why I latched on to you from the start."

That makes sense... I haven't spent much time contemplating my memory loss in the last month. It doesn't seem relevant anymore. I look at Shiah. "So you're saying you only want me for my memory reconstruction?"

She grins. "Who wouldn't? Your memory reconstruction patterns are dead sexy."

I chuckle. "I guess I can be grateful for losing my memory then. In all seriousness though, I *have* noticed that I think differently now. I do things that my past self would be up all night thinking, 'What the crap was that, Wendy?' but now... I go with it. Like telling Gabe how I felt... I mean part of it was him, how easy it is to be myself around him. But part of it is this invincibility. I can't put my finger on the hows and whys of it. It's like nothing seems all that daunting anymore..."

"Like letting me kiss you," she says knowingly.

Yeah..."

"You do want to know what it means, though," she says.

"I think I know, but I'm not sure."

"It means I love you and I knew that after the events of the night, you needed it."

"Why do you say that? If I was needing some love, you could have hugged me. That's what other people would do."

"I'm not other people."

"After our conversation, that is no lie."

"You put your heart out there for him, Wendy," she says. "And when you do that, and the person doesn't take it, it will stay out until someone either helps you put it back or hurts you. A hug is what people do when anything else comes with expectations attached. But a kiss is more. It conveys more love because of the level of intimacy."

"What made you think I wouldn't have expectations?"

"I didn't do it knowing you wouldn't expect anything. I did it knowing *I* wouldn't expect anything. If you had expected more, I would have given it."

"I still don't understand why you assumed I needed something more than a hug."

She laughs. "Are you arguing that you didn't need a kiss?"

"No. I—" I frown. "I don't know."

She reaches for my hand again. "Wendy, you love him. You love him so much that you would do crazy things. You've concocted reasons you need to follow him to California to find his wife. You want to figure out how to help him stay in contact with The Human Movement so that *you* wouldn't lose him entirely. And the outrage you felt toward Andre for taking Gabe's family helped drive you to pull that trigger at the airport. You wanted to do these things because you love him. And love will find a destructive outlet if you don't let it out. I kissed you because I wanted you to know of the depth of my love for you so you wouldn't be driven to do something crazy. I wanted you to have everything you've put out there reciprocated in some way. Are you saying it didn't work?"

"No, it did. It was beautiful. It made me feel safe and definitely loved." I frown again. "Except that I still killed Andre the next day. So maybe a little tongue next time so I don't go murdering people?"

"Ha!" she bursts. "You are hilarious. You can't handle the full Shiah and you know it. Besides, I can't have you falling for me. You're supposed to be with Gabe."

I lay my head on her shoulder. "I love that we can talk about stuff like this and it's not weird."

"I love that you let me love you. You don't overthink it. But I surmise it's because you are an empath. I don't have to spell out my intentions to you."

"Sometimes I do, like when I'm not around you and I start remembering that it's supposed to be weird. But when I'm near you, no issues. Everything makes sense."

"Remember what you told the crowd in Salt Lake?" she says.

"Mostly? But I'm betting you could tell me word-for-word."

Shiah pulls herself out from under me and stands up. She takes a stance on the other side of the table, and then lifts her chin. "When you wake up tomorrow, and you begin fretting once more over the events in the world, do not be fooled by your mind, by your memory. It *will not* give you this moment back. But that does *not* mean it never was. It is up to *you* to have faith that it was and allow that faith to guide you more confidently into each day."

She sighs, and her eyes fall to the floor without really looking at it. But a smile spreads over her beautiful face. "It was magnificent. So much truth. So much wisdom. It's my favorite thing you have ever said."

She comes back around and falls into the couch next to me. "Society's expectations will ruin how you reconstruct our moments together," she says. "It's yet another nemesis of faulty human memory. Don't let it strip your moments of beauty."

"Sounds like something Mikel would say."

"She was my apprentice."

I swear, nothing about Shiah surprises me anymore. "So what about you?" I say. "Do you want to have something with someone? You know, more than being my best friend and helping me navigate my insane life like kissing me when I get my heart broken?"

"Perhaps."

"Then *I* am going to keep my eyes peeled. Which way do you swing? Men? Women?"

"I already have someone in mind, and he's male."

I sit up, eyes wide with curiosity. "Who?"

"Down Wendy," she sniggers. "You can figure it out if you think about it."

I purse my lips, scrolling through probable men we've been around long enough for Shiah to have developed an attraction for them. Outside of our protection detail it's seriously limited. Which means it's someone *on* protection detail. And the problem is I don't see any of them as being good enough for her, if I were doing the picking. Except...

"Is it Mike?" I ask, trying out the idea. The more I think about it, the more I like it. Mike is my other confidant. Different from Shiah, more complicated, and to me, frustrating because he's so protective of his real feelings and motives. But for Shiah, that's an easy nut to crack.

"Very good," she says, patting the top of my head. "Your human brain has passed the test."

I swat her hand away. "Well I love it. Because I love Mike and I love you and there's nothing better than having two people you love find each other. Does he know?"

"Of course he knows," Shiah says. "I punched him at Co-op city, and I apologized afterward and told him it was my sexual frustration coming out in violent ways. He was surprised."

I burst into giggles. "I heard about that—the punching part. What did he say?"

"He said he was flattered but he was concerned about starting a relationship with someone when Gabe was in such close proximity, seeing as the two share some sort of mirroring. He didn't want to jeopardize your chances with Gabe."

I wrinkle my nose. "That's it? No angst or declarations of love or anything fun?"

She gives me a knowing half-smile. "I expected his reaction. But now I've got him thinking. Being so enamored with you has kept him in blinders. But now he's thinking and he's going to realize there are more women in the world besides Wendy Whitley. I'm quite enjoying being smitten with him and his quiet, unwavering commitment to duty, so the wait is not unwelcome."

I snigger. "You know, in normal people world, I'm supposed to be jealous of you thinking you're going to steal my backup plan and you're supposed to be jealous that Mike digs me. And then with you and I having kissed, the whole thing is supposed to be one giant awkward soap opera. If Gabriel ever decides to get with it and join the party, then in normal people world we'd have enough drama to fill a season's worth of Jerry Springer. Instead, in Shiah and Wendy land, it's going to be the best, most funnest love square ever!"

Shiah laughs.

"Seriously though," I say. "Tonight when I'm in jail and you're not around, my defunct human memory and susceptibility to cultural expectations is going to have me looking at it and wondering how I ended up in such a weird situation."

"It's unconventional," she agrees. "But that's because pure love, unencumbered by things like expectation, bias, fear, uncertainty, and judgment is unorthodox. I think if anyone can accomplish it, two men with a telepathic connection, an empath, and a robot can pull it off."

"You are more than a robot, Shiah."

"And you are more than an empath."

Forty-Nine

The clicking of the cuffs closing on my wrists is a satisfying sound. And maybe I'm in denial, but it doesn't feel real. It's a show. A formality. I'm fulfilling my obligation as an American citizen, and I feel good about it. Since I endured the paparazzi two days ago, I'm prepared for the barrage of cameras that greet us right on the tarmac. I'm careful to smile only in acknowledgement, but I hold my head high.

Shiah stays behind to make a statement on my behalf while I climb into the back of a cruiser. The door shuts, and I have a brief moment of panic. At first I'm not sure why, but then I realize, as I look around, that I haven't been so far away from at least one person from the Guild in… well since waking up in the hospital. I feel exposed. Alone.

"Miss Whitley, I'm a big fan of yours," one of the officers up front says as we pull away from the airport. "I used to be pretty skeptical about the Guild when they first came out, but I was one of the officers called in when a bunch of Primes were massacred right here in New York a few months ago. PHIA is a homegrown terrorist organization, and while I can't officially condone your version of justice, as a human being I can respect it."

"Thanks," I say, all fears dissipating. "I can't say I condone what I did either. But I've spent so much time thinking about protecting Primes that I didn't spend any time thinking about laws."

"Like you said in Salt Lake, that's your family," he replies. "I'd damn sure be tempted to shoot someone point blank who had been killing off members of my family."

I think about my brother then. Yesterday I saw Chase briefly, and he gave me a couple of ideas. He says he knows of an operative who can make a connection with someone and then he can locate that person anywhere. I remember reading about that ability, and I told Chase it wasn't going to help because he will have never met my brother to locate him. But Chase told me that the guy has been working on developing his ability more. He has figured out how to form secondary connections. So not only can he locate the person, but the people who are also strongly connected to them (say, someone who is missing). I looked it up and found out his name is Ben. He lives in Virginia, so I sent him an e-mail asking to meet.

The other promising life force ability was someone who can track down where people have been. A reverse trail. Her name is Hannah, and she's actually on the PHIA recovery team with Lainey. I asked Chase to handle the initial contact for me since I don't know how long I'll be out of commission. I'm hoping that Lainey will feel moved to return the favor I did her a few weeks ago, long before I killed Andre. I was just checking to see if she'd made progress. She wasn't forthcoming and instead felt at liberty to demand information from *me. Again.* But her question was odd… She wanted to know if I'd ever seen anyone *without* a life force.

I couldn't answer of course, since she's not in EWR, and the answer is no, but she was so serious about the question that I asked her what on earth would prompt it. She said she'd been working every angle to locate Andre using every possible life force ability available, but she wasn't getting anywhere.

I was floored: she didn't know about Invisibles—that Andre *was* one. All that time she was wasting looking for Andre with life force abilities without realizing they didn't work on him… It wasn't just a waste for *her.* It was a waste of Guild resources. It endangered Primes for Lainey to not have all the relevant information.

The Guild's policies and clearance levels can clearly be a hindrance—even a danger. What other ways are we obstructing our own progress?

Nevertheless, Lainey's intuition was impressive. She had drawn the conclusion that life force abilities likely acted on the actual life forces of others, and if an ability wasn't *working* on them, then that might mean the person had no life force to *be* affected by the ability. That's why she had asked, maybe because she'd heard the phrase often attached to psychopaths: they have *no soul.*

So I breached confidentiality, and I told her. 'Andre is immune to life force abilities, Lainey. I cannot tell you anything more than that.'

I thought she'd be grateful, but instead she seemed to cycle through surprise, embarrassment, and then defensiveness. Then she got really bitchy again and walked away. I'm hoping she's gotten over herself by now.

I perk up when I hear one of the officers in the front speaking to his dispatcher about our arrival, asking him if we're clear to take our exit. Why would we need clearance for that?

The dispatcher replies that the crowd has grown and they have to get additional backup in place first.

My stomach tightens. They need backup for a crowd? I knew there would be reporters, but this sounds like more than that.

After about fifteen more minutes, the dispatcher clears our arrival and the officers take an exit. We slow to a crawl as we approach a street with a crowd on either side. They have signs and they're shouting. With the approach of our vehicle the shouts become louder. It's a protest, I realize. But it looks and sounds to be two opposing protests going on at the same time, and they are mostly divided by the street we're about to drive down. I can read their signs from here.

On the right, the signs say things like:
Protect Our Life and Liberty. Protect The Guild.
Humans for Primes.
Guardian Angels Wear White.
Free Whitley.
Other signs on the left are very different:
Justice for ALL.
Murder is Murder is Murder.
We Support Accountability.
Humans for Inalienable Rights.

Upon the approach of the cruiser, something amazing happens. On my right, the protestors fall silent. They lower their signs. They stand still and raise their hands in the Guild Fist, their eyes locked on me—or my window at least—as we drive slowly.

Something hits the car, startling me, and that starts a new round of shouts. More people jump on board, throwing things at the cruiser, plastic bottles, someone's shoe, a takeout cup. A sign even slams into the windshield, words facing us inside. It says, *PHIA is a Prime Human Plot.*

To my right, however, they hold their ground, unmoving. Bound hands raised in determination, they do not retaliate even when debris thrown from the other side of the street hits them. Their eyes are on me, and I am humbled to my core.

The police doing crowd control suddenly have their hands overfull, pushing people on the left back. A quick glance behind us reveals that once we have passed, my supporters are breaking formation. They meet their opposition in the middle of the street, fists flying. Mayhem has ensued.

My heart pounds in fear because Mike isn't here. I don't know if I trust anyone else to have my back. This group looks and feels rabid. My head is locked in their war.

We finally reach the front of the police station, a five or six story building, and the entrance is swarmed by reporters. Four officers come through the doors toward the vehicle. They open my door, wave me out as reporters shout at me.

"Do you see yourself as guilty of murder?"

"Was it your idea to turn yourself in?"

"Have you heard about the riot in Chicago?"

That question captures my attention, but I'm being escorted through the doors, too quickly to find the person who voiced it.

What riot? Like LA, or is it Human Movement related?

I mull it over, itching for Shiah to show up so I can get more information, not that I can do anything about it...

I'm taken directly into booking where each of my fingers gets rolled in ink. I'm photographed from multiple angles while holding my booking number. And suddenly everything gets real. I'm in jail. Soon I'll be locked up. Because I killed someone.

I killed someone. Somehow that fact hits me in a different light suddenly, and I'm afraid, except I can't articulate why.

Shiah shows up, her hair in a high ponytail, her black bag hanging from the crook of her arm. She picked a pair of pointy-toed heels and a black pantsuit to wear. Everything about her appearance screams no-nonsense lawyer. Her ear is already pressed to her phone, her mouth barking at someone on the line, "Why am I speaking to you? You are not the lead on this. Contract militia always takes secondary command."

Her eyes tighten slightly. "Is that so? Well you are *not* authorized to use force. You need Prime operatives. There are plenty in your area."

She walks up and picks up the form I didn't notice the officer put in front of me to sign. Her eyes scan it as she says, "I am aware of that, Mister Daughtry. I didn't ask if they were comfortable with it. I'm not asking for their permission. If you call them up and *ask* if they'd *like* to help with crowd control, what do you think their response will be?"

She nods. "Exactly. Wording is everything. So when you call them, you tell them the Council has personally summoned them to assist with a priority Guild matter. *Do not let a question come out of your mouth!* Should they refuse, fine, but if you word it like I've told you to, only two will refuse, which will give you a team of ten. Pair each operative with someone from your team for protection."

She slaps the paper down in front of me and hands me a pen. Then puts a hand on her hip, a sign of exasperation. "Use the database that I gave you access to," she says with sudden amicability. It's her no-nonsense, this-is-your-last-chance-to-do-what-I-say voice. "I would recite their names for you, but as I said when you called, I am not in a secure location. Please do me the favor of remembering that. Aside from narrowing to Chicago, here are your search terms: reverse empathy—there are two, emotional dampening—there are two, emotional tracking, reverse telepathy, sound wave dampening, telekinesis, life force bond facilitation, time perception manipulation, hallucination generation. And the last one is the most important: amplifier."

The officer in charge of booking me stares at Shiah, open-mouthed.

Shiah nods impatiently. "Yes, yes. I know. This is why militia doesn't take point on Guild missions. I'm sending you contact info for a proprietary mission specialist in the area. They'll know how to best organize the operatives. Work quickly. I expect you and your team to be in the field within the hour. We need this under control. Immediately."

She ends the call and begins a text message as she says to the officer, "Speaking of riots, you've got one outside that will soon be out of your control, and both mine and Miss Whitley's bodyguards are already engaged with keeping things managed. Please inform your commanding officer that if the situation doesn't improve within the next fifteen minutes, I have an emergency injunction waiting to be filed to have Miss Whitley moved to a more secure location. Also, please let him know that I have operatives available to help manage the situation. We are at your disposal." She glances at him briefly over her phone.

He blinks at her for a second and then says, "Yes ma'am," as he reaches for his radio.

"Thank you," Shiah says, tossing her phone in her bag and turning to me. "A sit-in started in Chicago outside the stadium where THM is supposed to host their event this week. They were

Guild supporters. Human Movement supporters caught wind of it and showed up. A fight broke out. More people showed up. And now it's a riot. Several people have been shot, and law enforcement can't get control of the crowd. Reports are that Dumas went in to try to calm things down, but the media can't locate him, and I've tried calling. No answer."

I catch my reaction. "Mike?" I say.

"I haven't had the opportunity to question him. I got the call as soon as the car pulled up and he and Brad had to jump out to push back the protestors outside."

"Miss Whitley?" the officer interrupts a little timidly. "If you'll come this way?"

Anxiety assaulting my stomach, I hesitate until Shiah prods me in the back. "I have a press conference outside in ten," she murmurs. "I'll come see you as soon as I'm able. Hopefully with more to tell you."

I'm led into an elevator, and even before it moves, the noise of the holding cells above reaches my ears. I can smell it from here, too. The pungent concentration of human body odor is awful. I'm filled with dread, but I don't know if it's the realization that I'm actually going to jail or if it's worry over Gabriel. Maybe it's both...

The elevator doors slide open, and the officer leads me through a set of double doors. Beyond is a hall of raucous inmates hanging through the bars of their cell doors, shouting, catcalling, staring, goading as I pass by. They know who I am, and I feel ridiculous in my white jeans and white sweater tank, like an imposter. I've been stripped of everything I knew about myself only moments ago: Councilwoman to the Guild, the most influential organization in the world; seer of the energy world, the place where it all came to be; seer of souls; champion of peaceful Human-Prime Human coexistence. It's all meaningless here.

We stop in front of a cell. I scan the inside as the officer slides the door open. It has cement block walls, two hard benches, and a toilet. But what has my attention is that one of the benches is already occupied by another person. I'm about to open my mouth to say that the arrangement was for me to have my own cell, but that sounds like the complaint of a privileged celebrity who paid off someone to have jail be as painless as possible. I swallow my words, praying that the woman with the big, beautiful afro wearing tight jeans with rips in the knees and a cutoff T-shirt isn't going to give me grief. She looks familiar...

The door to my cell shuts behind me with a clang, and I become nothing to the world.

"It's the lady in white," someone says, and I whirl around.

The guy in the cell across the hall is walking the perimeter of it, looking up and then down the length of the walls. "It's the lady in white. She came. The lady in white is here."

He doesn't seem to be talking *to* me, just about me.

"Lady, lady, lady," he says to the bars. "White lady…"

I think he's either got some sort of mental problem or he's detoxing.

"I know who *you* is," my cell-mate says.

I turn around. The woman gives me a once-over, the kind that seems like disgust, but she's inside my empathic range, and she seems more curious than anything.

"You that crazy bitch who shot that guy in the face," she says, throwing a ball in her hands up toward the ceiling with one hand and then catching it with the other. "I watched that thing on repeat on the TV at my auntie's. We was like, 'That bitch done lost her mind.' Ain't never seen nobody kill in front of a crowd with so much confidence. And everyone at the airport jus' watchin'. Nobody doin' *nothin'*. Then you jus got in yo car and drove off." She shakes her head, tosses the ball up again.

"Then the camera must have cut away when I collapsed on the ground afterward," I reply, unsure if I should sit down, or even move. I also realize I haven't actually looked at the footage of my crime.

"Hmm," she says. "Guess so. Wouldn't want Miss White lookin' weak on national TV." She keeps throwing the ball.

"And you are?" I ask, trying not to sound defensive. It's been a while since I've felt so out of my element. I don't know if it's the emotions in the cell block or if it's the protestors below.

She catches the ball and holds it as she lifts her legs and begins doing crunches.

"Tonya," she replies in the middle of her set. She pauses for only a second to say, "Tonya Tranwick."

"Oh my gosh, you're—"

"Sick of seeing you in white, yeah," she stops me, sitting up and putting her high top-clad feet on the floor. "Ain't you got like, a person that picks out yo' clothes? White girl wearing white…" She shakes her head. "You don't see me wearin' all black, do you?" She glances at my stunned silence. "Nope. 'Cuz that'd be stupid."

"How'd you get in here?" I say, moving closer to the edge of the other bench.

"Broke the law. Ain't that what we all done?"

"What exactly?" I ask, perching on the edge of the worn metal, certain that I'm right about her. She's related to Porter Tranwick, Gabriel's bodyguard. I know there are more people on his protection team, but I don't ever see them. Mike says they all dress casually to blend in. It must be an event I've seen her at.

"Ain't you nosey," she says, then she nods her chin at me. "Can you catch?"

"Uh, yeah?" I say.

"Over here," she says, scooting to one side of her bench and pointing to the other side of it.

I sit where she indicates, which leaves only a couple feet between us. She throws the ball at the opposite wall. It bounces off and right at me. I fumble a little, but I catch it. It's a tennis ball, so worn that the green fuzz has been rubbed off. I throw it at the wall, trying to get the angle right so it will sail toward her, but I overcompensate and it sails too far to her left. Her reflexes are superb though, because she leans over and catches it one-handed.

Back and forth we go. I get better with my accuracy and she starts throwing it higher so I have to reach up to catch it. I miss it a few times, and I have to scramble around for the ball on the floor like an idiot. But Tonya seems patient, more interested in testing her own accuracy than mine.

She gets bored with that finally, standing up suddenly. Then starts tossing the ball upward and then kicking it back up with the side of her foot, like playing hacky sack. It looks a lot harder though, since the ball has a lot of bounce to it. Her skill is impressive.

I sigh heavily, and with nothing else to do, my thoughts cycle back to my trip here, the protestors outside—which I can hear if I close my eyes and listen—and to Chicago. There are people fighting because of what I did. It changed everything, and I'm starting to finally realize what a big deal it was. It scares me that it didn't occur to me sooner. It scares me that when I look back and remember the moment when Andre was on the ground, lined up in my sights, I didn't hesitate because I'd be taking a life. I hesitated because killing Andre meant killing the information he had. He wasn't human to me. In fact, I don't think I felt him in my head.

The sound of the elevator opening at the end of the hall ushers me to my feet and toward the bars at the front of my cell. Shiah comes into my view finally, accompanied by an officer, and relief washes over me. When she reaches my cell, she halts suddenly when her eyes rest on Tonya. Her eyebrows lift in surprise.

Grasping the bars in my hands, I look at her anxiously. Her emotions confirm that she not only recognizes Tonya, but she wasn't in on her being my cell mate.

"After the debacle outside I was planning to strong-arm the NYPD into stationing someone outside your cell at all times, but my data has been updated." She tilts her head slightly, her ponytail swinging. "Do you feel sufficiently safe?"

I lift my shoulders and give her a knowing look to indicate I've drawn similar conclusions: Gabriel or Porter Tranwick have planted Tonya. For what purpose, I can't say. But Tonya is trained in protection, and even though she works for THM, I do trust both Porter *and* Gabriel. Hopefully I can find out how it came about, and an officer outside my cell would inhibit that. "Yes," I reply.

"Help is available," Shiah says, nodding once.

"Yeah," I reply, knowing she's referring to my tracking implant that was updated before I came here. It now allows me to send a distress signal to the Guild if I get into serious trouble. It also constantly monitors my vitals now. "Chicago?"

Shiah places her hands over mine and steps closer. "Intel says he's too far away to know if he's in trouble. But he's alive."

I resist biting my lip in worry, instead resting my head between the bars. "This has gotten out of control really fast," I say quietly.

"It is about to get crazier," she murmurs so softly only my ears can hear. "Before the call about Chicago, the Council called and said to inform you of the latest information from the Grid: An event from Alaska down to Northern South America. And from Japan down to the northern tip of Australia. Another massive tectonic subduction they think. Most likely of the Philippine plate."

"Dear God," I say, lifting my head, eyes wide. My stomach drops into nausea.

She lifts her eyebrows and I know I said that too loudly. I lean forward again, rest my head on the bars, and she leans in as well. "California?" I murmur, struck suddenly with fear. If my brother is there and he's alive…

"Yes," she whispers, her head against mine. "A team is going to have to go in there and warn them."

"Timeline?" I whisper.

"Three months. They're certain this time."

My stomach is queasy, and I crouch down, gripping the bars to keep from falling over. Suddenly everything that's been bothering me about my circumstances washes away, exactly like what's going to happen to all those Asian islands in the Pacific. Tears eke out of my eyes. How much more can the Human race reasonably handle? The last subduction was not even a month ago. The Guild just used anti-quake technology in India last week that was only partially successful. Left unmanaged, the quake would have broken world records for land-based earthquakes. Instead, it was simply… really awful. What it revealed was that even the Guild has a limit. And the Ripple Effect is making it impossible to really fight this with everything we've got…

But now, with this latest event looming, it also tells me that the Guild is the only thing standing between mother nature and humanity. We don't have time for pathetic protests. Who cares about ideals when survival is in question?

I don't have time for what I've been doing. And quibbling over killing Andre? That's ridiculous. Prime Humans now have one less idiot gunning for them, which means the world has a little more of a chance than it did before. And speaking of Primes, I need to be devoting a *lot* more time to finding out if the energy world can reveal a cause of these disasters. I need to *use* what I've been given.

I've got to get out of here… Tomorrow *cannot* come fast enough.

"Shiah, you've got to make sure they let me leave the state. I've got to be in Chicago," I say, looking up at her.

She squeezes my hand. "You will be."

I stand up, and she wipes a tear from under my eye. "This is just as important," she says, answering my swarm of doubts. "I know it doesn't feel that way, but it is."

I look at her. "I don't know how to balance it anymore," I whisper, holding back the rest of the words I want to say, like how I know The Human Movement is a counterbalance for the Guild, but the weight of the world has shifted more precariously. Things like temperance go out the window, so I want to find a way to take The Human Movement down in a single event. In fact, that's what

I'm going to be thinking about while I'm in here with nothing else to do. These ridiculous protests need to end, and everyone needs to ban together to protect Primes so we can figure this thing out.

I'm pretty sure Shiah reads all that in my expression, astute as she is. And after giving me a critical look, she says, "The Grid technology functions on tracking humans. Their patterns of movement. When those patterns shift too far past predictability, that's when a disaster is bound to happen. Among the Grid's specialists, this is called 'survival shift.' Think about that during your time here tonight, Wendy." She leans toward me once more. "Odd, isn't it, that our opposition is called The Human *Movement*?" she murmurs.

I want to tell her I don't understand what she's trying to say, but this isn't the place. So I hold my breath and try not to cry.

She touches her forehead to mine, and emotionally it feels like a hug. "I'll see you in the morning," she says, releasing my hands and letting the officer escort her back out.

Fifty

I took a swing at an officer outside," Tonya says suddenly, after having remained silent all day. The lights went out a while ago, and the block settled and quieted along with it. Outside, however, it sounds like the protestors are waging a war of endurance to see who can remain at their post the longest. The chanting has cycled between the two groups, and at some point, someone on the anti-Guild side got ahold of a megaphone.

I've been sitting on my cot, bored and agitated. I can't remember any time in my life in which I've been this idle for this long.

"At the protest?" I say.

"Porter used to work with NYPD's chief of police," she explains. "He called in a favor."

"So you hit an officer so you'd be arrested and be put in a cell with me?" I say.

Her emotions confirm it.

"Why?" I say.

"You gotta lotta friends, Miss White," she says. "Even yo enemies is yo friends."

"Dumas," I mumble, unable to help the butterflies putting up a fuss in my stomach. He sent one of his people to jail to protect me? That's ridiculously sweet.

"Bloody hell, Tranwick! I put this on her. If she's harmed in jail I'll never forgive myself!" Tonya mimes in what I think is supposed to be Gabriel's voice, but she's leaning a little too much toward a British accent.

I chuckle.

"He knew that protest out there was goin' down," she says. "It ain't really jail he's worried about."

"It's still going strong out there," I say, hearing megaphone guy giving a monologue about The Human Movement ensuring that the Guild won't stop justice. "I guess they plan to stay all night."

"Did yo girl say somethin' 'bout things in Chicago?" Tonya says, and I can feel her concern. It must be because Porter's there. I wonder what their relation is?

"Just what you heard," I say. "Dumas is alive. That's all we can confirm."

"Damn," she breathes.

"It's probably under control already. They sent a team of Primes in there to help. I wouldn't worry." I want to add that there are bigger things to worry about, but the looming disaster in the Pacific hasn't been released yet. I forgot to ask Shiah when it would be.

"Hold on and I'll listen," I say. "Now that the place is mostly quiet I might be able to pick up a television. Cops watch the news, right?"

She replies by staying silent.

Eyes closed, I still my breaths so that I don't get distracted by the sounds of my own vitals.

The police station isn't as noisy inside as I expected, although that might be due to officers needing to be on duty outside to manage the protest. I do hear a few televisions though. One is tuned into a sitcom. Another the weather channel. Two of them have the same news station on, which is currently reporting on flood damage that happened in New Jersey after the continuous downpour a couple days ago. They talk about a few other local happenings, and eventually lead into the protest outside the police station where I am. It's being called a standoff between The Human Movement and Guild supporters.

Finally, they segue into Chicago.

I repeat what I hear aloud so Tonya can know what's being said, "The latest from Soldier Field: Under siege. Earlier today, upon the news that Wendy Whitley, Prime Human liaison to The Human Movement, would be turning herself in to New York authorities for shooting Andre Gallagher, alleged leader of PHIA, Guild supporters staged a sit-in outside of Soldier Field where a Human Movement event is scheduled to take place in two days. Their hope was to prevent entrance to the facility by Gabe Dumas or any of his supporters, but their plans were interrupted by the violent reaction of Human Movement supporters. Dale Jensen has the story."

"I'm here at the marina, and behind me you can see the number of flashing lights at the arena where law enforcement is still trying to gain control of the stadium. Earlier today, a fight broke out, resulting in the deaths of six people. The crowd grew in number, becoming unmanageable. Gabe Dumas himself came on the scene in an effort to calm his supporters. Guild supporters took advantage of the lull to begin storming the stadium while Dumas was speaking, and the crowd was once more caught up in a brawl. Suddenly, however, in the middle of police preparing to release tear gas, the crowd calmed on its own and began to disburse. We aren't quite sure what happened to cause the sudden stillness, but rumors have circulated that Prime Human life force abilities were responsible, and that the Guild sent in operatives to help take control of the situation.

"While the injured were being taken to local hospitals, Guild supporters took the opportunity to take the stadium by force. Staged at every entrance around the building, they are armed with weapons, preventing anyone from entering. Negotiations have met a standstill as Guild supporters assert that they will not leave the building until Wendy Whitley is cleared of all charges against her."

"Thanks, Dale. We've attempted to contact Mister Dumas for his statement on the events, but his team informed us he's unavailable for comment, so we have been unable to confirm his whereabouts."

Tonya blows a raspberry. "Not available for comment? Sound like Rita in charge. Dumas ain't never *unavailable* for comment."

"Why would he let Rita have the reins like that?" I say. "Everything has gone to hell since she started doing her own thing."

"I think he jus' busy stickin' his nose in the stadium business. Rita decided she'd do the talkin' for him—that bitch is a *bulldog*. But I think you right. He and Porter a'ight."

"Oh… hold on," I say when the words *breaking news* capture my ears.

"Coming to you live from New York at UN headquarters where dignitaries from member countries have been gathering inexplicably since earlier this evening," I say, telling Tonya what I hear once more. "We finally have information that an emergency meeting has been called. Three unidentified dignitaries arrived only moments ago, and our assumption is they are Guild Council members, supporting our suspicion that this meeting involves another major disaster prediction, and that it involves enough countries to warrant such a meeting—"

My words catch in my throat and my voice cracks. I stop, swallowing and putting my forehead in my hands.

"Oh shit. That's what you was all upset about wit' yo girl earlier," Tonya guesses.

A loud boom accompanied by the floor shaking shatters the air suddenly.

I put my feet to the floor and sit up. "What the heck was that?" I say, listening, but all I hear is incoherent shouting.

Tonya lets loose a litany of curses, hopping to her feet and straining to see beyond the bars.

The ambient lights in the hall go out, accompanied by the deescalating whir of the building losing all power.

The building shakes again, and I can hear debris raining down heavily somewhere in the building.

"Tonya," I say, leaping to my feet in fear. "It's a bomb or something."

But she's already doing something to the door of our cell. I can tell because she has her back to me.

I hold my left hand up and press my thumb into the center of my palm and my other fingers on the opposite side and squeeze to activate my tracking device distress signal. I feel it catch, confirming I did it right.

Tonya shoves the door open and motions me to follow her.

My mouth opens. How on earth did she do that? But I tail her, running down the hall, the other inmates shouting at us as we pass.

"What about them?" I say as we burst through the double doors to find the fish bowl housing check-in and the security desk empty.

"Ain't got time to deal with that mess," she says. "They ain't tryin'a bring the building down wit you in it. They tryin'a bus' you out."

"Human Movement supporters are going to get involved," I say. "They might finish the job."

"'Xactly. We ain't stickin' around f'dat. Let's go, Miss White." She stands by the door to the stairs, waiting impatiently.

I look back at the double doors.

"They got emergency unlock function on them doors," she says. "It'll let 'em out if the building gets in trouble."

I look back at her. "Really?"

"Yeah," she says. Just then the lights come on and we both look up.

I cross my arms. "You're lying. I'm an empath, or did you forget?"

She crosses her arms to mirror me. "Pfft. I ain't lyin,' bitch. I seen it in other precincts. I jus' can't confirm they got that here. Now move before I knock you out and drag yo ass down them stairs."

"Fine," I say, following her.

We're halfway down the first flight when an alarm sounds.

"Tol' you," she says. "That's the emergency system. Damn, you slow. Move, move, move," she urges, her shorter legs moving much more quickly than mine down the steps.

The sound of several gunshots followed by glass breaking pierces my ears, and I grab Tonya's arm, but even she heard the gun.

"Detour," she says, pushing through the door to the second floor, which is full of cubicles and offices, also illuminated by dim lights. It's also empty. We run toward a window at the back and look down.

"Perfect," Tonya says. "All the action's at the front." She begins unlatching the window. It's one of those old safety ones that opens outward but not actually enough to fit a person through.

That doesn't deter Tonya. She sucks in a breath and lets out a scream as her foot flies out and her heel hits the glass. It doesn't break the glass, but it dislodges the metal hinge that's keeping the window from fully opening.

She eases the glass open and looks down for a few seconds. "Come here," she says, motioning to me.

I look where she's indicating a tree next to the window. "We gonna grab on that tree and climb down," she says. "Easy. You scared?"

I give her a look, about to open my mouth when she says, "Oh yeah. You capped someone in they face. Never mind."

I roll my eyes as I follow her out of the window. The tree couldn't be placed more perfectly, plus, we aren't that far from the ground. I drop down beside Tonya, and she immediately pulls me over to the side of the building. We creep along the wall to get a look around the side, but right before we reach it, a group of rioters appear, bricks in their hands. I hope they're looking for a window and not a person to crush with it.

"Oh shit, you're out already!" one of them says.

"Back up," Tonya says, assuming a fighting stance.

"Hey, hey," the guy with the brick says. "Who are you and what are you doing with Miss Whitley?"

I step forward. "It's fine," I say, motioning for him to lower the brick, relieved that they appear to be Guild supporters. "She's protecting me. What's going on out front? What was that explosion?"

"Oh man," he says, throwing the brick down. "It's like crazy up there. Somebody brought in a rocket launcher. Shot it right into the front. Hey, you need help getting away? Place is crawling with THMs. If they see you, you're toast."

As soon as he says that, a much larger group appears behind him and his two cronies.

Tonya rushes them, pushing a kick right into the gut of the closest one. Our three brick throwers follow her lead, launching into the group of six or so with much less skill, but doing damage anyway with the bricks in their hands.

A brawl of arms and legs and grunts and cussing ensues. I back up several steps, wondering if I should make a run for it and find a hiding spot where the Guild can pick me up. This is insane.

Someone's arms wrap around me from the back suddenly, and I let out a scream, kicking my legs and squirming. It knocks both me and my attacker to the ground and we tumble around on the grass, me trying to land a kick or a hit and him trying to pin me down. He's a big guy though, so he overpowers me by sheer weight.

Fighting to breathe with his arm against my throat, I catch the glint of a knife in the yellow gleam of a faraway streetlight. He presses it to my cheek, but his indecision is obvious.

"You—don't—want—," I wheeze, trying to push his arm off of my neck with both hands. "Please." He presses harder and I'm seeing stars.

"Aiiyyyyyyyyy!" someone shrieks. A loud thwack meets the sight of my attacker's head jerking backward. The weight finally lifted from my neck, I roll over and cough.

"C'mon," Tonya says, pulling me up with one arm as I heave. As soon as I'm on my feet, she lets go of me and rounds a kick to the side of someone's head. Everywhere I look, people are fighting.

"We gotta get the hell outta here," Tonya says, shoving people out of the way and pulling me again. "I ain't fightin' these dickheads all night." She nods toward the fence surrounding the back of the police station.

I follow her, running at full speed, but my throat hasn't recovered yet. It hurts to inhale. The fence isn't that tall, and fortunately doesn't have any barbed wire. Tonya hoists me up and I ungracefully leap to the other side. My arm catches on the top of the fence, leaving a six inch gash, which immediately soils my shirt with blood.

"I tol' you white was stupid," she says, landing beside me. "Let's go."

We take off, hitting the backside of a neighborhood. We avoid streetlights and people. I stay close on Tonya's heels.

We pause in an alley, checking around the corner, when someone's hand touches my arm.

I don't think. I make a fist, turn, and round it into the person.

He catches my fist in his hand, grabs me in an embrace and I immediately recognize his smell.

"Mike!" I gasp, hugging him back. "About friggin' time!" My voice comes out barely above a whisper, and I cringe from the throbbing in my throat.

"Oh damn," Tonya says. "Scared the shit outta me."

"You suck at watching your back, Baby T," Mike says over my head.

"Don't call me that. You ain't family," she says indignantly.

Mike releases me, holds my arm up to look at it and winces. "Are you okay?"

"Alive," I croak.

"Looks like your adoring fans managed to break you out of jail just like they planned," Mike says.

"Idiots," I reply.

"What happened to your voice?" He demands, growing angry. "Did someone choke you?" He tilts my chin up gently with a hand to see my neck.

"Big, fat mutha fucka," Tonya says. "I broke his jaw."

"Hell yeah," Mike says. "Wen, are you having trouble breathing?"

I nod. "Mostly because it really hurts."

"Shit," Mike says. "I hope he didn't crush your windpipe. We'll get it checked out." Mike says into his communicator,

"Rendezvous on a hundred and fifteenth. And I need a medic." Then to me, "I'm sorry, Wen. They pulled me over for security at the UN when the police assured us the crowd was under control. I shouldn't have listened. I should have stuck around."

"It's fine," I whisper. "Tonya got me out." I shiver, partly from cold, partly from imagining what might have happened if I'd been in my cell when the crowd stormed the building.

Mike removes his coat and puts it over my shoulders. "It's not fine," he says, his hand on the small of my back, guiding me down the alley. "Jail or no. I left you vulnerable. Trusted the system when I know better. Let me know immediately if breathing gets harder."

"Is he okay?" I whisper, looking over my shoulder to make sure Tonya is following.

"Yeah. He called Shiah a while ago to check on you. That was before the riot here. Apparently, in exchange for asking Porter to make a call for you, he agreed to go into hiding until the event on Sunday. Porter was so pissed that he went into that riot and put all his people in danger that he threatened to quit. Gabe, the stubborn bastard, only agreed to lie low because he wanted Tonya to stay on the job. After seeing what happened in Chicago, he was right to assume things were likely to get ugly here. At least he did one thing right. The result, of course, is Rita has taken over speaking for The Human Movement to the media. Tensions are so high in Chicago right now that he's got a lot of people out for his blood."

We come out on a street, three cars waiting. A bunch of suits swarm us.

"Ya'll give me a ride to Jersey to my aunt's?" Tonya says.

I nod and hold the door open for her.

"They'll take her," Mike says. "We've got the other car. Shiah says I'm supposed to get you to police headquarters so that the whole thing doesn't look like an orchestrated break-out."

I sigh and lean down to peer inside the car. "Thanks, Tonya," I croak. "I'm alive because of you."

"Ain't no thang," she says, waving a hand. "Jus' doin' my job."

I shut the door and Mike escorts me to the rear car. I slide in and Mike follows.

"I'm not leaving your side this time," Mike says.

"Is Shiah at the UN?"

"Yep," he says, pulling a first aid kit out from somewhere and taking my arm to clean the gash.

My eyes are drooping; my body is crashing after all the adrenaline. It's sometime after one A.M., yet traffic is still horrendous, so we have a while before we reach our destination. With my arm still in Mike's lap because he's dressing the wound, I lay down in the seat, falling asleep almost instantly.

Fifty-One

I wake up with Shiah's arm over me. It looks like she came in and collapsed fully-clothed, on top of the blankets at some point. Couldn't have been that long after I was checked into the hotel around four A.M. Mike is sitting across the room, dozing in a chair, his elbow propped up on the table.

I reach up and grasp my neck gently. I wonder how big the bruise is. The doctor who came to check it out said it was just a bad contusion, but it sure *feels* like more. Maybe I should take those pain meds he gave me after all. My arm took a few stitches, and it's dully throbbing as well.

Shiah's phone rings, startling them both awake.

She sits bolt upright, reflexively snatching the phone from the nightstand without even fumbling.

After seeing the caller ID, she exhales, tosses the phone in my lap and lies back down.

I pick up the phone. It's Gabriel, which gives me the same thrill it always does. I tap the screen and put the phone to my ear. "Mister Dumas," I rasp, wincing.

"Wendy?" he says.

I close my eyes because the sound of him saying my name with so much concern makes my heart ache, especially in light of the miles and obstacles between us. This is torture.

So is my throat…

"Yes," I say, looking around for the bag that contains the pain pills.

"Heavens. You sound awful. Tonya told me what happened. I'm sure you've seen a doctor already?"

Mike appears next to my bed, holding the pill bottle and a glass of water.

"*Thank you,*" I mouth to him, taking the items. "Yes," I tell Gabriel. "My neck is just bruised. Stitches in my arm. Thank you for Tonya though."

I hear his breaths come more quickly, and he doesn't reply right away. "Gads," he breathes, his voice cracked. "I bloody hate this."

I don't answer, because everything inside of me is warring. On the one hand my heart keeps wanting to latch on to him, especially when I recognize in the tone of his voice how much he cares about me. On the other hand, I'm furious at him. I'm so over The Human Movement. Fighting over ideals that are irrelevant in light of what's happening in the world is insanity. He's causing so much strife and wasting our resources while he does it.

I set the glass down on the bedside table decisively. There's no helping it. I'm not going to rest until the words are said. "*You* hate this? This is all *your* fault! What are you even trying to do?" I snap at him, ignoring my throat. "Have you ever stopped to ask yourself that? You think you're protecting people? From what? You're helping them? How? At what point are you going to realize that the laws and government you're demanding we uphold are one disaster away from being gone, that the society you're 'protecting' from tyrant Primes has been destroyed? At what point are you going to realize people don't give a damn about justice and transparency when their homes are dropping into the ocean? What have *you* done to help those people? *Nothing*," I seethe.

"You're so wrapped up in keeping the voice of dissent alive that you don't care how it affects human life," I continue. "The Human Movement," I say scornfully. "That's a name you don't deserve. You aren't human. You put ideals above humanity. You put rules above people. You put a system over peace and you don't believe in exceptions. Well guess what, Dumas? Human Beings *are* exceptions. Every last one of them is an exception to *some* rule, *some* ideal, *some* belief. And you are a *fool* for believing that what you are doing is helping *anyone*. I'll see you in Chicago tomorrow, but I'll be announcing it as my last appearance. I'm not catering to your shenanigans anymore. I have much more important things to do. Like saving lives. And I'll do whatever it takes to make sure the Council pulls all funding and involvement from your events. The Human Movement is a waste. A bunch of people with lots of words and zero action. We are done with you."

I resist throwing the phone at the wall when I hang up, instead throwing it on the bed and putting my face in my shaking hands.

"He needed that," Mike says.

I look up, running my hands up to my neck. "So did I," I say, relieved that I'm not crying. I'm just shaking all over. "Can you turn the heat on? It's freezing in here," I ask Mike since he's right next to the thermostat.

Shiah sat up at some point during my rant. I took her by surprise again. I guess she's going to have to update her data once more. Surprise is replaced by realization and compassion though. "Don't let heartbreak rule your actions," she says.

I glare at her. "It's *not*. I meant exactly what I said. I'm done. I have to figure this out, and I'm wasting time by chasing THM all the time. I'm no better than Dumas if I put pushing my ideals over more practical things, like finding a solution in the energy world."

I feel her disagree as she swings her legs over the bed. She stands up and turns around. "The Human Movement is important."

"Why?" I say. "And don't tell me because the Guild needs someone to temper them. Maybe later. But what the Guild needs right now is unhindered liberty to get things under control. That's what the world needs, too."

She wraps her arms around her middle, stares at nothing. "Desperation causes people to do terrible things. A voice of dissent ties the heart with the head."

I sigh heavily. She doesn't get it. Maybe she has a little *too* much faith in humanity. "We can argue this all day, but I don't have time. I see the energy world, Shiah. *That* needs my time. Dumas needs... his head adjusted. When's my hearing?" I ask, changing the subject. Last night, the police were all too happy to release me into the custody of the Guild, fearing, I bet, the wrath of my supporters and risking another facility.

"I went to your bail hearing this morning," she says.

"Really?" I say, looking around for the time.

"It's nine," Shiah says. "They pushed the hearing up to seven."

"And I didn't need to be there?"

"No. I represent you."

"Bail?" I say.

"Quarter million."

"That's low, isn't it?"

"For someone with as many resources at their disposal as you have? It's laughable. But it was made on the concession that you'll remain in New York after your appearance in Chicago until trial, which we're pushing to accelerate."

I stare at her open-mouthed for several seconds. She was already *planning* on me not attending more events? "Didn't you just... I thought you wanted... What the hell, Shiah?"

She smirks. "I know you."

"But you still argued."

"Because you wanted to."

"Do you actually think the things you said?"

"Yes."

My face twists in confusion, but then I shake my head and exhale. "Whatever. What time is our flight?"

"Several hours," she says, opening her bag for new clothes.

"Then why are you bouncing around? You've been up all night. Go back to sleep, woman!"

"I'm fine," she says cheerily.

I watch her in confusion. "You're fine. And you need to be ready to go hours early because...?"

She turns around, clothes in one hand, her toiletry bag in the other. "I can't go back to sleep, Wendy. Mike kissed me when I got back this morning and now I need to go fantasize about him in the shower. I won't have time to later."

At first my jaw drops, but when I catch the look on Mike's face, I choke on laughter. "You go do that," I manage to say, unable to contain my hysterical giggles.

She grins, that beautiful, full smile she does so rarely, comes around and kisses me on the cheek before heading into the bathroom.

I collapse on the bed in a fit, eventually rolling over and propping my head on my elbow. "What's the scoop, Mike?" I croak, biting my lip to keep from laughing again.

He seems to have recovered shock, and is now playing it cool. "I got skills, Wen. You know that."

"Oooooh, right. You're a big player. So how did it go down, playboy?"

"I am *not* a player. And that is none of your business."

"Please," I scoff. "Shiah's going to tell me about it later. You don't want to give me your version first?"

He frowns.

"Okay, come on, Mike. The two of you are my best friends," I say, losing the mocking in my tone. "I need something to smile about on this awful day."

He tilts his head. "It's still a little weird for me. Knowing you and I…" The words get stuck.

"That we have the hots for each other, and you share Gabe's emotions, which means you are tied to me in a myriad of ways that may never go away," I say unapologetically. "I'm okay with it, Mike. The thought of you being with Shiah makes me so happy I want to kiss you, but that probably breaches boundaries or something."

"Ya think?" he says.

I bite the inside of my lip. He has no idea about Shiah kissing me, I think, and I'm not sure this is the time to bring it up if he thinks *this* conversation is weird.

"Are you going to let me revel in your happiness or not?" I say.

"The two of you have an odd relationship I still haven't quite figured out," Mike says.

I give him an expectant look.

"She came back from the UN earlier in a rage over the breakout. She checked on you, and I thought she was going to cry. But then she went into the hall and started calling the prosecutor's office, the chief of police, leaving messages that she was going to have their jobs for failing to protect you. Then she started barking at someone to get her a phone number for the White House. At that point she looked like she did at Co-op city with her father during your meeting with the Council, and I knew she needed some intervention. So I walked up to her and told her not to do anything she'd regret. She tried to punch me, again, but I stopped her. Brad got involved, because that's his job, but she told him to make himself scarce. So we sat down on the floor and had a conversation about you and then it just kind of happened."

"Oh geez. It 'just kind of happened'?" I say. "You're skipping the best part."

"I'm sure Shiah can tell you about all that. For me, it happened because I realized Shiah really seems to grasp what I go through being connected to Gabe. Never met a girl so clear on what she wants and so comfortable with this thing between Gabe and me. The fact that she knows it and seems to want something anyway made it a much easier decision to kiss her. I'm hoping that…" He hesitates.

"What?" I say, thinking this is exactly 'the good part' I was talking about.

"I'm hoping I can develop feelings for someone else and it will make it easier to be around you." He looks up and around.

"I didn't know you were struggling so much," I say softly, aching for him.

He looks at me. "I'm good at managing it when I'm on duty. It's the rest of the time."

"Oh Mike," I say, sitting up.

"He loves you, Wen," he says. "He thinks about you *all* the time. He struggles like I've never felt him struggle before. He argues with himself constantly. And just now, when you were talking to him, even from almost a thousand miles away, I felt him lose it. He's a mess. I don't think I've ever picked up on him from so far away, but ever since you met with him at his hotel the other day, his emotions have gained some serious reach. So when I'm around you, the object of his devotion… It's hard to keep myself in check, because I want to satisfy the urge to touch you, to tell you how much I love you and need you. I know *I* care about you a lot, but hell if I know how much. I couldn't tell you exactly how *I* feel even if my life depended on it. He's overshadowing everything."

I lay back on the bed, staring up at the ceiling, hating that Mike has to go through this, but also hating how much hearing about the power of Gabe's feelings for me can still make me come undone. "I wish he would have left to go find his wife already," I say. "I'll tell him that in Chicago. It will make things easier all the way around."

"He doesn't want to go. He's forcing himself. A month ago I never would have believed I would be saying this, but I think if you asked him, he'd give up The Human Movement for you."

I turn to look at him. "Really?" I say, shocked to hear Mike say such a thing.

"This thing with his wife… He's doing it out of a desperate attempt to hang on to The Human Movement. He worships you, and it's coming out more and more in public. He's handing it over to Rita because he realizes exactly what I told you from the beginning: obsession will lead to his undoing. He can't hang on to you and THM at the same time, so he's diverting his focus and distancing himself so he doesn't lose THM. But I swear, if you stood in front of him, asked him to give it all up for you, he wouldn't be able to say no."

I rub my face. "Why didn't you tell me this sooner?" I say, thinking I know the answer.

"He's my brother, Wen," Mike says, his voice cracking. "I'm telling you how to destroy him. I'm telling you how to break him. I'm not doing it lightly. Until last night, I couldn't justify manipulating him that way. It's wrong. But it's like you told him, sometimes you have to put ideals aside and make exceptions. I think this is one of those times. THM has gotten out of control in a matter of forty-eight hours. And it's because Gabe isn't reining them in. He built this thing, and now he's pawning it off on someone with a lot less sense. You're the only one that can put him—and consequently them—back in line."

"So you want me to ask him to give up what he believes for me?" I say, skeptical of that actually working.

He clears his throat. "Do you want to be with him or not?"

I rub my face again. I do. But I don't know if I like the terms. "I'd rather… make him see the error of his ways. And *then* be with him."

"I don't know if that's possible."

"*I* certainly couldn't give up the Guild for him and sleep at night. I'd essentially be asking the same thing of him."

"If you don't, more people are going to die, Wen."

"Great," I say. "You're using my words against me."

"He wants to be with you. He'd be happy to be with you. So what if he puts aside his convictions? They're wrong anyway. Love involves compromise, doesn't it?"

"This isn't compromise. This is… I don't know what this is. But it feels horrible."

"Just think about it. It's for the greater good. And having Gabe on our side? He's a force, Wen. My brother is the most capable person I know outside of Shiah."

"He wouldn't really be on our side," I say quietly. "That's the problem."

"Neither were you when you first joined the Guild," Mike says. "Shiah told me so. Sometimes you do the right thing first. The belief comes later. Gabe *does* change his mind, and he'd finally be able to see and experience first-hand how we work and he wouldn't think it was so terrible. And when Gabe changes his mind, he doesn't look back. He forges ahead."

I ponder that. How right he is. I have changed so much in my convictions, and it all happened because I took a leap of faith, choosing to do something against my nature and join the Guild. "You should have led with that," I say. "It makes the most practical sense and doesn't scrape against my conscience. I'll actually consider that."

Fifty-Two

How many people does Soldier Field seat?" I ask, looking at the ceiling where, directly above us, I've both heard and felt a massive crowd gather. I stand up for the twentieth time and tug my white skirt down. This is my most casual outfit yet. I'm wearing turquoise cowboy boots as my splash of color, and a white jean jacket. It's unseasonably warm in Chicago, and I kind of hope it's at least a little breezy up above. I feel like I can't quite inhale all the way. I fluctuate between dizzy and wired constantly, and we got here only half an hour ago.

"About sixty thousand," Mike says. "Are you going to be okay?" he asks when I totter unexpectedly to one side.

"Damn, that's a lot," I say. "The crowd is making me feel drunk."

"They're calling them rallies now," Shiah says, eyes on her tablet. "Dumas is making it more structured. They'll even open with a band. Then there's a string of speakers, including Dumas. Then you."

"Shiah, isn't this a bit much?" I say, asking in a roundabout way how much of the attendance is her doing.

"THM no longer requires our help," Shiah replies.

I see the monitor with new eyes. The camera is panning the stadium, and I am aghast. The Human Movement has broken the levy. How?

I killed one man on a sidewalk at JFK.

One singular moment… changed everything.

I did this.

That realization takes my breath away

"There are lots of reasons people showed up today," Shiah says, "and they aren't necessarily avid THM supporters. But Dumas has a reputation for being a powerful speaker, and since JFK, THM response protests have sprung up all over the country. They are all over the news now."

"Let's not forget they know Wen will be here," Mike says. "Did you see that group that walked in first thing doing Guild fists?"

"Right," Shiah replies. "You're speaking for the first time since being indicted. *Your* reputation is to say things nobody was expecting. You and Dumas are a duo that everyone wants to see. They got control of the stadium only yesterday so it's still a hot topic in the news. And since the UN is still in session and nobody knows what for exactly, this event has the entire media's attention."

I believe everything they're saying, but all of it still leads back to JFK. I killed a man, and I did it in such a way that made the entire world see the Guild and THM completely differently, whether they realize it or not.

Suddenly, I'm afraid to go out there. I know how *Primes* see me—the Guild is stronger than ever—but I no longer know how the world will receive me and therefore the Guild. I don't actually have a legitimate defense for killing Andre the way I did, and I suddenly realize that's probably the only thing the people in the stadium care about.

One speech, Wendy. You can do it.

But they have a band and a speaking schedule and lights and cameras… This is so not my stage…

"I am so glad I'm quitting after this," I say, leaning against a pillar. "They're turning it into a show. I refuse to be a musical number."

"Dumas was forced by his new donor to hire a consultant," Shiah says. "And so far, it looks like a good move. The place is filling up."

"Oh I know it is," I say, rubbing my temples.

"Seriously. Are you going to be able to handle this?" Mike says.

"I have to," I reply. "And fortunately, I only have to do it this once." My voice is also not yet back up to snuff, but it can't be helped.

"Would you mind mentioning quitting one more time?" Shiah says. "Just so we can all be *really* clear on it."

I glance at her out of the corner of my eye. "Mike, did Shiah just use sarcasm?"

"Pigs flew last night," he replies, propping his legs up on the coffee table. "And I also kissed her this morning. One of those is responsible for scrambling her brain. I highly doubt it was the pigs." He smirks.

Shiah looks at him from under her dark lashes and bites her bottom lip in her teeth. I've never seen someone look *that* sultry with such a simple expression. She doesn't say a word but returns to her tablet once Mike shifts in his seat. I know he felt the heat of her gaze as much as I did, and I wasn't even the object of her stare.

I whistle. "Mike, I've always had the impression that you can win any woman you want, and that you're used to pursuit, and that if you have ever been on the opposite end of that, it was by your choosing. How does it feel to finally be under someone else's power?"

"Who says I'm not the one pulling the strings?" Mike says.

I laugh. "Oh Mike. If you actually think that, you are much more naive than I thought."

He grumbles. "I wasn't disagreeing. I was just wondering what made you think that."

"Experience," I reply.

"Fine. But in answer to your question, it's hot as hell. I swear every time I kiss her she makes me think it was my idea. I like it when she owns me like that."

Shiah smiles, still concentrating on her screen as she types something in.

I smile back, but then I sigh, because pretty soon I'm going to be a third wheel. Of course, with this being my last THM event, we probably won't be together like this nearly as often. That makes me sad...

"You are the glue that holds us all together," Shiah says, finally lowering her tablet, and, as usual, preempting my doubts. "Mike can't forget you for even a second, even if he wanted to. And you are the reason I chose to pursue Mike in the first place. Not to mention the fact that all of my favorite memories involve you in some way. I have perfect memory, Wendy. It's impossible for me to neglect you and your feelings, even for a moment."

My eyes tear up, and I nearly fall into her while skipping over to hug her. She catches me. "This is not going to work," she says. "You can't even stand up on your own."

"Should I call someone to bring a walker for her?" Mike chortles.

I simper at him. "Shut your face. Why do I need a walker when I have *you?* You can hold me up."

His eyes widen. "No way. I'm not going out there, at least not on stage."

"Yes, you are," Shiah says.

"What?!" he says, sitting up and putting his feet on the floor. "I'm her bodyguard. I'm supposed to stay in the background so I can watch people. Going on stage will draw attention to me and make it harder for me to do my job."

"Relax," Shiah says with a half smile. "I'm talking about escorting her out and carrying a stool for her."

"Oh…" Mike says. "Yeah, okay."

"Just make sure you're really sweet with her. Put your arm around her when you walk out and hold her hand to help her onto the stool. The closer the better."

"Ugh," I say. "Are you using Mike to make Gabe jealous in front of sixty thousand people?"

"Wendy," Shiah chides. "If I want to pimp my boyfriend to make yours jealous, that's my prerogative."

I open my mouth in surprise.

"Plus, this is your last event as THM liaison. I'm pulling out all the stops."

"I know *exactly* what to do," Mike says, eyes bright, rubbing his hands together.

I throw my hands up, but teeter into Shiah again. "Fine. I'm in. Let's make this as epic as Prime Humanly possible."

凹

Dumas waves at the crowd, turning in a circle. He's back to using a comparatively small stage at the very center, one slightly bigger than the last time. The crowd doesn't just fill the seats in the stadium, but the field itself.

The cheers are deafening. In the stadium they stomp out a rhythm. I'm struggling to keep my eyes open now that I'm above ground. I had to practically be carried out here to my stool just inside a room attached to the tunnel leading to the field. I'm not tired. My head is so full that it hurts to add more stimuli. I'm gripping Mike's hand tightly because it gives me something to focus on. Everything is too much. Even my shirt is bothering my skin. And the noise of the crowd is piercing.

Once the crowd quiets—mostly—Dumas says, "Welcome to The Human Movement."

The crowd explodes again, and I flinch, letting my eyes fall shut. I lean heavily into Mike.

"Wen, I'm really concerned about you," Mike says. "Do you even remember what you're going to say?"

I purse my lips. "Mike, it's not my head that's malfunctioning. It's my body. The emotion is too much for it to handle."

"Do you need some tea?"

"Ugh."

"What do we do?" Mike asks, and I don't think he's talking to me.

"Today," Dumas says on the monitor. "Today is a new day."

More cheering. Good lord. He's never going to get through his speech.

"I've called in an operative that I think can help her. He should be here in ten minutes," Shiah says.

"We once called ourselves peaceful protestors," Dumas says. "We came together asking the Guild to reveal themselves. We came together asking the Guild to abandon their exclusivity. We came together asking to be part of the effort to save ourselves. And then we were assigned a liaison by the name of Wendy Whitley.

"For a time we felt like we might matter. We felt for a moment that our voices had not gone unheard." He turns slowly and his voice goes quiet as he says, "You felt it too, didn't you? That she belonged with us? That she was part of us? She championed us. She was our ally. She understood us and our cause. She even led by example, living her life in transparency, telling us who she was. She was… exactly what we so desperately wanted from the rest of the Guild."

The crowd goes deathly silent. It's bizarre to see so many thousands of people in one place and nary a word is whispered. But I feel them shift states, and it's like the whole crowd feels the affection that Dumas infuses into his voice. But I know where this is going. I know it and I can hardly believe he's been relegated to what is surely playing out to be a personal attack on me.

"We fell in love with her, didn't we?" Dumas says.

"Oh hell," Mike says quietly from beside me. But the crowd doesn't seem to realize what Dumas has admitted.

Dumas forges ahead, "Three days ago she stood over Andre Gellagher with a gun in her hand."

"Oh no," I say when the footage of me at the airport comes to life on the jumbotron above him. But I knew what this whole thing was going to be about, didn't I?

"She didn't look up to see who was watching," Dumas says, the video playing over his head corroborating his words. "She didn't care. She had Andre at her mercy. She looked into his eyes."

The crowd explodes. I grip Mike's hand, trying not to cry as their outrage forces its way through my body.

Dumas raises his hand for silence, and they obey as if he holds a remote control to their voices. "She never looked up. Not once. She never took her eyes off of Andre, even as she pulled the trigger."

The gunshot of the video reverberates through the stadium. The crowd is out of control.

Again Dumas silences them with one gesture. How does he do that?

"In that moment we realized that no matter how much she walked and talked like us, she *wasn't* us. Her rules were different. She was confident because she was above the law. She shot him without thinking because she didn't *have* to think. She didn't really belong with us. She was an imposter."

"He's lost it," Mike says to himself, but I hear him over the noise.

"I've been asked by the media, 'Why are your supporters suddenly so violent?'" Dumas says. "It's because we have been betrayed by false hope. It's because we realize that the Prime Human label is not merely a label. It's a mentality, one that peaceful protest will never change. But you know, I'm not bitter. This is who they are. Miss Whitley will go to trial for her crimes, but it won't be a fair trial. It's already rigged in her favor. Her counsel is a Prime Human, and no doubt she is possessed of life force abilities that will allow her to cheat the system, ones we can't know because the Guild won't disclose it. It's all a formality intended to make us believe they will submit themselves to the law."

The crowd's anger bursts forth.

I sigh and glance at Shiah. She built THM, and now it has exploded out of anyone's control. And I... I can't blame Gabriel for using my act as a springboard. If I'm upset that people are focusing on me killing Andre instead of the world's problems, the only person to blame is me.

Shiah does not appear to be bothered though, watching the monitor. I wish I knew what she was thinking.

"You know what I realized this week?" Dumas says. "Prime Humans exist. I don't know why it didn't occur to me before to ever address that fact. Perhaps it is because until this past week I'd never had occasion to directly see them in action. I watched a riot move from bloody and violent to still and peaceful in a manner of fifteen minutes because of them. ... They exist, and some part of me wanted to ignore that fact in the interest of more imminent problems."

He sighs. "It's clear that I can no longer ignore it: Prime Humans exist among us. The rules *are* changing, and we would be wise to recognize it, because we're running out of time. My fellow humans, I'm afraid that by spending our outrage on their upheaval of our society, we have inadvertently allowed them to rule us. We have relinquished that liberty we so desperately wish to protect."

I put my free hand over my mouth. Is he doing what I think he's doing?

"By our acts of rebellion... our demand that they share their resources... our fight to expose what and who they are... By these things we have unequivocally asserted that it is the *Guild* that has what the world needs, so we demand to have it for ourselves." Dumas taps the side of his head as if having an epiphany. "We protest, we cry, we shout, we make noise, pleading for our lives like children petitioning a god that does not hear them."

He stills his hands, clasping them behind his back as he turns slowly. "As much as we claim otherwise, that's exactly how we see them. Because that's how we treat them."

He makes eye contact with the bewildered faces. "What else *can* we do?" he asks, shrugging. "What else is to be done when the earth comes for our lives? ... Humans against the earth? That's ludicrous. What can *we* do in such a fight... but petition our god?"

He bows his head. "Our god. The one that can know this:"

On the jumbotron is a shot of the GDNS website landing page, a clickable map of the world. A mouse selects the US, revealing a more detailed map complete with flashing points revealing impending calamities.

"Our god," Dumas says, "who can do this:"

A line of Prime Humans stand at the edge of a collapsed building, and hand in hand they lift a massive piece of cement with their minds with more precision than any piece of heavy equipment. They are likely in search of earthquake victims, and I believe it happened after one of the first public Guild predictions: an earthquake in Tokyo. Not everyone evacuated as they were warned.

Another video plays, this one of Prime operatives mounting greenhouse globes through the mountains of Afghanistan. They were installed only a couple weeks ago. Their purpose is to slowly warm the valley that has been locked in the coldest winter on record.

Scotland: Operatives in gas-masks on the tops of buildings in Edinburgh, surrounding Castle Rock, preparing to release the chemical that will bond with the toxic gas in the air and make it heavy enough to fall out of the sky.

"Our god, who can see this:" Dumas says next.

The original preliminary map released showing the areas to be affected in the Carribbean crisis. Red highlights Florida, the Carribbean, the northwest coast of South America, and the western coast of Africa.

Then, the satellite map that was shown after the subduction, sped up to show Florida and the islands sinking into the sea.

"Our god, who can save them:"

Aerial images of boats, hundreds of them, fleeing the Carribbean. Photos of the never-ending refugees disembarking on foreign soil. Faces of the refugee treks. Men, women, children, babies. Lines and lines of people, on foot, searching for a place of refuge.

"Our god," Dumas says, "who can make this:"

A hand holding a tiny bottle of Purus.

"What else are we to do when faced with the power of our god...but to demand more?"

In silence above him, the jumbotron highlights THM protests: bouncing, shouting, moving crowds. Signs. Fists, screaming faces. But no sound.

He turns, slowly, asking for the answer. The silent video sets the mood, and agitated quiet prevails throughout the stadium for several minutes.

Dumas finally stops turning. "What are we to do when we realize the limitations of our god?"

Faces of misery appear on the screen. Tear-streaked. Mourning. Aerial views of fires, earthquake rubble. The unprepared aqueducts in California. The endless churned landscape. An underwater probe, skimming through a neighborhood that bizarrely managed to remain mostly intact when it was sunk into the ocean. Refugee camps for miles, some of their shelters nothing more than trash piled up.

Image after image of seeming unending destruction and suffering flashes above Dumas who does not look up, but at the crowd surrounding him, his eyes piercing, his mouth still and expectant, as if watching their reactions.

The screen goes black.

"This is what we can see when we look around our world," Dumas says. "But instead, *this* is what we choose to fight:"

He throws a hand up to indicate the jumbotron again, and on it is the still image of me, standing over Andre.

"Because the Guild is real. Prime Humans are real. But this monster?"

The jumbotron flashes through the destruction again.

"We don't know how to fight it."

All eyes are on Dumas.

"Or at least, we think we don't, because we are too busy watching all that *they* do that *we* can't."

The crowd inhales in synchrony.

"*Stop*," Dumas orders abruptly.

The crowd does stop, not just physically but mentally they take pause as well. It feels as if… as if time has stopped. It feels like when I watched him in the energy world, but I'm not there. At least I'm not seeing it. But I know it's happening. They have wound themselves around him. They are one.

"Look here!" he says, turning in a circle, arms outstretched. "Look around you! Stop looking to your god to save you! They won't because they *can't*! Don't you see that? Why do we wait on their permission to move? Why do we demand their attention when we have nothing to show? Why do we beg for their power while ignoring our own? They may be a few thousand or a few *hundred* thousand! But *we* are *seven billion!*"

The crowd erupts in excitement, and this time Dumas lets that excitement run it's course while I simply endure its intensity.

"Soon," Dumas says once they quiet. "Soon this moment will pass. The UN will release the latest Guild prediction, and we will be devastated. We will be afraid because the earth will once again show forth her power. In the midst of it, the Guild will flex their muscles before us, and we will be tempted to stand still in awe…

"But We. Will. *Not*. Because we are *not* Humans Stand. We are *not* Humans Watch. Neither are we Humans Talk. We are… The Human *Movement*. And we *will fight* the forces of nature bent on our destruction by *moving*. Lifting. Carrying. Sharing. Helping. If you are daunted by the task, I urge you not to look to your god. Look to your fellow humans, and I promise you will see a task before you that you *can* do. We have a world-wide community that beats with human hearts that have not lost hope in this world! And that community believes exactly what you do: that the Guild has sold us short!"

The stadium is filled with thunder. Pounding feet. Booming voices. I can't move underneath their power, but my eyes are pouring. I wish I could reach out and touch him. I wish I could whisper in his ear.

He listened. He listened to me!

"Time to move," Gabriel says. "The Human Movement is spearheading it's very first relief effort. In California our fellow humans have been neglected not only by the government, but by the Guild as well. We are going to fix their aqueduct first. And then we will push onward into Los Angeles county and see what holds them captive. I urge you to join us. Tell us how you can contribute. We have space for you. But so do your neighbors. So do ten million refugees. We can win. I promise you we can. And the Guild? They can finally watch *us*. Our trek will be broadcast at our rallies, which will continue under the direction of my associate, Rita Long. But this is only the beginning."

The crowd, to my surprise, is riveted. They are under Dumas' spell—in a good way I think.

Gabriel's eyes are piercing, his expression stern, demanding. "Let us show the Guild what they have sorely underestimated."

He clasps his hands together in front of him tightly—my Guild fist. The camera moves closer to him, and I can make out the veins of his arms as he presses his hands together tighter and tighter. "Let us show them and ourselves what can be accomplished when Humans *move!*" He explodes both of his hands outward.

The resulting roar is ear-splitting. People come to their feet, screaming at the top of their lungs as if they are about to march into battle. I come to my feet because I can't hold still. I want to run. I want to run straight out there and into Gabriel's arms. But I can't. I won't. This is his moment. These are his people. And I am no longer needed.

Someone starts stomping in a rhythm, and it swiftly fills the entire stadium in time with "*Hu*man, *Hu*man, *Hu*man!" It's deafening. It's powerful. It's intimidating and terrifying. It's an army of Humans who will not be stopped.

"He has joined the Guild and he doesn't even know it," Shiah marvels from next to me.

"No. He's finally fighting us for real," I say, now gasping for breath to expel as much emotion as possible. I'm going to pass out at this rate.

Shiah squeezes my arm. "I meant the *real* Guild," she says. "Let's get you below."

I shake my head. I need to see him in person, not on a monitor. I pull open the door and walk to the tunnel's entrance. A barrier and a line of protection prevents the crowd from access to the tunnel, and I perceive Mike's presence behind me. I stand at the edge, peering over their heads, my eyes finding Gabriel standing at the very center, his face to the sky, his arms outstretched as if embracing the whole world.

I have super vision so I can see the nuances of his face. The abandon. The complete… release. I've always thought it was Dumas who owned the crowd, but now… I think it's the other way around. Gabriel Dumas belongs to *them*.

The sky, which has been pregnant with dark clouds all day, rumbles suddenly as if answering the call of thousands of human feet. It can barely be discerned but for the fact that it's out of rhythm with the pounding beat. A few droplets of rain wet Gabriel's face.

Mike couldn't be hovering any closer, so using his life force, I blink my eyes and bring myself into the energy world.

The pull of sudden inertia has me staggering back into Mike. He catches me but I cannot keep my feet, instead sinking to my knees.

I hear Mike calling my name from somewhere far away, but I must see Gabriel. I lift my face, searching for Gabriel's life force. But in front of me is light. I can't see past it or through it. I notice, though, that I can see my hands bracing me against the ground, which is fluctuating in blues. *I see my actual hands.* Not just my life force which always obscures my skin. My life force is still attached to me though. My strands still cling to me by my skin, like tiny glowing purple hairs covering every inch of me. The hairs themselves extend away from me, as if seeking. I follow them where they blend into the light that surrounds me. I finally can see what it is though: life force strands, just like mine, but an infinite number of them. I cannot see their beginning or end. I cannot see the people the strands belong to. They're everywhere, surrounding me on all sides. I'm buried in a sea of life forces.

A form emerges from them, a life force assimilating itself out of the surrounding strands until it resembles a person—or at least the shape of one as I always see them in the energy world. It's strange, because even though the form and function—swirl at the head and chest—is the same as every other life force I've seen, this one is familiar. The smell… Every life force has a defining scent, and I know I've met this one before…

Suddenly, I'm knocked off of my hands and knees. The light disappears in an instant, and I see feet in front of my face. I hear echoes of incoherent shouting.

"Wendy!" Shiah gasps just as her wide eyes appear in front of me. She's crouched on the ground next to me, leaning down to peer into my face.

I blink, cough, feel the grit of dirt and cold cement beneath my hands. "Why am I on the ground?" I say, struggling to find my balance and sit up at least. The person… where is that person I saw? My head is spinning, but I have to see. There are people everywhere though. No one stands out. Except…

"Mike?" I gasp, sudden adrenaline giving me control of my body again. I quickly crawl to where he is lying on the ground.

"He's okay," Shiah assures me from somewhere over my shoulder just as I reach his side. He's breathing deliberately, eyes closed. He's got two medics near him, one who keeps trying to give him an oxygen mask. But he keeps pushing them away.

"What happened?" I demand.

Hearing my voice, Mike's eyes pop open and find me. "Wen! You're okay. What *happened* to you?"

I shake my head, confused.

"The energy world," Shiah says quietly from beside me. "You went there, didn't you, Wendy?"

I glance from her to Mike. "Yeah," I whisper. "To see. It was friggin crazy. It has never looked like that!"

"Mike touched your hand, trying to bring you back," Shiah murmurs so that only Mike and I can hear.

"Felt like… getting jerked right out of my skin," Mike gasps, and I can see now that his hands are shaking. He shudders as he sits up finally, but he rests his forehead in his hands, elbows on knees. "That was… not pleasant."

I don't know what to say or think. Mike touched my skin and got knocked out?

"Get the bloody hell out of my way!" shouts a familiar voice from nearby.

Mike and I look up at the same time, but a wall of bodies prevents us from seeing Gabriel, who sounds like he's trying to break through the line.

"I will *not* calm down!" he bellows to whomever is trying to talk him down. "The entire stadium saw exactly what I did! I am not leaving until I see her standing in front of me, unharmed!"

Mike braces a hand on the wall, pulls himself to his feet. Shiah helps me stand, and I try to brush myself off, but a dirty ground is very unforgiving of a white outfit.

It sounds like a scuffle has started, and Mike hears it at the same time as me.

"Gabe, take a breather, she's fine," Mike shouts as he pushes a path through our line of operatives. I fall in behind him, and Mike puts a hand out to stop me just before we reach Gabriel, who is backed by an army of reporters, hungry for a scoop. Tranwick has disarmed three of our men already, but they've gotten control back by aiming ten stun guns at him at once. Gabriel is being held back by two men. It's quite the scene.

"The camera that was supposed to film your entrance to speak caught you a hitting the pavement instead," Shiah murmurs inconspicuously in my ear. "And it happened again. You were out for thirty minutes this time. Until Mike touched you. Fortunately the cameras missed him getting knocked out because our operatives were blocking you by then. Now would be a good time to come up with something trademark Wendy. Break the tension a little."

I step out from behind Mike's arm, and the relief on Gabriel's face sends my heart fluttering.

I look from Tranwick to the reporters to Gabriel, and then back at my line of men. I only just notice that every single person, Gabriel and the reporters included, is soaking wet. Beyond the tunnel's entrance the rain is so heavy I can't even see the seats across the stadium. I guess the sky must have opened up moments after I saw that raindrop hit Gabriel's face.

"Well," I say, turning back to the wet group. "I did warn you people that if you got uppity my men would take you down." I shake my head. "I guess I should have had an object lesson." I flick a hand at my men. "Release them." They obey, falling back into our line behind me.

Gabriel blinks at me several times, totally confused, but then he laughs, immediately assuming a casual stance. "I am relieved to see you are indeed unharmed. I was about to make a scene in front of the media again and Rita would have my head." It's fortunate that the reporters with cameras are behind him, because the look of pure affection he gives me would be hard for anyone to miss.

"Miss Whitley! Can you tell us what happened?" one gutsy young reporter blurts. "You collapsed right when you were supposed to speak. Did someone from THM sabotage you?"

My instinct is to cross my arms protectively. I'm not used to giving unplanned statements to the media. I force my hands behind my back though, nod at Mike to alert him that I'll be leaving the safety of the line.

He takes his place at my shoulder as we pass Gabriel and approach the young reporter. Police have the group of them held back, and they scramble toward me now with their microphones at the ready.

"I collapsed because I was overwhelmed by the emotional energy in the stadium at the close of Mr. Dumas' remarks. I am an empath after all. The larger the crowd, the more difficult it is for me to cope."

"Given the growth of the Human Movement's following, and the expected attendance at their events now, will you be able to continue to perform your duties as liaison?" another reporter calls out to be heard above the others.

The question stops me. I hadn't even considered the possibility of using this as an excuse as to why I won't be present at THM events anymore. It would have been a convenient way to bow out without sounding like I'm surrendering.

But I refuse to be opportunistic, especially when Gabriel won the day. I do not want to take any of that away from him or his following. Today was a victory for *all* of humankind.

"No, it would not inhibit my ability to perform," I reply. "I was using my life force abilities in conjunction with one another. I was observing the crowd in the energy world when I was already emotionally overwhelmed. This was a mistake, and that is why I collapsed."

Several more questions battle for attention, but I raise a hand to silence them. "The reality is that this event was intended to be my final appearance at THM events anyway. But for other reasons. Namely because I now have far too many other demands as a Councilmember to continue to devote time to it."

More shouting, everyone trying to get their question in. Shiah has appeared behind me, and she gets control of them and selects one person to speak. "We're glad you are uninjured," a young, Asian woman with geek chic glasses says, "but I think everyone is disappointed that you never had a chance to deliver your final remarks, especially now that we know it was going to be your final appearance. Can you perhaps summarize for us what you had intended to say today?"

I bow my head for a moment, thinking. By the time I went out into the tunnel, I had decided I wasn't actually *going* to speak. I wanted Dumas to have the last word. But I can't actually *say* that. THM cannot glean that what they have been charged by Dumas to do is what the Guild has *wanted* them to do all along. They still need the fight. But they also need this victory.

I turn so that I may face Gabriel when I speak. He *is* THM after all, so it's like speaking to his constituents. His eyebrows are raised, but his mouth is still. He's been standing with his arms crossed, his feet spread, this entire time. He looks kind of like Mike standing that way.

I still don't know what to say though. Words just aren't coming to me. In my mind's eye I keep seeing him put his hands together and then exploding them. Although I know what he intended by it, and I know what his constituents understood, to me it meant something more profound.

I walk up to him and clasp my hands in front of my face. I lift my eyebrows, nod slightly to him to indicate my meaning.

He follows, clasping his hands together in front of him.

I nod again. He explodes his hands apart.

I fall back a step as if I've felt a shockwave. But I keep my hands together. I nod at him again.

He clasps his hands. Explodes them outward.

I fall back, this time letting my knee hit the floor. But when I stand, I still have my hands bound.

I nod at him as I approach. He brings his hands up again, but before he can clasp them, I shove my own between them. His hands wrap around mine, and we stand that way for a tense moment.

I look up into his face, my hands locked in his. And he gets what I'm trying to say. I can feel his emotions.

I begin to fight him, shaking my hands, trying to extract them. But he holds fast. I twist and turn, pull and push. Locked in this figurative battle, I spread my feet for more leverage, but to no avail.

Then I pause to look at him, shake my fist in his hands as if it is vibrating.

He nods at me, begins to shake his own hands in tempo with mine. With as much strength as I can muster, I yank my hands apart. He explodes, sending his own hands further and wider than ever before. We are both driven back, gasping, staggered from the metaphorical blast.

I look down at my hands, open, separate. I stand up, raise my open hands.

He looks at his own free hands. He steps toward me confidently, laces his fingers with mine in the air.

I can hear Gabriel's heart beating loudly as we stand feet from each other, staring, hands wound together. Finished.

The clicking of cameras is joined by voices, but I do not hear them. I don't think Gabriel does either. We have eyes only for each other, and I try to convey, with mine, how honored I am to have shared this light with him. Our time as rivals is over, and we are, as Shiah said, both in the real Guild now.

I give Gabriel's hands a light squeeze before letting go. I turn around and head back to my line, ignoring the questions meeting my back. I have said what I wanted to say. Who knows how well it translated, how the media will spin it, but a little ambiguity might be the right move in this situation. It lets people understand what they want to understand. See what they wanted to see.

Mike has returned to his post at my back, and Shiah is ready, my bag in-hand, to lead us down the tunnel and through the secure entrance to our caravan. Hope fills my chest. The next era has begun.

Shiah hands me my phone on the way. On it is a text message from Debra:

Announcement from the UN in 30 min. Secure conference call in 10.

As quickly as it came, the breath leaves my chest. I fight to keep my feet moving. I fight to see past the tears that have already begun. It's happening. I don't know if I can do this... I stumble. Mike catches me under my elbow. Shiah moves closer to me, clasps my hand in her own. She wipes my tears with her other.

And we keep moving.

Fifty-Three

*S*t. *Louis, MO* - Supporters of The Human Movement have gathered by the hundreds on the tarmac of the St. Louis International Airport for the past three weeks, preparing for their departure that will commence in one week. The team, which had originally planned to repair the aqueduct system feeding southern California, are now on a much bigger rescue mission. The golden coast must be evacuated due to warnings delivered by the Guild's Disaster Notification System: an Oceanic Subduction predicted to impact all Pacific coastlines and islands, world-wide.

While evacuation efforts have commenced in earnest, worldwide, it's anyone's guess whether Gabe Dumas and The Human Movement will manage to convince the estimated twenty million residents remaining in California to leave, and whether they will accomplish it within the two-month safe window of time allotted before the subduction is expected to begin. Prior efforts to offer assistance to California have been met with hostility and violence. National Guard were pushed back by armed residents in the desert. Helicopters have been shot down. Relief caravans have met the same treatment. Communication has been ignored.

In the last couple months, satellite images have revealed that all roads into both southern and northern California have been blocked off. As the severe drought continues, reserves are nearly depleted, likely forcing residents to travel further and further north to obtain water. The most imminent threat to residents, however, are the widespread, spontaneous brush fires, which have already taken seventy percent of the Central Valley, the agricultural heart of California, which joins the north and the south, while simultaneously cutting off water transport routes.

Gabe Dumas has been almost universally criticized for choosing such a dangerous and monumental task as The Human Movement's first official relief effort. Many believe that THM has bitten off more than they can chew, and that their trek into California will result in the ultimate end of THM. Gabe Dumas has offered little official comment, but when questioned, his answer has been the same: "Humans lead from the front. It is the Guild that leads from behind."

I sigh, sliding the computer off of my lap and resting my mug of ginger tea on the arm of the couch. I lay my head back. I know better than to read this stuff. My head starts going crazy with all the awful possibilities. This is out of control. California has become... the North Korea of America, but way worse.

Gabriel may not come back from this...

It's a struggle to believe in him in the midst of the facts. I know I should, but he's so far away. The memory of what I witnessed in Chicago three weeks ago has faded, so it's growing too easy to fall prey to my own doubts. If I could just see him... one last time. Experience his emotional rhythms coursing though me again. I think I could regain that faith in him. I could endure the next two months if I could just see him...

But it won't happen. I'm not just stuck in New York; I'm stuck in this apartment. My weeks have been far from idle though. I've spent most of it in the energy world working toward answers. I have a penthouse apartment, with wide windows on three sides. The energy world view from up here is stunning, and my one major discovery is that life forces shine with varying brilliance. It's not noticeable up close because it's like having two light bulbs right in your eyes and trying to determine which has more wattage. After spending several hours watching pedestrians from here, I've noticed on three separate occasions life forces so dim they're easy to overlook entirely. I wonder if these life forces would look any different up close, but without being able to leave, answering that is out of the question.

When I'm not in the energy world, I'm in conference calls with the Council. The issues are never-ending. The details to be worked out at the end of every conclusion just keep piling up. It's the most stressful, most exhausting thing I have ever done. The endurance I now know it requires has softened me toward my fellow Councilmembers though. They've been doing this for years with no break, and this job is easily a hundred times harder than being a public speaker. It's fortunate that the media was in such a frenzy over the latest Grid prediction, because they didn't hound me too much for interviews at first. That first week here was so hard, and I wasn't in a good mood for most of it.

But once the dust settled and I got up to date on most things happening with the Guild, I consented to a handful of interviews in my apartment. When asked about The Human Movement, I would reply: "we'll see." Because I couldn't answer honestly. They still remembered Chicago though, mostly thanks to the ten-page spread that appeared in TIME Magazine exactly one week ago. Still photos of what is being called 'The Fist Dance' between Dumas and me were captured by one of the reporters present. They're beautiful, and every time I look at them them, they move me. My explanation when asked about it has been that it was intended to relay a story and not necessarily a single idea. "I leave the rest up to you," I tell them. Video of the famous moment has been spread far and wide, but TIME's wordless article was my favorite. The cover even featured a stunning profile photo of Dumas and myself at the end, facing one another directly, our fingers laced. I would probably hang it in my apartment if I could get away with it.

The thing nagging me the most has been my brother. I want to find out what became of him, and it's strange and unsettling and even outrageous to what's left of my old self to realize that I have zero resources to look into his whereabouts. I am the most famous Prime Human in the world both in and out of the Guild, and I own nothing. I have nothing. I relinquished even my past. I have become as Shiah ordered me from the beginning: I am the Guild. All the power that I have is consecrated toward protecting them and furthering our mission. To breach the trust of the Prime Humans who affirm my position by commandeering Guild resources for my own personal endeavors is out of the question. My only hope is that one of the few operatives I contacted about finding my brother can work a miracle as a favor, or that the PHIA recovery team can track down what is left of PHIA, and therefore lead to Ezra.

This has been an awful realization, and I have not struggled like this with my Guild membership ever. Even after St. Louis, my struggle was more about ideals and conscience. This is about my own flesh and blood. Until now, I have not had a moment's regret over killing Andre. But it is *because* I killed Andre that

I am now stuck here in an ivory tower, unable to use the only thing I can call my own—my own body—to go find Ezra myself.

I sigh. Except it's not really mine. I chose to bodily turn myself in rather than run so that the Guild would not have to take the backlash of my actions. Even my body belongs to the Guild...

I hear the front door unlocking and I turn around eagerly. Shiah went to bully the prosecutor and then the court about my trial date this morning, and I have no doubt she succeeded in finally hammering it down. I need this over. Like yesterday.

"Good Morning, Wendy," Shiah says brightly. "Someone is here to see you." She opens the door widely and steps to the side.

Through the door walks a man, maybe in his thirties, brown hair, clean-shaven. He wears a pair of trendy wooden, square-rimmed glasses, which he adjusts before extending his hand toward me and saying, "Councilwoman Wendy. It's an honor to meet you. I'm Ben Feldt."

I jump over to him. "Oh! Ben! Yes, hi! I was just thinking about you!" I meet his hand with my own. "Thank you for coming all the way out here."

"My pleasure," he says, and I can tell from his emotions that he's slightly intimidated by me, but he's making a concerted effort to not let that show. That's pretty much how *all* Guild members treat me.

"Sit, sit," I say, motioning toward a chair and taking the nearby couch.

He does, sitting on the edge of it and adjusting his glasses again.

"First of all," I say, "I want to state up front that you have no obligation. This is a personal matter, and I've been on the hunt for someone with the ability to help me. Your name was brought up to me by my dyad, Chase. He was the one that told me that you had been working on expanding your capability. I wouldn't have known otherwise."

"I understand," Ben says, and then he laughs nervously. "But I hope you won't mind me saying that the obligation is still there. I kind of feel like you've taken the fall and the flack for all of us in public, and so I was actually really excited at the prospect of being able to return the favor."

My angst this morning over all that I have given up fades in an instant. "Thank you," I say genuinely, meaning it deep in my soul.

"Okay, so my understanding is that you believe your brother may still be alive," Ben says. "You want me to use you to try to establish a secondary connection to him so that we can pinpoint whether that's true. That should be fairly easy, although there are limitations."

"There always are," I sigh, taking my mug back up for comfort.

"One, of course, is if he is on the water, or very near the water, it will make it very hard if not impossible to pick up on him. The closer he is to water, the closer I have to be to *him* to pick him up. If he's in another country outside of North America, impossible."

"That's not surprising. But if you learn he is alive, will you be able to help locate him?"

"Maybe. We'll start with the first goal for now."

I nod eagerly. "Okay."

"First, I need to take an emotional sample. I need you to tell me about your brother, things that draw out a strong emotional reaction on your part."

I put my tea down, searching my cobwebbed memory for something that will do the job.

I start off by telling him about how Ezra ended up being my responsibility, what it felt like after my mom died and I realized it was just him and me. I tell him about Ezra's obsession with finding ways to make my life easier without me catching on. And maybe, because I was just thinking about giving my life up for the Guild, I tell Ben about getting in a huge fight with Ezra when he accused me of revolving my life around him. I started sobbing in the middle of it, because to me, Ezra was everything. He was my reason, my motivation, my purpose. And maybe that wasn't healthy, but it had saved me from a cycle that was even *more* unhealthy. And he was telling me to stop the thing that was keeping my head above water. Ezra hated it when I cried. It terrified him. So he dropped it and never ever mentioned it again.

I sigh, and I wipe a tear from my eye. "People would probably say I raised my brother," I finish. "But *he* raised *me*."

Ben, I realize, has his eyes closed. I don't know if I should keep talking, but he's concentrating intently. I suppose he'll cue me if need be. Shiah has been standing at the window, her back to me, hands clasped behind herself, silent. Listening no doubt.

"He's alive," Ben says finally.

I jerk my head back in his direction, eyes widening, heart pounding.

He's nodding. "Definitely. I know your next question is whether we can find him. I'm new at secondary connections," Ben apologizes. "So while normally I can tell how far away someone is, I am not nearly so accurate with secondaries. I think it's because the emotional bonds between people vary and I easily confuse them with distance. In your case, I can tell you he's west." Ben points out the window where Shiah stands. "He could be close with a very weak bond, far with a very strong bond, or any variation of that. That's why I can't really tell you distance. Does that make sense?"

My chest inflates with so much hope that it overflows my eyes again. I wipe them with the heels of my hands. I nod, because I haven't found my voice yet.

He's alive. Ezra is *alive.*

I nod, trying to get it together, but relief keeps rushing at me and I can't rein it in. Shiah is nearby suddenly, and she pulls me up and wraps her arms around me because I'm sobbing now.

Relief becomes gratitude and gratitude becomes happiness. The unexpected outpouring of emotions doesn't seem to be anywhere near completion. I let go of Shiah and come at Ben, pulling him up so I can hug him and sob out incoherent thank yous.

Then I'm laughing and crying. Smiling and wiping my eyes repeatedly.

"You don't know..." I gasp finally. "You can't imagine what this means to me, Ben. Thank you. Thank you so much."

"You are very welcome," Ben says, stunned and uncomfortable with my outburst.

I go over to the window, put my hands on it and look west. "I promise I will find you," I whisper, imagining my brother somewhere far away, maybe looking up because he feels Ben's 'eyes' on him.

"You work in agriculture research?" Shiah says to Ben from behind me. "Why?"

I turn around to find Shiah standing next to Ben, looking down at her tablet. Ben is adjusting his glasses again. "That's actually where my education is. There aren't a *whole lot* of applications for my life force ability. I get used in provisional missions sometimes. I started honing my life force ability in hopes that I could help refugees locate family members they'd been separated from."

I come back over to Ben and Shiah, about to make that hope happen right here and now, but before I can speak Shiah says, "That is an admirable cause, and one that we can most definitely make happen at some point in the future. For now, we have a greater need you can fill that will utilize your life force ability directly. What do you think about another provisional assignment?"

"I'm always up for a change of pace," Ben replies.

"How long can you retain emotional trails of secondary connections?"

"Depends on how much of an impression they left on me. Two weeks to a month."

"Good. I'm recommending you to Councilman Kasappa for the PHIA recovery team," Shiah says. "Councilman Wendy's brother was known to have been abducted by PHIA, and we have reason to believe he is still being held captive. I believe if you follow his emotional trail and find Ezra Whitley, you will also find PHIA. Are you up to the task, Mr. Feldt?"

Ben is blinking in shock. I'm staggered. A mission like that would most likely take him right into California, and the man works in agriculture, not the militia. I can only imagine what's going through Ben's head right now. A favor to me just turned into a job offer, although with how Shiah is using her 'do what I say' scary voice, it sounds less like an offer and more like an order that will involve punishment if he refuses.

"There is every possibility that the trail will lead into California," Shiah says without even looking up as she types something one-handed. I'm sure she said it because she discerned his reservations—as well as my own—using that disturbing mind-reading thing she does. "You'll be teamed with extremely capable operatives. Lainey Flynn and Hannah Somerset have already captured five moles within the Guild using their abilities, which are similar to yours. Kiera Johnson is new to the team, and she has proven invaluable during interrogations, but her skill set is widely applicable. I believe, Mr. Feldt, that you are the missing link we've been looking for. Your contribution will finally allow us to close PHIA's chapter once and for all."

She lowers her tablet and looks at him and then me. "Councilwoman? What do you think?"

I almost laugh because it doesn't actually matter what I think. Shiah will do what Shiah believes needs to be done, regardless of anyone else's opinion.

I glance at Ben as if sizing him up. I nod thoughtfully as if approving of what I see. "You are suited to the task, Mr. Feldt. The Council would agree, therefore you are summoned to assist with this priority Guild matter. Do you accept?"

Ben's eyes dart between me and Shiah. "Yes," he replies. "Whatever you need. Shutting PHIA down would be amazing for the Guild."

"Report to Councilman Kasappa at the Vault tomorrow," Shiah says. "I've emailed your flight itinerary and advised your supervisor of the temporary reassignment."

"O-Okay," Ben says.

I hold out a hand and smile. "Thank you for ensuring the safety of the Guild, Ben."

He shakes my hand and then Shiah escorts him to the door.

I'm sniggering and shaking my head when Shiah turns around.

She lifts an eyebrow.

"I'm pretty sure he's in the elevator on the way down, wondering what just happened to him," I say. "He's pretty timid. You sure he's cut out for the PHIA recovery team?"

"Oh no. He's about as adventurous as vanilla ice-cream," Shiah says. "And naive to boot. Tracking down missing family members of refugees? Such a mission is *equally* if not more dangerous than this one. He simply said it to impress you."

I look at her with confusion. "Then why on earth did you put the poor man on the recovery team and then send them into California? He's going to wet himself."

"How else would you be allowed to put forth Guild resources to track down your brother?" she says. "He doesn't have to do anything but lead the way. He might wet himself, but he'll return a hero when PHIA is extinguished. And most importantly, you will have your brother back."

I pause, overcome. "You did that for me," I state.

She turns and walks back over to the window, looking west as I just did.

"Shiah?"

When I approach her I sense reservation, which is an odd emotion coming from her.

"What is it?" I say.

"I have something I need to tell you," she says, bowing her head. "You may think less of me, and I don't like that prospect."

She frowns in consternation. "This is an uncomfortable feeling."

"When have I ever thought less of you? Sometimes you say things that bother me because I don't understand them, but I know that if I'll just be patient, they will eventually make sense."

"This... may not fit that bill."

"Why so?" I say, starting to worry.

"Because it still does not entirely make sense to *me*. I have never been so uncertain in my whole life." Her brow furrows. "No wonder people shy away from uncertainty."

"Oh boy," I say nervously. "You're freaking me out. Can you just tell me already?"

She reaches for my hand and pulls me over to the couch. She presses me to sit and then perches on the edge of the coffee table in front of me, her knees touching mine.

"I lost six years, just as Mike did," she says.

My breath leaves me.

"I know for sure that I became Mike and Andre's direct superior during at least some of that time. I have spent considerable time piecing together evidence and the accounts of others. I have an easier time making sense of very little, so it would not serve you to ask how I know these things. You only need to know the conclusions, which are these: I assigned Mike and Andre with the task of locating you. I chose them because of their personalities— Andre because of his willingness to work outside the system, Mike because of his compassion and obedience. I also know that I was the one to erase the Guild servers as well as all electronic evidence of your past. I know my own handiwork and it is unmistakable. And it is clear, based on the chalk-lines of missing information, that I was out to erase *you*."

I shudder, eyes wide. The obvious response is 'Why?' but this is Shiah. She knows what my next question is. I don't have to do anything but sit here and wait for her to conclude.

"I don't know why," Shiah whispers. "And I know that answer doesn't satisfy you. I was obviously out to find you for a long time, and it appears that once I found you, I then purposely lost you. If I am the one that erased memories, I have no idea how I would have done it. I don't know if I was working with someone else, but evidence points to me collaborating with Andre in some way."

Shiah looks down at her hands clasped over her knees. "I know what I hope. I hope that when Andre defected and began murdering Primes that I erased you in order to protect you." She looks up at my face finally. "I know you want to know why I didn't tell you of my memory loss. The answer is that I knew from the start that, in the very least, I'd had a hand in the missing data. I felt at the time that if I had done that, it must have been for good reason. I do not… question myself as other people do. Whatever I had left behind, I trusted that I ought to leave it. I suppose you could say I trusted my past decisions."

"What made you decide to tell me?" I ask.

"The Detritus Benefit Mike mentioned is when my memory loss began. I did not oversee Mike at that time, but I knew we had operatives there, in search of someone on the missing Primes list. I wasn't involved in that. But I was there because I had gotten a call from a certain high-profile Prime Human who had never joined the Guild. He wanted to meet with me there, so I made plans to go. But I have no recollection of what transpired." She looks at me meaningfully. "The Prime Human I went there to meet was your uncle, Robert Haricott."

My mouth falls open.

"When Mike mentioned that he met you there, but at the time didn't know your true identity, that's when things came together. Mike was there looking for the daughter of Carl Haricott. I was there to *meet* with Carl's brother… The coincidences just would not be ignored. I couldn't *help* drawing conclusions with so many interconnected facts staring me in the face. If I'm going to tackle the past, however, I can't do it halfway. So that is what I have been doing since then. Wendy, the memory loss revolved around you. I am certain of that. I have deduced that the Councilmembers lost the memories that related to or touched on you, which means that at some point they must have known your whereabouts. At some point, you were no longer missing."

"My uncle was at Detritus six years ago… Do you think he…"

"Knew you were there?" Shiah says. "I'd say so. Robert Haricott was nothing if not purposeful in all that he did. But I wouldn't have known it at the time. As I said, I wasn't aware that our operatives were there searching for Robert's niece. But based on my belief that you were the memory that was erased, I think that night began my interest in finding you. That is when I took over Andre and Mike's team. Six years later I erased everything I had found, everything relating to you. I am… afraid to know why I would do something so drastic."

I stare at her, unblinking. "Wow," I say.

"But I will uncover the truth, Wendy, one way or another."

I look at her. "I don't expect you to do that. I've let go of the past."

She smiles softly. "I know. But once I began to uncover pieces, I realized something: If I had wanted to completely eradicate knowledge of your existence, I did a poor job. I had to have known that as I was leaving a trail. Which means that though I erased you, I expected that one day I would be faced with the need to find you again. I know I did not intend the knowledge of the past to be gone forever. So I am uncovering the truth because it is the right time. And today, upon learning that your brother is indeed alive, and then witnessing your relief, I was faced with the reality that your suffering was most likely caused by me. To find him is my act of contrition. I *will* make this right."

I reach out and put my hand on top of hers. "I trust you, Shiah."

She blinks back tears. "Believe it or not, that matters to me. Especially now. Thank you."

"You're welcome."

Fifty-Four

*T*his moping Wendy is my least favorite version," Shiah says from the kitchen behind me.

I ignore her and continue staring out the window at nothing, chin on the back of an armchair.

"I agree," Mike says. "You'd think the fact that she's going on trial for murder in four days would put a smile on her face."

I turn my head to give him a derisive look. "You are not as funny as you think you are."

"Awww, come on, Wen," Mike says apologetically. "Give me some credit for *trying* to put a smile on your face."

"*I* know who would put a smile on her face," Shiah mocks.

Mike snorts. "We *both* know that, Shiah. I was trying not to bring it up."

I sigh, but my chest is full of rocks. Each day it gets harder to breathe than the last. The countdown to Gabriel's departure is excruciating. We're in what feels like the final seconds until a standoff. He will leave Missouri in two days. I wonder, will this anxiety go away once he's gone?

I don't think so. It feels like it's never going away.

"Why?" Shiah says. "He's leaving, and she's going to have to bounce back."

"Damn, Shiah. Have a little sensitivity. She has a right to be worried. Even I'm on edge. I might lose him. I'd like to go there and slap some sense into him, tell him how stupid this is for him to go into a place that would rather kill him than let him get five words out. But I can't. And he won't listen anyway. Nothing about this situation is easy."

"The Guild needs her," Shiah replies.

Her answer makes me angry. They don't just need *me*. They need the version of me that doesn't feel like the world is out of her control. Gabriel's distance is changing my entire landscape, and pretty soon he will be in another world altogether. Why does everything around me matter less and less? When he's gone will I care at all? The Guild needs me. But I need him.

I stand up abruptly and turn around. "I've got to say goodbye, Shiah."

Her spoonful of yogurt stops halfway on the way to her mouth. "You know you can't leave New York," she says, not missing a beat.

I watch her spoon resume travel to her mouth. "I know you can make this happen."

She turns the spoon upside down in her mouth and pulls it out with slow exaggeration. "You're asking me to break the law for you," she says. "I have been under the impression you want to do this legitimately."

"This is totally legitimate," I say, crossing the floor of the apartment and putting my hands on the counter. "I've been indicted for murder. I want you to help me sneak out so I can see my boyfriend. And I'm not asking you to use the Guild's clout to circumvent the justice system. How much more legitimately normal can you get?"

She lifts an eyebrow. "Your boyfriend? Is he aware of his status?"

"I doubt he would argue with the terminology," Mike says from the chair next to Shiah.

"Your words. Not mine." I stare at her with undaunted expectation.

Her shoulders slump in resignation.

I throw my hands up and squeal. "Thank you!"

"For the record," Shiah says. "There is likely nothing I wouldn't do for you. But thank you for making it at least appear that you had to work for it."

I come round the counter and throw my arms around her. "You are the absolute *best.*"

"I know."

Mike laughs.

"How long do you think it will take you to come up with something?" I say.

"I already did. I have a disguise for you already in the bathroom, and the operatives to help should be here within the hour. Don't worry about the Council. I've got it covered."

My eyes go wide. "Agh! I hate you!"

Mike sniggers. "Shiah nails it again."

She grins. "I was getting a little worried you weren't going to ask though. You sure waited until the last minute. It's a good thing I prepared or there would be no way to arrange to get you to Missouri before tomorrow on such short notice."

I look from Mike to Shiah, realizing their conversation was a setup to bug me on purpose. "You guys totally wanted to see me beg for it, didn't you?" I say.

"I don't think you know *how* to beg," Mike says. "You only know how to demand."

"Shut up," I say, simpering at him. "You guys just want me out of here so you can have the whole apartment to yourselves."

Shiah chuckles. "I have an assignment for Mike while you're gone. Now go change."

I push off the counter and over my shoulder say, "He's *my* employee, Shiah. All provisional assignments go through me."

"Not this one," she says.

I laugh and close the bathroom door behind me. I stop short when I see the disguise Shiah picked out laying on the counter. I have a moment of flashbacks, but then I shake my head and change. I wouldn't expect anything less from Shiah.

When I emerge from the bathroom, I pull the tan, knee-length, leather trench coat up over my shoulders and say, "It's weird. I even *feel* like the old Wendy Whitley." I run my fingers through the wig's tresses. "You even got my color and texture matched perfectly."

Mike gives me a once-over. "You had long red hair?" he says, shaking his head. "Damn, woman. Gabe is going to flip."

"What do you think of the clothes?" Shiah says, the corner of her mouth curving.

"You mean these exact replicas of what I showed up at the hospital wearing?" I say holding out one boot-clad foot. Combat boots. Skinny jeans. A white tank over a black bra. And the trench coat of course. "Genius," I say, fingering the coat. "I'm disguising myself as... my old self."

She folds her arms, tilts her head, her hair swaying silkily like it always does. "If I knew you before, I wish I remembered," she says.

"I used to wish that as well," I say. "But I like this version of myself. A lot. My past self can't possibly compare. Although evidence supports she was probably more capable with a gun than me. But that's easy enough to rectify."

"There can never be too many versions of Wendy Whitley," Shiah says. "You would be incredible in every one of them."

I throw my arms around her again. "I love you, Shiah. I don't know how I deserved to have you think so highly of me, but I swear the whole reason I have fought so hard to be where I am is because I didn't want to let you down." I pull my face away from her shoulder. "I'd follow you anywhere. I'm kind of obsessed with you, actually. I'd do anything you asked."

"I know," she says, holding my hand. "That's why I don't tell you what to do as often as possible. That being said, I *am* going to ask something of you this time."

I lift my eyebrows expectantly.

"Return from your visit," she says. "Because you're going to want to go with him. And you have important things to do here. The Guild is still in need of solid leadership, and you're on the Council. That's not a small thing. He'll be back. I believe this, and so should you. And by then you'll be a free woman. It will be a lot easier to sneak you out to see him then."

"I promise," I say.

"Also, try to live through the next two days without getting killed or kidnapped or injured," Mike says. "And don't murder anyone either."

I snort and laugh before throwing my arms around him. "Only for you, Mike. Don't want you losing your job—oh wait, I'm the only one that can actually fire you now."

"Also," Shiah says, standing up and going over to where her bag is hanging in the closet. "This is for Dumas." She holds out a manilla envelope.

"What is it?" I ask, taking it from her.

"The DNA results from the samples he provided."

I test the weight of the envelope in my hand, expecting it to feel heavier.

I also expect her to tell me the results, and when she doesn't, I say, "Do I want to know?"

She shrugs. "I don't know. I haven't looked at them."

"Why?" I say, furrowing my brow.

"Because I'm not on the Council. You are. I'm handing over custody of the information. I'm sure I'll find out once you share it with the Council. But I thought it would be nice if you could share it with *him* first. It belongs to him, after all."

"Sure took a while to get them," I say.

"I've been holding them for weeks," she says. "Waiting for today."

"God, I love you," I sigh, tucking the envelope in the backpack Shiah has ready for me.

"I'll see you in two days," she says. "I have your schedule mapped out by the minute. Follow it."

Someone knocks on the door.

"Ready?" she smiles.

"Totally."

Fifty-Five

I step off the small plane under an umbrella, adjust my fashion geek glasses, and follow the line of passengers toward the terminal. It's pitch dark and pouring rain in St. Louis where The Human Movement has been gathering for the last couple weeks. They'll be traveling in buses to a second gathering point in southern Utah. It's there that most of them will stay to organize the first of several camps to receive evacuees. Gabriel will lead a second team into California.

Supplies have been donated from all over the nation and are being transported by trucks to follow the massive caravan carrying some five hundred volunteers. More trucks will follow as food and supplies are collected at Human Movement events happening in the meantime, nationwide. For the next two days, however, THM's gathering grounds are actually here at the airport on one of the airstrips. I'm traveling solo, under the guise of taking part in The Human Movement's exodus.

No one has looked twice at me on this trip, and my story has been that I'm from West Virginia, and I spent my savings to be here. There are signs directing THM volunteers, and I follow them, my heart in my throat.

My phone rings suddenly, startling me. I dig in my bag for it, knowing it can't be Shiah or Mike. They know not to call. And Shiah said the Council won't bother me either. I look at the caller ID to see that it's Ohr. I panic for a second, thinking he must know I'm here, but he can't possibly. I bet this is about my egg donation last week. He actually came *to* New York to harvest them.

I recede from the main thoroughfare, into a secluded corner of the terminal. "Hello," I say into the phone.

"Greetings, Councilwoman. How is New York treating you?"

"Pretty good," I say. "What's up?"

"I wanted to ask a favor of you."

"What's that?"

"First, I have some information for you that you may find… upsetting."

"What's that?"

"Every one of the ovum you donated is non-viable. You are, in-effect, sterile."

My mouth opens in surprise. *Sterile?* How? I gave birth when I was sixteen. I obviously wasn't sterile *then.*

"I'm sorry to be the one to break the news. I know it can be very difficult for some."

"I… um… Thank you for telling me," I manage. "Do you know the cause?"

"A Guild-manufactured fertility drug. It's something we give terminal hypno-touch patients to protect their reproductive systems so that their gametes are not compromised by their end-of-life medications. It's powerful, and cells must be harvested within six months to maintain their viability, which it will eventually destroy entirely."

"I'm guessing there's no record of me getting it," I say.

"Correct. But the damage it did to your reproductive cells is unique to that drug, therefore unmistakable."

"Is there some other reason I would have had it?"

"Not that I can imagine. The drug is designed to protect your reproductive system, particularly against drugs that would destroy it, like chemotherapy. Remember I told you that seed-generation sickness often manifests as cancer. Councilwoman, I believe that's your answer. You remember having hypno-touch almost three years ago, and I told you that it usually affects Primes within a year. If I were to bet money, I'd bet you were ill, and you took the drug to protect your eggs. Perhaps you even had them harvested. I don't know. But if you had seed-generation sickness, yet you are alive, the only explanation is that you cured yourself. It would be the first and only case we have record of someone surviving such a thing."

It's clear from his voice that Ohr is impressed. I'm impressed, too. And it rejuvenates my commitment to researching all I can in the energy world, because if my past self learned how to *undo* life force manipulation yet kept my hypno-touch-given abilities, (like enhanced senses and channeling), intact, then I must have had some serious knowledge about the energy world. It means I essentially gave myself new abilities. It means I can give anyone abilities that way, in the same way Ohr plans to use stem cell technology.

"I am sure you can read into the significance," Ohr says.

"Yeah," I say, although my ultimate conclusion is of far more importance than his obvious interest: Unlike now, I knew what the hell I was doing in the energy world before I lost my memory. I am now in a competition with my past self. Answers are out there. I just have to work harder to find them. Hope surges through me. "Thanks for telling me," I say.

"You're welcome. And now, my favor. I'd like to harvest some of your non-reproductive stem cells."

So... he's going to figure out how to use my DNA to give other people my ability one way or another. I still haven't figured out how I feel about his plans to give people abilities at will. Unlike last time, when donating my ova was a duty spelled out in writing, this is entirely at my discretion. So I better figure out my stance. No passive decision-making this time.

"I'll consider it," I say.

"How long should I expect?" he asks.

Great. He's going to nail me down. "Until after my trial."

"Very well. Thank you for your time, Councilwoman. You're in good hands with this trial."

"I know," I say. "Have a nice day."

I hang up, and stare at the floor, revisiting the conversation in my head. A new, extremely comforting thought comes to mind: Andre was definitely lying about a child. If I'm sterile, there's no way I had a child.

"Suck it, Andre," I say victoriously under my breath.

"I like the look," a deep voice says from nearby.

I nearly jump out of my skin.

"Porter!" I say, recognizing the giant black man with the bald head and epic beard, leaning against the wall about ten feet away. "Scared the junk out of me."

"What you doin' here?" he says in a quieter voice, coming closer until all six and a half feet of him is standing right over me. "And without Big Mick? This place ain't exactly friendly to Primes."

"That's why he's not here," I murmur. "And why I'm dressed like this."

"Long way to travel alone," Porter says, eyes twinkling. "You here to see somebody?"

I give him a look. "You know I am. Quit playing dumb and help me get him alone."

He scratches his beard, eyes narrowing in consternation, as if he's not sure about my motives. It's a total show though. He has every intention of helping me. And he nods his head at me as he turns around and starts walking.

I scamper after him, gripping the straps of my backpack under my thumbs. We don't go far. A large group is gathered at the end of the terminal, most of them camped out on the floor, and at the very center is Gabriel.

My pulse jumps and I stop next to Porter, watching Gabriel locked in conversation with the smaller group at the center. On television, where I usually see him, he is movie-star attractive, but television, to me, is grainy compared to my own vision. So in person, even from this far away, the details of his features make him more… real. More present. And the reality of him… My heart once more overcomes my head, which likes to talk me into believing that my memory is distorted, that he's not as wonderful as I've convinced myself.

The group he's in has a map spread out on the floor, laptops and tablets in everyone's hands. I listen to them for a moment and realize they're planning backup routes to get into LA. I just had a virtual meeting with the Council earlier this week about this. The fires are out of control. The place is burning to the ground. We were discussing having THM's route cleared of fires ahead of time. The helicopters with flame retardant will be dispatched tomorrow, but the entire effort is being kept secret so THM doesn't get resentful of the help. There are actually several Prime Human operatives already planted to take part in the exodus and to report back to the Guild. THM *definitely* does not need to know that.

Gabriel's eyes shift around the terminal when someone else starts talking. They stop abruptly on me and his entire being goes still as he stares. I guess my disguise isn't *that* good if both Porter *and* Gabriel recognize me immediately in it. Maybe I should switch back to sunglasses even though it's dark outside. I even wore a lot more makeup than usual to help my disguise.

"You're welcome," Porter says.

"For what?"

"Getting his attention."

"You didn't do anything but stand there," I say, now worried that everyone in the room can see through my disguise.

"Exactly," he replies. "You should go sit down somewhere out of the way. You look suspicious next to me."

"Whatever," I grumble, hoisting my backpack higher and making my way to a far corner and plopping down. If Gabriel wants to see me, he now knows I'm here. For the first time I worry he won't *want* to see me. What if I traveled all this way and the best I get is a stare across the room? He hasn't called Shiah even once since Chicago. I spend a few minutes drowning in self-doubt when suddenly, a pair of familiar high-tops appear in front of me.

I look up into Tonya's face. She's pursing her lips, looking like she's suppressing a laugh. "Another Gabe Dumas fan girl? Ya'll needs ta start a Facebook page or somethin' instead'a comin' out here. This ain't The Bachelor. I ain't gon' have time to spend keepin' yo asses outta trouble."

"Seriously?" I say dryly.

"New arrivals. Over here," she says nodding her head to the side.

I hop to my feet as she mumbles, "Least you ain't wearin' white fo' once."

Afraid to look around lest I make myself appear even more suspicious, I follow Tonya with eyes on my feet, playing the part of docile new arrival as much as I can.

We head back the direction I came with Porter. Tonya unlocks a door, which leads to a hallway. She leads me down it, stopping and pushing open another door to what looks like an employee break room. "Wait here," she says, and then gives my outfit a once-over. "I like this," she says, nodding. "More you." Then she leaves without another word.

I look around, noticing that it's more than a break room. There are beds made up on the floor at the far end, belongings arranged in various locations. I perch on one of the chairs, anxiety threatening to become nausea.

Needing to give my hands something to do, I stand up, pull off my coat, and grab a rag from the sink. I start wiping down the tables, and then the counter by the sink. I open the fridge next to it and start wiping out the inside, grateful for something to keep me busy, because it seems I'm going to be here for a while.

I rinse my rag and start scrubbing the sink itself.

Once I'm done, I search the room for something else to do, and it's only then that I realize I'm not alone. Gabriel Dumas is leaning against the closed door, watching me, a slight smile on his face.

For the second time today, I attempt to jump out of my skin. "How long have you been standing there?" I say, wondering why it is I can't multi-task with my super senses. That would be really useful...

"I don't know," he says. "I lost track of time watching you."

Butterflies. Lots of them. I bite my lip, unable to prevent myself from looking longingly at him. He's dressed casually in jeans and a fitted dark green T-shirt. I've got to stop gawking...

"I have something for you," I say in a rush, nervous for who knows what reason. This is Gabriel. Why am I acting like we don't know each other?

"Aside from the surprise of a personal visit?" he says.

I walk over to my backpack, which I left on the table. I unbuckle the flap and pull out the envelope. I put it on the table between us.

"Your DNA results," I say. "No one on the Council has seen them yet." I want him to know I respect him enough to let him see them first.

His eyes rest on the envelope for only a moment before moving back to me. He's out of range, so I don't know what his reaction is. His face reveals nothing.

He tilts his head. "Why are you so nervous?"

"Hell if I know," I say, pushing my glasses up again and wrapping my arms around my middle and looking up and away.

"Did you only come to deliver the results?"

"Of course not. I broke my bail agreement by crossing state lines. I disguised myself and lied about my identity and made my people lie so I could get out of New York without anyone knowing." I look at him finally. "Are you going to call the cops on me?"

He bows his head and rubs the back of his neck with a hand, looking at me charmingly through his eyelashes. "Why would you do such a thing?"

I smile. "Because I make exceptions. So? Are you going to turn me in? Or will you make an exception for me?"

His face goes serious. "Wendy, you *are* my exception."

My breath gets caught in my throat. "Would you break rules for me?" I whisper.

"With the exception of violent crime, I would break *every* rule for you. If you asked."

I lean against the fridge, hands tucked behind me, struggling to breathe when my heart is taking up my entire chest. "I wouldn't ask you to do that," I say, knowing it's true.

"That's why you're my exception."

Our eyes rest on one another, and it's like the last time we looked at each other this way, back in Raleigh. I come unglued, wishing with every particle of my being that I could be in his arms and that I'd never have to leave.

"This isn't fair," I whisper pathetically.

"What do you want to do?" he asks.

A hundred things come to mind, most of them not right to ask. Actually, none of them are. "I came to see you off," I say, ignoring his question. "I don't know when we'll see each other again, and I didn't want you to leave without me telling you, face-to-face, how much Chicago meant to me."

"I've wanted to call. A thousand times."

"Why didn't you?"

"I'm afraid of you."

"Why?" I say, surprised.

"Because you're my exception, and the things I'd do for you scare me." He looks up and around. "These people? They're a bunch of inexperienced zealots with no idea what they're getting into. They see this as summer camp, and me their camp director with inexplicable magic skills beyond simply speaking boldly. They give me far too much credit, and I'm afraid it's going to get them killed, or mutinous in the very least when they realize I'm no sorcerer. I'm taking them into hostile territory. I have no guarantee I can feed them long term. Shelter them. Protect them. I have no clue what I'll find in LA. So many unknowns..." He looks at me. "But I don't care. I commit myself to crazy things in hopes that you will look at me with those eyes that can weigh my soul and... I'm determined to prove myself to you. Every day. It's all I care about. And you know what is so ironic it kills me? These people think it's me they're following. But it's really you." He laughs. "We're all working for the Guild now. And they have no idea." He looks at me again. "Isn't that insanity? But I don't care. Why do I not care? I don't know. And I don't care about that either."

I clear my throat, wishing I had some water to relieve the dryness. I knew he took my advice, but I had no idea... no idea that my hold on him was this strong. And even from across the room I can feel it. The power I sense he's given me frightens me. No wonder Mike told me Gabriel would give up THM for me.

"I thought Humans led from the front," I say softly.

"The Guild is always behind. *You* are the Guild. And *you* are behind everything I do." He laughs without humor. "Why are you doing this, Dumas?" he mocks. "California? Of all the places you could help, you choose the one that doesn't *want* help. Why not North Carolina? South America even? It just doesn't make sense. The only explanation is you're crazy. You're delusional..."

He clasps his fingers over his head, and he closes his eyes. "The logic has left me, so I must be as crazy as they say."

"Then should I leave now?" I say. "So I don't compromise you?"

His eyes pop open, he lowers his hands and shakes his head with exaggeration. "Please don't go."

"I have to leave tomorrow," I say. "My trial starts on Monday."

He puts his forehead in his hands, shakes his head again. He crouches down.

"Don't you want to see the results?" I say, my eyes falling to the untouched envelope on the table. All of that and no mention of his wife...

"No," he says abruptly, looking up. "Can we forget you brought that? At least until you have to go?"

"Okay..."

He stands up again. "Wendy, can I take you out?"

I furrow my brow. "Take me out? Where?"

"St. Louis. I have somewhere I want to take you."

"It's not a good idea for us to be seen in public," I say. "If I'm recognized I'm in big trouble."

"I can make a call. We'll have privacy."

"Where?"

"It's a surprise. Will you go? Just for tonight, can we pretend that none of this is happening? No Guild. No Human Movement. No apocalypse. Me. You. Out on a date. I want to have this one good thing to remember while I'm traversing California, proving myself."

"Yeah," I say, nodding. "I'd like that."

"Allow me a moment," he says, excitement creeping into his voice. "I need to cancel my meeting later, confer with Tranwick. You'll wait?"

"My flight is tomorrow night. I have nowhere else to go," I say.

"Excellent," he says, opening the door, about to go through it but looking back at me like I might change my mind and disappear.

"I'll wait," I assure him.

He nods, shuts the door behind him, and I all but collapse against the fridge. I take off the glasses and rub my face, push my hair back and wish I could take the wig off. It's way too hot in here.

And Shiah was right. I want to stay. I want to travel with him. I want to give up everything I have at the Guild so I don't have to leave him. And for a moment I concoct all the many ways they don't really need me.

My eyes catch on the envelope though, and I remember that Gabriel is married, or was. He had a child. He can't actually be mine until it's all resolved. In fact, he can't be mine at all. Not while the world is falling apart. We both have duties to fulfill. We both hold the loyalties of so many. We have a responsibility to them. And I have the mystery of the energy world. The world needs us, both of us, to give up what we want to save it.

But tonight? Tonight we can have this one thing for ourselves.

Fifty-Six

This is unexpected," I say, staring up from under our large umbrella at the giant concoction of… stuff. Steel wires, beams, tree branches, cement, an airplane fuselage, stone, and all kinds of metal… all pieced together into a playground of sorts—I think. It looks like a hippie's treehouse town, but *huge.* "Is that a giant praying mantis on the roof?"

Gabriel chuckles. "Probably."

"What *is* this place?" I say as we approach the pell-mell entrance under the dim lights. Porter holds the door open for us.

"The City Museum," he replies. "The owners are huge supporters of mine. They shut the place down early and gave me the keys, no questions asked. I don't ever ask such frivolous favors, as a rule. But as you know, you're my exception. We have the place as long as we want."

I squeeze myself to his arm more tightly as the sound of our shoes echo on the floor just inside the entrance. A huge staircase is to the left, ascending several stories. A slide runs the length of it, going three stories up I think. Above is a balcony and eating area next to a concoction of coiled tunnels. Directly ahead is a lot of tile art, a giant whale. A bunch of fabric tassels hang from the ceiling. Even further, a tree house of sorts. Everywhere is something to see, and everything has some personal touch intended to give it character, such as the railing on the stairs: each rung is hand-painted, and totally unique, no rhyme or reason. It's an artistic and architectural wonder.

"Here I was thinking maybe we'd be having a private dinner somewhere," I say. "Instead you take me to…"

"A functional junk yard?" he says. "Would you prefer something more standard?"

"No," I scoff, taking off my coat and wig and glasses and throwing them on the nearby unoccupied check-in counter. "I would prefer everything exactly *not* standard. Let's go!" I take off for the stairs, intent on making a trip down the slide. I expect Gabriel behind me, but instead I hear him shout, "See you at the top!"

He's not at the top when I reach it, but I hear him somewhere. I lean over one of the many balconies, spotting him climbing one of the spiraling iron coil tunnels. It looks like he's crawling through a human-sized slinky.

"I could go down the slide twice before you make it up here!" I say.

"Challenge accepted," he calls.

I run for the slide, throwing myself down its metal surface, and squealing with delight as I descend several stories. Not that the slide is thrilling enough to warrant it, but doing something so childish and free is. I leap up at the bottom and dash for the stairs again, sweating by the time I reach the top. I don't look for Gabriel, certain he's hot on my heels. Instead, I throw myself down the slide again, hooting as I go down.

I'm about to shout my victory at the bottom when I see Gabriel standing above me, holding out a hand to help me up, grinning. "I win."

I take his hand and jump to my feet, and he pulls me toward the whale room. We head for the tree house, and we have to crawl, hands and knees, up to the top of it, which then guides us behind a wall and then into a small dark room with a hole in the floor.

Without warning, he hops into the mouth of the hole with a whoop. I think it's another slide, but man it's steep. And dark. How far does it go? I stick my head down into it, but I can't see a thing.

"Wendy Whitley, the most adored woman in the nation, isn't afraid of a hole in the ground, is she?" Gabriel's voice says barely above a whisper from below, which makes it impossible for me to tell how far down he is.

"Hell no," I say, leaping into the hole without a second thought. "Eeeek," I say as the unknown steals my stomach. But I emerge rather quickly from the chute into another dark room with fabricated cave walls. It's disorienting to have expected a much longer trip only to come up much sooner. Gabriel is nowhere to be found though, and there are two different directions to take. One is a small cave, ascending upward. The other is a larger cave, large enough to walk through slightly hunched. I choose that one.

Dim light shines down on me through glass tiles above my head, and eventually I enter a larger cave room with a gap near the ceiling and several steps to reach it. I climb up through it, coming out of a hole under the whale's belly.

Still no Gabriel. I put my hands on my hips and look around, utterly impressed with the intricate pathways above my head, visible through the curtain of fabric fringes strung from every inch of the ceiling.

So, Gabriel thinks he can hide from me in here? That's funny. I close my eyes and hear footsteps far away and above. I head for a cave opposite the tree house. There's a waterfall and a massive tank of fish here. I go past it and find a sign at the entrance to a dark cave, telling me it's the way to the Enchanted Caves and the ten-story slide. I head that way, which empties into a huge room of fabricated rock walls, wrought iron platforms… and organ pipes? The only direction to go is up. I begin my ascent through the platforms, which spiral around a rock column. I reach a sign pointing me to a three-story slide, and I stop and listen.

The first thing I realize is that this place is absolutely massive, and there are literally openings everywhere, obscuring my directionality. But I'm determined, and with the museum empty of other human sounds I bet I can locate him if I concentrate.

He's climbing. Not here though. Below. I wait to see where he stops, which he does on this level. His footsteps echo across a cavernous space. I give him another minute to find a hiding spot before taking the exit from the caves on this level. It spills into another cavernous hall. To the right is a skate park. To the left, some exhibitions with neon lights, old arcade machines, a train track, a cafe, a giant rocking chair, a statue… basically a random smorgasbord. I stop and listen again.

I pass the arcade, more tubes and tunnels headed who knows where, bound for the far end of this floor. I'm certain he's up here somewhere. He's no longer moving, but I strain over the sound of the rain outside and hear his heartbeat. I stop at a giant wall of old doorknobs under glass. I've never seen so many doorknobs in my life, all different. And definitely old.

I keep walking and finally get why this is called a museum. The room is massive and filled with pieces of stone architecture. Key stones, corner stones, pillars, cornices, and decorative stones of all sizes and shapes. There's even an old elevator car, so ornate I actually pause in my search to marvel at its detailed metalwork. I stop and listen again, certain I'm heading for where Gabriel is. I walk slowly and carefully so as not to alert him I'm near. I want to sneak up on him if I can. I round the corner and find a large bar. It's old and beautiful, mirrors lining the wall behind it.

He's behind it. I'm sure of it. So I creep up slowly, put my hands on the bar's counter and hop up and lay over it. "Boo," I say, startling him crouched behind it.

"Good heavens, Wendy," he says, standing, a look of awe on his face. "I assumed you'd hear my footsteps, but I wasn't moving. Don't tell me you heard me breathing from three floors down."

"No. I heard your heartbeat," I say, propping my elbows on the bar, chin in my hands.

His jaw drops. "Even over the rain?"

"The place is empty. It echoes. Not like rain outside," I say. "If you really wanted to make it hard, you would have hid in one of those gazillion interconnecting tunnels. Or worse, kept moving so I'd have to figure out my way around in order to intercept you. This place is a labyrinth, and you seem to know it well, so that would probably take all night."

"That doesn't sound like any fun at all," he says, coming around to take my hand. "I didn't bring you here to not get to see you."

"Just to test my senses?" I say, grinning.

He looks sheepish. "Admittedly, I was curious."

"There is nowhere in this building you could hide that I wouldn't be able to track you down," I say as our steps echo across the floor. "Unless of course it was full of people. You'd have to be talking then for me to pick you out."

"That's astounding," he says, amazed.

"Where to next?" I say.

"Where would you like to go?"

"Ten-story slide?" I say.

He chuckles. "You have a thing for slides?"

"I have a thing for *you*," I say as we push through the door leading to the caves.

He stops and turns toward me in the dim light. The mix of our emotions has me swaying on my feet. I reach out for him to steady myself, and he catches me up in his arms, holding me close to his chest. I inhale his scent, thinking this date would be complete if we stood here like this all night.

"Aye, Wendy," he breathes. "Holding you is even better than I remember." He brings our joined hands up to his face, resting the back of my hand against his mouth.

"Gabriel," I say against his chest. "I'm letting you know up front that if you don't kiss me before the end of this date, I'm going to hit you."

He chuckles. "Are you? Then what?"

"I'll seduce you inside the whale's rear end," I say matter-of-factly.

He bursts out laughing, hugging me more tightly.

"So?" I say. "You already have a place picked out, right?"

He pulls away to look at me. "Absolutely not. That would imply I've premeditated intimacy. How ghastly."

"I have *definitely* premeditated kissing you," I say. "I visualized it in every dark corner on my way to find you. Right here where we're standing even. And then I imagined locking us in that super cool elevator car and having my way with you."

"You are quite the lorelei, Miss Whitley," he says, raising an eyebrow at me. "And your vocabulary of allurement is expansive. One minute you're fumbling words, and the next you're explaining how you plan to assault me in an elevator car."

"It's you," I say, following the sign that leads us toward another room, one as tall as the building itself. The rain is much louder here, and in the darkness I can make out the massive skylight many stories above us. We begin our ascent up a spiral staircase. "I get around you, inside your head, and it's easy to let my thoughts come out of my mouth. When you're out of range and I have to guess what you feel, I'm a wreck, second-guessing, feeling inadequate. It totally sucks."

"It always intrigues me when you do that. You know how I feel. What am I doing wrong that makes it so easy for you to forget?" he says, trailing me.

"It's not anything *you* do," I sigh. "I've had to hold myself back so much in the media where you're concerned that I worry you'll hate me for denying you in public, for making everything into a strategy of words. For making you look silly on Good Morning America. To you, that's not being true to myself. You, on the other hand, basically spell it out for people. But they don't actually believe it. They think it's some kind of metaphor or strategy. It's so over the top when you talk about me in public that people don't see it for what it is. So I feel bad for not giving you the same public treatment that you give me."

"What about Chicago?" he says. "My words were far from kind."

"I barely remember that part," I say, noticing that the slide itself runs next to us, in a spiral like the staircase we're climbing.

"I called you an imposter. I accused you of being oblivious to the rules. Of staring into Andre's eyes, unflinching, when you shot him. Of cheating the system. Just to name a few."

"It was all true."

He puts a hand on my arm to stop my ascent.

I turn around, one step higher than him so our eyes are just about level. He analyzes my expression, searching for something. He was hoping he was wrong.

"He kidnapped me in my own car," I say. "And then he proceeded to show me footage of my little brother working math problems, locked up somewhere in California. It was timestamped that same day. He said he had Ezra. Alive. He said if I wanted him to stay that way I had to announce to the world that the cause of natural disasters was Prime Humans. He wanted me to start not just a war, but a slaughter. I got the pistol out of my boot that he had overlooked, and when we stopped at the airport, I pulled my gun on him, made him get out of the car. I shot him, brought him down as he ran. I wanted to kill him right then and there. And it wasn't the idea of ending his life that made me hesitate. And the legality sure as hell didn't cross my mind. It was the things he said. 'Your brother will die if *I* do. *I'm* the only one that knows what you forgot.' I was so torn, and I hated that he had that hold over me, that he knew exactly what to say. It felt so violating. And then the last thing he said, 'You'll never see your child if I die.' That's what sealed it. That's what made it easy. Because it didn't matter what, of anything he said, was truth. I'd never know. Nobody would. And I was especially vulnerable because I didn't remember. And he was trying to remake my memories, trying to plant ideas that would give him a hold over me. I have a responsibility toward the Guild, toward humanity. I'm in a place to make a difference. I am a voice of progress on the Council. I'm the key to the energy world. I know my importance. And I couldn't let him compromise me. If I did, it would compromise the whole world."

He's been holding his breath. "Memory... You lost some too then. How much time?" he asks.

"Two and a half years, a little less time than you. It doesn't matter though. I've moved past it."

"Gads," he says.

"If you're hoping I have an ounce of remorse, I don't," I say. "And I fully intend to cheat the system because the world doesn't have the luxury of locking me up. I have an integral purpose. And Shiah is the most powerful Prime Human I've encountered. She can win my case with her eyes closed. As for being an imposter? I was. I did everything I could to make people see us as ordinary people. To make myself seem that way. When people think of the Guild, I want them to think of my face. They know me, so it makes them think they know the Guild, too. But you're right. We're not like you. That's why you've always been wrong. You wanted to change who we are. But who we are? The exclusivity? The secrecy? The mentality that we go by different rules? That's what makes us successful. It's a perception of ourselves, Gabriel. I'm outside of the system, and I full well know it. I take advantage of it. I'm not afraid of anything because of it. It's how, at twenty-two years old, with zero experience, I faced you down at events. It's how I finagled my way onto the Council. It's how I shot Andre and then got in my car and drove away. I'm not afraid of murder charges. Nothing holds me back. I have no rules outside of those within the Guild I swore allegiance to, only trust in my heart, that what I'm doing matters, that it will change things."

He stares at me, wide-eyed, transfixed.

I turn and start my climb again, breathless with the confidence I feel in my own words. "I am the Guild," I say.

"I admire your conviction," Gabriel says, his footsteps falling behind me. "Thank you for helping me understand that part of you."

"But?" I say, picking up his reservation.

"There's no but. There's only me, wishing I could reside in your sphere. You're quite intimidating, did you know that?"

"I've never felt you intimidated."

"Whenever you're near I lose my head and as soon spout poetry than take you on in an argument about ideals. I care nothing for my cause then. I can't even remember what it is. When you are afar, I see you as royalty. Untouchable. Poised. Ready. And completely put together from the inside out. And I think to myself, 'How on earth can I combat someone like that? She's a goddess and everyone knows it.' I feel like you could burn me to the ground with your eyes if you wanted to. You scare me. But I'm a moth to your flame."

I glance over my shoulder. "I feel the same way, you know. You're like… ridiculously brilliant. How many languages do you speak? Twenty? I don't even have a bachelor's degree—I think—and you have two doctoral degrees. And your voice… you have this way of speaking that makes the sound more important than the words. I don't really know how to describe it. Crowds love you. You do something to them in the energy world, Gabriel. They're like… like extensions of you. Or maybe it's the other way around… But it's the most beautiful thing I'ver ever seen there. I have no idea what it means, but you have followers by virtue of *you*. I have followers by virtue of my connections. And good marketing. And Shiah is a PR genius. Well, she's a genius in every realm, actually."

"Shiah…" Gabriel muses. "I'm afraid in my head she's a stern figure lurking in the background that I've subconsciously resented. She's your handler, so I see her as controlling you in that way. And I don't like that."

We reach the top, which is nothing more than a metal cage. The rain is deafening up here, and I turn around. "Shiah is…" My throat catches and I look up as all the emotions I have surrounding Shiah rush forward too quickly for me to catch them. I'm not even sure how to describe Shiah. I have too many words I want to use, but none of them seem quite accurate. I put my hand over my heart. "This is Shiah," I say, patting my chest. Tears come to my eyes anyway. I make incoherent gestures with my hands, striving for words to express how I feel, but they won't come.

He seems to grasp the depth of what I'm trying to communicate, in part. He'd have to know her like I do to really get it though. He's surprised by my intensity though, curious about its origins.

I slow my breathing, regaining my head after letting my feelings carry me away. I struggle for a metaphor to help explain. He takes the final step to get closer to be able to hear me over the rain.

"If people were beverages... like iced tea, apple juice, coffee, etc," I say. "Everyone would be different then, right?"

"Right," he says.

"Shiah is water."

His brow furrows. "Tasteless?"

"No," I frown, worried this metaphor is going to fall flat. "You can't make iced tea out of lemonade. But you *can* make iced tea with water. You can make *anything* with water. It's the starting point. It's unobscured by anything else. And water is miraculous. It's the one thing necessary to all life. Everyone has water, but it's hidden by all the flavors. But when you're around Shiah, you realize you're actually made of water, too. You're just... flavored. Ideally built for certain situations. Hot chocolate for a winter night. Lemonade for a summer day. But underneath it you're water. And like Shiah, you can become anything. You're limitless."

"That's... quite an endorsement," Gabriel says, captivated.

"You are the one that made me want to step out on stage," I say, "but with Shiah... I do it fearlessly."

"Does this have to do with her life force ability?

"Life force abilities aren't separate characteristics of a person, Gabriel. They're as intrinsic as personality traits. They're inseparable from a person."

My conversation with Kiera comes back to me, one where she said to me exactly what I just said to Gabriel. It wasn't that long ago. I have changed so much...

"I wasn't implying that your esteem was based on something tenuous. I'm simply curious," he replies.

"You can ask her next time you see her. I think you'd probably grasp who Shiah is even better than I do. Everything she says has layers, and a lot of it I only understand instinctively."

"She sounds fascinating."

"Your brother thinks so, too," I say, walking over to the slide, which is nothing more than worn metal chute winding around a iron column, bars on the right and overhead.

"Are you implying...?"

"That they're an item? Yes."

"Hm," he says. "It sounds like you have quite an intimate group. By the way, the slide is more fun in theory. Watch your back and the back of your head. The ridges between the metal sections can hit you in all the wrong places. And the lean toward the center makes it hard to compensate."

"How does that work? It's not like I can sit up. The bars are too close overhead."

He shrugs. "It's the novelty."

"Fine. I want to experience the novelty with you. We'll go together."

He chuckles. "We won't go very fast that way."

"Sounds like the perfect solution to the back and head problem. Come on," I say, stepping over to the slide and positioning myself and looking over my shoulder at him.

He assesses the slide for a moment, thoughts whirring. He finally steps over to me and sits down on the edge, not yet behind me. "If we go together, you sitting in front of me, we'll be scooting down the whole way. The pitch of the curve won't accommodate our combined length," he says. "Lay on my chest. I've been down this slide enough times to strategically angle myself to go fast and avoid the brunt of the metal. Then, you don't just get the novelty. You get the thrill, too."

"You want me to lie on your chest?" I smile at him teasingly. "Well okay. But only because it's strategic."

He waves me out of the way and lies down, holding himself in place with a foot on one of the metal bars. "Your chariot awaits, Love," he says, grinning up at me. "Your chest on mine. Your cheek by my chin. And bend your knees so your feet stay out of the way."

I grip the bar above as I put a foot on either side of him. "Why have you been here so many times?" I ask as I lie down on top of him, thinking the thrill of this slide is *not* going to be the speed. "I thought you were from California."

"I taught at the local university for a time," he grunts as he pulls me higher on his chest and a thrill moves through me. "I always brought my physics classes to the museum for a field trip. This place is nothing but people and the laws of physics getting acquainted."

"Are you saying I'm not the first girl you've taken down the slide?" I tease, because right now we are both totally turned on by our arrangement, and a little humor is good for handling that kind of heat.

"I sense you are implying a double-meaning with that question, but I will answer by saying I'm sad I never thought to use this particular exercise as a demonstration. My kids would have lost it over watching a woman straddle Dr. Dumas down the ten-story slide. Their reaction to the lecture afterward would have been priceless."

"How so?"

"They would have already been thinking about sex, and physics is already *very* sexy," he says, moving my legs between his knees and locking them in place. "All those curves… acceleration… friction…"

"Did you just physics dirty-talk me?" I say, bringing my hands up to his shoulders.

"There's a gorgeous woman lying on top of me and we're talking about physics. It comes without effort."

"Are we going to go already?" I say.

"Now that you've noticed I'm stalling, sure," he says, putting his arms around me and pushing off.

I tuck my face into his neck as we shoot down and around the curve at a rapid speed, but only for a few seconds. We slow suddenly, and then stop.

I lift my head, looking through the bars to see where we are. Not at the bottom. "We're stuck?" I say.

"Yes," he says, unconcerned.

I look behind me, down the slide to see. Nothing but a curved slope ahead.

I look back at him. "On what?"

"Friction," he replies. "It's every slide's nemesis." But heaviness gathers in my chest, his intentions made abundantly clear.

I bring my hands under my chin. "Did you premeditate this intimacy?"

"No. I realized we were halfway down the slide, and the thought hit me that it was almost over," he says, his voice lower. "I wanted to stop time."

"Stopping on a slide doesn't stop time," I say, reaching for his hand on my back and lacing my fingers with his.

"Stopping on a spiral slide has the best chance of at least slowing it."

"Why is that?"

"The steeper our descent, the greater our mass, the more our gravity pulls on the fabric of spacetime, which changes our point of reference for perceiving the velocity of matter around us. Stopping in the middle of our descent creates inertia, which tricks our body into thinking it's still moving when it's not. The effects of inertia can linger, and perception is everything where time is concerned. That's the science. But I also have a theory that our perception of time moves cyclically, in the same type of motion as a planet in orbit, so physically traveling along a helix with the force of gravity would enhance our awareness of time passing. The more keenly aware you are of something happening, the more you can alter it. Thusly, we have the ability to slow our own perception."

"Whoa," I breathe. "I didn't follow most of that, but it sounds… beautiful."

"That was to impress you with the size of my brain. I have a simple demonstration I use when I teach a class. I can show you one day. In any case, I told you physics was sexy." He brings his free hand up and strokes a finger from my temple down and around the edge of my jaw.

My eyes fall closed in pleasure. His finger trails across my cheek and over my bottom lip. Goosebumps dot my arms.

"Wendy," he whispers.

"Hmm?"

"May I kiss you?"

A lot of probable responses come to mind, like pointing out that me straddling him on a slide implies permission, or that I already *told* him I want him to kiss me, or teasing him by saying no. But in the end, the sincerity behind his question melts my heart. He's so open and vulnerable to me in this moment—but I recognize that's *every* moment with him. My usual tactics are for a usual guy. And Gabriel is exactly *un*usual.

"Yes," I whisper back, lifting my face up above his, otherwise he's going to find it awfully hard to kiss me.

He touches my lips again, caressing my face up to my ear, his eyes staring into mine and holding them like magnets. I love his eyes. I think they are my favorite feature of his. He can look at me from across a room, and if I stare into his eyes I swear it's as communicative as my empathic ability.

Remembering how much he likes longing, I'm afraid he's going to draw this out. But I think the fact that we couldn't get closer together if we tried has heightened the chemistry between us to unbearable levels much more quickly. I feel like I'm going to burst from it, and my lips physically ache. I read his mind as soon as he gives in, and he doesn't have to pull my face closer. I've already met his lips with my own.

Heat builds instantly, and I meet his intensity at the same time he delivers it, and I marvel at how easy it is to kiss him, no awkward adjusting to the way each other's mouth moves. No miscommunication of one being more excited than the other. It's like we've choreographed it, or like we've done it a hundred times before. When he moves his lips from my mouth, I have already lifted my chin, knowing he is going for my neck. I put my hands in his hair and gasp as he goes straight for a spot behind my ear as if knowing already that it's the exact spot that will drive me crazy.

I come at him with even more vigor, totally consumed with wanting him. He responds, running his hand under my tank, over my back, his fingers pulling at me. But I'm already here.

I start to cry because a nameless emotional energy rears up, overwhelming me suddenly, and I cling to him as his hands run everywhere he can reach. And I want him to. I want him all over me. I can't articulate anything, and it's not lust. It's this sensation through my whole body that latches onto the cells of his being, like magnets. I'm drawn to him. I want to meld with him, but I can't get any closer and the pull is maddening and humbling and beautiful all at the same time. The only way to express it is to cry. The power of it takes me over like a wave and I sob as his kisses move up my neck.

He stops at my chin, and then pulls my face to his chest, grasping me in his arms, and we are both gasping and crying. There are no words. Neither of us knows what to say. Neither of us knows what to call what we feel. But we both feel it. Maybe time really has stopped. Everything around us, beyond this space, is fuzzy.

Who am I?

I only know that I'm his.

So I close my eyes and feel. I let the energy thrum through me for the several minutes of absolute stillness between us. The waves of emotion still to more peaceful waters after a while, and I can think again.

"Wendy," Gabriel quavers, not as a question, but I

translate the words behind it. It's a declaration of his feelings—which I share. They transcend what we knew a person could experience.

I interlock my fingers with his again. "I know," I whisper. "And I don't know."

"I can't leave," he says. "I can't. And I won't."

"You know you have to," I say, his certainty scaring me.

"No. I can't. I physically can't."

"You can do anything."

"Not without you. Not anymore."

I lift my face. "Yes, you can. You can do it for me."

"Why do you want to be apart? After that? We can find a way."

"Gabriel," I whisper. "It won't be forever."

"How long? Give me a timeline. Give me a date. I can't do it on ambiguous terms."

"Six months?"

He panics. "The world could end by then. What if you die in New York from some oceanic disaster? Bloody hell, Wendy. I can't believe I put you in such a compromised position. You shouldn't be in jail. You shouldn't be on trial. I cut off my own foot. No. I cut out my own heart. All for upholding the senseless laws of a crumbling society. And I'm going to lose what little time I might have had. I give up. I give it all up. No more Human Movement. Let me join the Guild. I'm a Prime, aren't I? I have rights."

"Shhhh," I say, putting my hands on either side of his face.

He puts his hands over mine, his eyes full of fear. "Don't leave me," he pleads.

"I'm not leaving you," I say, looking into his eyes. "I'm not leaving you. Never. You're mine. I'm yours."

"I can't be apart from you."

"You can. We'll figure out a way to communicate. I'll be with you. Just not next to you. Gabriel, I wish time really had stopped. But it hasn't. Out there, people are dying. They need help. And you're not a quitter. Neither am I. We have to fight for survival. And for right now we have to fight for it in different places. If you want to ever be together, we have to fight on different battlefields."

He closes his eyes and exhales heavily. "I don't understand this. It doesn't make sense. We're supposed to be together, Wendy. I can feel it as certainly as I feel air in my lungs. So why has everything separated us? Why is it *still* separating us?"

"So that we fight harder," I say. "To give us something to go to war for. Don't you feel it? Like you could move a mountain? Like you would if you thought it would bring us together sooner? You said earlier that you didn't know how you were going to succeed. I didn't either, I admit. But now... aren't you ready?" I put a hand over his heart. "I know you are. I can feel it in you. You'll do whatever it takes. So will I."

He wraps his arms around me again, and I can tell he agrees. His determination builds itself, layer by layer. Once it's constructed, and I marvel at his strength, the strength of a thousand men, the strength I have come to associate only with him, we begin to move. We're sliding again, faster and faster, reaching the bottom in a few seconds and slowing to a stop. He stands, pulling me up with him and not letting go.

He touches my face again, cradling my cheek. "Thank you for believing in me," he says. He hugs me again, his hand on the back of my head. He kisses the top of it, and that simple act builds the heat between us once more.

"Mi encantadora doncella," he gasps. "I want to kiss you again. But there's nothing to prevent me now from removing all your clothes. And I have a rule of not doing such things on the first date."

"And I have a rule of not sleeping with married men," I point out.

He waves a hand. "I was afraid of that envelope before, but not anymore. I'm ready to face whatever it is. As long as you're with me. Will you?"

"Of course," I say, intoxicated with his newfound conviction and confidence. I love this version of him. It's such a turn-on.

"Then let's go be fearless," he says, locking his fingers with mine and pulling us toward the cave's exit. And then he laughs.

"What?" I say.

"You said you have a rule," he says. "About sleeping with married men. But apparently not one against making out with them on slides."

"That slide transported us to another dimension," I say. "Totally different rules."

He stops as we emerge into the whale room. "You mean I can make love to you on the slide and it's off the record? I can make that happen. I'm a physicist after all. I know all about matter... and motion... curves... and reducing friction."

I open my mouth. "You are a dirty physicist, Mister Dumas!" I reach out to smack him.

He leaps away. "That's Doctor Dumas to you, Miss Whitley," he laughs.

"And that's *Councilwoman* Wendy to you, Doctor Dumas," I say as we reach the entrance hall.

He doffs his imaginary hat while taking a bow. "At your service, Councilwoman. Allow me." He snatches my coat from the counter and holds it open for me.

I turn, put my arm in a sleeve and then the other. But he doesn't pull the coat up. He touches my exposed shoulder. "I meant to ask you about this. It's a nasty scar. Fairly new?"

"A tree fell on me. I was caught in a lightning storm, here in Missouri actually."

"What on earth were you doing in a lightning storm? Surely the Guild knew it was coming."

"I don't know," I say, tapping the side of my head. "That's where I woke up after losing my memory."

"Such an odd circumstance," he says. "So many memories being flushed at the same time."

I'm about to explain that what's even more odd is that the missing memories all correlate with lightning storms, but the words get caught in my throat when he slips the sleeve of my tank over my shoulder and plants a kiss lightly over my scar. He makes a trail of them, all the way up my neck and I suck in a breath, frozen. He lingers behind my ear. "It's after midnight," he whispers, "And I can officially call it our second date. So many slides here..."

I shiver and turn around, pull my coat up over my shoulders and grab my wig. "Focus, Gabriel. You're a married man."

He watches me put the wig in place. "Is red your natural color?" he asks.

I nod. "And this is actually almost exactly what I looked like. Before. I don't remember what prompted me to cut it off. "

He utters a low growl. "Red hair," he says, shaking his head. "You have natural red hair. Could the universe torture me any more?"

"Probably," I say as he snags the umbrella. "Don't tempt her."

"Oh I'll tempt her," he says, pushing the door open. "I have the love of my life beside me. I can take anything the universe rains down."

Just then, the rain gets heavier, pounding violently on the awning we stand under. I look up at Gabriel. "Uhh?"

"I'm no recreant," he says and runs out into the courtyard, sans umbrella. He holds his hands outstretched, facing the sky and getting completely soaked in two seconds. "Give it to me!" he bellows into the dark sky.

I smile at watching him embrace the earth, just as he did in Chicago. I hope after he opens that envelope he's still so buoyant.

Fifty-Seven

Gabriel appears at the door in a white undershirt, sweats, barefoot, and with a towel around his neck. I swear every time I see him he's hotter than the last time. He's also annoyed about something.

"What's up?" I ask, lying back on the sleeping bag on the floor of the conference room where Gabriel has taken up residence until his departure.

"Rita," he replies. "She reams me if I so much as breathe wrong."

"She's here?" I say, worried.

"No. She's in Omaha. I was supposed to record something tonight for her to use at the rally. I opted for other endeavors this evening so I sent over footage from earlier in the week. She noticed."

"Forget her," I say. "Let's get this over with. I'm exhausted."

He eyes my sleeping bag and frowns. "You're so far away from me. I'm going into the California front, Wendy. Can't you see me off with a proper night of cuddling? What's the harm in spooning?"

I roll my eyes. "You are trouble, Dr. Dumas. Grab that envelope already."

He slides it off the table and gives me a pouty look, sitting cross-legged on his sleeping bag. I start to scoot toward him but he holds a hand up. "Nope. You made your choice."

I roll my eyes again and lay back on my pillow.

I hear the tearing of the envelope, the slide of paper as he pulls it out. And then silence as he reads. I've noticed that I have a much wider range for him as far as my empathic ability is concerned, so even at eight feet away, I can feel him, and I pay close attention for his reaction.

First, intense relief. "The blood used to write the note," he says. "it's not related to me…" He sucks in a breath. "El Cielo," he gasps.

I wait, knowing he's going to reveal whatever it is that's so astounding.

"It belongs to a male. Twenty-four-point-seven percent related to… "

I turn my head to see him staring at me. I raise by brow questioningly.

"You," he says. "The blood is from someone related to *you.*"

I sit up abruptly, my mouth open in shock. "Wh—what does that mean?"

"Around twenty-five percent shared DNA. That would have to be either an uncle or nephew," he replies.

My uncle is the first person that comes to mind. What on earth?

"Could also be a half-brother…" Gabriel says, pensive. "Do you—?"

But I've already launched myself at him and snatched the paper. "Ezra is my half brother—most likely," I say, trying to see, but my eyes have already blurred with tears. Did Andre use Ezra's blood to write a note to Gabriel? Or was it Robert Haricott? Is the note that old? Why would he do that?

"Female, fifty percent DNA related to Ralph Gonzales…?" Gabriel murmurs to himself in consternation.

"What?!" I snap, wiping my eyes so I can see the paper.

"You know the name?" he asks. "It's the girl Mike and I found dead with our parents. Her DNA isn't on file, but it looks like her father's is. It says he was in the Navy."

I put my hand on my chest, head spinning. I hope I'm wrong. I hope this is just a huge coincidence. "My best friend in high school was Letty Gonzales. Her father's name was Ralph." I say, holding back a sob. I look at Gabriel. "She had a tattoo of her grandmother's name, Dulce, inside a heart, right here:" I point to the inside of my left wrist.

Gabriel nods slowly, shocked.

The sob escapes my throat, and I put my hand over my mouth. Andre killed Letty? How many people connected to me did that psycho murder before I got him? And what does any of it have to do with Gabriel?

He flips to the next page, and this time I scan it with him. It's the report about the satellite phone. It lists the phone's serial number. Below that, who it was registered to…

More shock.

"Robert Haricott," Gabriel says, lost in drawing some conclusion. But then he sees my expression.

"Wendy," he urges. "Tell me what you're thinking."

I gasp for breath. "First, tell me why you weren't surprised at reading his name."

"Robert Haricott's estate was the first donor to the Human Movement," he replies.

I catch my breath again, floored.

Gabriel waits, clearly dying for an explanation for my reaction, but I can't string my thoughts together in a sensible way. Too many questions are fighting to get out.

"But he's dead! And you— Wait. Did you start The Human Movement *before* you lost your memory?" I clarify.

He puts the paper down on the sleeping bag. "Yes, The Human Movement existed before my memory loss," he says. "When I was looking for clues to my past, I discovered it was created by me as a nonprofit within a month before waking up in Bakersfield with missing memory." He clears his throat. "It was also endowed with fifty million dollars. An anonymous donation. But I hired someone to track it back, thinking whoever had donated that much money must know something about my past. It came from a trust account linked to the Haricott Estate. The trust account was created *before* Robert's death, but the donation was, of course, *after* his death. From what I've been able to glean, the lion's share of the Haricott estate was being moved into someone else's name prior to his death, and it was completed *after* his death. Quite recently, the investigator I hired said the name of the heir had disappeared, as if they were completely erased. There were no contingencies. The estate is in limbo until they can track down physical records or until someone steps forward to claim a right to the inheritance. My investigator believes, and logically so, that the heir was killed, possibly by PHIA. Maybe they hoped to gain control of his estate? I don't know, but Haricott himself was a Prime Human, which I found to be a fascinating fact given the donation."

Everything he says keeps knocking the air out of my chest. Please let this be the last earth-moving revelation tonight. My body can't handle the constant shock...

"Robert Haricott was my uncle," I say finally. My head... it's full of incoherency.

It's Gabriel's turn to lose his words, and he stares at me, intellect going a thousand miles an hour.

"Are—Are you—?" he starts.

"Am I serious? Yes! But I don't remember knowing him. I only know I did because when I woke up, I had three guns on me, all registered to him."

"No, I'm asking, are you his heir?"

I blink, and the probability of that comes crashing down on me. There was that letter... *Oh gosh.* Robert Haricott sent me that letter two and a half years ago and I was supposed to go see him. Ezra joked about him leaving an inheritance...

"I don't know," I say. "It seems possible. And he—" I pause because I'm not sure if Gabriel will think I'm crazy for the next part... Who am I kidding? It's *me* that thinks it's crazy. But now it makes a lot more sense. "Did you see the interview I did with the girl that can see the dead?" I say.

"I've seen everything you've ever done in a public sphere," he replies.

"After the interview she told me she saw someone hanging around me. She described the person, but they didn't sound familiar. Shiah recognized it though, and she brought a picture up of Robert Haricott. The girl said that was definitely who she saw. My uncle's... spirit has supposedly been hanging around me."

Gabriel blinks. "Extraordinary," he breathes. Then he looks at me. "You do realize that if you are his heir, then you are the one that kickstarted THM?"

"That's the first realization that actually makes sense," I say. "I told you I thought like you once upon a time."

Gabriel suddenly pauses all thought as if he has come to a sudden and shocking realization. He jumps to his feet and digs through a bag at the other end of the room. Then he runs back to me and kneels down in front of me. He opens his hand. On his palm is a ring. A wedding band. He stares down at it. Then at me. "Will you try it on?"

I leap to my feet and back away. Try it on? What about his wife? Why? Oh gosh. Does he think—? Married? Me? No freaking way! This is way too far beyond belief. It's not possible. He's got this *all* wrong.

Everything in me is at war. I stare at it. I can't get my brain moving...

"What if you're wrong?" I plead, unable to tear my eyes away from the ring. "I will have tried on some other woman's ring. Hoping I can take her place. It'll be like Cinderella's evil step sisters, trying to make the shoe work. It's wrong…"

He remains on his knees, looks down at the ring.

"If it's mine," I say more quietly, "why wasn't I wearing it?"

"I don't know," he croaks, fighting his memory for the answer, for a flash, for a reason. I've banged my own head against that metaphorical wall enough times that I know the feeling well. He's grasping. That's what this is.

"If it *was* mine," I say confidently, "it's not anymore."

He chokes on a sob.

"This was a bad idea," I say. "You've got a past to sort out. I'm sorry. About the kiss. About coming. Everything." I look around for my belongings.

"No, no, Wendy! Please!" he begs. "Don't go! I'm sorry. It's not my place to—I just—I wanted—I didn't think—"

"It's not your fault," I say, finding my bag and digging through it for jeans so I can leave here *not* in pajamas. "It's mine for coming here."

"Don't go!" he pleads. "*Please don't go.*"

I turn, my cheeks wet already. "Gabriel, I have to. We were wrong to think we could put it all aside for a night. You never have let it go. Look at THM. It exists because of a past you can't remember. You want your life back. Everything you've done is a testament to that. And that's *okay.* Find the past if that's what you want. But you can't have both. You have to decide who you are going to be *right now.* And then you have to live with it. The past doesn't matter to me. Only *now* matters. That's why it was so easy to kill Andre. I killed the possibility that he could remake me. I didn't want that past always pulling me back. I choose *me,* Gabriel. *This* me. Right now. If I was your wife, it might mean something to you, but that ring is irrelevant to me. Because *I* didn't choose it, regardless of what the past says that I can't remember. If I have to choose to be her or me, I choose me because this is the only Wendy I know, and this is a Wendy I love being. You have to choose who you want to be, too. You can't hang on to what if's."

He sinks onto his heels and sobs, the ring cradled in his hands like an oracle.

I resist the urge to touch him, to comfort him. As I stand there, watching him fight with himself, his desire to be with me fighting fruitlessly with past promises, I can fathom what might have separated us. This power he wields to hang on to what he believes… It's unmatched. And I have seen with my own eyes that his power is more than tenacity. He moves people. He *is* the mover. He is the messenger. And I know I have the power to aim him. He has given it to me. And I think… if by chance I was his wife before, he gave it to me then as well. I wouldn't break him now, and I don't believe I would have broken him then either. It might have been our ideals, even then, that separated us. He has to find his past. He will not be able to fully embrace the future until he does.

I am about to kneel down to tell him so when my exceptional vision catches on a mark on the bottom of his foot. I lean my head to get a better look. It's a tiny tattoo, about two inches long, right beneath the ball of his right foot…

Promised to Wendy

in every world

I suck in a breath. "Gabriel," I say. "Do you… have any tattoos?"

He look up, fists clenched, eyes red. "Tattoos?"

I nod. "To your memory, do you have any tattoos?"

He shakes his head slowly, confused. "I would never have gotten a tattoo. To permanently imprint myself with one of innumerable possibilities? I could not possibly choose one or two or a thousand images to portray the sum of my life. So I choose none."

I'm partly in shock, partly amused, partly… everything else. This is unreal. All this time… He's been walking around with my name on him… This is the most insane turn of events I've ever heard of.

"Are you certain?" I say, and I kind of laugh when I say it. "Is there no exception to that rule?"

His eyebrows lift curiously. "I believe you are leading me somewhere with this… But if I'm supposed to guess where… I'm sad to say my intellect isn't keeping up."

"Look on the bottom of your right foot," I say.

He does so immediately. "Gads!" he exclaims, staring at the words. Then he looks up at me with wide eyes, questioning. Then back at his foot. Then at me.

"Every world…" I say. "That's an interesting choice of words…"

"You call it *interesting?*" he says. "I call it revelatory. Wendy—Surely you can't deny—"

"That I was once your wife?" I say. "I never denied that. I simply questioned it. I pointed out that there was doubt."

"So you're saying… What are you saying?"

"I already told you, this is me. Right now. Whoever that Wendy is on your foot, she's gone."

"So you... don't wish to be married to me anymore?" His words are rife with dread and sorrow.

"I didn't say that."

"Then..." He leaps between several confused trains of thought. Then his shoulders slump. "I am so confused. Please clarify. With the evidence before us concerning our past together, how does this knowledge affect us going forward?"

"It doesn't affect *us*. It only affects *you*. I don't know any other way to say it: I have let go of the past. I am no different now than I was yesterday. I still love you. I still want to be with you. But I can't be with someone who is always asking the past who they should be *now*."

I think he's finally grasping it, little by little. He looks down at his foot again. "The past says I belong to you. To me that is enough to stop asking." He looks up at me, reaches his hand out to me.

I step forward and take it.

"Wendy," he says, still on his knees, "I have always *been* yours. I want to always *be* yours. Will you be mine?"

"Yes," I say, touching his face with my free hand. He closes his eyes and pulls me to him, his face against my stomach. He sighs into me.

After a few moments of stillness, he opens his other hand, reveals the ring, hesitant because he's unsure how I feel about it still.

"You know you want to ask," I say. "Since when do you let what I might say hold you back? Be you. Not who you think I want you to be."

He doesn't hesitate then. He looks up at me, brings a knee up so that he's kneeling. He presents the ring in his palm. "Wendy, will you be my wife?"

I pick it up, holding it up between thumb and forefinger. It's an ordinary silver band, but my eye catches on the engraving: *Body and Soul.*

Goosebumps crawl over my skin. I look over my shoulder instinctively, as if my past self is watching me. It kind of feels that way.

I look back at Gabriel. "Forever?" I ask.

He swallows, more afraid of my rejection by the moment. "Yes," he replies.

"Are you certain?" I say, handing the ring back to him. "Evidence indicates we separated once. If it was me that instigated it, I have already let it go, no matter what it was. I am starting over with you. But it could have easily been you that instigated it… and I am not convinced that you have let go of the man you once were. Does he have a hold over your promises now?"

Gabriel looks at the ring, ponders it. Then he looks at me. "I cannot fathom what drove me from you, but I have decided. *You* are my exception. To my present *and* to my past. I am certain." He looks me in the eye, more fervently than ever. "Will you be my wife?"

"I will," I reply.

He slips the band onto my left ring finger. It fits perfectly.

We share in elation, staring at it with unveiled relief.

"It fits," Gabriel says. He kisses the top of my hand before burying his face in my abdomen once more.

I push him to the floor and straddle him aggressively. And then I kiss him with total abandon. This day… It's the best day of my entire life, and I tell him that in the way I kiss him. I want every bit of him on every bit of me. There is nothing to hold us back. I push my hands under his shirt, over his chest, and he growls, pulling me down and kissing my neck. I marvel at how destined the moment feels, and it makes my heart emerge from my chest to wrap more securely around him.

"I love you," I whisper in his ear after he removes my shirt.

He pauses, grasps my face lovingly in his hands while staring into my eyes, and we share in the moment of realizing, at the same time, how unlikely logic says this moment should be. Yet circumstances orchestrated it anyway. Something has driven us together. If someone had asked me the possibility of being Gabriel Dumas' wife even a day ago, I would have said the mere question was ridiculous. The founder of The Human Movement married to one of the twelve most powerful individuals in the Guild? Ludicrous. But then add the fact that we both started from ground-zero, having lost well over two-years' worth of memories? He managed to build and I managed to climb to the top of the two most influential organizations in the nation! And all of it… it must have happened just so we could find each other again. Because what if we hadn't become who we are? I woke up in Missouri. He woke up in California. How else would we have found each other again if not our opposition?

"El Cielo," Gabriel breathes, in line with my sentiments. "I thought… It felt like everything was keeping us apart. But it wasn't at all…"

"Nothing, not even lost memories can separate us," I say.

He sighs in awe, caught once more in the surrealism of it all. "I don't ascribe to fate. But you and me? We reek of esoteric words like destiny."

I shake my head. "Gabriel, in the energy world there are forces that move between people. I've seen you use them. And you saw that crowd in Raleigh after the announcement of Purus. There are connections as real as this one." I hold up our entwined hands. "So there is no reason to think that your soul and mine aren't what moved the world around us to orchestrate our reunion. I don't think there's a hand that moves us across a chessboard. I've certainly never seen any indication of that. But between the pieces themselves? That's where things happen. And it's as solid and real as our skin touching."

He caresses my face and growls against restraint. "Wendy... You talking metaphysics like that while lying on top of me is so arousing. I'm about to rudely interrupt our conversation with my mouth in places on you that will render any further words out of your mouth incoherent. So if you wish to continue polite conversation, we're going to have to put some distance between us."

I respond by pushing his shirt up and putting my tongue from his abdomen to his chest.

Incoherency takes over.

Fifty-Eight

'm going to lose my mind in California," Gabriel says in a rush as soon as I open my eyes. "I can already sense it starting. The thought of leaving you makes me want to vomit."

I grimace because I can feel it. It's anxiety unlike any I have ever personally experienced and it totally sucks to wake up to. Gabriel's emotions are more powerful than most. I think that's why I feel him so far away. I also think they're strong because he doesn't typically suppress them. He embraces every part of himself.

"I was watching you sleep, torn because I was dying for you to wake up so I could see your eyes, but dreading it because it means we're that much closer to when you have to leave. I've been driving myself crazy."

I glance up to a wall behind him to see that it's around nine AM. My flight leaves tonight at ten-eighteen. We have thirteen hours left. I pull him down next to me so I can lay my head on his chest. "You will be too busy to lose your mind," I say.

He tugs the sleeping bag up over my bare shoulder. "Do you think there was a child?" he asks timidly.

I pause, remembering Ohr's phone call. The relief of it is still readily available. "There couldn't have been. I can't have children."

He takes several deep breaths, expelling the worry he has been building up.

"Why that tactic then?" he says finally.

"It was Andre's ploy," I say. "The note in your pocket. Andre's words to me at the airport. He wanted us to *think* there was a child. Because he knew we didn't remember, so he planted the suggestions so he could hold it over us. If I'd believed him, it's the one thing that might have motivated me to negotiate."

"What did the Guild know about your past?" Gabriel asks.

"Nothing," I say. "Except for what they knew about my parents. I had been missing since I was a child, according to their files. But as you know, a bunch of data was erased along with the memories. Shiah believes the things that were erased had to do with me."

"You are the correlation? Because of your life force ability, I take it. So the energy world business must be a big deal…"

I snort. "It's *the* deal."

He ponders that, intrigued.

"I'm positive that I knew much more about it before I lost my memory," I say, thinking about Shiah's confession. After speaking to Ohr about my probable ability to undo seed-generation sickness, I wonder if it was my knowledge of the energy world Shiah was trying to get rid of? We had that conversation about giving life force abilities on demand, something that even to her is alarming. She is *adamant* about stopping her own genetic line right where it is. Of the members of the Council, Ohr lost the most time. What if I was working with him to accomplish his goal of giving everyone life force abilities so that we could better combat the disasters? And what if, instead of washing her hands of the decision like she has this time around, Shiah was opposed? What if she believed life force abilities should not be unleashed to the masses…? It sounds disturbingly similar to Andre's philosophy…

But Shiah is *not* a ruthless murderer. I am certain of that.

I realize that Gabriel propped himself up on his elbow again at some point, chin in hand, staring at me. When I turn my attention to him, he says, "That brain of yours never stops. I love watching you think."

I laugh. "Me staring blankly into space is a turn-on?"

"You are the sharpest, most articulate woman I know. When I see you thinking, I wait with bated breath to hear what wisdom will proceed next from your lips."

Conflict intercepts my ready smile at the compliment, because it is clear that Gabriel is asking to know my thoughts. To what do I owe my ultimate allegiance? Despite trusting Gabriel, he is not a member of the Guild. I accepted to be his wife, but what does that mean in this scenario? How did I not think of that when he asked?

What if I tell him all that I know? I will then owe it to the rest of the Council to be truthful, especially concerning my relationship with Gabriel. What will happen then? I could be removed from the Council on solid grounds, for violating classified information without Council approval. I have jeopardized everything by making promises to Gabriel…

Gabriel puts a finger over my mouth, and in his eyes and emotions I can tell that he knows what's going through my head. "Stop thinking so much," he whispers.

I'd like to point out that he just told me he loves to watch me think, but I know he's talking about a different kind of thinking. "Gabriel, my life is not mine to give you," I say, tears springing from my eyes. "And I—"

"I know," he says, resting his hand on my cheek.

"I want to though," I say, putting my hand over his. "I want to give you all of me, inside and outside."

"And I want to never talk about California ever again. I want to join the Guild and be with you. Do you want me to?"

"Want? Yes. Need? California needs you."

"I don't care what California needs. I exist for you, not them. What do *you* need?"

We stare at each other, my thoughts leaping back and forth between my duty and my heart. They refuse to be squared. "I don't know," I whisper.

"Wendy, you told me last night that you are the Guild. And I told you before that when I think of the Guild, you are who I see. You *are* the Guild. And I fell in love with you, as you are, your loyalties, your beliefs, your conviction, your duty, even your exasperating *confidentiality*. Why then would I ask you to give up any of those things just because you wear my ring? It earns me no rights. Instead it demands that I place no conditions on my love for you. I will always make exception for you."

"But all I do is take and give nothing," I say.

He looks up and around, then back at me. "Not to be patronizing, Love, but I think you ought to look where you are right now and recall all that you told me you did to get here. There's also Raleigh, New York… Any time you and I have seen each other face to face, it's been because *you* bent some rule to make it happen. When I met with your Council, everything I learned about my memory loss there was because you advocated for me when you had no obligation to do so. I know you put aside your loyalties to do that. The information you brought concerning the samples I gave to the Council… You said no one else had seen them when I am *certain* that's not how it should have worked. You have given more than I ever expected to receive."

I'm crying again. "It's not nearly as much as you deserve. I don't *want* you to come second."

"I have to," he says solemnly. "The fate of the world is more important. The Guild *must* lead from behind. I will tolerate no one but you as that force." He reaches for my left hand, holds it up to display the ring. "I asked you to be my wife, but we're not actually married yet. So this is a promise that one day, when the world finally rests, and the Guild can relinquish its hold on your loyalty, you will be my wife and I will be your husband. I will look forward to that day, and it will drive me to work harder and faster. I can wait. I will wait. As long as it takes."

I pull him down to kiss him. "I will, too," I whisper. "I will not rest until I am standing at a press conference and announcing to the world that I am marrying Gabriel Dumas."

He considers something carefully, hesitates, but finally says, "Could I... ask you a question?"

"You need to *ask* if you can ask me a question?" I say.

"I feel like I have no business asking."

"If I am at liberty to answer, I *will* answer."

"Have you dated anyone else? Since our memories forced us into new lives, that is."

I chuckle. "We've barely been engaged for a day and you're already jealous?"

"I am not jealous!" he says defensively. "I only... want to be sure while I'm gone that there won't be any old flames for you to contend with. I'll be out of sight, out of mind... Lots of longing and no way to satisfy it. Since we aren't actually married..."

I sit up and look at him with amusement. But he's completely and suddenly distracted by my body.

"I can't believe I have Wendy Whitley naked, in bed with me, and with my ring on her finger," he says, tracing a finger from my neck down between my breasts. "My fantasies of you were never this incredible. It was never in the realm of possibility."

"You fantasized about me?" I say.

He gives me a dry look. "That cannot possibly come as a surprise to you."

"I guess it doesn't," I laugh. "And no. I tried to start something with Mike, but that didn't work out. I never even got to kiss him." I purse my lips in disappointment.

My expression jars Gabriel, bringing him instant insecurity, an emotion I never associate with him. "You *want* to kiss Mike?" he asks. "Just how strong *are* your feelings for him?"

I don't like the accusation in his voice and I glare at him to express as much. "Mike is one of my best friends. I would go through hell for him. I love him fiercely. That's how strong."

"You're going to have to say a lot more than that," Gabriel says, getting upset.

"Why? It bothers you that I love other people? *Actually* married or not, I chose you. I choose you. My fidelity is yours. That's all you should care about."

"I care because Mike and I share a connection that makes it exceedingly difficult to—"

"Yeah, yeah," I say, holding up a hand to silence him. "I know. But you act like *you're* the one that has to suffer. He feels what *you* do. Not the other way around. He and I have been in close quarters, in danger, and we've had moments of serious chemistry. I love him, Gabriel. It's impossible not to with how much he sacrifices for me and especially for you. But I also know I don't ultimately want to be with him. I also love Shiah. I love her so much it leaks out of my eyes every time I think about it. And none of that should threaten you, especially when the two of them have spent so much effort in bringing us together. If anything it should bring you comfort. I have two people at my back who would do *anything* for me."

Gabriel puts his hands over his face, full of instant regret. "I'm sorry," he says. "I know you're right. It's our history. It's not pretty. My reactions are purely instinctual, so give me a little time to retrain myself."

I reach out and squeeze his hand. "Also, there was a guy I worked with named Jonas. I lured him into the shadows outside my residence building and seduced him out of his shirt. It would have gone farther if Mike hadn't shown up. But it wasn't a flame. It was revenge. Also, Shiah kissed me once."

He blinks at me, mentally leaping back and forth and he fumbles over a few pronouns before saying, "Can you give me more details, please?"

There's a knock on the door. "Mister Dumas, you're needed out here," says a muffled female voice.

"I told you to phone me, Lelani," Gabriel calls back, annoyed.

"We did. Several times. You didn't answer. What on earth is going on in there? Tranwick said the room is off-limits."

"Then why are you *outside of it*?" he says brusquely.

"Because Tranwick isn't my boss. What is your problem? Did you give in to the fan girls?"

Gabriel rolls his eyes. "Yes. I had an orgy with fifteen of them last night. Please give me a moment to put my clothes back on."

"Are you serious?" she asks, her voice full of disgust.

Gabriel chuckles and says in a low voice to me, "Sometimes I wish I was better at lying. I could have so much fun with this."

"No," he calls toward the door. "But I *am* naked. So I'll need a moment."

"Ugh," Lelani says. "I did not need to know that!"

He throws his hands up and gives me a look of exasperation as he yells, "You asked what was going on! If you don't want to know, don't ask!"

I cover my mouth and giggle.

He watches me and smiles. "I love the sound of your laugh," he says.

I lean forward and pull his lips into mine, which gets him excited and his hands start reaching for my body again. But I pull away and stand up, looking around for my backpack.

He huffs and crosses his arms, still laying on the sleeping bag. "I'm going to make a call and have your flight cancelled."

"No, you're not," I say, sitting in one of the conference table chairs to pull on my jeans. "You don't have that kind of clout."

He raises an eyebrow at me. "I have my entire operation based inside the city's airport and you think I can't pull off one flight cancellation. Do you know who I am?"

I snigger. "You know what's funny? You may never know how much of your perceived clout is your own doing and how much of it is the Guild making you *think* you have clout," I say, pulling my bra on.

He gives me a look of outrage. "St. Louis loves me. I booked an entire museum for you."

"St. Louis…" I say in a faraway voice, looking across the room at nothing as if trying to recall something. "Oh that's right. St. Louis is actually the *birthplace* of the Guild." I pull my tank top over my head. "The organization was ratified into being in 1976 right underneath the *Gateway Arch,* which was partially paid for by the Guild. Did you know that?"

He looks like he has something sour in his mouth. "I hate you," he says, sitting up, and snatching his T-shirt from a nearby pile. "It's a good thing you're leaving. You're a Prime Human plant with a love potion ability, intended to subdue me for your own purposes. You're a femme fatale." He pulls on his jeans. "Never mind. I'll get my head back once I'm free of your noxious influence."

"Awww," I laugh, coming over to him and locking my arms around his waist. "I'm kidding… Well, only partly… Most of it's true. Except the museum and the airport. I don't *think* the Guild had a part in that. I'd have to check."

He already has his arms around me though. "I don't care," he whispers, kissing my forehead. "I don't bloody care. You are my femme fatale. Beautiful. Dangerous. Alluring. And I am perfectly content to be under your spell."

Another knock on the door. "Dumas!" Lelani yells. "Get your ass out here! We have a situation and you are needed!"

He grumbles and releases me. He grabs his phone from the table to find it dead.

"Lelani!" Gabriel calls. "My phone is dead. Where is my charger?"

"How should I know?" Lelani says. "And here's a tip: If you're going to tell your people to call you if they need something, make sure your damn phone is plugged in!"

"She's getting as bad as Rita," Gabriel mumbles, rummaging around for his charger while I pull my wig on and smooth it. I complete the look with my glasses. I can hear that it's still raining heavily, so sunglasses are still not going to fly.

"I'm going to leave you here," he says, pulling shoes on. "Tranwick will come by to get you once it's clear. You can go get something to eat. Restaurants are at the other end of the terminal. Do you need money?"

I cover my mouth and try not to laugh, but I can't help it.

He stops and then rolls his eyes. "Nevermind. I was being considerate. But apparently you're too wealthy for such gestures to matter."

I hold up my hands. "First of all, let's get one thing straight. *I* am dirt poor. I don't have a thing to call my own. And second, I laughed because… this. The normalcy contrasting with outlandishness. We're engaged. You spoke to me like it's a normal day of being almost married, and it feels totally familiar until you think about where and when it's happening. I can't seem to get past it."

"Oh yes," he says. "The paradox of our life has not escaped my notice. Frankly, I'm insanely curious about exactly how all of this is going to play out, what other twists of fate will be thrown in. We have over two years' worth of memories missing. That's a lot of time unaccounted for. Pieces of our past could show up unexpectedly at any time and create even more madness."

"Don't say that," I say, throwing my backpack over my shoulder and sitting on the table to wait. "I really do have things to do. I don't need things any more complicated than they are already."

₪

"So ya'll is like, together now?" Tonya says, sitting across from me at one of the tables in the dining area. "How's that work?"

"I have no idea," I say, opening my orange juice. "I have no friggin' clue."

"You leavin' the Guild?"

"No," I reply.

"He leavin' THM?"

"No."

Her face scrunches in confusion. "You tryna unite the kingdoms or somethin'?"

I give her a look. "No. THM won't like that. And the Guild won't tolerate it."

"So it's gonna stay secret then?"

Tonya is a lot chattier than the last time I saw her. "Yes," I say. "I'm leaving tonight to go back to New York. Dumas is leaving for California with THM."

She puts her chin in her hand, amused. "You know you wearin' a rang, right?"

I curse, jerking my hand into my lap and yanking the ring off. I totally forgot I had it on.

She laughs. "You aight, Miss White. You ain't so stuck-up as I thought you was. I get the white now. You dangerous 'cuz how you look ain't how you is. Ain't nobody ever guess the game you throwin' down."

I shove the ring into my bag. "That sounded like it was trying to be a compliment, so thanks."

She pauses for a second and then puts her hand up under her hair and touches her ear. "Copy," she says. Then to me. "We gotta go back."

"What's going on?" I ask, wishing I'd listened in on her communication.

She shrugs. "Ah dunno. Porter said bring you back to the conference room."

I stand and put my bag over my shoulder, nervous. Something has happened. I don't know what, but this is way too soon. Gabriel knows he can't hole up with me in that room all day or his people are going to get seriously suspicious. So this isn't him trying to get more alone time.

I follow Tonya back up the terminal. There's as much coming and going as earlier when I passed through here. I don't see Gabriel anywhere, or anyone else from Gabriel's team that I recognize. The only thing I can think of is someone found out I'm here.

We meet Porter in front of the door to the conference room. "Shit's goin' down in there. You ready?" he says to me.

"Do I have a choice?" I say.

"Sho' do. I can take you to the utha terminal. You can chill until you gotta go. But I think you better off dustin' off your Guild lady shoes and kickin' ass in there. 'Fact," he says, looking over my shoulder. "Take that hair off and those glasses. Everybody in there knows who you are. The less guilty you look, the better."

I look over my shoulder, but Tonya's blocking me from anyone seeing me down the hall. So I pull the wig and the glasses off, crouch down, and put them carefully into my backpack.

Porter opens the door for me.

I see Gabriel first, and he looks furious, standing on the other side the table, arms crossed tightly, making his muscles bulge. He reminds me of Mike that way. Then I see Rita, blonde hair in a high ponytail on top of her head, arms crossed as well, a look of pure obstinacy on her face.

I thought Rita was in Omaha…

Lelani is here and so is Soren, whom I rarely see. He handles THM's social media and communications. Shiah interacts with him fairly often.

Also, Lainey and Kiera.

What the hell is going on?

Porter was right. Time to go Councilwoman Wendy on these people.

I put my hands on my hips and look sternly at Kiera and Lainey. "I would welcome you to Missouri, but you aren't assigned to be here. Explain yourselves, please."

Fifty-Nine

*L**ainey's*** expression changes so quickly I have trouble not laughing. She goes from smug to indignant in under a second, a gasp of outrage passing her lips as her arms come uncrossed and her hands go to her hips. "Me?" she shrills. "What about *you*? Secret meetings with Dumas? A secret affair with him? What do you call that? *Negotiating?*"

The one face I see in my mind is Shiah, and I tap into everything I have learned about and from her to choose my next move.

I remove my backpack calmly, set it on the floor and step forward, hands clasped behind my back. I look at Lainey directly, unflinchingly. "Miss Flynn, as someone who has tried desperately for nearly three months to get more Primes comfortable with thinking outside of the Guild, I am *so* pleased that you've obviously taken some initiative, pushing the boundaries of your assignment. Your clear efforts to protect the Guild are highly commendable. And I understand that being caught outside of your assigned area would make you defensive, but I need you to put that aside and explain to me why you are here with high-profile members of THM."

Lainey's mouth opens as her outrage surges through my chest.

"Ah," I stop her, holding my hand up. "I think you should take a moment to calm down. You seem to be forgetting who you are speaking to." I turn to Kiera. "Miss Johnson, I apologize, I forgot to ask if you could answer freely. And I hope that you haven't forgotten confidentiality while with the other individuals in this room."

I haven't seen or spoken to Kiera since I accused her of manipulating me months ago. But she, unlike Lainey, looks and feels like she's been caught with a boy in her room. "I haven't forgotten, Councilwoman," she says deferentially. "But, um, the cat was kind of already out of the bag. Didn't really allow for thinking through what might and might not be considered classified. If we've screwed up, I'm sorry. It wasn't intentional."

"That sounds reasonable," I say. "Continue."

She clears her throat nervously and she glances quickly at Lainey before saying, "I don't mean to argue, but in Lainey's defense, we aren't exactly outside of our assigned area. We were given a new mission as of two days ago. We were told it was handed down by the Council directly and it was to take top priority. We've been working with Ben?"

I restrain a gasp. I momentarily forgot that Shiah assigned Ben to PHIA recovery earlier this week, and they're supposed to be tracking Ezra. I guess I just didn't expect it to happen so fast…

Oh my gosh… Did they track Ezra here?!

Calm down, Wendy. Be patient.

"Yes," I reply. "I'm aware of the mission."

"Good. So we set off yesterday, and right off the bat, Ben flipped out on us. He kept talking about 'scent interference' or something like that. He was getting all bent out of shape because he was worried it was going to make him lose the scent memory or whatever. Hannah's the only one that even remotely understood what he was talking about, but you know, we haven't even worked with him a week so we don't know the ins and outs of what he can do. We were just told we were on a deadline so there was a lot of urgency we were dealing with, too. Ben just would not shut up about needing a scent reminder, that it was a bad idea to go if his scent connection was already getting screwy. Tensions were really high, and Lainey was losing patience, and long story short, she told him we should follow whatever was screwing up his 'scent radar' because if he could isolate it, maybe it would help him differentiate it from the 'right' trail. He seemed to like that idea a lot better, because I think he was embarrassed about the whole thing and didn't want to have to go back to the source and memorize it again."

She looks at me knowingly. I, of course, am the 'source' she's talking about. And I think I'm starting to get where this is going. I arrived in St. Louis yesterday, and the Vault is not too many hours south of here, which is where they would have 'set off' as Kiera puts it. It sounds like my sudden appearance so close to where he was at the Vault confused Ben's focus on Ezra's trail. He *expected* me to still be in New York. Dammit. This whole thing is my fault.

"When we arrived, Ben did his sniffing around thing and sort of got sidetracked… *again.* This time it was a girl standing in the registration line, holding a child, maybe a year old. Ben said, 'The source of the interference is a little further away, maybe down the road, but that girl and the child have a similar emotional scent.' I don't think I can properly communicate the level of frustration Lainey and I were experiencing at that point, because the guy just couldn't make up his mind and couldn't be clear about anything to save his life." Kiera huffs.

"Anyway, Lainey watched the girl and was almost immediately interested. She realized the girl did have some *odd* connections, but to the PHIA moles we have in custody directly."

I lift my eyebrows, surprised. I had heard that Lainey was getting pretty skilled with her ability to see connections between people. She sees them in a projection of sorts, like criss-crossed lines between people when they're close. She can also tell how strongly people are connected, just by the line between them. No doubt she sees the one between Gabriel and me. I'm sure that's exactly what she based her accusation on. But as for spotting someone related to PHIA, she's gotten good enough that she can memorize tags of some kind on people such as those of Garrett Stimple and the other PHIA moles. It means she can look at anyone and know if they were ever connected to those members of PHIA even if they aren't anywhere near each other.

"Okay," I say finally. "You began watching her then?"

"Yes," Kiera replies. "We didn't approach her because…"

"You wanted to know what she was doing here since she was tied to PHIA?"

"Yes. At first."

I lift my eyebrows.

"Like I said, she had a child with her, and at the registration desk last night she asked to speak to Mister Dumas. They refused, because I guess that's what everybody wants, since he's the celebrity and all. But she kept insisting. Finally, she got really frustrated and said something to *her*," She motions at Lelani. "And it seemed to change everything all of a sudden. They escorted her somewhere, and I followed while Lainey stayed behind to keep a lookout. She sent Ben back to our hotel because he was going to blow our cover with how nervous he was, being surrounded by THM.

"I could only follow them so far, but I pulled up a schematic that showed they had taken her back to where the holding cells are. It seemed to be causing a stir though, and Lainey pulled out the long-range microphones to hear what was being said. Basically, what we gleaned was that the girl claimed to know Dumas before his memory loss and that the child she had with her was his."

For the first time I glance up at Gabriel, who is staring back at me. He's on the edge of my empathic range, and with the other emotions in the room I can't tell what he's thinking other than that he's frustrated.

I don't let my eyes linger though, instead focusing back on Kiera.

"This morning the other woman showed up. Rita," Kiera says. "That was who Lelani was speaking to on the phone last night. We were in the process of listening in when their security caught on to us. And we were taken to a holding cell. But um, we told them we were only interested in the girl because we knew she had something to do with PHIA. They started asking us questions about how we knew, but we didn't answer, and then Lainey said if they didn't let her speak to the girl, she was going to make sure the world knew about her and what she had claimed about the child. Lainey also threatened to reveal that Dumas was tied to PHIA unless they let us speak to him directly."

I look at Lainey with disappointment. "You threatened The Human Movement, Miss Flynn? Under what authority? Because it certainly wasn't sanctioned by the Guild."

She looks like she would like to spit in my face. "Is *your* presence here sanctioned by the Guild?"

I straighten my shoulders, hands behind my back once more. "I am on the Council, Miss Flynn. I am sanctioned by the Guild wherever I choose to be. And every relationship and interaction I have is also sanctioned. Because whether personal or public, my dealings are all consecrated toward the advancement of the Guild's interests. We are part of the world, not separate from it. The future for us is continued blurring of those lines of demarcation. Go read the long term goals contained in the Guild Charter to refresh your memory. I think you'll realize your outrage stems from old habits of secrecy and exclusion and does not take into account our new initiatives. Further, your lack of clearance understandably makes it difficult for you to put my actions into a satisfying context."

Gosh, I sound like Shiah...

Lainey is staggered. Eyes wide as I've spoken, her emotions have vacillated between suspicion and conciliation, finally settling on the latter. The good thing about dealing with members of the Guild is that they will always lean toward obedience, particularly to Council members, even if it doesn't involve a clear understanding.

It both makes the Guild the effective machine that it is as well as holds back progress. It's a double-edged sword that Shiah has taught me how to wield.

"I'm sorry, Councilwoman," Lainey says, mirroring my open stance. "I shouldn't have jumped to conclusions."

Someone, Rita I think, makes a sound of protest, which I completely ignore. Instead, I say, "Again, I admire your initiative. I probably would have done the same thing."

Lainey seems relieved as she clears her throat and says, "I realized you were here because I saw you come in late last night with Dumas before we got caught by security. Yes, I was the one to issue the threats. I told them they had wrongfully kidnapped us, and that wasn't going to look good in the media when it came out. That's what had them bringing us in here. Dumas showed up finally, and from what I could tell, his team had kept the girl's appearance from him until this morning when they couldn't decide what to do with her or us. Everyone was throwing around accusations and we were getting nowhere so I said they had better bring you in here or I was going to activate my tracking implant and bring the entire Guild in and they'd never get any information about the girl." She grimaces. "That, uh, wasn't my best move. I had assumed that Dumas' people already knew you were here. I played the card because I was hoping that I could vicariously use your status to get them to take me seriously about getting information from the girl. So now here we are."

I finally look around the room and sigh as if disappointed in all the unruly children, but inside I am *dying* to meet this girl and take a look at the child. "Where is the girl now?"

"That's not your business," Rita snaps. "She's here to see Gabe. Not you."

I turn toward her slowly and narrow my eyes, grateful that I don't have to be conciliatory toward her. "It is *definitely* my business," I reply venomously. "Especially when I find out you've been keeping the girl all night in a *holding cell* like a criminal."

"Exactly," Gabriel says. "And now that we are all up to speed, let's have the young woman brought in. You people have gone mad." He looks around at his team. "I don't even know what to say to you right now. So the three of you can get out of my sight. You've lost my trust and confidence, therefore none of this concerns you."

He walks over and opens the door and says, "Tranwick, have the girl brought in, please. And have someone pick up some food for her."

His three people begin to file out, and Gabriel says, "Rita, you need to do some serious introspection. I know you set the others up to this. I'm about to be a thousand miles away, and if I can't trust you then this isn't going to work."

She spins around, a look of disgust on her face. "*You* can't trust *me*? You're cavorting with Guild prostitutes in secret and I'm the one with a trust problem?"

"That's enough!" he barks. "You will not speak about Miss Whitley that way and you bloody hell won't accuse me of not being honest with you. You have been privy to *every* detail since the outset, with the exception of things other people have specifically asked me to keep in confidence. As for telling you about her appearance here, she hasn't even left yet! The conclusion of our visit isn't even in the books! Get your jealousy in check, Rita. It's skewing your judgment, and I'm tired of navigating it."

Rita's fists balled at her sides, she turns around and stomps off.

Gabriel slams the door behind her and puts his forehead in his hand.

"Councilwoman," Kiera says. "Tracking down PHIA members is our proprietary mission, and knowing who this girl knows would be *so* helpful. I would be so appreciative if you'd allow us to remain in the room when you question her."

I look at them, considering it. I have *no* clue how this is going to go, but whoever this girl is may already know about my marriage to Gabriel if she's not lying about knowing his past, which means sensitive things may come up. And then Lainey and Kiera are going to know even more about things I haven't shared with the rest of the Council. They don't know that, and I think I can assume they'll keep all of that in confidence, but I don't truly know. It will be a tangled web for sure.

But if there's one thing I know about trust, you get it when you give it. And I could use a few more allies in the Guild whom I can trust so implicitly. They're good candidates. Plus, they've been assigned to track down my brother. I want the people doing something that important to trust me.

I nod. "Yes. But let me state up front that everything you learn is to be kept in confidence. I am your direct line of authority from this moment. We will discuss at a later point what can and can't be shared with your direct superior. I will personally inform Councilman Kassapa of what you discover."

"Yes, absolutely," Lainey nearly gushes, clearly relieved and grateful. She was obviously not expecting me to agree.

"And you will be silent unless I ask you something," I say. "Mister Dumas and I will do the talking."

They both nod and I wave them to an end of the conference table just as a knock sounds at the door.

Gabriel glances back at me briefly before he opens it wide.

Porter stands behind a young girl with dark brown hair pulled back in a ponytail. And she's holding a little boy with olive skin and thick, almost black hair that reaches his shoulders. He stares at Gabriel with big eyes as he grips the girl's T-shirt in his small fist.

The child's clothes are stained, but his face is clean. By the smell I can tell it's been quite a while since the girl has seen a shower. They're destitute. That's my first impression. My second one is that she must be a fraud. She saw the GMA interview about Gabriel's memory loss and decided to see if she could capitalize on it.

I step back because I have no idea how to handle this. I look at Gabriel, and he looks equally skeptical.

The girl seems to pick up our distrust and she wraps her arms more firmly around the boy.

"Won't you have a seat?" Gabriel says, motioning to the conference table.

She stands there, her dark brown eyes shifting from me to Gabriel and back.

I feel like I shouldn't even be here, so I back up and sit on the edge of the table.

"Don't be frightened," Gabriel says to the girl. "We aren't going to harm you. But I was told you wanted to speak to me. Wendy is a friend of mine, so I hope you don't mind that she's here."

"I know who she is," the girl blurts, almost offended. "And I was locked up by *your* people all night, so I'm a bit short on trust."

Gabriel grimaces. "Yes, I'm sorry about that. I wasn't aware."

Tonya shows up next to Porter, a paper bag in hand. The girl leaps to the side at the sound of crinkling paper behind her.

"Are you hungry?" Gabriel says, giving the girl a wide berth as he reaches for the bag. He nods at Porter and Tonya.

"Yes," she says. She holds out her hand and Gabriel puts the bag in it. Then she walks over to the end of the table furthest from the rest of us.

Gabriel shuts the door and leans against it. Stress is written all over his face.

An arm wrapped firmly around the child, the girl shimmies out of the large pack she has on her back. It looks like a hiker's pack, complete with sleeping bag; a rolled up, discolored tarp; and a pot and flashlight dangling from the bottom. A coat is bunched up with some kind of elastic and attached with a clip to her waist along with an empty knife sheath. She's wearing jeans, a T-shirt, and cowboy boots. She dumps the contents of the bag on the table, fries and all, and sits down, shifting the boy into her lap.

"What's your name?" Gabriel says, pulling a chair out, away from the table and sitting down, an ankle crossed over his knee.

"Kaylen," she replies, not looking up. She rips off a piece of her burger and places it on the table in front of the child who reaches for it eagerly.

"Where are you from, Kaylen?" Gabriel asks.

"Where are *you* from?" she replies.

"Bakersfield, California. But I was born in—"

"Pasadena," she says before shoving fries in her mouth.

"Yes," he replies quietly.

"Well at least you haven't forgotten your *whole* life," the girl says. Her eyes train on me now, and beneath the dirt I can tell she has beautiful skin. Her cheeks have reddened since she got here. "And where are *you* from?"

"That depends on what you mean by 'from'," I reply. "I moved around a lot."

"Because your mom was paranoid," Kaylen says. "She was running from your father, Carl." She pauses, her eyes blink rapidly, and she stops mid-chew. She swallows too soon and coughs several times.

Her words jar me, but I keep my composure. "You knew him?" I say, reading sorrow on her face.

The question seems to upset her more, and now her eyes begin to water. She wipes them quickly with the edge of her sleeve. "Yes, I *knew* him," she says, insulted. "I know *you,* too." She shoves the burger in her mouth.

I don't know what to say. She's awfully aggravated and close-lipped for someone who made such a concerted effort to find and talk to Gabriel. I'm certainly not revealing any cards until I know whether this girl is legit. I'm getting really worried that the reason she's not really saying anything is because she's wanting us to speak first, so she can figure out the best way to respond. I've already had Andre trying to screw with my head, and I can tell by the way Gabriel seems enraptured by the child's every move that if we can't determine her credibility quickly, he's going to let Kaylen screw with his own head, too.

I stand up and put my hands on my hips. "Kaylen, everyone in this room is truly sorry for how you've been treated since you got here, but we need to get to the bottom of this. You came here to talk to Mister Dumas, and you claimed to Lelani that this child was his. We're willing to listen to you, but my operatives have determined that you are *tightly* connected to PHIA, which means that we can't afford to trust your word. That means you're going to have to say something to convince us that you're not here making false claims to gain something. It's harsh and it's not fair, and I can tell you've been through a lot, but that's just how it is."

Kaylen, who has seemed awfully distracted the entire time, finally looks at me with unwavering attention. She smiles with just the corner of her mouth and it slowly goes wider. "I've missed you, Wendy."

I'm about to reply that I wish I could say I missed her, too, but she holds up a finger. "Hold on. I'm absolutely starving. Lemme finish and I swear I will answer all your questions."

I lift my eyebrows in response as she shoves the rest of burger in her mouth.

Gabriel looks over at me, gives me a slight smile as well. I have somehow broken the ice with this girl. Apparently all it took was a heavier hand. She claims to know me, but also that she has Gabriel's child... Something doesn't add up. I sit back down on the edge of the table and watch the little boy shove french fries in his mouth one-by-one. He's awfully cute, and his eyes are pretty enchanting, completely focused on what he's doing as if it's the most important thing in the whole world. Could he really be Gabriel's child? His features all support the possibility. Was Gabriel involved with this girl while we were separated? I test how I feel about that, and based on what I know about Gabriel, it's really hard to imagine. He was still holding his ring for goodness sake. Was he really so different before that having a child while he was still technically married to me was okay to him?

In that case, seducing me on a slide when he knew he was married, even though he didn't know who he was married to, didn't seem to bother him that much.

Kaylen pushes a few more fries in the child's direction before licking her fingers, wiping her hands, and looking up. "You'll have to correct me if I'm wrong, but over the past few months it has *seemed* like you both lost a big portion of your memories, right? I mean, I know Gabe has. He said as much on GMA. But Wendy, you act like you don't remember either."

"Correct," I say. "I did lose some memory. Is there anything you can tell me that will help me believe the things you're going to tell us? I've had people use my missing memory to their advantage before, so I'm pretty gun shy when someone I don't know claims they know something about me."

"Probably," she replies, thinking. After a few moments, she brightens and says, "Ezra. I know you remember him. Mostly. I'm not sure how *much* of him you remember, but I can tell you who his favorite superhero is."

I can't help my hands clenching at Ezra's name falling from her mouth, and I'm keenly aware she referred to him in present tense, which means she knows he's alive as well.

She looks at me confidently. "Catwoman. It's a secret though. He always claims Batman. Embarrassed about liking a girl superhero or something stupid like that." She smiles to herself.

I'm proud of myself for holding it together as she talks about him like an old friend, and she's spot on, but I'm still not buying. She's been with PHIA one way or another, and Ezra was taken by them, which means they could have gotten that information from him for just this reason.

"You're going to have to do better than that," I say, crossing my arms.

Gabriel looks over at me questioningly.

"You know you can tell if I'm lying if you'll sit closer," she says. "Or did you somehow lose that skill?"

It's a good point, so I come around the table and put her in my range. My first impression is that she's desperate, racking her brain for something to say that will convince us of her legitimacy.

"How about this," Kaylen says, leaning back in her chair and crossing her ankle over her knee like Gabriel and creating a sort of cradle for the little boy, who seems used to this routine. He's already laying his head back on her abdomen, staring intently at the fry in his fist. She rocks forward and back as she says, "You said you can still see the *energy world*." She wrinkles her nose. "Well *we* called it the colorworld. For obvious reasons. I can tell you what it looks like. Souls are purple. They're composed of strands, thinner than spider silk. The average person has around thirty billion of them. There is a swirl over the chest and head in the pattern of a Golden Spiral." She makes a swirl motion with her finger over her chest and then her head to demonstrate. "Souls glow and some are brighter than others. Really terrible people have practically no glow. Their life force abilities stop working then because they don't have light to power them. Really amazing people have really bright souls. Like you and Gabe. And like Uncle Moby." She frowns and my heart catches on her sorrow.

"You probably don't remember him either..." she whispers, seemingly to herself before looking at Gabriel and then me again. "You might know his name as Robert Haricott. He was the most amazing man on the planet. And this little munchkin," she says, looking down at the child lovingly, "was named after him for exactly that reason. Robert Gabriel Dumas, but we call him Robbie."

The child she calls Robbie is in the middle of falling asleep, his eyes fluttering, his french-fry fist falling to his side.

"Anyway," she says, still rocking gently. "Prime Humans have a head over chest ratio—wait, hold on, I'm getting ahead of myself. The spirals are where strands go into the body, so at the chest and head. The ratio between the two is the Golden Ratio. I don't remember the number, but that's what Ezra says. For regular humans, the ratio is reversed, chest over head. Hypno-touch is lethal because it pulls strands out of the body. The more strands you pull, the faster the person dies. The only way to save them is to shove those things back in. Both of you almost died from hypno-touch sickness, did you know that?"

I just stare at her, and Gabriel shakes his head.

"Wendy, you had leukemia. T-cell something or other. It's a really long name. Gabe, you had small-cell carcinoma. I'm getting off-track here, but the point is we figured out how to get the strands back in. Yours and mine and a bunch of other people. I would tell you how but I don't trust the Guild, like at all. And you have those two girls behind you that you said are operatives. You once said that protecting information about the colorworld was worth dying for, so I'm going to assume, if you could still remember, you wouldn't want me saying anything. I've already said more than I ought to anyway."

I exhale. She's got to be the real deal. With information like that… Telling me things I don't even know about the energy world but that make total sense… "Why don't you trust the Guild?" I say.

She has to think about it, but finally she says, "They hide everything for one thing. For another, I have a hard time separating Andre from the Guild. I still don't know how much the Guild knew about the terrible things he did to us while he was working for them." She looks at me purposefully. "And lastly, *you* never trusted them. In fact, I seriously wish I could see the expression of the Wendy I knew when she realizes her future self is now a Guild big-wig." She laughs and it fades into pondering. "I get a kick out of that every time… Always cheers me up."

She might find it odd, but I believe that one hundred percent, even without my empathic range to confirm her honesty. I have forgotten the struggle I had when I first encountered the Guild, but it all rushes back to me now.

"Kaylen, Wendy seems satisfied that you are who you claim," Gabriel says. "So could you enlighten me about the child? You said he's mine. Were we an item at some point?"

Kaylen bursts into laughter, startling Robbie awake, but he fades again quickly. "Gosh no," she says, and then her attention moves from Gabriel to me in utter disbelief. "Robbie isn't mine," she says. "He's yours and Wendy's."

My eyes dart to Robbie's sleeping face, searching for evidence of Kaylen's certainty. I shake my head slowly. "That's not possible. I can't have children."

"Okay…" Kaylen says, amused. She runs her fingers through Robbie's long hair. "Well. I saw you pop him out in a bathtub at Uncle Moby's house. You don't have to take my word for it though. A DNA test should do the trick." A new idea occurs to her and she looks up. "You don't even know you're married, do you?"

I don't answer.

"You *do* know!" Kaylen says. "I can see it on your face."

Gabriel clears his throat. "We figured it out only hours ago, actually."

Kaylen seems prone to fits of giggles over our situation. When I look at her with annoyance though, she says, "Okay, here. You conceived Robbie while you were dying. The Guild had fed you a drug without you knowing to preserve your reproductive system. They were betting you would die and they wanted to get their hands on your eggs in the autopsy room. Make little colorworld-sight babies to take over the world. The problem is that it causes mutations, so in normal cases they have to pick out the viable eggs. But if you're conceiving naturally you don't get that luxury." Her expression and emotions go dark and vengeful. "So Robbie has Duchenne Muscular Dystrophy because of the drug. You say your eggs aren't viable, but I don't know the ins and outs of the drug. Maybe it kills your eggs slowly. Maybe you think you're sterile because the eggs they tested were just the bad ones. I have no idea. But this is Robbie. He is your son. If you don't want him, I will be glad to keep him. Frankly, after watching you guys on TV, I've gone back and forth on bringing him to you at all. It makes me sick that you're working for the Guild. That's actually why I came to Gabe instead." She looks at me disdainfully.

Gabriel leans his head back and rubs his face. "Gads," he says. "This is absurd to the point of insanity."

All I can seem to find is indifference. I can tell she's being truthful, but there are *so* many unanswered questions.

Kaylen tilts her head curiously. "So are you guys together or not? I mean, Gabe obviously totally worships you. Per the usual—although that last Chicago thing was pretty harsh. It was true though, which is Gabe's MO. But you're both here, and from my understanding, Wendy, you're supposed to be in New York on trial for murder. By the way, watching you shoot Andre was the thing that solidified getting Robbie to Gabe even if it meant bringing you into the picture. I freaking cheered inside the electronics store. My plan was to get to Gabe and tell him everything he needed to do to seduce the crap out of you and get you away from those brain-washing freaks."

Kaylen's animosity toward the Guild is genuine, and it seems to be growing every time she mentions them.

"Alright, Kaylen," Gabriel says. "You have me convinced. I have only a thousand questions, but I think my most preeminent ones are how you ended up with Robbie and what Wendy and I were doing just prior to our memory loss. Based on evidence, we suspect that we were separated."

"Separated?" Kaylen says, pondering. Then she puts her hand over her mouth. "Where's Mike?" She looks at me accusatorially. "Wendy, are you with Mike? Like romantically?"

I frown in aggravation at her continued disdain for me. "No. Mike is in New York. We were never together."

She exhales in relief. "Oh thank God. That would have... sucked." Then she smiles to herself. "Go, Mike." She glares at Gabriel now. "You should really give him more credit. He is so loyal to you."

Gabriel holds his hands up. "I'm not arguing."

"Of course I don't get why Mike hasn't told you all this. Unless he went back to working for the Guild and was keeping everything secret... I have no clue. I swear, watching you guys it's like everyone has been living in an alternate reality. I've had to refuse to think about it. Nothing makes sense and there was no way to figure it out without actually talking to you."

"Mike lost memories as well," I say without regret because I empathize with her confusion. I know *exactly* what that's like. I hesitate but finally say, "Kaylen, the memory loss was Guild-wide. The commonality was that everyone's memories were wiped of *me*. Even our databases were wiped of anything relating to me."

Understanding washes over her face and she nods. "That's the most believable thing I've heard in a while. I can't believe I didn't think of that... Maybe because someone with a life force ability capable of doing something that big doesn't seem possible... Of course, someone who can make chunks of continents disappear under the water *also* doesn't seem possible, but that was always the assumption."

I catch my breath. "You know what's causing the disasters?"

"No. We were trying to figure it out, and that's what everyone thought. I don't know if you figured it out or not before you lost your memory."

"Oh," I say, deflated.

She shifts gears. "So Mike lost his memory as well, which means he didn't know you were married to Gabe... He was Wendy's bodyguard and you guys never got it on..." She looks at me in disbelief. "Are you lying?"

I make a sound of outrage before I can catch myself. "I have not slept with Mike! I haven't even kissed him!"

Her eyes widen in surprise and she believes me. "Wow. That's a really good thing." She turns to Gabriel. "And if you could remember, you would probably be cheering over what a big deal that is."

"I can only imagine," Gabriel replies.

"Oh man. This is awesome, you guys," Kaylen says. She turns to Gabriel. "And I know exactly why you were separated even though I wasn't there when it happened. The writing was on the wall when I left. It's because you were convinced Wendy was supposed to be with Mike instead of you." She rolls her eyes. "Sometimes you get stuck on the dumbest stuff. Anyway, we found out that in order to save you from SMA when you were a kid, Mike gave you like nineteen billion of his own life force strands without realizing it. That's why you guys are connected, why he feels what you do. And since Wendy loved Mike, too, you thought the only part of *you* she loved was the part Mike gave you. And you were being a real dick about it."

Kaylen leans back, still rocking, and wags a finger. "If I had to bet money, I bet it went like this: Gabe, you gave them an ultimatum. If Wendy wanted to be with you they had to move Mike's strands back to prove Wendy actually loved you and not him. Otherwise, you would leave. Wendy would never risk your life for a reason like that and neither would Mike."

She claps her hands victoriously and then looks at Gabriel. "Seriously, why do you have to obsess like that? Ezra totally called it. Before I left, right when things were starting to look bad, he said, 'Kaylen, it's happening all over again. Gabe's going to get stuck on this one thing and he's not going to let it go until he gets his way. I want to punch him. Repeatedly.'"

"Wait, *all over again?*" Gabriel says, sitting up. "I left her before?"

"Well, technically she left you. But you drove her to it. But that's a whole other story."

Gabriel groans and leans his head back again. "It terrifies me that I can actually imagine all of this happening exactly like you're saying."

"Kaylen?" I say hesitantly. "Where is Ezra?"

Fear and guilt hit her immediately and she hangs her head, running her fingers more quickly through Robbie's hair. "I don't even know if he's alive," she whispers. Then she looks up. "I'm going back. My plan was to get Robbie to Gabe and then go back to find out. I've wanted to go back for months but I couldn't justify putting Robbie at risk like that."

Knowing how much she obviously cares about my brother makes me immediately latch on to her. "Kaylen, I confirmed only a few days ago that he's alive."

Her eyes go wide. "Really? How?"

I give her a look. "The Guild is comprised of a lot of talented people. We have ways."

My eyes fall to Robbie, and I wonder why I have no compulsion to hold him to see if he feels like my child. I imagine Kaylen handing him to me, and it terrifies me. I don't know him. And he doesn't seem to know me either. Kaylen has been caring of him for four months. It sounds like she was close to Ezra, but she prioritized Robbie's safety over Ezra's.

"You say go back," Gabriel says. "Go back where?"

"Andre's nasty hovel," Kaylen says. "He probably moved it after I escaped with Robbie, but that's my starting point."

"You escaped with Robbie?"

She nods and then sighs. "Okay, so in like… June of last year, Andre shot missiles at us in Redlands and killed a bunch of our people. He shot Mike twice and nearly killed him. He kidnapped Farlen and Uncle Moby. He tortured them and beat Uncle Moby to death. Then he dumped his body and Farlen on the ground in front of Wendy. Right after that I realized nobody was going to do anything about it, I decided I was going to find Andre and kill him myself."

Sixty

've done a lot of things since the last time you saw me that you'd look down on me for," Kaylen says a little too proudly, but it doesn't match the shame she's feeling. She looks at me as she realizes the emotions she's passing me. "I did what I had to. I did what was necessary. And if I hadn't Robbie would be dead, Ezra for sure, and so would you and Gabe." She waits, expectant, ready to defend herself.

"Nobody is judging you," I say. "We're here to listen. You're the one with all the information."

She crosses her arms haughtily. "Exactly. Another thing you wouldn't have if I hadn't done what I did."

"Which is what?" Gabriel says.

"Long story short, I found Andre and got into his inner circle," she says. "So when he managed to take Jessie, Paul, Corben, Maris, Dan, Robbie, and Ezra, I was there." She looks up at the ceiling. "God, if I'd only had my telekinesis… I could have taken the whole place down, ripped all of them end to end and got everyone out."

"You're a Prime Human?" I say, intrigued, pulling my GIT out of my bag nearby to look her up.

She scowls at me. "Yeah. But not anymore. When you fixed my strands my life force ability went away. I could have really used it this year."

Her words are riddled with accusation, but her explanation doesn't make sense. She's saying I fixed my own life force after hypnotouch, but I still have my abilities. I did the same for her, but she doesn't have hers… She said only terrible people lose their life force abilities.

I type her name into the database. Nothing comes up. So instead I search by telekinesis. It's a fairly common ability, so it lists twenty-seven results.

Kaylen is curious about what I'm doing and she lifts her chin to see.

I cycle through the results, looking for something that seems like her. Everyone is active. Except for one. If she's telling the truth—and I think she is—this has to be her.

"Unaccounted for since nineteen ninety-eight," I say. "Abducted from your Guild foster family. Suspected telekinetic. Mother died from seed-generation sickness. Update: Hypno-touch performed by... Pneumatikon." I pause over the familiar name for a moment. "Father unknown."

"Sounds about right," Kaylen says, but I can tell she's jarred by the information. She wasn't aware of it for the most part.

"Once you realized my parents, Robbie, and Ezra were taken, what did you do?" Gabriel says, getting us back on track.

"Creative negotiation," she replies. "I went there to kill him, but once I was there I realized how many people worked for him. So I was going to take the whole thing down. That would be a lot harder, but someone needed to. I learned a lot about him. Andre kept most things close to the chest, and he had clearance levels for everything. Basically, he ran PHIA like the Guild. Totally secret. Nobody knows the whole scope. He'd have rallies to get people pumped up. He'd mentor people that might be straying, further the indoctrination. Everybody did their part, and he'd make it a point to regularly lavish people with attention, from the cook at the mess hall to the commander of one of his nasty cleanse operations. He was also a fan of changing plans spontaneously. I don't know if that's just the way his head worked or if it was a strategy to keep people from double-crossing him. It worked either way. And that's what made it so hard to figure out how to bring PHIA down. In the end, that's why I failed."

She takes a few frustrated breaths. "Andre was latched on to promoting this idea that Prime Humans were the cause of natural disasters. When he kidnapped everyone, it was really only Robbie he was interested in. He took everyone else as a show of power and control. He was hoping Robbie had Wendy's ability to see the colorworld, that he could use it to prove that Primes were causing everything. But one of the first things that happened when the team arrived back was that someone went to take Robbie from Maris and died on the spot." Kaylen smirks.

I stare at Robbie in shock.

"I don't follow," Gabriel says.

"He's a channel," I say in disbelief. "A lethal one."

"I didn't know there were non-lethal ones," Kaylen says. "In any case, nobody was going to touch him. So I volunteered. Nobody argued. That's when Andre killed Corben suddenly and without warning. He went at Ezra next and I got in front of him. Talked him down. I told him there was still a way and that if he killed all his bargaining chips he'd have to rethink everything. I told him you had your abilities back, which he didn't know until that point. I told him he could get *you* to find out the information he wanted. He had Robbie and he had Ezra and you'd do anything for the both of them."

My hands have grown clammy. It's sick. All of it. And as much as I see her logic for tricking Andre, I have a hard time imagining doing it myself. Why didn't she kill him right then? "Who was Corben?"

"Part of the family," Kaylen says. "Protection detail. Handpicked by Uncle Moby. All your people were. Even after he died, they worked for you because of him. That's how much everyone loved Uncle Moby."

"You said I had my abilities *back*. I didn't have them before?"

"When you fixed your strands you lost them. We realized we must have done the configuration wrong. That's why I don't have mine either. Dad—I mean Carl—did hypno-touch on you again to bring them back, which nobody agreed with. But that was kind of how you rolled, Wendy. You did whatever felt right even if it wasn't logical. And that's why I had the courage to leave you guys when I did. I knew nobody would like it, but I had to do it. I wanted to be like you." She looks at me searchingly, wondering if that same person she esteemed is in me.

It occurs to me, however, that I'm on a timeline most likely... I'm a Prime and I had hypno-touch. Again. It tried to kill me within six months, which means I'm not immune. How long has it been since Carl supposedly performed it on me again? It was at least four months ago, but probably longer.

"So he blackmailed Wendy," Gabriel says. "Can you give us a timeline? When was this?"

"Some time after mid-October. Last year. So five months ago."

Not long before I woke up in the woods.

"He gave her two weeks," Kaylen says. "She had to find the cause of natural disasters or everyone would die. That gave me two weeks to figure out how to get everyone out."

She sighs and resumes combing her fingers through Robbie's hair, this time separating out a section and beginning to braid it.

"He changed his plans, didn't he?" I say, reading it in her emotions.

"He did," she says, and her voice catches. She looks up at the ceiling to keep her tears in. "I don't know why..."

We wait for her to continue. She cycles through confusion and bitterness, a pattern that's familiar to her. She's done it so many times before now, to no avail. She finally lets it go as she has every other time and says, "I had to be really careful about taking an interest in the prisoners, even Robbie, who generally stayed with Maris and Dan. I didn't visit them, didn't ask about them. About a week in though, Andre told me I needed to go to Dan and Maris' cell and take care of Robbie. I didn't ask why. I just went. When I got there Dan and Maris were gone and Robbie was in his crib alone.

"I was afraid to ask questions, so I had no idea what had happened to them. I tried to stay focused on the fact that Robbie was okay, but I was freaking out about Ezra. Was he gone, too? Had Andre killed them and sent their bodies to Gabe and Wendy? Maybe his plan all along was to kill them off one-by-one. I realized I had no way of knowing if he'd told me the truth about the timeline. I had no idea what kind of threat he'd actually made. Paranoia took over and I had to know if Ezra was still there. So I went to the room where they were keeping him, which was empty, but there was blood on the floor. Not a lot, but it was still blood. The game was off at that point for me. I had to get us out of there. But first, I had to know if anyone was still alive."

My chest hollows with her residual fear and I lean forward without realizing it.

"I confronted Andre. I asked him where the prisoners were. I framed it like someone had busted them out, like someone had betrayed him and I was going to help him figure out who. All he said was that Ezra had been moved to a larger space because he was proving useful. Then he looked at me funny and I realized suddenly I was holding Robbie. I was holding a loaded weapon as far as Andre was concerned. And Andre was unarmed and alone.

"It was the moment I'd been wanting. But I hesitated. I was pretty certain Andre wouldn't survive, but what if he did?" Kaylen pauses in regret.

"Why were you certain?" Gabriel asks.

Kaylen looks at him and shakes her head, in disbelief once more over our lack of knowledge. She clears her throat. "Channels are only lethal to people who don't have enough life force light to endure them."

"Ahh," Gabriel replies.

I'm stunned, which seems to be the norm now. Kaylen is so knowledgable about life forces and the energy world. I must be right about my past self knowing a heck of a lot more about all that than my current self does.

I'm also relieved. Hugely so as the memory of killing Ezra with my skin that I dredged up with Mikel dies once and for all. I could not have hurt Ezra with my skin. He is alive. Ben was not mistaken.

"I apologized," Kaylen says, grimacing. "I backed way up, said I'd return Robbie to his crib. Told him I'd forgotten and my instinct was to not leave babies alone. I think it was that moment that Andre finally trusted me, like for real, because when I turned to go, he said he wanted help with something and he didn't know who else to ask. I asked him what. He said, with his son. I was floored because I had no idea he *had* a son. Turns out Andre had brought him back to the base from wherever he was living and the kid was freaking out. He was thirteen, totally indoctrinated by the Guild, didn't see Andre as his father. Andre was really upset about it; I'd never seen him like that before. I told him I'd be glad to help if I could, but inside I was like, crap, now I have not just Ezra to bust out, but this kid of Andre's as well."

I sigh, knowing about the kid. Andre has several, but they're not his kids in the usual sense. They're children born to surrogates using his sperm donation as part of the population increase initiative. And the one she's talking about was abducted in one of PHIA's cleanse operations.

"So Andre took me to the kid, Avery," Kaylen says. "He didn't want anything to do with either of us and Andre's temper kept getting away from him. I told Andre to leave me alone with him, and he agreed. Once Andre was gone, I did my best to convince Avery I was on his side. But he wasn't having it. By the way, that's another reason I don't trust the Guild. It didn't matter to the kid who I was. He'd been raised to see everyone outside the Guild as the enemy. He was also certain that he was going to be rescued by them. He wasn't going to go with me because he'd rather wait for someone he trusted. Can you believe that?"

I can. But Kaylen's basing her judgment on what a *kid* said. Kids know practically nothing about how the world works. They see things in black and white, and Guild children are taught that the Guild is a haven for them, that it's the only place they're safe, but that's to keep them from revealing their life force abilities to people outside of the Guild. It's intended to protect them from people who would exploit them. I'm about to correct her thinking when Gabriel says, "Did you manage to get him to go with you?"

"Yeah," she huffs. "Only after I told him Andre was going to kill him if he didn't fall in line. I said Andre killed people he couldn't use and Andre was losing patience. That got him moving."

"Prime children are taught that the greatest danger to them in the world are other people exploiting their abilities," I say. "He recognized that he had to avoid that at all costs. That's why he went with you even though he didn't trust you."

Kaylen stares at me with open-mouthed distaste. "Sometimes when you talk I picture your past self somewhere in your head chained up and gagged."

I've done a pretty good job of not letting Kaylen upset me, but that stings. A lot. She has no idea what I've been through. She's in no place to judge me. She's romanticizing a version of me that no longer exists. I can't afford to cry, certainly not in front of Lainey and Kiera, so I opt for my Councilwoman Wendy persona and say, "I have never silenced her, Kaylen. After I woke up from my memory loss, my past self used to think and say things just like you, and I would remind her that she was the one that lost everything. She couldn't argue with that, so she skeptically decided to give the Guild a shot. And why not? She had already lost everything there was to lose. That's when things started to change for her. She sacrificed a past of arrogance, sorrow, and fear. In exchange she received perspective, courage, and the love of those around her. She found a way to balance the strengths of her past with her vision for the future, and it made her unstoppable. And now, she is on a Council of twelve people who have the power to make the future. She is the most recognizable Prime Human in the world. Tell me, Kaylen, would my past self have had a prayer of influencing the future in such an immeasurable way? Would she have even imagined it? I doubt it. Based on what you've said, it sounds like she didn't change much from the person I remember. With the exception of knowing more about the energy world, having unusual taste in clothing, and wielding a gun, of course."

Kaylen actually considers what I've said, and for the first time she seems a little conciliatory, amused even. "I hope we can figure out how to get your memory back," she says. "Because I think you're selling yourself short. There's a lot to what you're saying, especially your position now, but you don't know my Wendy. And if my Wendy merged with *you*… Well let's say the Guild wouldn't know what hit it."

I smile. "My friend Shiah says my memory loss is what has allowed me to be so successful so quickly, but she'd also agree that our experiences are invaluable. So you're probably right."

"Avery came with me and Robbie to find Ezra," Kaylen continues. "I found his new cell and he was passed out, but alive, thank God. Right then, the craziest lightning storm I've ever seen started. It knocked the power out, which was a godsend because if I could get Ezra up, we could probably get out while everyone was distracted. I was freaked out, trying to get Ezra to come around because there was no way I'd be able to carry him. The building next door caught on fire. Ezra finally woke up, so I dragged us toward the entrance. On the way I saw two guys passed out. No idea why, but I wasn't going to look a gift horse in the mouth. It was like everything was playing out to help me. Until we got to the end of the hall. To the left was the closest exit, but it was the main one and we'd have a lot of people to avoid, especially if people were evacuating the building. I decided we'd go to the right, take the route that went by the main control area, and if I ran into Andre, I wouldn't hesitate to use Robbie this time. But Avery took off suddenly, headed left.

"Ezra stopped, told me to go ahead, that he'd be right behind me after he found Avery. I begged him not to…" Kaylen's eyes get misty again. "I begged him, 'Just leave Avery. He's going to get us killed.' But Ezra wouldn't. I said we were staying together then, that I'd go with him. But he said, 'If we get caught, I have the best chance of staying alive because I'm useful. You and Robbie have zero chance because Wen isn't going to figure this out in time. Andre will kill you both. You have to get out.' He ran, and I knew he was right."

She lays back, closes her eyes, her hand resting on the top of Robbie's head.

"He never caught up to you," Gabriel says quietly.

My heart is racing, my hands are balled up. Ezra… Andre really did have him. But Andre's dead, so who has him now?

I have all these crazy ideas in my head. I need to go to California. I need to find out if Ezra's out there. Ben has proven way too skittish. How on earth can I trust that he will follow through all the way? This is *my* brother and I can't leave him in the hands of so much inexperience.

"I'll find him," Gabriel says, reading my face. "You know you can't go, Wendy. You'll jeopardize everything."

Crazy. I gave *him* that talk this morning.

"Wendy," he says when he sees my skepticism. "*I'll find him. You know I won't stop until I do. I won't give up. You know me.*"

I bite my lip. I *do* know him. But this is so backward. I'm essentially putting the Guild ahead of Ezra. I hate it, and on this my past self and I are in total alignment. My old friend, Guilt, sneaks up and assaults me with guilt.

Gabriel turns in his chair and stands up. He walks over to the table, puts his hands on the center and leans over it toward me. He demands my attention with his eyes.

"You have *nothing* to be ashamed of," he says softly. "The world needs Councilwoman Wendy. You can depend on me. I won't fail you."

Then, he feels. First, the rush of determination, like a fierce wind washing through my soul. The exhilaration of it gives me goosebumps. Then, adoration, so heavy it makes my eyes fall shut. He's got my heart physically in his hands, protecting it, admiring it, like the feeling I get when I watch him speak in public. Awed, humble.

"You are my exception to all," he murmurs so softly I don't know that anyone can hear him but me. "Let me do this for you." He's physically aching for me to say yes, to be able to do something for me that matters so much.

I don't know how anyone, after feeling that kind of veneration, could say no.

I open my eyes and sigh. I nod.

"We'll go, too," Lainey says from behind me suddenly. She's standing, eyes intense and determined. "This was our mission to begin with. We serve the Guild, which includes *you,* Councilwoman. If Councilman Kasappa does not approve, I will resign from Proprietary Missions and serve your cause on my own." She decisively claps her hands together in front of her in the Guild fist.

Kiera stands next to her and does the same.

I stare at Lainey with surprise to see her express her loyalty in such a way.

"We can do this," Lainey says. "Ben can be managed. I will take responsibility for him. We'll go undercover as THM if need be so that we don't disrupt their mission. Kiera is the best undercover asset there is. She will make us invisible."

Invisible... She can't possibly mean the official term for a Prime without a life force ability—I never did tell it to her so she must mean something else. I realize in that moment that despite having access to all information, I never have looked into what Kiera's life force ability actually is...

Gabriel grabs my attention with his own. "You see? There is no need to betray any part of who you have become. What you have given has returned to you in full."

"I'm going with you as well, Gabe," Kaylen says. "I know where to start and I know how to survive in California."

All eyes are on me, and I am humbled by the readiness of everyone to leap into action. And my trust in Kiera and Lainey has paid off immediately, even with all they have learned about my ties to Gabriel and the ideals of THM. I have always believed in truth, and I am starting to get that the more confidently you hold it, the more effective it is.

"Thank you," I say, sighing. "To all of you. I don't know how else to express how much this means to me."

Gabriel pushes off the table and takes his seat again. "The most important question now," he says, "is what to do about Robbie." He looks at me.

I cross my arms. He's right. Robbie can't go with Gabriel. He has to go with me. But there are all kinds of problems with that. How do I go to trial, act as Councilwoman and a spokesperson, while being suddenly thrust into motherhood? I don't know how to be a mother even under normal circumstances. And further, the public can't know I have a child with Gabriel Dumas for the same reason they can't know I'm married to him.

The room stays silent. No one has any ideas and I think they're leaving it up to me to decide. After a while of thinking about it and getting nowhere, I reach for my bag, pull my phone out, and call the person I always turn to when I have no idea how to handle something.

Sixty-One

Shiah stays silent the entire time I relay the story to her. Even when I finish, she doesn't speak, and I know she's assembling all the information. When she finally does talk, she asks a question, "What is the child's life force ability?"

"He's a channel," I say.

"Of what?"

It didn't occur to me that it would be anything other than my own ability, but Kaylen never actually said...

"Kaylen, what can Robbie do outside of channel?"

"He has Mike's ability," Kaylen says. She glances at Gabriel. "Another thing Gabe was sooooo excited about." She looks down at Robbie. "Even not being fully developed, it saved me more than once on our cross-country quest."

"Mike's ability," I say to Shiah.

"Really..." she says, intrigued.

"Why do you ask?" I say.

"If he'd had your ability, I was going to suggest you bring him back *not* as your own child. He would be too much of a commodity, and we've previously discussed not relinquishing your monopoly on the energy world right now. If you brought him back as your child but with Dumas' ability, that would be a lot better. Sticky. But a lot more manageable. But you're saying he has Mike Dumas' ability?" She laughs. "That's perfect. Hold on."

The line goes silent for a moment and then she comes back on. "Mike agrees. You'll bring the child back as his."

"*What?*" I say, floored by her suggestion.

"Think about it, Wendy," she says.

I do, cycling through all of the facts, imagining how it will all come across to the Council and also to the media. It'd be a little scandalous, but at least Mike and I are on the same team.

Unless… "Shiah, are you suggesting I present him as mine and Mike's child? Or just Mike's?"

Gabriel makes a noise and I glance up to see him leaning forward, his expression heavy with skepticism and a little aggravation.

"Yours and Mike's. It will protect Dumas. It will protect you. And it will ensure you can keep the child close to you."

"Shiah…" I say, frustrated, "It's a bold-faced lie."

"Wendy, I have assessed this from all angles. There is no version of the truth that will allow you to keep the status quo. Unless you want to put him with a Guild foster family, there is no strategy that will allow you keep him close to you without lying. The Guild is only going to care about his life force ability, and claiming he is Mike's child is going to make it really easy to not stir suspicion. With your combined memory loss, it seals the deal."

I keep visualizing it, me showing up in New York with a baby in tow. I'll have to reveal my memory loss, and consequently, probably the wide-spread memory disruption… That's going to be hard enough to navigate… And then I'm going to say I have a child with my bodyguard and I didn't know it because neither of us remembers?

But one day… one day it will have to come out, won't it? And then what will that mean for me? For the Guild?

I really expected Shiah to do better than this. I can't believe she's suggesting such a blatant lie.

"The Guild can't handle the backlash of the truth right now," Shiah adds. "And neither can THM. Especially THM."

My insides rebel. "If Robbie had had *my* ability, what would you have suggested then?" I ask, starting to get really upset.

"To protect the energy world, you need to lie about who he is. Or disappear with him."

I can't believe she's saying this. That's disowning him.
To protect him…

Just how far would Shiah have me go to protect the integrity of the Guild and THM?

"Besides," Shiah says, "It sounds like, in a very real sense, the child is as much Mike's as Gabe's anyway. On a life force level. So, if you think about it, it's not the bold-faced lie you imagine."

"It's a lie!" I snap, coming abruptly to my feet.

"Before finding out about the child, were you planning to reveal your marriage to Dumas to anyone but Mike and me?"

"The Council."

"Why?"

"Because— Because—"

"You know how to handle them."

"Right! I can't control how the rest of the world would handle it."

"Why does the child change that reality?"

"Because I can't hide a child!" I say, panting because the words sound ugly and I didn't want to say them. Tears come to my eyes for the eighty-seventh time today.

I catch Gabriel's eye then and he's watching me. He's too far away for me to tell what he feels, but then, I don't have to. He would never lie. Gabriel would face whatever the backlash was, even if it meant endangering THM. He's going to divert his attention to find my brother even though his task already seems near impossible under the circumstances and with the limited resources he has. He loves me that much.

Let me do this for you...

And I would deny our marriage to the public simply because it would be easier to hide it? I would deny *him*?

"Lives are at stake," Shiah says in my ear. "The balance is precarious. This is what you gave up your life for. Don't let the obstacles make you turn back now, Wendy. I believe in you."

I barely hear her as my eyes rest on Robbie, and I realize, with disgust, that I've kept my emotional distance because I was afraid of caring too much. When I was sixteen I gave up a child because I didn't want to ruin my life, my plans. And I thought she'd be better off that way as well. So I shut my eyes, tried not to let myself care too much, and handed her to other people.

I am *not* doing that again.

"Forget it, Shiah," I say, slamming a decisive fist on the conference table. "I'm coming back to New York, with *my* child, with a ring on *my* finger, and I will announce that the matched pair is on Gabriel Dumas' finger. The Guild can handle this. THM can handle this. If one child can bring the whole thing down, then we stand no chance at all against the Apocalypse. We all fail. It was *you* that told me people will ultimately do the right thing. They won't do it without an example. *I* am the Guild. And the Guild does not lie!"

I hear Shiah's breathing quicken and she makes a sound I don't translate. She does it again and I realize she's crying. "That's my Wendy," she whispers, voice quavering.

My mouth opens in surprise.

"I knew you," she says again. "Before it all started. I knew this was who you were. My Wendy."

I hear a muffled sound and then Mike's voice further away, *"What did she say?"*

"Wooooooooooo!" Shiah shrieks in the background now. "That's my Wendy!"

Mike comes on the line, "What did you do to her? She's jumping on the bed in what I *think* is a touchdown dance... She just put on her Aaron Rodgers championship belt."

Music comes on. Heavy bass, hip hop.

"That's right! That is my *Wendy!"* Shiah whoops in the background. *"Let's do this!"*

"She tricked me," I say, flabbergasted. "She tricked me again! I swore I was going to catch it the next time."

"Ummm," Mike laughs. "She's dancing. On the bar. Naked."

"Was she naked before or after I called?" I say.

"Wouldn't *you* like to know," Mike says.

"Jerk."

He sniggers. "I gotta go," Mike says. "Naked woman... Bar... Congratulations to you guys, by the way. Tell Gabe I'm sorry I couldn't throw him a bachelor party. He should have told me sooner." He laughs.

"Have fun, kids," I say, rolling my eyes.

After I end the call, Kaylen is grinning. Gabriel is leaning forward in his chair, elbows on knees, mouth hidden under his hands clasped into a fist, but his eyes... They're like magnets again and I can't look away. For the second time today he communicates a level of reverence toward me that takes my breath away. It stops up my throat, and I can't help my eyes watering. Again. Dammit, since when did I become such a waterworks?

He comes to his feet and around the table. He reaches for my hand but I stand up and put my arms around him, my head on his chest.

"You guys," Kaylen sobs, and I turn my head her direction. "This makes me so happy. You have no idea... The things I've gone through to get here... The number of times I thought maybe I should give up because you guys were so... consumed with your causes. I thought, everything is a waste. I should keep Robbie, because the family I had was gone... This makes every second worth it."

"Thank you, Kaylen," Gabriel says. "For not giving up."

I let go of Gabriel, but glue myself to his side with my hand in his. "I wonder why it is that you are the only one who didn't forget?" I say to her. "Everyone else did, down to the smallest memory. Did Andre... save you from it?"

"You think Andre erased everyone's memories?" Kaylen says, her brow furrowing.

"I'm not sure. But I *do* know Andre didn't lose his own memory. Which means it's likely he at least had the ability to prevent the memory loss."

She shrugs. "I don't know... When exactly *did* your memory loss happen?"

"October twenty-ninth," Gabriel and I say in unison.

Kaylen's brow furrows as she thinks and mouths something silently. She counts on her fingers several times. Finally, she says, "I'm might be off—I wasn't exactly keeping a strict calendar—but I think that coincides with the day I escaped with Robbie. So if Andre's the one that did it, I don't know why he would have spared me. What would be the point? If his reason was that he didn't want you to know who you were... why leave one person to one day find you? Someone who knew you as well as I do? Andre wouldn't have overlooked something like that."

Why indeed? That makes no sense. And it could not have been because Kaylen was out of reach. The memory loss wasn't hindered by distance in every other case.

"It also sounds like Ezra's memory wasn't disrupted," Gabriel says pensively.

"Except Kaylen found him passed out," I say. "That seems to be the common theme. Passing out and then waking up with no memory? When Ezra woke up, he didn't seem confused?" I ask Kaylen.

"Come to think of it..." Kaylen ponders. "He did seem disoriented when he was coming around... Didn't know where he was for a few minutes. I had to convince him of what was happening, and with the lightning outside and the power being out, he didn't spend a lot of time arguing, but then—"

Kaylen's eyes go as wide as saucers. She looks down at Robbie and then back up, clearly resisting the urge to leap to her feet. "Guys!" she hisses. "Robbie! That's why I didn't lose my memory!"

Her excitement is palpable, and I am totally confused.

"If the day I escaped was the same day you guys had your memories wiped, I was *holding* Robbie practically the whole day!

And then you asked about Ezra and it all makes sense! He *was* confused when he woke up. Didn't know who I was, *where* he was. I just figured it was temporary trauma, whatever. I didn't have time to like, diagnose him. I just needed him to get moving. I told him, 'Get it together, Ezra! We have to move or we're going to die!' I shoved Robbie into his arms just to like, motivate him, told Avery to stay put so I could go check the path and make sure it was clear so we could get out. I didn't want Robbie putting up a fuss and giving me away. I actually met Ezra in the hall on my way back a few minutes later, and he was totally back to himself."

"But you said Robbie has Mike's ability," Gabriel says, as confused as I am. "My understanding is that Mike exerts some sort of mental influence. What does this have to do with preserving memory?"

Kaylen shakes her head vigorously and holds up a hand. "Okay, first of all, you have to understand that you have nineteen *billion* of Mike's strands. That's more than half of his life force. Life force strands are what *enable* an ability. Your presence actually *neutralizes* what Mike can do, evidence that Mike's ability is stunted in some way overall because of this. We also know that Mike's ability involves physically *moving* life force strands. Dad—Carl, actually saw Mike's mom, Alma, do it in the colorworld years ago, so that's more evidence. Then there's Robbie, and he allows anyone who touches him to move their own strands in the colorworld. Robbie is actually how Wendy saved herself from Leukemia. But again, another story. Look, I don't know exactly how strands and memory are interconnected, but considering your life force is basically your *soul,* the essence of who you are, and memory is how that essence is made, then ergo, life force strands and memory are connected somehow. And if Robbie can allow anyone to manipulate them then… Hopefully you see where my logic is going now. It's the *only* plausible explanation right now for why I never lost my memory and Ezra seemed to gain his back."

My eyes have fallen to Robbie as I've listened to Kaylen. Her ability to draw that connection is astounding, and it must be due to a wealth of experience with the energy world. It's not just cut and dry knowledge. It's an intuitive understanding, something I sorely lack.

"Kaylen… that is a brilliant intuitive leap," Gabriel says, deeply impressed. "So… do you believe Robbie—"

"Can give you your memory back?" she says excitedly. "I'd be willing to bet money. It's certainly worth a try!"

As if on cue, Robbie starts to stir in Kaylen's lap, and she looks down at him and then back up at us, eyes bright with anticipation.

"How would that work exactly?" I say. "Does it just take touching him?"

"Who knows?" Kaylen grins. "We'll start there."

I nod, biting my lip nervously. Gabriel grips my hand harder, but I'm oddly less nervous about the possibility of gaining my memory back and more nervous about whether Robbie will start screaming when I touch him.

Kaylen leans forward and scoots Robbie up onto her lap, shifts him to her hip and stands up simultaneously. She steps closer to us, looking down at him, but he's staring at Gabriel again. He reaches his hand out and makes a grabbing motion toward Gabriel's face.

Gabriel's heart lurches and he releases my hand. Robbie lets out a shriek. I think it's an excited sound. He's reaching as far as his little arm will go, kicking and squirming and nearly pushing himself right out of Kaylen's hands. I can even feel his hazy, baby emotions. He's frantic, but out of curiosity, not upset.

"A warning," Kaylen laughs, adjusting him so he can't get away. "He has a thing for noses, and he's got yours in his sights, Gabe." Then she thrusts him into Gabriel's waiting hands.

Sure enough, Robbie goes right for Gabriel's nose, gripping the end of it in his fist and pulling, his expression so enthralled it's hilarious. A smile spreads over my face to watch.

Gabriel sinks down to sit on the floor and I follow, clinging to his arm, my eyes not leaving Robbie who is testing the durability of Gabriel's nose. I reach out to touch him, but Gabriel places him in my hands while simultaneously yawning. "Heavens," Gabriel says. "I suddenly can't keep my..."

I don't hear the rest of his sentence because Robbie is in my arms, his brown eyes staring into mine with a kind of intensity that has Gabriel written all over it. He's utterly still, and his emotions, which were once laser focused on testing Gabriel's nose, are now laser-focused on my face. He reaches out, and his hand brushes across my cheek in the most un-baby-like manner. It's like he's testing to see if I'm real.

"I'm here," I answer, my insides melting into a puddle. He's mine, the certainty growing more strongly by the moment. I know this feeling, and I grasp it firmly, determined to pull it out of obscurity.

"Gab—" I start, but the breath gets pushed back into me somehow, taking with it the words I was going to say. But it doesn't stop. It's a powerful wind, and it blows through my being as if I'm hollow. It leaves me inescapably exhausted suddenly. My eyes fall closed against my will, and though I hear muffled speaking and movements outside of me, I can't respond, and they are growing fainter anyway. I fall a thousand leagues, into a place much deeper than sleep. The fall is so swift that it strips away parts of me, though I have no idea which ones. It's terrifying at first, but I can't seem to care once they are gone.

And then, having left everything behind, and reaching the bottom, I begin to ascend back up the way I came.

August 2015

Sixty-Two

"*This* was the best idea you've had in a while," Ezra says before jumping out of the SUV and running up the stone steps of the log ranch house. 'House' is probably too small of a word, though. 'Estate' is more accurate. And 'sprawling estate' would be even better. From end to end the house is probably the size of an average indoor mall. It's also set against a gorgeous backdrop: the rugged landscape of northern Wyoming. And the sun is setting, casting the dusty earth in purple hues.

I'm with Ezra. I feel about a hundred pounds of stress lighter. I wish I'd done this sooner: chosen a base of operations instead of traversing the continent constantly and living out of hotel rooms.

As I drink in the beauty and wonder if it's possible to hide out here until everything blows over, my thoughts turn to Uncle Moby. He picked this place out and signed an agreement to purchase it mere weeks before he was killed. He knew. Like always, he knew we'd need this. I don't, however, think he did it to give us a place to bury our heads until the Apocalypse was over.

"Wen!" Letty's head pops up from one of the SUVs. She holds up her phone. "Check it out!"

I recently assigned Letty the task of keeping me informed with what's happening in the media. She was already doing it anyway, so I figured I'd make it official.

I come to her side.

"It came out fifteen minutes ago and is already *all* over social media!" Letty says as she restarts the news clip on her phone.

It's a press conference, and at the microphone is a man I don't recognize.

'*Good evening,*' the man says after clearing his throat. '*My name is Dave Renfrau, and I'm speaking on behalf of an organization, which, before now, you were unaware existed. We are a collaborative of individuals committed to technological, societal, and environmental improvement. We are known, collectively, as the Guild. Individually, we are known as Prime Humans.'*

"Whoa…" I say as the air explodes into camera flashes and questions. The Guild just came out of the closet. Holy cow. It's about time though. PHIA, or the Prime Human Insurgency Alliance, has been out terrorizing people for a while now. Right after Andre killed my uncle, I guess he decided he liked torturing and murdering innocent people, so he gave himself a name and started committing mass murders in seemingly random communities around the country. In each place they leave their symbol painted in blood and carved on the bodies. And they leave hate messages such as 'Give up your Prime Humans or pay the price!' and garbage like that. Wild speculation abounded, but nobody could really answer the question: What was a Prime Human and why was this crazy cult seemingly hunting them?

They get the crowd under control, and Dave continues, *'The Guild has existed for forty years, working toward the global good. Recently, as you know, a terrorist organization known as Prime Human Insurgency Alliance began hunting and killing our members. The leader of this outfit is Andre Gellagher. He was once a member of the Guild and defected two months ago, taking with him our technology as well as data that would allow him to track down vulnerable Prime Humans and execute them.*

'We are, as yet, unsure of Andre's motives, but the high profile, serial nature of the homicides has drawn attention to our membership, which confidentiality has protected until now. Our purpose for making our existence public information at this time is two-fold: First, to speak out against the defamation of Prime Humans and correct the rumors circulating about what and who they are. Second, to offer our help with the problem of escalating natural disasters.

'To the first purpose: A Prime Human is an individual who is born with superhuman capability. Such capabilities include above-average cognitive, emotional, and physical talents. These abilities originate from the energy world, a layer of reality that was discovered by one of our founding members. Details and information on this reality are of strictest confidentiality due to the danger of abuse. For further details about the scope of Prime

Human abilities, please see our website, which will be referenced at the conclusion of this press conference.

'To the second purpose: We have been actively engaged in tracking natural disasters since before the problem was recognized by world governments. Our most recent technological development in this area allows us to predict, within a reasonable margin of error, the occurrence of natural disasters, world-wide. At the conclusion of this meeting, a comprehensive list of upcoming disasters will be freely available on our website, to be updated minute-by-minute, twenty-four hours a day. I'll take questions now.'

"Well then," I say, noticing that everyone is crowded behind Letty and me.

"Game on," Mike says. "It's going to be interesting. Primes don't know how to exist in the open."

"Actually, I listened to all the questions," Letty says, and our large group naturally moves into a circle. "And they basically aren't giving away a thing more than what you heard here. They basically said they'll help, but their business is still their business. This one reporter asked, 'How do we know you are what you say?' And Mister Dave was all haughty when he answered, 'When the predictions we make come true.'"

"They're leveraging themselves right off the bat," Gabriel says, arms crossed, thinking-mode assumed. "It's bold, but it's probably going to work, and when it does, the public is going to fall at their feet."

"You're right," my father, Carl, says. "But their aggressiveness isn't for the public though. It's for the membership. They need to believe in the strength of their leadership."

"Is this what Andre was after?" I say, looking at Mike because he used to be Andre's partner at the Guild, so he would be most likely to know. "He basically egged them into the open."

"I think it was," Mike says. "Because now that people know Primes are a real thing, Andre can force a division. Create a rivalry."

"I don't get what that dude wants," Ezra says angrily. "What's the point of destroying Primes?"

"He lost his ability," I say, "so I guess he feels like a reject and he wants to kill everyone that makes him feel that way."

"That's a pretty strong grudge," Ezra says. "Andre lost his ability so he decided to slaughter all Primes? You don't get that sick all of a sudden."

"You also don't lose your ability all of a sudden," I point out.

"My understanding is that members of the Guild, especially those raised within its confines, see it as their family," Dan Dumas says. We all turn to look at Gabriel and Mike's father, because he doesn't speak all that often, and when he does it's always something of substance. "My understanding is also that one cannot become a member of the Guild without these life force abilities. It is the thing that defines them as *part* of that family. It is then logical to imagine that when Andre lost that which made him a Prime Human, he saw himself without a family, alone. I don't know how they handle their members losing their abilities, but I surmise that no matter how it was handled, he saw it as rejection. And to be rejected by your own…" Dan shakes his head. "It would be a traumatic experience that easily could negatively shape your future."

"I would second that," Carl says. "The psychology of Guild membership is a powerful driving factor. The culture breeds a strong sense of belonging. To lose that is to lose your identity."

"To a point," Mike says. "I wouldn't say Andre saw himself as belonging. Instead he was superior. His ego was extreme, and he had no qualms about crossing boundaries, breaking the rules, to get the job done, and he believed he could make those decisions because his motives were noble. I would say he saw himself as a secret mercenary for the Guild, their protector. The Redlands incident outed him. So he found some reason to reject the Guild before they could reject him. That way he could preserve his own ego."

That gets all of us thinking.

"I'll keep up with how things go down over the next couple days," Letty says after a moment.

I nod and then clap my hands. "Alright, everyone. What the Guild is doing is irrelevant to our cause. I'm still hoping they give me what I've asked them for, but I'm not holding my breath. For now, our job is to fortify this place against Andre and any other crazies and to make it Apocalypse-ready. So go forth and be productive!"

The group disburses and Dwight, who was once my uncle's assistant but is now mine, appears next to me. "Over there," he says in his quiet African accent, pointing to the south. "The surveyor said that would be the best place for the warehouse."

"And the other side of that ridge for the solar farm?" I say, pointing to the north. The property is rimmed by huge rock formations, a natural protective barrier against… Apocalyptic things.

"Yes," Dwight says, and he and I start walking toward the eastern edge of the property. I look over my shoulder as Gabriel pulls suitcases out of the back of an SUV. Maris is nagging him in Spanish, and Dan is holding Robbie. Gabriel should be here with me, listening to Dwight, especially because he's going to head up the property upgrades. The only reason he isn't is to avoid being near me.

It fills me with familiar angst. How is it that a person who once made your heart too large for your chest can also so easily create such sharp feelings of resentment?

I turn back to Dwight, who is describing the plans for an irrigation system linked to the nearby reservoir. I hope the world doesn't get to the point where I need a supply warehouse, a solar farm, and self-sufficient irrigation system, but Uncle Moby picked this place for a purpose, and I'm not going to take that for granted.

"The men are concerned…" Dwight says once we reach the stream that borders the property, putting us out of range of any of the members of my protection team.

"So am I," I reply. I turn to face Dwight. "But there's nothing I can do that I'm not already doing."

He bows his head slightly. "I know. But you need to be aware. Take extra care to keep their morale up. Their loyalty is strong, but all loyalties can be broken if not nurtured."

I sigh, trying not to get irritated. That nobody who actually *is* concerned will come to me directly is inconsiderate and disrespectful. "I wish I'd sent Darren to be with Farlen instead of Mark," I say. Mark led the team, with Farlen as his second-in-command. But Farlen is in a rehabilitation center to help him relearn the speech and motor functions he lost from having a smashed skull, courtesy of Andre. I sent Mark as protection for Farlen, because I am *not* giving Andre a chance to finish him off. The result is that I get Darren as my team's lead, who too easily sees me as my late uncle's pet, ill-equipped to make well-reasoned decisions. And a female, which apparently makes me too weak or something.

"You can swap them if you need to," Dwight says.

"No… Then everyone would know I'm getting rid of Darren because he got to me. He's good at what he does… He just can't seem to trust my judgement. And not getting anywhere for the last month…" I exhale disappointment. "I'm sure that's solidified his opinion."

"I understand, but you don't want that attitude infecting everyone else," Dwight says.

"I'll figure something out," I say just as my phone rings. I pull it out of my pocket, look at the ID. "Duty calls," I say, accepting the call.

"Ohr," I say into the phone. "I see the Guild is going for the bold approach."

"It did go well, didn't it?" he says as if patting himself on the back.

"No turning back. Are you worried it's going to backfire?" I say.

He laughs, slightly giddy. "Isn't it interesting that the only living Prime Human the public knows about with any degree of certainty is our spokesperson, Dave Renfrau himself? They have a website with free disaster prediction newsflashes, and that's it. The website itself is hosted on a remote server, should someone actually manage to hack it. We are just as invisible as before. Should the initial experiment go well, we may add more public figures, reveal a handful of consenting high-profile Prime Humans."

I'm surprised by Ohr's boasting. It's not usually his style. I also wonder why I didn't see that as the strategy. Of course, I haven't looked at the website or anything, but Gabriel is right. They're operating on the assumption that their disaster prediction will gain them a positive reputation, daring the public to question them and thereby assuming leverage right off the bat. "Clever," I say.

"Yes. My daughter is quite the bold PR genius."

"I didn't know you had a daughter."

"Yes. I hope you get to meet her one day."

"Right. Well, please tell me you're not just calling to brag about your public prowess."

"I wouldn't dare," he says, back to his usual amicable cadence that always seems to be on the verge of joviality. It makes it seem like everything he says has an inside joke he won't share. "But I do want to congratulate you on owning your first home. Cody has such a delightful landscape, wouldn't you agree?"

"I'm not in the mood today," I tell him, and truly I'm not. I usually endure Ohr's creative taunting with my own version of humor. He has the people and technology and scale to be able to keep up with my every move without me knowing, and he likes to remind me of that every chance he gets.

"I left you a little gift," he says. "I hope it doesn't upset anyone, so I'm telling you ahead of time."

"Weeeeenn!" I hear Ezra's voice echo across the property. "That dirtbag's been in the house!"

I roll my eyes. "Seriously, Ohr? You know I'm the only one that even comes close to liking you. My people get out of whack every time you preempt them or leave 'little gifts.' And then I have to explain why I put up with you. I'm running out of reasons."

"One *would* have thought curing your diabetes would have earned me a little more grace."

"Humans are fickle."

"I'm aware," Ohr says. "Which is why today you get your way. The Council has agreed to provide you with all of the data we've gathered on the disasters in exchange for having one of our operatives personally shadow your efforts."

I smile widely. This truly is good news. This day might turn around yet.

"The operative should arrive in one week," Ohr says.

"That's generous. Figured you'd have them here before we even arrived."

"You just moved in. I assumed you'd appreciate some time to get settled."

"And the data?"

"Already in your brother's hands, I should imagine," Ohr says.

"Weeeenn! Where are you?" Ezra yells. "He left a flash drive! In the lab. Crap, do you think that's the data? I'm afraid to plug it into my computer!"

I shake my head. "Now that's more like the Ohr I know," I say.

"May this be the start of many civil negotiations between us," Ohr replies.

"Don't hold your breath," I say. "Once I figure this crap out, I'm so done with you and the Guild."

"The Guild is the future, Mrs. Dumas. You will never be done with us."

"Now you see there?" I say. "We were doing fine until you started talking about your world domination plans again."

He laughs. "You confine yourself to too small of a pond, Mrs. Dumas. Fish in small ponds never grow as large as fish in big ponds. Move the fish from the small pond to the big and he thinks all the larger fish there are out to eat him."

"They *are*," I say.

"Then you better grow quickly."

₪

"I wanted to talk to you about Jessie," Darren says, first thing the following morning. "She's planning to bring her boyfriend. And Louis is bringing his aunt."

"Okay," I reply, not looking up from the email on my laptop that Dwight told me to look over. It's from my lawyer, the estate planning one, and it's a proposal for an insured holding account for my liquid assets. It doesn't gain interest, but it's supposed to hold value if the dollar tanks. It's backed by commodities, real things like oil and agriculture. All these new words I've had to learn... I think I'm starting to get the hang of it, but things like this... I need to talk to Gabriel. He's got more experience in this area. And I'm ever the skeptic. I'm not convinced any organization can reasonably claim to be able to back up my assets if the Apocalypse really hits the fan and the economy implodes. And to give up the interest I'd accrue before then... that's a *lot* of money for such a sketchy promise of return.

Darren apparently expected a different reaction because he's still standing there, waiting.

"I think it widens the invitation too much," he says when I don't say whatever it was he was expecting. "We should stick with immediate relations."

I narrow my eyes at him over the top of my computer. I told my team they were welcome to bring their families here. Only two of them have wives and kids, but they all have somebody, and the world is getting really dangerous. Especially California since the riots began almost two months ago. It's getting harder and harder to go there safely. Some places, like LA, you can't get into at all. Not to mention Andre is still out there. It's not only a cheaper solution for me, it's also the one that tells everyone I care about them and their families. I need their loyalty, now more than ever.

"I'd like to bring everyone I know," Darren says, now set on making his argument in earnest. "But the more people we have here, the more it's going to take to protect them."

On my tongue are a lot of retorts, such as pointing out that Darren tried to get his ex-wife here so he could have his daughter safe, but she refused. I know this because I have super-hearing, so he's a hypocrite at best. And I'd say he's trying to crack down on who can come because he's bitter.

But instead, I clear my throat and say, "I'll take your thoughts into consideration." I smile wanly at him before dismissing him by returning to my email.

I hear the frustration in his sigh as he turns and walks out. I've got to do something about him. This questioning of my direct instructions is getting more frequent.

Sixty-Three

I catch myself from angrily slamming the door to Robbie's room behind me. Yesterday I asked Maris to let me get Robbie out of bed in the mornings from now on, but it looks like she chose not to listen. We're not living out of a hotel anymore so Robbie has his own room, but I like to be the first face he sees in the mornings. He's the most content then, and I love sitting in the rocker with him, letting the sounds of the morning filter in, letting my brain slowly wake up.

But Maris has now stolen that time from me, and I really needed it today. Last night, our second night here at the ranch, Gabriel officially informed me he'd be taking a separate room from me. I guess it was expected; while in hotels he has been sleeping in the second bed in our shared room. But I had hoped that being in a new setting might change things between us for the better. That was apparently never in Gabriel's plans.

"Maris," I all but snap when I reach the kitchen where I find her giving Robbie his morning bottle, "I told you I wanted to be the one to get Robbie out of bed in the mornings. What part of that didn't you understand?"

She looks at me with her wide doe-eyes as if I've struck her and she's about to cry, one of her typical tactics. It might work on the rest of her family, but it doesn't work on me. She deliberately went against my wishes!

"Mija, it wasn't my intent to upset you. You and Gabriel have not had a moment alone, having Robbie with you all the time. I thought you might appreciate one morning to laze about."

I'm rendered speechless, wondering how oblivious she actually is to the state of my marriage to her son. I haven't told her, but I had assumed Gabriel would have at least given her a general overview at any point.

I'm irritated enough at Gabriel for making me the bearer of that news that I take it out on Maris, saying, "I'm not sure what delusion you're under, but your son refuses to share a room, let alone a bed with me. My nights are just as lonely here as they were in hotels, so if you could please let me share my son's first morning moments with him, it would help me start my day in a slightly better mood."

I don't wait for her answer, I spin on my heel, headed for the cabinet to start making Robbie his morning cereal. I haven't gotten used to the layout of the kitchen yet though, so I bang through the cabinets, looking for the box. Ezra, who is also in the kitchen, finally comes up next to me and murmurs, "Pantry, Wen." He points to a door on the other side of the room.

Right. The place has a walk-in pantry.

"Morning," Mike says, emerging from the hall. He makes a beeline for the coffee-maker.

"Are you alright?" Ezra whispers worriedly, having accompanied me into the pantry.

"No," I growl, scanning the rows of boxed items. "Which is why I don't need meddlesome mothers-in-law making things worse." I slam down a box that ends up being raisins instead of baby cereal.

"Sorry, Wen," he says. "Is there anything I can do?"

I finally find the right box. "No," I sigh. "Just find something in that data the Guild sent over. I need all this crap to be over already so that maybe I can have the luxury of dealing with things like my marriage."

I leave Ezra behind in the pantry and begin digging through the cabinets again, this time for a bowl.

"Wendy?"

I turn around immediately at the sound of Gabriel's voice saying my name. It's not just that he's saying it, he's *asking* for me, and I can tell by his tone that it's not strictly business. My heart pauses on hope that he's going to ask for something that will begin to close the vast distance that has grown between us.

"Do you know what happened to my books?" he asks.

My hopes falter. "Your books...?" I say. I know he visited the Cody library yesterday in preparation for his work with Ezra concerning the disasters. I also know he complained about the selection, so I wasn't aware of whether he'd brought back any books at all...

"Wen," Ezra says from the table, and I glance over at him. His expression turns into an exaggerated scowl. "He's looking for... his *Preecciooouus*!" he says in a raspy voice. Then he pulls his bowl of cereal toward himself possessively and shovels a spoonful in his mouth, glaring at me from over it.

Mike makes a choking sound from over by the stove, and I look over to see him grinning at Ezra's obvious—and near perfect—effort to sound like Gollum, from Lord of the Rings, although I haven't quite gotten the context of the joke as Mike seems to have.

Gabriel, after giving Ezra a disdainful look, says to me, "My book collection. I've not been able to locate it among the boxes delivered by the movers. I was wondering if you'd seen any of my books while unpacking."

"Oh…" I say, disappointed. The concern in his voice was for his prized collection of books, which has nothing at all to do with me. As petty as it is, I have the sudden urge to burn those books. I'd like to say something like, *No, but while we're on the topic of missing things, do you know what happened to my marriage?* It's a good thing there are so many people in the kitchen with us or that would most definitely come out.

"We wants it, we needs it. Must have *Precious*!" Ezra mutters, hunched over his cereal and stabbing it violently several times with his spoon.

I can't help grinning now at Ezra's strikingly good impression, now getting that he's totally making fun of Gabriel. "I haven't seen them," I say, carrying the warmed cereal in my hands over to Maris, who's putting Robbie in his high chair.

"Maybe the movers stole them," Maris suggests, scooping the cereal and expertly keeping the spoon away from Robbie's reaching hands as she deposits it in his mouth.

"That's likely," Gabriel replies. "They're quite valuable. The one signed by Einstein is worth over ten thousand dollars by itself."

"If I got a dollar for every time I've heard him talk about that damn book…" Mike says from behind his mug.

I knew Gabriel had such a book, but I wasn't aware it was that valuable—though I might have guessed, it being signed by Einstein and all.

Ezra pounds the table with a fist. "Curse us and splash us! My Precious is lost!"

Mike can't help crowing again at Ezra's display, and I pinch my lips together to keep from laughing, and then say, "I'd ask around before jumping to conclusions. We've barely been here two days, not nearly enough time to unpack everything. It more likely ended up with someone else's things."

"What has it gots in its nasty little closetses?" Ezra growls. "Filthy little Hobbitses. They stole it from us..."

Gabriel rolls his eyes at Ezra. "I am not amused." Then, to me, "Thank you. I'll ask everyone to be on the lookout."

Ezra hops out of his chair like an ape, trailing Gabriel when he turns for the exit. "Come on Hobbit. Long ways to go yet. Smeagol will show the way." Then he looks over his shoulder at the rest of us, an evil grin on his face as he whispers, "Follow me..."

Mike guffaws, sets his mug of coffee down. "Oh hell, I need to see this."

Gabriel seems intent on ignoring Ezra as the two leave the room, but I'm with Mike. Ezra is only getting started, and I'm just miffed enough at Gabriel to enjoy seeing Ezra use him for entertainment.

Mike and I follow at a distance, but Ezra takes to Gabriel's heels down the hall, crouched, arms swinging like a Neanderthal as he sings, "The rock and pool, is nice and cool, so juicy sweet. Our only wish... To catch a fish... So juicy sweet..."

Gabriel stops in the main common area connecting the two wings of the estate and turns around, arms crossed as he looks down at Ezra, "What is the purpose of this spectacle?"

Ezra hops from side to side. "We swear to serve the master of the Precious. We swear on only the Precious!"

Mike is about to lose it next to me, and I drag him by the arm as Gabriel puts his back to Ezra once more and moves down the hall where he knocks on the first door, which I know is the room Letty chose.

"Pardon, Letty," Gabriel says when she opens her door. It's obvious she was sleeping. "I'm on the hunt for—"

"Myyy PRECIOUSSSS!" Ezra wails, wringing his clothes behind Gabriel.

"Oh for the love of humanity, stop it, Ezra!" Gabriel says exasperatedly.

"Uhhhh, Wen's not here," Letty says groggily.

"Wicked. Tricksy. False," Ezra seethes, hunched over and peering at Letty from behind Gabriel. "She wants it, Master. She wants the Precious. We mustn't let her haves it."

I wheeze in suppressed laughter, pulling Mike back behind the corner and out of sight, tears leaking out of my eyes as I struggle to hold it in. Mike's right there with me, hand over his mouth, his face growing red to restrain himself.

"Books!" Gabriel exclaims to be heard over Ezra's continued murmuring. "I'm looking for my rare book collection! If you come across a box containing books will you let me know?"

"Uhhh, sure," Letty says, baffled. "Can I go back to bed now? My shift was super late."

"We ought to wring her filthy little neck. Kill her! Kill her!" Ezra exclaims wildly.

"My apologies," Gabriel says. "For waking you *and* for *that*." He jabs a thumb over his shoulder.

"Whatever," Letty says, shutting her door.

"Go *away*!" Gabriel says, continuing his trek down the hall toward the kitchen in the other wing.

"Yes, Precious... Once it takes a hold of us it never lets go…" Ezra wails sadly.

Mike and I watch them stop at the entry to the second kitchen. "Excuse me," Gabriel says to the room. "Have any of you—"

"My Preciouuuuusssss!"

"Be gone, Ezra!" Gabriel demands, swatting at him.

Ezra leaps away and hisses at Gabriel.

Mike and I fall against the wall in the hallway, no longer trying to hide our laughter.

"I have a rare collection of books that should have made it here with the movers," Gabriel says in a rush, blocking Ezra from the room. "But I can't locate them. If any of you come across some books, will you let me know?"

"Sneaky little Hobbitses! We wants it!" Ezra screams, bobbing from one side behind Gabriel to the other. "PRECIOUS!"

"Ezra!" Gabriel yells. "By the stars! Stop acting like an imbecile!"

Mike hoots, and I'm howling. We fall against the wall and then sink to the floor, totally overcome.

"We will kill him," Ezra seethes evilly. "We will wring his filthy neck. Then the Precious will be ours. And then *we* will be the master! Yes! Yes! Yes!" He dances around Gabriel on all fours.

"Oh this is simply ridiculous," Gabriel says, now staring at Ezra and then glancing down the hall at us. "Honestly. Don't you all have better things to do than pester me?"

"Nope," I manage to gasp amid my giggles.

"Those fat Hobbitses know…" Ezra snarls, pausing in his maniacal dancing and staring down at us with a death glare. "Eyes always watching. We will stabs them out. We will put out their eyes. Yes... Yes... Kill them both."

Before I know it, Gabriel is standing over us, arms crossed, eyes unflinching. But it only seems to infect Mike and me with even more laughter. My eyes start streaming and I can't even make out Gabriel's stern expression anymore.

"Oh my gosh," I gasp to Mike. "I think I might have peed on myself…"

"Where is it?" Gollum, I mean Ezra, demands, standing over Mike and me as well. "Master, The fat Hobbitses stole it from us!"

Gabriel shakes his head and sighs. "Do let me know when the charade is over and we can go back to behaving like adults."

"Curse them," Ezra says, pacing behind Gabriel, eyes locked on Mike and me. "We hates them! It's ours, it is, and we wants it! My Precious!"

"*Yours*?" Gabriel says, looking down at Ezra.

Ezra shrinks as if he's just been struck. "We didn't means it, Master! *Ours.* The Precious will be *ours.*"

Amid my tearful mirth, I don't miss the fact that Gabriel just played along. And I think he may be smiling, just barely.

"Come, Smeagol," Gabriel says. "You will lead me to the black gate."

They head back toward the other wing, Ezra trailing Gabriel and saying, "Yes, Master. We know the way. Soft and quick as shadows we must be!"

Mike and I slowly recover. "That was... the best," I say.

"That kid is a riot," Mike agrees, putting his hand out to help me off the floor.

"I don't remember the last time I laughed that hard," I say, rubbing the remaining moisture from my eyes. Thank goodness for my brother. My heart clenches, knowing Ezra only did all that to cheer me up. To see Gabriel lose his unapproachable exterior, if only just briefly, makes me feel slightly lighter.

"Wen, it'll be okay," Mike says, noticing my expression.

"What's he feeling right now?" I ask in a small voice.

"Happy that he had a hand in making you laugh," Mike says. "As much as he tries to distance himself, at the end of the day he can't help wanting your happiness. And eventually he's going to realize that all of this with me and him and the life force strands we share doesn't matter. He's going to realize that the only thing that makes *him* happy is seeing *you* happy. That's when he'll come back to you."

I look into Mike's brown eyes, caught in his contrast of wills: both meaning what he says while yearning for me at the same time. I almost ask, *what about you?* But I know for Mike the solution will never be easy. He's tied to Gabriel as long as Gabriel has some of Mike's life force strands. He never gets to escape. He's forced to deal with it, head on. That Gabriel acts like the victim is infuriating.

"It'll be okay," Mike repeats.

His sincere concern wrings my heart. It's so hard not to touch him. I don't want to push Mike's boundaries, so I keep a physical distance. But sometimes I want to tell him with more than words how much his friendship means to me. He's always cheering me on, and just knowing he's in my corner makes it easier to face the gulf in my marriage each day.

He suddenly steps toward me and puts his arms around me. At first I have to endure the excessive amount of energy his touch always brings, but once it settles, I exhale and lean my cheek against his shoulder. There is no doubt that a lot of chemistry exists between us, but we're both aware of it. We've talked about it and that has made it much easier to navigate. I love Mike. There's no denying that, but I want to throw up every time I think about him spending his life worrying about Gabriel and me. I'm going to find someone for him, someone who won't be afraid to love him, who won't be intimidated by his connection to Gabriel and consequently to me. She's got to be out there. I swear I'm going to find her.

Sixty-Four

I watch Gabriel's eyes flick over the page at lightning speed. In under five seconds, he has memorized it and will be able to recall it for perusal whenever he chooses. He can memorize any piece of written material that way, but I can't fathom how he holds it all in his head.

"My dad is the one you need to consult if you want the best source of advice," he says, handing the printout of my lawyer's email back to me. "I have told you before that securities law is his specialty."

"Right…" I say, struggling not to feel dejected that he has already returned to the book and map spread in front of him on the bed. I'm not sure why I forgot that about Dan Dumas. Maybe because the term 'securities' didn't mean anything to me when I first met Gabriel's dad. Or maybe I just wanted to devise some excuse for Gabriel to speak to me.

I can do this…

I close the door behind me and lean against it.

He looks up questioningly now that I've enclosed us alone. For the moment he spends in worry over my intentions, I imagine changing my plan and seducing him, but I don't think I can take the rejection. So I refocus on my actual reason for closing the door: to not be overheard.

"Gabriel, I need you to take the reins on the protection team," I say.

His first answer is to return his attention to the book. Jerk. Then he picks up his pencil, which he had previously placed in the book to look at the email I showed him. "I'll be busy assisting Ezra with mapping," he says. "Mike can do it."

"No, he can't. Mike used to work for the Guild, and even though the guys like him, they'd see me promoting him over Darren as a betrayal."

"Then don't. Darren does a thorough job. And you know how to assert yourself. The problem is you don't do it enough because you think you don't have a right to. They're *your* people now. Not Robert's. Act like it."

Resentment bubbles hotly in my stomach. The Gabriel I used to know would have jumped at the chance to take away some of my stress. This Gabriel wants to stay in the background. My problems are no longer his problems. A sense of isolation moves through me even more than usual.

"I *have*, Gabriel," I say. I gnaw the inside of my cheek, struggling to keep from lashing out, but it's getting harder everyday. "You'd know that if you were ever around to see it."

He looks up finally. "You act like I don't have responsibilities, like I don't contribute. I already agreed to take over the construction supervision here. I handle your logistics and scheduling. I even handle the grocery shopping. And now I'm working with Ezra on developing a map that should allow him to deconstruct the pattern of the disasters and find the origin. It's a monumental task."

"I never said you don't do anything," I shoot back. "But everything you do is aimed at being as far away from me as possible."

"This should not come as a surprise to you," he replies, leaning over his book again. "We discussed as much when I told you, a month ago, that I needed some distance."

"I've given you that," I shoot back, struggling to keep my voice even. "At what point am I allowed to start closing that distance back?"

He doesn't reply. He's too far away to read, which was purposeful when I came in here. That's something I've also given him the last month, and I did it without needing to be asked. I've fought to be understanding. I've held my tongue. I've been patient. So patient. Every time he's done one more thing to separate himself from me, I've never complained. I've wanted to do that for him, because he said it would help, and I wasn't going to violate that even with my emodar—my ability to sense the emotions of those around me. I was hoping all of this would communicate my respect for him, my willingness to do what it took to get through this thing with him sharing some of Mike's life force. But it looks like I've accomplished nothing at all. He must know that...

I cross my arms, waiting and growing more upset with every silent moment. He can't even do me the favor of answering! "If your goal all along has been to make me hate you, it's working."

He seesaws the pencil between his fingers, not yet looking up, but at least he's doing *something* different. He finally puts the pencil down on the bed and then snaps the book shut with two hands.

He stands up and comes over to me, his own agonizing restraint attacking my chest. He comes very close to me, reaches up to touch my face with a hand, exhaling with relief at the contact.

I hold my breath, because it has been *so* long since he has touched me. Anticipation builds without trying, and he caresses my face from my temple to my chin. Then he brings his hand to the back of my neck, resting it there as he leans down and runs the tip of his nose over the curve of my neck, stopping at my chin. His need for me builds, but he doesn't move. It reminds me of when we couldn't touch, and he'd stare at me from mere feet away, letting his emotions communicate how much he wanted me. It's intoxicating and passionate, and I wonder if this is his answer. Is the separation over? Is he not asking to kiss me because he wants to take this slowly?

"Right now," he says, "my brother is present for every bit of this. My hand on your skin, the need to put my lips on you, the desire building in me... If you reciprocate any of that right now, it is a desire for *him,* not me. If the situation were reversed, I would feel none of it. If the situation were reversed, you would be wholly his. And you... you wouldn't feel what you do for both of us. What you think you love in me? What you think you want? It's him. This moment between us... It's your head tricking you. It's Mike satisfying you through me. It's fake. Why would you want that?"

I gasp and shove him off of me, glaring at him with shock. His face is passive, waiting. He expects his demonstration was so clear I can't possibly disagree. It doesn't even occur to him what was so wrong about what he just did. I shake my head in disbelief and loathing and pain.

I bring my hand up and slap him across the face.

"Don't you *ever* touch me like that again," I seethe as he recovers and looks at me with outrage. "Don't you *ever* manipulate my emotions to make a point. It's disgusting. It's violating. You might be trying to shed pieces of yourself to figure out which ones are Mike, but what you're replacing him with is ugly, Gabriel."

"Why do you refuse to see this how it is?" he says, raising his voice. "You love me. You love Mike. I have Mike's strands. Ergo, you love Mike. It's bloody logic, Wendy! Every time I look at you I feel like an imposter. I've been trying to do right by you—keeping a distance. I've been giving you the opportunity to get your emotions directed to the right person without me in the way. Why don't you see that?"

Am I hearing what I think I'm hearing This can't be... He's crazy. He's absolutely lost his mind over this.

I fumble behind me for the doorknob, wishing anger wasn't turning into tears. I get the door open and practically fall through it.

Someone catches me. It's Darren. I find my feet quickly and straighten my shirt, embarrassed. "Sorry, Darren," I say, wiping my eyes quickly. "I wasn't paying attention."

"Yeah, no problem," Darren says in a rush, uncomfortable. "Did you take your communicator out? I've been looking for you."

"Uh, yeah," I say, struggling to get myself out of the hole Gabriel dumped me into so I can get back on task. "Sorry about that. I was um..." *Don't apologize, Wendy. You're the boss.* "Nevermind. What's up?"

"The Guild plant is here," he replies, but his pity is clear.

"Oh, good," I say. "Where are they?"

"*She* is in the kitchen."

"Okay," I say, fumbling through my upended emotions still, so I start walking toward the double doors. "Thank you."

"*Your* kitchen," Darren calls after me.

I stop and turn around. "*My* kitchen? Why?"

His ears grow slightly red. "Nobody knows her. She's here to shadow you and your brother, not my people. Figured she'd be better off in your wing."

I grind my teeth. He forgot to add his real reason: because she's a woman.

I don't have time for this argument with him. I *shouldn't* be having this argument. I already told him where the Guild operative would be staying, even picked out the room.

I need to get his face out of my sight before I make my second bodily assault of the day. So I turn my back to him and set off down the hall toward *my* kitchen. "*She* will be in the *east* wing, Darren!" I bark over my shoulder.

I hear him jog after me, but I don't pause until I round the archway into the kitchen, and there, sitting on the counter, one leg—not just crossed, but *posed* perfectly—over the other, is a woman.

She hops off the counter as soon as she sees us. "Hello, dahhhlings!" she says, raising her hands excitedly up by her shoulders with a flourish.

I don't at first notice any particular part of her very extravagant outfit because there's just so much to *see*. Greens and blues, ribbons and lace and satin.

"Are you Vendy? You are adooorable," she says with a very heavy accent. German I think.

"Yes," I reply, holding a hand out. "You are from the Guild?"

"Ya! Ya!" she says, taking my hand, but using it to leverage herself closer to me, which makes everyone else in the room flinch. She kisses one of my cheeks and then the other, saying, "Muah! Muah!" as she does it. She steps back, puts one of her nails—which I notice are painted in alternating green and blue—into her teeth pensively. Except she stands as if modeling for an ad. "Soh kute," she says. "Luk at your hair! Zey showed me pikture, but eet vas looong."

I don't know how to react to this person. I'm finally getting an eyeful of her now that she's not getting in my space. The most outrageous part of her getup is her hair. Her head is shaved on both sides but long on top. It's dyed green and blue and wound into a six-inch roll on her head. She's wearing a knee-length dress with a green pattern on it; fishnets; black, Mary Poppins shoes; a black corset; and an extravagant choker with lots of intricate beaded patterns. And her eyeshadow… Greens and blues and yellows that kind of look like peacock feathers painted over her lids. It's the kind of fancy job they use for advertising eyeshadow that nobody *actually* does. Except this woman, apparently. She is an eyeful from head to toe.

Someone is running down the hall and I turn to see Ezra emerge, but he skids to a stop. His mouth opens. "Whoa. What. Is that?"

"Ezra!" I chide, tempted to face-palm myself.

"Eeeee!" the woman says, making a tiny claps. "Eeezra! Even leeetle boy genius ees gut aussehend!"

"Uhhh… what?" Ezra says, scratching his head. He looks at me, at a loss. But I'm as clueless as he is.

"She said you're handsome," Gabriel, who has appeared behind Ezra, says. He bows his head slightly at the woman. "Greetings, Fraulein. Wie lautet dein Name?"

"Ahh, Herr Dumas! Halloo! I am Rowena," she replies. But she makes a face. "But you vill *not* call me zat. I go by Roe."

"Pleased to meet you, Roe. Willkommen."

"Danke," she replies, clasping her hands together in front of her. She turns to me. "I dun't plan to be ah speektator. Pless, put me to verk, ya?"

"You'll be spending most of your time with Gabriel, Ezra, and Letty," I explain. "I'm sure they can use you."

"What is your background?" Gabriel asks.

"Geology," Roe replies, smiling. "Relevant, ya?"

"Höchst!" he says, smiling and nodding excitedly. "Sie warden von unschätzbarem Wert."

I don't know what he said, but seeing him smile so genuinely at someone after what he just did to me is infuriating.

"Awesome," Ezra says, dragging his hands down his face. "Why? Why do I get stuck with the non-english-speaking weirdos?"

"What's wrong with Letty?" I say.

"She's always pinching my ass. And I swear she talks dirty to me in Spanish."

I lift my eyebrows, fasten my lips together to keep from laughing.

"Don' you know, Eeezra? Genius comes out best among ze freaks," Roe says, putting her fists on her hips in a pose of determination. "So! Let your freak flag fly!"

Sixty-Five

Let me take him," Mike says, reaching for Robbie, who has been fussing for a couple hours now. He should be asleep this late, but he's teething. I tried going into the colorworld with him, because when I touch someone while there I can feel not only their emotions but everything else, including pain, and I can take half of it on myself. But Robbie seemed to get more upset with me.

I relinquish him to Mike, resentful when Robbie not only calms but starts cooing. Why can't at least Robbie like me? It would be nice if the times I get to spend mothering would give back a little. But like everything, they just take. Like everything, I come away a failure.

"You okay?" Mike says, rocking from foot to foot.

"Yeah," I say, unpacking Robbie's meager things from the suitcase on the bed so I can put them in drawers, a task I've been putting off since we arrived a week ago. "Still frustrated about Darren. He tried to tell me who should and shouldn't be allowed to come here."

I pull out a pair of pajamas that look like they might be too small. I turn around to hold them up to Robbie, but I catch Mike staring at me, and he's moved to the other end of the room, out of my emodar range.

I endure brief awkwardness, but it doesn't last long; I've kind of gotten used to this: Mike looking at me wistfully, his attraction hitting me at inopportune times, and then flirting our way to laughing about it. He doesn't usually move away like that though. Sometimes, like Gabriel used to do, he'll let his feelings fester near me for the fun of it. Other than Ezra, who always has a joke ready to make me laugh, Mike has been the easiest person to be around in the whole group.

"Don't lie to me," Mike says, now swaying and bouncing Robbie at the same time.

Not wanting to violate Mike's purposeful distance, I put the pajamas aside and pull out something else. "Shouldn't you be hating me right now?" I ask flippantly. "Seeing as you share his emotions and all."

He stays silent, but the look on his face says he's thinking hard, maybe fighting against saying something, or maybe *to* say it.

I'm not going to push it. Mike is the one that has to fight Gabriel's emotions all the time, not me. It's not his fault if Gabriel rubs him the wrong way toward me.

"No, Wen," he says finally. "Hell no. It's times like these I know that the love I have for you isn't just a reflection of Gabe. Because while he pushes away, it only makes me want to be closer to you. So I can make you smile again."

I keep my hands busy, going between the suitcase and the dresser. His words are pulling at me dangerously.

Until today, Gabriel has never directly done anything *to* me. He rejects me in small ways, avoiding meals with me, taking a different vehicle when we've gone to disaster sites to look in the colorworld, not speaking to me unless necessary. But it all still hurts, and the space has grown so wide that I often look at Mike and wish I could have him. And after today I wonder why I'm fighting so hard for Gabriel now that it's clear he has no plans to come back to me.

"What did he do?" Mike asks. "The emotions were… confusing. I know he touched you, and he hasn't done that in a while. And then… did you hit him?"

I don't know if it's good idea to go into this with Mike, but I don't have anyone else. Even Letty, my long-time friend, who has remained with us since Mike and I ran into her back in June, doesn't grasp the difficulty. She's constantly experimenting with her own complex sexuality. A long-term relationship is not something she has ever had. She sees Gabriel's avoidance, and she offers to take me to a club so I can gyrate with some well-muscled hotties to let off some steam.

Maybe I *should* do that…

"He pretended to want me," I reply simply. "As an object lesson."

Mike groans. "Holy mierda…"

"He has no intention of coming back." I slam the drawer without thinking. Robbie starts crying. I look over; Mike almost had him asleep. *Stupid, Wendy.* I cross my arms over the edge of the crib and lay my forehead on them. I suck at this. Maris was right: I have such a hard time with Robbie because I don't spend enough time with him. And Robbie is probably an empath like me, which means he picks up my impatience with him, my distraction, and then my guilt. He picks up my worry, my stress, and now this thing with Gabriel. Robbie will never get happy emotions from me again, which is a travesty all on its own. Robbie has such a short life to live because he has Duchenne Muscular Dystrophy. The least I can do is be a happy influence on his life...

The sound of his shrieking drills into my head, shattering my composure. If I don't let myself sob I'm going to vomit instead. So I sink down to the floor and weep against the crib bars. I never should have given Gabriel space. I should have stood my ground, told him to get over himself, told him the only thing distance would create would be estrangement. But now... now I've given him that inch and he's turned it into a mile, like he always does.

Shouting from somewhere further away brings me around and I sniff and look up to find myself alone in the room.

"*Come on. Hit me. Please. Because I am really going to enjoy kicking your ass!*" I overhear Mike's voice echo from somewhere in the labyrinth.

Maris is shouting in Spanish. Robbie is crying.

"*You're being ridiculous,*" Gabriel says. "*Back off.*"

"*Or what? You're gonna twist my head the same way you twist hers? You sorry piece of shit.*"

"*You know nothing,*" Gabriel replies. "*And I'm not interested in helping you vent your simple-minded impulses.*"

"*Michael! Mind your own affairs!*" Maris says.

"*Step away from me, Mike,*" Gabriel warns.

"*No,*" Mike says.

Robbie is whimpering. Ezra says worriedly, "*Guys... Let's all chill out.*"

"*Should I tell them, Gabe?*" Mike taunts. "*What you did?*"

Silence.

He scoffs. "*You don't care if I do, do you? That's how fucked up you are. You figure you did her some kind of favor. Made it real simple for her to understand?*"

"*You know it wasn't my intention to cause her pain,*" Gabriel says. "*But the truth hurts. I have no control over that.*"

"*You make me sick,*" Mike replies, and then I hear a grunt and a crash. I scramble to my feet, going for the door as more thuds and smacks echo down the hall. I don't see them until I round the corner into the recreational room of the the west wing.

Mike is staggering back into a wall, and Gabriel is coming at him again. Mike kicks him sharply in the gut and Gabriel falls back into an end table, which clatters to the floor. Mike is already on top of him, sending his fist into his face, again and again as Gabriel grabs his shirt and tries to throw him off, finally leveraging himself and dislodging him with a blow to the side of his cheek

Maris is now screaming at them to stop, but Dan seems to know it's fruitless, taking Robbie from Maris' arms and carrying him into another room.

Gabriel leaps at Mike to straddle him, but, lying down, Mike catches him around the arms, taking him in a bear hug, and shoving his knee into Gabriel's stomach.

I stand with my fists at my side, horrified and confused. I expected the fight to be over quickly. Mike should have gained the upper hand from the start. I've seen him use his body enough times to know he far exceeds Gabriel in skill, quickness, and sheer strength. But I remember suddenly and sickeningly that Gabriel is only having a chance because every blow he receives, Mike mirrors it. As Mike grounds Gabriel's face and draws blood, he's feeling it as much as Gabriel is.

Gabriel slams into the coffee table, which must be pretty solid because it barely moves. Mike puts his knee on Gabriel's chest to hold him down and delivers a blow to the side of his head. Mike staggers over him at the contact, which gives Gabriel the opportunity to make a comeback, but Mike twists out of the way in an instant, coming to a crouch several feet away, eyes on Gabriel, who is not as graceful, staggering to his feet.

They stare at each other.

"Mike," I plead. "This is only going to end like the last time," I say, reminding him of the last fist fight he told me he had with Gabriel some six years ago.

Mike glances at me, and I regret my words because the distraction allows Gabriel to come at Mike again. He delivers an uppercut to Mike's chin. Mike reacts so quickly it looks instinctive, grabbing Gabriel's opposite arm and using it to fling him right into the wall, face and chest first, except Mike doesn't release his arm soon enough. I hear a muffled pop.

I bring my hands up to my mouth just as both of them roar in agnoy. Mike is lying on the ground, holding his arm tight to his side. Gabriel is staggered against the wall, doing the same, and both of them have expressions of agony.

Maris utters a stream of Spanish, rushes to Gabriel, puts her hands all over him. "Mijo! Is it broken?" But she doesn't wait for an answer, turning and scolding Mike in rapid Spanish. Then she's back at Gabriel again. "We have to get you to a hospital. Can you walk?"

But he's in too much discomfort to answer, sitting slackly against the wall. I survey the room. Ezra and Letty are here. Letty has her hands over her mouth, eyes wide. Behind Ezra and in the doorway to the lab is Roe, her lips pursed in surprise, hands on her hips.

Paul and Jessie and Corben, from my protection team, are at the opposite end of the room, near the hallway that leads to the other wing where they all stay.

I look down at Mike again, knees bent, hand over his arm, eyes closed. He's conscious though, so I don't think he needs medical attention.

"Will you unhand me, woman?" Gabriel drawls to Maris. "It's merely dislocated. Stop prodding me!"

"Paul, could you go find my father?" I say. "Maris, there should be ice packs in the freezer. That's all you can do right now." Gosh, someone get her out of here...

Thankfully she takes my advice, scampering off. I go over to Gabriel, crouch down. "Are you sure it's just dislocated?"

He nods, his face starting to swell up in various places. It looks like he caught the edge of the table; blood is pouring from a wound on his forehead.

"Are you lightheaded?" I say, concerned about a concussion—that's what happened last time the two had a knock-down, drag-out.

"I'm fine," he growls. He looks at me finally, one eye already closing to a slit. "And you'll keep him away from me from now on or I'm leaving. I won't be subjected to his bouts of childish aggression."

My mouth tightens, and when I look for my heart, my chest is empty. When I look for a response, I can't think of a single thing that will make a difference. And I'm tired of trying.

So I stand up and go over to Mike. "Do you need help getting up?" I say, kneeling beside him.

He shakes his head, eyes still closed. He looks to be in much better shape than Gabriel. "Stayin' right here," he says.

I sigh and sit down on the floor by him. Maris comes back, starts fussing over Gabriel again. I reach for Mike's hand and the familiar surge of energy pierces its way into me. The brilliance of Mike's life force defies all records; I can't even look at it directly when I'm in the colorworld unless I'm touching him. We assume the light inadvertently came from Andre, whose ability, before he lost it, was to enhance the life force abilities of others. The only way to do that is to give them life force light. So over time, after working with Andre for years at the Guild, Mike gained an excessive amount of light. When I touch him, he shares that light with me. It literally takes my breath away at first but eventually settles out. And it gives my senses a huge boost. I can see the molecular level of things, and with my own voice, I can use echolocation to visualize the room around me. I can even read a person's emotions based on their tone of voice and smell. The detail I'm capable of perceiving with Mike never ceases to amaze me.

I pull us into the colorworld, though, because I have to be there to alleviate Mike's pain. It's a good thing Mike has spent so much time with me there during our trips to disaster sites. When the colorworld is boosted by Mike's light—which we call Mike's colorworld—it's nearly impossible for an unpracticed person to endure due to all the bombarding stimuli. I keep my eyes closed to keep it to a minimum. I'm here to take on a portion of Mike's suffering, not do research.

"Mija, you go get Robbie," Maris' voice invades my ears. "Put that poor baby in bed."

"Leave me alone, Maris," I say sharply, having heard the censure in her voice. I can smell her disapproval from here. She's giving me grief because I'm giving Mike attention instead of Gabriel. She doesn't understand the things going on between Gabriel and me, and she assumes my attachment to Mike, our open flirtation and honesty, is some sort of infidelity. I've tried to explain it, but her traditional Catholic views make her only see things one way.

She makes a sound of protest. Carl, my father, asks Gabriel what happened. But I can hear in his voice that he knows. Gabriel makes small sounds as Carl tests his arm.

'*Shit, Wen. I didn't mean to dislocate his arm,*' Mike says to me telepathically—another thing I can do with the people who touch me while in the colorworld. '*That really hurt.*'

'*You think?*' I reply. '*You're an idiot. You knew it was going to go like this. You're probably feeling twice what he is because you're suffering for both of you.*'

'*I don't care. Kept me from doing something stupid.*'

I see it in his mind: me crying in Robbie's room, him taking me in his arms… things escalating because I'm hurting and he's desperate to take that away. Mike and I are close friends. I've shared more with him than Gabriel in the last couple months simply because Gabriel refuses to be around. Such a moment would be easy.

'*I hate him making you feel like shit,*' Mike thinks bitterly '*I wanted to fix it. I needed to. And I was afraid you were in a place that you'd let me do something we'd regret. So I instigated a distraction.*'

'*Mike, did you just beat yourself up so you wouldn't kiss me?*' I think to him. '*That's so sweet. But only in our world, where weird things abound.*'

'*I'd do anything for you. Even beat myself up.*'

I squeeze his hand and sigh with familiar angst over his plight. '*I don't know what to do about him.*'

'*Pursue him like a desperate prostitute,*' Mike thinks. '*But the thought of him touching you after what he did makes me want to hurl. He doesn't deserve you.*'

'*This isn't him,*' I say.

'*Why are you making excuses for him? That's what victims do, Wen.*'

'*If I'm a victim, and he's ultimately a bastard, why do you care about whether or not you make a move on me?*'

That stumps him for a moment but he replies, '*Guess I'm hoping he's going to have an awakening. And you know if I breach my boundaries, it's going to kill him even if he won't admit it aloud. I'll get the after-effects. I'll feel him die inside. And that would kill me.*'

'*Why does he not get that?*' I wonder even though we've broached this topic many times. '*Why doesn't he understand that you're happiest when* he *is?*'

'*Because he doesn't make decisions on emotional logic like that.*'

'*What does that mean? The only cure is to take your strands back from him,*' I reply fearfully. '*He hasn't made the ultimatum, but it's coming. He's going to make us all miserable and when we're desperate he's going to throw it down.*'

He thinks about it for a while. Meanwhile I'm thinking about his first suggestion: pursuit. I know how to do that. I've never had to do it with Gabriel, so that will be new, but I *do* know how to gain a hold over a man. In this case, I'm trying to save my marriage, so that makes a little lustful manipulation okay, right? I don't see another choice, and my past, maybe fortunately, qualifies my expertise in that area. I come up with several ideas off the top of my head.

'*Um, Wen. You're turning me on with all these visuals. It's a good thing I hurt all over,*' Mike thinks.

'*Crap! Sorry,*' I apologize, embarrassed. It's easy to forget how much of my thoughts transfer here.

He laughs aloud, but it causes a pain under my ribs and he stifles himself. '*And yes, you have every right to seduce your husband against his will. If he argues, tell that bastard I gave you permission. I own half of him after all.*'

It's my turn to laugh.

'*I'll let you know how it works on him,*' Mike thinks. '*They're about to pop his arm back in place, and it's going to hurt like hell. Maybe you want to go over there? Touching him is like touching both us. Kill two birds with one stone.*'

I cringe as I let go of him and look to where Darren and Carl are gathered around Gabriel. I sit near his feet while Carl explains to Darren how they're going to turn his arm to pop it back in. I put my hand on Gabriel's shin. He flinches, looks up, protesting internally. But I give him a look of pure challenge, and he withholds comment.

We go into the colorworld, and I suck in my breaths again to adjust to the various pains. It's hard not to reach up to hold my own shoulder. Geez, somehow he's feeling worse than Mike.

I keep my eyes closed, grip Gabriel's leg harder as Carl and Darren talk through synchronizing their actions.

'*Thank you,*' Gabriel thinks to me right before they rotate and push his shoulder.

I make a small sound, but it's more out of expectation than actual pain. It's far easier to endure than it would have been without me. Gabriel's words of gratitude are genuine, and he gasps in relief, having expected much worse as well.

I open my eyes to the colorworld, Gabriel's swirling soul mere feet from my own, my life force not just entwined but bound with his where my hand touches his skin. I close my eyes again and purposely inhale his scent in the colorworld, desperate to remember why I chose him. It easily takes me back to when I met him, to one particular day not long after I arrived at Pneumatikon's hypno-touch compound. He was lying on that rock out in the woods, having volunteered himself as my subject so I could experiment with my newfound ability to enter the colorworld.

He smells now as he did then: like wonder and awe. A dry mouth aching for a kiss, or like standing on an overlook along the Pacific Coast Highway and trying to inhale the expanse of the ocean. You feel like you can't quite get enough of the air, but you keep sucking it in anyway. I had fallen in love with him before then, but it was that day, inhaling his essence, that I understood the breadth and width of Gabriel. And even though I'd never touched him, I felt I had been more intimate with him in that moment than I'd ever been with anyone physically before him.

'*I love you,*' I think, unable to help the words I know he doesn't want to hear. '*I love you so much.*'

He moves his leg out of my grasp, taking the colorworld with him, and stands up, but I can tell he felt some of what I was sending him. I can tell that for a moment, he was right there with me.

It was small, and it was more for me than for him, but that was the perfect start to what is now my aggressive plan to win Gabriel back.

Sixty-Six

"*Cooooofffffeeeeee,*" Ezra moans, holding his hands out like a zombie and shuffling over to the coffee maker.

"You want eggs?" I say, hurriedly spooning the last of Robbie's baby food into his mouth and handing him a teething biscuit.

Ezra's arms flop to his sides when he comes to a disappointed stop in front of the empty coffee pot. "Weeeeennnn," he wines. "Whyyyy?" He holds his hands out to the pot. "Surely, with all your billions, you can hire someone to make sure there's coffee at all times." He turns around. "You're sabotaging the mission. How am I supposed to work with no coffee?"

"No. *You're* sabotaging it by sprinting right out of the gate. Barely a week in and you're already staying up two nights in a row." I pull eggs out of the fridge. "Besides, I'm not spending money to pay someone to do things you're too lazy to do. Money does run out. Even billions."

"It wasn't my fault," Ezra says, banging through the cabinets in search of coffee grounds. "Gabe stayed up mapping the wall, so me and Roe couldn't go to sleep, otherwise we'd be super behind on logging."

I crack eggs into a bowl. "Gabriel is used to pushing himself to extremes," I say. "Don't expect to keep up with him. He can do his own logging—whatever that means."

"I don't know how and when to make adjustments to the graphing formula in the simulation," Gabriel says, striding easily into the room as if he didn't get beaten to a pulp two nights ago and is functioning on little to no sleep. Even his voice sounds refreshed. "And we had to backtrack to take into account the new information Roe gave us on the geological aspects. It's necessary to collaborate through each step."

I hop lightly to where he is, standing right at his back,

hands clasped behind me as he decides what he wants out of the open fridge. "But you have a point," Gabriel says, still not turning round. "Ezra hasn't built up endurance."

He grabs orange juice and butter awkwardly in his one good hand and turns. "I'll keep that in mind and—" The butter flies out of his hand, but I catch it. "Heavens, Wendy. What are you doing standing that close?"

"Good morning!" I smile, blocking him between the fridge door and a getaway. "Do you want eggs?"

He gives me a head to toe. I'm wearing a tight, low-cut camisole and very short pajama shorts. I even painted my toes pink using the nail polish I found in the small stash of Kaylen's things we've been lugging around.

I take the orange juice out of his hand and hold the tub of butter near my face, blocking my words from reaching Ezra at the table. "You want me to butter your toast?" I ask. "Or something else…?"

The innuendo isn't lost on him. I take it a step further and reach past him for the fridge, which is still slightly ajar because I haven't let him move. "There's jam in here, too." I reach for it, biting my lip and letting my breasts brush his arm. And then, before he tries to duck away from me, I turn around and put everything on the center island. I lean over it to snag the bread, grateful that fate has it in such a strategic location.

I look over my shoulder when he doesn't answer, pleased to find him looking. "What do you think?" I say.

He struggles for an answer.

I hop up on the counter, cross my legs and lean back on my hands. "You could try both. One with jam. One without?"

He glances over to the table, looking for Ezra I think. But Ezra's gone. He even took Robbie with him. I spoke to him yesterday, warned him I was probably going to act like a seductress any time Gabriel was in the room, and he should do me the favor of leaving if it made him uncomfortable instead of complaining about all the things he doesn't want to see me do. And this is only a warmup.

Gabriel's eyes would probably narrow if they weren't already so swollen. "I know what you're doing. I'm asking you, if you have any respect for me or yourself, please don't."

I raise an eyebrow, start swinging an ankle, because there was a hint of begging there that he's stifling, which only fuels my determination. Gabriel hiding his emotions? So he *can* be a typical guy after all… I hop off the counter and drag the bread over to the toaster. "I'm making you breakfast. Why is that a problem?" I throw two pieces in, but when I turn around, he's gone. As I expected.

I quickly fry some eggs, butter the toast, one with jam and one without. And then I go to Mike's room.

He's coming out of it when I arrive. "Help me find him?" I say, inhaling Mike's freshly showered deliciousness.

He gives my outfit an appreciative look. "Clocking in early?" he titters.

"You know it," I say, walking next to him down the hall toward the east wing, which belongs to my team. I laugh. Gabriel thinks I won't follow him in there wearing this? *Oh Gabriel... you are making this so easy.*

"Hold this," I say to Mike, handing him the plate.

He takes it. I pull my shorts off to reveal the spandex workout shorts I have underneath. I couldn't decide between them and the pajama shorts this morning, so I wore both in case of necessity. Subtle usually works better. Except when you're sending a clear message, like now. I tug my light blue camisole down further until it shows the top of my lacy black bra.

I take the plate from Mike, and he chuckles at me. "He's not far. Twenty feet or so. The other kitchen, I bet."

"Thanks," I say, glad Mike's connection to Gabriel allows him to locate Gabriel no matter where he is. The eggs would have been ice cold by the time I found him in the Labyrinth. Although I'm probably going to have to heat them up anyway.

"Confession," he says, before he leaves me, using our cue word. We say it when we need to tell the other person something in the interest of honesty but it might create chemistry or discomfort. "You got him bothered already this morning, and it looks like more is coming. I'm going to go take another shower until... you're done with all this." He motions the length of me.

I smile at him and push through the double-doors. I smell waffles wafting from the kitchen. Ugh. How can any of them possibly be in the mood for waffles when we've been living out of hotels for nearly two months? It's a staple of continental breakfasts. I've eaten enough of them for a lifetime.

When I enter the room, there are probably six guys crowded around a table. Gabriel is over by the sink, rinsing a plate, one-handed.

Standing by the waffle iron, with her back to me, is Roe, wearing a black satin robe, matching pants, and furry black monster feet slippers.

Someone at the table notices I've walked in, and the murmuring stops. All eyes shift to me in succession. I'm confused by the emotions in the room, which are at first abashed, as if I've caught all of them at a peep show.

"Guten Morgen, Vendy!" Roe says, and I look back to see her holding a waffle on the end of a long fork, which she walks over to the table and plops onto a larger plate at the center. But that's not what has my eyes widening. The woman's robe is open, and she has nothing on underneath. Her breasts swing to the side as she leans over the table, quite near Louis' head, and he is enjoying every moment. All six of them are.

I flounder for about seven seconds. And then, observing that Roe is not oblivious to her state of apparel, I have to assume there is a reasoned explanation. Besides, all things being equal, she's actually got more on than I do. I couldn't have picked a worse time to walk into the east wing kitchen wearing what I am. This situation has the likelihood of descending into the kind of awkwardness that will go down in infamy.

Or… I might be able to use this.

Two guys try to duck out as I come to this decision. "Not so fast," I say, giving them a warning look. "Get back here."

Gabriel's holding a mug of coffee, leaning against the counter next to the sink. I can't read his expression that well, what with the state of his face, but I'd like to think he's amused, or maybe he's smug. I don't know. I turn to Roe. "Good morning. I came here to seduce my husband, who decided to hide from me in here, thinking I wouldn't follow him. What's *your* excuse?"

The corner of her mouth curves upward. "Oooh. A ket and mousse game. Sexy. And you look smashing, dahling. You vant help next time, you come see me. I meek you look so hot he von't remember how to find his vey here. But! Now you vant to know vy I have my breasts uncovered, ya?"

I walk over to one of the two microwaves in the room and put Gabriel's plate in. I start it and turn around. "I might take you up on that. And yes. You have the girls moving and shaking, so if you're a spy, and mind-controlling my people was your goal, you're doing a pretty good job."

She laughs and pours more batter onto the waffle iron. "Eh." She shrugs. "Now, zey see sex. Give it two months. Then zey see Roe." She turns, spatula still in hand, and holds her robe open to show me her apple-sized mounds. "See? Vat is big deal? Zey sink sex because culture tells them. Zey are taught as children to vant ze sings dat are hidden. In nineteen hundred, ankles make men sooo hot. Now? Zey juus see ankles."

I hear movement from the table and point at them without looking. "Sit *down*." I lean over the island, putting my own breasts on display for Gabriel who is almost directly across from me, and my butt for... everyone else. "Good point. But I think it's going to take more than *your* breasts to desensitize them. Aaaand I'm already struggling for them to take *me* seriously."

She bites her lip sheepishly. "I might... also be hoping zey trust me some. When vooman uncovers, she makes herself vulnerable. Ven she acts comfortably with her body, ze seductive mystery disappears and men act like humans. I read about Robert Haricott. He was goot man. He mek goot people. I trust you all. I treat you as I do my own femily, breasts and all. I hope to earn ze same."

The microwave beeps. I seductively but naturally push off of the counter and pull the plate out. Then I walk over to Gabriel. "Your eggs and toast. Sorry it's a little limp... You should have stuck around and had it while it was fresh and hot."

He's stunned and confused. I wait until he takes the plate from me, and then I walk over to Roe. "You need help?"

"Who still vants vaffle?" Roe calls to the table of wide-eyed men.

ℸ

Letty falls back on the bed, laughing uncontrollably.

"And then," I giggle breathlessly, "Roe put on some kind of German dance music—and we started getting down in the kitchen and tossing waffles to the guys as they came out. The whole team showed up because of the music—even Darren."

"Santa Maria!" she exclaims. "What did Gabe do?"

"Stood there, brooding and eating his eggs the whole time. I figured he'd make himself scarce, but he couldn't make himself leave. His jealousy always gets the better of him."

Letty's mouth opens in outrage. "What the hell? Just stood there?"

I smirk. "Until the end of the song, when I was leaning across the table to take up plates. He smacked my butt on his way out of the kitchen."

"That's wassup!" Letty hoots, clapping her hands. "Jealous as hell, watchin' all those guys eying you."

I roll my eyes. "Idiot. I'm taking him down."

"I know you *are*, girl. Just like old days." We high five each other.

I sigh and lay down on the rug.

"Would you be mad if I came on to Little Mickey?" Letty asks.

"You haven't already? Don't you guys have some sort of gummy bear romance going on?"

"That's kid stuff. Flirting. I mean for real."

I can't help grimacing.

"I see that look. Nevermind."

I come up on my elbow. "It's not what you think. For you, 'for real' means you make him your booty call for a while. You don't mean something serious."

She makes a sound of protest.

"Come on, Letty... Mike's head gets messed with enough."

"Joder, Wen. You act like all I do is whore myself."

"Last I checked, you weren't getting money for sex. I'm just saying I want to see Mike in a committed relationship."

"Maybe I'm turning over a new leaf..."

"Liar."

She rolls toward me. "Aaaaagh. Wen, my libido can't handle abstinence," she whines. "And he's *hot*."

"You're a mess," I say. "Do what you want. But I might not like you much anymore if you hurt him."

"Want me to ah... get Gabe worked up while I'm at it? Mess with his head a little?"

"Oh my gosh! Are you seriously asking if you can come on to my husband?"

"I won't let it go anywhere. Just get him a little hot and bothered. Then he'll want to take it out on someone..."

I put my hand on my forehead. "Oh geez. Get a vibrator, Letty."

"I'm serious, Wen. We can tag team. I'm gonna see him all day. I need an outlet anyway."

"I don't know, Letty... That's not really playing fair."

"Pshh. Like *he* is. Besides, using everything you got is totally fair," she says. "And you got me havin' your back."

"Tell you what. I'll keep it in mind. In case things get desperate."

"Kinda figured they were already," she sighs.

I wince. All joking and fun aside, things *are* desperate. I'm purposely reverting to a person I thought I had shelved for good, so things must be dire. I'm a billionaire with superpowers. I survived leukemia and being married with a death touch. I decimated a fleet of Andre's Guild deviants and helicopters with a rocket launcher from a rooftop. After all that, I'm back to shamelessly using my body to gain power over a man.

What. The hell.

"You either gonna own this all the way, or you gonna half-ass it and lose," Letty says.

This kind of behavior should be beneath me, shouldn't it?

But what if I lose him because I didn't do everything I possibly could out of principle?

"You gotta do it, Wen," Letty says. "For women everywhere."

"Uh. Okay?"

"If you consider the time men spend obsessing over women and their bodies, it's a wonder we don't rule the world already," Letty says, her hispanic accent becoming more pronounced because she's getting riled. "But somehow we always have the bottom end of everything. Oh we getting somewhere. Little by little. Now they realize we aren't so stupid. Now we have all these movements that talk about not objectifying us, not sexualizing us. Now it's this emphasis on brains and personality, on trashing the gender roles. That's cool. I'll take all of that. But you know what? I still got a fine ass, too. Sayin' I can't use it to get ahead or it makes me a whore is just more of the same oppressing shit that has kept us on the bottom."

She props herself up on her elbow. "You know I don't want to steal your man. But you're mi hermana. You're also a woman. And women gotta have each others' backs. That's why we've been failing for thousands of years. We don't combine forces. Instead we fight over who has perkier breasts and better shoes. Fight over guys. Not me though. I have your back. No matter what. That bastard's trying to set all the rules, trying to tell *you* how it's gonna be. You bore his son. You warmed his bed. You let him have you when you could have had anyone. And this is how he's gonna play it? Hell no, Wen. Don't take that shit lying down. You own him."

She lays back on the bed. I like her enthusiasm. I like the idea of joining forces for each other. She's right. That's how it should be.

"You can own that dick, Darren, while you're at it," she adds. "That guy has some serious issues workin' with women. Shoulda seen him telling me I was holding my gun wrong. Pshh. I've been firing a glock since I was five. Then he always wants me on backup instead of the point team." She scoffs. "Thank *gawd* I get a break from that dumbass."

I chuckle. "Glad to know it's not just me. Does he do that to Jessie, too?"

"Oh yeah. Jessie and me, we stick together. Sometimes we twerk behind his back when he ain't looking. Funny as hell."

I laugh, picturing it. I sit up. "Alright. You're on. I bet I can even get Roe in on it."

Letty pushes herself up, bouncing up and down. "Yesssssss. Hey, tomorrow is Sunday. It's gonna be a hot one and there's a pool out back. I say we start Skimpy Swimsuit Sunday."

"I'll make sure it coincides with my new policy: Lock the Lab Lunchtime," I say. "Because you know Gabriel is going to try to work through it."

"Lock the Lab Lunchtime…" Letty says, nodding. "Definitely. It's for the good of the team. Can't be skipping lunch, after all."

Sixty-Seven

*I*t's beautiful here," Carl says, coming up beside me to admire the view of the river far below us.

"Hey, Dad. I guess we had the same idea this morning," I say, thinking the title finally sounds normal. It was awkward the first time I called him Dad, but the constant threat of the Apocalypse and Andre had me wanting to forge a stronger bond with my father, who was not that long ago my enemy.

"Have I ever told you I'm sorry?" he asks, glancing at me out of the corner of his eye, the sheepishness in that look reminding me of Ezra, not to mention his dirty blonde hair would be exactly the same shade were it not for the grey.

"Only every other day," I say, smiling over at him.

"Good," he says, folding his arms and following my gaze across the gulch.

Since Mike and I found him in Chicago, I've curiously watched Carl. He wasn't around my whole life, and I was raised by a woman who wasn't biologically related to me. I've been fascinated every time I've caught him doing something and realized I do the same thing. Just yesterday I went to find him in his room to ask a question and found him in a corner, sitting on the floor, typing on his laptop. Being close to floors and walls had always been one of my inexplicable quirks, until that moment. About a week after Carl joined our group, Ezra pointed out that we purse our lips the same way when we're annoyed.

The other thing Carl and I have in common is dedication. We take forever to change our minds, to make up our minds, but when we do, the change is ironclad. I accepted his proclaimed turnaround in Chicago and haven't worried about him since, somehow subconsciously recognizing that I saw myself in his drive to do what he said he'd do: follow me and help in any way he could.

He once murdered people. He once kidnapped me. He once manipulated me. He once made me harm people without my realizing it until it was too late. He lied to me over and over.

The crazy part is how every time I think about that, I can only find gratitude for his being such a consistent force in my life. I don't know what I would be now without it. We were always at war with each other, but now I realize it was my proving ground. It wasn't the real battle. Some people have fathers that nurtured and encouraged them. But my father taught me to fight.

"Have I ever told you I forgive you?" I say.

"Sometimes," he replies.

"Oh…" I frown. "Well, I do."

"It doesn't matter to me. It doesn't make me any more or less sorry. Do you think Kaylen will be okay?"

I sigh. Kaylen has been gone for nearly two months. After Andre murdered Uncle Moby, Kaylen left a note that said she was going after Andre, something I consider a stupid idea. But I also consider Kaylen capable of making her own choices.

Most likely though, Carl is especially on edge about it because of the news this morning: Last night, PHIA massacred the residents of an apartment building in New York. The apartments were owned by a technology firm that provided housing to its employees. It's evident that the Guild or a member of it owns that technology firm, and it employs Primes. It was the largest-scale attack yet, and graphic photos show the greek symbol, Phi, painted in blood inside the apartments of the victims—PHIA's sign. One hundred and eight men, women, and children were killed as PHIA went from apartment to apartment and quietly executed them. The fact that it was done so seamlessly and without anyone realizing what was happening is what has disturbed so many. No one even knew anything was amiss until someone was spotted quickly spray-painting the sidewalk in front of the building with PHIA's symbol. The Guild spokesperson confirmed that thirty-three of the victims were, indeed, Prime Human. Humans are left wondering just how safe they are, since none of them knows if who they work for or live next to is a Prime, whether it will cost them their own lives.

"Andre is doing a good job sowing dissension," I sigh. "As for Kaylen, every day I don't see her body dropped off in an unmarked van, I feel a little more confident. Every day I don't hear from her, I feel a little more afraid for her. I think I'm still at the same place I was months ago: I have to let it be. It's *her* life."

"She's not you, Wendy," Carl says with a gust of fear. "She learned who she is from me. She learned…" He shudders. "How to come second to the person that should have cared more. But you… Sara taught you the exact opposite things. I worry… I worry Kaylen will end up like I was. Consumed with retribution."

That's a legitimate worry I sometimes share, but what can I do about it?

"It's in the past, and she has to figure out who she wants to be," I reply. "But you know, our attitudes toward the people and things around us have visual manifestations in the colorworld. I think believing in her really does help. Doubting her can only hurt."

Silence prevails for a while, and I'm about to continue my run, but Carl says, "I need to tell you some things… some ancient history."

I look at him. He's never offered to share his past before. And I didn't press because I don't think it's relevant anymore, and it's obviously a deep source of pain for him.

He clears his throat nervously. "When we arrived here, and I saw that massive house, all the preparations to make it self-sustaining, I recognized it was a result of Rob's foresight. He knew the future would be dangerous. And I recognized there was no guarantee that I'd make it through. I dislike the idea of dying without you knowing all that I know—or at least what I think I know. I don't want to tempt fate."

"Alright," I say.

He sits down on the ground, and I follow.

"I honestly don't remember anything I've ever told you in the past. There were so many lies, they were hard to keep track of. But right now I'm going to tell you the truth, as best as I can recall it. I swear this on my life and on Regina's memory. I am done lying to you."

I nod, knowing that there is no one Carl has ever loved more than my mother—my biological one—Gina.

"Eric Shelding was Louise's father. He discovered hypno-touch in the fifties. The romanticized story within the Guild is that he had a vision about the energy world and it inspired him to discover hypno-touch. (I can neither confirm nor deny that account.) He was of course excited by the results, performed it on everyone he possibly could. Even Louise's son, who had a blood disorder."

"Oh… man," I say. Louise was the woman that Carl used to work with at Pneumatikon, the compound I lived at after I had hypno-touch. She is the same woman that abducted me when I first discovered I could access the colorworld. She had to have seen hypno-touch kill her child, yet she headed a compound dedicated to it?

"Louise killed her father for that," Carl says simply.

Well, okay then… Looks like Louise's son was to her what Gina was to Carl as far as motivation.

Carl waves a dismissive hand. "But again, the Guild touts it as a story of martyrdom: Someone didn't want the world to have Eric's dream of life force abilities. His research was in shambles until the early seventies, when children of his past victims caught on to their capability and looked into their history to learn the source. Reinventing the history of Eric Shelding began, sanding his rough edges and burying the probable controversies; assembling the theories of the energy world; tracking down all his past subjects… This was the Guild when it began."

"And you?" I say.

"Mine and Rob's biological parents were among Eric's victims. That's actually how they met. Everything that followed… I've hesitated to share because it could be pure speculation as easily as it could be truth."

"Then why does it matter?"

"Because… It made me into what I became. And I guess… I don't want you to make the same mistakes. I don't want you to rely on a history told through the eyes of others over what your heart tells you. And for me this is where I erred, relying too heavily on a legacy to guide my actions."

"I guess that makes sense."

"Our mother was the first to see the energy world. Our father had foresight like Rob. He could stand in a place and see flashes of its possible futures. His name was Samuel Pruitt and he predicted that the world would end and that it would happen within a lifetime. He was one of the founding members of the Guild."

My mouth opens in surprise.

Carl looks at me questioningly. "Bearing in mind that he was not a Prime, and if the world weren't headed where it is right now, what would be your gut reaction to that?"

I purse my lips, thinking. It's hard to let go of what's happening right *now*, but even so… "Sounds a little far-fetched. Hypno-touch abilities are *not* that strong. Seeing that far in the future and he wasn't even a Prime…? Sounds more like he might have used the prediction to garner support from Primes to start a club. Assuming he could wow them with some sort of demonstration of his capability."

He grunts, "Like father, like daughter."

"Is that why you never joined?"

"Partly. Here's the way I saw it: If he was right, then we should be pumping out Prime Humans as fast as technologically possible. We need them everywhere, in all realms, in all cultures. Diversify their upbringing and experience to give us a better chance of solving the upcoming problem. If it was all a lie, however... we should do the same thing. Because if it was all a lie, then what was the purpose other than exclusion and ultimately power? To me, the choice was so easy, so perfectly logical. I had to perpetuate Primes outside of the Guild. It was the only way to fight either of those possible futures."

"I see that..." I say. "But Uncle Moby would say that predicting the future always does that. It causes you to either fight it or make it. And both things always backfire."

"Yes. Although he was not as wise back then. He and I held similar ideals for a time. However, we used our talents to attack the problem differently. He grew an empire, which he used to recruit Primes away from the Guild. And I built Primes through hypno-touch, which I didn't at first know was lethal. We were raised by a Guild family, and the prediction of the end of the world, and our place in saving it, was the basis of our indoctrination. You look forward to becoming eighteen, the age when you finally get to take part in the thing you were born to do. Only in certain positions are you privileged to learn the Guild's actual origins—of the hypno-touch of Eric Shelding. Because I never chose to join, however, I was forced to learn all of these things through trial and error."

"Louise," I say. "She taught you hypno-touch."

"Yes. Until then, I knew I was supposed to be able to access the energy world, and I knew the energy world was where Prime Human abilities came from. Every Prime Human child was taught about that place, the place where they came from. It was all presented in a very mystical light. Prime children consider themselves chosen by that place to take part in the fight for mother earth. So imagine the perception I had of myself... the one person alive capable of actually seeing it. The age of eighteen, when I could finally be trained, would be the most important day of my life. But I knocked someone unconscious by touching them and it was found out that I was a channel. And then another person fell victim. I was afraid, but I trusted in what they told me, that this meant I was destined for even bigger things. But then, at ten years old, I killed someone."

I put my hand over my mouth and shake my head. I remember how much it haunted me to kill Dina, and I was nineteen by then… What an awful thing to endure at ten.

"That's when everything began to change," Carl says. "Because nobody could explain it to me and no exceptions were made, like letting me start early in training how to use the energy world. I became jaded little by little, and the prediction began to look different to me. Everything looked different. So when activation time came, I would have no part of it. It helped that Rob stood with me. He had rejected activation himself, as an act of blackmail on my behalf. But it failed, and by then he was already building his empire, and using his ability to recruit Primes right out from under the Guild. Rob got closer than I ever did to taking them down—and probably would have if he had continued—but the death of his wife changed the direction of his life, and he didn't care about what the Guild was doing anymore."

"He told me about his wife," I say softly.

"We Haricotts do crazy things when our loved ones are in danger, don't we?" Carl asks, smiling knowingly at me. It's nice that we can joke about the past like this. He and Louise tricked me into doing hypno-touch on Gabriel only a couple years ago, which gave him lung cancer. I was in a race against time to save him, which was what Carl intended. He wanted me to cure hypno-touch sickness, and he knew Gabriel's probable death was the only way to motivate me.

"It does seem that way, doesn't it?" I grin.

He looks back at the ravine. "Louise found me after I graduated medical school—a career I chose, in part, because I could wear latex gloves constantly and nobody would notice." He smiles in memory. "She was the daughter of the famed Eric Shelding, and she said he had never envisioned the Guild. She said they stole his legacy and remade it to suit their purposes. To me, the moment felt like destiny pulling me back on track. Her appearance out of obscurity, to me, someone who viewed the Guild so differently from everyone I had grown up with, was a sign that I had been right, that the Guild operates on perception. That is their power, their draw. They give their people something to believe in, something to work toward. And they do it *so* well.

"Louise and I became a team, motivated by a need to take down the Guild. We began Four Winds Energy Clinic. We churned out life force abilities under secrecy, not to hide it from others, but to hide it from the Guild. That's why we had the compound, to *teach* energy therapy, hoping to perpetuate it."

"To perpetuate it? But I was taken to the compound blindfolded. We signed an agreement to keep the methods confidential. There were patents…"

"Yes," he says, "To recreate the same perception Guild children grow up with about the energy world, to impress its importance. The secrecy was all a show intended to make people desperate to share it."

"Ah. That makes sense," I say. "But what happened to them? I mean I know some of them I cured, but the others?"

"The Guild got to them," Carl says. "Louise and I were fools to think that we could hide from them. The list I gave you were the ones they *allowed* me to give you. They were as anxious as I was to find out whether you would find a way to cure the sickness."

"Ugh," I say. "No doubt they were more than happy to have a bunch of new blood to harvest reproductive cells and make new Prime babies without getting their own hands dirty."

"They are nothing if not opportunistic," Carl replies.

"Before all that though, you learned that hypno-touch was lethal. *After* you did it on Gina. Louise had to have known what she was doing in teaching you, right? What made you stick around with her once you figured it out?"

Carl sighs. "Yes, we're getting ahead of the story. I did perform hypno-touch on the love of my life and others without realizing I was killing them. And I was seemingly good at it. My subjects had abilities far more powerful than anything Louise could do. When it became apparent what was happening, Louise begged innocence. And then she backpedaled and claimed she didn't know my version of hypno-touch was even *more* lethal. Her hope had been that I was an exception because of how powerful I was… So on and so forth. Eventually she broke down and told me about her son, what her father had done, which, to me, was even more fitting of what I believed the Guild to be by then. The heart of the Guild, the energy world, was founded on a scumbag like that? No surprise to me. My partnership with Louise became… more like a convenient alliance against a common enemy, but trust between us no longer existed."

I pick up a handful of pebbles and toss them toward the edge of the ravine, thinking what a stressful existence Carl chose to lead being so close to someone who could and would easily kill him if she chose. I met the woman. I know.

"But how…" I start, unsure if I should ask this. I really want to know though… because we are so alike. And I never want to find myself on the path that he once chose. "If there was no trust, no respect, how did you let her strip you of goodness?"

Carl's thoughts cloud over. "She didn't. I did. The way I saw it for so many years after Gina was that I was fallen. I had already hurt so many. I had already sacrificed all there was to be sacrificed. Lost all there was to be lost. Once you finally realize how low you have sunk, the pain of it becomes so heavy that you lose the strength to care. You cannot earn forgiveness. You cannot redeem yourself. It is a place… of no escape."

We sit in stillness, me pondering that place he describes. It sounds like… what people feel when they die from my skin, and it is the most misery I have ever endured.

"Justify. Justify. Justify," Carl whispers. "Lower. Lower. Lower. Down there you have been slowly stripped of your senses. You don't feel anymore. And hurting people doesn't stir anything. And killing becomes easier."

My hands are clenched in my lap. It's terrifying to me to see the progression of Carl's life and realize that perhaps the only difference between us is in our circumstances. I have the fate of the world hanging over my head, but at least I have people all around me whom I trust. I am never alone. Not like he was. He had no one. I wonder… was it better or worse for Carl that Sara took me away from him? I don't know. But I am… *so* relieved that we are all in his life now.

I reach over and put my hand over his. "You found your way out."

"No. You pulled me out," Carl says, his voice catching.

After a while, I say, "So, the prophecy. It was true all along?"

"Things do seem to point to that," he says reluctantly.

I wonder what that means… The Apocalypse is inevitable? Is there even a way to stop it?

"I know you disagree, but I am still convinced this is all the Guild's doing," Carl adds. "I'm looking forward to seeing Ezra's finished schematic. I believe he will be able to deconstruct it to reveal the source."

"At this point, I'm open to any possibility," I say. "Your idea to map the disasters… really genius. And I really appreciate what you did, giving Ezra confidence that he could be the one to do it."

"I got the idea from Sara, actually. We were on a road trip once, back before GPS, and she was holding the map. She kept flipping between pages, back and forth, back and forth. She must have spent an hour doing that, and the sound was driving me crazy. I finally asked her what she was doing. She said, 'Testing myself. I look at the full map, pick one of the major cities, and I predict the close-up layout of that city based on the roads of the larger map. There's a pattern to it. *A signature.*'" Carl smiles to himself. "Realized how much genius she had underneath the surface. And Ezra is capable of far more."

"One would think the Guild would have people of similar genius," I point out. "It baffles me that they haven't figured this out already."

"Why would they if they were the ones to make it?"

"If they made it, why do they care about *me*?"

"Because they want you in their collection. The energy world is the basis of all they believe. They can't have the person capable of seeing it on the *outside.* How would that look to the new recruits? That's like Jesus coming back and disowning the Christianity movement."

I laugh at the analogy. "Good thing I have no intention of ever joining."

He exhales exasperation. "Small ways, Wendy. First is negotiation. Then collaboration. Before you know it, they will take credit for what you do. And when you die, they will distort your history just as they did Shelding's. Future generations will never know who you really were and what you really stood for. They will have erased the real you."

This isn't the first time Carl has fed me this line. Though he is committed to my cause, he still hasn't let go of who he thinks the Guild is and what they're after. And maybe he's right. But does it really matter? I'm just trying to fix a problem: out of control natural disasters. I don't have time to be suspicious every time Ohr sends me gifts—such as the cure to my juvenile diabetes a couple of months ago, among other things.

"I apologize," Carl says, frustrated. "I didn't intend to rehash things we've been over before. Revisiting history has that effect on me, I guess. I actually had something else to tell you."

Still sitting cross-legged on the ground, he pivots to face me and I copy him.

"I've figured out how to go into the energy world without a subject," he says.

I lift my eyebrows. "Really? I didn't know that was possible."

"I didn't either, but I couldn't think of any reason it shouldn't be. So I started experimenting."

"Wow," I say. "So that's what you've been doing that's had Darren in a fix. 'I think he's doing *energy things* again, Wendy…'" I roll my eyes. "Tried to convince me to assign you a chaperone."

He laughs. "Not a bad idea. I wouldn't have blamed you. I've always felt you've given me more trust that I deserve."

I shrug. "I think I'm more motivated to disagree with Darren out of pure spite since telling me what to do is on his daily to-do list."

"Well I want to teach you how to do it."

"That'd be awesome," I say, excited by the prospect. "Going into the colorworld whenever I want… Even alone? I can totally get behind that. Never know when it will come in handy."

"It's not what you think… It's not the same as the colorworld you're used to," he says, and behind his words is the gravity of awed anticipation. "My vision is grossly inferior to yours, but even I marveled at the change. To say I'm thrilled to find out what you can do with it is an understatement."

Taken aback, I stare at him, doubtful that anything could rival Mike's colorworld—which Carl has never seen. *That* place is where incomprehensibility and comprehensibility reside at the same time. It reveals the stitches of reality.

Carl translates my look. "I've heard you talk about seeing the energy world with Mike. And I am sure it's astounding. Incredible. Beyond real description. This is different in a marked way."

"What way is that?"

"My theory is that by using a life force to channel in, you are limited by the perception of a life force. With the method

I'm going to teach you, you use the other living matter around you."

"So like… a tree or something?"

"Yes. Eventually. But to learn, you start with something much simpler. What do all living things have in common?"

I purse my lips, thinking. Grass, trees, shrubs… Like people, those things have static colors in the colorworld. Inert matter is always shifting hues. It's what makes the colorworld disorienting. "Their colors don't change," I say.

"No, I mean in *this* world," he says. "What gives them all life?"

"Water and sunlight." I stop, mouth open. "Water. Oh my gosh. *Water?* You access the colorworld using *water?* But you can't even *see* water there! It's invisible."

His eyes shine with a fervor I've never seen on him. "Not when you use it to channel in."

Sixty-Eight

This is going to be the fastest way to learn," Carl says, facing me in the shallow end of the pool. "But I promise, once you have this down, you'll be able to do it using a bathtub, then a sink, and then the grass if you like."

"I figured…" I say, grimacing and waving my hands through the water. It's a salt-treated pool, but the reminder brings the smell of chlorine to my nose. I can still feel the remnants of exhaustion that overtook my body little by little until I couldn't sit up for more than a couple minutes as the leukemia tore apart my body from the inside. "Me and pools have a long and sordid history," I explain. "I thought the affair was over."

He chuckles. "Just think of it as training wheels. As soon as you grasp the idea, you get to leave the pool behind again."

"Wonderful," I say, pushing off and paddling toward the middle of the water. "Then let's get this over with."

Carl takes long strokes to follow and says, "You'll need to be where you can't touch, not the floor and not the walls. Completely buoyant. Floating on your back will work best because you won't be distracted with having to stay afloat. Relax as much as possible, exactly like you would if you were about to access the colorworld using a subject."

I lay back, spread my arms out, and close my eyes, letting the sunshine fall on my face directly. It takes some time to relax the way he's asking. It's been forever since I've had to actually *think* about how to access the colorworld. I've gotten so good I only have to blink to go there—provided I'm touching or next to someone, of course. Very rarely am I in such a state that I can't immediately go there.

I start by thinking about breathing, letting my breaths move in and out smoothly. I do that for a while, not sure if it's accomplishing anything. I move on to step two, which is visualization. Except it doesn't work, because what I would usually imagine would be the sensation of someone's life force against my hands. Imagining it—expecting it—would bring it forward.

"A little help?" I say. "I'm stuck on trying to feel a life force touching me. Except there isn't one."

"I didn't say try," he says. "I said relax."

I come up, treading water to find him sitting on the pool's edge. "How long do I have to do that for?"

"Until you actually are," he laughs. "If you're thinking about how long it will take, that definitely means you aren't relaxed enough. I'll prompt you. For now, *relax*."

"Fine," I grumble, laying back again and closing my eyes and thinking the word *relax* over and over.

Relaxing is hard. My brain won't shut up. Instead I get stuck on thinking about the serial failures of the last couple of months. After I escaped the Guild and my uncle died, we began traversing the United States, visiting disaster sites and observing them in the colorworld, specifically Mike's colorworld where you can see things interact via what we call 'change events,' which are basically the domino effect between molecules. It's best summed up in the philosophy that the flapping of a butterfly's wings could realistically create a hurricane on the other side of the world. Except in Mike's colorworld you realize that it's basically irrelevant, because the domino effect begun by the flapping of wings would affect and be affected by trillions of other paths of movement on its way to the other side of the world. And the flapping itself was influenced by trillions of precursors.

Basically, there is no end or beginning to reality. This fact became solidified the more we looked for the 'source' of the change events created by a disaster. In a word: impossible. Something as big as an earthquake or a forest fire or a tornado has numberless contributing change events and numberless effects on everything around it.

We also spent time looking at people. Gabriel, with his ability to count to, as yet, infinite numbers, had observed in Mike's colorworld that life force strands are all unique. They have crystalline structures, which are always changing. In Prime Humans, we saw, those changes happen more slowly than they do in Humans. We still have no explanation for that, but in trying to discover it, we found out that life forces are two-toned. Some strands are brighter than others. Darker strands go in the chest; lighter strands in the head.

This was actually the biggest breakthrough. Because when we fixed my life force after hypno-touch almost killed me, we couldn't figure out why I lost all of my abilities, which should have been natural, since I'm a Prime Human. I had to have hypno-touch *again* to get my abilities back, which put me in danger of illness again. But knowing that chest and head strands can be differentiated, that they have to go in the right location for a natural ability to work, we now know we can put them back in the proper place. We haven't yet because I don't want to lose my channeling ability, which I only have because of hypno-touch. Undoing it would most likely strip me of the ability to channel, not to mention diminish my senses somewhat. And I need both of these things to continue to address the state of the world.

My refusal to fix my strands, thereby risking my life, resulted in a nasty argument I'd rather forget, which is probably why I find it hard to view as a success. I don't think it's a coincidence that right after that argument with Gabriel, he issued his request for distance.

Great. Now my heart hurts all over again. I am definitely *not* relaxed. I blow air out through my lips, hoping that maybe thinking about these things will get the stress out of me. I should have spent more time reflecting before now. That's probably why I'm having so much trouble. My life has so many demands now.

Inheriting my uncle's fortune might have given me practically an unlimited budget, but it also takes a huge chunk of my time in exchange. Uncle Moby set things up so that all of his holdings would systematically liquidate. Even his twenty or so businesses are set to sell themselves off little by little, a process that will conclude in another two months. In the meantime, though, I am on-call. I've had to fly from east coast to west coast and back to attend meetings and speak for my interests in front of each board of directors. I've had to meet with portfolio managers, insurance people, lawyers, and more lawyers.

Meanwhile, hurricanes and flooding have hammered the east coast, mass panic and fires have consumed the west coast, bizarre weather of all kinds has rained down in the mid and mountain west, and mudslides and earthquakes and tsunamis have terrorized the rest of the world. So my other project has been this ranch my uncle purchased for me, working with various experts to make it a place that can withstand mother nature. The date of October twenty-eighth, which is in less than two months, when my uncle's arrangement to have all of my assets become liquid concludes, cannot be random, so that's my goal for finishing.

I'm exhausted... But that's not all.

The next thing we need to do is look into understanding Mike's life force ability more. Carl said Mike's mother, Alma, moved her life force to touch people when she would put suggestions in people's heads. Mike's ability works with a longer range. He can make things happen by meditating on what he wants to happen. Short range, he can affect the way people move and act, as long as they are open to suggestion.

I think, however, that everyone has conveniently forgotten curiosity about Mike's ability, because once we discovered that he was short about nineteen billion strands and that Gabriel had an overage of that same number... well, Mike's life force is something nobody wants to become any more complicated than it already is. I know *I'm* afraid of it. Not for me, but for Gabriel because of what he might do if we learn something about Mike's life force ability that strips Gabriel even more of an identity separate from Mike. We already know Mike's ability is stunted when Gabriel is nearby. So Mike's ability is connected to Gabriel in some way as well.

I sigh. I should probably work on that now. Things can't really get much worse between Gabriel and me, and my responsibilities have eased slightly now that we have a centralized location...

I open my eyes and have to immediately shield them from the sun. "This isn't working, Dad. I'm a head case." I swim to the side near him.

"I noticed," he says. "You know, thinking about breathing is the quickest way to empty your mind."

"Yeah... I've been trying." I bite my lip. "But I don't think I'm capable of regulating my breathing when I feel like I can barely breathe all the time."

He frowns in compassion. "Wendy, something needs to change. This thing with you and Gabe..." He shakes his head disapprovingly. "You have too much to do to be under marital stress also."

I struggle not to cry. "If only it were normal married things. On this, I can't change his mind. The best I can do is manage it."

He thinks for a moment. "Massages and purely therapeutic energy work were things we often prescribed for people who had trouble reaching hyper-alert at the compound. You might think about hiring someone. I would say daily at first. We can work together right after to capitalize on the endorphins."

"Whatever it takes," I say.

"Hoooolaaaa!" Letty chirps from behind me. I turn to see her standing at the patio door wearing a bikini. I temporarily forgot our agreement to have Skimpy Swimsuit Sunday. Jessie files out after her. And then topless Roe.

I turn back to Carl, embarrassed. He looks as uncomfortable as he feels, caught between glancing across the pool and back at me.

"Ummm, yeah. Sorry, Dad. I forgot the girls planned a pool party of sorts today. And um, Roe is... she's ah... German. Oh man. It apparently doesn't matter how old you get. Having your dad and your half-naked friends in the same space is mortifying."

He bows his head, now purposely avoiding looking. He even puts a hand nearly over his eyes and begins shaking with laughter. "I agree," he says. "And on that note, I'll leave you girls to it."

He keeps his head turned away from Roe, Letty, and Jessie for his entire trip around the side of the pool and through the patio door.

Letty looks like she's going to die from holding back laughter, and as soon as Carl slides the door shut, she bursts like the top on a champaign bottle, bowed over and holding her stomach, hooting with uncontrollable laughter.

"Auwwww! Your Vater ees kute!" Roe says, unfolding herself onto one of the patio lounge chairs, hands stretched above her head, toes reaching out as far as they'll go. Aside from the topless aspect, she's wearing the tiniest swimsuit I've ever seen. Her outrageous sunglasses are bigger than that piece of cloth, round lenses in cat-eye frames. Very retro. Her hair is tied up in a bandanna, her lips are painted bright red as if she just did a shoot for a topless, fifties housewife calendar.

I pull myself out of the pool and snag my own sunglasses off the ground on my way to take a chair next to her. Letty appears to be planning out a dive from the side of the pool, but she's striking all kinds of provocative poses to do it, probably to show off the fact that she's wearing a thong.

Jessie chuckles from next to me.

"Hey, Jessie," I say to her. She's thin and tan and blonde like a Barbie doll—which probably aids in Darren's stereotyping of her. But she's the most tech-savvy in the group. She handles the set up and maintenance of counter-surveillance wherever we go, and technology upgrades and troubleshooting for the whole team. She keeps them out of the dark and running at all times. Her job is never done. Except when I tell Darren she gets a few hours on Sunday with nobody bugging her. "Welcome to our plan for female domination."

"Thank you," she replies. "Letty sold me. When do we get T-shirts?"

Letty, meanwhile, seems to have decided against diving in just yet, instead going over to the bar. Moments later, salsa music with a sultry bass floods through the speakers. She motions me over with an index finger and I know exactly what she's doing. Frustrated over my failure at Carl's simple relaxation lesson, I'm eager to do something I *know* I'm good at.

"Go time," I say, pulling myself out of the chair and hopping across the hot concrete to her side.

"He's making himself lunch," she murmurs as her body begins to sway. "You know he won't be able to resist lookin' out here. Remember how we do?"

But I'm already there, letting the music take over my body. Hands up with Letty's, we move together, at first a sort of slow and sizzling gyration toward and away from each other that Letty calls The Tease. We don't touch, but we flirt, making wanton eyes at each other, coming closer and closer to touching as we move. We try to coordinate but inevitably have to improvise as we go. I feel a little rusty at first, and it may be partly because we aren't in a club surrounded by bodies and emotions. But I'm not failing a second time today.

Roe joins us, which adds a new dynamic, making it more naturally playful and less sensuous. But I think that in this setting, in the bright sun by the pool, more playfulness is in order. That brings in Jessie as Letty's playlist moves to the next song that's more hip hop than Latin, but not too fast, still sensuous. Letty smacks my butt, which is the cue for The Oven—Letty's naming, not mine. We move way more provocatively, touching each other whenever we get close. When Letty and I were clubbing, if a circle hadn't formed around us, it was only because the dance floor was too full. But we always had the attention of the room. Letty and I got really good at dancing together, even practicing new moves between going out. We're totally comfortable with each other as a result, so we can get really hands on and not feel like we're violating unspoken boundaries.

I don't hold back, aggravated for the first time that I don't have long hair to use anymore. So instead I use Letty's. I find new moves like wrapping it around both of us to bring us so close that anyone watching has to wonder what we're doing underneath it. I put my hands on her in ways that surprise even her, but she considers it a challenge and responds in kind.

Letty spins aways from me, signaling the last phase, The Catch, which is when we'd pick out whoever we had singled out. With no other options out here with us, I take Jessie, and Letty takes Roe. Jessie starts off a little embarrassed by my attention. I doubt she's ever danced with a woman this seductively. While Letty would come on stronger than a freight train, my specialty was always easing them out of their shell, and women and men are basically the same in that. By the end of it they didn't want to stop dancing.

I help Jessie by coordinating myself to her moves, even demonstrating easy things she can follow. She gets more comfortable in her own skin, less self-conscious of me touching her—which I do much less of since she's not Letty. It helps that I know she *wants* to let go, because if she didn't I'd have to figure out how to gracefully let her out of dancing without her feeling foolish.

The song ends, and Letty puts her arms around me. "That's my good luck, bruja," she says, and we don't let each other go. It's a good moment. I'd forgotten what it was like to live in the moment with Letty like that.

The door slides open and Mike appears, shirtless; tawny, rippled chest gleaming in the sun. *Oh hell, he's hot.*

"Little Mickey, you are my hero," Letty squeals, bounding over to him and taking a tall glass of something from the tray in his hand. She walks her fingers up his chest and I hear her say quietly, "Right on cue, Señor. Remind me to reward you later."

She hands a glass back to me, and Roe and Jessie crowd around for theirs.

"I sink ze two of you hev past in exotic dancing, ya?" Roe says.

"Wen and I have a past in being the hottest bitches on the prowl," Letty says. She gives me a sexy look. "Right, Wen?"

"Anything else, ladies?" Mike says, catching my eye, and I wish I knew what his look meant. He's too far away to read.

"Poolside hot dancing and shirtless Kellner," Roe says. She wipes the actual and metaphorical sweat from her forehead. "Zey vill not believe me ven I tell zem. Best provisional assignment ever."

"You guys are something," Jessie says. "I'm with Roe. You seriously aren't trained dancers?"

"Pffft," Letty says, gulping the rest of her drink.

"We really aren't," I say. "But we practiced a lot." Letty and I give each other a look.

Letty shoves her empty glass into Mike's chest and purrs at him, rolling her r's provocatively. "Practice makes perfect, doesn't it, Little Mickey?"

"It certainly does, Violeta," Mike says, brushing the length of her arm to her hand as he moves to take the glass.

She sighs whimsically, turns and sashays to the poolside, her voluptuous, bronze, Latin backside moving enviably. She executes a slow motion, arched dive into the water.

"Next!" Roe says, jumping in feet first. Jessie follows.

I look back at Mike, caught up again in how ridiculously attractive he is. "Confession," I say, crossing one arm and propping my glass on it with my other. "I think I'd rather stand here and look at *you*."

"Your hair is so cute all wild on end like that," he says.

"You just saw me gyrate against a hot hispanic goddess and all you have to say is that my hair is cute?"

He bites the inside of his cheek, glances up and around, looking adorably boyish. "I don't think my other compliments are appropriate," he says in a low voice.

"Better," I say, taking a sip.

"Damn," he breathes. "That was hot. "

"Hot *enough*?" I ask, hoping he catches my meaning.

He makes an odd sound and laughs, but it's too dry to develop fully. "Couldn't tear himself away. He's pacing right now. And if you don't mind, I'm taking a dip in the pool now. It's cold, right?"

I hold out a hand toward the pool and step to the side. "Solo swim with three hot ladies—one of them topless. You are the best, Mike."

He hands me the tray and bounds for the pool. Meanwhile I hop onto one of the bar stools, sit back, and imagine Gabriel. In fact, I listen for his footsteps in the house and chuckle at the number of heartbeats close to where I am. I wonder how many of Darren's people snuck a look through a window? I locate Gabriel's pacing finally. I cling to every footstep, hold my breath when he stops. Then the sound of him throwing himself on a bed. Then a door opening. Shutting. More pacing. A drawer opens, then the door again. Footsteps. Another door. And then running water. A shower.

I down the rest of my drink and reach for my phone. An in-house massage during Lock the Lab Lunchtime sounds like a great idea. I'll treat all the ladies, I think. I doubt Cody is big enough to cater to my need for four hot male masseurs, so I may have to fly them in. Pricey maybe… But I'm a billionaire. Frivolous maybe… But I have my marriage to save.

Sixty-Nine

There's a ship in her hair," Ezra murmurs, plopping in the seat across from Letty and me.

"Three on-point disaster predictions so far," Letty says to me, showing me the Guild's disaster prediction schedule on her phone. "Two minor ones. A forest fire in Montana. A storm of tornados in Texas. The last one is two back-to-back hurricanes. The first made landfall yesterday."

"Guys, there's a ship in her hair," Ezra insists.

I glance at him as I reach down and hand Robbie another slice of banana. What is he talking about?

"So the speculation has started," Letty continues, ignoring Ezra. "Because there's also a decent-sized earthquake or something predicted for Japan, right through Tokyo."

"Will they or won't they evacuate," I say, nodding.

"They'd be stupid not to," Letty says. "Because if they don't and something happens... Gonna be a lot of pissed off people."

"But if they go through the trouble and *nothing* happens, they're still going to be pissed off," I say.

"Yeah, Tokyo is *not* small. Still though. If they evacuate and nothing happens, they can just blame the Guild. Settle it once and for all."

"I hope they do," I say. "Unfortunately the Guild is *not* full of hot air."

"Yeah, and by the way, another PHIA attack," Letty says. "This one... freaks me the hell out. Basically, they painted the symbol on a few houses outside DC at night. Then, they just waited for people to freak out. What do you do when you wake up and realize you live next to a Prime Human? Burn the house down, apparently. Know what's crazy? The Primes had already left. And thank God. All it took to have people acting like savages was graffiti. They knew they were gone. They were just afraid they were next, so they burned the houses to like... ward off the cooties."

I grimace. Andre is not just a psychopath, but one that understands psychology and takes advantage of it.

"Guys!" Ezra hisses.

"What?!" Letty says, slapping her phone down on the table, irritated at being interrupted.

He nods toward the other end of the kitchen where Roe is making Spätzle from scratch. "She's got a *ship* in her hair."

I look from Roe's back to Ezra. "Yeah. So?"

He throws a hand up, eyes wide, frustrated. "A ship!" he says between his teeth. "Like the Mayflower? But smaller? A wooden ship. She's wearing it in her hair. Like it's a barrette or something!"

I wrinkle my nose at the scent wafting off of him when he moves. "Oh my gosh, Ezra. When was the last time you showered?"

His mouth opens in dismay.

I wince. "Or brushed your teeth?" And then it occurs to me that this is the first time I've seen Ezra outside of the lab in a week. "Dude, you need to go take care of your hygiene. Like now."

"What?" he says. "Why does nobody care that Ray has a ship in her hair!?"

"Her name is *Roe*," Letty says.

Roe turns around. "Vy, thank you, Eezra!" she says, daintily touching the bow of her ship with a finger. "Just a leetle somesing I've been verking on, in my spare time. You keep me suh busy! Barely time to get dressed in a new outfit each day!"

He blinks at her, then back to Letty and me. "This is real, right? I'm not dreaming?"

"Yeeees," I say slowly, wondering if I should start worrying about him.

"Did wearing wooden toys in your hair become fashionable and I've somehow totally missed it?" he says, crossing his arms— thank goodness. The boy *stanks.*

"What's more surprising is that you've been working with her for over a week and you can't remember her name," I say.

He purses his lips to the side, unable to argue with that.

"She's had the ship in her hair since breakfast," I say. "Then she was with you in the lab *all day.* Yesterday she had spiders in her hair. The day before that, seashells. So a ship is... more substantial, but still normal."

Ezra sits back, baffled.

"I think I need to check on you more often," I say, torn

between humor and horror that Ezra looks and feels like he just woke up to the world after checking out for a week.

"Seriously," he says. "It's really Roe?" He looks at Roe's back again. "Why didn't you correct me?"

"When leetle genius boy ees on verge of a breakthrough," Roe says, turning around while kneading dough in her hands. "you don argue when he says name vong."

"I bet you could have gone into the lab topless after all," I say. "He wouldn't have noticed."

"Why didn't *you* notice?" Ezra says to me. "I've been sleeping in the lab not showering and you never came to check on me? Hovering is one of your special skills."

I furrow my brow. I'm not sure… Gabriel is in the lab, but I don't bother him there. I let Roe and Letty accost him—which I hear they've managed quite well.

"She figured you were staying out of the way while she's been workin' it for Gabe every chance she gets," Letty says.

"Wearing lingerie to dinner," I point out.

"Dance lessons after lunch!" Roe says.

"Squeezing Roe's tiddies during breakfast," Letty adds.

"She said she was worried about a lump," I say. "She wanted a second opinion."

"It occurred to her suddenly in the middle of eating her yogurt at the table," Letty adds matter-of-factly.

"Surrounded by five men who were already ogling them," I add.

"I had to do it right den vhile I vas thinking about it," Roe says. "My memory is terrible!"

Letty elbows me and mocks, "'I don't know, Roe, let me feel both at once, to compare…'" She giggles and leans down to pick Robbie off of his blanket on the floor.

I roll my eyes but can't help my grin. "Comparison is important."

"Breast exams vait for no one!" Roe booms while pointing a finger to the ceiling declaratively.

"Spidey's tights," Ezra says. "What the hell has been happening out here? Have you people lost it?"

"Ezra," I chide, "It's the end of the world…"

"As ve know it!" Roe sings.

"And I… feeeeel… finnnne…" Letty finishes in a gentle melody to Robbie. He reaches for her nose in response.

"Wow. Um. I'm not sure whether to be disappointed I've been missing it or not," Ezra says. He holds up two hands like a scale. "On the one hand, *breasts*." His left hand sinks the scale. "On the other hand… my sister touching them…" His right hand sinks and then surpasses the left. He shakes his head. "Nope. Totally ruins it."

"Have you seriously been completely in the dark on what's been going on?" I say.

"I'm only out here because I started to smell myself and I figured it would be a good idea to venture out into the world and make sure it was still standing. Didn't want to be killing myself for nothing."

"You could have taken care of the smell *first*," I say.

"I've been spraying him with Lysol when I pass him," Letty says. "I didn't want him to start growing things."

I give her a look. "You couldn't poke him toward the shower with a stick or something instead?"

That makes Roe laugh.

"Wen, your brother is scary as hell when you bother him in the middle of thinking," Letty replies, "which he's *always* doing."

"All the more reason to use a stick. For defense." I turn to Ezra. "Wait a minute, have you been *inside* the lab during LTLL?" I say.

"LTLL?"

"Lock the lab lunchtime," I say.

Ezra scoffs. "You have an acronym for it? I treat it like nap time when the lights go out."

"You should see him, Wen," Letty says, standing with Robbie. "He stops, throws his head back in the chair and he's out in like three seconds."

"It's actually really helpful," Ezra says. "I get my second wind after that. Figure all kinds of stuff out."

"How do you get Gabriel out then?" I ask curiously.

"Start stripping in front of him," Letty replies.

I burst out laughing. "You strip in front of Gabriel *every day*?" I say, surprised at her dedication.

"No. I threaten first. Only took a couple days of following through. Now he just gets out."

I burst out laughing. "Surprised he doesn't stick around then."

"I told you he's loyal. He wants to look, but he knows he'll pay the price later. When he's alone. All alone. No Wendy to carry out his sexual fantasies with."

Robbie yawns.

"Will you take him?" I say.

"Sure," Letty says. "But he makes my ovaries hurt every time he falls asleep on me."

"Me too," I sigh, reaching for his hand and putting it on my mouth. "But he's the last and only."

For the first time in a while, that recognition smarts. Robbie has a primary doctor that visits regularly, and several specialists that check in on his condition wherever we are. It's too much of a hassle to go *to* all his specialists involved in treating his Duchenne Muscular Dystrophy, which still, as yet, has no visible manifestations. He's healthy so far, developing normally. But some days, like today as I watch Letty carry him out, I spend time dreading the day when I'll notice something that will steal the air in my lungs as I realize that he's declining.

"Are you sure you're not taking this flirtation thing overboard?" Ezra says in a low voice once Letty's gone and Roe is back to rolling out Spätzle.

"No, I'm not. But I'm meeting Gabriel's extremism with my own," I say.

"I'm not talking about just Gabe. Letty said you felt Roe's boobs in front of five men? Uncle Rob's guys? What's up with that? You're making me worry."

I look at Ezra confidently. "First of all, they're *my* people. And second, I know you're thinking about what I did before Mom died. I did similar things, but to dominate and humiliate guys. This time… it's not about tricking them. It's been about destroying their false perceptions. I think sometimes when people choose to see you a certain way, the only way to convince them to see you differently is to *show* them something so far outside of what they're used to that they have to stop and ask themselves if what they thought they knew about you was right. You shake them out of their assumptions. That was my goal. And it's working. It's been days since Darren questioned something I've told him to do. He looks at me differently—but not like you're thinking."

Ezra raises a skeptical eyebrow.

"You're missing my point. *Yes*, he likes looking when I'm putting myself on display, but when it's all said and done, he realizes he has no idea what to expect from me. Now I'm unpredictable, calculating, capable. I command his attention and therefore respect. He's been looking at me for months, but not really seeing me. I wave something he *does* want to see in front of his face, and now I've got his attention. You follow?"

He looks up, biting his cheek and considering it. I'm glad I've spent some time reflecting on things, to be able to answer Ezra. I didn't start out so clear on the outcome. But talking to Roe made me start to see it differently. Roe and Letty are on two different extremes that way. Letty feels that because she *can* manipulate using her body, she should. It comes too easily, and she doesn't think she needs a reason or a purpose. It was from Letty I learned the skills I have with flaunting my body, but Roe taught me that it's possible to use seduction in a positive way.

"Roe says when a woman reveals her body purposefully, she's being vulnerable," I say. "She's demonstrating trust. And giving trust gets you trust in return. I need my people to trust me, something they've lost little by little the last couple of months."

That does the trick, and I feel him wrap his giant brain around that easily. "Counterintuitive," he says. "I like it. But I think I'll stick to the lab anyway. *No* interest in seeing you fondle breasts."

I chuckle. "So, a breakthrough, huh?"

"Maybe," he says, his lips pressed together in a line. He sits back, sort of checks out for a minute while he thinks. "I'm missing something in the data. Something that will support… what I'm seeing." He waves a hand, thoughts spiraling suddenly into frustration. "I don't want to talk about it right now."

"Take better care of yourself," I say. "I'll make sure Letty or Roe get you out of there periodically."

He nods. "A good idea. Sometimes I look up and everyone is gone and the clock says it's been eight hours since the last time I looked. I don't even know what day it is right now…"

"Friday."

"By the way, I think either Gabe is not as smart as I remember or whatever you're doing is working."

"Oh?" I lift my brows enthusiastically.

He nods. "He'll be calling out data entries to me and he'll lose his spot. Or I'll explain the formula I want him to use for the simulation. I'll think he's got it, so I go back to what I'm doing, but then thirty seconds later he's asking about what some variable represents. Stuff I already spelled out. Easy stuff."

"Hmm," I say, smiling to myself. Thank you, Letty and Roe.

"Either that or his brain doesn't work very well when he's tired. I have no idea how much he's sleeping."

"Nobody's brain works very well when they're tired."

"Mine does. It actually works better. I've noticed I get to this point of exhaustion, and I used to just go to sleep, but I started pushing past it. And then my brain will suddenly light up like it never does when I'm rested. I can go for hours and hours after that, and I can think more quickly. It's crazy. I'm like a zombie. But a really freaking genius one. The intuitive leaps I can make then surprise even me."

I raise an eyebrow. "I'm looking forward to the resulting breakthrough."

"I have something," he says. "I think. It just needs backup..." He frowns. "I'm going to go shower now." He scoots his chair back.

I watch him leave, analyzing his residual emotions. He leaps between being stoked and confident about his work to totally doubting it in the same mental breath. Is he manic because he's sleep deprived? Or is there something else? I need to talk to Gabriel about where they're at. I've been so consumed with my other endeavors that I haven't tried to find out.

I can wait a bit longer to ask Gabriel though. I don't want to ruin what I've been doing, which is to make myself as a sort of ethereal fantasy for him. If I talk math and apocalypse things, it's going to ruin the perception. Letty told me she's come on to him strongly twice, and he's refused her both times. The second time, he told her she was crazy and asked why she was acting like he wasn't married to her best friend. What would Wendy say? To which she replied, 'Wen says you're fair game because you don't see yourself as actually the one married to her.'

That was genius logic. He's got to be totally flummoxed about the whole thing. And after tomorrow, I think he's going to wonder where I stand on my own fidelity. And I'm going to keep it up until he breaks and talks to me, demanding to know. And that's when I'll win this stupid stalemate.

Seventy

The following day, the girls and I have our second Skimpy Swimsuit Sunday. The pool is a *lot* fuller this week. Word gets around. I'm glad I don't have to worry about Maris showing up because she thinks it's family pool time. It turns out, Mike, ever vigilant for my cause, encouraged her to find a church in the area, so she and Dan take Robbie to Mass for a good chunk of the day. I doubt we'll be doing this next weekend though. It's September, and the weather is already cooler, plus, I'm turned off by the idea of making my patio into a weekly dance club for the wanton eyes of my men. I need to keep changing things up. I don't want to risk the guys starting to *expect* the women to be available as eye candy on a regular basis.

But I want Roe and Jessie to have a chance to flaunt their new skills. Letty and I have been giving them daily lessons during our aerobics workouts in the gym in the mornings—something we chose to do because Gabriel works out there at that time. Carl gave him a schedule of exercises to do to help the shoulder he dislocated heal faster. It turned into a spectacle in and of itself though, as morning workouts are popular for everyone. Letty and I decided to choreograph a dance that incorporated all of the moves, and we've practiced *that* part with Roe and Jessie secretly each day.

They nail the performance, and this time 'The Catch' involves the men of our choosing. Roe takes Darren. Letty takes Mike. I take Paul. And Jessie takes her boyfriend, who actually arrived this morning, lucky him. She promptly disappears with him right after.

Meanwhile, my afternoon is off to a less-than-enjoyable start when I get a call from one of the board of directors for Qual-Soft, my uncle's primary software company.

I'm told I'm needed immediately because they need to evacuate their facilities in California, overnight preferably. The

National Guard is currently in Los Angeles, trying to bring order to the streets, but it's escalating into a war. It's creating a domino effect of fear, and even in northern California, where most of Qual-Soft's offices are, society is crumbling. Employees are demanding to be transferred to the east coast. The problem is there's only one office there.

I really don't want to care. The company is slowly transferring out of my hands anyway, but the board is talking about laying everyone off, reorganizing in another state, and then rehiring. But that means everyone is going to be stranded there, many without means to escape California to *get* rehired. And how will they survive in the meantime? I have to go. Sort out a solution with the board.

I hang up, dejected, in direct contrast to the festivities going on. "Darren," I say, walking up to where he's having a conversation with Roe. She's put on a coat, because it's actually pretty chilly out if you aren't wearing anything. Her coat looks like it came straight off of a llama's back, long hair coming out of the sleeves and collar, exactly as eccentric as I'd expect. Darren is finally *not* looking at her suspiciously for being from the Guild.

He looks up, shielding his eyes.

I move to the foot of his lounge chair so he doesn't have to squint. "I need you to assemble a team to go with me to Monterey for a few days. I have to meet with the board. It's an emergency."

"Sure," he says, sitting up, swinging his legs to the ground and immediately moving into task mode. "You're wanting to leave tonight?"

"Yeah," I say. "ASAP."

He grumbles suddenly in irritation, but not at me, surprisingly. He looks around for his phone. "I'll have to call now to have the jet prepped in time. I had them put it in the hangar just yesterday..." He stares across the pool at nothing, letting loose more profanity before turning back to me. "I really apologize that I didn't ask you about it. Wasn't my call to make. And I obviously didn't think it through anyway. But I'll make it happen. Give me twenty minutes and I'll get you a takeoff time and a team. Who do you want as your lead?"

"I trust your judgment," I say, pleased at his easy apology, not to mention his can-do attitude. In the past he'd tell me all the reasons the schedule would be put behind and why I needed to rethink my plans. And then I'd respond by giving him even more explicit instructions and stripping him of any opportunity to act autonomously.

This plan could not have gone better. Now, if only I could say the same for my relationship with Gabriel. I need to find him though, let him know I'll be gone and he's got Robbie, who has two doctors coming in this week. I step from the patio into the kitchen, making a mental list of the things I need to do before I go… I need to call Dwight. He's off-site with his family this week, but I need him to meet me in Monterey. Where is Gabriel? It's LTLL, so he's not in the lab. His room maybe? I don't have time to hunt him down in the Labyrinth. Mike might be easier to track down. I didn't see him by the pool on my way in…

I take a brisk pace through the kitchen and into the hall where I run right into Gabriel.

He catches my elbow. "Whoa there," he says, but his voice is husky, and his emotions… Holy hot and bothered mess. They take me over easily, because I wasn't expecting them. And *he* wasn't expecting *me* either. With his powerful presence in my head, reason has totally left me. What was I doing? Oh my gosh he smells good. Before I know it, I've let him put me against the wall and I've grabbed him around the waist and pulled him into me.

"Oh my," he gasps, putting his good hand against the wall to the side of my head, then he starts rambling in Spanish. I lift my leg and hook it around the back of his and push my hands under his T-shirt and over his back. I want more of him on me, so I push the front of his shirt up, too, pressing my chilled, nearly-naked body against the warmth of his skin.

He only has one good arm, but that hand moves immediately underneath my raised thigh, lifting me up easily, and I wrap both of my legs around him. I twine my arms around his neck, and he buries his face against my skin as he breathes me in.

"Wen! Wen! Where are you? Holy hell! He made me point! He made me the mother-effin' point!" Letty shouts just before she rounds the corner and nearly runs into us. "Ooooopsie!" she exclaims, backing up as a grin spreads over her face.

Gabriel, meanwhile, has not moved from where he has me against the wall, his face still buried in my chest. But he groans disappointedly.

"Sorry guys," she says, backing up even more. "Pretend I wasn't even here!" She flits back around the corner, and I hear the patio door slam.

I quickly assess my two choices in the situation, and with my head back, I opt for the smarter one. I let go of Gabriel, tap his shoulder, indicating I want him to put me down. He does, setting me down gently, but not without significant effort. He backs up two steps.

I adjust my swimsuit, and, still shaking from the unspent desire in my body, I clear my throat and say, "I was just looking for you. I'm leaving tonight for Monterey. I have some emergency business." I look up to see him staring at me, bottom lip in his teeth as his eyes rake over me. Apparently, Letty's appearance did not shake him out of the moment at all. I don't even know if he heard what I just said.

"Gabriel," I say, trying to catch his eye with mine, which works, but when he sees me, he's not really *seeing* me. He's thinking now, which invites indecision. He's back at war again with himself. I don't have time for this.

"Did you hear me?" I say.

"Pardon," he says, his voice hoarse. "Yes. Monterey. Are you taking Mike?"

My brow furrows. I don't *feel* the intent behind the question, but it sure sounds exactly like the kind of thing intended to encourage me to get with Mike. "I don't know," I say. "I left choosing the team up to Darren."

"Please take Mike. He's still, by far, the most capable. It would ease my mind."

My brow lifts now. I think he means it exactly the way he said it. This simple but obvious display of concern strikes me so powerfully it has me wishing I'd opted for my other choice and taken him into one of the empty rooms.

"Okay," I say. "It's fine with me, but I'd like you to be the one to talk to Darren about it. I just told him the whole thing was in his hands, and I don't want to backpedal on that trust when I've come so far with him."

"Absolutely," he agrees, nodding. "I'll do that."

"I'm not sure when I'll be back, but Robbie's appointment schedule—"

"Is posted in his room. I know. I'll take care of it. I know I've been absent from his life a lot recently. I'd apologize to him directly, but he's too young to understand, so I'm apologizing to you instead. I have excuses, but none of them are any good. I'm grateful that the situation has necessitated my involvement, else I might still be wrapped up in my own endeavors."

More surprise on my part. He hasn't spoken this much or this honestly to me in a long time, and I wait before replying, hoping that maybe it's going to continue, but when his emotions indicate he's concluded and is about to go, I say, "Apology accepted. I'll keep you updated on when I'll be back."

He nods and heads into the kitchen, the door to the patio sliding open and then closed. I guess he's going to speak to Darren.

Was that progress? I don't know… Gabriel is a good person, above all, even when he's driving me crazy. So even if he doesn't think *we* should be together, he's not going to all of a sudden treat me badly out of spite. He's not going to disrespect me or stop caring about my welfare. It's been easy to forget this through the weeks of avoidance.

It's also easy to forget how Gabriel operates. There's no such thing as 'progress' with him. He either makes a complete turnaround or none at all. So that was… just a moment of weakness for him. And the caring was simply Gabriel being Gabriel.

In that case, I'm glad I made the smarter choice.

₪

When the jet is finally in the air and sailing toward California, I prop my feet up and lay back in one of the luxurious chairs on the main level, organizing my thoughts, settling my nerves. I always get anxious when I have to meet with company big wigs. I'm not many years out of high school, and these are high-powered executives who remain baffled as to why Robert Haricott, the most influential counter-surveillance technology mogul of the day, left not just his fortune but his power over several hundred-billion dollars'-worth of companies to a veritable nobody.

I don't get to think about Uncle Moby as often as I'd like, but with my upcoming task gnawing the inside of my stomach, I send out a plea to him, if he's out there watching, to help me do this. It's been a couple weeks since I've been on the plane, and being back on it, his scent, which had previously faded from over-exposure, now hits my over-sensitive nose. It twines with the barest hint of ginger—his favorite tea and always his choice over coffee. He told me once that he drank so much ginger in order to settle his stomach, which suffered from regular anxiety over the constant gravity of his knowledge and power. My beloved uncle could see the future, in more detail than anyone ever really knew. He was constantly faced with what to do about the things he knew, often having to resist using his skills to change the reality of people's lives around him. Among a myriad of other things, he taught me the value of ignorance, a thing he infrequently enjoyed.

The effect of his scent is immediate. My eyes fill with tears, and I put my feet to the floor and bring my seat back up so as not to cry on my skirt-suit, something that I would never wear in any other scenario. But I've got to dress the part, to at least not come across as young as I am, to do my uncle's confidence in me justice. I fumble around for something to wipe my face with. I even put makeup on, and it's now going to smear everywhere. The closest thing is a blanket, and I pull it onto me, weeping into it as the floodgates let loose all of the emotions I have surrounding my uncle's memory.

And then, hatred. The day his mangled body was thrown at my feet constructs itself far too easily in my mind. If Andre were here right now I would murder him. I would do it while looking him straight in the eye so he would know how thoroughly unfazed I would be over extinguishing his life. I could do it easily, too. Just one touch. My skin is still lethal, but only to people like Andre whose souls are dry chaffs, empty of all goodness, nothing but drains on the light around them.

I hate him, and hate feels like too weak of a word. How is it only one syllable? Love is one syllable, but only because it's bigger than words. It's emotion meeting action, and actions cycle back to emotions. It perpetuates itself, and it grows each time. Hate, though… Hate is a pit, a never-ending one. That's why it's so unsatisfying to say. It doesn't *go* anywhere.

My eyes stop leaking finally and I sigh as I intuit my thoughts as exactly something my uncle might say. Love floods me once more, easily pushing the loathing aside. I put my hand over my chest, feeling strongly that if he really is around here somewhere, he was speaking to me while I was in the pit just now.

"Hey, you alright?" Mike says from over my shoulder.

I look up. "Yeah. I was just thinking about Uncle Moby… Smells like him in here."

He takes the seat across from me, and I see that he's holding a legal-sized, white envelope. "I wish I'd been able to know him longer."

"Me too," I say. "I honestly don't think any amount of time would have been enough. I always needed him. I still do, even more than before. More everyday. So sometimes I'm mad at him for letting himself die like that. He already knew it was going to happen. He also knew the world was going to go to hell. So I'm stuck asking myself why. Why did he have to die *right then?* Why did it have to go the way it did? So violently. So abrupt. I have no good answers, and it's frustrating, and it hurts too much, so I try not to think about it."

Mike sighs. "I'm sorry, Wen. And I know that doesn't mean jack, but I don't know what else to say."

"I don't expect you to say anything." I lay my head against the headrest. "I'm just telling you because you're here and it's on my mind."

"I wish I'd killed Andre any of the times I'd had a chance," Mike says. "It all seems like such a waste now. And a lot of Primes would still be alive…" He exhales heavily. "I have a confession. But this isn't the usual kind."

"What?"

"Andre and I started off like I told you—searching for missing Primes. But not long after that task was assigned, about the time we started looking for *you* specifically, someone else took on overseeing us. She wasn't *on* the Council, but damn near close."

He frowns in consternation. "In fact, sometimes it seemed like she had just as much power as them. She didn't have to get clearance for anything because everyone treated her orders the same they would a council member. She was more progressive-minded than the Council though, and often undermined them. She didn't care about any of the other missing Primes on our list. She wanted you and only you, so she'd allot resources and people, assign tasks without ever informing the Council—like infiltrating Louise's compound for instance. She knew they'd shut it down as soon as they knew about it, but she wanted you, so she sent someone in to find out what they knew about your whereabouts. Our operative was killed, but still she didn't tell them, because Carl was your father, and he was looking for you. Chances were good you'd turn up there one way or another. Two teams searching for you were better than one."

"How on earth did the Council not know what she was doing?" I ask.

"Because she was brilliant. She designed the data security systems, so she could tamper with whatever information she wanted and no one would know. I still have no idea what she actually reported to the Council as far as our progress. Sometimes I wonder if they knew anything at all. I didn't question because she wasn't trying to take the Guild down. In fact, she was hyper-protective of it, and that was the whole reason she undercut the Council. Less red tape. Less bureaucracy. She got things done that would have taken the Council ten times the amount of time. But the Council is in place for a reason, and I should have reported her to them. But I didn't. If I had, Andre wouldn't have been able to do the things he did."

"I thought you said Andre was a dirtbag way before he killed my uncle," I say, something missing to this story that's got me confused. "You're saying you were on board with this woman circumventing the Council, but it sounds like she was the whole reason Andre had resources to begin with. So that must mean she agreed with his methods, right? If you wanted to take Andre down, it seems like the easy solution would be to turn her in, too. Why didn't you?"

He clasps his hands on top of his head, props his feet on the other side of the ottoman between us. "Andre was involved with her for a while, early on. It was basically the two of them that had this vision for the Guild—they both wanted it to be out in the open, a kind of beacon to the rest of society. She broke things off with him after a while, and he started blackmailing her about her actions against the Council. Not only for resources, but for other things. He was obsessed with her, wanted her back, and he took her back the only way he could: by threatening the thing she cared most about: the Guild."

Just thinking about it makes me ill. *"Why...?"* I say. "Why would she let him rule her like that? And why didn't... you..." I grimace, because I have no right to judge his answer, whatever it is, let alone even ask the question.

"Why didn't I kill him?" Mike says, obviously knowing exactly what I want to ask. "I thought about it, pictured it, dreamed about it, planned it," he says brusquely. "Eighty times a day. But she said you had to be found. It was more important than anything, and if Andre died, she couldn't bury that with all the hacking in the world. He was too widely known. And if he died, we'd lose progress because I'd be taken off the assignment. Andre was point. I was simply tactical muscle. They'd put a new operative in place, and she said there were no other probable operatives willing to circumvent the Council's priorities without questioning. She'd hand-picked our dyad for the job."

"And it was that important to you to do what she asked? I don't know Mike… I probably would have faced the music if I'd been you. Just to save her from herself."

"You'd have to know her…" Mike says, a faraway look on his face. "I don't know how to describe it to you, but she knew things she didn't say, planned things you didn't realize until they happened… She wasn't a damsel in distress. She was calculating. She weighed her options and made decisions on logic. Paying the price for trusting Andre was a given because to her the bottom line was that the Guild was more important. It didn't cause her the kind of stress you'd think. The only person I've known that rivals her drive is Gabe. So I know you know what I'm talking about."

"Wow," I say, finally grasping this woman's personality.

"It was an effort to help her accomplish her goal once and for all that I sent Gabe to the compound. I didn't tell her I had because I didn't want Andre knowing. I didn't want him doing something stupid to endanger Gabe's life. Turns out though that I did just as good of a job doing that. I didn't know about hypno-touch, the dangers of it. It's not something you get to know unless it specifically pertains to your job. But it was her I went to after I found out he was in the hospital. Told her I found you. Told her about Gabe. And she's the one that said you were his only hope. I was prepared to beg her to leave you be so you could save him, but she already knew—that's how she was. She gave me the diabetes treatment for you, set up the autograft procedure to keep you alive. Andre found out though. Set up the ambush at the compound and got a bunch of guys killed. It was a mess."

He looks at me now. "The Guild was a way to escape Gabe, but ultimately, when my duty started clashing with my personal life, I had to decide. I chose the Guild because of her. The things she sacrificed for it… I was having to give up far less by comparison. I couldn't let what she was sacrificing go to waste. Plus, when push came to shove, she had my back. She chose to save my brother by leaving you be, even after everything."

His angst over events so long in the past can only mean one thing. "Mike, did you have feelings for her?"

He glances at me, the question not surprising him. "Yeah. But there was no way I could really explore them. I couldn't let myself feel more for her than I already did. The thing with Andre was already killing me. Watching him use her and her letting him like it was a contracted exchange." He shudders. "That's probably the reason I turned Gemma Rossi into a beacon of hope. I kept her on my mind as much as possible to keep myself from getting too invested in what was happening to Shiah. I had to put my head down and work."

Gemma… Mike now knows that Gemma was me. We met six years ago, but we never saw each others' faces. "Her name was Shiah?"

Mike nods. "*Is* Shiah. She's still with the Guild. When we captured you… I expected that it would be over finally. She was the kind of planner that I expected she knew exactly what she needed from you and how to get it. But I went to her about what Andre was doing to blackmail you, what you were willing to do to save your son… And she… cried."

"She cried?" I say. Mike feels the significance of it, and even though I have no idea why that would be a big deal, I can tell that it is.

"I'd never seen her cry," Mike says. "In all those years I knew her, all the shit she went through with Andre. Even her mom's death. She didn't cry. She wasn't emotional. She was always on top of everything. Most people you can see when they might be cracking a little inside. Shiah didn't know the meaning of stress. And she also wasn't afraid to fail. So many failed attempts to get at you. She barely looked back at them. But that day when I told her I wasn't on board with what Andre was doing, it's like she read my mind. She knew what I needed to do for Gabe, for myself. She helped me get you out. After everything she'd gone through to find you… she just… let you go."

"Who *is* this person?" I say.

"She's Ohr's daughter."

My jaw drops. Ohr actually mentioned his daughter to me. He told me she was the one that designed the strategy for the Guild to come out to the public. "Seriously?"

"As far as I know, she's still in the same position. The day Andre blew up Redlands, I was both thrilled and horrified. She was going to be free of him, one way or another. The price ended up being bigger than intended though. So that's why I say it all feels like a waste."

"Everything matters," I say, repeating words that float up from somewhere forgotten, "Every choice. Every act. Every thought. Every *one*. Nothing is wasted." I don't know why it comes to me so easily, but it probably came from Robert. I like it.

"Shiah would probably agree," Mike says, tilting his head.

I wrinkle my nose. "That's nice. But I'm not sure if I should like this girl or not."

He gives me a look. "Are you jealous?"

"No. But she obviously put you through a lot of hell. And I don't like people doing that to you."

"You're jealous," he says, sitting back and crossing his arms.

I roll my eyes. "I just have high standards for you. I'm totally willing to share you, but not with just anyone."

He laughs. "*Share* me? Which part is yours?"

"Nineteen billion life force strands," I fire back. "That means I have the majority."

"Touché," he says. "And since we're touching on that topic…" He grabs the white envelope he showed up with and hands it to me.

I take it, testing its weight and thickness. It's not that substantial, several sheets of paper maybe. It's also sealed. "What is it?" I ask, ready to tear it open.

He holds a hand up to stop me. "Gabe asked me to give it to you."

I see the legal-size envelope with new eyes. Fear grips me. Oh my gosh… Is this divorce papers? Is that why he hesitated to give it to me?

"Calm down," Mike says. "I'm pretty certain I know what it is, and if I'm right, it's not what you're obviously thinking."

"What do you think it is and why shouldn't I open it?"

"Well…" he struggles for an answer.

"Mike!" I say. "We talk about everything. The most ridiculous, most awkward, most difficult things there are. How can this possibly be harder than that?"

"Because I'm trying to figure out how I think you'll take it. I feel like it could go either way."

"Oh my *gosh*," I say impatiently, putting my finger under the lip of the envelope and tearing it open.

"Whoa, whoa," Mike says, standing up. "It's sealed for a reason. I'm going to sit this out. I'll leave you alone with… that. I think I'm going to miss Letty's meeting if I don't go now anyway. She'll slit my throat if I don't show up." And then he disappears.

I've already got the thing open though, and I reach in, pulling out the small stack of paper. I thumb through it briefly.

They're letters. To me. From Gabriel.

Seventy-One

My face is hot, my heart is beating faster, and my hands are shaking before I've even finished the first letter. They're *dirty* letters. Unbelievably erotic and extremely detailed, as if I'm reading a book, about him and me.

I throw them on my lap and blink through my hedonistic thoughts that result from visualizing the things he's describing. I pick up the pages again, not lingering on the words too much as I scan them for *why* he has given me these. They are all directed to me, and they all start out with describing something I'm doing— things I've done in the last week—and then describing whatever fantasy he has that results. I think, and I don't let myself get too caught up in the specifics that want to suck me in, but he's telling me what he *would* have done had he let himself act on what he knew was my attempt to seduce him.

I don't know why he gave these to me... I really don't.

I dig in my bag for my phone. I dial Gabriel.

He answers on the first ring. "Wendy! Are you alright? What's wrong?"

I don't understand his frantic tone until I remember I'm calling from my satellite phone and he can tell from the number. And he knows it's for emergencies.

"I'm fine," I say tersely. "I am calling to find out why you gave me these... whatever they are. I wouldn't exactly call them letters."

"Oh..." he says, relieved. "I gave them to you because they belong to you."

I rub my forehead with a shaking hand. "I don't understand. Can you... be longer-winded? I'm not interested in deciphering your psychological tactics."

"It's not a *tactic*," he says. "I don't use tactics and you know it. Did you or did you not intend all of your... performances to be seen by me? Or at least to have me hear about them?"

I'd like to argue that yes, he *does* use tactics, but it looks like he's going to address the elephant in the room finally and I don't want to sideline him. Maybe we can actually get somewhere now.

"Yes," I reply.

"Which means that you expected them to affect me, correct?"

"Yes," I say, starting to figure out where this is going.

"The letters are how they affected me. You achieved what you intended."

"No. I didn't," I say, getting more upset. "Maybe if you'd actually *done* some of the things you describe in these letters *with me*, I would have. But this is..." I grit my teeth and narrow my eyes. "This is your way of throwing it back in my face."

"Wendy," he says, frustrated, "you flaunt your body from one end of the house to the other, purposely manipulating my sexual appetite when you *know* I can't be intimate with you—"

"Excuse me, you *can't*?" I interrupt. "That's a *lie*! You *can*. You just *won't*. So don't twist this as something *I'm* doing wrong. *You* have chosen this. This is me trying to change your mind in the only way I have left!"

"And the letters are the only way I know how to give you what you're asking for," he replies.

Hot tears fall down my cheeks as I seethe through gritted teeth, "Because if you write it down that means *he* can't possibly be part of it, right?"

"It's not about that," he replies. "It's never been about that. Why do I have to keep explaining this to you? I write it down because the feelings you're creating by manipulating me don't belong to me. But they're there, and I can't do anything about it except write them down to get them out of me. I gave them to you, because they belong to you."

I rub my face, frustration pressing so heavily on me I just want to scream at him.

"Gabriel," I say with restraint, "what is it you want from me? Truly? Spell it out, please. Because at this point all I keep hearing is how much of a victim you are in all of this, and it makes me want to punch you right in your stupid face."

"I want you to take Mike's strands out of me."

Rage consumes me and I stand up. "THAT WILL KILL YOU, YOU IDIOT!" I scream at the top of my lungs into the phone.

He doesn't reply, and I'm heaving with fury anyway.

Letty rushes in through the doorway. "Wen! You okay?"

When Gabriel still hasn't said anything, I end the call and throw the phone across the room where it thunks against the wall. And then I yank my wedding band off and throw that as well. It pings against the wall and falls among the furniture. I let let loose a scream, as loud and as high-pitched as I can manage, because anger is bottle-necking everything else.

I fall into my chair and let my head fall into my hands, lightheaded.

"I um," Letty says, swallowing, "You want me to get Mike?"

"Of course you would ask that," I say, standing again and swaying on my feet. "Because when I'm upset, who *else* are you going to get? Certainly not my *husband*! Because he's a jackass!" I pace down the cabin toward her. "He's lost his damn mind, Letty! He's lost every bit of sense in his head! He needs to be admitted somewhere! I'm not even kidding! How?" I say, holding my hands out. "How can this *possibly* be such a big deal that he would want to throw his *life* away to get rid of it? And it's not just *his* life. He's my *husband*! He's Robbie's *father*! He's Maris and Dan's *son!* He's Mike's *brother*! And all of us, every single one, is willing to do what it takes to make this work. And he won't even *begin* to compromise! Why?" I look to Letty for an answer, but she just stands there, eyes wide at my rampage. "Why, Letty? Why?"

She shakes her head. "I don't know."

I catch my hand on the seat next to me as the plane dips down, starting our descent. We're nearly there.

I huff and tug my dress down and take off the matching coat. It makes me look like I'm trying too hard to fit the business lady mold, plus, I feel like I'm being strangled by it. The dress is simple and classy on its own, fresher.

Why am I thinking about my wardrobe at a time like this?

"Well," I say, holding up a finger, "I'll tell you two things. One, there is *no* way in *hell* I'm giving him his way on this. He can divorce me. He can hide for the rest of his life. But he's keeping those strands. And two, the board is in for it if they think they're going to bully me into laying off those people. Not today. I'm not messin' around. You and your team ready?"

"Si," she replies, her mouth curving slightly. "You mind if I grab your ring though? I seen that look on you before, and I'm pretty sure you're gonna want it back eventually."

"You keep it," I say. "I'm not putting it back on until he's on his knees begging me to."

Seventy-Two

Three exhausting days later, we're driving back to the airport to make our return to Wyoming. I'm still not quite sure if I can consider what happened a victory or not. After two days of negotiations that were going nowhere, my lawyer pulled me aside and said the only way employees were going to keep their jobs was if I bought back most of the company. The board wasn't going to vote to throw money at employees to sustain their livelihoods until Qual-Soft could assemble new offices. I considered it. The surveillance industry is becoming even more relevant, particularly to governments, but my uncle had it set up to sell off for a reason. And that was the only thing that kept me from pulling the trigger.

I felt like a failure. I came here to do one good thing for the people who worked for my uncle, and I wasn't able to do it. But then Ohr called. The Council would be making an offer. They sent over a proposal, which was that if I would sign over my share of the company, they would purchase the additional shares necessary to achieve a majority vote, allowing people to not only keep their jobs, but to be relocated on Qual-Soft's dime.

I didn't bother asking how they knew what was going on. I just asked Ohr why. He said because Robert employed Primes, and they took an interest in protecting their own.

I then had to weigh the nearly one billion dollars I'd be losing by *giving* my shares away with the livelihoods I want to preserve. I broke down and called Gabriel, because he's the one person I know savvy enough about corporate culture whose judgement I also implicitly trust. After quickly pulling his dad on the line and explaining the situation, Dan immediately told me to counter, because Qual-Soft is the forerunner in the industry, and offering nothing for such a huge portion of shares was insulting. Gabriel agreed and said there's no way the Guild hasn't had owning the lion's share Qual-Soft on their wish-list. So I did. I offered to sell my shares at seventy-five percent of their value. They countered with sixty. And the deal was made.

I'm satisfied with the deal, but it also aches. Qual-Soft was Uncle Moby's baby. He built it from the ground up, and that's where he spent most of his time. He used it to give people second chances at life on a regular basis, and he was proud of being the guy who had unbeatable surveillance tech.

I'm thankful I called Gabriel. I'm thankful he always answers the phone, no matter how difficult things are between us. I'm thankful his sense of duty always outweighs his pride.

We pass a familiar road, the way to get to my Uncle's Monterey home—which is now mine. It's on the market, but nobody's buying homes right now, certainly not multi-million dollar homes in California. And I'm secretly glad. The Monterey house has lots of memories. I spent most of the last two and a half years there.

Tugged by all of those memories, I sit up abruptly and say, "Turn around. I want to go to the house."

Letty, who's sitting in the front, taps her communicator and issues the order.

"Picking something up?" Mike asks from next to me.

"No… Just memories," I say. "I realized there's a possibility I might not see it again. If people start really pouring out of northern California like they have in the south, it's going to be owned by squatters."

The neighborhood is several miles down the road, secluded and away from the more bustling areas of Monterey. I know every curve, and when we reach the circle drive at the front, it feels like coming home. Mike, acting as my personal bodyguard, waits in the car with me while Letty disburses the team to check things out. Once they're done though, per protocol, they gather in a group behind me and I put my ear to the door, listening.

I give the all-clear by punching the code on the door and opening it.

Mike goes inside with me, and I stand in the middle of the cavernous foyer, unsure where to go next. The grand staircase ascends to my right, and the hall toward Uncle Moby's office and bedroom reaches to my left, next to the living room. The kitchen is ahead. We took a few things from the house for traveling a few months ago, and I had the contents of our bedrooms packed up and brought to meet us in Wyoming. Everything else was left here because the ranch is fully-furnished.

Mike waits in the foyer while I walk through the kitchen. I stop when I round the island, which puts the bar in front of me. I can see Uncle Moby perched on a stool on the other side of it, having arrived after everyone has already had dinner. I've saved him a plate, and I chat him up while waiting for the microwave to ding. Kaylen walks in behind him, a newborn Robbie plastered against her shoulder. She's patting his back and telling me the precise volume measurement of milk he's had. It's an ounce less than yesterday… Should she start logging it so I can let his doctor know?

I smile and chuckle. In one of his rare moments of humor, Uncle Moby pulled a napkin out and started writing something down. "No need, Kaylen. I'll save you the trouble." He handed her the napkin, which had a calendar of the week ahead. Beside each date he'd written the number of ounces Robbie would consume during Kaylen's dinnertime feeding.

Kaylen took the list, skeptical that he was joshing her, but awed when Uncle Moby insisted it was accurate. After she was gone, I gave him a look. "I'm on to you, Uncle Moby."

He looked up from his freshly-steeped, post-dinner ginger tea, eyes sparkling. "Oh?" he said. "About what?"

"You aren't that good and you know it," I said.

"I beg your pardon," he replied, aghast. "I am, too. Just wait and see."

"I'll see alright," I told him. "I'll see Kaylen keep that bottle in Robbie's mouth until she reaches the exact measurement you gave her and then stare at it, dumfounded that you 'predicted' it. That's not fortune-telling. That's tricking her into making the future."

He hid his face behind his mug.

"In fact," I said, pressing, "I bet that's what you're really doing half the time you're calling the future, huh?"

I was halfway joking about the last part, but there was genuine surprise on his face. That was during the time I didn't have my life force abilities, so I couldn't read more. But he looked into his tea then, pensive about it for a while.

I can't remember what he said next… It bugs me that I can't, and I stare at the empty spot at the bar, the entire memory now going fuzzy, as memories do when you try too hard to get at them.

I bound up the stairs next. The first room on the right is mine and Gabriel's room. Connected to it is Robbie's room. Both are empty of course. I tour quickly through the rest of the upstairs, deciding that saying goodbye to a house is silly, especially when all the most meaningful places are empty. I save Uncle Moby's wing downstairs for last. His bedroom suite and office should be empty as well, so I don't expect to find anything other than stale smells that might make me cry. I had everything of his brought to Wyoming, and it's still sitting in boxes in the garage. I haven't had the heart to go through his things yet.

His space echoes, empty of course. I make a stop at his bathroom on my way through. I told the movers to leave all of the bathrooms. After discussing the move with everyone, what to have brought and what to leave, Gabriel made the suggestion that we leave the bathrooms as they were, full of toiletries and such. Being near the coast, the house might end up being needed to house disaster victims, and it would be nice if they had access to some of the basics immediately. It's typical of Gabriel to think that far ahead, and it was so thoughtful everyone readily agreed. But I just want to make sure Uncle Moby didn't have anything important in his bathroom, photos or anything like that.

His bathroom space is immaculate, so the large box on the counter makes me wonder if they packed it up and then remembered they weren't supposed to. I open drawers and cabinets. Nope, they're still full. I look at the box, about an eighteen inch cube. It's taped shut, and on the top is Gabriel's name, written in marker, in my uncle's unmistakeable scrawl.

What in the world?

I pick up the box, and it's really heavy. I shake it, but the contents only shift a little.

I reach for the knife in the holster at my waist—which, along with a pistol at my ankle, I've kept on me whenever I'm away from home—which is now Wyoming. Or dressed to take on executives of course. I'm about to slice through the tape but pause because it isn't *my* name written on the box. It's Gabriel's. This isn't my box to open, and even though I know my uncle's handwriting and I'm *dying* to know what's in it, I can't. Uncle Moby even wrote Gabriel's name *across* the tape sealing the box.

I can't help shaking the box again, but it doesn't help.

I step back, fold my arms, staring at the mysterious box like it's an oracle. Actually, it is. I am one hundred percent sure it was purposely packed up and left here in my uncle's bathroom *by* my uncle just so it would be found *right now* and not simply among the other things the movers took. I know my uncle. This is his MO.

I turn around in the bathroom, like there might be an explanation written somewhere. The walls and the mirror are clean. There's not a shred of paper anywhere. Uncle Moby left this just so it would be found. By me? Or was Gabriel supposed to find it? Does it matter? If I didn't have lots of experience with my uncle's ability to tell the future, I'd have a much harder time accepting this as a direct message from him in the past to Gabriel in the future.

"Miiiike!" I call.

He bounds into the bathroom a few moments later. "You okay?"

I point to the box. "Will you carry that to the car?"

"Sure," he says, noting Gabriel's name, but not thinking anything of it as he picks it up. "Sheesh," he says. "What's in here? Books?"

My mouth falls open. I think I know what's in the box. "Hang on," I say, catching up to him. I put my nose close to the edge of the box's flaps and inhale deeply.

"Oh my gosh," I marvel. "It *is* books. Mike, it's his books. The ones that didn't show up with the movers!"

Mike looks down at the box and then at me. "The *preecciooouuus*?" he says, mimicking Gollum's voice from *Lord of the Rings*.

I snigger. "Yeah. The one book to rule them all," I say, referring to the first edition by Albert Einstein.

I touch the box, wondering what had Uncle Moby put these aside to be found later. They are Gabriel's most prized volumes. Some of them are over a hundred years old. First editions. Some are by his favorite philosophers written in their original languages. And of course, the Precious. When no one had seen them, our assumption was that one of the movers must have known their value and taken liberties. I felt so bad for him then, but he said they were just things. Inside though… I could tell losing them was a blow.

I don't know if there's more to it, but for now, I'm excited to be the one that gets to deliver them, to see the look on his face when he realizes they aren't lost. This is a gift from Uncle Moby to me as much as it is to Gabriel.

"Let's go," I say to Mike. "I think I have what I came for."

Seventy-Three

Letty moans evocatively. "Dulce madre de Jesús del bebé…" she says.

"Und die zwölf Apostel…" Roe sighs.

"Et son culte, le pape," Jessie chimes in.

"Say vat, Jessie? Parle vous Français?" Roe says, lifting her head, the wildflowers she placed in a nest she made with her hair still holding fast. What does she hold those things in with? Super glue? They even made it through our festivities in the kitchen this morning where we turned out a killer breakfast.

"Un peu. Sobre todo español. Und ein wenig Deutsch," Jessie says.

I recognize that not only has Jessie referenced three different languages, but she claimed knowing them somewhat. I pat myself on the back for picking up that much. I raise a hand. "Hey! I speak English. Isn't *that* awesome?"

My masseur, Dominic, moves around the side of me to work on my shoulder, blocking my view with his bare abdomen. Not an unwelcome sight, if only I could turn off the knowledge that he's enjoying putting his hands on me a little too much. Sometimes being an empath sucks.

"Girl, you're the billionaire heiress who runs the whole ish. You could be a mute and be awesome," Letty says. "And remind me to thank your papi for giving you this idea when we're done. I might forget with all the pleasure rippling through my nethers."

"It's a massage, Letty. Nethers aren't involved," I say.

"My nethers are always involved," Letty replies.

Roe laughs. "Letty ees vat ve call erregbar."

"My gosh, and we get this for an entire *week*?" Jessie says, audibly sighing. "Best job *ever*."

"I know, right?" Roe says. "I say this eevery day!"

My phone rings and I grumble. "Dominic, can you grab that for me?"

He hands me the phone and then runs his hands down my back and over my butt. I'm distracted by it for a moment and the ring trills at me again before I process the name on the caller ID. I do a double-take when I realize it's Gabriel.

I can't decide whether to answer. I wonder if he's watching. We're in the east wing common area. I keep all of my over-the-top shenanigans to this wing and away from Dan and Maris. I can only imagine what her opinion would be.

The phone trills again.

I send the call to voicemail and hand it back to Dominic. "They can wait." Then I turn to Letty, who's at my right. I mouth Gabriel's name to her.

Her eyebrows lift. She bites her lip, thinking. Then she pulls her phone out, which she has apparently kept next to her, and makes a call.

"Hola," she says quietly. "What's the story?"

I listen in.

'*I seriously can't talk to you right now,*' I hear Mike say.

"Why not?"

'*I'm busy.*'

"I don't care," she says, indignant. "He just called her. We need you to tell us what's up."

I hear a frustrated sigh in reply. '*Letty, I don't like what you're doing to her. You're taking this way too far.*'

Letty makes a disgusted sound and props herself up on her elbows. "*Me*? You act like I'm forcing her. The boob exam? Her idea. The massages? Also her. But no. I'm the puta de mierda. And Wen's still the saint. Used no sabe nada de mierda! Usted no sabe su—"

"Letty," I interrupt loudly, realizing this is only going to end badly. "Let me have the phone."

"Gladly," she huffs, shoving her phone at me and flopping back down angrily.

"Mike," I say, coming up on my elbows. "What's the problem?"

"This isn't you, Wen," he says. "You know it isn't."

I pause in confusion over this sudden change of heart. This was all basically *his* idea—

Oh. Man. I know exactly what's happening.

"Mike, he's giving you a hard time, isn't he?" I ask gently.

He heaves several staggered breaths.

"He's overpowering you, isn't he?" I say.

Silence fills the line for a long time, but I feel him struggling through heavy breaths. I worry he's going to hang up, but then he whispers, "I'm sorry."

"Don't be sorry," I beg. It's not fair that he has to suffer through Gabriel. "Don't be sorry, Mike!" I'm nearly crying and I'm not entirely sure why this is hitting me so hard. Mike sharing Gabriel's emotions is nothing new. I think it's knowing he's having to fight them right now.

"Don't you dare be sorry," I repeat.

I hear a clatter, like he dropped the phone, and then coughing and retching. Throwing up?

I sit up abruptly, grab a towel and wrap it around me. "Where are you?" I ask. But he doesn't answer. I'm frantic for a couple of seconds before I remember to listen. So I close my eyes and do so.

I hear him easily. He's in the house and he's close, in this wing, actually. I head toward the sound of him gagging and spitting.

"Wen?" Letty asks, but I don't stop.

Near Mike is the clatter of weights, confirming my suspicions that he's in the gym, which is all the way on the end of the east wing where I am. I get there within moments and find the gym full of men. I glance around for Mike but he's not here.

"Where's Mike?" I demand.

"Uhh, bathroom, I think?" Darren says, placing a set of barbells on the floor at his feet, his eyes scanning my outfit—or lack thereof. I'm only in a towel.

Right. Of course he's in the bathroom if he's throwing up… I turn on my heel without answering and go to the bathroom connected to the gym. I don't knock, testing the knob, grateful to find it unlocked. I push the door open carefully and spot Mike sitting on the floor at the end of the bathroom, leaning sideways against the wall, elbows on bent knees, head in his arms. His phone is on the floor near the shower. I shut the door behind me silently. I don't smell vomit, so maybe he was just gagging. He's sweaty though, and shaking barely, visible only to me.

I pad across the cold, tile floor and kneel silently beside him. At first I'm not sure whether I should touch him, because the emotions coursing through him are so strong it frightens me. Pain, frustration, fear, panic, fury. I don't know how one person can contain so much, and maybe that's why Mike was gagging. It's nauseating.

I swallow, determined to be here for him even if it makes me feel like the worst person on the planet.

I reach out and touch his arm, which pops his head up immediately. His eyes are red, his jaw slack. "What are you doing here?" he demands, but he's more afraid than anything all of a sudden.

"Mike," I say, forcing him to look at me. "I'm here."

"Get away from me." He scoots closer to the wall, shaking off my hand.

"No," I say. "I'm not going anywhere."

"That's the problem," he says, and the nausea of his disgust forms a lump in my throat.

I reach for him again, this time caressing his hair.

He stands up. "Don't *touch* me," he growls, eyes wild.

"Mike," I quaver. "This isn't you. You know that, don't you?" Please let me be right about that...

He glances around in a vague haze for a moment, but it concludes quickly. "After everything, he tried to make this easy for you. He tried to—" He blinks, losing his train of thought. Then he looks at me, and for a brief moment his emotions take a back seat, as if they've been pushed to the side momentarily. "Wen..." He looks at me as if suddenly seeing me differently.

I stand, tug my towel up, which catches his attention and he finally realizes what I'm covering myself with. It seems to enrage him all of a sudden, and he stands. "So this is really you..." he says in disgust. "Using your body. Using it to control." And then he pulls the bathroom door open and leaves.

Without his influence, fear takes center-stage. And maybe in any other scenario it's irrational, but I'm afraid this really is Mike, that the betrayal he feels is his after all. Surely part of it's Gabriel, but what if Mike feels that way, too? I've been jerking him around just as much as Gabriel. It's inevitable because of their connection. The confusion he must endure... What's him and what's Gabriel... And me... He must wonder if I care at all when I flirt and flaunt and then expect him to tell me what's going on in Gabriel's head all the time. I take for granted how it affects Mike. I know how jealous Gabriel gets. Today, with the massages, it took things too far. Gabriel is overwhelming Mike.

The thought that I've inadvertently hurt Mike has me tearing out of the bathroom after him. "Mike!" I say, scuttling to a stop in the gym because I didn't hear him leave it entirely. Darren and everyone else is looking in my direction. Expectant, worried, anticipating, questioning...

Mike, I find, is at one of the benches, pressing a bar with an enormous amount of weight. He's removed his shirt somewhere between the bathroom and the bench, sweat now beading all over him as he gasps through the set, veins and muscles popping.

Up. Down. Up. Down. He throws the weight in the air with seeming otherworldly strength.

"Hey man, that's your set," Paul, who has moved over to spot him, says.

Mike ignores him, pumping the bar several more times, but I can see his arms shaking. "Paul, stop him!" I cry, stepping toward them, worried he's going to push too much and drop it on himself. Darren takes the side of the bar opposite Paul, and the two coordinate to take it from him, but Mike practically throws it back onto the stand. His lays there, heaving, arms hanging slack at his sides. The room is silent.

I move to stand over him, unsure of what to say that will convey how much I value *him* and not just what he's been doing for me. The tumult of earlier has receded, but numbness seems to be what's left, profound, lonely, empty, hopeless. He's doing a really good job of ignoring me, even sitting up and taking a towel from Darren and wiping himself down while I stand inches from him.

There's nothing to say, I realize. Because no matter what I say, every time I toy with Gabriel, Mike will feel it and he'll have work through how I feel about him all over again. It will change him because emotions are real things. They *do* real things. Can I keep justifying what I'm doing to get Gabriel back if Mike has to suffer so much?

I don't know.

But I do know I love Mike. He takes care of Gabriel and me and everyone else. He puts everything he wants and feels aside for the rest of us. And with all the conflicting emotions he endured, it's a wonder he stays so even-keeled most of the time. He deserves more. Actions speak louder than words, and I want Mike to know without a doubt how much he means to me. This calls for vulnerability. For risk and accepting whatever consequences may come. For thinking of only Mike and no one else for once.

He tosses the towel at the hamper across the room and is about to stand up when I put my hands on either side of his face. His energy rushes into me with a vengeance, but I'm prepared for it. I welcome it. I make him look up at me from where he's sitting. He moves his hands up to take mine off of him, but I lean down and put my lips on his before he can, taking him completely by surprise.

He jerks from irritation to disbelief to confusion, and then worry. He makes a pitiful attempt to pull away, but with the slightest pressure on his mouth I convey without words that I've thought this through. The shift to pleasure comes easily then, and instead of reaching to take my hands away, he's putting his fingers gently on my neck as I caress his lips with my own. I convey affection with them, not heat. Because I don't want him to see this as manipulation, or a moment of weakness, or lust. When it's over I don't want him to think it was a mistake, so I stay in control by letting my heart brim with the love I have for him and letting it spill into the movement of my mouth on his salty lips.

I let my heart off of its leash. I let it go wherever it wants and shove my reservations and fear aside. I don't care. For Mike, right now, I don't care about any of it, only in embodying every bit of how I feel in this simple, but beautiful dance of my lips against Michael Dumas, who has loved me far better than I ever had a right to expect.

He pulls away first, but not entirely, just enough that I can put my forehead against his. I keep my hands on his face, stroking the side of his cheek with a hand as I stand over him. I breathe in his heady scent and let things settle into all the right places, mainly, how Mike feels about it all. I won't shy away, won't entertain regret. This was for him and no one else. As I follow his emotional trek, I think he grasps that for the most part. But of course, he can't help entertaining worry. Worrying about Gabriel is what Mike does a lot of the time, it seems.

"No," I murmur. "Don't." I pull him to his feet and wrap my arms around him, my cheek resting near his collar bone.

"That wasn't necessary," he says finally. "He wouldn't have been in a rage forever."

I ignore him, keeping my eyes closed and basking in his closeness.

"You also picked a helluva place to do it, too," he says. "Look at all these people... *Everyone's* here."

I shrug against him to indicate I still don't care.

"Wen, did you know your father was in the room, too?"

"What?" I startle, eyes popping open. I twist around to look, and at the same time my towel comes loose and falls. With reflexes only Mike has, he pulls me back to his chest and catches the towel before it hits the floor. He throws it over me.

My backside is covered at least…

"Well then," Mike says as awkwardness settles over both of us, the eyes in the room literally glued on us. "Your boobs are on my chest. I have to say, I did *not* see my day going like this."

I laugh.

"And by the way, I was kidding about Carl."

"You!" I punch him, but it doesn't work so well since I'm using him pressed against me to cover myself.

He sniggers. "Wanted to see what you'd do."

"Give me my towel," I say, clumsily covering my front with his chest while simultaneously grabbing the sides of the towel to wrap it back around me. I tuck it tightly and put my hands on my hips. "If you'll excuse me, I have to go tell Gabriel I kissed you before someone else does." I wave at the room. "Carry on, guys!"

When we reach the privacy of the hall and the sounds of clanging equipment resume, Mike stops me. "Wen, I don't think it's a good time to do this."

"Will there *ever* be a good time?" I say.

"Preferably one where you aren't wearing a towel and when Gabe's not throwing a tantrum about seeing another man put his hands all over you after you've been working him into an oversexed fever for weeks. He's not in a good place to even *begin* to hear you if you tell him why you kissed me—why *did* you kiss me?"

"Because I love you and I appreciate you and I wanted you to know it."

"Oh hell. He is *definitely* not going to like that reason." Then he puts his hand over his neck uncomfortably. "I'm sorry you felt you had to do that."

"Please don't do that," I say. "Stop apologizing. You haven't done anything wrong. Never. In all of this you've done nothing but try to make things right between Gabriel and me. It's *his* fault you hated me. It's *his* fault you blamed me. *He* is why you're going through what you are. And frankly, it pisses me off so bad that he doesn't even *try* to care about what he's passing to you. He only conveniently remembers when it involves *me*. Then it's like he can't stand the idea of sharing an iota of our relationship with you. He's okay with pouring on the angst though, and he uses it to punish you, as if anything is your fault."

"You're just mad. I get it. You were excited to show him the books when we got back yesterday, and he was already hiding from you. I thought the three day break while you were in Monterey would help, but it's like he had all that time to think about you without being afraid you'd show up and catch him off-guard. Wen, I'm telling you, the more of an ass he is, the more you're affecting him. And it's because he loves you."

"That's supposed to make me feel better?" I snap. "He's mean to me because he loves me? No, thank you. I hate him. He infuriates me, and I swear the only reason I'd give him even half a chance of getting back with me one day is because I know it's what you want."

"Don't say that."

"It's true," I glare. "That's how far he's pushed me."

Now both his hands are on the back of his neck and he sighs. "I shouldn't have let you kiss me."

I throw my hands up. "Gah! Shut up! This is not about kissing you!" I shout. And then I turn around and start walking again. "Where is he?" I say.

"He left," Mike says.

"Left?" I say, turning back toward him.

He nods and then sees the panic on my face. "Not like, permanently. Although it's nice to see you actually care after everything you just said—not to mention considering you aren't wearing his ring anymore."

I flop against the wall and look up at the ceiling, crossing my arms. He's right. I do care. The thought, even for that small moment, was suffocating. "I can't do this anymore," I say, so wrung-out. It's like the massage I was getting not that long ago has already worn off. Which sucks. I was really hoping today would be my breakthrough with Carl in the pool. Gabriel ruins everything.

"Stick to the plan," Mike says. "It's going to be okay."

I roll my head over to look at him, thinking the only reason I'm going to is because he asked me. But telling him so apparently bugs him, so I just nod.

"When he gets back, tell him about the kiss. Then give him the books. And be nice about it."

I give him an exhausted look.

"Come on," he says, urging me back down the hall. "A massage should help get you ready."

"Fine," I grumble reluctantly.

"I didn't realize having a buff dude rub you down was such a terrible thing."

"Eh. Having a stranger rub me down is actually not as relaxing as I expected."

"In that case, what if I was there? I'd actually like to learn how to give a good massage. Think your gigolo would give me some instruction?"

I stop and look over at him right before we reach the doors to the common room, because he's totally serious. "He's not my gigolo."

Mike sniggers. "Whatever you say. But you're a billionaire that flew him in here to rub your naked body for a week. Don't tell me he hasn't been thinking about the possibility."

I wrinkle my nose. "Yeah, that's kind of why it's not that awesome. Letty and Roe and Jessie though, they get to be oblivious to all their horny thoughts. I am actually glad you offered. Maybe you can pretend like you're my jealous boyfriend, and that'll put a cap on it."

"That's kind of why I offered," he says.

My shoulders slump as his thoughtfulness warms me over. "Oh... Mike..."

He rolls his eyes. "Stop. I already regret it. Being too nice is working against me. Let's talk about something else. Like the fact that Letty might end up running a tab with these guys. You know she's already got one picked out for the evening."

"*Oh...*" I grimace. "I totally did not think about that. Although I have no idea why. Letty was just complaining about being sex-deprived." I look at him, curious about something but not sure if I can or should ask.

"No," Mike says, apparently knowing me well enough to translate my expression. He waves his hands in front of him. "No way. This love triangle is complicated enough. And there are at least three guys on Darren's team, including Darren himself, who are perfectly willing and available to satisfy her needs if she wants. I already gave her their names."

I can only laugh, picturing Letty purring at Mike to lure him into bed, and him holding her at bay, saying, 'I can't handle this job right now. But here are some names. Tell 'em I sent you.'

"Confession," Mike says, watching my expression.

I lift my eyebrows expectantly.

"I love to see you smile."

"Ditto," I say.

"And your boobs on me. I love that, too. That moment is going to be permanently imprinted in my head."

We push through the doors. "Good lord," I say. "I don't even know how I'm going to explain that one to Gabriel, let alone make it sound believable. 'I needed a shirt! He was the closest thing!'"

"Hola!" Letty calls, spotting us, and it looks like she's recruited Dominic to work on her as well as her own masseur.

"Remind me to check the contract later, to see what's included in the 'incidental charges' section," I murmur to Mike.

Seventy-Four

*D*on't stress about it," Carl says, putting a hand on my back.
I pull the towel tighter around me, thinking I should
have had an indoor pool installed. I never would have guessed
I'd need a pool in this way again. What *is* it with water and the
colorworld anyway?

"I'm running out of time," I say, hating that I've failed
again. "The weather is changing too quickly." I've tried three
times in the last four days to access the colorworld using water. I
can't get myself to let go.

"You can have a beefier heater installed," he replies. "Turn
the thing into one massive hot tub." He grins knowingly at me.
"That should help maintain morale during the winter…"

"Yeah, but it won't help to be in a hot tub if your face
is freezing off. Maybe I can have it enclosed…" I grimace. I
really don't want to spend money on something like a pool. It's
ridiculous when the world is falling apart. Yesterday a tsunami
hit a four hundred mile stretch of the Baja strip. The Guild had
already called it on their website, and the area was evacuated
after all previous predictions had come true. The Guild has earned
themselves an ironclad reputation in less than a month.

Mister Dave Renfrau, spokesperson for the Guild, has been
keeping busy as the only contact the world has with the Guild,
but he's been extremely close-lipped. Nobody has a clue *where*
they are, how *many* Primes they comprise, but the one thing he
did explain was the Council, a group of twelve Prime Humans
who make decisions for the Guild as a whole. He emphasized the
need to keep their membership secret, and that was reinforced
yesterday as well, when another massacre took place in Chicago
and five Prime Humans were murdered by PHIA. Like the Guild,
PHIA is a phantom. People know they exist, but the scale and
scope of both is a complete mystery to the world.

"I don't know, Wendy…" Carl says after a while. "This should be easy for you. Maybe the fact that your colorworld comes so easily to you is a hindrance. You've never had to really try like this…"

I don't agree. I think it's my state of mind lately. Most of the time I feel like I've got it together. I stay busy, taking care of Robbie and spending hours on my computer and my phone with Dwight, handling the day's latest issues across the Haricott empire. And I visit the construction sites daily now, because Gabriel kept upsetting the foremen with his overly-meticulous oversight. I had to take him off the job because it was taking too much of both his and the crew's time to argue over every detail of their work. But when I get alone, long enough to think about something that isn't right in front of me…

"I'll see about getting an extra heater for the pool," I say, standing up to go inside.

"Have you spoken to Ezra lately?" Carl asks, following me across the patio.

"Some. Why?" I ask.

"Wondering how he's making progress…"

I slide the door closed behind us and look at him, because there's more behind that question than he lets on.

"He won't talk to me," Carl replies.

I frown. "I'm not sure if he *will*, Dad. Not anytime soon anyway. Have you tried visiting him in the lab?"

"I have. He ignores me. And I'm not looking for a father-son relationship; he owes me nothing. But I may be able to help him with what he's doing."

"Help him with advanced theoretical math?" I say, skeptical.

"No… Everything else. Math is just a language. Ezra's life force ability is not mastery of a language. It's a particular enhanced perception of the world. All life force abilities are. If Ezra confines himself to mathematical language, he is likely shortchanging his full capability. I did say *may*, but I need to know what he's thinking. To do that, he has to talk to me."

I lift my eyebrows at Carl's assessment. I used to think all my father ever did with his life was obsess over hypno-touch. But more and more I'm realizing how much knowledge he has in other areas. He becomes more multi-faceted all the time. "I'll see what I can do."

On my way to my room, I decide there's no time like the present to visit Ezra. I have a small window before I have to go out to the construction sites anyway. I stand in front of my closet, deciding what kind of understated but alluring outfit I can wear since Gabriel will see me. I've kept it slightly toned down lately, more out of a need to keep from establishing a pattern of expectation for everyone else. I've accomplished what I wanted to there. And Gabriel has been actively avoiding me anyway.

I've failed with Carl again today though, and Gabriel is a huge reason I'm so stressed out...

I choose a pair of stretchy, bright pink running pants and matching racer back tank. I pull on my tennis shoes, too, planning to also attack my stress with a run detour on my way to the solar farm site.

As soon as I exit my room, however, hushed voices capture my attention and I stop. I don't make it a habit of eavesdropping, but it's Dan, and I've never heard him speak in anything but a calm and clear voice—except for that one time he reprimanded Gabriel for disrespecting his mother.

"*You may want to consider it,*" Dan says. "*I cannot see another way around the situation at present.*"

"*I know it seems that way,*" Mike replies. "*But you haven't spoken to her. She hates him, Dad. If it weren't for me being around to soften the blow, she'd recognize just how much. She doesn't even want to do this anymore with him. She's only doing it because I keep begging her not to give up. Gabe can't know how far he's pushed her, because if he smells a victory, he's going to bring it home. If I leave, that's what happens. She won't have a reason to keep trying.*"

"*You don't know that, Michael,*" Dan says. "*People say a lot of things, especially when they are upset. And besides, my reasoning is less about how your leaving would affect her, and more about how it would affect Gabe. Your mother and I would go with you. You wouldn't be alone, but there are things that must be worked out between them without the rest of us in the way.*"

Mike laughs mirthlessly. "*By 'the rest of us,' you mean me, don't you?*"

"*No, Mike. Please do not read into my words. All of us. The three people that have tried repeatedly to bring Gabe to his senses. He does not hear us. He builds a wall because of our relentlessness, and it shuts Wendy out as surely as it does you, me, and your mother.*"

Mike huffs several times. I think he's not going to answer, but finally he says, "*You know, I take a lot of shit from you and Mom about my friendship with Wen, and I think to myself, 'Maybe they're right. Maybe I'm only making things worse. I mean, Gabe sure as hell hasn't put up a fuss about me talking to his wife, so that must mean that I'm giving him exactly what he wants.' But then you say things like that, like 'He builds a wall. He shuts us out,' and it knocks me back every single fucking time. Why the hell am I listening to you when you obviously haven't got a clue? He can't shut me out! There is* no wall *he can build that will keep what's going on in his fucked up head out of mine! It's never going away. There is nothing he can feel that won't find its way to me one way or another! Fuck, Dad. At least Gabe is smart enough to realize there's no escape for me.*

"*It's like you are totally oblivious to what's going on. I'm not here for me, or for you, or for mom, or even for Wen. I'm here for Gabe. Because he needs to see that no matter what, I can reside within the same four walls as her and keep my damn hands to myself. I can handle myself. I can handle her and him and the whole shitty situation without running away from it. And I can be happy with how things are with her without needing more or without turning my back on her to get away from feelings I can't control. You think distance is going to help me do that? There are only two outcomes to this situation: Gabe is either going to accept this and take Wen back, or he's going to find a way to give my life force strands back to me. That's it. There is no in between. So I'm not just trying to save his marriage, Dad. I'm trying to save his fucking life.*"

I've fallen back against the wall as Mike's words take my breath away. He's right of course. I've known as much about Gabriel's conviction from the beginning, but it's never been spelled out, cut and dry. What really strikes me is that I've never stopped to question why Mike stuck around to put himself through so much stress and struggle, especially when I was the one putting him through that. I did ask him before, why, if he saw Gabriel's actions as so unpardonable, it mattered whether or not he, Mike, respected the fidelity of my marriage to Gabriel. My guess is he must have realized it all then, but he was afraid to tell me because of what it meant he would have to put himself through—things I *never* would have agreed to do to him if I'd known. But that's the moment he decided just how far he'd go.

That's when he told me to flaunt myself. It was as important for his own mission to prove to Gabriel that he was capable of handling any temptation as it was for me to try to win Gabriel. Mike put *himself* through everything Letty and Roe and I dished out to prove to Gabriel that he wouldn't break. He even turned Letty down, to prove he didn't need an outlet.

All of it. To save Gabriel.

"Oh Mike…" I whisper, wrapping my arms around myself. His love for Gabriel leaves me speechless whenever I'm confronted with it like this. Now that I know exactly what he's been doing… what do *I* do?

I'm not sure. I'll have to think about it when I'm not so furious at Gabriel. For now I'm too upset that Gabriel has forced Mike to go to such lengths.

Returning to my mission at hand though, I head back down the hall and stop at the edge of the door to the lab, curious suddenly what Gabriel looks like when I'm not around. The lab is a huge room, the result of tearing the wall down separating two bedrooms. The wall visible directly through the doorway is abnormally long because of that, but it serves to accommodate a huge map of the world that has been marked up into near unrecognizability. At least to me it seems that way. But it still gives me the distinct impression of ordered chaos. It means something, just not to me. To the far right is a massive, six foot monitor on the wall. It's connected to a cluster computing system, which was set up by Qual-Soft. It's this computer Ezra uses to run simulations: from individual disasters, to a region of them, to a schematic nearly identical to the map on the wall, but more dynamic and with the ability to enter different experimental variables.

Ezra is sitting with his back to me at the computer controls, and next to him is Gabriel, leaning forward with his hands on the table. They're locked in an intense argument, and I don't understand a word of it. The argument pauses at one point because Ezra has brought something onto the screen. It's a spherical graph with a bunch of data points. He draws lines between points by wrapping the lines around the sphere. He cross-sections the sphere, rotates the sections until they look like two circles, and then superimposes them on one another.

I have no idea what it means, but Gabriel makes an exclamatory sound of recognition. He ruffles Ezra's hair, which makes Ezra reach out to smack him. But Gabriel leaps away, laughing.

A smile finds my face at watching them interact, but it's followed by a frown. Gabriel keeps claiming that he doesn't know who he is or how to behave, but the confusion obviously only surrounds *me*.

I feel eyes on me. It's Roe, dolled up as usual: full makeup, corset, and a Chinese dress, which she told me at breakfast is called a cheongsam. She changed her hair color a few days ago; she's going through a red and gold phase. She's sitting at one of the other, smaller computers, but she's not using it, instead holding a tablet in her hands. I've come to learn the tablet is how she communicates with the mothership. Her brow lifts and she gives me a soft smile.

"Hello, Wendy," Gabriel says.

I turn back to him, step out from behind the door. "Hi," I say. "Just came to make sure my brother has bathed recently."

"You don't have to explain your presence. You own the place after all," he says amicably.

I don't know who I owe for influencing Gabriel to look at me that way, but I find myself bothered by it. That he can go from completely ignoring me for days to being upbeat and *nice* is yet another way he keeps me stressed. Because later I'll spend way too much time analyzing his words and actions.

I turn away from him without answering, instead looking at my brother, whose eyes are wide, maybe expecting a fight between Gabriel and me.

"Ezra," I say firmly. "I'm assigning Carl to work with you. I want you to get him up-to-date on what you're doing."

Ezra's mouth falls open in protest. "*Whaaat*?! No way, Wen."

"Yes way," I reply.

"I can't work with him around. I just can't."

"Why?"

"Because I don't trust him. And he likes to lurk, wearing that creepy look on his face like he does when he's thinking. Then, totally out of the blue, he'll say something totally irrelevant. The only explanation is he's scheming. I know you like him, that you trust him because you're a mind reader, but I can't stand him."

I purse my lips in annoyance, and I realize after I do it that it's the same look Ezra says I share with Carl. "So you're still stuck on his past?"

"Stuck on it? He twisted your life so he could fight the Guild. He still sees the Guild the same way, which means he hasn't let go of it. Which means he plans to use you if he isn't already. He's going to disappoint you."

"Just let him in on what you're doing. I'm interested in his insights. All this was his idea after all. Can't you put aside your feelings to do that for me?"

"It's *because* of you I can't put it aside. If he doesn't jeopardize us with all his scheming, he'll jeopardize us because he'll stress me out being in the same room and me wondering what he's up to."

I narrow my eyes. That is so bogus. "Is that so?" I say, putting my hands on my hips and stepping further into the room. Ezra flinches, obviously knowing he's in for it. "You work with Gabriel just fine," I point out. "He treats me like crap on a daily basis, makes it impossible for me to work in the colorworld because I'm so stressed out about our relationship. And he does it *right in front of you.* He doesn't even hide it so it's not like you have to wonder! He jeopardizes me and therefore all of us because he does it. Yet you have *no* problem not only putting it aside, but getting along *swimmingly.*" I hold my hands up. "And I'm not complaining. You both have the brains, so you *should* work together. But I'm telling you, you *can* work with Carl. Your actual fear is that you'll like him, that you'll see yourself in him. And then you'll have to figure out how to deal with it."

Ezra stares at me, stunned.

I clasp my hands in front of me and straighten my shoulders. "I'm making an executive call here, because I *own the place, after all,*" I say, simpering at a wide-eyed Gabriel. "Carl is going to be in this room, looking over your shoulder. So. If you don't want him to watch you in creepy silence and make inopportune comments, I suggest talking to him. That's the best way to figure out what someone's up to. Got it?"

Ezra glances up at Gabriel and back at me. But I am strictly ignoring Gabriel. "Ah, um, okay?" Ezra says finally.

"Lovely," I say, turning on my heel and striding out.

I'm almost to the outside door when I hear jogging footsteps accompanied by Gabriel's voice, "Wendy! Hold on!"

"I have somewhere to be," I say, reaching the door and stopping in front of the coat rack, undecided about putting a pullover on. I won't need it while I'm running, but once I'm talking to the foreman in the cold I'll probably wish I had it…

"I'll go with you."

I look up and grunt softly. Yet another Gabriel flip-flop. Avoidance followed by insisting on accompanying me. I lean against the door, hating the fact that with such a simple request he can stir anything at all in me. I hate that he still owns so much of me that he can abuse me continually and I keep coming back for more.

I don't want to do this anymore. I am so done with Gabriel living by a set of rules that don't ever have exceptions. Not even for me. And certainly not for Mike who lives his entire *life* around making exceptions for Gabriel. I don't understand why I still have such strong feelings for him… How can I look at him and not be utterly disgusted? How have I even *wanted* him to touch me the past few weeks?

It hits me suddenly: it's because of Mike. They both told me once that whatever woman one of them was involved with, she would inevitably end up mirroring her feelings for one brother onto the other, and vice-versa. What Mike just said moments ago, I now understand. Gabriel has shattered my heart over and over, but Mike keeps picking the pieces up and putting me back together. Mike told his dad that if he left, I would realize how much I actually can't stand Gabriel. It's because of Mike that I keep giving Gabriel credit emotionally. Mike's love for me outweighs all of Gabriel's abuse. And so I'm stuck in this cycle.

Gabriel is watching my face, and I could swear he knows what I'm thinking. But I can't do this right now. My head is in such a bind that I'm on the edge of screaming at him just for standing there. And I don't want to sabotage all that Mike has been trying to do, especially when I'm so emotional.

"Not right now," I say. "I really need a run. And I need to check on Greg. He's pouring concrete today."

Gabriel nods. "Later then? I need to visit the grocery store. Can I find you after that?"

"Yeah," I sigh, feeling in my core that this is the beginning of the end. Of something.

₪

I watch Gabriel's back, bucking up courage. At least I had enough to find *him* instead of waiting. My run did a world of good for my state of mind. And Greg, the foreman in charge of the solar farm construction, was so friendly and upbeat about the progress of the project, it was hard to cling to my bitterness. Happy people who enjoy their jobs can really dull the edges of life.

Gabriel's putting away groceries, so it's not long before he turns to grab another bag and he spots me standing against the archway.

"Hey," I say.

"Hi," he acknowledges, putting his back to me once more.

"I have something to give you," I say. "I also have to tell you something."

"Oh?" he says, arranging things in the pantry.

"I kissed Mike a few days ago."

He pauses only briefly, a box of crackers in his hand. Within a few seconds he's put them on the shelf and is reaching into the bag again, as if what I've confessed only produced minor surprise. He's much too far away for me to read. "Why are you telling me?" he asks.

"Because I'm married to you. I owe you honesty. And besides, Darren and a bunch of other guys saw it. I wanted it to come from me and not them."

He makes a sound of acknowledgement, but doesn't speak. Did he change his mind from earlier about wanting to talk to me?

I slump. Gabriel was once the easiest person in the world to read and talk to. He is now one of the most difficult. He and Mike have exchanged places in so many ways, because it wasn't that long ago that Mike was the difficult one. He changed when he found out my alter ego was Gemma Rossi, a girl he met six years ago at an art benefit, that he'd been searching for ever since. The other thing that changed him was when I was able to discover what exactly connected him to Gabriel in the colorworld. He'd spent his whole life not understanding why he was tied to feeling Gabriel's experiences. He'd spent his whole life running away from it. Now he spends his life getting *Gabriel* to accept it. The two have made respective one-eighties.

I was sixteen then, and I don't remember meeting Mike. My daughter had recently died and the entire night was a blur. Supposedly Gabriel met me as well, but he doesn't remember either. He also doesn't remember his fight about it with Mike afterward. I realize I've never talked to Gabriel about Mike realizing I was his long-lost dream girl because he became so distant right after I learned of it. The one thing everyone *does* remember is the cloud sculpture I made for the fated benefit, which Gabriel and Mike had purchased for their mom. Nobody knew it was actually mine until

I recognized it at their parents' house. That was such a bizarre moment...

"Gabriel, did you know Mike remembers the Detritus Benefit?"

He stops in the middle of facing out and reorganizing all of the cans in the pantry. He's kneeling, working on one of the bottom shelves, and his hands fall to his sides.

"He remembers me as Gemma Rossi, and finding me in a wooden crate. He remembers fighting you afterward," I say. "Why do you think neither of *us* remembers?"

"I remember," he replies, so softly there's no way I would hear him if I didn't have super hearing.

My brow furrows. "You told me you didn't."

"When I told you that, I *didn't*." He comes slowly to his feet, puts his good hand on the casing above the door, exhales. "That's... ironically what I wanted to talk to you about." He turns to fully face me, his expression slightly strained. "I was stalling, but I suppose you bringing it up unprompted is my sign to crack on with it."

When I exhale, it makes me lightheaded, so I sit on the floor. "Let's talk then."

He follows my example, sitting on the tile, leaning back against the cabinets, maintaining a distance from me, which is fine. When serious stuff is about to go down, I'd rather have just my own emotions to deal with.

"I hadn't thought about it for a while," Gabriel says. "Until you went to Monterey last week. After we had that moment in the hall I was confronted with the fact that my attraction to you wasn't going away. I was... desperate to reciprocate everything you'd been offering for the past few weeks—also part of the reason I gave you those letters. But of course that backfired. I'm not withdrawing the thing I asked of you—that I be able to give Mike's life force strands back to him. But I realize neither you nor Mike are of a mind to do that. So I began searching for an alternative while you were gone. I broke everything down. I let go of the conclusions I'd drawn, specifically the one that says the life force you are bonded to is Mike's and not mine. I went back to the beginning, looked at everything."

I bring my knees up, wrap my arms around them. "So the beginning was Detritus when I was sixteen. How did you remember?"

He shrugs. "I really don't know. I fell asleep thinking about that cloud sculpture you made, remembering how serendipitous that moment felt when we realized we'd met a long time ago. I think maybe I forgot that night until now because I wanted to. This was the first time I actively *wanted* to remember. When I woke up the memory was there, like I'd repressed it all along."

"So you remember you and Mike talking to me in the crate? The fight?"

"Yes. Except that the account Mike gave you wasn't complete."

"How's that?"

"Afterward, when I implored Mike to refrain from making you a sexual conquest, he got upset. It wasn't the first time I'd accused him of being a philanderer, so it wasn't that. He was more defensive than I'd ever seen him about any woman, ever. I wondered how deeply his sudden attachment went, so I began to goad him, which sent him into an absolute frenzy. That's how the fight started, and to be honest, I welcomed it. I was finally seeing him want someone that clearly had no interest in me. I *wanted* him to care like that. I wanted him to fight for you. Because up until then, all he'd ever done was fight *me*."

My stomach hollows slightly and I think I'm beginning to see where this is going.

"Somewhere in all of the flying fists, I told him I wasn't going to fight over you. And I wasn't. Sure, I found you intriguing— as much as I could considering you stayed inside that crate and never showed your face—but unlike Mike, I wasn't interested in conquest, in winning. I wanted someone that chose *me*. And I wanted Mike to have the same. So I promised him. 'I won't interfere. She's yours. As far as I'm concerned, I never met her.' And it provoked him all over again, probably because I put you in the context of a trophy. So he knocked me out. The rest is history."

I have my cheek in one of my hands, elbow in my lap. *Gabriel made a promise...* I groan internally. Blessing and curse. Just like Maris said. But at least the insanity of Gabriel's behavior is starting to make sense.

"Wendy," Gabriel says gently, "you met us both at the same time, and you clearly chose him. You were clearly drawn to him out of the two of us. I *know* you don't want to hear it, but that supports my theory, that the life force you fell in love with was Mike's, that I'm merely his second vessel."

He takes a concerted breath while I get a hold of my reeling thoughts. "I'm not oblivious to Mike's plight," he continues pleadingly. "I know that everything I feel is transferred to him. Both good and bad. I don't purposely inflict him. When I suffer, I am well aware that it's not simply my own. And I know that's why he believes it's in his best interest to see you back with me. He believes that if I'm happy, he will be, too. If I'm heartbroken... so will he be. Therefore *my* happiness first and foremost rather than his own is the thing he has committed himself to."

Gabriel holds his palms out. "But I'm not. I'm more miserable than ever. After remembering what really happened at Detritus, and what *should* have happened between the two of you but didn't... The guilt is drowning me. I married you before he ever had a chance to really meet you. I made a promise to him and I broke it. I took away his opportunity to fall in love with the one woman he ever demonstrated caring about."

He hangs his head, shoulders drooping. "And now I'm stuck between the two of you. I want to do right by both of you, but I've been condemned from the start, accused of wanting nothing but to make your life a hell." He looks directly at me. "That could not be further from the truth. I am desperate for his happiness. And for yours. Wendy, you're good for him. He's gentler, more selfless, more patient. He worships you, so much he'd cast his own feelings aside to give you peace over your inability to reciprocate. And he's embracing himself honestly. I've never *ever* seen him so unguarded with anyone like he is you. Not even with me has he ever been that way, and I share a part of his life force! *You* are his best friend. How can I live with myself as your husband? How?"

His tone pleads for the answer, but I don't have it. He's right. I've painted him as the bad guy. I've made him the opposition when in reality he has been doing the same thing Mike has been doing. They've both been trying to make each other happy. And failing.

Where does that leave anyone?

"I realize the difficulty," Gabriel says, reading my expression. "And by the heavens I know you are in a more difficult place than anyone. And of course Robbie makes what are already hard decisions, much harder. But you know, even Robbie is tied to Mike. He shares some version of Mike's life force ability. They may not be genetically father and son, but they are life force related. Look at how easily Mike quiets him.

"You confessed kissing Mike, but that's only a revelation to *you*. Considering the fact that Mike not only feels my emotions but the sensations against and under my skin, he has already been even more intimate with you than I was when we were first married and were restricted from actually touching each other. The lines have already blurred between the two of you, Wendy. You already belong to each other. Neither of you will admit it because propriety and loyalty hold you back."

Gabriel sighs heavily. "I'm not here to plead my case. I just want you to know to what lengths I've gone to consider the situation from all angles. I want you to know that everything I've tried to do has been an effort to do *right* by you and my brother. I admit, I stumbled through it when we first discovered the life force connection. I have unnecessarily strung you along. I haven't wanted to make hard decisions. And heaven knows I haven't wanted to explain all this to my family or anyone else, frankly. But when you came to the lab today and admitted what was happening with the colorworld, I had yet one more thing to add to the list of reasons I should stop delaying making a decision."

I already have my arms wrapped around me, and I squeeze harder. Oh God. My chest is being torn from the inside. I'm being sheared right down the middle. Maybe when the split finally happens I can give half of myself to each of them. I want to. I want them both. I want Gabriel for never shunning hard things. I want Mike for making it easy to breathe. I want them both for such an incredible ability to sacrifice their own happiness for each other and for me.

I slip off the bed again, come close and bend down to lift the box, desperate not to feel him, but it's impossible. By the time I've got the box in my own arms, I'm already crying. I shove it into him.

He seems equally eager to get away, and I shut the door behind him. And then I listen to his footsteps retreat.

"Within two weeks I'll be leaving here," Gabriel continues. "I'll help Ezra finish up the mapping—he is very close being able to lay out his findings—but once that's done I need to put some *actual* distance between us. There's no way for the three of us to reside in such close quarters without things continuing to be torturous. This isn't me attempting to force you to be with Mike. I'm done doing that, coercing people to do what I think will make them happy. It only results in misery. So I'm trying something new; I'm going to do what I can feel at peace with. And I'm hoping it will end up benefitting everyone."

His rubs his face, up and down. "Wendy, I promise you, this isn't manipulation. I hope you don't see me leaving as another method of forcing you into something."

I shake my head. I don't see it that way at all. Not anymore. After all that, there's no fight in me. Only compassion.

"Thank you," he says. "For not making this hurt more than it already does."

I struggle not to cry. I sniff back tears, get control again. "You're welcome," I croak.

He swallows and sniffs. "You said you had something to give me?"

I blink. "Yeah." I stand up. "It's in my room. Kind of heavy…"

His brows lift and he follows. My room is really close to the kitchen so we don't go far. I sit on the bed so as to keep myself as far away from Gabriel as possible. On the one hand I want him to hold me while I fall apart. On the other, I think it will only make me feel worse.

He appears in the doorway and I point to the box on the floor. "I found it at Uncle Moby's in Monterey. It was in his bathroom. Sealed like that and everything." I give him a knowing look. He should recall that the bathrooms were purposely left behind.

"What is it?" he asks, crouching next to it.

"You want me to tell you and ruin the surprise?" I say, struggling to be lighthearted, but it's not coming out in my voice.

"You know what it is then?" he asks, glancing at me.

"I'm ninety-five percent sure."

He tests the weight of the box with his free hand. "If you can lift it into my good arm, I should be able to carry it."

Seventy-Five

What do we do?" Mike says, his hands on his head. He has refused to sit down the entire time he's been here. He showed up early this morning, woke me up, clearly having been awake all night, not knowing what was going on, but knowing Gabriel wasn't in the house. He decided to stay at a hotel in town until he leaves more permanently.

"Nothing," I say. Even though I explained everything Gabriel told me, Mike is *not* pacified. So far he's taking this much worse than me. And after all his effort, I can't say I blame him.

"Nothing?" Mike says, confused. "You're throwing in the towel? How can you do that?"

"I love him too much," I reply simply, honestly. It's the one thing I know. It's the *only* thing I know. It's the only determination I made while discussing it all with myself last night.

"What?" Mike says, even more confused.

I sigh, thinking that Mike won't really understand no matter how I put it. After hearing him talk to his dad, I understand that protecting Gabriel from himself is what motivates him. I also know from experience that it won't work. That's why I separated from Gabriel the first time—to protect Gabriel from himself, and it nearly ruined everything. As much as I admire Mike's dedication to Gabriel, I can see the error in his thinking.

All of these realizations have come over me now that I've stopped and *listened* to Gabriel. After being so vulnerably honest as only Gabriel can do, I couldn't find an iota of resentment toward him. Even hours later. He has literally made it impossible for me to do anything but ache *for* him, not *over* him. He has made it impossible for me to do anything but give him what he asks.

"I'd do anything for him," I confess, sort of mystified by that fact, staring down at my hands, "whatever he needs to be happy, even if it means not being with me."

"That's so fucked up. How do you not see that?"

I flinch and lace my hands over the back of my neck, having a hard time not getting upset with him. "It's love, Mike."

"No. I don't know what it is. But it's not love."

I lay back against my headboard. "I've done everything else. And all of it sucked. Hating him was betraying myself. Being angry distracted me. Plotting took all my time. Desperation consumed me. But listening to him even when I don't understand it, trusting him when he says his heart has told him this instead of telling him he's stupid and broken and horrible... I can finally breathe. Maybe it doesn't look like love to you, but it feels a hell of a lot easier than what I was doing before."

I'm hanging on to that reasoning like a life preserver. Without it, I know I'll drown.

"What about Robbie?" Mike asks.

"We'll figure it out."

"What about Andre? Gabe's not safe out there by himself."

"I sent Paul to look out for him for now. Longer term, I'll figure something out."

"I'll go."

I give him a questioning look.

"Longer term. He needs protection, Wen. It's not that I don't trust your guys, but Gabe is probably going to give them problems. He always thinks he's invincible. I not only know him, but I can keep track of him better than anyone. And you know I'm capable. Plus, maybe you've given up, but I haven't."

"Mike... I don't want you harassing him. He needs healing."

"I won't. I swear to you. But if I'm with him and not you, it will tell him exactly where I stand. I won't have to say a thing."

I bite my bottom lip.

"Wen," Mike says, irritated, "I'll lay off of him, just like you want. I'll respect your decision in that. But on this, you don't get a say. He's my brother. I can follow him wherever the hell I want. I don't need your permission."

I lift my eyebrows.

"It's settled then," Mike says, crossing his arms and spreading his feet in a stance I haven't seen him use toward me in while.

"I guess so," I reply, and I have to admit, I feel better having Mike with him as well. Not just because Mike is the best at protection, but because I see a lot of lonely nights ahead for me. I'd prefer to stay lonely over using Mike as a crutch. I need to survive. I need to heal. From all of this. On my own.

ℵ

I catch Dan alone in the kitchen once I venture out for breakfast. "Good morning, Wendy," he says, stirring creamer into his coffee.

"Hi," I say, looking through the pantry and seeing nothing I want. I think the problem is I'm not actually hungry. I just came in here because… breakfast is what you do when you wake up. I'd leave except Dan is still in here, and he'll figure out that I'm wandering around without a purpose.

I snag the bread, thinking I can probably handle shoving down some toast.

"I looked into that investment recommendation from your lawyer," Dan says. I always find the slight French lilt of his voice soothing.

"What did you think?" I say, pressing the lever down on the toaster.

"It doesn't matter what I *think*," he says, taking a seat at the island. "I can tell you that the i's are all dotted and the t's are crossed as far as legality is concerned. The real question is, where do you see the state of the world in six months? Worse, better, or the same as it is right now?"

The first thing that comes to me is the prophecy, which would indicate the answer is worse. But do I believe the prophecy or not? Does it matter if I do? Will my belief change anything? Or does asking myself these impossible questions constitute trying to 'outthink' the future? I know that never works, but I still have to *do* something. I sigh. "I have no idea. But I trust my uncle, and he bought this place before he died. Even laid plans for the solar farm, irrigation, the warehouse… So I guess I'd lean toward hell in a handbasket."

"Then focus on putting your money into physical assets rather than securities. Land, equipment, textiles, energy. Invest as if currency will become meaningless."

I nod. "Thanks for the advice."

"You're welcome," he says. I expect him to retreat now. He's not one to invite drama or to stick his nose in it unless he's forced to, and I'm pretty sure Gabriel broke the news to at least his dad already. I couldn't help hearing Gabriel after he left my room last night. He asked his dad for a private word, but I didn't listen after that.

"I have recently acquired some information you might find interesting," Dan says. "I'm not sure what to do with it myself, who to share it with, but you seem like the most logical person to be able to make use of it. It may shed a little more light on Gabe and Mike's connection—or it may make things more complicated. I suppose it depends on how you choose to take it. Are you interested?"

I turn around with a piece of toast in my hand, considering it. What information could he possibly have about their connection that I don't already know? Last I checked I was the only one able to even *see* their connection. Well, at least he's not offering me advice...

"I guess so," I reply.

He nods. "I'm not sure if you are aware of this, seeing as we don't talk a whole lot, but Gabe inherited his inquisitiveness about the world from me. I have a great many interests as a result. So when I learned that Mike and Gabe shared a one-way mirror due to a life force strand donation, I wanted to learn what I could. I don't see the things you do and likely never will, but I do have an understanding of genetics. I made it one of my interests when Gabe was diagnosed with Spinal Muscular Atrophy as an infant.

"I took a sample of Gabe and Mike's DNA after Mike told me what you explained about his life force. Mostly out of curiosity. But I think you'll find what I learned rather shocking. First, I know you are aware that Mike and Gabriel are technically first cousins rather than siblings. In an ordinary scenario, first cousins share around twelve percent of their DNA. That can get as high as fourteen percent, but that's the upper range. Siblings, however, who have the same parents, share around fifty percent. Gabe and Mike, I have learned, share fifty-six percent of their DNA."

My mouth falls open. They're genetically related even more than brothers?

"Curious, I went a bit further, took samples from Maris and myself. Mike is still around twenty-five percent related to Maris, which is in normal range for a nephew-aunt relationship. He is also, as expected, not biologically related to me at all. Gabe, however, as our biological son, ought to share fifty percent of his DNA with each of us, give or take a couple percentage points. However, tests show he is only thirty-seven percent genetically related to Maris and twenty-seven percent genetically related to me."

My hand came up to my cheek at some point, and I am speechless.

"Given the evidence, it appears that Gabriel's DNA has altered itself to align more with Mike's. There is no other biological scenario in existence to explain that kind of relation, with those kinds of percentages. He was tested after he recovered from SMA and his genes no longer carried the SMN1 mutation despite previous tests that diagnosed him. I pulled his old genetic profile, taken when he was an infant, and none of it matched his current profile. His DNA has mutated drastically. That much is clear."

I rub my cheek now, amazed, although I suppose I shouldn't be. Gabriel *told* me that after he recovered from SMA, he no longer tested as positive. That meant something in his genes changed. "So Mike's strands altered Gabriel's DNA beyond simply the SMA," I say. I pull myself up to sit on the counter, totally lost now in pondering what it means. "It's logical when considering the fact that Gabriel took on nineteen *billion* life force strands. That's something like a sixty percent increase in the original number of strands."

"Mmm, yes," Dan agrees. "And not to disturb you further, but to put into perspective just how much change we're talking about, it's worth knowing that SMA is caused by *one* protein-coding gene. There are somewhere in the neighborhood of twenty thousand of those, but those twenty-thousand represent only one and a half percent of the entire human genome. We have no idea what most of the human genome biologically does though. Gabe's genome has drastically changed, *far* beyond repairing his survival motor neuron gene. Since he was so young when it occurred, I have no clear before and after picture other than genetically. I couldn't begin to describe the myriad of ways such a dramatic mutation would have affected him and his development. Genes are illusive and mysterious even in normal circumstances."

"Well… my first conclusion is that abilities must be DNA driven. But DNA itself is actually life force driven…"

"They are interwoven, it sounds like," Dan says.

I think about it for a while, and I begin to somewhat grasp the DNA-life force relationship, but I can only go so far. It's going to take me a while to nail down how exactly it impacts the situation with Gabriel and Mike. And at this point I'm so exhausted over the whole thing that I need to take a step back for a while.

I sigh and shake my head. "You've got something, that's for sure."

"Do you believe I should share it with the other two people involved?" he asks.

My gut reaction is no. Gabriel will take this information and find some way to use it, some way to convince me he needs to shed Mike's strands. I'm not ready for that argument. But I also hate the idea of keeping things from him.

I snort softly. That's something I would think I owed him because we're married. But we're not anymore. At least not in any way but on paper. I don't owe him anything. And vice versa.

"Dan," I say, looking at him directly finally, "that's not my call to make. Gabriel and I are separated. He is leaving. Since you're the one that sought out the information and discovered it, I'd say it's up to you to decide what to do with it. I'm out of it." I hold my hands up for emphasis.

Dan doesn't seem surprised by my announcement, so I think I'm right and he already knows. "You're right," he says. "I apologize for trying to put it on you. I guess I'm afraid to make the decision myself."

Knowing that struggle, I slump, hands clasped between my knees as I look down at the floor.

I hear Dan get up, but I don't hear him leave.

"Wendy?" he says after a few moments.

I look up.

His brow furrows. "For all of his life, I have believed without proper reason or evidence or authority that Gabe is no ordinary man. And I don't mean that in the typical, cliche meaning."

I stare at him. "I know," I whisper.

He nods. "Gabe loves to claim that his decisions are always based on logic, but he neglects that logic itself is highly subjective. It is a slave to observation and perception. Although the spheres of our experience cross in a myriad of ways, allowing us to adequately relate to one another, the reality one person experiences will never compare in exactness to that of another. We are, essentially, walking around in our own self-made reality. But Gabe's reality falls somewhere even further outside the normal derivations. He has a sense, an awareness of the world around us that the rest of us don't have. He is like you in that way: seeing the world through lenses of a different color. I don't think he can articulate it, doesn't even recognize let alone acknowledge it, but I know he does act on it. He may be here, in this world with the rest of us, but he is really there, in that place that the rest of us can't see. Unlike you, he can't step out of it and see the world as the rest of us do."

I bite my lip, an inexplicable understanding trickling over me. He's hit the nail on the head. I have seen and felt what he describes, but I have never been able to put it into words like that.

"Knowing what I know about first his life force and then his biology now," Dan says, picking up his mug, "I have a solid reason for what I see in him, and I find myself more capable of trusting that his actions are based on more than simply... arbitrary facts. I find myself more forgiving of the things I don't understand."

He walks out without another word, and I slip off the counter, my conversation with Mike this morning coming back to me. I've been fighting so long for Gabriel, and felt nothing but resistance. Sometimes, no matter how you explain something to someone, they are simply not capable of understanding, because like Dan said, what we see are two different things. Words do fail. And in our case, even actions have. There is nothing to do or say or demonstrate anymore. Gabriel is somewhere unreachable. The only thing left for me to do is accept him, exactly as he is. I can yield. I can surrender. I can love him, maybe not with action, but like water. Water can reach places that other things can't. And maybe, if I'm water, I can reach Gabriel in his reality.

It's easier said than done though, mostly because control is a hard thing for me to let go of completely. I pull the dishwasher open to empty it, trying to imagine myself as an incorporeal being, relenting to whatever is thrown my way. Hopefully all it takes is practice.

Carl walks in, holding Robbie. He makes a beeline for the coffee maker, and I pull a mug out of the dishwasher and slide it his way.

"Thank you," he says. "How are you this morning? Did you sleep well?"

I lean over and kiss Robbie on the forehead, formulating a response, but after being straight with Dan, I feel more confident that I can break the news to people without falling apart each time.

"Crappy," I reply, building a stack of clean plates. "Gabriel and I agreed to separate yesterday. He's leaving. So I didn't get much sleep."

Carl doesn't respond immediately, so I say, "I don't want to talk about it. I'm telling you so you don't have to wonder."

Carl takes a pensive sip of his coffee. "Is there anything I can do? To help you cope?"

"Yeah. Help me use water to go into the colorworld." I pause with the cabinet door open. "I need to accomplish something today."

"The usual time?"

I shut the cabinet, decisive suddenly. "No. Now, if possible. Before people start looking at me pityingly. Before the girls start interrogating me about the separation. Before Maris loses her ability to speak English to me. Before Ezra starts freaking out... Right now I'm calm. I feel good about it, at least relative to how I've *been* feeling."

"I understand," Carl says. "And by the way, yesterday I went into town and bought an extra heater. It should be warmer today. I knew you were probably too busy."

I look at him, that small gesture sinking like warmth into my cold bones. I step forward and hug him and Robbie both. "Thanks, Dad."

"No problem," he says, but I can tell it pleases him. "Robbie and I will head on over and wait for you... He's such a contented baby. Maybe his quiet influence will help you." He smiles.

"Maybe," I say, bounding out of the kitchen.

Within ten minutes I'm in the pool—which *is* slightly warmer than yesterday—and Carl is sitting on the edge, holding Robbie. I'm more convinced each day that Robbie's an empath like me, and he's quiet and calm because Carl is.

"I've been thinking a lot about your inability to clear your mind," Carl says before I lay back in the water. "I realize there are a lot of external factors preventing you from focusing. So instead of fighting that again, we'll try something different. Instead of relaxing, I want you to embrace emotion, which I believe you're good at managing. Despite feeling what others feel, you don't often allow it to overwhelm you. You are able to separate yourself from it. Likewise, you can draw it into you. This entire exercise is about control, and we are driven by emotion. So this time, I want you to control your mind by controlling what you feel. Find something that pulls a strong emotion forward and hang on to that feeling. Raise your hand out of the water when you've got it, and I'll prompt you what to do next."

I push off into the middle of the pool like usual. I lay back to float and close my eyes, wondering what's going to be the easiest thing to feel right now. With everything happening between Gabriel and me, I'm naturally drawn back to the last time we were separated. It was when I couldn't touch people—or believed I couldn't. Gabriel threatened to make himself the guinea pig, to touch me as a way to prove his theory—that only bad people were in danger from my skin. To me there wasn't enough evidence of that. It was too much of a risk. So I left him because he left me no choice.

I was a different person then. Afraid. That's the main emotion I associate with that time period. And I had been looking for a reason to run ever since I had met him anyway. Gabriel couldn't possibly be who he seemed... so it was all a mistake. As a result I missed all of the signs that were pointing me to him, trying to bring us back together. Instead, because I was looking for it, everything seemed like it was working against me, conspiring to torture me.

A sliver of that sensation touches my soul suddenly, like a ray of light piercing my being. Gravity takes effect, pulling more details into a memory that has gone fuzzy. I was in front of the mirror in our hotel room in San Francisco, and it was right after Gabriel and I had not only reunited but had touched for the first time. Finally. And I was standing there, in awe over the events of my life, which suddenly looked dramatically different now that I was on the other side of them. *I* looked completely different. The change was almost incomprehensible. Impossibility had become possible right before my eyes and deep down inside of me.

Oh how similar circumstances are now... All of these unknown, unanswerable questions. All of these things that have pointed Gabriel away from me. It's a repeating cycle...

I laugh, suddenly empowered by this realization. I'm exhilarated by it, and I exhale, feeling myself open up fully, pushing out darkness and letting in the light. I am fearless. I don't fear today, tomorrow, or any moment that will follow. This is going somewhere, and even though I have no clue where, I *know* it is. Every bit of it is going to make sense. This is orchestrated. I've seen Mike's colorworld. Everything is moving, cycling, changing. *Becoming.* Every molecule of the earth is doing it under the influence of a trillion molecules around it. And I am no different. *We* are no different. We are woven *into* that reality. Not apart from it. When we resist the path, we are fighting the forces around us. And we are grossly outnumbered. I'm done fighting on the losing side. Instead I'm going to see where reality takes me. Just like water.

Inhaling invincibility, and remembering what I'm supposed to be doing, I lift my hand for Carl, but the action feels odd. Disembodied would be my first descriptor. I don't perceive my body. I feel the sensation of leaving my stomach behind, but less jarring and more constant.

I open my eyes instinctively. Above me and around me is a swirling mist, curling and bending and burgeoning, folding in on itself and pushing outward all at the same time. It's a mesmerizing dance of chaos. Colorless. Devoid of permanence. Devoid of purposeful direction.

Confusion and fear make a grab for me, but I hold them in reserve. If I didn't have so much experience visiting the alternate and often overwhelming reality of the colorworld, I would probably be terrified. Everywhere I turn is the churning mist, and none of it has any sensical form.

And then it hits me suddenly; I've done it. Holy cow. *This* is the colorworld without touching a life force? But there's no color at all! It's water vapor. Nothing but water…

"Wendy?" Carl says, but I ignore him because I can finally make things out: the house, a couple trees, the pool chairs. But it's not these objects I actually see; it's their outlines as the mist envelops them.

My eyes are drawn down, to the water of the pool itself. It's doing what the sky was doing but with far more solidity. Not like a mist, but exactly like it is: water. Only I can see its movement in more detail: spiraling in on itself while simultaneously dispersing outward. It's churning. At one depth it's moving one way, while above and below it's moving another. Frictionless. Fluidity in perfect, unhindered disorganization.

I don't see the cement walls or floor of the pool. I see the *shape* of the pool, because the water has conformed to it. Beyond the pool… in the ground? I see water there, but it's almost static, creeping at a snail's pace. Now that I'm looking harder, things are taking shape, gaining depth. I examine one of the trees again. It's the shape of one, except unlike the house, the movement of water is happening within as well as without, but at different speeds and patterns and paths. Veins of water creep upward and downward, and within the leaves the water whirls slowly, sometimes escaping into the vapor coiling around the tree.

The dimensions of this world are limited to the characteristics of water. The solidity of anything here is only apparent by its impression on surrounding water, which is bent on continually finding entry into every available nook and crevice. It's relentless. Pervasive.

The nature of it's transparency allows me to see *through* things, as long as I'm trying. Like looking *into* the tree. Like seeing past the walls of the house. The plumbing system is entirely visible. Within the house are people. And each person is a ridiculously detailed circuitry of water. The shape of the pathways are what enable me to make out the shape of organs, although the sheer number of veins reminds me of when I saw Louise die in the colorworld from my channeling touch. Her entire vascular system was lit up for a short second. Here though, I can stare at every bit of its intricacy as long as I want. It's marvelous.

Water. It's absolutely everywhere. In the colorworld, water is absolutely invisible. Here, everything *else* is invisible. This is the *inverse* of the colorworld.

"Holy. Crap," I say to Carl, whose water form is nearby, holding Robbie's water form.

"You did it," Carl marvels, and from his mouth emanates more mist and chaos, as if he's a water-spewing dragon.

I'm totally dumfounded. I hold my hands up, slightly horrified at how impermanent they look. "This isn't the colorworld, Dad," I say, a cloud of vapor spiraling out of me as I speak. "This is the waterworld."

Seventy-Six

*O*ver the next few days I am dedicated to mastering entry into the waterworld rather than analyzing the usefulness of the place itself. It's getting colder every day, so I can't be dependent on the pool. It doesn't come to me nearly as easily as the colorworld, and for a couple of days I can't do it outside of the pool.

It requires two things: A floaty impermanence gained by letting go of anything solid. Suspension in the water achieves this. The second thing is not just *actual* buoyancy, but mental buoyancy. So far that means immersing myself into moments I've had in my life where I've felt bulletproof. Pretty soon though, I'll become emotion-blind to my own memories, having delved into them too often to manufacture old feelings.

I'm hoping to get to the point where I can blink my eyes and go there, just like I do the colorworld. But four days in, even in my large tub, the difficulty remains. The waterworld is going to fight me each time. Figures. The place is not nearly as orderly and beautiful as the colorworld. To me, the waterworld is the skeleton of the colorworld. It's always been there, covered up by the more beautiful 'flesh' of colors and lights. It's creepy like a skeleton, too. Skeletons sort of take away the mysterious beauty of the human body by appearing so practical and mechanical. The waterworld, likewise, has stolen some of the colorworld's majesty. Going back and forth, I now can't look at the colorworld without mentally superimposing the forces of the waterworld on it.

That's why I am committed to cracking it. It's the missing link. It's the element upon which the colorworld is dependent.

The waterworld is trickier to leave as well. I have to be out of the water, for one thing, and I have to close my eyes and grab something solid, imagining the physical properties of the thing until it materializes. I can't unfocus my eyes there in order to see the normal world either. Once there, I'm stuck there until

I work to get out of it—or until I touch someone. Because I also can't channel it. If I touch someone while there, (so far I've only tried Carl and Robbie), I get yanked into the colorworld, which is actually the easiest way to leave the waterworld. It's a stubborn place, all the way around. So I tend to think of it as a entity rather than a place, and sometimes I even wonder if it's sentient. And I'm far less hard on myself for taking so long to figure out how to access it to begin with. It's a miracle I managed it at all.

Carl, on the other hand, is baffled by my difficulty. He finds the fluid nature of the waterworld comforting, and he describes it as a guilty pleasure to spend time there.

I don't get it. I guess it's a difference in personality. But I'm hell-bent on dominating it, one way or another. So I work every day, most of the day, training myself to go in and go out. I've been freaking everyone out a little, having not explained to anyone what I'm doing, while spending so many hours floating in the pool and then more hours locked in the bathroom. I'm getting better, but I have to start off each day in the pool to remind myself of the exact sensation of physical buoyancy in order to revisit it later in the tub.

On day five, I finally manage to access the waterworld with nothing but a sink full of water. I cheer and dance around the bathroom until a knock sounds at the door.

I fling it open, a wide grin on my face, ready to yank whoever it is in to celebrate with me. It's Gabriel, and I beam more widely, because I can actually tell him about it, and he'll surely appreciate my accomplishment. "I did it!" I gush, putting my hands on his arms and shaking him. "I freaking did it!"

I spin around, jump onto the edge of the tub and strike a superhero pose. "I.. am the master… of *all* worlds," I boom. "I made the waterworld my friggin' we-otch."

I know he doesn't know what I'm talking about, and I'm about to explain myself when I remember our circumstances… I forgot. And then it occurs to me that the sight of him didn't cause a single twinge of difficult emotion. I'm acting like everything is completely normal between us. It surprises me. *Shouldn't* I feel something?

"Congratulations?" Gabriel says, curiously baffled but genuinely pleased to see me so upbeat. "This has to do with your obsession with being in water lately? We've been theorizing that you might be willing yourself to become a mermaid."

I laugh, happy, hopeful, and victorious, and, to my satisfaction, still convinced as I was days ago when I first viewed the waterworld, that things between Gabriel and me are going to work out somehow. This is just... a hiccup. I haven't been face-to-face with him in days, but there is no one I'd rather live up this achievement with than him. I leap off the tub and throw my arms around him, causing him to stumble backward and into the bedroom. I ignore his shock as well as his discomfort while he hugs me back with not nearly as much gusto.

I let go of him and kick the door shut, plopping on my bed, bouncing. What has come over me? I don't know. And I don't care. "The waterworld," I explain quietly, "is the inverse of the colorworld."

"Waterworld..." he says, leaning against the dresser, becoming far more curious than uncomfortable with being in my room alone with me. "Water is invisible in the colorworld... But it influences the forces there. So you must be seeing water, but in greater detail than you do here...?"

I clap my hands. "Yes! It's nothing *but* water. It's the water in your body, the tiniest concentration of water in the floors and the walls, in trees and grass. In the air. Everything else there is invisible. It's exactly what the name means. Water. Everywhere. In everything."

His eyebrows lift in amazement. "That is... *most* intriguing." He leaps into analysis, then shakes his head in wonder. "The possibilities..."

"I know!" I gush. "Carl told me about it. Taught me how to access it. But it's *way* harder. That's what I've been doing for days."

"Fascinating..."

"But," I say, suddenly serious, "don't mention it to anyone else. I don't want it getting back to the Guild. I doubt they know anything about it and I want it to stay that way. So if anyone asks, just tell them I've been working on accessing the colorworld without a subject. That's basically what I thought I was doing, but once I saw it, I knew it was definitely not the colorworld I was dealing with. Carl just sees the colorworld in such poor detail..."

"Of course," Gabriel says. "What a find! Heavens, I forgot for a moment why I came here looking for you. Ezra is ready to present his findings."

I jump off the bed. "Seriously?"

He nods. "Yes, it would appear that Carl has been extremely helpful to both of you."

I clasp my hands together again. "This day is epic. Would it freak you out too much if I hugged you again? Sorry about not asking earlier. I just have all this energy and it's making me act crazy!"

His brow lifts again. "Your excitement is rather infectious, so I think I could handle that. But would you mind answering a question honestly first?"

"Anything," I reply.

"Are you on any mood-altering drugs? Recreational? Prescribed?"

I laugh again, unsurprised by his question. I'd wonder myself. I *do* wonder. "Definitely not," I say. "It might be that I've spent the last five days meticulously reliving only the most enlightening and happiest memories I have in order to access the waterworld. That's a lot of positivity to dwell on. Kinda leaks out." I smile at him.

"Oh…" he says. "I admit I was worried. The reclusive behavior…"

"Hold on," I say suddenly, eyes widening. I dart back into the bathroom, thrust my hand into the sink of water again. This levity I'm experiencing is the perfect emotional medium to try again.

I focus on the sensation of my hand, even stirring the water a little to increase it's movement against my skin—I've found that helps.

"Bam," I say, triumphant as the liquid reality meets my eyes faster than ever before. "Personal best," I say to Gabriel's alien water form in the doorway. "I think real-time emotions work *way* better than remembered ones."

He takes a step back, intimidated. "My word, your eyes…"

I instinctively turn to the mirror, but of course I can't see it here. "What?" I say.

"They're black…" he says. "Not *actually* black. It's just how dilated your irises are. I didn't know they could do that." He shudders. "You look a little vampiric, Love." Then he catches himself, sucking in a breath. "Apologies," he says, immediately guilty. "I didn't mean to… I got caught up…"

"Stop rambling," I say. "It's fine. We have an extensive history. It's bound to come out. Not like you can erase it." Then I bare my teeth at him, playing on my 'vampiric' appearance.

It works because his water form flinches. "El cielo, I can't think of a more descriptive word for that than 'creepy.'"

I giggle. "Okay, time to see what Ezra's got. Can I get that hug now? Touching someone is the easiest way to leave."

This time he approaches *me*. He wraps his arms around

me and sighs, pulling me into the colorworld, and subsequently himself there as well. That means he gets to feel what I do the same as I do him. "Congratulations on making the waterworld your personal playground," he says, unable to resist inhaling the clean smell of the colorworld. Smells are powerful here, and I know mine is having an effect on him. As soon as he recognizes it, he lets me go, which thrusts both of us out of the colorworld.

"I can't channel it," I say. "The water world is a miserly old man, set in his ways. Things always have to be just so."

Gabriel stares at me, and I can feel his emotions for me building. "Happiness becomes you," he says softly. "Seeing it on you brings me such comfort after such a stressful week."

"And you?" I say, tilting my head questioningly.

"Coping."

I put a hand on his shoulder. "It will be okay. You can handle this. You can handle anything. I believe in you."

He's confused by the gesture, by my words, by my attitude, as I would expect.

"So. Ezra?" I say. "I'm dying to find out how all your hard work has paid off."

He returns to himself, leads the way out of the room. "Carl," he says as we walk down the hall toward the common room separating the wings. "He seemed to know Ezra was holding himself back. Pushed him to accept things he was seeing intuitively. Ezra was having trouble trusting them because he didn't have the mathematical language to back them up. He'd been pigeon-holing himself for weeks, developing all these new equations and variables to explain things. Carl convinced him there wasn't time to do all that. They got into quite a row, but Carl didn't back down. Reminded me of you, actually. And Ezra saw it, too. Seeing Carl behave in such a familiar, trust-your-instincts way that Ezra's come to appreciate in you gave him the courage to place the bet. The result... Well, you're about to see it."

We emerge into the common room, and both doors to the lab are blocked. Louis catches sight of us and motions for the people further inside to make way.

"Coming through," I announce, squeezing in between Darren and Jessie. Looks like the entire household is present, which is probably a good thing. "Man, did Skimpy Swimsuit Sunday get moved into here? Or have you all just missed me that much?"

"Wen, finally," Ezra says, standing near the head of the long table in the room, upon which are piles of open books, stacks of papers, and two laptop computers.

I wave to the room. "Nobody panic. I have arrived." I turn to Ezra. "Commence mind-blowing announcement."

He gives me an open-mouthed questioning look.

"On screen," I order impatiently, catching Mike's eye. He's standing in a corner near the giant screen.

Ezra gives up, turns around, punches a key on the main computer, and a map of the world appears, similar to the one on the wall.

"Red lines are fault lines. Blue lines are oceanic currents," Ezra says, arms crossed, staring at the map. "Yellow are atmospheric or meteorological. Green are other significant geological formations. That's the simple stuff. But our findings took into account a host of other variables, and not just on earth: temperature variances... electromagnetic pulses... magnetic fields... lunar movement... heliophysical events..." He counts them off on his fingers. "Of course none of you care about any of that, but I'm saying it because it sounds fancy and it shows we covered all the bases."

He turns around to face everyone and sits on the edge of the table. "The orange bursts you'll see are the disasters, and their size is determined by their scope. Before we even start, here's revelation number one." He gives Roe a look. "I had Roe tell the Guild three weeks ago that they hadn't given me all the data. I could tell something was missing. *They* denied it. Repeatedly. So I drew them a nice little map, showed them exactly what was missing, and told them they could either send me all the numbers or I would send the map out into the cyberworld for the media sharks to pick apart." He breathes on his knuckles and polishes them. "That got their attention."

"Aww, you threatened the Guild?" I say. "I'm so proud! I guess I've done something right."

"Eet vas not ze blackmail that moved them," Roe interjects from where she sits off to the side. "Zey were impressed with your skill and vanted to see vat more you could do."

"What did they leave out?" Darren asks.

"Ze Guild hass been diminishing or preventing many disasters," Roe says. "Even though zey did not happen, Eezra saw gaps in ze progression. He vas able to tell zem approximations of vhat vas missing."

"They've been *preventing* disasters?" Jessie says, awestruck.

"Yes," Roe replies. "However, zis is best kept classified. Most disaster prevention technology is in experimental or prototype phases. Ze Guild cannot accommodate 'requests' if zat meks sense. Zere are still many problems associated with prevention technology."

Ezra frowns at Roe. "Says you." Then to the rest of us, "Back on track, purple bursts are the missing disasters."

"Why do missing ones matter?" I ask.

"Good question," Ezra says, widening his eyes expectantly and turning toward Roe with an exaggerated motion. "I'd like to know, too. Why did they pick the ones they did?"

Roe draws the corner of her mouth in and narrows her eyes at him.

"What kind of disasters have they been preventing?" I ask.

"Freaktastic stuff," Ezra replies. "They seem to be focused lately on earthquakes. Before that it was volcanic eruptions. Tectonics. But they've just started venturing into changing weather patterns."

I cross my arms. "Whoa."

"Alright," he says, rubbing his hands together. "Ready? FYI, this is time-progressed. One second equals about two weeks. The start date is four years ago, but for the record, I think this has been progressing a lot longer than that. I still want to calculate that, but I ran out of time this round."

He reaches forward and punches a key.

It's like a small fireworks display at first, orange bursts with the rare purple burst thrown in. The fault lines glow brighter from time to time, creating a smattering of orange. Blue current lines sway in continuity with other yellow atmospheric lines. I'm most impressed with how much the variables move like a dance, responding to and influencing each other. It reminds me of Mike's colorworld. There's so much to see going on though that I don't notice a particular pattern except the gradual increase in the prevalence and scope of disasters. Purple bursts also begin to happen more frequently. The lines don't mean much to me except that they criss-cross disaster areas, and I wonder if it's the convergence of these hot zones that initiates a disaster.

The background of the map, which has been black until now, flashes to white, and Ezra punches a key to stop the simulation. He turns around.

"Everything you saw has already happened—or was supposed to. It was at this point that I began to see a pattern. A direction? I don't know what you'd call it. But there's a definite outcome to this thing. An end-point."

"An end-point?" I say. "What—"

He punches a key.

The screen lights up again. Orange bursts of varying sizes all over the place, like pin-pricks on the map. It's a light show, growing in magnitude as it reaches the climax. One after another, fault lines grow red like infected cuts. Blue lines shift direction with yellow lines. And then the red lines *move.* One near the Caribbean begins to converge with another. And that's when I realize that the shape of the land masses have changed. Florida and the Caribbean have disappeared. I'm staring at the empty space in shock for far too long and getting distracted by the chaos of blue and yellow lines, because when I finally look elsewhere on the map, the collection of faults in Asia have grown active. The Eurasian islands disappear. And that seems to create a domino effect. The fault running along the west coast lights up with a string of orange bursts, and then it eats a portion of California. And then half of Mexico. They just... dissolve.

No one speaks. No one can tear their eyes away as the massacre of continents continues in earnest over the next ten minutes. New faults form as plates get sheared every which way. With all the action, I don't at first notice that the continents have begun creeping toward each other as their shapes are remade. The Atlantic ocean shrinks smaller and smaller until Africa collides with South America and Antarctica; the Pacific brings North America to China; and Australia gets pulled into the tip of Africa.

My mouth is open in shock.

"Pangaea?" Mike says, aghast.

"How can you possibly tell that?" Darren says.

"Actually," Ezra says, turning around to look at the new map, "I call it Novapangaea, not to be confused with *Novo*pangaea—which is someone else's configuration for the world in ten million years or so. But anyway, yeah, it's a supercontinent like Pangaea."

"I thought you were *deconstructing* the disasters, finding the source," I say quickly, totally shocked. "But this is a prediction. I thought the Guild could already do that with the Grid technology."

"Well, well, another good question," Ezra says, crossing his arms and drumming his fingers on his biceps. He looks deliberately at Roe again. "Turns out, either the Guild *isn't* as good as everyone thinks, or they're a bunch of big, fat, liars." He shrugs and looks at the screen again. "I'd say a little of both though."

"Tell them how you've arrived at this," Carl urges.

Ezra glances at him, thankfully not with animosity, and then leans against the table again. "Once I'd mapped everything that had *already* happened, I saw Novapangaea right off the bat. It was just... the movement of the disaster points over the globe that hinted at it. I can't explain that part to you. But I figured, 'if I'm right about this thing, then there's other evidence of it happening. The most obvious evidence would be continental shift. And bingo. I was right. North America and Europe, for example, in the last two years, have moved apart about ten feet. Doesn't seem like much, I know. But contrast that the 'normal' one inch per year. That kind of discrepancy basically renders the data from historical cycles completely useless. These things usually take millions of years. By my estimation, it's going to happen within a decade."

"Supercontinent..." I say, letting the size of that idea settle over me.

"Directionally speaking," Ezra says, "every bit of continental shift I found record of supports Novapangaea as you see it here."

"Ezra has made the Grid obsolete," Carl says, and the pride in his voice is evident. "Using Novapangaea, he has reverse-engineered the map, plotted out all of the major impact disasters that will occur, and in the last month, has watched his predictions come true. He's proven Novapangaea's viability by testing its data output against the Guild's."

"Using the specs of the supercontinent to plot the disasters to test it was actually Carl's idea," Ezra says, visibly embarrassed by the praise. "I got caught up in trying to prove Novapangaea deductively. That's what took me so long."

If I weren't in total shock over what to *do* about this information, I'd pat myself on the back for forcing Ezra to work with Carl. But this is truly incredible. I find a seat, plop down and put my chin in my hand. How have I never known Ezra was this capable? "How," I say. "How does the Guild have ten thousand Prime Humans and hasn't figured this out?"

Roe sighs. "First of all, contrary to your belief, ze Guild does *not* have unlimited resources. Zey must prioritize jus' as you do. Zeir priorities are precise prediction, targeted disaster alleviation, and humanitarian aid advancement. Ze end vas predicted long ago. Eezra jus' defined it. Zat is all."

"It was predicted?" Gabriel says.

"She's talking about the prophecy," Mike replies. "Made by Sam Pruitt in the early days. Predicts the end of the world happening in a lifetime."

"It's why the Guild was founded," I say. "Which is why it doesn't make sense that the Guild wouldn't want to know exactly what they are up against. If they're actually *preventing* disasters, looking at a map like this could help them target strategically— have the most impact."

Roe huffs impatiently. "First of all, Eezra's intuition about ze end-point vas not supported by nearly enough data. He might as vell hev picked it out of a hat. I do not understand how he vas able to see vat he did. If ze Guild vas able to do ze same et any point, zey could have made disaster predictions in ze same way, rather than relying on forward Grid predictions."

Ezra clears his throat and says, "Point is, so far this model has worked, and I feel comfortable using it as a point of support for the next part, which is figuring out what the actual cause is. This supercontinent formation is happening at an insane speed. So fast, in fact, that I'm convinced we can rule out any sort of geological evolution."

"So you agree that someone is causing it," I say.

"Yes. Look behind me at the map. What do you see?" he says.

"*Not* something that one person could cause," I say.

"It's way too big," Darren says.

"Something that would take god-like skill to accomplish," Mike adds.

"If this is the end-point, it's not just about causing chaos," I say. "That makes this a *way* more dangerous problem. If there is actually someone out there capable of doing this...? Like whoa."

"Like mother-effing whoa," Letty says.

"It'd have to be a group," Ezra says, nodding.

"A really *smart* group," I say.

"Yeah, with a very specific set of necessary skills," Ezra says. "Basically, mad crazy knowledge about how the natural world works. You'd have to be the top expert in geology, meteorology, oceanography, tectonics. And that's what's necessary to even *begin* to have the knowledge of where to hit in order to initiate and accelerate this kind of continental shift. The hows... that's a totally different problem. I don't know what the hell kind of skills you'd need. Telekinesis *way* beyond anything Kaylen ever did. Or maybe some sort of crazy mining technology allowing you to travel to the edge of the earth's crust and screw with plates. Screw with magnetic fields... the orbit of the moon. There are a lot of possibilities. At this point, I couldn't tell you exactly how it's being done, only that it is."

"The Guild," I say. "Which is why they claim ignorance about the supercontinent idea."

"Unless it actually *is* God," someone says, and I look to see that it's Louis. "I understand you guys want to find someone to blame for this," he says. "But Mike D just said, it takes god-like ability. Even the Guild doesn't have that."

"Sí!" Maris pipes up, somewhere behind me. "The end of the world has been prophesied in scripture, through His holy prophets since the beginning of the world."

I hear Gabriel groan.

"Gabriel Daniel Dumas!" Maris snaps. "You have evidence right in front of you that this is far too big of a problem for the hands of men to have accomplished. What more evidence do you need? There is obviously nothing that can be done, so you'd be better served dedicating your time to easing the suffering that will follow the destruction of—"

"God?!" Gabriel says. "Mamá, the formation of a supercontinent over the course of a decade is an extinction-level event! You're not talking about destruction of the wicked! You're talking about the destruction of ninety-five percent of the earth's population, *if we're lucky.* If that's the doing of some divine being, they bloody deserve to be in that hell they so pompously created!"

Maris makes a cry of outrage.

"Alright!" I say, holding my hands up and turning toward the group. This is about to go nowhere fast, and I know Maris isn't the only religious person in the room. "We are *not* going to go there. We're just not. No. An argument about whether this is God's doing is actually irrelevant. If you are in the camp that believes it's God, and that helps you sleep at night, awesome. It also means you have no dog in this fight against the elements or even against the people trying to stop it, so you can go about your business. Be my guest. I won't judge you, but let the rest of us do what our conscience dictates. If you're right, however, and we're destined for death, I personally would rather go out fighting anyway. So it should be all the same to you, therefore we're going to stick to non-religious discussions. Thank you!"

Maris harrumphs and clicks out of the room, but everyone else stays.

I turn back around. "Where were we?"

"Why would the Guild want Pangaea—I mean *Nova*pangaea?" Mike says.

"That's easy," Carl says. "For one, a centralized population is easier to control. Second, if they know how this will progress, they can preserve Prime Humans while simultaneously eradicating Humans."

"Ze Guild is *not* interested in zee eradication of Humans!" Roe says indignantly.

"That leads me to the purple bursts," Ezra says, ignoring Roe's scene. "Now the Guild *claims* that the disasters they've prevented have been chosen based on their perceived population threat and their ability to actually *prevent* them in those particular circumstances. Lots of variables, blah, blah, blah. They can't possibly police *every* disaster, so they have to pick and choose. That's the claim. But the interesting thing about the prevented disasters is they have a way of feeding other events elsewhere, as if the 'prevention' was the trigger for something else. A lot of times it's causing groups of disasters, a bunch of simultaneous tornadoes in different places or a bunch of mini-quakes. It's like the disasters are all energy-linked dominos. These preventions aren't doing anything but causing bigger or more successive disasters."

"Exactly vat I expressed before," Roe says, flustered. "Disaster prevention is more complicated zen it at first seems. Ze Guild scientists call vat Eezra has described, ze Ripple Effect."

I exhale heavily. "I'm still having trouble believing that the Guild has *known* the apocalypse was coming for years but has never figured this configuration out. I've been to one of their facilities. These people are smart. They cured my diabetes with a single shot. They brought Farlen out of a coma that the doctors said he'd never wake up from. They have *seven* Grids that can spy on and identify people anywhere in a twenty mile radius they choose." I point at the map. "They *know* this is happening. The question is why are they playing dumb!?"

Roe's eyes dart back and forth over all of us staring at her. She seems at a loss, not that I would expect her to actually know. Transparency among their own people isn't how the Guild operates. "But… vhy vould zey give you all this data if it incriminated them?"

"They didn't think Ezra could do it," Carl says. "They encourage practical thinking, practical data assessment. Trusting instincts is not something they train their people how to do. Instincts can't be quantified or reproduced. It is their own hubris and rigid control of life force abilities that prevents them from doing more with them. They are afraid of losing control, so they discourage excessive experimentation."

"Zat is completely untrue!" Roe says. "Plenty of life force abilities are demonstrative of such instincts."

"Sure," Carl says. "But not the ones categorized as intelligence-based. An ability like Ezra's is simply pattern recognition to them. They'd limit it with mathematical language. They'd pigeonhole him—which they did to their detriment this time."

"And ze energy world? Vhat of it? A place none of us have ever seen, but understood as ze basis of all. In zis vee trust. In zis, vee know zere are no limits!"

Whoa. Is praising the energy world just a Roe thing, or is it a Guild thing?

Carl waves a hand. "They may believe in the energy world, but they know nothing about it. What parcel of data they may have, they have no idea what to do with it, how to actually apply it in any meaningful way. The energy world that the Guild believes in doesn't exist. The Council made it up to feed the egos of Primes, to keep order and control. The actual energy world moves, oblivious to human or Prime human. It does not choose or act or care."

Roe looks like Carl has slapped her.

"We're getting off-track again," I say. "There's one major hang-up to this theory, guys. Life force abilities. They don't work if you're evil. Eradication of humanity… sounds pretty evil."

Silence all around for a while. And then Gabriel says, "For the person orchestrating it, sure. But the people actually doing the work? They could be doing it and not realizing what they're doing."

"Yeah…" I say. "They do operate like a terrorist organization." I steal a look at Mike, who rolls his eyes. I told him this exact thing when he first told me about the Guild. "Exploitation," I say. "It'd be the only way around it."

"The hierarchical system of the Guild would *easily* allow members to be exploited," Carl says.

"I guess the next step is for me to speak to Ohr," I say. "Ezra, is there anything else to share?"

"Yeah, a request."

"What?"

"That you fix your life force. Now that we've got a direction, and we know the problem, I think we can risk going without your channeling ability. That's the main reason I've worked so hard on this—so you don't feel like it's all on you and the colorworld."

I look at him with surprise. I can't but be impressed all the way around with that. He's been thinking about this a while, but he's kept his mouth shut about it for months, instead working to help me instead of against me. And he's probably right. It only took six months after getting hypno-touch the first time to fall ill. I don't know how much time I have this time, and it's already been three months. Besides, I'll be concentrating on the waterworld for a while, which I can't channel anyway.

"Okay," I say. "You've sold me."

He fist pumps the air and then hugs me.

"So what's the plan now then?" Darren says.

"Confront Ohr," I reply. "Then decide from there."

"Alright," Darren says. "Keep us posted. I need to get my people back on patrol."

I nod.

"Well done, Ezra," Gabriel says, reaching for Ezra's hand. "It's been a pleasure watching you work."

"What are you talking about?" Ezra says. "We're not finished. There's still more to do. I want to plot the safe zones we talked about. I want to work backward to find the smoking gun."

"Safe zones?" I say.

"Yes, places on earth that will see the least impact," Gabriel says, and then he clears his throat. "I'm afraid you'll have to proceed without me. I'll be leaving tomorrow."

"What?" Ezra demands, and his eyes shift between the two of us, but he knows. I can read it in his emotions.

"Gabriel and I are separating," I say when Gabriel hesitates. "He's moving out. I'm not sure where." I look at him. "What's your plan?"

Gabriel looks at me, in disbelief that I'm saying things so matter-of-factly. "Bakersfield," he replies. "My parents would like to return there. It's quite a ways out of the LA hot zone. I hope you don't mind my leaving the bulk of my belongings for now. I'll be looking for more permanent residence and then I'll send for them."

"What. The hell," Ezra says, flabbergasted. "You two. Gabe. This is bullshit. Is this about the strands? Get over yourself, man. Seriously?"

"Ezra," I say, holding up a hand to quiet him. "It's fine. And you haven't been part of the conversation so you can't jump in now assuming you know the details."

He huffs. Twice. Then he turns on his heel and walks out of the room, which has mostly emptied.

"Mike will be going with you," I say.

"He informed me," Gabriel says drily. "I obviously don't have a choice."

"You're the father of our very gifted child," I say. "You're the love of my life. And you're a capable genius in more ways than one. You are valuable to PHIA and the Guild both, even if it's only to blackmail me. Your attitude that you're only complying because you don't have a choice is narrow-minded, prideful, and selfish. In the very least, I'd think you wouldn't want to risk compromising me. You said so yourself: Mike is by far the most capable bodyguard there is. Therefore he's going with you into California, which you know is the most dangerous place in America right now. And I'll be sending Jessie with you as well to install surveillance. Also, Letty. She's been wanting to check on her family."

"Apologies. You are correct," Gabriel says, and then he observes me critically for a while. "Explain this excessively level-headed behavior you've been exhibiting concerning our separation," he says finally.

"The explanation would be wasted on you," I reply.

More long staring. "You know what this reminds me of? When we found out I had stage four lung cancer. And you were suddenly convinced you were going to fix it…"

"That's a good memory," I smile. "I'm not going to fix this, though."

"What *are* you going to do?"

"Aside from figuring out what to do about this Novapangaea thing, wait."

"Wait? For what?"

"Answers."

Seventy-Seven

"*Stand* behind me, Mike, to keep your light out of my line of sight," I say, adjusting Robbie higher on my hip. "Gabriel, I'm going to need help telling which strands are the brighter ones."

"Easy enough," Gabriel says, and then he chuckles. "Fixing life forces is always such a production. Mike's light to be able to see your strands in enough detail. Robbie to channel you the ability to move them. And me to verify."

"And Ezra to supervise," I say, glancing at Ezra sitting on a stool. We're doing this in the kitchen, mostly because we were already here following our last breakfast together; everyone else cleared out to give us privacy for our goodbyes. I'm taking advantage of it because I don't want prying eyes to see how we accomplish my strand repair. "Ready everyone?"

Mike touches the back of my neck, which requires me to close my eyes to equalize the excessive energy he sends into me. Gabriel takes my left hand in his own.Then I pull the four of us into the colorworld. Robbie makes a sound of delight, but for Mike and me, it's a little more jarring. The excessive stimuli of the version of the colorworld lent by his light can be piercing, and it's been a while since we were all here like this. Gabriel, however, never seems fazed by it.

"If you'll put your loose strands where I can see them?" Gabriel says after giving me a few moments.

Moving my strands is as easy as thinking it—but only when I'm touching Robbie who gives me that ability. I bring them around to my front, like cut ends of thread—microscopically thin thread.

"Eighty-two thousand, two hundred thirty-eight," Gabriel says. "Good. That's your displaced number precisely. Let's put bright strands to your right and the duller ones to your left." He begins pointing at strands and I move them. Sometimes he'll circle his finger around a group.

I move them where he tells me. But after a short time of watching them as well as perceiving my loose strands more and more like extra limbs, I say, "Hold on."

Gabriel pauses with his purple life force-clad finger above a small group of my strands. "You're starting to differentiate them," he says, having read the idea in my head before I've uttered it.

"Yeah..." I say, letting the intuitive discernment of my strands sink into me more surely. "Is it weird to think they're telling me where they go? I mean, not like *talking,* but more like being able to tell your feet from your hands even with your eyes closed."

"Not weird at all," Gabriel says. "I would have been surprised if it *weren't* possible for you to tell."

With that, I arrange my strands with barely more than a single thought, dividing them between my right and a much larger collection at my left.

Gabriel analyzes them closely and then shakes his head in amazement. "To think we used to have Kaylen use her telekinesis to move strands one-by-one... Robbie's ability makes that process seem as archaic as card-punch computing."

"Channeling..." I say. "It makes so much more possible."

"In my opinion, the ability to channel is the most powerful ability there is," Gabriel says.

"This might be your last time seeing this place," I say, remembering once more that I will most definitely lose the coveted channeling ability once I reinsert my strands.

"No love lost here," Ezra says from across the room. "I have had enough of that place."

"I can't say I agree," Gabriel says, his words laced heavily with emotions. This place has a *lot* of memories for Gabriel and me. They dance through our minds in flashes. Mike stays silent, and even if he weren't directly connected to Gabriel, he'd feel through my own telepathy that the intimacy I've shared with Gabriel here in the colorworld has been otherworldly. We have been able to share somatosense as well—or the ability to mimic each other's sensations on our own skin, to share pain as well as pleasure.

"I'd prefer if we didn't revisit all the particulars," Gabriel says when I begin to let my memories run rampant.

I sigh. "Okay. Well here goes then." I bring the collection at my left to my chest swirl and the one at the right to my head swirl. Then I push them into those respective locations simultaneously. I feel them wind their way inside of my body—a curious sensation because of how it seems to bring parts of my skin alive that I didn't know were dead.

Once they've settled into place, I expect to lose the enhancing effect of Mike's light, to return to a far less detailed version of the colorworld instantaneously and jarringly. But I don't.

"Well that presents a host of questions," Gabriel says, still in the colorworld with me. All three of us are. That means I'm still a channel…

"How?" I marvel.

"For the same reason I didn't lose my character memorization ability after you reversed my hypno-touch," Gabriel says. "It looks like when you reinsert strands in their proper place, it doesn't reverse the life force enhancements, only the damage."

I lift my eyebrows.

"Holy Batmobile," Ezra says, leaning forward. "That's exactly what Carl was wanting all those years. To make a way to give people abilities without killing them. So you can do hypno-touch on people to manifest abilities, and then you reverse it, and they keep the abilities but lose the shortened life span."

"So you and Robbie can *make* Prime Humans," Mike says.

"And you," I point out. "I can't see the strands well enough to put them back without your light."

"With the strength of abilities you can manifest…" Gabriel says, having let go of my hand. "Prime Human-level abilities. Not the weak ones made with typical hypno-touch."

"And you can give *Primes* extra abilities as well," Mike says, also letting go of me, and the brilliance of his version of the colorworld fades into my own, less busy but easier-to-handle version.

"For real superhumans," Ezra says. "At will."

"Guys," I say in a low voice, suddenly terrified of what we've just discovered, "this does *not* leave this room."

"No argument," Mike agrees.

"Pfft," Ezra says. "The trifecta is not only related to me but standing in my kitchen and you think you have to tell me to keep it on the DL?" He hops off his stool. "Which reminds me, I want to tell you what I didn't tell everyone else yesterday. Especially because we're about to be split up…" He casts a scowl Gabriel's way.

I listen again for anyone nearby that might overhear. "Go for it," I say, handing Robbie to Gabriel because it's almost time for them to say goodbye. Releasing Robbie—the only life force now touching mine—releases me from the colorworld as well.

"Two things," Ezra says. "So I told you the evidence is pointing at the Guild. I get that on some level it doesn't make sense. Roe sure as heck is ready to defend them tooth and nail. But then, if you remember Andre, how he's after Primes… I mean, it's totally messed up and all, how he's going about it, but… doesn't it make sense that maybe he found out what was happening to the world, maybe realized *who* was doing it…?" Ezra lifts his eyebrows expectantly.

"And chose to take solving the problem into his own hands," Gabriel says, nodding. "Yes, that makes perfect sense."

"He figured the easiest thing to do was to kill them all," Ezra says. "It's extreme, but evil always has some explanation right? So in a roundabout way, Andre's vendetta supports my theory that the Guild is behind it."

"I'm looking forward to chatting with Ohr," I say.

Mike puffs out an exhale, rubs his forehead with a hand. I can tell he is the most uncomfortable with the whole thing. It just doesn't line up for him. And I think that means there is much more to this story than Ezra has laid out. "If you all are right about this…" he says. "Well let's just say the everyday Prime Human has had no idea."

"I believe it," I reply. "There'd be no other way to keep their life force abilities intact."

"The second thing," Ezra says, "is I think the missing disasters were chosen for an additional reason: to protect pockets of Prime Humans," Ezra says. "To corroborate, almost all of the PHIA attacks have happened in places where disasters have been prevented. I think if I look into every purple burst, I'll find something in that location that the Guild wanted to protect. I'm going to use the missing disaster map to locate them—the Guild."

"Why?" I say.

Ezra gives me a derisive look. "Seriously? I tell you the Guild is causing Novapangaea and you don't think we should know all the places they hide out?"

"They're in the process of relocating people, Ezra, so that's probably wasted effort," Mike says. "Andre knows too much about where Primes are living."

"You're saying they moved everything? Even their big major bases?" Ezra says.

"Well…" Mike says. "No. Just the vulnerable settlements."

"Exactly. The main ones will be easy to locate," Ezra says.

"But knowing where the hives are is going to make it possible for me to figure out the smaller satellite operations."

"Ezra, I think it's more important for you to figure out the safe zones first," I say.

"Funny you should say that, because I'm pretty sure tracking the safe zones will actually lead me right to them." Ezra smirks. "If they know what's happening, and especially if they're causing it, they'd be smart enough to move their people to the safest places."

"Oh…" I say. "Yeah, I guess if you actually found them based on safe zones, it would do even more to prove they're behind it."

Ezra crosses his arms and nods at Gabriel. "What are *you* going to be doing?"

I look to Gabriel as well because I haven't allowed myself to ask him such questions. He wants to be separated, so that means his business is his, but I can't help wanting to know.

"I'm going to take on the Guild in a different way," Gabriel replies. "I'm going to design a campaign against them."

"They can predict natural disasters and save millions of lives," Ezra scoffs. "Have you seen the news lately? People love them. They're modern-day superheroes without the spandex. Actually, it's more like Men in Black. But either way, what kind of *campaign* could you possibly think would have any effect in swaying that kind of public opinion?"

Gabriel gives Ezra a look. "The Guild operates in secrecy, and that is the chink in their armor. That's where we start. With your help, eventually we'll put all the pieces together and be able to build our case from the evidence. We need to have a public force already in place by then with enough momentum and attention to deliver the message. Because the Guild is powerful enough to have the capacity to control the media if they choose. We have to plan ahead."

I fold my arms. "I think you need to stick with your track, Ezra. The trail leads to the Guild, but there's still something missing. It's hard for me to believe the Guild wants to eradicate humans. Why would they simultaneously save and destroy them? Why become public at all? They know more than they're saying, and that needs to stop. I agree with Gabriel. The scale of Novapangaea means we need a group. A movement."

"*We* need movement?" Ezra says, disgusted. "You two can't even agree to stay married for more than six months at a time. And you want to start a *movement* together?"

I give him a look. "I meant *we* like humanity," I say, ignoring his actual accusation. I don't want to say what I really think, which is that I have every intention of staying married. I need Gabriel to think this separation is according to his own terms of permanence though, so he doesn't think I'm simply placating him according to his demands even though I am…. It's complicated.

"Human movement…" Gabriel says after a moment, testing the words. "I like the sound of that."

"If you'll make it official, I'll make a donation. You'll need something to get started," I say.

"That would be appreciated," Gabriel says, bowing his head slightly.

"Ugh," Mike says finally, having been silent the whole time. He rubs his forehead. "You guys… I can't take any more of this gross civility. I'll be waiting outside, Gabe."

"Ditto, but I'm going back to work," Ezra says, following Mike out of the kitchen. Then, over his shoulder, "I'm not saying goodbye, Gabe. I bet you a Benjamin you'll be back. Once you're done being an ass." His back disappears.

I can't disagree with him, but I won't say it.

Suddenly, we are alone. The three of us. Gabriel, Robbie, and me.

Everything is about to change.

Gabriel looks down at Robbie, who has fallen asleep in his arms. Everything in him begins to ache at the moment finally being upon us. It hits me about the same time, and my throat is suddenly thick with tears. It's been pretty easy to put off thinking about this, and maybe I've lied to myself about how difficult it would be to let him *actually* go, but it's real now. He's *leaving*. Even though I'm not convinced it's forever, I still face the dread of time that will pass without him close by. The unknown… It's making this unbearable.

What do I believe will finally change his mind about us?

I honestly have no idea. My head is fighting with my heart and making it hard to breathe.

I put my hands on my hips, looking up and around, anywhere but at Gabriel.

Just go. Just go… Just go…

He clears his throat. "I feel like it would have been easier if I had just left unexpectedly."

"I was just thinking that," I say, wiping the corner of my eye and sniffing.

He's at a loss for words, realizing, I think, that nothing he can say honestly right now will mean anything to me. There is no comfort in what he believes about our relationship. What can he say? *It's been a blast, Wen. Sorry it's over.*

There are a lot of things *I'd* like to say though. And likewise, none of them will mean anything to him. We are on two different planes, and language fails me.

"Two weeks," I say, thinking there's nothing to do but skip over all of this and stick to practicalities. "I'll send Robbie out to you with Letty."

He steps closer to me to deposit sleeping Robbie into my arms, but he lingers. He puts his lips on my forehead, and I gain courage at his touch. He is still the same Gabriel. I feel that in my bones, and being able to trust that gives me confidence.

I can do this. I will.

"Be safe," I whisper, knowing the words are conventional, but not knowing what I'm allowed to say that's honest and heartfelt.

I can tell that he understands my struggle, so he puts his arms around me and Robbie. For his sake, I don't know if that was the best move. Somewhere, deep below us, the earth has shattered. A rift has formed, and sooner or later, if we aren't ready, it's going to swallow us...

I feel ready. I have already committed myself to a course I know will be difficult. I have hope. But Gabriel has nothing. He is giving up everything. I don't think he has any idea what he has signed himself up for. For the first time, this hits me and I am afraid for him. What is left for him to care about?

I grit my teeth, fighting for determination. Do I believe in him or not?

I exhale. This is Gabriel. He is power and conviction and limitless endurance. If I can't believe in him, I can't believe in anything. If I can't believe in him, then I never knew him in the first place. And if I never knew him in the first place, he's been right all along.

Seventy-Eight

*F*ascinating," Ohr says as if the accusations I've made are new scientific discoveries. "Yes, I see the problem. It does present us in a rather damning light, doesn't it?"

I'm at a loss for words. I told Ohr that Ezra's findings point to the Guild instigating the progression of natural disasters. I was expecting denial, indignance... annoyance at least.

Finally, I respond with, "Yeah... Yeah, that's what I was thinking. Did you... I don't know... want to defend yourself?"

"Hmm," he says. "No. No, not really. Did you *need* me to defend myself?"

More confused silence on my part.

"Yeah," I reply. "I kind of do."

"Okay. The Guild is in no way causing or escalating natural disasters. We only have an interest in stopping, slowing, and preventing them."

"Uhh... I'm supposed to take your word for it?" I say, totally in the dark as to where Ohr is going with this.

"I certainly don't have anything else for you to take."

"Ohr. The evidence is against you. You're going to have to give me more than your word."

"At the moment I don't have more than that. That's the reality. I would suggest that you look elsewhere for answers. Your brother is missing a crucial variable, one that will prove our innocence."

"It's not my job to prove your innocence. That's why I'm talking to you."

"But you don't actually believe we're behind this."

"How do you know what I think?"

"You are neither naive nor stupid."

I'm not sure how to take that...

"I'd rather not waste time on this line of conversation," he continues. "What do you plan to do now?"

"It was actually kind of dependent on how this conversation went."

"And?"

"I have a duty to share what we've found with the rest of the world. Let *them* be the judge."

He's silent.

"It's so damning, in fact," I point out. "that I don't have to spin it. People are going to draw the same conclusion as me without my help."

More silence, which frustrates me.

"What do you expect me to do?" I demand. "Put yourself in my shoes…"

"Wen! Weeeeenn!" Ezra yells. "WEN!"

I nearly jump out of my skin at the panic in his voice, and I come flying out of my office, nearly running into Ezra.

"What!" I gasp. "What's wrong?"

"Something happened! It just disappeared!" He flies past me and around my desk, bringing my computer to life. He jabs the keyboard, the worry on his face lit up by the screen. "Please, please, please," he murmurs, his eyes wide and scanning, expectant.

He slams his fist onto the desk. "No!" he booms. He stands up, rubs his hands through his hair. "The entire system has been wiped," he yells. "Even the backups!" His eyes fall to the phone in my hand, which I realize I've let fall to my side. "This was *them*, wasn't it?" The look of devastation on his face sinks my stomach to my feet.

I bring the phone to my ear again. "What did you do?" I say just above a whisper.

"You should know that I don't actually believe you are capable of carrying out the threat you just made," Ohr says serenely in my ear. "You wouldn't be able to live with yourself. Knowing what you know about life force abilities, how they work, their limitations… You know you don't have all the necessary information to pass that kind of final judgment. You know what will happen if you do. Nevertheless, it's my job to be prepared for every eventuality. Even this one."

I grip my phone and look around my office like some sort of alarm is about to go off, notifying me that our defenses have been breached. They erased everything remotely? How?

"Mrs. Dumas?" Ohr says, and his voice grows more authoritative. "The Guild is not to be trifled with. We do not tolerate even idle threats. We have extended our trust, put our membership and the world at risk for your sake, but it is clear you are out to prove our villainy one way or another rather than focusing on the problem at hand. What do I expect? I expect you will follow in your father's footsteps after all. In the end you will fail at what you have set out to do."

I barely hear him. Ezra's data... This is my fault. I sold Qual-Soft to the Guild. I *gave* them the means to do this...

Dammit, Wendy.

"You tell him," Ezra growls, and there is a fire in his blue eyes that I haven't seen before. It's an odd moment to notice, but it strikes me how old he looks. "Tell him that he has not won. I don't *need* his data anymore. And even if I did, Gabe has memorized it. He's memorized my formulas, my calculations. A little time and I will come back with even more evidence. The only thing he's done is delayed the truth coming out." He turns on his heel, fists clenched at his sides as he heads back to the lab.

"Tell me one thing," I say. "Did Andre come to the same conclusion as us? Is that why he's out to eradicate you?"

"Ahh, you wish to use Andre's motives as support for your theory," Ohr says. "I'm afraid I don't know what Andre believes."

I roll my eyes. "Well do you know why it is my eighteen year-old brother was able to come up with a supercontinent projection and your Guild of geniuses couldn't?"

He chuckles. "Rowena made quite a production about young Ezra's intuition. We have no Prime Human in our membership who can compete with what that young man can do with his mind. The beauty of life force abilities never ceases to give me a thrill!"

"Wonderful," I say drily. "But that doesn't answer my question. Two heads are better than one, so they say. And you have like, a bunch more than two. Even if Ezra is just plain smarter, a team should have been able to get to the same place."

"No, no, no!" Ohr urges. "He is not just smarter. He is the grandson of Samuel Pruitt, who did indeed predict the apocalypse. Ezra has some version of foresight. To have 'seen' a supercontinent as the goal of a smattering of points on a map is not something you do with mere intelligence. Ezra's capability... I shudder in awe to imagine its scope. I have no doubt that he will do exactly as he said a moment ago: reconstruct the data I erased. He is correct. I have merely delayed him."

"Foresight?" I say, and strangely that sounds more right than wrong when I think about what my brother actually *did*, what I *felt* when I saw Novapangaea and then learned Ezra was using it to predict disasters even further in the future than the Guild.

"Yes. A most unusual kind that involves direct visual input to produce output. Of course, Sam's worked that way, too. He had to stand in the place to see it's future. Robert, of course, had to either see or visualize the thing he wanted to know. Ezra's ability is so very similar to theirs, but with some of his mother thrown in. We think of foresight as a sort of nebulous, magical thing, but it is always based on something a lot more solid than we imagine. For Ezra, this is patterns in the natural world."

I'm going to have to spend some time on that idea, but right now I'm getting totally off-track.

"Tell me about your daughter," I say. "What was her obsession with me?"

"My daughter?" Ohr says, and for once I have said something he didn't expect. I wish I was there to feel his emotional reaction...

"Yeah, Mike told me she supervised him and Andre. She broke all kinds of rules to hunt me down. Why was she so obsessed with me?"

There is silence for a little bit too long, telling me that Ohr wasn't prepared for my question. "My daughter is not prone to 'obsessions.' She took interest in you, just as the rest of us did. We *still* have an interest. Mike and Andre were overseen directly by another Council member. They were responsible for recovering missing Primes, and on occasion they sought my daughter's help. The 'obsession' you speak of is solely Andre's."

I lift my eyebrows. "I'm not going to take your second-hand word on that. I trust Mike a lot more than you or your daughter."

Ohr laughs again. "Andre is the culprit. He duped everyone. Mrs. Dumas, I have no interest in defense. Only in—"

"Mike wasn't duped," I interrupt. "He knew Andre was nuts. Why didn't you listen?"

"Dyads are difficult for everyone. We expect complaints. If Mike was indeed so innocent, then Andre *did* fool him as well. You are grasping at straws. Andre is not the Guild."

I sigh. "I see you're taking your usual scapegoat. Must be awfully convenient to have an unpredictable psychopath like Andre around to blame everything on. You should just start saying 'the devil made me do it.' That's pretty much all I hear now anyway."

"At *any* time, you are welcome to join the Guild, Mrs. Dumas, and see for yourself what exactly we *do* do and how we do it. If you are frustrated by the lack of information I give you, it is by your own choice."

"In your dreams."

Seventy-Nine

From the very first time I saw the colorworld, I was immediately convinced that its secrets were likely endless. Why were the trees blue? Why was the sky a menagerie? Why did inanimate objects change hues so drastically when I altered my point of view even the slightest bit? What did the colors *mean*? There was so much to see there, so much complexity that I had to accept that learning its mysteries would have to come in steps.

By contrast, the waterworld is simple. The only thing to see here is water and its movement. Ironically, it's this simplicity that has me so enthralled. It's such a bizarre thing, so devoid of obvious, useful information. It's water, the most common element on the planet. And for whatever reason, my vision allows me to block everything else out to see only water.

I had a short conversation with Ezra about it earlier this week. I wanted his take. Ezra stared at me like I was crazy for a good five seconds, and then he kept asking if I was joking with him. When I finally convinced him that I was dead serious, he said, "Wen, that is the *dumbest* superpower I've ever heard of. What do you even do with that?"

That's when I realized why I've been so obsessed with it in the last week since Gabriel and Mike left: the absurdity.

What is the point of being able to see it? It offers nothing. I've been perfecting my waterworld access skills, watching the shape and movement of water as it fills out the world, convinced there has to be a purpose. And unlike the colorworld, the purpose of the waterworld *is* the secret. It's that simple. I'm convinced it's on the tip of my tongue, and one of these days I'm going to see something and it's going to click.

I sigh. Not today though. The river near my property snakes through the mists below as the most 'solid' thing around.

I like watching it; it moves more purposely than anything in the waterworld, making it look so animate. I've even tried speaking to it a couple times, to see what would happen. It ignored me, intent on obeying gravity that urges it forward in a never-ending procession.

I wonder if I'm inventing its importance. Maybe the waterworld, inverse to the colorworld, is as meaningless and useless as the negative for a photo. Sure, it looks kind of cool, but it doesn't serve to capture life as it really is.

I think I had this same impression of the colorworld shortly after I discovered it. I was obsessed with undoing my lethal skin, certain the colorworld was going to present the solution. But the crazy part was I ignored the actual clues, talked myself out of them, mistranslated them to serve my own fear. Because it turned out the solution wasn't in the colorworld at all. It was in me.

What if that's what's holding me back this time? I don't know how well I'm handling my life right now, and I don't have anyone to give me feedback. Kaylen was the one that shook me out of my obsession with the colorworld last time. She got my head back on straight. But she's gone. Gabriel and Mike are gone. Roe said goodbye yesterday with a two-cheek kiss. Letty went back to patrol duty for Darren so I don't see her as much. Dan and Maris are gone. My Uncle Moby is *really* gone.

Perhaps this obsession with the waterworld is to distract myself. I've basically refused to acknowledge my separation from Gabriel, pretending like he's on a temporary journey of self-discovery. I'm waiting on… something. But I have no idea what.

I wonder if there is anything short of transferring Mike's strand donation back that will convince Gabriel of the error of his ways? Is *that* the answer that I'm looking for? Am I blind to it because I won't entertain it?

My conversation with Dan comes back to me. After I fixed my strands for the second time, (this time the *right* way), I didn't lose a single part of my abilities. If abilities are DNA-driven, and DNA is life-force influenced, then me keeping my abilities implies that changing my life force didn't change my DNA back to what it was before I first had hypno-touch. It implies you can't *reverse* life force-influenced mutation. And that at least hints at the possibility that Gabriel's DNA wouldn't revert if Mike's strands were taken out of him. But nineteen billion strands… Taking them out would *have* to have *some* effect. Yet another thing for me to make a decision on.

And then there is the Guild, the disasters, Ezra's findings, Andre... I've been thinking about all of it since my conversation with Ohr nearly a week ago, trying to read between the lines, searching for something I've missed. Nothing but more confusion has resulted.

Round and round my head goes, desperate for direction, and I get nowhere. Did I make a wrong turn somewhere and that's why I've met a dead end in every part of my life?

"You are never going to guess who just showed up," Darren's voice says suddenly in my ear, jolting me. I forgot I was wearing my communicator.

I tap my ear, on sudden alert. "Will I like it?"

"Yes."

I wait for him to elaborate, coming to my feet. "Who is it, Darren?" I say impatiently.

"I thought you were going to guess," he laughs.

I roll my eyes. "I'm on my way."

"Meet you in your office," Darren says.

I start walking carefully down the path toward the house, which is not so easy because I'm in the waterworld. The rocky ground is so devoid of moisture that the only way to judge where my foot will fall is to watch the shape created by the moisture in the air above it. In the waterworld, the air here is more opaque and therefore more solid-looking than the earth, so I often feel like I'm walking through a wall.

I wonder who has arrived? Since I was thinking about him, my thoughts go straight to Gabriel, but it can't be him. Darren wouldn't have worded it the way he did if it was Gabriel.

I know who I wish would show up: my Uncle Moby. I feel the whisperings of desperation lapping at the edge of my sanity. For the last three months I've had no choice but to trust myself because I no longer have anyone around to tell me if I'm doing things right. And so far I have nothing to show for my faith. In fact, I have even less than I did when I started out...

"Calm down, Wendy," I murmur as come over the hill and the house is in view. "Freaking out is definitely *not* helpful."

I can't seem to let it go though. Anxiety that has been lurking in the background each day, begins to build in earnest. I need a sign or something. I need to know I'm not wandering aimlessly. I wish more than anything that the colorworld would let me see the souls of the dead. If I could simply smell my uncle's life force, that would make all the difference.

I stop when I reach the side of the house, and put my hand on the exterior wall. I close my eyes, focus only on the sensation of the wall so it will pull me out of the waterworld. It works, and I open the patio door that leads into my bedroom. In the hall I find the door to my office open already. I stop at the threshold, and stare in shock at the lean, dark-haired man sitting in one of the armchairs.

"Farlen!" I gasp.

The sight of him fills me with two contrasting emotions: elation and dread. He's in the middle of placing his cane just so, in order to come to his feet. He glances at me once, his face wearing the usual reserved smile I'm used to seeing on him. But his obvious handicap yanks forward all of my horror-filled memories of seeing him flung onto the sidewalk in front of me at the hospital in Redlands. And next to him was Uncle Moby, already dead.

I try to be stalwart, but I've got my emotions in a chokehold. My hand grips the door jamb as I fight the memory of exhaust mixed with ginger. And blood.

I notice Mark nearby, rocking on the balls of his feet. He gives me a jowly smile. "Wendy, aren't you a sight," he says good-naturedly. "Glad to see you kept Darren in one piece."

I grin at Mark, grateful for a moment to rein my emotions in with a little humor. "I almost didn't."

"Hey now," Darren says from nearby. "I think the actual gauge of performance is the fact that I kept everyone *else* here in one piece."

Farlen has managed to find his feet, his slender form swaying only slightly.

"Dang, Mister Spock," Ezra says, having come up behind me, using his nickname for Farlen whose dark hair, thin eyebrows, and demure attitude resemble the Star Trek character. "You're lookin' good."

Farlen gives Ezra and me a little salute.

"He isn't able to speak still," Mark says. "But I kept telling him he was too young to be in a nursing home like he was. Don't think he liked that much, so he pushed himself harder. Blew all the therapists away with how quickly he's managed to start walking again. That's why we're back so early."

"You're walking with just a cane?" I marvel, watching Farlen place his feet carefully, one in front of the other, toward me.

Last time I saw him, he was in a wheelchair, practically paralyzed. The doctors told me he had almost no chance of walking again.

He nods at me, and I close the distance between us, putting my arms around the tall man, careful not to knock him over. He returns the hug only briefly, impatient. Farlen holds the cane in place with an elbow and taps his chin with each of his index fingers in succession.

"He wants to talk to you," Mark translates.

Farlen holds up his right index finger, turning his wrist.

"Privately," Mark adds.

"I don't know sign language," I say. "You'll need a translator."

Farlen looks at me, taps his head with a finger.

I lift my eyebrows in understanding. Farlen is one of the only people outside of my immediate family that I've shown the colorworld to, and he knows we can speak telepathically there. When he finally came out of a coma in the hospital, I tried to communicate with him that way and he ignored me, despondent. I didn't want to press him on something that was obviously so traumatic.

He nods once with knowing eyes, and I'm sure that's what he's asking.

"Okay," I say. "Darren, can you let Mark know which rooms are available?"

Darren nods. Ezra offers Farlen another greeting, and Mark shuts the door behind them.

Farlen takes his seat once more, and I scoot the office chair around to his side.

He holds an open palm out to me on the arm of his chair eagerly. I take it and unceremoniously pull us into the colorworld.

'*Mrs. Dumas, I apologize. I'm two weeks late,*' he thinks to me.

'*For what?*' I reply.

'*Robert told me to wait three months before I spoke to you about our time with Andre. That day occurred three months and two weeks ago.*'

I pause, surprised, never having guessed that the reason Farlen wouldn't tell me about his and my uncle's abduction was because Robert directed him. But I should have. And Farlen recalls exactly how much time has passed since my uncle was killed… That's a miracle in itself.

'*Oh...*' I reply. '*I figured you either didn't want to or you forgot—brain damage and all.*'

'*I remember it well. Robert told me to pay close attention at the time.*'

A whirlwind of emotion upends my stomach. And a little excitement. Please let this be the signpost I've been waiting for. '*Okay,*' I reply, steeling myself. I haven't prepared myself for staring the past in the face like this. I know both Farlen and my uncle were tortured, and I don't know if I can stomach hearing details.

'*No, that's not important,*' Farlen replies to my internal turmoil, drawing the correct conclusions. '*What's important are the words and the whys. Andre's first demand was to know whether the prophecy was true. I'm still not sure what prophecy he was talking about, but Robert did—and I can tell you do, too. Robert told him yes. Andre then demanded to know "how to stop it." To which, Robert replied, "You can't." Andre didn't like that answer and he let it be known, demanding over and over with incentives. He believed Robert was holding back, and then he got a lie-detector. Not the usual kind. This one involved voice-analysis. After re-questioning Robert and getting the same answer, Andre stopped and said, "Wait. You said, 'You can't.' But who can?" Robert said, "If you give your word to spare my bodyguard, I'll clarify."*'

Farlen pauses with heavy emotion, and I experience it with him, both of us feeling our way through it until it finally recedes.

'*Andre agreed.*' Farlen continues. '*Robert seemed satisfied and said, "A prophecy will always be fulfilled. That is their nature. They are inescapable. This one is no different."*'

I take a moment, letting that sink in. Armageddon is inescapable... How can that be? I spin the wheels of my intellect for a bit, wanting to reject it. Desperate for hope, I search for an explanation.

But Uncle Moby said it... And I trust him. He wanted me to know this, but what good is knowing of the world's demise? Why would he burden me with knowledge like that?

'*It feels like you are having the same reaction as Andre,*' Farlen notes. '*Andre argued with him for a while, about how the future worked, insisting there had to be a possible alternative. But when Robert wouldn't be swayed, Andre asked, "Then what are* we to do?" Robert replied, "Oh I suppose you'll choose sides, naturally.'"

I bite my lip, frustrated by this one-sided conversation with my uncle. What sides?

'*This next part, I cannot guarantee word-for-word,*' Farlen thinks. '*I have done my best to preserve it in my memory, and if I err in his exact words, I hope that I have at least preserved his meaning.*'

'*Do your best,*' I think, hungry for my uncle's wisdom, even if it has to pass through a filter.

'*Robert said, "The truth of any prophecy means that all actions will either fight or facilitate it. I know what you're thinking. Everything devised to fight the prophecy has failed. The Guild has failed. After all they are capable of doing, they fail, which bewilders you. To you, it means only one thing. But I warn you, this is the downfall of man, falling prey to the polarizing nature of prophecies, of inevitabilities. Kindness is the only sure course. Samuel's prophecy will come to pass. Whether we fight it or facilitate it, neither will change the outcome."*'

My head is in knots, but it's a welcome feeling, one I haven't experienced since before my Uncle Moby's passing. I don't fully understand the words, don't know how to put them into action. But I repeat them in my mind, to make sure I can recall them.

'*He was mad because he didn't get it, wasn't he?*' I ask.

'*Enraged,*' Farlen thinks. '*Assumed Robert was stalling him, to confuse him on purpose. He then claimed Robert was a fraud, consumed with delusions, and that's why his words were showing as truthful. Robert became very... amused at that point. He said, "Frustrating, I know. I'm telling you to determine 'right' when no matter what you choose, the ultimate outcome is still the same damnable prophecy. What is right then?"*'

I sigh. It *is* frustrating. But... it's a familiar frustration. It actually sounds a lot like something Robert said to me before. He said death is the sure future for everyone. Yet most of us waste so much time fighting it, worrying over it. That was the reason Robert didn't mess with life and death when it came to his ability. It was his number one rule. This... prophecy of destruction... is death in a different context, a grander scale. To fight it... I only know that's not the answer.

'*I think Andre... wanted to erase him,*' Farlen says. '*Whatever the prophecy was, Andre would do anything to make sure it didn't happen. I believe he didn't set out to kill Robert initially. But he snapped. And if the news is any indication, he has never snapped back.'*

"Knowing the future," I sigh aloud. "It's the worst. Turns good people bad and bad people into murdering psychopaths—" I stop. My eyes widen. My mouth opens.

'It feels like you've had an epiphany,' Farlen thinks.

"Farlen, I think…" I reply, testing the idea, seeing how it feels… "I get it," I breathe. "The Guild *is* behind it all."

I look at Farlen, eyes wide. "Andre had to know. He had to. And he wanted me then for the same reason he wants me now: to prove it so that more people will jump to his cause, to his *solution*. He asked Robert how to stop it, but Uncle Moby said it couldn't be done. Andre though… he decided to translate Robert's answer as 'no *acceptable* solution.' Which means, to Andre, mass murder presented itself as the only *logical* solution."

I shake my head in wonder. "Uncle Moby warned him, Farlen. Falling prey to the prophecy would be his downfall. *Oh Andre…* You started out only trying to prevent the destruction of the world… The future took advantage of your good intentions."

'The prophecy is the end of the world?' Farlen asks, disturbed.

I nod. "But there's no way they know—the majority of Primes. They're being used…" I furrow my brow. "Why though…? That's the missing piece. But I guess it doesn't matter anymore…"

'Then… What is all this for?' Farlen asks.

"All? In the long run? I have no clue," I reply. "I'm sure there's more to it, but I only know that for this moment, the purpose is for me to understand that Andre is murdering Primes because he can't accept the inescapability of the prophecy. And most important of all, I am to understand that the Apocalypse is happening. There is nothing we can do to stop it."

Eighty

*M*y thumb is hovering over Gabriel's name. I want to hear his voice, but…

I sigh, letting the phone fall back onto the covers. I rub my face, and suddenly my throat tightens. My shoulders shake, and I'm crying gentle tears that have been slowly gathering day-by-day. I miss him. At least I think I do. I mostly miss having someone I can talk to about anything and everything. But it's been a *long* time since Gabriel was that person. Even before he left. In fact, he hasn't been that person since before Mike kidnapped me earlier this year—over four months ago? My marriage has been a mere shadow of what it once was.

That's what I miss. But it's hard to remember exactly what it was like. I know we were blissful once. Now that Mike is also gone, and he's not buffering Gabriel and making it difficult to actually be upset at him, emptiness is growing within me. I wonder how long I can do this? How long can I hang on to memories? How long can I be separated and not completely forget what I used to love about him? I'm slipping a little each day.

My phone rings, startling me.

It's Mike.

I scramble to scoop it up and accept the call.

"Mike!" I say into the receiver.

"Hola, Mija," Maris' voice says, and it's one of censure and definitely not greeting.

What the hell is she doing using Mike's phone?

Maybe because he and Gabriel are the only ones with satellite phones to contact you…

Oh. Right. California has no cell phone coverage.

"Hi Maris," I say. "How are you?"

"I have been better," she replies. "But it's been nice to be among neighbors and friends again."

"Bakersfield seems pretty isolated from the LA madness," I say. "I take it there's not nearly as much migration happening out of there?" This week the news has been covering the retreat of the national guard out of California. With so many other places in the country being declared in a state of emergency, the government has basically given up on regaining control of LA and San Francisco areas. That means people are leaving—the ones not consumed by... whatever has taken hold of the people in LA.

"A bit," she says, "But it makes for much quieter streets. Less busy stores."

Maris asks about Robbie, and I give her the run-down of his most recent doctor's visit. I ask about Dan and about her church, but the whole conversation is superficial.

The line goes silent for a little while, but the elephant couldn't be more obvious. To her credit, Maris has kept insanely quiet about the whole separation, but I think sometimes silence can speak louder than words.

I look heavenward, considering outing the damn elephant. The first time Gabriel and I were separated, Maris called me up to offer encouragement. This time she's calling to... I don't know.

"What do you expect me to do?" I say finally, my voice breaking. "I can't force him to love me. I can't force him to stay. I can't do anything. And I know you don't approve of my friendship with Mike, but if you truly understood, you'd get that the only reason I still even *like* Gabriel after everything he's put me through is because of Mike."

"I know, Mija," she sighs in a small voice. "I know."

"Then why do you treat me like an adulteress? Why do you act like this is all my fault?"

"Because I was looking for blame," she blurts. "Michael told me finally—the real problem. I know now what Gabriel is demanding. I don't know the things you do about souls, and I have been in denial about all of these supernatural things for a while. It is testing my faith, and I have spent a lot of time on my knees, asking for understanding. The answer I have received is that the mind cannot grasp the things of God when the heart is closed. And that is because I have not treated you as my daughter. I called to apologize but my pride wouldn't let me bring it up. It took you doing it for me. I thank God for you, Wendy..."

Her voice is quavering by the end, but I'm at a loss for how to react. It turns out I don't have to, because she continues, "I thank God for what you have done to change Michael. Sometimes you don't realize how harrowed a person has been until they no longer are. His attitude is like night and day. He is unburdened for the first time in his life. At peace. You can see it in his countenance even when he isn't speaking. He told me it was because you helped him understand his connection to Gabriel and because you helped him see the world differently, how to act on morality without fear of consequence. How to have faith.

"I thank God you came into Gabriel's life, that you have had the strength and patience to endure the energy of his convictions. He is special, Mija, and God has set him apart for a special task. I have known this from the time he was born. He has tried me in ways only you can imagine. Were it not for the fact that I am his mother, our relationship would not have endured. You are a stronger woman than me, because for you it is voluntary. I praise God that he made you with such enviable steadfastness. I am sorry, Wendy. I am sorry I ever treated you as any less than the awe-inspiring woman that you are. I think, perhaps, I was jealous of you."

I've been twisting a stray thread sticking up from the comforter on my bed. I'm crying again, but it's for a different reason. I needed her words, and I didn't realize it before this moment.

"I am a prideful woman, Wendy," she admits. "It is my favorite sin. I imagine myself a godly woman, superior in my relationship to my maker. I live a blessed life. I have never wanted for anything material, secretly believing that my righteousness has earned me the things I have. And I have left all the things I didn't understand to God. And then you married my son. Ever since, it seems that my prayers have been nothing *but* 'help me understand.' I'm slowly coming around to the notion that God can only help you understand the things you're *willing* to understand.

"It was only after the world started to collapse that I was willing. That's how stubborn I am, I suppose. Dan has been telling me for years that Gabriel is exactly like me, but I didn't believe it. But the other day, Michael told me, 'Mamá, for years Gabe was always here with me, and he would never go away. Now? I am always *there*, with *him*. Seeing it that way has made such a huge difference.'

"Gabriel and I are the same. We are both ruled by our beliefs. To the death. Regardless of consequence. We drew lines long ago and we have stuck by them. Decisions are not emotional. They are tested against what we know, what we accept. We don't make excuses. We don't second-guess ourselves. We act. It is just easier to stick by our rules than it is to question all the time whether the rules we have chosen to accept are the right ones. Once I saw this parallel—saw Gabriel's system of decision-making in the same way I see my religion—it all clicked. Seeing it that way changed everything."

She exhales heavily. "I didn't mean to be this long-winded. I was just going to apologize…"

"It's okay," I say, finally getting a word in. "I'm glad you told me."

"This week has been quite revelatory for me," she says, breathless now. "I have you to thank for it. Were it not for what you did to change Michael, he would never have been as open with me as he was, and it never would have had me seeing things the way I do now. Thank you. You are such a blessing to my whole family. I couldn't love you more."

"Um. You're welcome," I say, amazed at Maris' speech.

"I feel moved to offer you some insight into Gabriel. With your permission."

"By all means," I say, although I'm pretty sure there's nothing she could say about the working of Gabriel's mind that I don't understand. I've spent a lot of time in there.

"My husband has never seemed to have much trouble dealing with our son. I always saw this as their special father-son bond, that Gabriel respected him, saw him as an authority, and that's why they argued so little. But I now know that Dan has been handling Gabriel's antics in the same way he has handled mine. When Dan disagrees with me on something, he becomes overly conciliatory. He will go so far as to facilitate whatever it is I've argued for." Maris laughs. "Every time, without fail, I start to doubt. I think it's because I like to argue. I like to disagree. I like to defend my version of truth. And when none of that is present, the whole idea loses its appeal. Dan has been agreeing with me for years and getting me to change my mind that way."

"Well… Dan *is* a lawyer," I say skeptically. "I'm sure there's more to it than agreeing."

"You didn't fight Gabriel on leaving, did you?" she says.

"No, but that was because I knew there was nothing I could say to change his mind."

"Exactly. Nothing you can *say*. That was always my problem with him. We like to argue about everything. It's a sport. But for us it almost never got anywhere, especially once he was grown and out of the house and liked to imagine he no longer needed me. Look, I'm telling you you did the right thing. You're *doing* the right thing. Keep it up."

I don't reply. I don't have the heart to tell her this isn't the type of disagreement she might have had with Dan about interior design choices. Or how to deal with obstinate neighbors. Or where they would spend Christmas.

Maris seems to read the doubt in my silence, and she says, "Michael told me Gabriel is more disquieted than ever. His system is failing him, Mija. My system was failing me, too. It is at that point that we are forced to remake some of the rules. It will be okay. I sensed when we left that you were unafraid, and at the time I saw it as hubris. But now I know what it really was. You have faith, Mija."

She's actually right about that part. Before she called I was having trouble remembering that though.

"You know you are right," she says, "so you are willing to let that conviction be tested. You know truth doesn't need a defense."

"I've run out of ways to defend it," I say, thinking that's true all the way around. I've run into a weird impasse with the natural disasters. The Guild has been, in a way, my opposition. But now the war is going to have the same outcome no matter how the individual battles go. So why fight them and have casualties? I think I'm *supposed* to do something. But what? Why?

"You've done your part. God will do the rest," she replies.

"I don't know what that means, Maris," I sigh.

"I believe, in your language, that means the universe has your back, Mija," she laughs.

"Ah," I reply. "Well I'm curious then. If you believe the universe wants me to be back with Gabriel, but you also believe the apocalypse was orchestrated by that same universe, what's the point? If we're all slated to die, why does it matter if Gabriel and I ever get back together?"

She pauses, but I can hear her breathing. I think I mean the question not just for her but for myself. If what my uncle said was true, what am I fighting for? The lessons my uncle taught me keep pressing questions into my mind, specifically the one that helped me come to terms with Robbie's illness and his shortened life-span. I said it didn't matter how short he had to live. I said he was privileged to know how much time he *didn't* have. I said he was going to make more out of a little than most people make out of a lot.

Time doesn't matter. Quality does. That's what I've come to believe.

But even knowing that, when placed in the context of the life span of the world rather than the life span of a singular person, I'm having a much harder time understanding the point of it all.

"I don't know, Mija," Maris says finally, "but I believe if God—or the universe—wants you and my son to be together, then there *is* a purpose."

A purpose... That's the thing people say, but it's basically meaningless. Something needs to change. My spirits are sinking really quickly. I think maybe I wish Farlen had never told me what he did. It's like he erased my hope.

I hang up with Maris, contemplating again whether I should call Gabriel. I haven't shared what Farlen told me last week with anyone. Why ruin someone else's life with inevitable predictions of destruction? But I desperately need someone to talk to about it.

I miss Gabriel. My heart feels like it's being dragged over rocks all the time. I am so lonely. I am so lost.

That seals it. I dial Gabriel.

"Hello, Wendy," he answers, and I want to imagine that the lift in his voice is a result of getting an unexpected call from me.

"Hi," I say, and behind that simple greeting is a crowd of words, all of them begging him to come home. My heart starts coming apart at the seams. I nearly hang up, because knowing this can be nothing more than a phone call to arrange the logistics of Robbie's visit makes the whole thing unbearable.

"How are you?" he asks.

I'm not fine. But that's what I'm supposed to say, right? I can't say it...

"Crappy," I answer. *Oh God...* I can't do this anymore.

After a moment he replies, "What is it?"

"Everything," I reply, fighting to keep my voice even, but I'm already digging my fingers into my eyes and swallowing lumps. I mouth the words, "*I need you.*" But he can't possibly hear that.

He clears his throat, and before he can speak, afraid of what he'll say that will crush me into oblivion I add, "I called to talk about Robbie's visit. I've got a take-off time scheduled out of here tomorrow. Darren and three others will accompany Letty and Jessie with Robbie. Ezra is also coming. Anyway, they are scheduled to arrive at the Bakersfield air strip at three twenty P.M. Does that work for you?"

"Yes," he says, but I hear—or maybe I *hope* I hear—the restraint of words and emotion behind it. Maris told me he was falling apart, so I should be right about that, shouldn't I? I don't know. It's hard for me to imagine why he would continue to inflict himself if he feels as badly as I do.

I think of a lot of things I could say to keep him on the line. I could ask him how things are going with The Human Movement. I could ask him how things are looking in California. But I now want to get off the phone with him as badly as I wanted to call him only moments ago. I don't care about any of those things, and acting like I do might kill me. I called thinking I might talk to him about the prophecy, about Robert, about *purpose.* But the longer I stay on the phone with him, the deeper the knife in my chest buries itself. Any deeper and I worry the damage will be irreparable.

"Good," I say. "I wish he could stay longer but he has—"

"Doctors coming," Gabriel finishes. "I know."

"Alright then. Please call me when they arrive. So I know they're safe."

"Will do," he says,

I lower the phone and tap the 'end' button just as I hear him say my name through the receiver. It's too late to reply though. The call has ended, and I'm left staring at the call time of one minute and forty-eight seconds. I nearly panic and call him back, but what's the point? Talking to him is obviously not going to do anything but torture me.

I drop the phone to the bed again and put my forehead in my hands. "You can do this," I whisper to myself, desperate to believe it. "You *need* to do this."

Need to? Why?

God. At this moment, when shrapnel has taken up the space in my chest, I don't know why. I don't know what I'm doing at all.

In the waterworld, in the colorworld, in the world-world, I have no clue what I'm *supposed* to be doing. Gabriel and I are separated. Indefinitely. I'm alone. I'm purposeless. The only thing I have left to cling to is faith that something is going to come out of this. I have no indication of that though. My circumstances have never looked so bleak. And I want out.

"Why, Uncle Moby?" I quaver as sobs begin to fill my chest. I'm in for a torrent. "Why did you want me to know the future?"

Eighty-One

There is a future," Carl points out, sitting on the ground beside me along the trail I usually take on my runs. Here the trail rests at the same elevation as the river, and we came out here so I could practice switching between the waterworld and the colorworld without anyone watching. I also came here to talk to Carl, who, of all people, might be able to give me much-needed insight concerning the prophecy and what Farlen told me my uncle said about it.

"For a small portion of people, sure," I say. I lean forward and touch the surface of the moving water at the river's edge, closing my eyes to better influence entry into the waterworld.

It's nighttime, and the view of the stars is incredible out here, but I chose to do this at night because I see lights and details in my colorworld more clearly in darkness, and I want to see change events, the domino movement between matter. I want to transition my sight between water and colorworld and compare the movement of change events to the movement of water—to see if there is a connection.

"Yes," Carl says. "But if the Guild is only taking an interest in Prime Humans, someone else needs to take an interest in the Humans. I think that's where you come in. I think that's what Rob intended by telling you."

"Why me in that case?" I say, eyes still closed. "Gabriel is already working toward that with The Human Movement. Uncle Moby always had a very specific purpose for telling me the future when he did. This… What you're saying doesn't fit him."

"He wasn't perfect," Carl says. "And he died over three months ago so his past actions intended to speak to you now would lose their potency. You're looking for an answer wrapped in a neat bow, but I don't think there is one."

I shake my head. "Doesn't feel right. And I need to be quiet now or I'll never find the waterworld."

Carl replies by staying silent.

I already know change events, or energy vapor as we sometimes call it, are tremendously influenced by water. They aren't really *things,* per se, but they are chains of movement, and earlier today I observed that this movement seems to get pulled toward water. It's sort of a… termination point. To revisit the movement of a butterfly's wings, if the chain reaction of that movement came near this river, the chain would dissolve here. The river takes it. The water dominates everything.

This isn't all that surprising to me. We've seen life force abilities facilitated by change events, and we've also seen those change events nullified by water. Kaylen, for example, was telekinetic, and we watched it in the darkness in the colorworld once. A stream of energy vapor left her, enveloped the object, and animated it, which is what caused it to move without her physically touching it. But we also learned she couldn't move things surrounded by, or with a high concentration of water. When we watched her try, the vapor that left her dissolved when it hit the water. It made the process of repairing hypno-touch-damaged life forces long and tedious, because at the time water was the only way we had to single out displaced strands—it spreads them out like hair. But that made it nearly impossible to retrieve those strands *out* of the water and insert them back into the subject's head or chest. It could only be done a few at a time, and it wore Kaylen out quickly.

But now I have not only seen Mike's colorworld, but my own vision has improved enough to allow me to see more of the behavior of change events. Water disintegrates order. It can pluck the telekinetic or empathic intentions of a person right out of the air and render them useless. It's like interference in radio waves. The message never makes it to the intended receiver.

Finally experiencing the lift in my being generated by entering the waterworld, I open my eyes into the mists.

They're different… I had worried I wouldn't be able to see the waterworld as easily in the dark. I'm not sure what lights the place so I had tentatively assumed it was the light of the normal world—sunlight. And maybe it does, partially. But like the colorworld, it seems that sunlight obscures some of the more subtle lights and therefore details of the waterworld. But with the sun down, it takes on a new look.

Excitement gusts through me. The mists are luminous in the moonlight, similar to silver spray paint mixed with water. This effect is most noticeable in the river itself, which is nearly-opaque, gleaming silver. If I stare up into the sky, the silver is far more transparent, therefore darker because it seems like the silver is the primary source of light here.

As I let the furling motion of the mists and the forceful current of the river captivate me, I wonder what the silver is made of. While staring at the river, I reach over and lay a hand on Carl, transitioning into the colorworld while keeping my eyes glued on the silver of the mists hovering above the river's surface.

The answer to my question is immediate. The silver transforms before my eyes, becoming the energy vapor common to my colorworld, accentuated into stark visibility due to the darkness of nighttime. In Mike's colorworld, I know these are change events.

That means the silver is the waterworld's interpretation of change events…

"The level of detail you see is astounding," Carl says, reminding me that by touching him I have taken him into the colorworld—*my* colorworld. The version he sees on his own is comprised mostly of colorful blobs with nearly no distinction between objects.

As I watch the change events, I think I wouldn't call the water a termination point anymore. It's actually more like a magnet and delivery system. It's pulling the energy vapor—change events—silver—toward it and then carrying it… somewhere. To the ocean, I'd guess, since that's where all water ends up. I realize I have never observed a river in the colorworld at night, otherwise I would have noticed this long ago. I've seen a pool at night in the colorworld, but that water is stagnate, trapped. This water is on the move, and it's taking with it the change events—energy vapor—created by the millions of life forces around me: plants, animals, humans.

I lean forward again and hold my hand close to the water's surface, observing how my own energy vapor gets sucked away from me and into the river like a vacuum. What an odd phenomenon… What does it mean?

I've said that energy vapor is the stuff created by living things that affects other living things and surrounding objects in real ways, but from what I'm seeing, it looks like that effect might be diluted by earth's water. Or maybe water makes sure it's more evenly distributed. Maybe the waterway system of the earth is the means to connect people and things all over the world. It's humbling to imagine, and it makes me think of the earth's rivers and lakes and oceans as a vascular system that mirrors our own. Its job is to both distribute nutrients as well as cleanse out impurities, rendering them less concentrated and therefore less potent. Does it have a filtration system, too? I wonder what it is…

I begin to feel the dirt beneath me as animate in a way I haven't before. I'm in awe. Gabriel is right. Cycles repeat on multiple levels and we are all part of a larger system. It's beautiful, and it changes my perception suddenly and irreversibly. The earth is a living thing. And whatever is happening to it right now is a sickness. It just needs to be diagnosed.

"I don't know what all of this means," I say, "but I finally feel a heck of a lot closer to figuring it out."

"And I'm not sure what you're referring to," Carl says. "But of course, I think this may only be the third time I've witnessed the energy world through your eyes. Seeing its vivid detail, it's hard for me to imagine that you *can't* figure it out."

My phone rings, jarring me.

I let go of Carl, coming back to the visible world and the nighttime chorus of crickets.

The phone trills again as I tug it out of my jacket pocket. It's Ezra.

"What's up?" I say into the phone once I accept the call.

"Something is going on with Mike," Ezra says in a low voice. "I'm not sure what… Have you talked to Mike or Gabe?"

"Gabriel texted me that you all got there two days ago, but other than that, no," I reply. "Can you be more specific?"

He makes a frustrated sound. "I'm not exactly sure. But Mike has been sick since right after I got here. Like, laid up in bed unconscious most of the day kind of sick. Everyone is freaking out about it. Gabe is… just sitting there with him, all night and all day. They got a doctor, and he says Mike's vitals are all fine and asked what he was doing before. I overheard Gabe tell him Mike went to bed normally and then hasn't been the same since. I heard Mike wake up a few times today, and anytime he does, he starts speaking Spanish, so I have no idea what he's saying. But then… Wen, does Mike speak any *other* languages?"

I'm in the middle of processing what he's describing while suppressing my instantaneous need to be there with them to see for myself what's going on that I barely hear Ezra's question. Only when he says, "Wen? Are you listening?" do I remember what he asked.

"Um, I think Mike's only bilingual," I reply, my heart pounding in fear. "Why?"

"Because he hasn't *just* been speaking Spanish. I'm no expert, but I think he might have been speaking Russian or something, too."

"Russian?" I say, totally flummoxed by that idea. "I'm pretty sure he doesn't know Russian... Gabriel does though. What does Gabriel think?"

"He's been almost as bad as Mike, Wen. I can't get him to talk to me. He stays in the room with Mike. He ignores me when I ask him questions. He ignores everyone for the most part. Honestly, I think he knows something about what's going on. Or he suspects something. His look does *not* say he's clueless."

A hundred unmatched pieces of various scenarios flash through my mind, the worst being that Gabriel has done something to hurt Mike. I can't fathom that, but the possibility remains with the evidence at hand. Why is Ezra the first person to call me? I'm suddenly terrified. Whatever is happening is going to send my already upside-down life spinning into oblivion. I can't handle more complex problems. This has complication written all over it.

I close my eyes, and I can't help thinking about it though. Sleeping all day? Waking up intermittently and mumbling incoherencies? *No, Wendy. Don't. That can't be...*

Life force repair. That's what this reminds me of. *Dear God, no. He didn't.*

How?

It's Gabriel. He always finds a way.

No. I won't think about this. I can't.

Everything in me stumbles backward. I feel myself running away even though I'm still sitting in the same place.

"Do you want me to bring the phone to Gabe?" Ezra says. "Maybe he'll talk to you?"

My first thought is absolutely not. I couldn't say why, but I instinctively know without a doubt that the only thing that will come from speaking to Gabriel will be to have what remains of my world pulverized. I'm not ready for that.

Without thinking, I blurt, "What if I'm not strong enough?"

The line fills with silence for several moments. I didn't mean to say that... But I haven't felt this afraid since... since the moment I realized Uncle Moby was gone. Ezra has called me because he thinks I can do something to fix things, but his faith is misplaced this time.

God, I'm so tired. When will I rest from the constant upheaval of my life?

"Wen?" Ezra says finally.

"Ezra," I reply. "I'm sorry. I can't."

"What are you *saying*?" he says. "You're giving up?"

"I'm saying... I'm not getting involved this time."

"What the hell does that mean?"

"It means I'm at my limit."

He exhales loudly. "Wen... That's not true."

"You say that because you're not me, " I say, tears now falling down my face. "Years, Ezra. For *years* I've had one thing after another. It started with Elena, and it has never ended. And it always gets harder. Bigger. More impossible. And I lose more people each time for different reasons. One day even you will be gone, and I'll look around and realize I'm absolutely alone. That's where this track is leading, and I'm getting off. Everyone has a limit. This is mine. If Gabriel caused this thing with Mike, then Gabriel is the one that needs to fix it."

"I don't believe you," Ezra says, matter-of-factly. "You're tired of struggling, I get that. But you're not done. Wen... You're a fighter."

A hand lands softly on my shoulder, reminding me that Carl is still with me out here in the darkness. My father is here. Concern creases his already careworn face.

"You've lost. We all have," Ezra says. "But you also keep gaining people. Kaylen became part of our family because of you. Mike was with the Guild, even kidnapped you. People died because of him. And now he's with us because you won him over. Because you overlooked every crappy thing he did to you and us. Even Carl..." Ezra's voice cracks. "All that shit he did to you... All the people he hurt... You're still cleaning up his mess. You brought him back with you though, didn't care what any of us said about it, made him one of us and never looked back. Wen..."

Ezra clears his throat, heaves in deep breaths to keep his voice from cracking. "It's just hard right now, but you're winning like you wouldn't believe. Uncle Rob meant a lot to all of us, but I know to you he was more than special. Nobody got him like you did. But it didn't really matter. Because what Uncle Rob was to you, is exactly what you are to the rest of us. Look at Darren and everyone that worked with Rob. They were castoffs. Uncle Rob made them part of his family though. And you know he *never* had it easy. His whole life was a fight. His life force ability never gave him peace. The crap never ended for him either. Right up to the very end he was fighting. If Rob thought that a life like his was such a terrible thing, he never would have given it all to you. He believed in you. Wen, *everything* Rob worked for his entire life, even the people whose loyalties he won, he gave every bit of that to you. He put all his eggs in one basket. Don't you realize what that means? That's how sure he was. And that's how sure *I* am. You can do this. You know how to fight. You've been training your whole life."

With tears now streaming down my face and my uncle's legacy resting upon my shoulders just as surely as my father's hand, I know that Ezra is right. I'm past the point of no return. I imagine quitting, and I realize I don't know what it looks like. Somehow, I have bought into this path of life with so much of myself that I am nothing without it. Whether that is a good or bad thing, I don't know. It's just who I have become. Apocalypse or no, I have not been given the option to give up any more than Robert was given the option to give up his ability to see the future. Robert knew the future, and he lived. He lived to be the greatest man I have ever known.

"You're right. I'm sorry I forgot for a minute," I say to Ezra. "Please, let me talk to Gabriel."

"You got it," Ezra says.

I hear his footsteps through the phone, and I wait.

A door opens. More footsteps, shuffling.

"Gabe, here," I hear Ezra murmur. "Wen wants to talk to you." Silence.

"Take it," Ezra says.

"Let her speak to Mike," Gabriel replies.

Ezra comes on the line, "Wen—"

"Put me on speakerphone," I say.

"Okay. Go."

"Gabriel," I say. "Talk to me. What's going on with Mike?"

"Wen?" Mike says accompanied by rustling and grunts.

"I'm here, Mike," I say. "What's up?"

"Where are you?" he asks.

I pause at his question.

"I'm in Wyoming, Mike," I say carefully. "You know that."

"I thought you would have come…"

"Do you need me to come?"

"I always need you. But he needs you more."

"Gabriel?"

"Yes. I've felt it all," Mike says. "Every moment. Every touch. It's all I can think about. They think I'm sleeping, but there's just so much. I was just thinking about that time in the fridge. At the compound? Your hair… I wanted to touch it so bad, wanted to bury my face in it. I would have gladly died, so long as I could do it with my hands in your hair…"

My chest hollows. How does Mike remember that? That was *Gabriel* in the fridge with me.

"I don't want them to leave," Mike says sadly. "I want to live those moments over and over. But they're fading. Gabe says that's how memory works. You don't get to keep it forever. Not exactly like it was. Instead it becomes part of you…"

I'm speechless. What is going on?

"Wen," Mike says, his voice changing to his usual gravelly timbre, and if I had to guess, I'd say it signals a sudden change in his mental awareness. "Gabe did something. The memories. Oh God… the memories. Wen?"

"Mike," I say. "I'm here. What memories? Gabriel's? How do you have them?"

Mike starts speaking in rapid Spanish. Then French. And then another language I don't recognize.

He's lost it. "Gabriel!" I shout, hoping to be heard over Mike. "You talk to me this minute!"

"Sit with him, Ezra," I hear Gabriel say, and then Mike's babbling fades into the background.

I hear a grand sigh, and then Gabriel says, "I think you've ascertained what I have."

"That you screwed with Mike's life force somehow?" I snarl, the heat in my chest building. "Yeah. I picked up on that. That he's remembering things he shouldn't? Yeah, I picked up on that, too. What did you *do?*"

"I have no way to verify, but I can only deduce that I have successfully returned Mike's strands to him. I can't verify whether or not it has removed Mike's empathic connection to me—

considering his state, but the side-effect is his memory. It appears that life force strands record memory. I don't know the scope, but it seems extensive. I hypothesize that Mike has access to every memory I have ever made since he gave me his strands to begin with. The good news is that he seems to be improving."

I blink at the rock-strewn ground, my mouth open, no coherent words coming out. Gabriel figured out how to move strands by himself? How? And Mike has *every memory*? How does that work? How do you take on someone else's memories? What does that do to your head?

"Improving..." I manage. "You call that improving?"

"You should have seen him yesterday. And he's now aware of what's happened. He's slowly assimilating the new memories, and I believe once that's done, he will return to normal."

I nearly choke on my own disbelief. *Assimilate* the new memories? He makes it sound like... like Mike is some android that has just had his hard drive replaced with a refurbished one. "Normal..." I gasp. "Normal? You can't be serious, Gabriel. He will never be what he was before. Not with a new set of memories overlaying his own! What? How? Gabriel... I..." I can't breathe for one thing. I don't have enough air in my lungs to keep speaking. I think I'm about to have a panic attack, so I bring my knees to my chest, wrap my arms around them, tuck my forehead.

"I used Robbie," Gabriel says quietly. "He channels his ability to move strands. I got the idea when you fixed your life force, and I've been mulling it over the last few weeks. If Mike was the one that moved his strands over to me in the first place, then it stood to reason that Robbie could do the same. And with him being a channel, it seemed worth a shot. And it was quite simple, really. I just closed my eyes and concentrated on it. I felt them leave... such an odd sensation. I didn't see any change on Mike's end until he woke up the first time."

I'm too busy heaving to answer. My head is spinning. My hands are sweaty. And Gabriel... He's crazy. But really, did I expect anything less? I called this, didn't I? I said he'd find a way. But I swear sometimes it's hard even for me to believe the lengths he's willing to go to.

"I didn't expect the memory transfer though," Gabriel continues. "That is... a complication. And—"

I wait.

Nothing.

"And *what*?" I snap.

"It appears that the mirror has become two-way. Now I also feel what *Mike* does."

I don't know what to say. I don't know what to do, what to think. I don't know what this means. But as silence settles over the line, and it becomes clear Gabriel isn't going to say anything else, my breathing settles, and bewilderment is replaced with rage. How could he do this? Without telling anyone? He basically tampered with Mike's life force without consent. He violated Mike. He violated me. He desecrated everything we've shared.

To top it all, he's put himself at high risk of death. Without those strands... will his DNA revert? Will the SMA return? If so, he'll likely die even before Robbie.

How dare he do this... To me. To Mike. To Robbie who has so little time in this life. Rage builds until it becomes an inferno, so powerful that it consumes everything. I combust from the inside, leaving behind a shell, hollow, empty, emotionless.

"Your selfishness astounds me," I say once I find my voice. "I didn't think it was possible to ever feel genuine hatred toward you... But it looks like I was wrong. Usually I have all these words, all this outrage pouring out over the things you do that push my limits. I want to yell at you just so I can get it out of me, somehow knowing that on the other side it's all going to be okay. But this time you've crossed a line that I didn't even know I had, probably because I just never imagined you were capable of this kind of betrayal. You have broken every promise you ever made to me that mattered. You've demolished all the goodness I used to see in you because you've destroyed yourself so thoroughly."

"I know," he says.

"You *know*?"

"Yes. I've hit the reset button. I've returned what was not mine. I never expected you would understand."

"You're right," I say. "I *don't* understand. I don't *want* to understand. The day I understand is the day I find myself capable of being as much of an egomaniac as you. We're done, Gabriel. I'm flying out there tomorrow to pick up my brother and my son and everyone else. I don't know when I'll ever find it in me to forgive you, certainly not the day your mother calls me, weeping that you've died of SMA. Just remember when you're all alone at night, wondering what happened to everyone in your life, that this is what you wanted."

I hang up, dropping the phone into my lap and staring into the darkness. My only explanation for the stillness in my head is shock.

"It sounds like Gabe has declared his independence," Carl says.

I look at my father. "Is that what you call it?"

"Me? No. I'd call it self-sabotage. I, myself, have been there."

"I've never seen Gabriel as the self-sabotaging type," I say. "He's too calculating. Of course, what the hell do I know? Nothing about him, apparently. I never saw him being so reckless where his and Mike's lives were concerned." I shake my head. "Never. He's torn his life force apart. He's eviscerated it. Was it really so terrible?" I look at Carl for an answer. "He must have truly believed that I never loved him. His denial was so complete that there is nothing in this world I could have done or said to change his mind. *Nothing.*"

I come to my feet, but nausea hits me as soon as I do. I was right to dread speaking to Gabriel. I was right that this was the end.

"I don't know what's next," I say, stumbling down the path toward the house. The rage from earlier burned out my sense of balance as well.

"I don't know either," Carl says, coming to my side. He puts his arm around my back to lend support. I don't fight him. I let him walk me all the way to the house and to my bedroom.

He sits me down on my bed, crouches in front of me. "Can I get you anything?"

I blink at him. At this exact moment I can't think of anything I want. I feel like I am dead already. The only thing left to *do* is die. The world is ending, so why the hell not?

I recognize fear in Carl's eyes, but I don't feel it. I don't feel anything, actually. I lay back on my bed, staring at the ceiling, unsure if I'll ever feel again, but not caring one way or another.

Eighty-Two

The sound of my phone ringing wakes me briefly, but I don't reach for it. Thankfully it only rings once. I hear a door open and shut, then mumbling. I invite the haziness of slumber back into my head, curling into a ball on my side.

I nearly reach unconsciousness again when the sound of Carl's insistent voice jerks me uncomfortably back into reality, "Wendy! Wake up!"

I reluctantly turn over, rubbing my eyes and blinking into the half-darkness of my bedroom.

"Robbie and Ezra have been taken!" he says.

It takes me a second to process his words, but when I do, I sit up abruptly. "What? By who?"

"Andre! Maris and Dan, Corben and Paul were taken as well. Jessie and Luis are dead."

"Andre took them?" I repeat, struggling to regain my head. "Jessie… Luis… They're *dead*?"

Carl thrusts a phone at me. I stare at it for a long second, processing the name on the ID before putting it to my ear. "Gabriel?" I say.

"Wendy, he has them. *All of them*," he says, panicked. "I'm so sorry… This is my fault. I wasn't on alert."

I throw my legs over the side of the bed, my eyes widening more fully, *finally* grasping the situation. The terror in Gabriel's voice is enough to send my pulse into overdrive.

"Mike, Darren, and I are the only ones left," he chokes.

"And you know it's Andre?" I say, my throat going dry. Oh no. Please no.

"The PHIA symbol is carved on their foreheads."

Shock has me frozen in place.

I can hardly hear Gabriel's guilty pleas as visions of what Andre will do to my family begin to crowd forward. This can't be.

No. Andre cannot have taken *all* of them just like that… And killed Jessie and Luis? Not with Mike around… No. Wait. Mike is down. In some sort of semi-conscious catatonia. Because of what Gabriel did… That bastard. No wonder he's begging for his own guilt.

"Did he leave anything else?" I ask, although I think it doesn't really matter. Andre is a cold-blooded killer. My family is as good as dead.

"No."

The words strike me in the chest. Cold sweat breaks over my forehead. I dissolve, slipping from my bed to the floor. My head spins, and I can't see.

My chest is moving in and out, but I'm suffocating. I'm in full hyperventilation. The phone falls from my hand and I come to my hands and knees, trying to gain control.

"I'm so sorry…" Gabriel whispers over the line, followed by a sob.

"Your apologies mean nothing to me," I reply, heaving hot breaths through my nose.

"What do I do?" he begs.

"You can go off yourself for all I care." I pick up the phone and throw it, sinking to the floor, my lungs winning the battle for control.

I have no doubt Andre will show no mercy. He is ruthless.

They are all dead.

ןּ

"You can predict worldwide natural disasters, even prevent earthquakes, and you can't find *one* psychopath?" I nearly scream into the phone at Ohr, pacing in the common room.

"PHIA has brutally massacred seventy-two Prime Humans and one hundred and four Humans with no indication of stopping and you think we aren't expending every effort to find Andre? Mrs. Dumas, I am not the enemy here, and it was not my oversight that caused this. You sent twelve of your people into a hostile area and didn't inform me or my operatives who could have offered you backup."

"Tell me what the Guild is really after," I snarl. "Ezra has *proven* this can't be anyone's doing but yours. And Andre believes it, too. That's why he's killing you people. My family is paying the price because of you."

"It's not true," Ohr says thinly. "Whatever conclusions Ezra has come to about the origin of natural disasters, it's wrong. We've already talked about this. It doesn't make sense, and you know it."

"He's going to kill them," I say. "I can't just sit here and let it happen."

"What is it you would like me to do that I'm not already doing?"

"FIND HIM!" I scream and then collapse onto the couch with a sob. I know I'm acting crazy. I feel crazy. I'm absolutely frenzied. Ohr was my last hope. If the most powerful group on earth can't find Andre, nobody can. Everything inside of me is scrambling, desperate for something, anything... a hint of hope.

"I'm sorry," Ohr says. "I wish I could help. The search for Andre is ongoing, and as I told you before—"

"He's invisible," I say. "Yeah, I know."

Why? Why are the the most horrible people like Andre completely immune to life force abilities? That's just not right.

"If you think of any way we can assist, don't hesitate," he says.

I end the call and lay back on the couch. I reach up and dig my palms into my eyes, exhaling exaggerated breaths through my lips. On the verge of hyperventilation again, anxious nausea has increased to excruciating levels. I wish I could just throw up already. Then maybe it would go away and I could think.

"He took them. He didn't kill them," Carl says, pacing nearby, thinking. "That means he wanted them alive."

My phone rings. I lift it up to see. Gabriel.

"Dad," I say, hardly able to breathe. I hold the phone out. "Talk to him."

Carl takes the phone from me while I try to hold myself in one piece.

'*Tell Wendy he's made contact,*' I hear Gabriel say after Carl answers.

I nearly fall off the couch trying to get the phone back, but Carl has already put it on speaker and set it on the coffee table.

"What did he say?" I ask breathlessly.

"He wants proof that the Guild is causing the disasters," Gabriel replies, his voice dead. "And then he wants it publicized. When I asked him how, he said, quote, 'she has enough resources to buy airtime.' He said you have two weeks. None of us here can leave until you've finished."

It takes me several seconds to get my brain out of panic mode and into thinking mode. Ezra's data. All of it is gone, thanks to Ohr, and Ezra's the only one that can recreate it—and he's with Andre. Plus, I am nowhere near proving anything about the disasters in the colorworld whatsoever.

My final thought is the most devastating: how can I possibly give in to a demand like that? If I prove the Guild is behind the disasters, Humans will hunt down innocent Primes and kill them.

A couple minutes pass. I don't even know if Gabriel is still on the line until he says, "Wendy, what do you intend to do?"

"I don't know," I say in a small voice.

Gabriel begins to sob suddenly, and it does nothing but inexplicably enrage me. Afraid I'm going to say something awful to him, I hang up.

I sit up, elbows on knees, eyes staring at the striped rug at my feet. My head goes everywhere and nowhere at once.

"You have two options," Carl says, sitting on the coffee table in front of me. "Find Andre, or do what you've been intending all along and expose the Guild. I believe if you did that, Andre would spare them."

I stare at Carl.

"You have nothing to lose," he replies. "The world is ending, one way or another. There's no right in this situation. Nothing else matters now but the people you love. You have to do what it takes to save them."

"When have you *ever* known what was right?" I snap, glaring at him angrily before leaning forward and putting my elbows on my knees again, and my face in my hands. I need to think, but the panic is crowding my chest again; imagination is suffocating me.

Uncle Moby... Uncle Moby... Where is my Uncle Moby? Tears come to my eyes. Resentful tears. Desperate ones. Lonely ones.

"I haven't, and that's why I gave it up," Carl says quietly. "Everything I did before? What I did to *you?* To your mother? God, if I could take back the things I did... It was all in the name of the illusive *Right*." He sobs on the end of his words. "The idea of 'right' is a red herring, Wendy."

He scoots back on the table.

"It doesn't exist. It's a fantasy," he pleads. "Fighting for Right through the course of history has yielded far more bloodshed than peace. More oppression than freedom. The worst crimes against humanity have all been done in the name of Right. Right will always betray you. Right is dangerous. Right seeds evil. Just look at Andre. Wants to prevent destruction because it's *Right*. Only way he sees to do it is to murder Primes. So what do you do, Wendy? When no matter which way you turn, the rules of the Right you have come to accept will be violated?"

When I don't reply, he says, "You'll reinvent Right. You'll have no choice. And that's what proves my point, that Right is a foolish dream invented by men to lead them. But you'll be too far in to recognize it. Unconscious of your own insanity. Just like me. I wasted my time. I wasted my life worshipping Right, fighting for it. I lost reason to it. I lost kindness. I lost Gina. I lost you and Ezra. I should have fought for *you* instead. I should have worshipped Love. I should have *loved*. Don't lose yourself to Right, Wendy."

I hear him swallow back sobs. "Forgive me if this crosses a line, but Right is ruining your life, too. That's why Gabe left, isn't it? Not because he doesn't love you, but because he thinks it's *Right...*"

I bite my lip. My father has never spoken truer words. That's exactly why Gabriel left.

"I care nothing for Right anymore," Carl says soberly. "Right was the thing that ruined me. You and Ezra and Robbie are the things that have saved me. Don't lose the things that will save *you.*" I hear him stand and his footsteps retreat from the room until I am completely alone.

There is a war in my head because so much of what my father has said feels like an exhale of relief. And with the people of the world facing a future of death, his logic is not just an idea. It's a reality. Faced with a future of destruction, what is left to matter?

My people. It's an easy answer. Left with nothing else in this world, Right is meaningless. Logic is meaningless. And humanity... the idea that there is something in us that raises us above the rocks... above animals... I don't know what that even means right now. And how can I care? How does it matter anymore?

"*Uncle Moby...* Help me!" I plead in a whisper, closing my eyes and begging with everything in me. "*Help* me!"

I lay on my side, curled up, wrapping my arms around my knees. When Uncle Moby fails to appear, when he fails to show himself, the chill of betrayal moves through me.

"Did I not say I would follow you into hell?" I cry to my uncle who, if he is even around, has chosen to be silent. "I would follow you… I would endure anything… And I would! I trusted you… I would do anything you said. You only had to tell me what it was!" I burst into sobs. "You only had to tell me… I would do it."

I can't breathe. I can't think. I can only feel the most intense loneliness I have ever endured in my life.

Abandonment. My uncle has abandoned me. He was the source of my Right, and my father spoke the truth: Right will always betray you.

Eighty-Three

Fight or facilitate... Fight or facilitate...

As I blink my eyes into the dim lights of the common room, those words repeat in my mind and I can't remember where they came from at first. I try to recall my dreams that must have been happening only moments ago while I was sleeping, thinking the words must be lingering from a fading conversation had by my subconscious.

Everything has failed.

More words dredged up from somewhere.

The Guild... The Guild has failed.

Recognition. Finally. Consciousness grabs a hold of me, tries to yank me fully into reality, but I'm on the verge of something important so I hold it at bay, closing my eyes again and inviting the words that are slowly leaking up from memory.

This is the downfall of man, falling prey to the polarizing nature of prophecies, of inevitabilities... Kindness is the only sure course. Samuel's prophecy will come to pass. Whether we fight it or facilitate it, neither will change the outcome.

I know these words. Farlen told them to me. They were my uncle's. Oh please, let me remember the rest...

Frustrating... I'm telling you to determine 'right' when no matter what you choose, the ultimate outcome is still the same damnable prophecy. What is right then?

Fight or facilitate. My uncle said when you know a prophecy, you will either fight it or facilitate it, but neither will let you escape the ultimate outcome.

Why would he want me to know the truth of the prophecy?

Why?

Why?

Why?

I'm awake enough to remember now… *Robbie. Ezra.* I put my hand over my mouth to hold back a sob of fear. It doesn't matter what I choose now. To give in to Andre's demands or to let my family die. Both will ultimately yield the same thing for humanity. Does it truly not matter what I choose then? Is Carl correct and there is no right choice?

So what if I didn't know about the prophecy? What would I have chosen?

That's easy. I would never have given in to Andre. Never. Because it's clear that if the world could have been saved, Primes would be the ones to do it. Ezra proved as much. That, I realize, is why I had so much trouble accepting that they were behind it. Before the inevitability of the prophecy, the fate of our world rested on them. I could never, in good conscience, take away our only hope.

But now…

I sit up suddenly. Oh my gosh. I get it. I know why my uncle wanted Farlen to tell me what he did. It seems so backward though… But it's the only explanation. And it's exactly something my Uncle Moby would have thought of.

He was freeing me from conscience. From consequence. From *Right.* Uncle Moby is telling me to do what Andre wants, which is to prove that Primes are causing the natural disasters.

A chill moves over me. Goosebumps dot my skin, and fire, sudden and nearly overwhelming, fills my soul.

I know my course.

Does that mean the Guild truly is out to destroy Humans?

I shake my head. I don't know, but I can't overthink this. I'm not going to like where logic takes me and it's going to make it harder to act. I can't go back to that place of confusion.

"Thank you," I whisper into the emptiness. I can save my family. I only know that much. What will happen once I do what Andre wants, once I prove Primes are behind this? I have no idea. But I have a direction. Time to move.

₪

"So he has a tap on this line?" I ask, putting the phone on speaker so Carl can also hear both sides of the conversation. I've called Gabriel's cell phone from an unprotected line to be sure Andre has more than adequate opportunity to hear what I'm about to say.

"That's my understanding. He claimed he would be listening in to get your updates on progress," Gabriel says.

"Good," I say. "So that means I can talk to him."

"You've… decided how you'll respond then…" Gabriel says, and I know he's holding back, considering everything he says will be overheard. I wonder for a moment what's been going through Gabriel's head the last twenty-four hours? I wonder what he would do if he were in my shoes?

"Yes," I say. "I'm going to do what he asks. If the Guild is behind the natural disasters, I *will* prove it. And then I'm going to expose them for it. I sense Andre is the type of person who holds up his end of the deal, since he let Farlen live, which was according to Robert's wishes. So he won't kill anyone if I do what he asks. I'm counting on that. If he betrays that, I will hunt him down and I will *not* fail at finding him. I will kill him by whatever means necessary."

I'm speaking to Andre more than Gabriel. I want him to know that I know what my uncle told him. I want to take away any risk that he will hurt my family. I want to convince him I am committed to doing what he wants and why.

"You're making quite the gamble…" Gabriel says, "Trusting that he will keep his word. Don't act out of desperation."

"I know exactly what I'm doing. I've made my choice based on the outcome, which you know nothing about. So don't assume you understand my motives. To Andre, however, they should be very clear. He knows what *I* do, which is that my choice has zero bearing on anything. The future is still the future, even though he wishes it were otherwise."

"I don't know about the outcome? Then please enlighten me. I have a right to know. Because this isn't just your call…" Gabriel says, frustrated.

"Yes, it is. I'm sorry you think you get a say. You relinquished any right to decide things with me when you left. When you betrayed me. When you hurt Mike. When you chose yourself over everyone else."

"That's not fair, Wendy. He has *my* parents, and Robbie is mine as much as he is yours. *I deserve to know what's going on.*"

"Fair? You're delusional if you have the gall to talk about fair. And deserve…?" I say. "You deserve everything you have created. You chose this. But look, I'm not calling to get into some tit for tat argument with you. This is between Andre and me. And I'm here to tell him I'm going to be calling you to update him. I also assume the Guild is listening in since I'm not using a protected line, and I'd like to tell *them* if any of their people get in my way I can't promise I won't use lethal force. If they aren't truly behind all of this then they have nothing to fear. I *will* uncover the truth, one way or another. I'm on no one's side but my own."

"This is a dangerous game you're playing..." Gabriel says, and I can hear how much he's holding back.

"This is nothing more than truth or dare," I say. "Andre chose dare because he denies truth. I choose truth because you are the one that taught me not to be afraid of it. Now, I need your help on something."

He lets out a grand sigh. "I thought you didn't care about my input."

"Stop being petty," I say. "Ezra said disasters were energy-linked. How exactly?"

"The transfer of energy varies depending on where the disaster happens in the first place. Ocean disasters use oceanic currents. Land disasters use mainly atmospheric currents. Tectonic events that are land-based are a bit more complex and can spawn a lot of events at once and use different means to do so."

"They're the most destructive then?"

"Yes, but that's expected, isn't it? They do the most damage, so their energy gets more fully disbursed. Energy can neither be created nor destroyed. But it *can* transform."

"What's the biggest contributor to spawning an earthquake?"

"Ezra's theory. He calls it branching, and he's been working on a formula to define its parameters. But the concept is fairly simple. A single point of concentrated energy—like an earthquake—explodes outward, branching out to cause multiple events all over the globe. The resulting energy of *those* events is brought back together again via the means we talked about— currents mostly—gathering even greater energy along the way to a single point once more: earthquake. The point of explosion. Energy disbursal again. Branching out to mini-events. Then they gather back in. Another, bigger earthquake. Then branching out and gathering in. The cycle repeats, growing in intensity each time."

"Okay..." I say, visualizing it. "I get it, but where does the excess energy come from that's making the events more violent each time?"

"That's the missing variable."

"Ahhh," I say. "That's what I need to focus on then."

"How do you presume to do that?"

"I'm not sure…"

I think about what I saw last night in the waterworld and then in the colorworld. The earth is an organism. So disasters are… immune responses. It actually makes a lot of sense to think of it that way. Tornadoes, hurricanes, heavy precipitation, even earthquakes. All of them could resemble some sort of human immune response. I was just looking on the Guild's prediction website, noticing in particular how many fires are happening in California. It's out of control, and it sort of reminds me of inflammation and fevers, something intended to burn out infection.

"I swear I can hear you thinking over the silence," Gabriel says, questioning in his tone.

"What about wildfires?" I say, the inkling of an idea beginning to take shape.

"Fires?" he says. "What makes you bring up fires?"

"Ah! You first," I reply, sensing I've hit on something.

"Ezra said fires are an exception to the cycle. He called them dead ends," Gabriel says. "Atmospheric conditions create them, and they burn. They digest excess energy. They don't transfer it."

My eyes widen. "And you didn't… think that was significant?"

"Of course. But I tend to think of it as the earth's attempt to purge excess energy that has no immediate outlet. The source of the extra energy, as you said, is where the answer lies."

"Would you say fires do nothing to accomplish Novapangaea?"

"It would be accurate to say that they most likely slow it. Wendy, what are you thinking?"

Fire slows it. It terminates the cycle? Didn't I just say that about water? Except I realized I was wrong. In reality water is the transportation system. But all transportation systems have a main hub. In people, that's their heart. On earth, what would that be?

I stand up suddenly as an idea plunks right into my head. I restrain myself from speaking until I can frame my question the right way. I now wish I had a secure line to speak to Gabriel. It can't be helped though. I'm just going to have to word this right.

Considering I suspect the Guild is behind things, I don't need them preempting my plans. With a nonchalant tone, hoping Gabriel will read into my words and answer accordingly, I say, "I have no idea... I'm just throwing things out there."

I rustle some of the papers in front of me to make it sound like I'm rifling through things. Then, I say, "I've been looking at Ezra's notes in the lab, and I notice he references natural springs a lot. What's that about?"

Silence. Just long enough. I know him well enough to read into it. Natural springs are significant. That's what he's telling me.

"You recall Ezra's been pinpointing safe zones, correct?" Gabriel says, nothing in his voice indicating I've unsettled him, but he's already told me what I needed. "It turns out natural springs and their immediate surrounding areas are the first and most obvious safe zones."

I suck in a breath. Safe zones? I'm close. I'm so close. In reality, I have no idea where I'm *going* exactly, but I'm on my way somewhere important. "Ah. That's interesting. I'm guessing that's not something they'd want to broadcast," I laugh. "They'd be overrun then, wouldn't they?"

"I see you've easily grasped the dilemma. Springs are also the most consistent source of fresh water. Overpopulation would easily contaminate it. Announcing natural springs as apocalypse safe zones would very likely negate their ability to preserve people altogether. There is no easy answer to whether safe zones are a worthwhile endeavor. It would force humanity to choose who lives and dies."

I shudder. The difficult moral questions behind the idea of safe zones is not something I've considered. And I'm actually glad that's not my question now. I think the fact that springs are safe zones is merely another piece of evidence in favor of my real theory. I have some research to do, so I need to find a natural way to end this phone call.

"Okay," I say. "I'm going to keep looking through the lab. I'm sure I'll have more questions. I'll call you."

"Very well," he says, and I can hear reluctance in his voice. "Good luck."

As soon as I hang up, I yell down the hall for Carl while dialing Dwight at the same time.

Fire is the end and water is the beginning. Those are my clues. I have travel plans to make.

॥

"So fire is invisible in the colorworld, too," I conclude, although I expected as much. I once saw a lighting storm over the San Francisco Bay, and in the colorworld neither the clouds nor the rain nor the lightning was visible. It stands to reason that fire would not be visible in the colorworld either.

Carl pokes the wood in the fireplace in the common room with an iron rod. The sparks that fly look like multi-colored confetti. The wood itself fluctuates between colors continuously. It kind of reminds me of the sky.

"Do you think that means there's a fireworld, too?" I ask.

"You touch life forces to see the colorworld, and you touch water to see the waterworld," Carl says. "If there is a fireworld, I doubt you'd be able to access it given that pattern."

"True," I say, thinking, desperate to calm my thoughts that are going a mile a minute. It's partly due to panic. My family is in the hands of an evil psychopath. He could kill them on a whim at any moment, and though I'm only one day into my two week deadline, it already feels like the last thirty seconds before the bomb goes off. I'm in a hurry to figure this out. The other part is anticipation. I'm on pins and needles waiting for a call back from Dwight, confirming he's found a way to fly me to Missouri, incognito.

I was fortunate enough to find the location of all the major natural springs in the United States in Ezra's lab in hard copy rather than going to the internet—which is likely being monitored by Andre or the Guild or both. I'm still giddy over the fact that I figured out the significance of natural springs on my own and that my own deductions were confirmed by the fact that Ezra had taken an obvious interest in them, too.

According to his notes, Big Spring is currently the largest natural spring in the United States. It's in southern Missouri, in the Ozarks, just outside of a town called Van Buren. So that's where I'm going. And if Dwight can pull it off, the Guild won't realize it until I arrive.

I'm going to find something there. I just know it. But I need to sneak in without anyone the wiser, especially the Guild. So that's why Dwight is having to come up with a creative travel solution.

"Walk me through this again," Carl says, absentmindedly poking the wood. "You want to visit a natural spring because you believe springs are the *hearts* of the world's vascular system. Which means that if the Guild is behind the disasters, they would be dumping excess energy into the springs, which is what's creating progressively more intense disasters. You want to investigate the area to see if you can figure out how they're doing it. How exactly do you 'dump' energy? And how does that allow for coordinating disasters in such a way that they create Novapangaea?"

I let go of Carl's arm and let the colorworld fade. I sit cross-legged on the rug and reply to Carl, "Remember how Ezra said geological evolution actually predicts the formation of a supercontinent in millions of years? And then he said, this is basically doing the same thing, but in ten years."

"Yes. *Oh.*" Carl's brow lifts in instant recognition. He figured it out even faster than I thought he would. He's no mental slouch. Behind my father's generally quiet exterior is a man with an extremely quick intellect. "I don't know why that didn't occur to me... They aren't *determining* how the continents will merge. They're simply speeding up natural geological evolution! Wendy, that's brilliant! It makes the whole thing much easier to believe possible."

"I can't take credit for it," I say. "It was actually one of the last things Ezra was working on before he went to California. That's even why he went there, to talk to Gabriel about it. So he was a step ahead of me. You know what totally blows me away? The cycle of the earth's surface moving between supercontinents and continental drift isn't new. Like he said, it takes millions of years, but it's a likely future that has already been determined by geologists. If Ezra had considered that from the start I bet he would have worked that much quicker because he wouldn't have been looking for proof for his intuition. He would have jumped right into deconstruction"

I shake my head. "I realize it's a major oversight, that he took the long way, but it's evidence of how extraordinarily capable he is. I just can't get over it. All this time we've been worried about Andre having access to me and the colorworld. But I have to be honest, I'm actually growing more terrified that Andre's going to wake up and realize he's got the real prize right there. I'm kicking myself that I mentioned Ezra at all in my phone call to Gabriel earlier. I just hope Andre is so focused on me and what I can do that he'll completely overlook everything I said about

Ezra, because Ezra may have the ability to give Andre whatever he wants. He's just a few math problems away from figuring just about anything out."

"You're correct. His scope seems to broaden all the time," Carl says. "I'm not sure what his limits are."

After another moment, he says more solemnly, "I realize the danger of having Andre realize Ezra's capability, but in reality, it's that same capability that may save him. Andre most likely won't kill someone he can use."

I hold my breath. He's totally right. But where does that leave everyone else Andre took? What if, in realizing what Ezra can do, he ditches his plans for me and kills all the dead weight?

My heart pounds. I've got to hurry… I glance at my phone, willing it to ring.

"On another note," Carl continues, "you have to wonder why it is Roe didn't suggest a supercontinent to begin with. She actually *is* a geologist."

"True. The evidence is not in the Guild's favor. At all."

"Let us hope we can prove it in Missouri, one way or the other, once and for all," Carl says.

"That brings me back to your other question," I say, glad for something to distract myself from urgency. "How do you 'dump' energy? I'm not sure. But Gabriel said springs are also safe zones. I think I know why. Change events are the manifestation of energy movement. When Ezra says 'energy,' I'm almost positive that in the colorworld, it manifests as change events. They look like a vapor around living things, and it's the kinetic movement between molecules, something we don't get to observe. I also know that they can be controlled by the flow of water. And as far as fresh water and landmasses are concerned, springs are where that flow starts. Then it branches out, supplying the freshwater system of rivers and streams for thousands of miles.

"That's basically mirroring exactly what Gabriel described for disaster progression. The gathering would happen as clouds form, pulling moisture up along with change events. Clouds are the perfect atmospheric disaster breeding ground. The cycle starts all over again. The springs are safe because they aren't *gathering* energy in one place. They're pushing it away as soon as it gets there, down the rivers and streams. A spring would be hard-pressed to collect energy long enough to see a major disaster at its own location."

Carl's impressed. "That's a beautifully simple idea. And in my experience, simple is—"

"Usually the answer," I finish. "Yes, Gabriel taught me that. But it was the waterworld that made me start to think of the earth like an organism. That made think of the disasters like a symptom of disease. I didn't tell Gabriel this because I didn't want to be overheard, but that's also why I got hung up on what he said about fires. They're inflammatory responses. They're burning something out—the extra energy. The earth is trying to heal itself. It just can't keep up with the constant energy dump. We stop the dumping, and I think the earth will be able to heal itself."

His brow furrows, and he thinks for several moments. "It sounds simple enough. I'm on board. But I have to ask, what of the prophecy? You seem to believe Rob, that it is inevitable. How do you square that with your mission to stop it?"

I put my chin in both hands, elbows on my knees. The heat from the fire has made the space cozy, and the crackling is soothing. How odd that something so simple could still feel *pleasant* amid the circumstances. I'm slightly less frenzied, too, now that I've laid my ideas out for Carl. They sound even more realistic outside of my head. But he's right. The prophecy is the one piece of this story with no resolution. One minute I'm using it to justify why I am going to meet Andre's demands. The next minute I'm pretending it doesn't exist for the benefit of my theory.

"I'm not squaring it," I say finally. "I only care about proving the Guild is behind everything so I can have my family back. I'm taking your advice and choosing them. I think that's what Uncle Moby was telling me to do, too."

We sit together for a while, both in absolute stillness, the flickering of the fire the only movement in the room. With definite plans for how to handle Andre, there is only waiting for the means to carry them out. I know Dwight will come through. I'll need fake but flawless identification to travel without the Guild knowing where I'm going, which will take time. And with time comes room to think. I refuse to entertain what might be happening to Robbie, Ezra, and the others, so that leaves thinking about things that are, surprisingly, less stressful. Like Gabriel.

My stomach recoils anyway though, and I mentally stagger back as soon as I revisit the nuts and bolts of what he's done. I have to force myself to analyze it, and it's like learning about a heinous crime and then being forced to hear the grotesque play-by-play.

He has complicated the situation to the status of a gordian knot. But unlike before, when the news was fresh, and I just wanted Gabriel to disappear from my life entirely, I actually wonder what he thinks now that he's had time to process it. Does he regret it? How will Gabriel cope with a Mike who remembers everything he himself has ever lived? He thought it would be a simple thing, that Mike would have his strands back, they'd lose the connection, and then he could continue his life sans Mike's leash. Instead, he has intertwined himself with Mike even more tightly. Memories make us who we are. And Mike is now…

It makes me nauseous to think of it. It's not that imagining what Mike might be now is so terrible, but it's the fact that Gabriel has erased the Mike I *knew*. When I think about it too long, sorrow begins to build, as if I need to mourn his death. Except he's not exactly dead. I don't know what he is. I get confused and anxious and upset all over again.

My phone rings. Thank goodness. I snatch it off the floor next to me.

"What have you got for me, Dwight?" I ask.

"Four days," Dwight says. "That is the soonest I feel is safe."

"*Four days?*" I say, anxiety building again.

"I need to establish some sort of travel history for your alter ego before you use it. They're going to be looking, at least at a most recent paper trail. And I'm going to fly you into Memphis rather than direct. If Van Buren has been an important location to the Guild from the outset like you say, they are most likely monitoring incoming air traffic to the area because of PHIA. You'll get in with less trouble by car, which I'll have waiting for you as soon as you land."

I sigh heavily. How am I going to survive four days? But Dwight is right. I need to lay low and look extremely busy here at the ranch for the next four days, give them no reason to suspect I'm about to leave, to get their guard down. "I agree," I say. "You'll send me the itinerary?"

"I will bring it to you in person as well as your new credentials. I have papers for you to sign anyway, which we can use as a guise. The less of an electronic trail, the better. The Guild now owns a large portion of Qual-Soft, and the people who designed the counter-surveillance you enjoy. We have no idea how long it will be before they can crack it. It is perhaps overkill, but this will be the last electronic communication we will have about this topic. You will wait until I speak to you in person. In the meantime, look occupied."

"Understood," I say, although I fear they already *can* crack it. "Thank you, Dwight."

"My pleasure. To confirm, you will be going by Gemma Rossi? The background looks good. I don't often work with preexisting aliases, but on short notice I believe it is a good idea."

"Yes. The Guild was never aware of the alias."

"I'm going to make her a California refugee. There are more and more of those. She should fit in nicely."

"Great," I say. "Anything else?"

"Look busy."

"You said that already."

"On purpose. What you do over the next few days is very important. It's best if you don't even think about the fact that you're leaving."

"I can handle it."

"I will see you tomorrow evening then, to deliver instructions."

Eighty-Four

*W*endy," Carl says, standing in the foyer, fear in his eyes and a tablet in his hands as I come in from my run.

I shut the front door behind me. "What's wrong?" I ask, although I expect he's found a new way to express his concern about me going to Missouri alone. Dwight didn't have time to develop a second alias, but more importantly I need someone to stay behind who knows where I am and what I'm doing should things go wrong.

Carl flips his tablet around to show me. It's the GDNS, (Guild Disaster Notification System), website. Carl has pulled Missouri up. The entire lower east quadrant is highlighted.

"Whoa," I say, taking the tablet into my hands and tapping on the highlighted section. Very rarely does an event cover so much ground. Is it an earthquake or something?

The description reads:

Estimated Time Frame: October 29; 4:00 PM - October 30; 10:00 AM

Event Type: Atmospheric Disturbance - Level 8

Recommended Actions: Evacuation

"The state issued mandatory evacuation of the area earlier today. Everyone has to be out by noon tomorrow," Carl says.

"Craaaap. I need Dwight to move my flight up to tonight," I say, shoving the tablet back to Carl. "I have to get in there before they shut the roads down." I snag my phone off of the table to find that I've missed several calls from Dwight.

"Wendy, you can't go into a disaster zone!" Carl says, trailing me into the kitchen.

"I'm going into a safe zone," I say, holding the phone to my ear.

"Mrs. Dumas," Dwight says in my ear. "Have you seen the GDNS?"

"Yes. Can you get the flight moved? Tonight, please. I'll drive in overnight, find a place to hide until it's clear."

"I've already arranged it. Courier has been moved up, and your flight leaves Cody in an hour and a half. I will meet you with your credentials in the same place we discussed. Hurry."

"You're a life saver, Dwight," I say.

"Return safely, Mrs. Dumas," he says.

I glance at Carl's worried face. "I can't make any guarantees, but I'll try my best."

After I hang up with Dwight, I dash to my room. Carl follows. "Wendy... either the safe zones aren't really safe or the Guild knows what you're up to."

I pull my leather coat out of my closet along with my combat boots and throw them on my bed. Thank goodness I already packed my carry-on. "I trust my brother. So I think it's the second part. If this disaster thing is a ruse to keep me away like I think it is, then they don't know me very well." I take a pair of jeans and a tank into the bathroom and shut the door.

"What will you do if they ambush you?" he says through the door.

"Unload my weapon for one," I say, *so* relieved I decided to ship my weapons ahead of me. They'll be delivered by courier to meet me at the rental car agency.

"Please," Carl says. "Let me go with you at least. You're flying into Tennessee and PHIA just made an appearance there this morning. Thirteen confirmed Prime Humans dead in Nashville..."

I open the door and pause, chilled with disgust. Andre's got my whole family kidnapped while he spies on my efforts to prove his case, and he's still got time to murder people?

"*I will kill you, Andre, one way or another*," I whisper under my breath.

I turn to look at my father, hating that I'm about to put him through an incredible amount of nail-biting uncertainty. And now that I'm going into a supposed disaster zone, it's almost *certain* that the Guild knows I'm going there. If I were him, there's no way I'd stay behind...

"I'll have Dwight get you the next flight after mine," I say, shoving my feet into my boots and yanking the laces. "I'll make contact tomorrow by midnight. If I don't, you'll know something happened. Then it will be up to you to finish what I started."

Carl nods as I throw my bag over my shoulder and my coat over my arm. Before I move past him for the door, I take him in a hug. "But if I have anything to say about it, I'll be fine. I'll get exactly what I went there for. Then, it will be time for Wendy Dumas to take the public stage and tell everyone exactly who the Guild is."

Not quite letting me go, Carl looks into my face. "I know you will. I look forward to the call."

"I love you, Dad. Thanks for leaving Chicago that day and coming with me."

He smiles. "The second best decision I ever made in my whole life. The first was letting Gina convince me to have a child."

I pause. "Convince you?"

He nods. "I didn't want a child to share my abilities and be burdened with the pressure I faced."

I lift my brow.

"Gina said, 'You need a child so they can pick up where you leave off. To be a better version of you.'" He cups the side of my face as if I really am a child. "I love you, Wendy. You are far more than the woman your mother promised you'd be."

ℼ

I glance at the time on the dash of my rental car.

4:59

It's well past the cutoff time for evacuations, and I can tell by listening that the town is absolutely abandoned. I rolled into Van Buren late in the night and found a spot behind a school to park the car and wait out the rush to evacuate.

I didn't sleep much in the back seat, worried as I was about everything. Mostly I was thinking about Andre and hoping that my sudden disappearance hasn't caused him to do anything rash. I need to be *at* the spring before I call him. I have a burner phone with me, but it's the only means of communication I have. The only people that know the number are Carl and Dwight. Gabriel has no idea what I'm doing. He's called the last few days, but he hasn't pressed too much, especially when I express I don't want the Guild knowing what I'm up to. He's agitated though. That's for sure. It must be torture to be on house arrest and unable to help do anything.

Speaking of the Guild, it's an hour past the start of their prediction timeline and the skies are completely clear. It's looking more and more like the whole disaster thing was intended to either scare me away or trap me. Too bad for them that I'm not even a little bit afraid of them.

Sunset is in about an hour, and I'd like to visit Big Spring in the dark. It will give me the best shot at seeing what, if anything, is going on at the spring that shouldn't be. I'll call Gabriel about that time, deliver the news to him and consequently Andre. At this rate, I can almost guarantee that the Guild will show up. It will turn into a showdown, and they will get to reveal to me, once and for all, whether they will stop me with lethal force or not. No Andre to blame for their bad deeds. I don't know to what lengths they'll go, but with my family's lives at stake, I don't intend to allow anyone to lay a hand on me.

There is one small worry: What if I find nothing at the spring?

I don't know. I have no backup plan.

ℵ

So far, so good.

I shut my car door and check my weapons for the fifth time, just to test that I can reach them quickly. I scan the empty parking lot. The first thing to grab my attention is the sound. Water. I hear it everywhere, in the distance and beneath my feet. A muffled whooshing and gurgling. Ahead of me is the mouth of the spring itself. I can see and hear it from here, not very large on the surface, but I know the real story is beneath the ground.

At the moment I'm more interested in possible human sounds though. To my sudden alarm, I hear a faint heart beat. It's coming from the direction of the ranger station. And then I'm slightly disheartened because that's *all* I hear. It'd be nice if I could catch the Guild in a big energy-dumping operation. Of course, I have *no* idea what said energy-dumping ought to look like, so I'm certainly not losing any hope yet. Plus, the Spring is actually a tourist spot. They wouldn't have something going on so close to a place people frequent. There's no reason it needs to be right at the mouth of the spring anyway. I'm going to hike down the river until I find something. But first, I want to know whose heartbeat that is.

It's not that chilly out, but I put my leather trench coat on to conceal the weapons I'm carrying. I have two pocket pistols and a larger glock. Plus my favorite knife in case I need stealth. I buzzed my hair yesterday, too. I've kept it on the shorter side all along, but I haven't buzzed it this close since I was on the run with Mike. Buzzing my hair always gives me an edge of fearlessness, which I need right about now.

I cross the parking lot, and the smell of wood smoke fills my nose, plus smoke of a different kind... It's been a while since I've been around it, but I think that's marijuana. What on earth?

I follow my nose, passing the ranger station to a mostly fenced-in area at the back with a utility shed next to a wooden shack. It's modest and quaint and definitely the origin of the smells. Is it the ranger? Still here despite the GDNS? Maybe he hasn't left because he's high. Or maybe he got high because all the witnesses left. I hesitate, listening hard as I try to decide what kind of threat the guy might be. I decide to hold one small pistol in my pocket to be ready.

Nervous, I knock lightly on the door. I expect to hear scrambling inside as whoever lives here tries to hide the evidence of illegal activities from their very unexpected visitor. Instead, a set of confident steps reach the door, which opens to reveal Santa Claus in overalls. That's what he looks like anyway, long white beard, twinkle in his eye, but with much less of a belly, and taller than my childhood self imagined him.

He's got a pipe in-hand, the traditional kind, and it looks like he's carved it himself. He's a weed-smoking santa in overalls who knows better than to gorge on cookies.

"Hallo," he says, taking a puff of his pipe, eyes going squinty as he unabashedly takes a hard pull. "You lost?"

He blows his smoke upward.

"No. I came to see the spring. And I wanted to ask you some questions about it." I put my hand out. "Gemma Rossi. Are you the ranger?"

He looks a little amused as he shakes my hand. "Park closed at eight. But there's a mandatory evacuation anyway. You miss the memo?"

I'm not sure how to respond. He's telling me about the evacuation yet he's standing right here in front of me *not* evacuated.

"Ain't you been keeping up?" he says. "Stuff like that, figgered everyone was keepin' in the know."

I shrug. "I have reason to believe it's a safe zone."

"Safe zone?" he laughs. "Whole south-east is under alert,

and you think the dead center of that mess is safe?"

"*You're* here," I point out, although I very much doubt this guy is a Guild operative.

"Eh, you gotta point there, Miss." His pipe is hanging out of the corner of his mouth, his hands tucked behind the bib of his overalls as if it's a pocket. He gives me a once-over, beginning to suspect that I'm here for more than a tour. "Ah'm stayin' b'cause I live 'ere. And I want to see it," he mumbles past his pipe.

I let the gun fall to the bottom of my pocket and cross my arms. I like the man. He's genuinely friendly, but maybe because he's high. In fact, I bet he's puffing away for bravery. "Is that right? Sounds a little foolhardy."

He pulls the pipe from his mouth. "Prolly so. But I ain't no spring chicken. Time comes for us all. Goin' out with the woods ain't a bad way to kick the pail." He leans against his door jam, crosses his ankles and puffs away like we're suddenly good friends shooting the breeze on a cool autumn night. "What's *yer* story?"

"I came to see the spring. For research."

"At night? In a hot zone?"

I shrug. "Its the best time for me to gather data. Do you get a lot of people here? For the spring?"

"Campers mostly. River tours. Hiking. What kinda data you after?"

I consider how to answer that. I am almost positive he's just some park ranger who likes to smoke a bowl to relax in the evenings. But he might actually know something about this being a place of interest to the Guild, likely unwittingly. If I can ask the right question…

"I'm studying the disasters," I say. "They function like a network, and I suspect this is an important place in that network. So I didn't come for any specific reason other than to look for anything that stood out."

He waves a hand the direction of the spring. "Yer welcome to it. Careful though." He scans the sky. "Looks clear now, but they almost ain't never been wrong."

"No thoughts?" I say, not caring in the least about his warning. "Anything in particular you think I should take a look at?"

He considers it. "Sounds like you know better than me. Storm oughtter be pretty interestin'. Ain't had nothing like that madness out this'a way 'til now. S'pose it was gonna happen sooner or later though."

I analyze his emotions. He seems truly clueless. "Has anyone else been out here to check out the spring for non-tourist reasons?"

"O'course. It's a big spring. Major freshwater source and all that. With all these calamities, important people take an interest in how it's affectin' groundwater."

"Alright..." I say, doubting this guy has any relevant information to share. "I'll go check out the spring then. Thanks for your time."

"Sometimes those things don't fit the timeline exactly," he says as I turn to leave. "I ain't gonna make you leave, but you should get outta here."

"Thanks, Mr...?"

"Name's Claude," he says. "Lemme know if you need anything else. I'll be here."

"Thanks, I will."

I trek back toward the spring, keeping my ears open for any sounds outside of the roar of underground water and the usual forest noise. I pull my phone out of my coat pocket. Might as well call now. If the Guild already knows I'm here, there's no point in hiding anymore. Plus, I need Andre to know I'm working. Before dialing Gabriel, however, I crouch down and put my hand in the water, closing my eyes and releasing my emotions to the river to encourage the waterworld to take over. Thank goodness I've practiced so incessantly or the situation with my family would make it impossible.

Once there, I turn my eyes on the spring. It's absolutely massive. It's not that large on the surface, but it's linked to a myriad of underground waterways that stretch out as far as I can see. Beneath my feet, to my right and my left, water runs along the underground cave system that comprises the spring. The tangle of subterranean caverns and veins fan outward to collect water from all parts of the Ozarks. It's beautiful. And expansive.

To my vision, I'm standing on an enormous web of silver, which comes to a head at the spring, furls up with force, and then expels itself almost entirely toward the Current River. Being able to see so much of it at once... It's monolithic. No less awe-inspiring than the Grand Canyon, and perhaps more impressive, because it's something people don't get to see. It's underneath their feet, and they don't realize it, can't even conceive of what it looks like.

This is one of the earth's hearts, collecting underground water for hundreds of miles, and then sending it upward and outward. If I were going to infect the earth with a disease, this is definitely one of the places I would do it. Is it just the size of this organ, or is there really more concentrated silver here than in the river by my ranch in Wyoming? I can't be sure... There's no accurate way to measure how 'silver' it is. I stand for a while, enthralled by its scope and beauty in the waterworld, which is far more mysterious, intimidating even. Nothing is familiar here. I'm on an alien planet where nothing is solid. It's nothing like the colorworld where things still retain a sense of unchangeability. In the waterworld, *everything* is moving. The only variables are speed and direction.

I begin walking along the edge of the spring's mouth, toward the river, ready to walk along it all night in the waterworld if that's what it takes. I keep my eyes peeled in every direction, searching among the water shapes of plant life for anything foreign. About ten minutes in, I decide I'm deep enough into the woods to find a quick and easy hiding spot if I need to, so I pull my phone out but keep walking and looking.

"Wendy! Finally!" Gabriel answers.

"I'm at Big Spring, in Missouri," I say. "After our conversation about safe zones, I had a theory about the energy that's powering the disasters. I couldn't say it then because I didn't want the Guild to preempt me. Although I suspect they might have already. In any case, if the earth is sick like I think it is, then natural springs are the point of infection. Can you think of—"

I stop because I hear grunts followed by the clattering of furniture over the line. Mike's voice is in the background, saying something about wanting the truth. He's demanding to talk to me, and Gabriel is trying to calm him down. Are they in a fight?

I stop in the darkness and hang my head, hand on my hip, deadlocked once again over Gabriel's sin. Why now? Why did Gabriel have to screw with Mike's life force *right now?* Sure, he couldn't have known Robbie would be taken, but he knew the state of the world and our place in it. He knew the importance of Ezra's work, of mine. He couldn't have just... waited?

I don't need this. I'm in the middle of what might be my only hope at meeting Andre's demands. Gabriel has mentioned each time we've spoken how much more cognizant Mike is each day, and I've told him I don't want to speak to Mike. I don't want to be reminded of what Gabriel's done because I can't afford the distraction of my ready rage toward him. Let Gabriel wallow in it for a while. There may be a solution to help Mike in the colorworld, but not right now. They are under veritable house arrest until we have Robbie and the others back.

"Wendy, I haven't told him what's going on," Gabriel says, coming back on the line. "I didn't need him getting worked up in his state, but I think he may be back finally. A hundred percent. I know this is the worst time, but he's demanding to speak to you. He can easily overpower me and I need him to stay put."

I plop on the ground and sigh. "Fine. Speakerphone, please."

"Wen, I'm thinking about murdering my brother," Mike says, and Gabriel's right. He sounds one hundred percent like himself.

"No need," I say. "Depending on how quickly SMA deteriorates an adult body, he's going to be facing an untimely death anyway. How are you handling your new-used life force?"

"Gah," Mike gasps, and I hear him breathing heavily as if struggling through something for a few moments. "Like I'm on the verge of losing myself every moment. I have two voices in my head. His and mine. It's not Gabe. It's a shadow of Gabe, like he split himself and shoved half into my brain. You know how everyone has that internal voice? Well I have two. And every time I hear it I have to figure out which one is 'the most me.' But I gotta do it while the voices are arguing. I can't even take a piss without getting confused about how I usually unzip my pants. And then there's the memories... they pop up as soon as I so much as wonder about something. They're all there. If I didn't know what Gabe did I'd swear I've slept with you. I remember it like it was me. My brain's already fudged everything to make sense, taken it all and dissolved it into one big pot. I can't pick out what's mine anymore. What's his. I don't know what the hell *I've* actually done for my entire life. Timelines are all fucked up. It's a blur. It's possession. That's what it is. I'm getting better at not letting him take over, but I spend the whole fucking time fighting him back. So if I say something that makes no fucking sense, it's because I don't know what's real."

I've held my breath the entire time he's been describing it. It's even worse than I imagined. Mike is himself, but he's on the verge of psychosis. This is dangerous, for everyone.

"I don't know what to say," I reply. "I'm... Well I'm totally lost on this one."

"Did we really never sleep together?"

"No. We haven't," I say.

"Do you think… it's basically like we have since I remember it? I mean, experience actually takes place in the mind, right?"

"That's what they say. But I think it's not the same because I wasn't there, Mike. I have no memory of sharing that with you." I have tears leaking out. Dammit. This is so messed up. How will we *ever* make sense of this? Can it even be undone? Gabriel… How could he?

"Please don't hate me for saying so," Mike says, and his voice, which has been louder than normal until now, softens and becomes almost a whisper, "but I wish you had… In my head, you are mine. I married you. I nearly watched you die. I saw you glow like a goddess after delivering our child. I held him through long nights without you. And then I remember where you were and that's when I realize it can't have been me. Because I remember that time with you on the road… I feel like I was in both places at once. Things like that… those are the only indications that things don't add up. Except I want it all to be real so badly that even those red flags are fading. I think the memories are changing so they make sense. I know it's a dream world, Wendy. But I don't want to leave."

I hang my head, dig my palm into one of my eyes. A sob pushes it's way up against my will.

"Please don't cry, Wendy," he pleads. "Just tell me what to do. I'll do it. I'm yours. It doesn't matter what's real. The strands that he's carried all this time are a part of me now, and *that's* real."

"Mike…" I cry, but I don't know what to say, what to do.

"I want to come back to Wyoming," Mike says. "I can't be here with him. I keep wanting to take my frustration out on his face. But Gabe says I'm not allowed to leave. He won't tell me why. He won't tell me why everyone left. I need answers."

"I know you do," I say. "What he's not saying is that Andre took everyone. Robbie, Ezra, your parents, Jessie, Corben, Luis, and Paul. Andre's going to kill them all if I don't prove the Guild is behind the natural disasters."

I swear I can feel Mike's shock in the silence on the line. It's like a vacuum. And I even have to take several short breaths as if the air has been sucked right out of me. I cough a few times to recover.

He curses several times. Then several seconds of silence. Then more profanity.

Finally, I hear him swallow. "Robbie…" he chokes. "Wen, we have to get him back."

"That's why I'm in Missouri," I say. "And you have to stay where you are or Andre will kill them."

"We *have* to get him back," Mike repeats, this time as if by his very words he can make it so. It comes to my attention at that moment that quite a breeze has picked up. I look up to see the furling silver churn violently though the sky in the waterworld. Is it really going to storm after all?

"I'm working on it," I say. "I was hoping to see the Guild up to something here, but so far it's nothing but me and the rushing water of the spring. I need ideas."

"No," Mike says darkly. "*I'm getting him back, Wendy.*"

"Mike, no!" I exclaim. "If you leave the house, Andre will know! He'll kill them all before you ever find out where he's hiding out!"

"You don't understand," Mike says. "I have my strands back. And I realized really quickly why it was my ability wasn't working like it should. *He* was the governor. Gabe was the regulator. Kept me from exercising what I could do at full capacity. And now he no longer has any control over my life force. And I'm plus a couple of thousand watts of life force light. Remember? Robbie *is* safe. *Believe me.*"

The sound in Mike's voice… I'm nowhere near him, but I swear I can feel its effect on me. Goosebumps dot my arms, and something in me shrinks to an unarticulated power.

Once again, I have no idea what to say. What am I feeling? Can he be serious? Is he right? What he claims about his ability makes sense, but I have no idea what his capacity is if he's now 'at full power.'

I vacillate. I want to believe him. But who is he right now? Is he even in his right mind?

"I have one question," Mike says, his tone full of authority I haven't heard there before. "For Gabe."

"If this is another question about whether some sexual exploit you recall having with Wendy was real, the answer is still the same," Gabriel says. "I'm more interested in how you presume Robbie is safe simply because you declare it."

"Shut up," Mike says. "My question is this: You've gotten your way. You've given back what I loaned you. And in my opinion, you've perverted this situation so thoroughly that even I can't guess what your next move will be. You've vaporized your entire life. What now? Wen deserves to know, and so do I."

I might deserve to know, but I'm not sure I *want* to know right now... I'm trying to save Robbie and Ezra and the others. Why are we talking about this?

I'd interrupt, but frankly I'm a little afraid of Mike right now. The phone is frozen to my ear.

"For me, there is nothing left," Gabriel says, but I know him well enough to hear the struggle woven into his tone. "But from the outset, I knew there would be no easy solution. That's the nature of it."

He releases a trembling sigh. "Wendy, I had to do it because it was where my reason continually ended up. I know you don't understand. I know you hate me. But doing what reason tells me is all I have! It's who I am! To act against it is to act against myself. I have no belief in a religion. In paradise or hell to motivate me. To me, what I observe in this life is all I can be sure of. The consistency of scientific laws, patterns of human nature... In these things I trust. What I know is the only basis I have to make choices, to determine right and wrong, to act morally. I know I'm different. I know that for others, there is something in them that allows for exceptions. It lets them make choices outside of logic. It's some kind of wisdom... I have seen you do as much and envied you. How often did I wish I could erase the part of me that binds me to a singular pattern of action. *Especially* now, in this situation. But the itch... the compulsion to act based on my knowledge could not be ignored. I had to return what was not rightfully mine. The drive was overwhelming. *It's just who I am.* By the gods, I have never wanted to eradicate myself more than I have the past few days. If I could just die everything would be easier for everyone. Logically, this is the best course for all: to eliminate the piece that complicates everything. I *should have* died years ago anyway..."

I hear him convulse into cries in the background, and my heart is once more drawn to him. His plight draws so much compassion out of me I feel like I might pass out from the weight of it. "But you didn't..." I say, so grateful that this is true. I must not hate him as I believed... "*Why, Gabriel?*" I plead. "If you can make an exception for yourself, to act against logic to save your own life, why not for others?"

"Robert..." Gabriel gasps and then sobs. "He bloody told me to live!"

"Robert?" I say. "He...? How?" But suddenly the box flashes to mind. The box of books that maybe didn't just contain books.

"I had to listen," Gabriel says, his voice cracked and broken. "I did it for him because he found a way to transcend death, to ask me to live at the precise time I began to think of my own death. I did it because you proved he knew things outside of what could be observed. Robert was and still is a law of nature which can be tried and tested. I didn't make an exception for him or myself. I acted on what I knew: The laws of Robert can be trusted."

I look up and around me, my tears giving no indication of stopping. The surface of the river has grown rough. The silver laps at the shore, so violently at times that it gets knocked back into the air, released from the grip of the ever-forceful water.

"I wish..." Gabriel says, and his voice become whimsical.

"What?" I ask, enthralled as I watch the silver batted back and forth between being airborne and waterborne.

"That we could turn back time," Mike breaks in. "I wish I could have had the chance to earn real memories with Wen. Not these knockoffs that are nothing more than dreams."

"Yes," Gabriel replies. "To turn back time to before things were decided. Before we found ourselves on this roller coaster that we now have no way off of. To instead have Mike meet you first. Not for me. For you. For him. To give him the chance to know you without me. Truly. As I promised him. But I would give up *everything* for you, Wendy. I would remake myself. I want so desperately to give you back the man unburdened by an identity crisis, the pitiful man that I am, unable to let go of my own nature. That same nature that says the only way to bring that man back is to give you the choice you should have had from the beginning. The worst part of this is knowing how much pain I have caused you yet being unable to regret my actions. Because I still can't fathom any other course, even now. For that I am sorry. I'm sorry I can't be the man you wish I was."

"Gabriel..." I sob. "I love you. I would undo it all just to prove that you are exactly who I want. I am not afraid of what ifs. I know who you are. And I know who I am. To give you that assurance... To erase it all and start over would be worth it. If turning back time were possible, I would give you that wish."

A powerful wind hits my back, so strong it feels like it could lift me without much more effort. It has grown darker in the waterworld, at least as far as ambient light. But no sooner have I thought that than the subterranean web of silver that comprises the spring beneath me begins to glow, not with light, but with the silver, heavier and thicker than any I've ever seen. I follow its path with my eyes, realizing that the thick silver has contaminated the entire river. It looks molten the way it slows the flow, choking back the current. I automatically reach out to touch the surface, curious if it feels as viscous as it looks.

Suddenly, I'm enveloped in it. I even feel it, manifesting like a great gust of wind sweeping though my being. It's so thick I can't see beyond it. I only feel myself crumbling to its force.

I'm loose like sand. The cloud of silver is picking me up and separating me, blowing me away. I'm not sure if it has left any of me behind until the silver begins to take a more definitive shape in front of me, a funnel. Silver is siphoned off of me and pulled in a stream upward into the sky. Faster and faster it spins, winding its way up, filling the sky until it's covered in a sterling blanket.

The flow linking me to the sky finally stops, and I fall on my back, staring up at it, that lustrous cloud. I watch it, mesmerized and confused... and then suddenly and inescapably tired. I fight to keep my eyes open, because it's just so incredible. I see a flash above, shaped exactly like lighting, branching out in a web, much like the underground spring below me, except it's silver. It looks like someone cast the lighting bolts from metal rather than ions or whatever lightning is made of.

My eyes... They refuse to stay open. But memory is screaming at me as I lose consciousness: silver lighting bolts. I've seen these before...

₪

The sky is in full assault mode as my eyes flash open. My God. I have never seen or heard of a lightning storm like this. It's right over me, and I watch it strike five trees at once, the crashes so loud I'm certain I'm going to be deaf after this. The sky is being fractured. The air is being shattered by the booming explosions. More white cracks criss-cross the entire sky at once. It's being ripped apart. The earth is breaking. This must be the end.

End or no, awe turns to panic when a tree not a hundred yards from me is splintered in two. I smell its singed wood, and a fire has started. I roll over, crawling at first, afraid of the lighting making *me* its next target. It's more open here by the river. I think I'd be better served being among the trees where the lighting will likely strike *them* before *me*.

I come to my feet, stumbling over roots and bushes, pressing into the woods. I'm surrounded though. Thunder and lightning is on every side. Which way will take me *away* from this storm?

Where am I?

I stop.

Oh my gosh, I have no idea how I got here. And where is *here*?

Another snap of thunder and a blinding flash. More cracks. Groaning.

I'm thrown to the ground by a rod at my back. My chest slams into the dirt, knocking every bit of air out of me. I can't find my breath. I grow lightheaded from the lack of oxygen, and then I pass out entirely.

April 2016

Eighty-Five

I hear lots of murmuring. Then beeping.

"She's coming around!" a woman's voice says.

I suck in a breath, blink my way into full consciousness. A face is over me. I don't know it. But she's in pale green scrubs. Then another face appears next to her. A head of tight curls.

"Kiera," I say.

She nods, and I notice her face is a bit tear-stricken.

"Miss Whitley, can you move?" says the first woman.

Miss Whitley... I let the title marinate for a minute, thinking it sounds both normal and abnormal. I can't place why.

I lift my hand though, to show the woman I can move.

"Councilwoman, are you hurt anywhere?" Kiera says, peering down into my face as if I'm a specimen.

At first I don't understand the question. I don't know why she called me that.

At first.

I slog through memories that come to me all mixed together, grasping enough that I am on the Guild Council. I hang on to that identity with an iron grip, certain I'm going to need it to makes sense of more things in a minute.

"I'm fine. I think. Where am I?" I ask.

"Hospital," Kiera says. "You were in a coma for several hours."

"A coma?" Why does that sound so familiar? More flashes. Looking around me, at the familiarity of hospital surroundings, I remember. Coma. Leukemia. Gabriel woke me up that time. "Where's Gabriel?" I ask.

I feel it before I see it on her face: worry.

I sit up abruptly. "Where's Gabriel?!" I demand.

"Also in a coma, Councilwoman," Kiera says timidly. "Lainey is with him."

More information I don't understand… Gabriel is in a coma?

It doesn't matter. I can reach him. I fling the sheets off, yank my IV out.

"Miss Whitley, lie down! You need to allow yourself time—" the nurse starts.

I ignore her, swinging my legs over the side of the bed and standing. "Take me to Gabriel, Kiera," I order. "Where's my phone? Get Shiah—"

A new blast of information hits me at once and I freeze in place. Shiah, my advisor. The Guild. The Council. Mike, my bodyguard. The Human Movement. Gabriel Dumas. My memory…

I fall to me knees.

Oh my God. I know what's happened.

I start panting as the details fall into place. The puzzle builds itself, but every new fact is a revelation. I grip the side of the mattress next to me, my other hand pressed to the floor, gasping from sheer incredulity. Reality becomes more unbelievable with every new piece of assimilated information that fuels the white-hot flame that has started within me. Understanding feeds into me in pulses, each one stronger than the last until my being becomes transcendent.

My memory is back.

I'm positive. So I start testing myself, looking for the gaps. But instead I'm shocked at the impossibility… Who I have become… I am… a duality. Wendy Dumas meets Wendy Whitley for the first time and gasps in astonishment. I made it onto the *Guild Council?* I'm a public icon? I speak to thousands? I *oppose* Gabriel in a public sphere? *Everyone* knows who I am. I killed Andre in front of hundreds… I am… so self-assured. Undaunted for such little experience. How?

Wendy Whitley, however, looks at Wendy Dumas and is shocked to find a battle-worn well of courage and faith. Her depth of experience, her unrelenting obstacles, her continual suffering, her dogged work in the trenches with almost no recognition. She is wise. She has such faith for someone with such small reach. She is, by comparison to Wendy Whitley, a nobody who *chose* to remain in the background.

They merge. These two parts of me, who both had such rare experiences, at first stumble through the contradictions. How do I square two parts of myself that held such different ideals? They both *became* something amazing though…

And then. Wendy Dumas laughs. Wendy Whitley laughs. *I* laugh. I pull in all the parts of me and I am… the luckiest woman alive. I won the lottery, except I never bought a ticket. The laws of time and space say I should not exist…

"I—" I gasp, kneeling.

I look around the room, seeing nothing and everything all at once. What might have been has become what is. I have lived two lives, and I remember them both. I *am* them both. I have seen my potential realized in two drastically different ways, and it makes me wonder… *do I even have limits?*

I don't feel them. Power. I feel *that*. Nevertheless I am *humbled. Grateful.* To what, I'm not sure. The earth maybe. The universe. Or maybe the entirety of reality, which saw fit to equip me with an overabundance of skills in such an extraordinary way. I am not a woman of singular experience, but double. I exist on two paths of reality… When comprehending this, time seems almost meaningless. How can this be?

Because of Gabriel. Who wished to turn back time. And somehow found a way.

Mike… He was the means. Once Gabriel forced Mike's strands back, Mike realized the full scope of his capability.

He and Robbie can alter memory.

Mike caused it, and Robbie undid it. Because Gabriel forced us over the edge, made us realize and then redefine our limits. Like always.

Tears begin falling profusely from my eyes, but I cannot move. I am dumfounded.

Is there anything that man cannot accomplish?

And Kaylen…

I sob. She saved us all… What she must have endured to do it…

I clasp my arms around myself, gratitude so heavy it may disintegrate me altogether.

Frozen in the depth of incredulity, in humility that shrinks what and who I am to nothing, I am suddenly swept up just as surely, caught in ecstasy, a sense of infinite power both heavy and weightless at the same time. It's like armor. I feel its weight, but it's counterbalanced by the fact that I am now invincible with it. Destiny has made a claim on me, called me to a path I cannot refuse now that I have seen at what price I have been purchased. How can I possibly even *want* to when I know the lengths that have been obtained to prepare me?

Prime Humans...

We *are* the cause of this. I saw it happen directly with my own eyes—the power of Mike's ability to erase memories on a massive scale made visible in the waterworld and then rained back down: a cluster of lighting storms all over the nation.

With tens of thousands of Prime Humans, we have exceeded what the earth can handle. But that fact cannot be changed. This outcome was put into motion from the time Eric Shelding discovered life force abilities. You cannot close Pandora's box.

The Prophecy is coming to pass.

The only option for us... To Survive.

I don't know how we will, but I am unafraid. I have a place in it, a task. And I will not fail. No matter the difficulty of the course I have been put on, whatever job I have been prepared for, I will do it. I am a warrior. I simply didn't realize I was being trained until now. But now... Now I'm armed and eager for the fight.

I am ready.

"Councilwoman!" Kiera cries. "Please, you'll injure yourself!"

I look up and around at the hospital room. Then down at my hospital gown, confused by how ordinary and plain it looks. I am the champion and leader of Prime Humans. There is a war to be won. I do not belong in a hospital.

This sphere of mortality is stifling. Everything around me is so dull... lacking depth. It's so... breakable compared to the invincibility in my soul. This world is a dream impersonating reality. Why did I ever cower from its phantoms?

This world is temporary and contrived. I can't seem to take it that seriously, making the irony of my situation suddenly hilarious. I see Kiera looking at me like I've come back from the dead, and I start laughing. I'm overcome with a fit of giggles. I'm Wendy Dumas. The Guild was my enemy. And I am now its voice, its keeper. I let my forehead hit the floor in a fit of laughter.

And Gabriel... He was my opposition. No. He still *is* my opposition. Except I basically *own* The Human Movement. I even named it. Both sides are *mine*. Some god or goddess out there has a wicked sense of humor.

I sit up suddenly. "Gabriel..." I breathe. I look up at Kiera, who is looking back at me with terror. I'm sure I look like I've lost my mind. But I haven't lost it. I've found it. All of it. All at once.

I stand up, determined not to fall on the floor anymore. It is time to be what I now see that I am. "Please, take me to Gabriel," I say, but I am on the verge of taking off into flight. I'm not of this world. This world is a cheap knockoff. I will bring it *and* that ridiculous prophecy to its knees.

The Council... They have lied to me, and I will make sure they answer for it.

What has come over me?

Power. It flows through every part of me, and I hold my hand up to see it, as if it will be visible. I blink my eyes, bring the colorworld into view. A voice in the back of my mind says I should not be able to do that without someone near me, but I laugh at that voice. I can do whatever I want. I command my eyes to see and my ears to hear, and they do it. The colorworld is always here. It only takes willing it to see.

My hand is shrouded in energy vapor so thick it obscures my life force. My whole body is cloaked in it, and I watch the energy vapor all around the room flowing my direction, attracted to me. I hold my hand out, inviting it to come. The cloud around my life force gathers, and then I absorb it. I watch as my own life force grows brighter before my very eyes. I'm a live wire. A filament. My capacity for light is far greater than I ever knew.

Kiera's emotions distract me. She seems caught in a battle in her head.

I shake off the colorworld and hold up a hand. "Stop worrying. I'm fine. I've simply remembered everything." I grin and shake my head. "And it's crazy to the point of hilarity. But right now, I need to speak to Gabriel. And—" My eyes widen. I've been so caught up in the most ironic situation in history that I've forgotten to ask about Robbie. "Where is my son?" I ask Kiera.

"He's safe," she replies, cowering from the command in my voice. "He's with the girl, Kaylen. I tried to arrange a hotel for her in the area, but she wouldn't have it. So I got the hospital to give her a room here, next to Mister Dumas. She's, um, confined there. But I swear we've been kind! Operatives have attended to her every need." Kiera bites her lip, afraid. Of me, I realize. "She wanted to be with you, but... the boy... we couldn't be sure..."

"Spit it out, Kiera!" I demand, taking a step toward her.

She shrinks. "Do you recall what happened right before you went into a coma?"

"Of course. Kaylen had found us. She was trying to convince us who we were, and she had Robbie with her. She figured out it was Robbie who could bring our memories back."

"Kaylen had also said he was a channel, even described that he had killed someone," Kiera pleads. "So when you and Mister Dumas fell, Lainey and I… We feared…"

"That it was his death touch…" I say, finally getting why Kiera's so afraid. They had to quarantine Robbie because they worried he had hurt me. She fears how I will react to, yet again, holding Kaylen against her will.

"It wasn't. And he didn't hurt me," I say. "Escort Kaylen to Gabriel. And take *me* to him. Now."

I don't wait for her to recover her shock. I walk right out of the room and stand in the hall. "Which way?"

Kiera grabs a bag off the floor and scampers to my side. She simultaneously pulls out her phone while leading me down the hall. There are protection operatives everywhere. The nurse seems to have given up on getting me back into bed.

Once Kiera is off her phone, and we stop to wait for the elevator, she says, "Shiah should be landing at any moment. But she's probably going to have a time getting here. I've wanted to keep things under wraps, but THM was hellbent on exposing the fact that you skipped bail. And I have your phone. I had to turn it off though, because it was going off nonstop and Shiah told me not to answer it."

"She knows what she's talking about," I say, retying the strings on my hospital gown as we step onto the elevator. "Once we get to Gabriel's room, you will leave me. Kaylen and Robbie are the only ones you will let in until Shiah arrives. In the meantime, I need you to get me some clothes. Something I can make a public statement wearing. White, please. Like you've seen me wear. Have it delivered to the room. Can you do that?"

"Of course, Councilwoman," Kiera says as the doors open.

"Thank you," I say. We round the corner at that moment, and there, only twenty feet away, is Lainey standing next to Kaylen in front of an open door.

I stop in my tracks and stare at the woman who looks almost nothing like the Kaylen that left all those months ago. She is older, in much more than years. The power emanating from her being reaches me all the way over here, perhaps because I have never been more in touch with the colorworld than I am at this exact moment.

I saw her hair float once, a couple years ago. She was dripping with energy she had saved up to make sure her telekinesis was as powerful as possible for a mission we were on. She looked alien then, like a celestial being who had come down among mortals to command nature.

As she stands here before me now, her life force pushing its way into my sight despite me willing it, I see that same being. Her power radiates from that world into this one.

For a moment I am intimidated to approach her, but then her mouth curves up just slightly. A sob escapes my throat and I run to her, throwing my arms around her. I can't speak, and I'm getting her shirt wet, but I can't seem to infuse enough of my esteem and love and gratitude and utter awe into my embrace. So I fall to my knees, my arms wrapped around her waist as I cry out the overwhelming emotions that have no words for this woman who spared no part of herself to save us.

"Thank you," I whisper finally. "Thank you."

"Wendy," she cries, pulling me up, but she's fraught with conflict and shame.

I know exactly where her thoughts are, and I will not have it. I put my hands on either side of her face, and I look into her eyes as I pull us into the colorworld.

"Look at your soul," I say to her.

She sobs.

"Look at it!" I command.

She holds up her life force-clad hand, crying and sniffling.

"You did not give any part of it away," I say.

She cries.

"Not one strand! Not one particle of light. You have only gained."

She nods, wordless, tucking her face into my shoulder.

"Don't trust your eyes," I say, cradling her against me like a child. "They lie to you because they have been clouded by suffering. Trust mine. I see exactly what you have become. And it is magnificent."

I spot Lainey over her shoulder then, holding Robbie.

My chest catches, and I reach for him. Lainey relinquishes him immediately.

Something I didn't realize I was missing clicks into place when his weight reaches my arms and his smell invades my nose. He bounces in my arms, tugs on Kaylen's hair. He knows.

"Let's do it, Robbie," I say to him.

I close my eyes and touch Kaylen's soul with my own. I let her life force speak to mine by feeling what she does with her own body, the somatosense that left when my memory did. I parse the strands of her life force, recognizing the ones that are numb. Those ones are in the wrong place. I coax them to withdraw, and I feel them leave her body.

"You were never powerless," I whisper in her ear. "And you were never without a choice. Own all that you have ever done and you will realize all that you have become. When you do, this ability that you have dreamt of having all these months will simply become a tool, auxiliary to your unstoppable power in here." I put my hand on her chest. "Will them back, Kaylen. They'll tell you where they go."

Having been caught by surprise as to what I'm doing, she takes a moment to get her perception properly channeled. But Kaylen has handled millions of life force strands. No one perceives their sensation and energy better than her. With a single thought, she commands them to return, this time to the right spot.

She gasps at the sensation that's like lights flickering back on in an abandoned building.

I let go of her to release her from the complex sensations of the colorworld.

I watch her with an expectant smile. Robbie stills in my arms.

Kaylen turns her attention to a wheelchair at the end of the hall behind me. I turn as it begins to roll toward us, faster and faster.

Lainey flinches and Kiera squeaks, but just before it collides with me, it sails up over our heads, crashing back to the floor and continuing down the hall where several nurses in a group jump back, shrieking.

I turn back to a beaming Kaylen.

She steps forward and takes Robbie from me. "Go," she says, nodding toward the closed door next to her.

I reach for the handle, and as soon as the air of the darkened room hits me, I perceive that Gabriel is already awake.

I can see him from here, his head turned away from the door, and I can smell his misery from here.

He does not realize I'm here, so I step through the door, and then I slam it behind me so that it echoes with a loud boom.

"Gah!" Gabriel jumps, turning my direction.

"*Wendy*," he says, lacing my name with guilt and penance.

I run over to him and leap to straddle him.

He gasps in surprise. His face is wrought with so many lines of agony that I can't help but trace them with my fingers, trying to erase the marks.

He remembers. He recalls how this all came to be. And then he weeps as I have never seen him weep before.

"Qué he hecho?" he moans softly. "Qué he hecho?" He reaches for his hair and I grab both of his hands to still them. He fights me, but I grip them firmly, hold them fast.

"I... I..." he sobs. "What do I say? What can I do?"

"Don't be sad," I whisper, my tears now meeting his because his pain is mine in this space we share.

He presses my palms to his mouth, penitent and sorrowful like I have never felt him. He scrambles for words but he can't form them, can't get them out.

"Don't be sad," I repeat as his tears wet my hands. "This was necessary. *Look who we are.*"

He squeezes his eyes shut, a keening sound coming from the back of his throat, holding my hands like lifelines.

"Do you remember our last wish? With Mike on the phone? We did it, Gabriel! We turned back time!" I whisper.

He chokes on a sob, harrowed. "Why?" he forces out between clenched teeth. "Why this cost?"

"All miracles come with a price," I say, stroking his hair with the one hand I've managed to get out of his grasp.

"Why must you always pay the price for my sins?"

I wait until he opens his eyes. I want him looking at me when I answer.

"*You* are a miracle, Gabriel. Your life was spared by your brother's love for you. And your existence at this moment in time when the world needs you and your ability to move them is no accident. Love does not cause accidents. Even immovable, tenacious, unwavering, miracles who would rather face death and hell than break a commitment."

I lean down and kiss him lightly on the lips, still stroking his hair to quiet his unrest. His eyes have left mine, his heart broken and aching. "You are a miracle," I say. "From the time Mike gave you his strands and spared your life. And I *willingly* pay the price for you."

He still won't look at me. "Gabriel," I gasp, "look who I have become because of your so-called sins." Tears fall freely from my eyes, but I see him finally turn his face toward mine. He reaches up and wipes the tears from my cheeks.

"Gabriel," I whisper, holding his hand to my cheek. "Look at me."

Epilogue

I'm out of paper. Where the hell is Andre? It's been like a week since he showed his face. Or is it two? I don't know. I lose track of days and nights, weeks and even months.

I really need to know the date. If I had Wen's senses, I could have kept track. I'd be able to hear when it got quiet in this place at night. If I had to guess I'd say I'm in a hospital, just like the last place we were, the last place I saw Kaylen... When was that? Months ago. I know that much.

Please, Ezra. You don't know what I've done, what I've sacrificed to get you and Robbie out. You're throwing it away over some stupid kid! The look on her face when she said that... It didn't hit me then what she meant. It didn't even occur to me to wonder until later. And then it was like someone was relentlessly dragging a rake through the gray matter in my head every time I let myself think about it.

If I had known, I wouldn't have gone after that kid, Avery. I sure as hell wouldn't have let Andre take me alive. I would have gouged his eyeballs out with my pencil the first time he let me have one.

I have to stop thinking about this. Kaylen made it out. That's all that matters. And I know she made it back to Wen, because Kaylen isn't like Wen. If someone looked at Robbie wrong, she'd slit their throat before she'd let them touch him, and she wouldn't look back. She scares me sometimes, what she's willing to do.

I stand up and kick the rolling chair out of the way. It slams into a wall and knocks some books off the shelf, which I ignore. I rifle through the stacks on my desk, searching for a blank scrap to write on, but I think I've written on everything, front and back. I shove the cot, then the desk. I already searched all those places, but what else am I supposed to do? I need paper.

I need a calendar more.

Where the hell is Andre?! How does he expect me to work if he doesn't give me anything to write on? I scan the room. The walls are covered in maps, and I've even written on those too. The only place left is the floor.

"Screw it," I mutter, plopping down on it, and with a nub of pencil I start writing on the tiles.

The truth is I already have what Andre wants: a way to locate all Primes Humans. I figured that out ages ago—a month maybe? I have no idea. But it was easy once I got all my notes and diagrams from Wyoming plotting all the disasters and got a fresh look at them. Primes are the cause. I finally nailed that down while I was going over everything again. Once I accepted that as fact, things got easy. Stuff made sense. Primes don't realize it though, which is why Ohr swore up and down they weren't doing it.

But they are. We all are. That's exactly why Andre's targeting Primes, although I don't think he has proof, and I'm scared as hell to give it to him. Of course, who knows who would believe my theoretical math anyway. Nobody would understand it enough to use it as proof.

Primes can be tracked, though, within a few miles, just by tracking the weather. Andre thinks that should be simple. But he's a dimwit. It's only simple because my math makes it simple. The formula is a thing of beauty, and if I could get my hands on a few more data sets, I could make it even more accurate.

None of these things I've given to Andre though. As far as he knows I'm still working furiously on the tracker.

Agitated, I throw my pencil across the room and run a hand through my hair. I can locate every Prime on the planet and I can't even figure out what day it is?

I hear the lock on my door and I jump to my feet and back up against the opposite wall. If I'm anywhere near the door when Andre comes through, he shocks the hell out of me with the dog collar locked on my ankle. Asshole.

It's Ricardo, not Andre. Dammit. Ricardo *always* shocks me. It's part of his standard greeting: *Bzzzzt. Oh hey, twit. How's it going? Bzzzzt.* He does it because he likes it, and I've learned to hit the floor as soon as I see him so I don't fall and hit my head.

For the first time, though, no shock follows his entrance. I don't even see the button in his hand. Instead he looks agitated, his eyes glancing around at the maps on the walls as if it's the first time he's noticed them. That's actually most likely true. He's always too busy laughing at me drooling on myself after he shocks me to notice anything else.

I need to get the torture over with though, so I goad him. "Where is Andre?" I demand. "I need more paper. Updated data."

I grit my teeth expectantly. Still no electricity though. Ricardo is looking at me like he doesn't understand what I'm asking.

"Paper," I say slowly. I hold my hands up to mime a rectangle shape. "To write on." I mimic writing on the imaginary sheet.

"Don't get cheeky with me, you little punk," Ricardo says finally. "'Specially when I'm tryin' to help you out."

I have no idea what he's talking about. Does he really not have his button with him? I try again, snatching a sheet of used paper off the desk. "Looks like this," I say. "But it needs to be white. Not written on? Oh wait. You didn't graduate kindergarten, did you? See, writing is where you form characters with a pencil, stringing them together to make *words*. This paper already has words all over it. I need to make *new* words, so I need blank paper. Know what? Never mind. I don't want your head to explode. Just send Andre in here. He'll know what I'm talking about."

"Pshh," the half-ton Mexican man says. "Smart-alecky twit. I'm tellin' you, go ahead and act like your usual self in front of the new boss, and you can kiss your testicles goodbye."

"New boss?" I say, still testing the waters. "You're too stupid to figure out how to best Andre, so I'm guessing Andre's on vacation and left you in charge. You been in his closet playing make believe again?"

Ricardo growls and makes his massive backside comfortable on my cot. I watch the frame bow, thinking I will *not* be able to control my laughter if it collapses. Mostly, though, I don't get what's going on, why Ricardo is acting like we're bros all of a sudden. Unless he's finally realized he doesn't need to shock me. He can take me out just by sitting on me...

"I've actually always liked you, Whitley," Ricardo says. "But you're like my Aunt's yappy chihuahua, just won't shut the hell up, even for your own good. Sometimes I'd have to throw that thing against the wall, too. Just to get it to listen for a second. You know how easy Andre woulda killed you? Kept you in line enough that he'd tolerate you."

Ricardo is trying to justify torturing me? Since when does he feel like he needs a reason to be a dick?

"Be my guest though," Ricardo says, waving a hand. "Test Horatio. He doesn't like the Primes that don't fall in line. He won't give a shit what kind of brains you have."

The goading in his voice has caught my interest, not to mention Ricardo actually has a name to go along with his claim: Horatio. I've never heard of him, so I seriously have no idea whether to believe this BS. Ricardo really could win an idiot award. Who knows what he heard that led him to that conclusion.

He leans over to get something out of his pocket, putting even more stress on the cot's frame, and I involuntarily wince. "You don't know this," Ricardo says, a phone in his hands now, "but most people here don't even know who you are—who you're related to. Pretty soon Horatio's gonna take a look at what Andre's been keeping down here in the basement. If I was you, I'd figure out what you're gonna say ahead of time. If I was you, I wouldn't let on who I was—who you are—you know what I mean."

I roll my eyes. What a dumbass, although he seems to have an angle. That's a surprise. I didn't think Ricardo knew what an angle *was.* "Why's that?" I press, leaning against the wall and crossing my arms defiantly.

He taps the screen of his phone a few times, then whips it around to show me.

I jump to my feet involuntarily when I recognize the person in white. Even with the less than stellar resolution, I know it's Wen. She's holding a gun, standing over Andre who is on the ground, holding a hand out like he's pleading for his life.

She fires. Andre's head flies back into the cement instantly. But I don't see any more because the video pans away, lost in the shuffle of bodies and screaming.

Ricardo laughs at my expression, which probably looks as stupid as I imagine.

Wen killed Andre. Holy Shit.

New boss... Ricardo wasn't lying.

"You didn't know, did you?" Ricardo says, shaking with laughter. "You didn't know Andre went to New York to mess with her head." Ricardo can't control his fit, wipes his eyes with a thumb and forefinger. "Ah, man. Funny shit. Your sister put him down like a dog, and then..." Ricardo sniggers, trying to get the words out. "She got in her limo, drove right onto the tarmac at JFK and boarded a plane back to her castle. Left his body on the ground like he was roadkill."

I watch Ricardo, totally shocked, speechless. I want him to keep talking. I've heard next to nothing about what Wen's been up to the whole time I've been locked up. After Kaylen escaped with Robbie I told Andre I'd work for him if he'd just leave Wen alone. I made him promises to buy me time to implement my own plan. But Wen... She took him out. Andre's dead, and Wen did it.

I don't realize I've sunk into my chair until Ricardo says, "Your sister is brutal, Mano. Horatio wants her. He'll probably try now that Andre's out of the picture, but my guess is she'll give him the same answer she gave Andre."

I decide to keep with the shutting up. Ricardo just wants to run his mouth, which is fine with me.

Sure enough, Ricardo continues, "Your sister runs the muthafuckin' Guild, dude. I know Andre didn't tell you that. Four months, total takeover. Whole fuckin' Guild loves her. Whole fuckin' world loves her. And what does Andre have right here in his very own basement? Her baby brother. Tried to use you to motivate her and she put a bullet into his face without even looking away. That bitch is hardcore."

I'm holding my breath, in total confusion. That doesn't sound like Wen at all. But I just saw the video. And Andre's not here so...

"Horatio wants your sister's attention bad, man. Thinks she's the fuckin' Prime Ghandi. He probably has a shrine dedicated to her somewhere. Jacks off to it every night. Has a blow-up doll with her face taped to it. Hell if I know. But if he finds out who you are, shit's goin' down. People get hurt. Maybe you. Maybe her. I don't think you want any of that."

It doesn't sound that way to me. It sounds like Wen is immune to blackmail. About time she stopped pussyfooting around these psychos always banging down her door. Now this Horatio guy? How much longer is the line of certifiables gunning for her attention?

And what is Ricardo after? I don't understand what he's saying about this Horatio guy.

"Why are you warning me?" I say suspiciously.

I can tell from here that he's sweating. Of course, Ricardo sweats over everything. Even breathing. He scratches the side of his chin with a finger. "Everyone thought Wendy Whitley was just a figurehead, a prop for the Guild—even Andre. But then she chased him down in public and executed him with hundreds of eyewitnesses, and now people realize she ain't just a distraction for the media. Nah, she's runnin' that joint. And the way things going out there, the Guild gonna be runnin' the whole damn world. That makes her the muthafuckin' empress. I'd be stupid to get on the wrong side of someone like that."

I stare at Ricardo for a minute, dumfounded. Can this really be happening? One of my guards is telling me he's changed sides? Is this a setup? PHIA isn't just anti-Guild, they're anti-Prime. They don't do politics.

But I think the guy's being truthful. Ricardo isn't a mastermind. He's the guy that will do what he thinks will save his own skin. This time that seems to be putting himself on my side—unless this is a new strategy to make me *think* I have an ally here, undercover. I glance at the door. An easy way to test this supposed loyalty is to try to walk out of here. But first, if Ricardo isn't holding anything back, I'd rather have information. Maybe I can even learn the date.

"Who is Horatio?" I say.

"Governor of the New California," Ricardo scoffs. "Best way to look at it. Until now, Andre had him under his thumb. Horatio's just more extreme in his ideas. Horatio thought Andre was working for him. Clearing the land so to speak, taking the Council out. Horatio wants to take over the Guild. Believes in Prime Human supremacy or some shit. Andre was using him for protection. Using his connections in the Guild. Horatio's been around a lot longer than PHIA."

I furrow my brow. Horatio is more extreme? How can you be more extreme than wanting to exterminate an entire group of people? And Prime supremacy? What the hell is he talking about? I rake my hands over my face. Trying to get coherent information from Ricardo is exactly as hard as I thought it'd be.

"Let's recap," I say. "You people hate Prime Humans. But Horatio hates *humans*? And somehow Andre convinced Horatio that they were on the same team?"

"Who hates Primes?" Ricardo says.

I suppress a groan. "PHIA, Ricky Ricardo," I say. "PHIA thinks all Prime Humans need to die. Did you skip reading the mission statement when they brought you on board?"

"Man, I don't know what you're talking about. PHIA is about getting rid of the dirty ones, the ones causing armageddon. What the hell? We aren't Nazis."

Wow. Members of PHIA don't even know what Andre was actually trying to do?

One thing becomes abundantly clear: Andre was a genius. It looks like not only did he dupe his own people into believing his Cleanse operations were only targeting evil Primes bent on world destruction, but he duped the king of the new California into believing PHIA's mission was to take down the Guild's government. Andre may be the most impressive liar I've ever heard of. He's also dead, so it looks like he rode that train of lies a little too long.

Andre is now irrelevant though. A power shift is obviously in the middle of happening, and instead of being the hostage of a Prime-hating scumbag, I'm the hostage of a human-hating scumbag.

Okay, that *sounds* like it ought to be more in my favor—me being a Prime and all. I'm also really smart, which has kept me alive. My plan was going to be a lot harder to implement under Andre, but with this new guy? Piece of cake. I just have to get the math right. I need more data. Ricardo should be able to get me what I need. I have an ally on the inside. I can work with this.

Ricardo leans to the side and lets out a chorus of farts, grunting in between the notes.

Nevermind. I'm probably going to die.

"What's the date?" I ask.

"February twenty-seventh," Ricardo says.

"Three months," I murmur to myself, determined to keep track this time.

"What's three months?" Ricardo says.

"That's how much time I have."

"For what?"

"Finishing my plan," I say, reaching under the desk for the pencil I threw earlier. I start writing on the tile again. Three months is a lot more than I thought. But I better plan on two, just to make sure.

"We gonna take Horatio out?" Ricardo says excitedly.

"If he gets in the way," I reply.

"What you want me to do, E?"

I pause and sit back to see Ricardo's eager expression. After the number of times he's tormented me, I'm baffled that he has chosen an allegiance to me so quickly. And all because he saw my sister shoot Andre? "I didn't realize we were on a first letter basis, *R*," I say snarkily.

"We're on whatever basis you want. Did I tell you she even turned herself in to authorities? I saw the coverage of her arrest. The smug look on her face was like she was doing society a favor. And you know what happened when she was in jail last night? A crowd broke her out. Blew a hole in the side of the police station with a rocket launcher. Seven people died in the brawl. Authorities are afraid to put her in jail again. She's untouchable."

I shake my head in amazement. Wen is in charge of the Guild... I'd kill to know exactly how she pulled that off. Knowing Wen, how she can win people over, I'm not that surprised.

"I need paper," I say, writing again.

"Paper?" Ricardo says.

I sit back and look at him. "We went over this already, Ricky..." I say. "Paper comes from trees. It's usually white. You use it—"

"Shut the hell up, man. I know what fuckin' paper is."

"I wouldn't suggest doing that with paper," I say.

Ricardo blinks, face red, back to sweating again. "Fuck you, man!"

I hold my hands up. "No thanks. You're pretty and all, but that's just not my jam."

"Smartass twit," Ricardo says under his breath.

"First get me paper," I say. "Then get me Horatio."

"Ah, you gotta plan," Ricardo says. "Why didn't you say that to begin with? I can help you."

I roll my eyes.

"Ohhhh!" Ricardo says, a lightbulb turning on. "You don't tell me 'cos you don't know whether you can trust me. Since I was the guy that held you in here. And Andre took you and your family and I worked for him. Bad blood. Yeah, I got it. Hey man, don't worry 'bout that. I told you, your sister is the shit. And if Horatio tries to mess with her, he's gonna end up just like Andre."

I totally get why Andre had this guy do nothing but sit in front of the cameras all day.

"You sure you can handle this, bro?" Ricardo says, fear in his eyes. "Maybe you should just kill him, you know? Take him out right from the start."

"You think he's going to take over PHIA?" I say.

"Already has," Ricardo says. "People here, they just fall in line, because that's how Andre ran it. And Horatio's been here lots before. People know him."

I nod. "And you're saying he's a Prime supremacist?"

"Yeah. Hardcore. Primes are the only ones he'll let into California alive. And all the humans here are Prime-worshippers. He calls it the Amalgam. But it's got a lot of different names on the street."

Andre, you crazy ass-backward genius. He used PHIA's ex-Guild Prime status to his advantage. Humans worshipping Primes? That sounds like some kind of cult thing. Andre was planning a Prime Human extermination right under the nose of Prime Human fan extremists.

If Andre can hijack this group—the *Amalgam* or whatever the hell it's called—then I can, too. Wen's a public figure who murdered Andre and runs the Guild. I can count on her if I need to. This should be easy.

"If you're telling the truth and he runs California, I need him alive," I say. "That's all I'm going to tell you right now. First paper. Then Horatio. Got it, Ricky?"

"Yeah yeah. I got it," Ricardo grumbles, heaving himself off the cot.

"Don't forget to lock the door on your way out," I say. "Horatio doesn't need to know we had this conversation. But *after* you get me paper, you tell Horatio about me, who I am, show your loyalty by giving him me, and you'll live."

"This is a dumbass plan," Ricardo says, heading for the door.

"Only because you're a dumbass," I say. "I'm trying to make this idiot-proof for you, Ricky. The less you know, the less you'll screw up."

Ricardo turns around. "You know who you sound like right now?"

"Ezra Whitley, boy genius," I quip.

"No. Andre."

I shrug. "Andre was smart. But I'm a hell of a lot smarter. Smart enough to know you don't reinvent the wheel if one already exists. You hijack it. That's exactly what my sister did. And that is exactly what I'm going to do."

LOOK FOR BOOK 6 IN THE COLORWORLD SERIES:

WATERWORLD

Visit the official site:

ColorworldBooks.com

Acknowledgements

A while back some friends of mine gave me a T-shirt that quips:
Careful or you might end up in my novel.
It turns out that some people weren't scared of that possibility and graciously allowed me to create characters based on themselves for this book, and I need to give them a shoutout!

    Chase Clark.
    Erin Brostuen.
    Meagan Kruenegel.

Thank you guys. It's always a pleasure for me to think about actual people when I write, especially those who have inspired me. Being able to integrate some of the awesome personalities from my own reality into the Colorworld story has been a privilege.

I would like to make it clear to readers, however, that while I did my best to portray the personalities of these people, I do not claim to know their histories and opinions. Any statements made by the fictional Chase, Erin, or Roe in this story do not represent the opinions or views of the people on whom those characters are based, nor do the events in this story describe actual events.

Thank you to my indispensable copy editors who make sure all my i's are dotted and my t's are crossed:

    Kristin Scadden South
    Samantha Dailey
    Heather Burns
    Bradley Kelly

Thanks you, fans. Every story is for you.

On February 24th, 2015, my husband, four kids, and I came to a stop in Kansas City Missouri. We were on our way to Colorado Springs for our next event, and our RV needed gas. We had a few dollars in cash and no money in our account. It was clear that we didn't have enough to make it. I have a lot of words to describe the feelings I had on that day and the day that followed, but those will have to wait for the memoir. Suffice it to say, we were stranded and destitute in the middle of winter.

I wrote a short Facebook post, trying desperately to humble myself and ask for help. I then sent that post out into the harsh world of social media and prayed that my pride would survive.
Help came.

And it never stopped.

Today, as I write this, since January 1, 2015, we have attended 116 events. By the end of the tour, (December 31, 2016), that number will be 119. We have travelled well over 200,000 miles and visited all but one of the states in the continental US. For two years we have survived on the generosity of fans. Not only have we survived, but we've built a Colorworld that can now survive—the book, the story, the team, the art, the idea. Because of all you've helped us build, the Colorworld Book Tour (#CWBT) is about to go to the next level in 2017. We will be taking the tour international, but most events will not be attended by me personally. I'll be busy writing more than I've ever written before in a year. I'll be writing about Wendy of course, but I'll also be writing about YOU and this tour, so that everyone knows exactly how Colorworld was made.

Thank you.

Made in the USA
Columbia, SC
20 February 2018